transcended

ingrid j. adams

three bees
— press —

Printed in Australia

Cover design by Bea Brabante

Illustrations in this book are copyright approved for Three Bees Press

Paperback ISBN 978-1-7635034-2-7

eBook ISBN 978-1-7635034-3-4

Distributed by Three Bees Press and Lightningsource Global

 A catalogue record for this work is available from the National Library of Australia

transcended

a love that spans lifetimes

For Dash.

Thanks for all the Matty material, babe. Don't ever lose your magic.

warning

Here we go again! You're about to step back into the 1990s, which as you know from *descended*, is an era of political incorrectness where anything goes.

This is a book about life, and life can be confronting and heartbreaking and pretty damned full on at times. The *descended* series doesn't shy away from the big stuff; it never has and it never will. These pages contain emotionally confronting content which some readers may find isn't productive for them to explore. If you're particularly sensitive, you might want to set it aside. I don't believe in spoilers, so please visit ingridjadams.com for a list of triggers.

not a child of the 90s?

One thing *transcended* definitely does contain is an epically nostalgic playlist. The QR code below will take you to a Spotify playlist (entitled 'transcended · two') so you can sing along at home.

re-meet the gang

(note: if you haven't read the first book in this series, this list contains spoilers, so stop right now, avert your eyes, and go read _descended_)

australia

indigo – Our MMC. Survivor of depression and conqueror of intense higher senses. Brutally hot Aussie surfer. Possessor of a light inside that illuminates everyone he meets. An empathic, telepathic, psychokinetic, clairvoyant healer. Currently nursing a broken heart courtesy of Cordelia. Age: 19. Quote: _"I loved Cordelia in another time and place when we were different iterations of ourselves; different, but fundamentally the same. I lost her then. I can't lose her now."_

cordelia – Our FMC. Indigo's one true love, and we hope, destiny. Ethereally beautiful Aussie gal and ocean lover. Fierce defender of friends and family. Dreamer of past lives. Age: 18. Quote: _"Indigo: the love of my life, or so I'd once believed. But that was then, and a lot has certainly changed since. In another time, another place, I'd say to hell with everyone else, with the rest of the world and run straight into his arms. But here and now... I can't. I never want to hurt Drew the way Indigo hurt me."_

robbie – Cordelia's twin brother and all-round drama queen. Conjurer of smart-arse comments, queen of snark. Age:18. Quote: *"If you can't say anything nice, come sit by me."*

drew aka pres – Indigo's ex-best friend and Cordelia's current boyfriend. Theorist of conspiracies, breaker of knees (but only his own). Age: 19. Quote: *"The truth is out there. To see it, you just need to open your eyes and your mind."*

reinenoir aka harper – OG baddie and high priestess of the most notorious coven of the 90s. Collector of many powers. Obsessed with Indigo and will do anything to make him hers. Age: 20. Quote: *"If I can't have him, no one will."*

the maiden aka orwen – Balinese warlock. Right-hand woman to Reinenoir. Lover of lizards. Telekinetic and telepathic collector. Age: 24. Quote: *"I serve in shadow. We shall stop at nothing to restore the timeline."*

artax – Addict of body-modification. Owner of forked tongue. A telekinetic, telepathic dome shrouder and collector. Age: 28. Quote: *"You move, you bleed."*

scarlett – Mum to Cordelia, Robbie and Matty. Bohemian goddess. Mother extraordinaire. Lover of books and holistic medicine. Age: 36. Quote: *"You're always welcome in my home but your shoes are not."*

joshua – Stepdad to Cordelia and Robbie, dad to Matty. Doctor. Man of science. Big-hearted sweetheart. Age: 42. Quote: *"Family comes first, second and third."*

matty – Baby brother to Robbie and Cordelia. Collector of not-so-imaginary imaginary friends… Age: 3. Quote: *"My other mother had short red hair and lived in a house made of sticks on a green hill. One day she stabbed me with a sharp thing, and now I live with you."*

essie – Best friend and colleague of Joshua. Most popular nurse at Manly Hospital. Currently in a coma courtesy of Reinenoir and her coven. Age: 33. Quote: *"Who's up for margaritas?!"*

sarita – Gatekeeper between worlds. Guardian to Indigo. Only he can see her. Ageless. Quote: *"You've always been able to see through the membrane between realms, and I've always been here, guiding you, watching over you, trying to help you find your way to the path you're destined to follow."*

edita – Nanny-cum-housekeeper to Indigo. Keeper of the Van Allen Estate. Lithuanian. Age: 44. Quote: *"You look hungry. I will fix you something to eat."*

lukas – Husband to Edita and groundskeeper at the Van Allen Estate. Top Aussie bloke. Age: 51. Quote: *"G'day, g'day, fancy a beer?"*

bernadette – Movie star/pop-sensation/Australia's most famous export. Self-centred ditz and absentee mother of Indigo. Age: 40. Quote: *"I'll see you in Aspen in January, kitten."*

peyton – One of Cordelia's two best friends. Loud, opinionated redhead. Lover of fun. Age: 18. Quote: *"Chicks before dicks."*

sian (pronounced sharn) – Cordelia's other best friend and girlfriend to Will. Assumes she's Eurasian. Desperate to know who she is and where she really comes from. Age: 18. Quote: *"Like, why didn't they want me?"*

sandy – Dealer of drugs. A loose unit. Massive toolie. Age: 19. Quote: *"It's totally fine to get high on your own supply."*

usa

raf aka diego – Leader of soul family, knower of many things mysterious. Has a secret life as illustrious author Sebastian Winters. Hosts the discarnate Micah. Abilities undefined. Age: 41. Quote: *"I'm only human, here, just like you on this lonely blue planet floating through space, trying to make sense of being in this world and in this body."*

nash aka blaze – Lover of the ladies and lead singer of the hottest band in Sedona. Cocky British redhead. Posh English boarding school survivor. A psychokinetic pre-cog. Age: 20. Quote: *"If I told you, you had a beautiful body, would you hold it against me?"*

aurora – Kicker of ass and taker of no-nonsense. An African American walk-in. Telepathic and telekinetic. Age: 27. Quote: *"I don't have time for your bullshit."*

sasha – The ultimate karate kid. Japanese-Thai surfer dude from Hawaii. Black belt in multiple martial arts, champion meditator and telepath. Expert bilocater. Age: 22. Quote: *"Yesterday's smoke in the wind, man, it's gone ya, you can't change it, so why waste time worrying about it?"*

dawn – Bubbly blonde empath. Master of healing and mentor to Indigo. Obsessed with angels, fairies and rainbows. Wife to Earl, mother to Reggie, Phoebe, and four sons. Age: 46. Quote: *"In this house we never apologise for our emotions, honey."*

wilson – Hollywood royalty, famous movie star. All round prick and father of Indigo. Age: 72. Quote: *"I want to thank the Academy and, of course, my public..."*

ana maria – Wilson's housekeeper and right-hand woman. Jamaican. Age: 59. Quote: *"Smarten up your act, young man, or I be telling your father."*

skeet – Inbred warlock. Kidnapper and stabber of Indigo. On-again-off-again boyfriend of Dawn's daughter Reggie. Stripped of his memories by Raf and banished from Sedona. Age: 31. Quote: *"Everythin' I know 'bout pleasurin' the female body I done learned from my sisters."*

matias – Father of Raf. Widower. Chilean. Ex-serial-philanderer. Age: 63. Quote: *"I loved your mother desperately... but there were days I didn't like her very much at all."*

total eclipse of the heart

toorak, victoria, august 1982

reinenoir

Harper threw open her wardrobe door with a squeal.

"Found you!" she cried, giggling as she spied her uncle's face peeking out from between two freshly pressed dresses. A look of disbelief marred his bronzed good looks.

"Again?" He pretended to scowl and grumble as he unfolded himself from his hiding place, smoothing the creases from his black trousers. "No fair, *ma petite reine.*" He smiled as he rolled down his sleeves, then fished a pair of gold cufflinks from his pocket, threading them through the buttonholes. "You're just too good at this game. Are you sure you're only *seven?*"

Harper beamed, hugging herself in delight. No one had ever been able to beat her at hide and seek. Then again, no one else had a super power like hers. When people were hiding, they hushed their lips, but they rarely hushed their minds.

Her uncle reached for his suit jacket draped neatly over the foot of her gauzy, mauve canopy bed. "We'd better get back downstairs."

"No!" she cried, crossing her arms and scowling. "I don't wanna!"

Her uncle sighed heavily and sat on her bed, patting the spot beside him. Harper reluctantly climbed up to sit next to him. "I know things are hard right now, *ma petite reine*," he said, putting his arm around her. She rested her head on his shoulder as he gently stroked her long, blonde hair. "But Mama and Papa need you by their sides today."

Her scowl deepened. Their house was full of sad, old, ugly people, all wearing black, all dabbing at their eyes and gazing at her with pity. The last thing she wanted to do was go back down there. The funeral had been bad enough, with those two small flower-laden coffins up there at the front of the Church making everybody cry.

Except her.

Harper didn't like to cry.

Her sisters were dead.

She was an only child now.

Crying wouldn't change that.

Harper smoothed the skirt of the black taffeta dress her mother had made her wear. It had a white Peter Pan collar, and Mama had laid it out with white tights and shiny black Mary Janes. Ugly. She'd wanted to change for the wake, but her mother said she wasn't allowed.

"Oncle Olivier?"

"Mmmm?"

"Can we play *one* more game of hide and seek, and then I *promise* I'll go downstairs with you?"

"No, Harper–"

"Please, Oncle Olivier? *Please?* I'll play fair. This time I swear I won't listen to where you decide to hide." The moment the words left her mouth, she realised what she'd done. She bit down hard on her lip.

Oncle Olivier jerked suddenly, his arm falling away from her shoulders as he turned to look her in the eye. "*Mon Dieu!* What did you just say?" He narrowed his gaze.

Harper felt her cheeks warm. Oops.

She hadn't meant to say that out loud. "Nothing!" She jammed her mouth shut and lowered her eyes. She slid off the bed and tried to scurry away, but he grabbed her arm and spun her to face him.

"You know you can tell me anything, *ma petite reine?*"

2

She stared into his eyes, then went deeper, went beyond, venturing into his mind to read his thoughts. He baulked sharply, then something happened, something that had never happened to Harper before. She felt herself being shoved out of his head, and then, even more extraordinary, a black curtain fell around his mind. She gasped, fought to push her way back in, but the curtain was impenetrable, like it was made of steel or stone.

"Hey!" she cried, screwing up her face in concentration as she continued to try and shove past it. "What did you do?"

"Something I didn't believe I needed to do around you, little miss!" He sounded angry. "Does your mama know you're telepathic?"

"What's telepathic?" She was ramming at the curtain now, but it deflected her over and over again.

"It means you can read people's thoughts."

She shrugged.

"What else can you do, Harper?"

She shrugged again.

As *if* she was gonna tell him. It wasn't as though he'd told her what he could do. She'd always loved him best, and now she found out he'd been keeping secrets from her! His power was super cool. She wanted to be able to do that! She had an idea.

"I'll tell you if you tell me," she countered. "What else can *you* do?"

He cocked a brow at her, and with a little half-smile, he flicked a finger towards her wardrobe. The doors banged shut in unison.

Harper gasped. "Teach me," she demanded, still trying to force her way into his mind.

"No, *ma petite reine.* Not today and not without your mother's permission."

"Who cares what *she* thinks. Teach me, Oncle Olivier!"

He stood up and slipped his jacket on. "We don't even know if you're capable."

"Please?"

"I said no."

Harper got to her feet. "Well *I* said yes!" Hands on hips, she glared at him.

He shook his head at her. "We do not speak to grown-ups that way, Harper."

Now he was making her mad. Oncle Olivier was always fun. He'd never told her off before, and he'd never said no to her.

She stamped her foot at him. "I wanna do what *you* can do! Teach me *now*! Or I won't love you best anymore!"

Right now she hated him! He was being so mean!

Luckily, Harper had other secret super powers. Like the determination to always get what she wanted. And she *really* wanted to be able to make things move without touching them, like he could.

Screwing up her face in concentration, she stood opposite him, feet firmly planted on the ground, and opened her arms out wide. The intense power of her want burnt white-hot through every cell of her being. It fuelled her. Focusing with all her might on what she desired from him, she summoned it to her, demanding it unapologetically. She didn't know what would happen. It was like she'd left her body, as if something else had taken over her and, whatever it was, it knew exactly what to do. All she knew is that she wanted it badly, and that was all she could see.

A strange expression came over his face, then it all happened so fast she couldn't have controlled it, or stopped it, even if she'd tried.

She took and took until he had nothing left to give.

When it was all over and she'd come back to her body, she was terrified.

Her parents must have heard the thud because suddenly the door burst open and her room was full of people. Everyone was crowding around Oncle Olivier lying there on the floor, his eyes were closed and he was very still, but through the haze she heard her father say he was breathing.

She hadn't *meant* to hurt him. She'd just really wanted what he had. She didn't even know what she'd done. She curled into a ball in the corner and squeezed her eyes shut. Jamming her hands over her ears, she tried her hardest to block out images of swirling vortexes and great black writhing hooks pumping, and sucking, and hijacking all his power...

They took Oncle Olivier to hospital, and Harper felt sad about that for a couple of days, but she soon found comfort in her newly acquired super power. Never having to get up to close a door, ever again, was really cool.

For as long as she could remember, Harper Valentine knew how to hit 'em where it hurt. She'd always had a special way of knowing what those around her were thinking, and it was true what they said, that knowledge was power.

Beautiful, magnificent, dizzying power.

Even as far back as kindergarten she'd ruled like the queen she deserved to be. She'd firmly established herself at the top of the pecking order on her first day of primary school by zeroing in on the prettiest girl in her class – the one all the other girls were fawning over. "Was that your mother who dropped you off this morning?" she'd asked. When the girl had beamed proudly and nodded, Harper commented, "She's so chic and beautiful, you must take after your dad."

Harper had a knack for knowing someone's weakness just by tuning into them. And using it for her own benefit. When she'd started at the imposing sandstone monolith of North Head Grammar in Year Seven, she'd shunned any attempts at friendship offered by those she considered beneath her (which was ninety-nine-point-nine percent of the population): no fatties, no sluts, no fuglies, no goths, no freaks, no molls, no dykes, no dweebs… and cankles were definitely a deal breaker.

Harper had a reputation to protect, a reputation she let precede her.

Her first day on campus, she made sure to casually saunter by the popular clique at lunchtime. These girls were the best North Head Grammar had to offer, the prettiest, most stylish and the wealthiest, the *crème de la crème* of the Northern Beaches. They were ensconced in their usual spot – the benches in the back corner of the lawn under the big Norfolk Pine. Their leader was a brunette named Chloe (apparently, all the boys thought Chloe was hot, but Harper couldn't see it; she was above average at best).

Harper observed them from the corner of her eye. Chloe was holding out her hand while the other girls gushed over the hideous ring she was sporting, a new acquisition from her boyfriend, an older guy from another school.

As Harper passed by, Chloe glanced up. "Hey, you're Harper, right?" she called.

As the most popular girl in the year ('til now), everybody knew who Chloe was, a fact she took great pride in. So Harper half turned, flicked her long hair silkily over her shoulder, furrowed her brow, and very pointedly replied, "Who's asking?"

Chloe's pencil-thin eyebrows shot up.

"Um, *hello?*" the striking redhead sitting next to Chloe replied. "This is *Chloe*. Chloe *Radcliffe?*"

Harper regarded Chloe blankly and merely shrugged. "Nice to meet you, Chloe," she said, turning on her heel and making to walk away.

She managed two steps before Chloe called out, "Wait!"

A sly smile pulled at the corners of Harper's lips; she quickly hid it as she turned, her eyes wide and innocent. "Uh… come sit with us," Chloe said, shuffling over to make room for Harper in the prime spot next to her. Harper glanced thoughtfully at her watch, then shrugged in resignation, settling herself into the offered spot.

They chatted casually for a while, Harper making an effort to compliment all the girls in the group, all except one. She made sure to sit with them for no more than ten minutes. By the time she told them she had to run, they were practically begging her to meet them at the mall after school.

"Wow, nice ring, by the way," she said to Chloe, glancing at her hand as she stood to leave. "Where did you get it? My grandmother's birthday is coming up and she simply adores gauche junk jewellery."

Chloe went bright red and subtly slipped her hand into her pocket. She never wore that ring again, and broke up with her boyfriend (who she suddenly decided was a loser with no taste) that weekend.

Harper was quickly accepted as one of them and from then on, it was relatively easy. Chloe hadn't been keen to give up her position as queen bee, but historically, Chloe, had a very unhealthy relationship with food, having battled eating disorders in the past, so it wasn't too difficult to destroy her.

It all started with a few innocent comments. "Oh my God, Chloe, you're SO lucky you can eat stuff like that," Harper would say, looking her nose down at Chloe's peanut butter sandwich and Mars Bar. "If I ate like that my thighs would be the size of tree trunks." A few days later she whispered to Jess, the biggest mouth in the group, that she'd overheard a group of guys calling Chloe "Thunder Thighs". This little bit of gossip had quickly done the rounds of the group and then the school before eventually making its way to Chloe.

When Harper found her crying in the bathroom she comforted her, saying, "The best revenge is a hot body." The next day, when Chloe came to lunch empty-handed, claiming she'd forgotten the brown paper bag her mother had packed for her, Harper found it hard to hide her smile. More so, the day after that, when not only did Chloe "forget" her lunch, but also spent the break running laps around the school oval.

A week later, when the girls surrounded Chloe after school and expressed their concern for her sudden aversion to eating, Harper stepped in and demanded they leave her alone, saying anorexia was a disease of the weak and the vain, and Chloe was neither of those. She gazed at Chloe with challenge in her eyes, daring her to say otherwise and ask for help. Two months later, when Chloe's parents admitted her to a clinic and the whole school was abuzz about her big relapse and her skeletal frame, Harper slid smoothly into Chloe's place. Her first order of business was to get rid of all the dead wood in the group.

She always knew when there was unrest in the group, when an uprising was coming and it was time to cull. When Saskia started having thoughts about challenging her, Harper pulled her aside and expressed concern about Saskia's relationship with Mr Gojkovic, the school gymnastics coach. Harper knew Saskia had never told anyone about the torrid affair she'd begun with Mr Gojkovic. He was married with two kids and Saskia knew her father would flip out if he ever found out, so she was frantic when she discovered Harper knew. She begged her not to tell anyone. For the life of her, she couldn't figure out how Harper had found out about her and Mr Gojkovic, because although he plagued her every waking thought, she'd never spoken of their love affair to anyone.

What she didn't know was it was guaranteed that if she thought about it enough, Harper would hear it.

Harper had always been able to hear what was going on in the heads of those around her. As a toddler, she never bothered with generic words like "Mama" or "Papa" or "more". Instead, she waited to speak until she was two-and-a-half, at which time she opened her mouth and spoke in fully formed sentences, her first being, "Mama, you should get rid of the baby in your tummy, I don't want another sister." And although her mother hadn't mentioned her pregnancy to anyone, not even her husband (who didn't want any more children), she knew the problem had consumed her mind.

That was the day Harper's mother, Helene, realised her daughter had the same gift she had. The same gift her brother and mother had, that her mother's father had possessed, and his mother before him had, too.

Unfortunately, Oncle Olivier was the only member of her maternal family Harper had ever met, and he'd been in a coma since she was seven. Harper had never been introduced to the only other family member on her mother's side, her estranged grandmother, Isadora DuPont. The more tight-lipped Helene grew around the subject of Isadora, the more Harper's curiosity about her grandmother intensified.

Helene never told Harper what she was, but it wasn't hard for Harper to figure it out given she could read minds. All she had to do was clear her thoughts and merely focus on someone to hear what was going on in their head. Thanks to Oncle Olivier, she knew how to shroud her own mind so the same couldn't be done to her.

Helene's mind was in constant turmoil, stressing about how similar Harper was to her grandmother. It was clearly her mother's biggest fear. Which only made Harper more curious about Isadora.

After catching Harper in her mind for the third time, Helene sat her down and tried to teach her the etiquette that came along with her gift, how it was deemed rude to barge into someone else's head and read their private thoughts. But as far as Harper was concerned, the rules didn't apply to her.

So she used it to her advantage, slipping into people's minds to discover their secrets and insecurities to be used against them when needed. A master of mind games, no one was safe, not even her own parents. The older she grew the more she recognised her parents' weaknesses, and Harper couldn't abide weakness.

And then, one day, when she was in Year Nine, a boy at school caught her eye.

Harper always had her pick of any boy she wanted. Not only because she was stunning and popular, but because she knew how to give them exactly what their unformed little brains wanted. But she grew bored easily and moved on quickly, never forming an emotional attachment.

Until Indigo.

Indigo Wolfe. He'd been a year younger than her, but certainly didn't look or act like it. He was as tall as the boys in Year Eleven and Twelve, and way hotter than all of them put together. And his smile! He had a smile that could light up the sky on a dark moonless night. A smile that managed to melt even her cold, jaded heart.

But it wasn't just that. There was something incredibly elusive about him, something irresistibly alluring. Effortlessly cool, incredibly popular, he didn't seem to care what anyone thought of him.

Everyone knew who he was because of his parents. His mother, Bernadette Van Allen, was Australia's most famous export – an actress and pop sensation, she'd famously married and quickly divorced Indigo's father, American movie star, Wilson Wolfe, who was bona fide Hollywood royalty. Indigo's parents hated each other's guts and neither of them had particularly wanted Indigo, who'd been raised by the hired help.

Indigo was sad, a lot.

Poor little fucked-up rich boy.

One day between classes, Harper ensured she ran into Indigo – literally. They started hanging out, and for the next six months they were hot and heavy. She found his energy, his attitude and his very essence, utterly addictive… not to mention the complexity of his mind which challenged her every day. She found his mind an incredibly interesting place to visit, a place unlike any she'd ever been. It was vast. She couldn't get much past the forefront, the rest a maze so very intricate that even she had trouble negotiating it, figuring him out, and she found it fascinating. Indigo was one of a kind.

She knew he was different.

The same way she was different.

Although she never let on.

She sensed great power within him, but he was out of control, with no idea of even a fraction of what he was capable of. Thanks in part to dear Oncle Olivier (who'd never recovered from their encounter that day back in 1982 and by then had finally succumbed to his vegetative state and passed on), she was an old hand at shrouding her mind and emotions, so Indigo only had access to what she allowed.

She loved the way she felt when she was around him. He quickly became an obsession. She wrote his initials in little hearts all over her school books. She sought him out in the halls between classes to sneak a quick kiss, to run her hands through his deep-golden hair, to grope that insanely beautiful body of his. She couldn't get enough of him, anywhere, anytime, any place.

He was so different to her, sometimes annoyingly so. His constant compulsion to go out of his way for other people was beyond irritating to her. Especially when it interfered with her day. They'd be running late for school when all of a sudden he'd notice some old biddy who needed help carrying her shopping, or a guy having car trouble who needed help pushing his ute off the road, or a mangy old dog limping down the middle of the street that needed rescuing. It drove her mental.

And, if one of his mates needed him? He'd drop everything to be there. Especially his best mate, Drew Prescott. Indigo had even cancelled on *her*, for Drew. Why did Drew's parents' divorce have to affect *her* life? She didn't care his skanky mum had run off with her lover, leaving Drew's dad to raise him and his two brothers. Quite frankly, she found it naïve of Indigo to let other people affect him so much. He only seemed to see the best in them. It was a real weakness of his, a pathetic weakness she had no time for.

And it was best not to get her started on Indigo's unnatural relationship with his nanny-cum-housekeeper, Edita. Edita – the human equivalent of a dry cheese sandwich on white bread – so plain, so boring, so dependable and stable. And her mind, so blank! When Harper delved inside, gaining easy access of course, it was like the woman didn't have a thought in her head.

Edita didn't like Harper. At all. And Harper despised Edita. The woman was a member of staff yet she didn't seem to know her station. If Harper spoke to Edita the way one was meant to speak to the hired help, Indigo got really upset with her. "That woman raised me, Harper," he said to her once after she'd snapped her fingers at Edita and ordered her to bring a Diet Coke with extra ice and a lemon wedge out to the pool for her. "You can't talk down to her like that, she's not your slave."

"*Au contraire, mon cherie*, that's *exactly* what she is!" Harper had replied.

He'd been so angry with her after that, he'd suggested she leave. She gathered she was no longer welcome there and could never bring herself to cross the threshold of the Van Allen Estate ever again. Which meant he had to come to her place instead, and of course he found out about her sisters, Ebony and Reign, about how they'd *died*. Then he found out about her dad's methods of dealing with his grief, about the drinking, about the way he took his anger and resentment out on her mum. She was the one driving, after all, when her sisters had been killed.

And Indigo finding all that out had changed things between them. It had forced her to let her guard down, forced her to open her heart to him. And she'd stupidly, naively, thought that was a good thing.

Their differences meant they fought – a lot. They'd fight and she'd end things with him. And then she'd miss him, and her heart would hurt, which made her angry. So she'd find out which party he was going to that weekend and make sure to turn up with some hot older guy with whom she'd flirt shamelessly right in Indigo's eyeline, which would piss him right off. So, by the time she'd abandoned her date to grab Indigo's hand and pull him into the nearest empty bedroom, he'd be more than ready to make up. And so the cycle would begin again.

But then came the night of the Carlisle twins' plebeian little karaoke party. She hadn't wanted to go, and not a day went by that she wished she'd listened to her instincts and forbidden Indigo from going. Because that night was the night that changed everything.

She'd had a bad feeling about that Carlisle bitch from the start. She should have kept Indigo away from her, and her family. Ever since the day Oncle Olivier had fallen into his coma, Harper had been plagued by vague visions, hazy and unformed. She only ever got enough information to know whether something or someone was going to have a positive or negative impact on her life, but no more. It was a tease really, a frustrating power she likened to a sneeze that tickled her nose, but never eventuated, and more often than not, left her with a headache.

Of course the party had been a disaster. It was karaoke, for fuck's sake, and of course Indigo had felt inclined to swoop in and save the day, making karaoke cool, as only he could. And after that night, he began spending more and more time at the Carlisle's homely little cottage – it didn't have a pool or any view to speak of – and less and less time with her.

Then one day he told her they needed to talk. No boy had ever told her they needed to talk before, so she was completely unprepared for what was coming. But the moment he arrived at her palatial Mosman home and her maid Fernanda sent him down to the pool house with its uninterrupted views of the harbour below, Harper had heard what was going on in the forefront of his mind before he could get the words out.

He wanted to end things with her.

No one had ever broken up with her before.

She quickly decided he wouldn't be the first.

He'd always been easy to manipulate because he was one of the most sexually charged people she'd ever met. Even when they ran out of things to talk about, they had that in common, and she had no complaints because he really knew what he was doing (which was another reason she found the thought of giving him up unfathomable).

So she tried to lure him back in with what she was best at.

But for the first time ever, it didn't work.

He pushed her away. Rejected her! Even after she pulled out the big guns and told him she loved him.

"You don't *love* me," he told her. "Some days I question whether you actually even *like* me. You're constantly trying to change me and all we do is fight! It's never gonna work between us, Harps, I'm sorry, I truly am, I never meant to hurt you..."

That was when her walls bricked up. "*Hurt* me?" she spat, standing up and glaring at him, fury coursing hotly beneath her skin. "Hurt me?! You wanna know about hurt? Oh you'll know all about hurt once I'm finished with you! You're an arsehole, Indigo Wolfe, a total fucking arsehole!"

"Ok, we're done here," he replied curtly, turning on his heel to leave.

"Just so you know," she screamed after him. "I'm telling everyone I dumped YOU!"

He stopped then and slowly spun to face her. She was breathing heavily, so angry she could hardly see straight. And then she saw it. Pity. Pity in his eyes. "You do what you gotta do," he said with a shrug. A shrug and pity in his eyes. He was *pitying* her? How *dare* he?

"If you think I'm ever going to forget this, you've got another thing coming!" she screamed after him. "I'll get you back for this, Indigo! I never forget! I'll get you back for treating me this way!" She wanted to hurt him, to scare him even. They were just words, she didn't even mean them, at least not all of them, but that's all she'd really had at her disposal back then.

After he left, she slammed the door shut behind him with a mere flick of her finger, then fell onto the couch and sobbed her poor, broken heart out. He'd made her cry! Harper hated crying; it was a pointless exercise that changed nothing. But, the hurt took her breath away, and the tears, they were unstoppable. The only boy she'd ever let in, ever loved, and he'd just walked out of her life, just like that. Gone, cold turkey. Didn't he know she needed him? She needed him to make her whole! When she was with him, she felt things she'd never felt before, things she needed to feel, things she'd spent the next six years trying to find elsewhere, from others.

Her whole life, people had left her.

Her sisters.

Indigo.

And then, her parents.

When Harper's parents died, it was splashed across the news day and night for a week. Apparently a grisly murder-suicide in Mosman was worthy of relentless media attention. Vultures.

And just like that, Harper found herself all alone in the world.

That winter, she received a letter from her grandmother, the mysterious Isadora DuPont, offering her condolences and inviting her to tea. Harper re-read that letter about a thousand times. She'd been kept away from Isadora her whole life. Her parents had considered the old woman a bad apple whose rot they wanted nowhere near their daughter. But forbidden fruit is always the sweetest, and Harper jumped at the chance to visit with the largely reclusive Isadora.

Isadora's house was in the middle of nowhere. Harper almost drove right by the entrance, so overgrown with privet and brambles, a mere break in the bushes marked by a rusted gate and a shabby letterbox. Frowning, she checked the address again. This was definitely it, but it looked deserted, abandoned. At the end of a seemingly endless winding driveway cracked with weeds and potholes, she finally came upon the rambling old house. The gardens were overrun, the stonework mossy, the mansion itself in disrepair. Harper climbed out of the car and gazed up at the crumbling gables, almost expecting to see gargoyles perched there. She shivered. It was a lot colder in the Southern Highlands than it had been in Sydney.

The front door creaked open, and there stood a striking girl in her early twenties with dead straight hair cut into a chic blunt bob. She looked Balinese. "Harper?' she asked, her accent thick. "Madame DuPont is expecting you."

She led Harper through the dim, musty house with its worn, dark wood and deep burgundy finishes. Faded paintings hung over faded wallpaper. The carpet was practically threadbare and dust motes twirled in the air. It was draughty inside, and cold – the kind of cold that seeped deep into your bones. They arrived in the sitting room where an unlit fire lay in the hearth. The heavy, moth-eaten drapes were drawn and, despite the cold, Harper itched to throw them wide and open a window. The house was in dire need of fresh air. Fresh air, a good vacuum, central heating… a wrecking ball, perhaps?

An elderly lady dressed in pastel green sat in an armchair in the corner, her pale mauve hair topped with an emerald satin turban bedecked with jewels. A silver cigarette holder was clasped between two fingers, and she was stroking something nestled in her lap. At first, Harper thought it was one of those repulsive hairless cats, but upon closer inspection she saw it was some kind of lizard, a bearded dragon maybe. She wrinkled her nose.

"Madame DuPont, your granddaughter is here," the Balinese girl said. Isadora looked up, her sharp blue eyes moving critically over Harper. "Do you want me to take Mortimer?" the girl asked.

Isadora nodded and passed the lizard to the girl. "*Oui.* Tea, please, Gede."

Gede nodded and plopped the lizard on her shoulder as she left the room.

Isadora took a small puff of the cigarette holder, smoke furling from her nose. "Don't just stand there, *petite-fille.* Sit down." Her French accent meant her words flowed quickly into one another, her vowels nasal.

Harper glanced around at the grimy, worn furniture, selecting the least offensive bit of couch to perch gingerly upon. Why today of all days had she worn white? She folded her hands in her lap and looked expectantly at Isadora.

"Well, you're quite the little snob, aren't you?" Isadora grinned, resting her cigarette holder in a chipped crystal ashtray and crossing her arms. "My house isn't good enough for you?"

Harper stared her down. "It could do with a good clean, for starters. I'd fire that housekeeper of yours – Gede, was it? She's clearly taking advantage of you. This place is filthy."

"Gede is not my housekeeper. She is my apprentice."

Harper narrowed her eyes. "Apprentice?"

Isadora gave her a withering look. "Your mama never told you what I am? What you are?"

Harper cocked her head to one side.

"We are warlocks, *petite-fille*. Although your imbecile mother spent her whole life in denial of that fact."

A slow smile spread over Harper's face. She knew it!

With the clink of crockery, Gede returned with a tray laden with a teapot and three small, floral teacups. Harper watched her intently. Who *was* this girl? Some kind of gold digger after her grandmother's house? Harper smirked. If she wanted this hideous mausoleum, she could have it. Gede slapped the tray on the table and busied herself pouring what smelt like chai tea. She thrust a cup at Harper.

Harper pressed her lips together as she eyed it. God only knew how filthy it was. That disgusting lizard thing might have touched it!

"I just washed it," Gede sighed with a subtle roll of her eyes. Harper did a double take. How had Gede known what she was thinking? And then she realised. Gede was her grandmother's *apprentice*, which meant she was a warlock, too. A telepathic one, obviously.

'*And no,*' Gede projected, '*I'm not here to manipulate myself into your grandmother's will. Do I look stupid enough to mess with the great Isadora DuPont?*'

'*I don't think Isadora has much for anyone to inherit, by the looks of this dump!*' Harper shot back.

"Now, now, *petite-fille*," Isadora interjected. "We're family, and family don't judge one another. We judge other people, together."

Harper's head snapped towards her. How had she heard that? She hadn't even been projecting it at her!

"You have a lot to learn, *ma chérie*. I'd like to step up and do what your *décevante* mother failed to do. I want to teach you our ways. I believe you can restore our family name, Harper. You are a true DuPont, through and through!"

Isadora waved her hand then, and just like that, the room transformed around them. Harper's mouth dropped open. Where there had once been damage and disrepair was now opulence and glamour. Decorated in pastel silks and velvets, the furnishings were rich, luxurious and beautifully maintained. Gilded mouldings and Swarovski crystals accented the room so it glimmered where the light hit.

Isadora waved her hand again, and a fire roared to life in the hearth.

"B-but... why?" Harper stammered.

"I do not like to draw attention. No one pays any notice to a ramshackle *maison* occupied by a reclusive old hermit."

Harper smiled. That was certainly one way to maintain privacy! She liked Isadora's style.

When she left later that afternoon, she wandered slowly through the old house, admiring its beauty. She stepped outside and gasped. The exterior was now just as beautiful as the inside, the immaculate lawn edged by rose bushes in shades of blush and champagne, a pond adrift with water lilies and swans at its centre.

Isadora swiftly became a big part of Harper's life. She started visiting her grandmother every week, and found she spent just as much time with Gede as with Isadora.

"What did Isadora mean the other day?" she asked Gede one afternoon after Isadora had retired to her room for a nap. "When she said I could restore our family name?"

"You realise your grandmother's a really big deal in the wiccan community, right?" Gede said, stroking Mortimer's horrid little head and feeding him a blueberry. "She was formidable. Until the... the incident."

Harper scowled at the lizard on Gede's lap. It was utterly feral. "Incident?"

Gede hesitated, frowning. "It's Madame DuPont's story to tell."

Harper didn't like many people, but she actually kind of liked Gede. The two of them even started spending time together outside of Isadora's home. "I want you to meet a friend of mine," Gede told her one evening when they were heading out for a drink together. "I've invited him along tonight."

They met Philip at a bar in Newtown. If ever there was a living breathing example of non-conformity, Philip was it. A great mountain of a behemoth, Philip wasn't one to follow the rules of his fellow man. Harper was actually embarrassed to be seen with him in public; he *so* wasn't good for her image. He barely looked human. Philip had shaved every strand of hair from his head to best show off the assault of tattoos covering his scalp and face – even the whites of his eyes had been inked black. He'd had two small horns implanted in the top of his forehead, and his tongue had been sliced in two lengthways so it was forked, causing him to lisp when he spoke. Spacers stretched his earlobes out so they hung halfway to his shoulders, and piercings filled his nose, chin and ebony-tattooed-lips. In fact, Harper could see glimpses of tattoos on every imaginable inch of flabby pale skin on his great hulking body.

He was truly revolting.

She said as much to Gede, who laughed and told Harper to trust her. So they'd hung out a couple more times, and Harper had gotten to know him. An amateur magician with a penchant for pyromania, most of the tricks Philip performed for the girls involved flames and setting things on fire, even his pet pigeon (which may or may not have been an accident but was funny as hell either way).

Philip was telepathic and telekinetic, meaning not only could he read minds, but like her, could move things with a single thought.

The thing Harper found curious about Philip was the fact that no matter how hard she tried, she found it impossible to get inside his head, even for a second. Thanks to Oncle Olivier, she of course knew how to shroud her mind, but only in response to intrusion, not as a constant defence. The funny thing was, when she wasn't around Philip, she practically forgot his existence until Gede mentioned him. It was like when he wasn't with her, he ceased to exist.

One day, about a month after she'd first met him, they were sitting on the couch in Gede's apartment, Philip playing with the flame of the candle in front of him, telekinetically shifting it from the wick to his palm and then back again. Harper sat beside him, trying desperately to tune into his thoughts, when he sneered at her. "Don't ssstrain yoursssself there, darlin', it'sss not gonna happen."

Gede laughed and Harper felt her face flush. Fuming, she quickly got up and left the room.

"I guess I should go soon," she said to Gede when she returned a few minutes later, a glass of sauvignon blanc in her hand. "You're getting your slut on again tonight with that grungy loser from HMV, right?" Instead of laughing, Gede turned red, her nostrils flaring as she glared at Harper.

Harper frowned.

And then she heard cackling laughter and jumped as Philip suddenly appeared beside Gede on the couch. "I hope you're at leassst getting sssome free CDsss out of it!"

Harper's mouth dropped open. She'd totally forgotten he was there. "How did you *do* that?"

"What, you've never heard of dome ssshrouding?" He yawned.

She wrinkled her nose and cocked her head.

"I'm a master of energetic camouflage, ssssweetheart. I have full control over the flow of information in and out of my biofield – and I can make my biofield pretty damned big when I want to."

"How big?"

"I can ssshield pretty much anyone or anything under the cover of my ssshroud."

As he explained his gift, she saw it in her mind's eye, a giant bubble of concealment hiding all he encompassed, to the point people actually forgot about his existence... all people except other witches and warlocks, unless they were actively thinking about him. It was then and there that Harper understood that Gede was right: Philip was the sort of person who could come in very handy. Very handy indeed.

Harper continued to visit Isadora's every week, where she was regaled with tales of the good old days, tales of how powerful Isadora had once been... Before.

"Before what?" Harper constantly asked.

"Before the incident that saw me shunned from both my family and the larger wiccan community," was all Isadora would say. "When you are ready to do what I could not, only then shall I tell you of it."

Isadora encouraged Harper and Gede to form a coven of their own – with Harper as High Priestess, of course. They invited Philip to join, and while he was certainly powerful enough to challenge her for the position of High Priest, he allowed Harper to lead them as he couldn't be bothered with the responsibility or politics that came with the title. Gede took the position of Harper's deputy, known in the world of craft as her Maiden.

They took craft names and only referred to each other in this way. Harper became Reinenoir, Gede became Orwen, and Philip was henceforth known as Artax.

It wasn't hard to find initiates. Reinenoir had her ways. But, as always, she was very picky about who was acceptable. After undergoing a rigorous screening process, each potential member had to undertake an initiation rite of passage, because this was the way it was done in Isadora's day. Initiates were made to ingest a potion of the psychedelic mushroom *psilocybe cubensis* and sent out on a nocturnal vigil into the bush. Those who returned from their Night of the Shrooms unscathed were considered worthy of the coven.

Isadora told them about the abandoned tunnels beneath Manly's North Head, and this was where they established their covenstead. Built by the government during World War II, the network of underground tunnels was originally dug to transport ammunition and was now largely forgotten... especially with Artax around to use his shroud to erase it from memory. There were shell rooms and engine rooms and even a hospital dormitory down there, which was a great hidden resource for the coven to have at their disposal.

Before long they'd found their full complement of thirteen members, each contributing their own gifts: from telepathy to precognition; telekinesis to psychokinesis; herbalism to astrology; empathy to healing. Reinenoir didn't stop there, quickly adding twenty-six more. But, most importantly, all thirty-nine members of her coven pledged to practice the dark arts and wholeheartedly shirked the bullshit premise of love and light and the greater good.

They summoned the discarnate for their own benefit, cursed those who crossed them... but at Isadora's urging, their most prevalent goal was to collect the life-force of others. They targeted those whose biofields were light and bright and full of delicious nutritious goodness. They found that those who were unaware of the power of their own energy were the easiest to steal from.

Although the accident with Oncle Olivier back when she was seven was but a vague memory, it had taught Reinenoir what happened when she went too far. So they just took a bit at a time, skimming a little off the top of this person's field and a little off the top of that person's. But, as the years went on, they grew greedy and careless, governed neither by the rules of man nor the universe. They began attacking the lightest and brightest they could find, feasting off their biofields like vampires, taking all their energy at once like she had with Oncle Olivier, leaving them with nothing. Because now, her coven was untouchable.

It was the greatest rush known to man. They hunted in small groups all over Australia and the world, never taking from the same place twice.

Isadora helped Reinenoir master the art of collecting, explaining that when the energy of the wiccan was stolen, their higher senses came along with it. Reinenoir then taught Artax and Orwen, and eventually the rest of the coven. They targeted powerful witches and warlocks, collecting their powers, adding them to their own, starting with those who'd applied to the coven, but hadn't made the cut. Reinenoir always fed first, allowing Artax and Orwen to go next, leaving the others to nibble on the carcasses of their cast-offs. Soon she was so powerful no one was willing or able to challenge her.

She was unstoppable.

Even Artax and Orwen feared her now.

That was when her grandmother sat her down and finally told her of the incident, told her what she'd attempted and failed, told Reinenoir it was up to her to restore their family name, to avenge Isadora's failure...

But before Reinenoir could, Indigo Wolfe returned to her life, upending her world in more ways than one.

Isadora told her she had to get rid of him, that if she didn't, he had the ability to destroy everything they'd worked for... But the moment she'd laid eyes on him again in the flesh, she'd known there was no way she was sticking to that plan.

She wanted him. Not just his power.

Him *and* his power.

Together, they'd be unstoppable. She'd seen how powerful he was, and she knew all of it was inherent, none of his gifts collected like so many of hers.

With him by her side, she'd be able to do what Isadora had tried and failed to do, she'd be able to do what Isadora had lost all her standing failing to do: Reinenoir would finally be able to challenge the Witch Queen for her crown.

And Indigo? He would be her king.

She'd asked him to join her. But he'd thrown a spanner in the works when he refused. He was so brainwashed by Diego 'Raf' Rafael and his Akasha tribe he hadn't even stopped to consider what she was offering. So, she'd given him a taste of what she was capable of and then left him to think on it.

Sure, Isadora didn't believe their world could be restored unless Indigo was out of the picture, but Reinenoir had a theory that turning him might just do the trick. And she was willing to risk it all on her hunch.

So she'd decided to give Indigo a little time and then she'd ask again. She could be very persuasive when she wanted to be, very persuasive indeed. Just like Oncle Olivier had learned, she always got what she wanted… in the end.

And she wanted Indigo.

And she wanted the throne.

And if he still wouldn't turn? If his ridiculous morals outweighed his will to live? Then, well, maybe collecting his power would be enough to fill the hole he'd left in her life, to give her back that feeling she'd been missing for so many years now… To give her the power she needed to rule the world.

Either way, she was soon to find out.

it ain't over 'til it's over

sydney, new south wales, november 1995

cordelia

Cordelia rummaged through her cesspit of a purse, mild panic rising inside her. Lip gloss, hairbrush, pen, pen, scrunchie, pen, lip balm, lip gloss, sunnies, pen, Rescue Remedy, apple, hair tie... She exhaled with relief as her fingers brushed paper.

She grasped it, yanked it out, and held it up in triumph... Short-lived triumph, because it wasn't her plane ticket. It was the drawing her baby brother, Matty, had pressed into her hands earlier that day between bouts of wrapping his small body around her leg, begging her not to leave him.

"Matty really didn't want us to go this morning, hey?" Robbie said from the backseat of the car.

"He certainly did not. But, unfortunately in life, people leave." Cordelia shrugged. "In fact sometimes they leave, they wait two years for you to move on, and then they come back to declare their undying love for you and turn your world upside down."

She saw her dad and Robbie exchange glances in the rear-view mirror.

"That's... oddly specific," Robbie commented at the same time as Dad said, "So we're allowed to talk about Indigo now?"

Robbie leant into Dad's ear. "I wouldn't risk it," he stage-whispered.

Cordelia set her jaw.

Indigo.

With the mention of his name, his image swam in her mind, tall, bronzed and golden blond. She squeezed her lids shut, but that beautiful, chiselled face of his tormented her, was burned on her brain. Her hands balled into fists as she thought of his eyes... Those captivating eyes, soft hazel flecked with luminous gold and green, eyes that had a way of seeing into her so deeply. Every time she thought of the kiss they'd shared a mere forty-eight hours ago, goosebumps scattered across her skin, only to be smoothed away by a swell of all-consuming, churning guilt.

Cordelia refolded Matty's drawing and clamped it between her teeth, as much for safekeeping as to save Robbie from a snarky retort. She dove back into her purse. At the very bottom of her bag, she finally located her crumpled ticket. Extracting the drawing from her mouth, she declared, "Got it!"

"Thank goodness." Dad smiled as he turned the car into the entrance of the airport. "Now, do you have everything else you need?"

"Uh-huh." She carefully slid the ticket into the inside pocket of her bag. "Hey, check this out," she said, unfolding Matty's crude colourful sketch. "Have you ever seen anything cuter?"

Robbie leant forward and snatched it from her hand. "Is this *us*?" he asked, rotating it from side to side, screwing up his nose.

Cordelia nodded and laughed.

He turned the drawing around, then pointed to the extra-tall, extra-skinny figure with a scrawl of dark hair. "It's like looking into a mirror," he deadpanned. "So who's that then?" He pointed to a shorter figure in the middle. Matty had ringed it with a scribbly black circle dotted with white.

"That's apparently Dad," she said with a wry smile.

Their father glanced at the picture and furrowed his brow. "I won't even ask why I'm trapped inside a black bubble."

Cordelia shrugged.

"Those two with the long yellow hair are obviously you and Mum... Oooh, and which of Matty's freaky imaginary friends do we have here?" Robbie asked, pointing to a figure in the background.

"I'm told that's a Care Bear," Cordelia informed him.

"Ah yes, a Care Bear, of course," Robbie said. "Matty seriously needs to work on his bear drawing skills, because his Care Bears never look anything like bears. I mean, this one's sporting what appear to be fuck-me-boots."

"Give him a break, he's *three*." Cordelia snatched back the picture and refolded it. She slipped it back into her purse, then turned to her father. "We're meeting the others inside so you can just drop us off up here, thanks, Dad," she said, pointing to the curb outside the Ansett domestic terminal.

He manoeuvred the car to the side of the road, shifting it into park. Robbie was out in a flash, grabbing their bags from the boot. Dad eased himself gingerly from the car, heading round to help him.

"Are you sure you're ok, Daddy?" Cordelia asked, teeth pincering her lower lip as she eyed him up and down. He'd lost weight recently and he looked almost… frail. He was pale, and he wasn't his usual jovial self. The two of them had this thing going lately where she constantly asked him if he was ok, and he constantly reassured her everything was fine.

He enfolded her in his arms and rocked her tenderly. "Stop worrying, my sweet girl. You and Rob have worked so hard this year, and I'm so very proud of you both. You deserve a week of fun." He kissed her forehead and squeezed her tight. "Just be careful, ok? Look out for one another." He looked pointedly at Robbie.

"Always," Robbie promised.

Robbie slung a bag over each shoulder and moved to embrace Dad, who kissed him on the cheek and hugged him hard. "You've got your medication?"

"Yes, Daddy dearest, and the bracelet Mum got me," he said, holding up his wrist to show him the motion-sickness band.

"You coming?" Robbie grabbed Cordelia's wheelie bag and started towards the terminal. "Let's get this flight over and done with, yeah?"

She glanced at her father one last time. "Promise me you'll get some rest, that you'll take care of yourself?" She reached for his hand.

He gripped hers tightly. "I promise," he said hoarsely.

She drew his hand to her lips and kissed it, then smiled brightly at him. "Love you."

"Love you, too," he replied, but his voice wavered and she swore his eyes were glistening. It was hard for him, she guessed, seeing the twins he'd raised since they were seven all grown up and easing slowly from the nest. She knew he was under a lot of stress at the moment, too. He was a doctor at the local hospital in Manly, and one of his dearest friends and colleagues, Essie Matthews, had recently been found unconscious on hospital grounds. She was yet to come out of her coma. And now he had other patients presenting with the same symptoms, all barely clinging to life, all impossible to revive from their comatose state.

Cordelia flashed him one last smile, then went to join Robbie, who was searching for their check-in counter. The twins had been looking forward to Schoolies Week for years. A week of pure debauchery, it was a rite of passage for every Year Twelve student post-final exams, heading en masse to Surfers Paradise, *the* destination of choice for seven days straight of partying.

"There's Peyton!" Robbie cried, pointing to the redhead in a bright green sundress struggling into the airport with two enormous bags. Cordelia went to help her, hugging her tight, then taking a bag from her shoulder.

"Sure you've got enough stuff, Peyts?" she asked, raising an eyebrow at her oldest friend. Peyton and Cordelia had met their very first day of primary school, when Cordelia had been sitting alone in the playground trying not to cry because she'd been told off for forgetting her hat. Peyton, a firecracker of a girl with untamed curls and a gigantic smile, had plopped her hat on Cordelia's head and then told her a joke about a know-it-all parrot belonging to a magician aboard the Titanic.

"It takes a lot more fabric to swathe these dangerous curves than it does yours, Cee," Peyton laughed, her voice deep and throaty as she looked Cordelia up and down, taking in her slinky, bronze slip dress, her platform slides, her long hair caught up in a high ponytail. Peyton linked her arm through Cordelia's and tugged her wheelie bag towards the check-in counter where Robbie was waiting in line.

"Oh my God, Peyts, I thought I was bad, but you've certainly outdone me in the luggage department," Robbie said.

"Yeah, and he has an extra bag just for his hair products," Cordelia added, playfully pinching his cheek. Robbie stuck his tongue out at her, his hand automatically moving to his dark hair, blow-dried and gelled to perfection. "Where're Sian and Will?" Cordelia asked, craning her neck towards the entrance.

"Oh, they're coming. Shi's dad was giving them a stern lecture about teen pregnancy and the dangers of narcotics, so I made myself scarce." She grimaced.

"Ew," Robbie said, screwing his nose up. "Poor Will, Mr Roberts would be the father-in-law from hell." He shuddered. Sian's parents had met when her father was transferred to run the Hong Kong branch of his office. Her Chinese mother had been assigned as his secretary. They'd hit it off, married, and adopted Sian's big sister Zara from China and Sian from Australia. Soon after, her mum had fallen pregnant with their little sister, Aubrey. Unlike Zara, Sian wasn't sure of her lineage. With dead straight jet-black hair and dark eyes, her fine features were a striking mix of Asian and, they guessed, European.

It felt like fate had intervened in the form of their Year Three teacher, Miss Day, when Sian moved to Sydney from Hong Kong and was assigned the seat next to Cordelia's in class. Their connection had been instant, and Cordelia, Sian and Peyton had been inseparable ever since.

"Here they come now," Peyton grinned. Sian was red-faced and flustered in a blue babydoll dress and matching Alice band. She was tugging Will behind her through the crowd. He was staring straight ahead with an expression that suggested dazed bewilderment, with a possible touch of violation.

"Fun chat?" Robbie asked Will as they shook hands.

"He told me if I so much as touched his daughter he'd drive me out to the Belanglo State Forest and make me wish I'd accepted a lift from Ivan Milat instead," Will mumbled, his brown eyes wide. Mr Roberts was arguably as scary as the notorious backpacker serial killer.

"Seriously?" Robbie replied. "He's warning you off touching her *now*? You two have been dating since Year Seven, I think the ship containing Shi's carnal treasure has long since sailed off into the sunset."

"Yeah," Will said, wide-eyed, "and I'm shit-scared he's gonna figure that out."

"Oh my God," Sian whispered to Cordelia. "I am *mortified!* I seriously hate my dad. He's like, *so* embarrassing!"

Cordelia hugged her tight, rubbing her back. "It's ok," she whispered back. "Surely Will's used to him by now."

"Drew still AWOL, Cee?" Will asked, leaning to give her a peck on the cheek. She looked up at him, sandy-haired and stocky, and nodded. Drew and Will had played in the same footy team until Drew had wrecked his knee last year, ending his rugby career.

The others moved forward in the line and she and Sian hung back. "Have you seriously still not heard from him?" Sian asked quietly as they reached the front of the queue. "Is he still meeting us in Surfers?"

Cordelia sagged and shrugged. She hadn't spoken to Drew in two weeks, since their big fight, when she'd told him they needed a break from one another. He'd been road-tripping up the coast with some of his uni mates and had originally arranged to meet Cordelia in Queensland for Schoolies.

She felt sick at the thought of their fight. At the thought of how things were between them. At the thought of what had happened between her and Indigo a couple of days ago...

Indigo, it seemed, was never far from her mind these days. As always, her stomach lurched at the very thought of him, heat rapidly spreading through her body.

Indigo had been everything to her for so long... And then Drew had come into her life. She found it hard to comprehend that someone could go from being your all-consuming everything, to nothing.

Well, not nothing.

Indigo could never be nothing.

"You ok?" Sian asked, squeezing her arm. She was peering intently at her. "We're all checked in. The others are headed to security." Cordelia nodded as Sian linked her arm through hers. They dawdled after their friends. "You worried about Drew?"

Cordelia nodded reluctantly.

"He doesn't know Indigo's back?"

"Nope," Cordelia said.

"You think he's like, gonna freak?"

"Shi," Cordelia sighed, finger twisting through the ends of the ponytail that hung over her shoulder in loose waves, gold and treacle-blonde, "I don't even know if he's gonna show."

"Do you want him to?" Sian asked with a pointed eyebrow raise.

"O-of course I do! I *miss* him. I hate fighting with him." Her face crumpled. "I was SO pissed off at him when we had it out the other day. I told him not to bother coming, that I needed space. I said we should take a break. He probably thinks we're over. I mean, he hasn't called in two weeks. And… it's not as though things have been amazing between us lately," she admitted in a small voice.

After the accident last year on the rugby field that had destroyed Drew's knee, he'd finally been getting back on track when he'd reinjured it skiing. His pain and suffering had been all-consuming and his method of managing his agony had somewhat divided him and Cordelia. Drew's best friend these days was Sandy Whitcomb, school-mate-turned-dealer, and the source of Drew's pain management.

Peyton hustled back to see what the hold up was. "What're we talking about?" she asked, leaning in conspiratorially.

"Inds and Drew," Sian told her, before turning back to Cordelia. "Do you want to work things out with Drew?" she probed as they placed their purses on the security conveyer belt. "Like, even now Inds is back?"

"I told Indigo I was with Drew, that I'd chosen Drew," Cordelia replied evenly. "Drew's been there for me these past couple of years. Indigo has not. Two-and-a-half-years-ago, Indigo told me he loved me then completely abandoned me." She exhaled heavily. "How can I ever trust him again?"

Peyton eyed her. "To play devil's advocate, Indigo hasn't exactly had the best time of it these past couple of years. I'm not sure it's fair to condemn his behaviour, given what he nearly did to himself."

Cordelia felt tears spring to her eyes. She quickly blinked them away. It still hurt her heart to think of the depression that had led Indigo to attempt to take his own life. It triggered a range of emotions in her, from all-encompassing fury he hadn't turned to her for help, to desolate sadness that the blackness had consumed him so completely, he'd felt he had no choice but to throw himself off a bridge.

"I know that, Peyts," she whispered. "I know that better than *anyone*. And I have so much respect and admiration for all the hard work he's put in to make himself well. But him coming back now, telling me he loves me, well, it's too little, too late." She walked through the metal detector then grabbed her purse, waiting for her friends to follow. "I had to move on with my life, you know that as well as anyone," she said as they joined her. She'd had to move on with her life because waiting for him had been killing her. "Drew and I have built something together and I'm not just going to throw that away for some rogue romantic notion of what Indigo and I could have been." They wandered through the terminal in search of their gate.

"As long as you're not cutting off your nose to spite your face," Peyton said, exchanging a look with Sian.

"What's that supposed to mean?' Cordelia asked, stopping dead. The girls turned to face her.

"All we're saying is, that, well, you've got such a good heart, Cee, and you're always putting others first. And w-we love that about you," Sian stammered as Peyton nodded vigorously. "But in this situation, well, like, sometimes what's *right* for us isn't the choice that's... umm... like, *morally* correct." She put her hand on Cordelia's arm, peering into her face. "Do you get what I'm saying?"

"Doing what you think is right now may not be what's right for anybody in the long run," Peyton reiterated.

Cordelia lowered her eyes to the ground. "Guys, please don't. Right now I just need you to tell me I made the right choice and support me."

Peyton sighed heavily. "Babe, of course, we're your gals, always." She moved in to draw Cordelia into a hug. Sian leant in and wrapped her arms around the two of them. "Chicks before dicks forever, right?"

"*Today*, people!" Robbie called out from where he and Will were waiting in front of a news stand. "They're about to start boarding us." He brandished a freshly purchased *TV Hits* magazine in her direction. Luke Perry brooded from the front cover in his signature James Dean kinda way.

"For someone who hates flying, you're certainly keen to get on that plane," Cordelia said as she gave her besties a final squeeze then disentangled herself from the group hug.

"The sooner we get on, the sooner we get off," he sniped, stuffing the magazine in his bag and wrinkling his delicate nose. A man walked by with a bag of McDonalds, the scent of rancid oil drenching the air in his wake. Robbie blanched and paled. "Oh my God," he muttered, fanning the air in front of his face. "I'm gonna hurl." He looked around for somewhere to sit, beelining for a bank of plastic chairs and dropping into the nearest one, putting his head between his knees.

"Maybe if you ate something, it would settle your stomach," Cordelia suggested, sitting beside him and rubbing his back. "I can go get you some crackers or something?" Robbie refused to eat before he flew, claiming that if his stomach was empty, he'd have nothing to bring up when his tummy inevitably started heaving mid-flight.

"Don't even talk about food," he said through clenched teeth.

"Oh no, not again," Peyton said, coming over and crouching down in front of him. "You ok, Robster?"

He shook his head.

"I love you, mate, but seriously, you are the only person I've ever met who gets air sick *before* getting on a plane! You're such a drama queen!" She laughed.

"I'm glad my idiosyncrasies entertain you so," he mumbled.

"I'll go get you some water," she said, standing up and disappearing into the crowd.

Their flight was announced and Cordelia hauled her brother to his feet. "It's only an hour flight. You've managed to survive flying as far as New York and London. Suck it up, baby bro," she said lovingly.

"Yeah but that's because I was flying with my own personal pharmacist – Dad."

"He gave you those pills. Where are they?"

Robbie fished around in his pocket and came up with a blister pack containing a couple of motion sickness tablets. He handed them to Cordelia who popped one out and handed it to him. Peyton returned with a bottle of water and Robbie took an unenthusiastic sip to wash the pill down, then promptly gagged.

He spent the whole flight staring straight ahead gripping the armrests tightly. He wouldn't talk or engage in any way, so Cordelia tried to read. But her mind kept turning to Drew and what the girls had said. She hadn't been able to concentrate on even one of Ken Follet's beautifully written words, so she'd ended up listening to a mix tape on her new Walkman, gazing listlessly out the window at the streaky clouds below.

Drew was the epitome of tall, dark and ruggedly handsome, with his sky-blue eyes, an adorable dimple that deepened when he smiled and his slightly crooked nose (a football injury Peyton had always claimed was sexy, a sentiment Cordelia had grown to agree with). He'd been Indigo's best mate once upon a time. After Indigo had moved to New York, he and Cordelia had bonded over their shared absence of him in their lives.

Cordelia had found Drew's quirkiness refreshing. He'd been captain of North Head Grammar's Firsts rugby team until his accident, yet he was a mad keen conspiracy geek. He'd distracted her from her worries and hurt with notions such as the human race was descended from aliens, that the US government knew about Pearl Harbour and allowed it to happen to justify their entry into World War II, and that the insecticide DDT was the actual cause of the polio epidemic.

She adored the unique way Drew saw the world, his open mind, and his passion for speaking up for what he believed in. He didn't care who thought he was nuts. She didn't always agree with him, but she respected that he looked outside the square and did his own research. He never blindly believed what he was told. And their conversations were never dull.

But ever since his accident, he'd changed. He'd lost some of that fire. He'd been consumed by his pain, and he'd been relying on speed to study and weed to sleep.

A couple of months ago, she'd arrived at his house to find him sitting in front of the TV, frozen solid and white as a ghost. When she'd asked him what was wrong, his whole body had sagged and he'd promptly dissolved into tears. When she'd finally calmed him down, she'd managed to figure out the problem: he was so stoned he'd accidentally just watched an entire movie on mute and had thought he'd gone deaf until the moment he'd heard her speak.

After that incident, she'd begged him to lay off the drugs, to find another way to manage his pain, but he'd been lukewarm on that idea at best. She heard herself nagging at him, and she hated herself for it. She'd never wanted to be *that* girlfriend.

And then she'd been consumed with her HSC exams and he with his first year Medicine exams, and they hadn't been able to see each other as much as they would have liked. He'd promised her things would be different over the summer, that they'd make up for lost time… But the day after his final exam he'd jumped in a car with his mates and taken off up the coast without a second thought. He hadn't cared that she was in the midst of the most important exams of her life and might have been counting on his moral support. He hadn't cared that they'd be apart. They'd had a colossal fight and hadn't spoken since.

But before all that, they'd had grand plans to spend this week in Queensland together. He'd booked them a room at a nice hotel, she knew that. But now she had a sinking feeling he wouldn't show and she'd end up bunking in with Peyton at the seedy Chateau Beachside.

When they touched down on the Gold Coast, she took Robbie's elbow and hauled him up. He looked peaked at best. She was so busy trying to convince him to eat something before they caught a cab to Surfers Paradise that at first she didn't see the boy standing at their gate, an enormous bunch of sunflowers clutched in his arms, his features etched with sheepish hope. But she heard her name – "Cee?" – and she turned at the familiarity of his voice, unclasping Robbie's elbow, her hands moving to cover her mouth as a lump formed in her throat.

"You came," she whispered, a smile blooming on her lips as she walked slowly towards him. He was a sight for sore eyes in baggy denim shorts and a faded black T-shirt that stated: The Truth Is Out There.

"Of course I did." His lips turned up shyly, that bloody dimple popping as he gazed at her, his eyes soft with emotion. "I love you, Cee." He shrugged. "I've thought of nothing but you these past two weeks."

"I love you, too," she murmured, allowing him to draw her into his arms. She rested her head on his chest, closing her eyes as she inhaled the musky scent of his aftershave.

"I'm sorry," he breathed into her hair. "I hate fighting with you, Cee, I've been feeling bloody sick to my stomach about it. You'll always be number one on my list of priorities, and I'm sorry if I made you feel like you weren't. What can I say? I'm an unevolved troglodyte." He pulled back so he could look into her face, his expression drawn with hope.

"I'm sorry, too. I overreacted."

"When you broke up with me?" he said, his eyes searching hers, and she could tell he was only half-joking.

Her tummy lurched and she nodded tersely. Because she hadn't wanted to break up with him, of course she hadn't. She'd just been so angry and frustrated and she hadn't known how else to express that.

"So we can go back to the way things were?"

She hesitated, thinking of what she'd done, how she'd kissed Indigo.

And damn, it had been some *kiss*.

Technically, she and Drew had been on a break. *Technically.* But she still knew it was a massive betrayal and he'd be crushed if she told him. The last thing she wanted was to hurt him, yet her guilt pulsed heavy in her mind.

Only she and Indigo knew what had transpired between them in his car that day – she hadn't even told the girls that part – and she knew Indigo wouldn't tell anyone. She pushed it from her mind as Drew leant in close and, as his lips brushed hers, warm and familiar, she melted into him, allowed herself to be swept away by the very nearness of him.

I'm a bad person, she thought. But she pushed that thought away, too.

chapter two

born to be my baby

manly, new south wales

indigo

Indigo gunned his motorcycle down Eastern Hill into Manly, the azure sea sparkling below in the spring sunshine. The sight of the red and yellow flags speared into the white sand by the lifeguards brought a smile to his face. He loved his hometown. Being back by the ocean invigorated him.

It made him happy.

And he needed to feel happy.

Three days ago, he'd told Cordelia he loved her and asked her for another chance. And for a moment there he'd thought she might feel the same way, that he was her world the way she was his. But it had only been a moment. A fleeting moment of unadulterated bliss, of a happiness so pure and all-consuming he was sure it could have lit the world's darkness, if only he'd been able to capture its luminescence.

But then it was gone, had slipped through his fingers, as had she. He'd stuffed up. He'd wrecked things between them, decimated them so spectacularly, that it really came as no surprise she wanted nothing to do with him.

Cordelia. The girl with the coral-sea eyes. The girl with the golden tiger's-eye hair. The girl who was the other half of him. If he knew anything, it was that he loved her beyond compare.

He frowned as he rode past the beach, remembering how poorly he'd treated her, how he'd cut her out of his life and hurt her. Back then, he'd believed it was for her own good, that he was toxic, broken, no good for her. But now, things were different. He'd spent the last couple of years slowly putting himself back together, growing strong and whole. Now, he knew himself, he knew his place in the world, he knew who he was.

He knew *what* he was.

If someone had told him three years ago that he was kind of a… *witch*, he would have backed slowly away from them, careful not to make any sudden moves. But now he knew better. And these days nothing much surprised him.

He'd been born different to most people. He possessed higher senses – psychic powers – that made him special: telepathy, clairvoyance, empathy and psychokinesis. Back then, before he'd learnt how to manage them, before he'd understood them, those higher senses, they'd almost killed him. They'd pushed him over the edge, quite literally. He'd been completely out of control until he'd found his soul family in Sedona, kin who'd taken him under their wing and taught him how to handle his abilities, enhancing and strengthening them.

Sasha was a bilocater; Nash, a psychokinetic pre-cog; Aurora was a telekinetic walk-in; Dawn, an empathic healer; and Raf… well, Indigo didn't have a label for what Raf was. His new family were fellow Warriors of the Akasha, an elite group of witches charged as guardians of mankind. Apparently, it was their duty to leave the world in a better state than that in which they'd found it. No pressure.

He now knew he'd been born to use his higher senses to protect and heal others. Something he'd supposedly been doing lifetime after lifetime, honing his skill with each incarnation.

It scared him, how lost and out of control he'd been before Sedona, seeing and hearing and *feeling* so many things that made him feel crazy, and made him feel scared, and filled him with a desolate melancholy he thought he'd never survive.

He sped past Queenscliff Beach and up over the hill, heading towards Harbord, towards the house that had once been a home to him, the house where he'd been part of a real family for the first time in his life.

The Carlisle home.

The home where Joshua and Scarlett and Matty and Robbie and Cordelia had welcomed him into their fold and accepted him as one of them. The home where he'd felt true happiness, back then such a foreign sensation. And he'd never wanted it to end.

But it had. It had come to a screeching halt, with his warring, movie-star parents using him as a pawn once more. And that's how he'd ended up in New York. His father had demanded Indigo be sent to live with him in an attempt to repair his reputation as a shithouse father. That had been a turning point in Indigo's life. Because it had all spiralled from there.

Before he'd met the Carlisles, he'd assumed he was destined to battle through life on his own. Which was fine by him: if he wasn't needed, then there was no one to need back. Simple. Except for the constant drumbeat, the inherent, desperate need to *belong* somewhere. And he'd found that somewhere to belong with them.

In fact, he'd wanted so bad to belong that he kept his feelings for Cordelia to himself, feelings that consumed him and burnt his insides to ash, feelings that had finally bubbled over the night he'd left Sydney back in 1993. The memory of her lips on his was imprinted there permanently. That night, he'd kissed Cordelia for the very first time and finally confessed his love for her, as he'd slipped the bracelet that had been a permanent fixture on his arm, black leather beaded with obsidian and tourmaline, from his wrist to hers. He'd worn that bracelet so long, he'd felt naked without it in the days and weeks that followed.

But not as naked and exposed and rudderless as he'd felt without her. Her warmth and support and gentle presence was something he'd come to rely on, depend upon even.

Once he'd arrived in Manhattan, he'd plummeted so far so fast, living with his father who despised him, feeling so lonely and alone. His higher senses had spiralled completely out of control. He was utterly consumed by the thoughts and feelings and excruciating agony of a city of souls in pain. And he was plagued by discarnates, day and night. That compounded with feeling so incredibly unloved, so utterly hopeless, meant he'd plunged into a deep, dark state of depression. A black void, that in the end, he could see only one way out of.

And he'd taken it.

Well, he'd tried to take it.

When he looked back on that time, it was like he was looking at someone else, watching it all on a movie screen. He barely recognised that boy now, so lost and damaged and desperate and consumed by shadow.

The Carlisles had flown all the way to New York for him, turning up at the facility he'd been admitted to after his failed suicide attempt. He regretted refusing to see them more than anything. His shame had been so great back then, his self-worth so low, the thought of facing them had undone him all over again. He still remembered Cordelia's beautiful face outside that hospital in upstate New York after he'd had them turned away, tear-stained, lip trembling, as she'd slipped his bracelet from her wrist and discarded it in the snow.

He pulled up at the curb and gazed solemnly at the two-storey, soft grey weatherboard. He had such fond memories of the cosy Carlisle home, with its white shutters and lush garden heavy on banana palms, birds-of-paradise, and pandanus trees. He climbed off his bike, running his palm through his hair, now so long it almost touched his shoulders. It was parted messily, and blonder than it had ever been, thanks to the harsh Arizona sun.

Frowning, he jiggled his keys in his hand as he pep-talked himself into approaching the house. It wasn't as though he hadn't been here since he'd gotten back; once on the night Cordelia was attacked by warlocks, and then again when he'd dropped her home after she'd rejected him at the beach a few days back. He'd seen Robbie and Cordelia, made tentative amends with them. But he hadn't seen Scarlett and Joshua, who'd been like parents to him, or baby Matty. Although Matty wouldn't be a baby anymore. He'd be three.

Indigo took a deep breath, fingering the wolf's tooth that hung low around his neck from a fine black leather string. He fanned his snug, grey T-shirt where it had sweated to his back, then slid his keys into the pocket of his worn, black jeans as he walked slowly up the driveway. Indigo kicked his biker boots off as he reached the front door, automatically reaching to open it and just walk in as he always had. He'd already turned the knob and pushed open the door before he remembered himself, but by then it was too late so he gave a little rap on the doorframe and called out, "Hello? Anybody home?"

He heard a squeal of delight from the kitchen, and Scarlett came bursting into the foyer, forever youthful in a short, olive dress with voluminous sleeves. Her creamy blonde hair hung loose to her shoulders, and she was barefoot as always, her nails painted a glossy dark purple. A small smattering of pale freckles covered the bridge of her nose.

"Hey, Scar," he murmured as she rushed at him, throwing herself into his arms. She'd always been a vibrant force of nature. He wrapped her up in a bear hug, squeezing her tight. A smile touched his lips. She still gave the best hugs.

"We've *missed* you," she breathed, leaning back to cup his face in her hands so she could examine him closely, her clear, blue eyes filling with tears as she eyed the small scar on the left side of his forehead, a remnant of his suicide attempt. "Why did you stay away so long?" She was as lovely as ever, the mother he'd always wished had been his.

"It wasn't by choice," he assured her, as she grabbed his hand and led him into the kitchen. "Nothing's changed around here, I see," he said, glancing around. The house still smelt of the Nag Champa incense Scarlett burned night and day.

A shadow flitted across her face, so briefly he thought he'd imagined it because it was quickly usurped by that bright smile. "Sit, sit," she beckoned, her silver bracelets jangling as she pulled a chair out from the kitchen table for him. "I'll make us a cuppa and you can tell me *everything*. I've just picked some lemongrass fresh from the garden and I have some ginger here somewhere." She was rummaging through the fridge. "By the way, I have a little friend up there if you'd like to take care of him," she said, gesturing to the enormous huntsman perched above the window. "I assume you still have a way with arachnids."

Indigo stood and approached the window, reaching up to coax the spider gently into his hands. He carried it out, placing it on a branch of the gigantic banksia tree that grew just outside the back door.

He headed back inside to sit at the table, watching as she filled the kettle from the water filter and put it on to boil. "So, Cora and Pres, huh?" he ventured. He knew the topic would hang over them if he didn't put it out there straight away.

"Oh, honey, I know," Scarlett said gently, leaning over his chair to wrap her arms around him from behind, resting her cheek on the top of his head. "But if it's any consolation, he's been good for her."

Indigo made a face. "That's the shittest part, Scar, I know he's a top bloke so I can't even hate him." He laughed hollowly. He'd never bothered lying to her. Scarlett always demanded the bluntest of truths.

She plopped down beside him. "Darling, I know it's tough. But you need to understand, Cora was completely cut up after you left, Rob, too. We all were to be honest." She smiled sadly, stroking his hand.

"Don't get me wrong, I know I only have myself to blame, that I stayed away too long. I've made some pretty massive mistakes when it comes to Cora… And I'm happy she's happy, I truly am, but…" He trailed off.

"You're heartbroken," she finished for him matter-of-factly.

He shrugged in resignation and emptied his lungs long and slow, a sad smile tugging at his mouth. His mind wandered back to three days ago in his car with Cordelia, to how the butterflies that had lain dormant in the depths of his belly for so long had been resuscitated by her very nearness. She'd smelled of the sea and of the ylang ylang shampoo she'd always used, a scent that carried so many memories.

"Cordelia feels wretched about all this, too, you know." Scarlett regarded him closely. "You know how thrilled I am to see you, Inds, but you coming back and professing your love to her after all this time… Well, it's dredged up a lot of stuff I'd hoped for her sake was long buried." She gave her forehead a weary rub. "My daughter is so strong in many ways, yet so fragile in others. She cried herself to sleep in my arms the other night. It's not an easy situation for either of you, honey."

A wave of nausea washed over Indigo. "I-I don't know what to say. The last thing I ever want is for Cordelia to hurt because of me. I'm sorry, Scar."

She reached to cup his cheek. "I know, sweetie, and I know how badly you're hurting, too."

Indigo forced a weak smile. "She's the love of my life, Scar. I thought we were… *inevitable,* you know? And now, I feel like such an idiot. It's a pretty major thing to be wrong about."

Scarlett tilted her head, stared at him solemnly. "Maybe we get more than one love of our life?" she finally suggested.

He frowned, because he couldn't in all his wildest dreams imagine that to be true. Cordelia was the only girl he'd ever loved and he couldn't fathom ever feeling for anyone the way he felt for her.

But she didn't love him back. So where did that leave him?

"No?" She smiled sombrely.

He shrugged. "I'm no expert on love. Clearly. I've managed to stuff it up over and over again. I abandoned her, I hurt her… I know this is my fault, and I'll never stop being sorry for what I did to Cora… what I cost us. But deep down I'm struggling to accept the fact it's over. How can I be wrong about something that feels so right?"

"Well, maybe it's just not right for now," Scarlett ventured. "You two are both so young and there's a lot to be said for divine timing."

"You know what, Scar? Someone very wise once told me that if it's not meant to be, it's not meant to be, and it's impossible to make someone love you if they don't. She's made it very clear that she doesn't want me. She's made her choice, and it isn't me." He swallowed hard over the lump in his throat. "So I have to back off, or so I keep telling myself. I have to let things go back to the way they were before, when we were all just mates, her, me, and Rob. And Pres," he added, with a resigned twist of his mouth.

"Can you do that? Just be her friend?"

"I'm going to have to, aren't I? Because it's that or nothing, and the one thing I can't cope with is nothing. One thing being away so long made me realise is that I need to be in her life, in all your lives, any way I can get it."

Scarlett reached for his hand again. "I know it hurts now, honey, but I promise you, and I'm speaking from experience here, that time is the best healer. What feels like the end of the world today, well, you'll look back on it as a turning point in your life. And it won't always feel so red raw. I mean, it may still ache a little when it rains," she said with a smile, "but it won't be a huge gaping wound forever. And who knows what tomorrow might bring?"

He stared at a spot on the table and shrugged despondently.

"So tell me, tell me," she said brightly, knowing, as she always had, when he didn't want to talk about something anymore. "I want to hear about what you've been up to. Cora tells me you've had quite the adventure and picked up a few new skills along the way? I'm *dying* to hear how the guy who branded me a hippie and just *loved* to pay me out about my, what did you call it now? Ah yes, my 'peace, love and mungbeans' practice," she teased, "has been living in the hippie mecca of Sedona, of all places? You know I've been pestering Josh to take me there for years, right?"

"Yeah, yeah." He grinned sheepishly, holding his hands up in resignation. "I stand corrected. I am a changed man."

"Tell me?" she said, standing up and wandering to the kitchen bench where she poured water from the now-boiled kettle over the lemongrass and ginger she'd chopped up and thrown in a teapot.

If anyone would understand what he'd been through, what he now was, it was Scarlett. She was incredibly open-minded and non-judgemental. With a background in naturopathy and psychotherapy, she ran a small practice from home, and had been the first person to introduce him to the importance of eating well and approaching health holistically.

He spent the next hour giving her the abridged version of the past couple of years of his life, focusing predominantly on the healing side of things she was so interested in.

"So yeah, when I moved to Sedona I made some amazing new friends," he said wistfully, his chest aching. He *missed* them. "And I found where I fit. I guess you could say I found my calling. I love working beyond the physical, I love helping people heal, being able to look outside the square to help them get well in ways no one else has thought of or been able to access. It's a real rush." He stared at her thoughtfully as she squeezed his hand. He was sick of talking about himself. "So how is everyone? Matty? Josh?"

A shadow crept across Scarlett's face again; this time he definitely hadn't imagined it. The high energy she'd been holding the entire time he'd been there suddenly seemed to drop away, leaving her exposed. And she felt *sad* to him. Just sad. Sad to the very marrow of her bones. He could feel it all, every bit of it.

"Matty's going through a kleptomania stage," she said with a roll of her eyes, and he knew she was trying to distract him. "But only for eggs!" She forced a bright laugh. "It turns out that for months now, every time I bought eggs, he was stealing one or two and hiding them away. I only discovered this when trying to locate the source of the horrific stench in his room and I opened his bottom drawer and found his stash – one of the older ones had gone bad and broken. I don't think I'll ever get the smell out." She shuddered. "He blamed it on his imaginary friend, Roger, of course, said Roger made him do it." She flashed him an exasperated grin that didn't reach her eyes.

"What's going on, Scar?" he asked, peering at her with deep concern. She averted her gaze and jumped up to clear away their teacups, turning her back to him.

She was saved by the sound of the internal door to the garage opening. "Darling? I'm home," Joshua called. He stopped short and gasped as he entered the kitchen and locked eyes with Indigo. "And who do we have here?" He detoured past Indigo to kiss Scarlett and hand her the bunch of freesias he was carrying.

Indigo's pulse quickened as he stared at Joshua.

His stomach dropped away and his palms began to dampen.

Because he immediately saw it.

And he knew.

He knew why Scarlett was so desperately sad inside.

His heart plummeted like a stone as he stared in shock at the thin, wan version of the man he'd not seen in over two years. When Joshua moved forward and wrapped his arms around Indigo, he was bombarded with a landslide of information that caused bile to rise in his throat. He pulled out of Joshua's embrace and peered into his face, past the forced smile, to the deep-set fear in his eyes.

"Oh, *Josh*... Oh God, Josh, how did this happen... To you of all people?" He felt tears spring to his eyes.

It was bad.

It was so very, very bad.

"What are you talking about?" Joshua whispered, paling further.

"Your pancreas first... then your lungs, your liver..." Indigo paused while he continued to scan him. "And now it's in your lymph nodes, in your blood, in your *bones*?"

"Where's Matty?" Joshua said tersely to Scarlett, squirming under Indigo's intense scrutiny.

"At my parents," she said.

"You *told* him?" Joshua said, his tone tinged with betrayal.

"No one had to *tell* me anything. I can see it. Does anyone else know? Cordelia? Robbie? They sure didn't act like they knew!"

Joshua's shoulders slumped as he fumbled for a chair, sunk into it. "The twins had their HSC this year. We decided it was best to let them focus on their final exams without adding *cancer* to their worries." He smiled bitterly.

"When are you planning on telling them? You're practically skeletal! I love you, Josh, but it's pretty hard to ignore the fact you look like hell. How have they not noticed?"

"Of course they've noticed. Cordelia's been at me like a dog with a bone, telling me I need to take better care of myself. But, uh, we told them my Crohn's was flaring up," he said, reddening. Joshua had always been one of the most honest people Indigo knew; he was obviously embarrassed at having been caught out in a deception.

"Which isn't exactly a lie," Scarlett said defensively.

"It's not exactly the truth either," Indigo said, incredulous. "You need to tell them!" He sat down at the table opposite Joshua. "They have a right to know. They *need* to know." His voice cracked. From what Indigo saw, Joshua was lucky if he had a few weeks. His family needed time to prepare themselves.

Scarlett moved behind Joshua and wrapped her arms tightly around him, resting her chin on his head. Indigo could see her face was wet with tears.

"We wanted to shield them from it for as long as possible. How am I meant to tell them I'm… I'm *leaving* them?" Joshua whispered helplessly. "Matty…" His voice wavered. "He's three years old, for Christ's sake!"

"What are your specialists saying?" Indigo asked softly. "You obviously decided against chemo." Chemotherapy left a very distinct imprint on the biofield and Indigo could see Joshua's was clear of it.

"Chemotherapy isn't an option for me. I was already stage four metastatic when they found it and what I have is… it's just *so* aggressive, Inds." He cleared his throat and swallowed hard. "It's too late." He shrugged helplessly, smiling sadly. "I've been a doctor for decades, I've seen the toll chemo can take… and I made the personal decision it was best to just enjoy the time I have left for as long as I possibly can." He glanced away.

"How did you know?" he suddenly asked, looking at Indigo. "That I'm… sick?"

Indigo felt his cheeks heat. In hindsight he realised he'd grossly invaded Joshua's privacy. He needed to learn to be more tactful, to shut his senses down when he wasn't working.

"Our Inds has spent the past couple of years studying to be a healer," Scarlett said. She regarded him closely, eyes narrowed. "Although I wasn't aware that he was *that* good. How *did* you know Josh has… cancer?"

The only way through this was with complete and utter honesty. "I could see it. And when I hugged you, I could feel the sickness, so I gave you a quick body scan – and I'm sorry about that, it's still a reflex I'm not entirely in control over yet. I was able to see the cancer, where it started, where it spread to, each and every tumour…" He trailed off, gauging their reactions.

"And where exactly *are* my tumours?" Joshua asked, ever the sceptical man of science.

Indigo regarded him solemnly, chewing on the inside of his cheek. "You have three in your pancreas, two in your liver, five small ones in your right lung, one on your lower spine… and one in your brain."

"There's not one in his brain," Scarlett said as she turned to look at Joshua who averted his eyes. "Josh?"

He nodded slowly. "I… I just found out today. I was going to tell you tonight." He shoved his chair back and stood up. "I need a minute," he choked as he left the room.

Scarlett squeezed her eyes shut and shook her head back and forth, her breath rapid. "Nooo," she moaned. She jumped up and stumbled to the kitchen sink, leaning over it. Gripping the bench tightly with both hands, she gulped in big breaths of air between dry heaves. Suddenly she straightened up and spun around, staring at Indigo. She rushed to him, falling onto the seat beside his and grasping both his hands.

"*You* can help him," she cried, her eyes pleading. "If you can do all that, everything you just said, then *surely* you can heal him?"

"Oh Scar…" Indigo breathed. "I dunno."

"Please, Indigo, *please*. Can't you at least try?"

Indigo had never worked on anyone in such an advanced state of disease. And Joshua was someone he loved. The stakes were so high. If he tried and failed, how would Scarlett ever forgive him? How would Cordelia? Hope was a fragile thing. If he agreed to do this, he would give them hope. And was that the right thing to do at this stage? As far as he could see, there *was* no hope.

"He's everything to me, Inds," Scarlett sobbed. "I can't lose him, I just can't." He pulled her into his arms and held her while her body shuddered with the force of her tears. He stared solemnly into space.

After a while, she grew still, quiet, but still she clung to him like a life raft. He continued to hold her. "What I said to you before, when we were talking about Cora," she suddenly said into his shoulder. "That maybe we get more than one love of our life?" She pulled back to look at him.

He frowned, confused about the tangent she'd taken.

"When I was your age," she said, "I thought… I thought Cora and Robbie's father was my soul mate, the love of my life."

Indigo froze. He knew from Cordelia that Scarlett never spoke about her first love. The column of her throat worked and her lower lip wobbled. "But he *died*, Inds. He was so young, and we had our whole lives ahead of us, and he *died*. And it was just so… so *final*. I went through hell on so many levels. His death, it made me question my life, my faith, everything I believed in. I mean, why would the universe be so cruel as to hand me my soul mate only to snatch him away so callously? If it wasn't for the twins, I don't know how I would have gone on. And then I met Josh." Her voice broke, and a tear zigzagged down her cheek. "And that man, that wonderful, beautiful, big-hearted, amazing man… I love him with everything I am, Inds."

She grasped his hands in hers. "And surely… surely this can't happen to me *again?* I mean, life can't be this unfair, can it? It just doesn't seem possible, which is why I can't believe he's not going to survive this. I can't go through this again, Inds, I can't, I can't, I can't…" Her hands were shaking and she dissolved into great wracking sobs again. "My h-heart can't t-take it."

Joshua. The man who had always been there for him, for all of them. Who'd pulled them together and made a family from their broken pieces. Who'd sat at the head of their household, who'd invited Indigo into the fold without a second thought, and accepted him, loved him, guided and supported him, as though he were his own. The man who had flown sixteen thousand kilometres for Indigo when his own father could barely be bothered to get up out of the director's chair he now favoured.

Indigo set his mouth in a straight line, his face grim with determination. Of *course* he'd try to heal Joshua. And, of course, there had never really been any doubt that he'd do everything he could to try to save the man who was, in every way but DNA, a father to him. The responsibility sat like an anvil on his chest so he could barely breathe. Joshua leaving them, it was unfathomable. What had he been working so hard for these past months if not for this?

"Ok, Scar, I'll try," he told Scarlett, who hugged him harder and cried and laughed at the same time. She had the hope she so desperately needed. "Let Cora and Rob enjoy their holiday. That will give us a bit of time to get the lay of the land."

"Oh thank you!" she cried, kissing his cheeks. "Thank you, thank you, thank you!"

"*But,*" he continued, pulling out of her grasp, "you have to tell them the minute they get home–" she nodded vigorously "–and you have to be realistic. He's very sick, Scar, you know it would take a miracle to cure him?"

She gazed deep into his eyes. "I'm hoping that miracle is you."

chapter three

beautiful life

surfers paradise, queensland

cordelia

A waiter strutted by clad in nothing but a pair of sparkly black hotpants that left very little to the imagination. Either he was smuggling a pepper grinder, or he was genetically blessed. Robbie hailed him, standing to whisper in his ear. The waiter nodded and minced off.

"What are you up to?" Cordelia asked, raising her voice so he could hear her over the pulsing techno music.

Robbie just grinned mischievously and winked.

She burst out laughing. It was three in the morning and somehow they'd ended up in a gay bar. Well, not somehow. Robbie had bitched for three nights straight about the dire lack of prospects at the clubs they'd been frequenting, so Drew had asked around and found this place and here they were.

Sian and Peyton were dancing their hearts out on the packed dancefloor, while Will looked on from his comfortable position beside Cordelia. Drew sat on her other side, his hand resting gently on her thigh. He was deep in conversation with an immaculately made-up drag queen who clearly knew more about make-up than Cordelia ever would. He was six foot tall and portly and had flamboyantly introduced himself as Iva Wang.

"Ok, beverages!" Sandy announced, having wended his way through the crowded club to the couches they'd procured. A large tray of drinks was balanced expertly in his hands. Cordelia scowled at the sight of his scrawny physique hovering there in the smoky haze. She'd thought Robbie was making a really bad joke when he broke the news Sandy had flown up from Sydney to join them for Schoolies. She could have done without him there this week. Drew had been excited to see him, which had only irritated her more. He and Drew had been constantly back and forth to the bathroom together all night, always returning with lazy grins and dilated pupils. Apparently, Sandy didn't live by the dealer's code – "don't get high on your own supply".

As he passed around beers and cocktails, the waiter Robbie had signalled earlier returned with a bottle of tequila, lemon wedges and a salt shaker.

"Woo!" Robbie cried, punching his fist into the air and sloshing the toxically green cocktail Sandy had bought him down the front of his vest, worn open over a pin-striped shirt.

"Ugh, Rob, are you ever gonna order a new drink?" Cordelia asked, handing him a napkin whilst screwing her nose up at the artificial melon fumes radiating from his sickeningly sweet cocktail. She adjusted the black tube top she'd paired with a black sequined miniskirt, then slipped her ankle-breaking-high stilettos from her aching feet, tucking her legs beneath her.

"If Indigo Alexander Wolfe, the most persuasive person I've *ever* met, tried for years to convince me to give up my Midori and *failed*, there's no way little old you has a hope. In. Hell," Robbie slurred, booping her nose. "The Midori Splice will always and forever be my signature drink." He took a large gulp and grinned widely.

"She's right, mate," Sandy said with a grimace as Robbie placed his cocktail on the table. "That thing's totally rank! I was embarrassed to order it. And we're in a *gay* bar."

Robbie raised his palm in front of Sandy's face. "Talk to the hand, *toolie*," he said with a roll of his eyes. Cordelia snorted, because Robbie had just branded Sandy with the worst possible insult anyone could dole out this week. A toolie was any sad, sleazy loser over the age of eighteen who gatecrashed Schoolies to crack onto drunken graduates.

Sandy flipped him off, grinning broadly.

"Anyhoo," Robbie said, throwing him a mock scowl and clapping his hands together. "Tequila for everyone! Who's up for a shot?"

"Pass," Cordelia said, staring at the bottle with distaste. She was so wasted her head was spinning.

"You're too young to be this boring, babe," Sandy chastised. "When I was your age I would have chugged the whole bottle and chased it down with a bag of coke."

"You're like, a *year* older than me, Sandy," Cordelia said, fiddling with the back of one of her large silver hoop earrings.

"Yeah, a year too old to be at Schoolies, *toolie*." Robbie chuckled.

Sandy just flashed them his gummy grin. "Yo, Robster, let's do this!" he said, pulling a crumpled pack of Winnie Blues from his pocket and lighting one as Peyton and Sian returned to the couches. They were both flushed and covered in a sheen of perspiration.

"Can I bum a durry?" Robbie asked, reaching for the pack Sandy had chucked on the table. Sandy nodded and threw him the lighter.

"Tequila?" Peyton cried. "I'm totally in!"

"Woooo!" Robbie, Sian and Peyton cried in unison, punching their hands in the air. Peyton squeezed in next to Sandy as Sian plopped herself onto Will's lap, kissing him enthusiastically then snuggling into his arms.

"So pour us a drink then," Sian said to Robbie. "Where're the shot glasses?"

"*Shot glasses?*" Sandy scoffed, taking a long drag on his ciggie. "Nobody drinks tequila out of *shot glasses* at Schoolies Week!" Smoke furled from his stubby nose. He turned to Peyton, dressed in white pants and a bright red, low cut top. "Let's show 'em how it's done, babe," he said as he passed Drew his cigarette to babysit. Peyton flushed with pleasure and lay back across Sandy's lap, face up, arching her neck dramatically. It hadn't escaped Cordelia's attention how excited Peyton had been by Sandy's arrival. She'd been aware her friend had been harbouring a secret crush on someone for a while now, and it was growing more and more apparent who the object of that crush might be. If Cordelia's suspicions were correct, Peyton needed to have a good hard look at herself and her taste in men.

Sandy placed a lemon wedge between Peyton's lips, then sprinkled a line of salt along the curve of her neck. He lifted her shirt and poured a generous slurp of tequila into her bellybutton.

"Chin chin," Robbie toasted, holding up his cocktail, puffing on the cigarette Cordelia knew he'd regret in the morning. Robbie only ever smoked when he drank, yet was guaranteed to bemoan the fact it made his hangovers that much worse.

Cordelia watched as Sandy expertly licked the salt from Peyton's neck, sucked the tequila from her navel and then bit down on the lemon wedge clamped between her teeth, stripping the flesh from the rind so all that was left was a sliver of bare lemon skin between her lips.

"You're next, pookie," Sian told Will, yanking up her gold cowl-necked top and draping herself seductively across the low table in front of him, her back arched, her arms stretched up over her head.

"My my, what would Daddy Roberts say if he could see this?" Robbie quipped, shaking his head in amazement. "He'd likely dust off his shovel and his shotgun."

Will shot Robbie a narrow look, then shrugged as he grabbed Sian's hips and pulled her closer so he could sprinkle the salt up the centre of her ribcage. "What Mr Roberts doesn't know won't hurt him," he laughed as he placed a lemon wedge between Sian's teeth.

"Live fast, die young, leave a beautiful corpse!" Sandy said, holding the tequila bottle high in the air.

"Live fast, die young, leave a beautiful corpse!" they repeated, holding their glasses high.

"Chin chin, Master Banks," Robbie prompted, taking a swig of his cocktail.

Will laughed as Sandy poured tequila into Sian's navel, the liquid spilling out and gushing over her sharp hipbones. And as everyone whooped and cheered, he went for it.

Drew's new bestie, Iva Wang, convinced Cordelia to partake in the body shots and the night turned pretty loose after that. An hour later, she was sitting on the couch with Drew, his arm slung around her as he nuzzled her neck, Robbie on her other side, while they watched their friends on the dancefloor.

"What fresh hell is this?" Robbie suddenly demanded, a look of fascinated disgust wrinkling his nose as he watched Sandy and Peyton grinding against each other in time to the throbbing beat of La Bouche's *Be My Lover.* "Are they like, a *thing* now?"

"Whoa," Cordelia replied, as Peyton suddenly launched her face towards Sandy's, their lips meeting in a very wet, sloppy pash, all drunken lips and teeth and tongues. "I guess so."

Robbie stared at them, his brow furrowed, his head tilted to one side. "I can't even imagine how all *that* would work," he finally mused.

"All what?" Drew asked, leaning over Cordelia to look at Robbie.

"All of *that*," Robbie said, thrusting out his palm and circling it to indicate Peyton and Sandy. "You know, the whole *sex* thing. He's practically an anorexic midget and she's a whole lotta woman. He'd be like a little piece of dental floss between her thighs, right?"

"Rob!" Cordelia scowled, hitting his arm. "You're such a bitch when you're drunk! Stop, ok?"

Robbie shrugged as Drew and Iva Wang guffawed. "I'm not being a bitch! I'm genuinely curious about the *logistics.* Sandy is a mini person. Peyton's gonna eat him for breakfast!" He looked at Cordelia. "You're super lucky Drew showed up. Imagine if you had to share a room with those two tonight?" He shuddered. They looked over to where Sandy and Peyton were now vigorously dry-humping each other against a wall.

Robbie's lip curled, his nose wrinkling. Cordelia pointed a finger at him in warning. "Knock it off, ok?" she said, sweeping her hair behind her shoulder. She'd straightened it so it hung sleekly down her back almost to her waist.

"I didn't even say anything!" he proclaimed, holding his hands up in defence.

"You didn't need to. Your face has subtitles." She shot him one last look then turned to Drew, who was regaling Iva Wang with his latest conspiracy theory: bilocation. He'd stumbled across a book about the superhuman ability in a bookstore in Byron, and hadn't stopped talking about it since he'd arrived in Surfers. He was coked to the eyeballs and talking a mile a minute.

"So explain this to me then," he was saying. "St Martin de Porres was a monk living in Peru in the 1500s. Although it was widely corroborated that he was reclusive and never *ever* ventured outside the walls of his monastery, he was frequently seen tending to the poor and infirm all over Lima, and as far away as France, Mexico, Africa, and China."

"Urgh, not this bilocation shit again, mate?" Robbie groaned, rolling his eyes so far back in his head only the whites remained. "Drew, I love you, man, but you're *craaazy!*"

"You need to open your mind, Rob," Drew said, his gaze intense.

"You don't believe this crap, do you?" Robbie asked Cordelia.

She kissed Drew's cheek, leaning in when he squeezed her knee. "I do, actually," she said defensively. She hadn't repeated the story to Robbie that Indigo had told her about his time in Sedona, about the friends he'd made… the friends he claimed had higher senses such as the ability to *bilocate*. Indigo hadn't asked her not to, but she kind of felt like it was his story to tell. And she certainly hadn't told Drew, who'd gone all weird and quiet a couple of days ago when she'd told him Indigo was back.

"Cordelia Evelyn Carlisle! My God, woman, you've lost it," Robbie gasped, clasping his hand over his heart. "I can't believe I once shared a womb with you!"

"When I was your age seven minutes ago, I had a lot more respect for my elders," Cordelia retorted.

But Robbie was no longer paying attention because a cute guy was approaching, dark and petite, his gaze trained on Robbie.

"Oh. My. GOD!" Robbie breathed, gripping Cordelia's arm and leaning into her. "Do you know who that IS?"

Cordelia frowned. He looked familiar but she couldn't place him.

"Robbie?" the boy said, smiling cockily. "Is that you?"

"Gino?" Robbie flushed, clamouring to his feet. "Of all the gin joints in all the towns… What are the chances?"

Cordelia's mouth fell open as it dawned on her who this was.

Gino leaned in close to Robbie and whispered in his ear. Robbie smiled bashfully, nodded, and allowed himself to be led off to the dancefloor.

"Who the hell was that?" Drew asked, frowning after them.

"You don't remember? Mardi Gras After Party? 1992?"

Drew raised an eyebrow.

"The year Indigo's mum was performing and got us tickets? Robbie met Gino that night. He was there with his older brother. He was Robbie's first kiss, and Rob was totally smitten, but Gino refused to give him his number because he was terrified of his mum finding out he was gay."

"That's not Hot Wog?" Drew gasped.

Cordelia laughed and nodded, because that was how Robbie had referred to Gino in the years since: the Hot Wog that got away.

"Good for him, looks like the fates have aligned," Drew murmured, grinning lazily. They turned their attention back to Iva Wang and the conversation they'd been having prior to Gino's appearance.

"So you're saying, honeybun, that these people, when they *bilocate*," Iva Wang said in his broad rural accent, patting his fairy-floss-pink bouffant, "that they're able to project their consciousness to the point they create a second version of themselves that can travel anywhere in the world?"

Drew nodded and pointed at him. "Exactly." He grinned, his eyes shining as they only did when he met a kindred spirit. "So I read, that an old mate of St Martin's fell deathly ill whilst visiting Mexico. St Martin visited his friend, staying by his bedside to care for him, not leaving until his friend was on the mend. Once recovered, the friend asked around for the monk, wanting to visit his accommodations in Mexico to thank him. He soon discovered that St Martin was in fact still in Lima and had never, ever set foot outside the monastery." He widened his eyes at them.

Cordelia couldn't help but smile. She loved how excited he got when he was sharing theories he was passionate about. She kissed his cheek and nuzzled into him. He was so handsome in his black trousers, his paisley shirt buttoned to the throat, his hair neatly combed.

Drew went on to describe St Martin's experiences all over the world, then moved onto a list of other saints with the ability to bilocate. He was yet to draw breath.

"Fascinating," Iva Wang said, pursing his heavily-lined lips, taking the cigarette Drew offered him and allowing him to light it. "And you're saying the Vatican has documented all this?"

Drew nodded, then lit his own ciggie, taking a drag before continuing. "The phenomenon is actually quite prevalent throughout history. It seems nearly every culture has documented cases of bilocation, practiced by mystics, shamans, saints, and monks amongst others, although would you believe the Catholic Church has the most predominant records of cases witnessed and corroborated by reliable sources?"

"Of course they do." The drag queen caught Cordelia's eye and grinned. She winked affectionately and grinned back.

"As the Church considered bilocation a gift from God," Drew explained, "the Vatican spent years investigating the supernatural phenomena, eventually declaring it a core miracle deemed worthy of sainthood."

"So learn to split yourself in two, become a saint?" Iva Wang smirked.

Drew shrugged.

"He's very convincing, isn't he, love?" Iva Wang said to Cordelia.

"He could sell ice to Eskimos," she agreed, leaning her head against Drew's shoulder.

"Believe what you will," Drew told them. "Alls I'm saying is that there's a lot more to the world than what we've been led to believe. In fact, we're only told what they want us to know, what will keep us complacent and easy to rule. Humans are capable of superhuman abilities, it's a *fact*." He took a sip of his beer and leant back in his seat.

Iva Wang nodded. "I believe you, handsome. Millions wouldn't, but I do. You see, when I was just a wee queen, I moved to Sydney from Gunnedah. I rented a room in Kings Cross from a lady who made her living telling fortunes."

"Was she any good?" Drew asked, leaning forward intently.

"If it wasn't for her, I'd be sitting here dead," Iva Wang dead-panned, bejewelled hand planted on his chest.

"Tell us?" Cordelia said, taking a sip from the bottle of water Drew had bought her.

"Well, love, it was Kings Cross in the seventies, and I lived with this fortune teller, Madame Carlotta she went by, but I just called her Mary. So I met her when I answered an ad she'd placed in the Trading Post for a room in her terrace house on Darlinghurst Road. She was a strange old stick, butch as a lumberjack but didn't have any interest in sex or relationships. Anyway, she made her living reading tea leaves from these wee china cups, although that was a gimmick I reckon cos she just *knew* things, you know? All kinds of characters rocked up day and night to see her, and of course I was curious." He raised his eyebrows, razor-thin painted arches.

"She read for me one day. Told me I'd never go back to Gunnedah like I was meant to. And deadset, she was right. My dad died, and my sister's half-wit husband took over the farm and ran it into the ground and Mum was forced to sell," he said wistfully. "Anyway, my friends all thought Mary was completely cuckoo. They didn't know her like I did. So one night I was going to a party with a group of them, my friend Trevor was driving. Just as we were about to leave, Mary fair dinkum grabs my arm and tells me, *don't go.* She had this look in her eyes, you see, the same look she has when she tells me I'd better take an umbrella because it's going to rain, the same look she had when she told me to sit down before I answered that phone call letting me know my dear old dad had passed. I deadset *knew* what she was saying. I tried to tell my friends. They laughed at me, called Mary a kook. Only one of them listened, my mate, Shane, a sensitive soul if ever I saw one."

"What happened?" Cordelia breathed, wide-eyed.

"They had an accident. Trevor was high as a kite, he misjudged a turn, rolled the car down an embankment. Not one of them walked away."

"Fucking hell!" Drew gasped.

"And then it was just me and Shane. I guess it wasn't our time."

"So answer me this," Drew said. "If it wasn't your time, does that mean if you'd gotten in the car you would have survived?"

"You know, I've always wondered that. But I guess I'll never know."

"Maybe you would have died," Drew mused. "Maybe in another timeline you got in that car and you died, too. With Mary's premonition, your life split off in a different direction than it could have if you hadn't listened to her."

"Or, maybe, you were always meant to meet Mary and she was always meant to stop you getting in that car," Cordelia suggested.

"I like that theory, love," Iva Wang said, smiling, his heavily made up eyes distant. Cordelia reached out and squeezed his hand.

great southern land

sedona, arizona

raf

The phone was ringing as Raf pulled his key from the lock and pushed the front door open. He strode into the kitchen and snatched up the receiver from its cradle on the wall. "Hello?"

"By my calculations, you've just gotten home from yoga," the voice on the other end said.

"Indi!" Raf boomed, the corners of his mouth instantly turning up as he tossed his yoga mat on the table behind him.

"How are ya, Raf?"

"Better now I'm speaking with you. The house is too quiet. I miss you, buddy." Raf felt himself choking up. He swallowed hard.

"I miss you, too," Indigo said, clearing his throat. "How's Sedona? How's the gang?"

But there was something in his voice. A forced casualness.

"What's wrong, Indi?"

Silence.

"Indigo? Talk to me."

A shuddery exhale.

Raf sat down at the kitchen bench, the receiver gripped tightly in his hand while he gave Indigo the time he obviously needed to gather himself.

"It's Cordelia's dad. He's really sick," Indigo finally whispered.

"How sick?"

"Stage four metastatic sick. It's everywhere, Raf, just… everywhere." Indigo sounded wretched; lost and scared. He had a lot of guilt around Cordelia and her family and had barely spoken of them during his time in Sedona, but Raf knew they'd played a big part in his life and that they were Indigo's family as much as Raf was.

"I'm so sorry, Indi."

"They've asked me to help, Raf. To try to heal him. But I'm scared. I'm so bloody terrified I can barely see straight. What if I can't fix him? He's so sick, man, I've never seen anything like it. I wouldn't even know where to start."

"Indigo," Raf said sternly. "Listen to me. You're spiralling. You need to get present. If you're not here and now, you're nowhere, remember?" Raf picked up his glass water bottle and took a big sip. "You won't be able to help him if you're wobbling all over the place like this. Cordelia's dad, he needs you to get it together. Ok?"

"Ok." Big exhale.

"Get out of your head. Trust your instincts; you'll need every single one of them firing to get through this."

"Thanks, Raf."

They chatted about it until he felt Indigo was calm and more confident. Then Raf asked, "What else is going on? Have you had any luck tracking Reinenoir down?"

"I refuse to call her that. She'll always be Harper to me."

"Well, Harper is dangerous. She needs to be stopped."

"I'm aware of that, Raf," he said tersely. "I'm trying, ok, I've just got a lot going on at the moment, you know? Cordelia's up in Queensland so at least she's safe, and I have Nash using his pre-cog skills to look in on her just to be sure. As for Harper, I have no idea where she is. She's completely dome-shrouded. No one can find her." He paused for a moment. "I'm only one person, Raf, there's only so much I can do and right now Josh is my priority." The stress was clear in his voice.

"That's not true, Indi."

"Huh?"

"You're not only one person. You have *us*, which means you'll never be just one person ever again. If you need us – *when* you need us – we'll come."

"Really?' Indigo breathed, and Raf could practically feel his relief.

"Of course we will, bud, we love you. You know we've got your back."

"Oh God, Raf." His voice broke. "Just knowing that…"

"You just let us know when, and we'll be there." While Raf knew Indigo was strong, that he could now handle anything life threw at him, he also knew that no one was meant to handle the hard times alone. Indigo was silent, and Raf knew there was something else. "I take it things didn't go well with Cordelia?' he asked gently.

"Nope. That's over."

Raf bit his lip and squeezed his eyes shut tight. *Dammit.* He knew how Indigo felt about this girl.

After he hung up from Indigo, Raf put a load of laundry on, then went to take the trash out. As he stepped outside, a sudden feel of unease washed over him, a prickle down his spine, the slither of unwanted eyes over his flesh. He froze, trash-bag in hand, frowning. He turned towards the backyard, gazing out at the forest beyond his property. All was calm, tranquil. He smiled to himself and shook his head. All this talk of Harper and her coven combined with thoughts of the past, was making him paranoid.

He went inside and made himself a cup of peppermint tea. He carried it into the living room and settled into his favourite brown leather armchair. He loved his home, with its cathedral ceilings and enormous windows that provided panoramic views of the woods and brought the outside in.

He propped his feet up on the coffee table and blew on his tea. It seemed Raf's past was coming back to haunt him more and more these days, things he'd pushed to the recesses of his mind because they hurt too much to dwell on; it felt like they were being jostled free.

Raf hadn't always been the person he was now. He'd known shadow and darkness just as much as the next person. But life was all about experience, and how could he regret the experiences that made him who he was today? Raf believed he was exactly where he was meant to be, doing exactly what he was meant to do. And his life, his past, it had led him here.

He felt for Indigo, he really did. He knew Indigo had made mistakes when it came to Cordelia, but he'd hoped Indigo would be able to fix them. Because the hurt of losing the person you believed was put here on this earth just for you, he knew that hurt only too well. For him, that hurt had had a purpose. It was what had pushed him out of his comfort zone, forced him to grow up, to find himself, to become a man.

Raf had never been into relationships when he was younger. Girls, yes. Relationships, no. He blamed his parents for that, because their marriage had been so volatile it had put him off dating.

His mother hadn't gotten along with her Italian-American adoptive family, and his dad was illegal with no family in America to speak of, so it had always just been the three of them... the three of them and Raf's twelve 'aunties' who were constant fixtures at the Rafael home.

Despite their dysfunctional marriage and the fact they drove him nuts, Raf had loved his mom and pop with all his heart. He couldn't say the same for school. He struggled to read because the words seemed to vibrate and jump around the page, and his teachers constantly criticized his writing, claiming his letters and numbers were either back to front or upside down. He was relegated to the remedial classes where he was bored senseless. So one day, he just stopped going.

He got a job, worked hard, and by the time he was nineteen he'd saved enough money to leave. For years, he surfed his way around South America and the Pacific, taking odd jobs here and there to pay his way: Mexico, Costa Rica, Hawaii, Fiji, Indonesia, Australia.

It was in Australia's Byron Bay in the late 1970s where it had happened. He'd finally fallen madly in love and had his heart broken for the very first time. The very first and the very last time. And broken wasn't the right word for it. Decimated. He'd had his heart decimated.

He'd never met anyone like her. Beautiful, effervescent, free-spirited, he was smitten from the first moment he laid eyes on her. And he'd never been smitten before. He fell. Hard. Jarringly bone-crunchingly hard. He was all in. He planned to give it all up and settle down with her in Byron. "*Il mio cuore é il tuo per sempre,*" he used to tell her. "My heart is yours forever".

And the two of them, they'd had seven months of bliss, seven of the best months of his life, seven months that would live in his heart forever. Until the day she'd turned up to meet him, distraught and tear stained.

They'd messed up. Badly.

And their relationship had ended. *Badly.*

So he'd left, walked away... no, he'd *run* away. He'd hitchhiked up to Cairns, where he'd drowned his sorrows in the warm tropical waters of the Pacific. When he eventually got restless, he ventured west to the Northern Territory, bumming lifts from strangers, letting fate decide where he would end up. Fate chose to lead him up to the top end of Australia, to Kakadu, where he got a job as a jackaroo on a cattle ranch. Life was harsh yet simpler up there in the tropics where there were only two seasons – wet and dry. It was sweltering twelve months a year, sometimes unbearably so; it was only the humidity that rose and fell.

The beauty of the landscape often stole the breath from his throat. The cattle farm was set on the floodplains where waterlilies flourished, so he felt like he'd stepped into a painting etched by Monet. Magpie geese and whistling ducks took to the sky enmasse when unsettled by human intrusion and the tiny jacanas walked on water, their fluffy chicks tucked up under their wings.

It was a land that time had forgotten. For all he knew he could have travelled back to when dinosaurs roamed the earth, for here they surely did. The first time he saw a saltwater crocodile in the flesh his heart nearly exploded from his chest. The beast must have been sixteen feet long and over two thousand pounds! The sickening sound its jaws made as he witnessed it snap down on a heifer that had strayed too close to the shoreline was enough to persuade him to approach all waterways with extreme caution. The power of the croc was not to be messed with.

When the bottom fell out of the cattle industry, he found himself jobless and aimless. So he kept running. He grabbed his pack and his swag and took off to explore the Territory. He wandered as far north as he could go, to the untamed Arnhem Land, where the boundless top end of Australia met the balmy Arafura Sea.

The land here was wild and desolate, completely unforgiving. But there was a haunting energy to it that he loved, a palpable ache in the rugged landscape, so vast and endless and empty. Here he felt man's true insignificance, the sheer power and size of Mother Earth in all her greatness.

Arnhem Land was like nothing he'd ever seen: wild bush, sprawling wetlands, jutting red rock formations, vast sandy beaches and azure seas. At night, a million brilliant stars blanketed the sky, so bright and beautiful that when he lay in his swag gazing up at them, he never quite knew if he was awake or already dreaming.

Because he struggled to read and write, Raf recorded his adventures on a Dictaphone. As time went on, he found himself also committing his dreams to tape, and then, like a fool, ideas for novels he believed he'd never have the skill to write. But once those ideas invaded his mind, he had to get them out or they'd drive him mad.

He lived alone for some time, just him, his broken heart and his swag, sleeping with only those brilliant stars for company, foraging off the land and fishing in the rivers and seas. Back then he'd been a carnivore, lost to the land, and he probably wouldn't have survived if he hadn't been. He'd made the decision to completely surrender himself to the universe, to fate, and so he lived day to day with no plan or worry. Under the blanket of quiet the wilderness provided, the little voice inside him, his intuition, grew louder and louder, deafeningly so. He learned to trust, to follow his instincts.

All instincts that is, but one. The one that came in the middle of the night, that invaded his dreams and tossed his belly, bringing images of her face, her name echoing through his mind like the wind through the mighty gums. The instinct that urged him to turn back, to head south, back to her. It was almost like he could hear her calling for him. While at night he lay awake entertaining that instinct, in the light of day he pushed it from his mind, berating himself for living in a past that was not meant to be.

Food was scarce and it didn't take long for him to realise he was no match for the wild tip of Australia. He decided it was time to make his way down to Darwin and start heading home. He hadn't eaten in a couple of days, so when he stumbled upon a small billabong full of silvery barramundi swimming listlessly close to the surface, he couldn't believe his luck. Although the small voice inside him told him not to approach the billabong, his hollow belly overrode it and he reached in to pull a slow-moving fish from the water, quickly building a fire and cooking it. After he'd eaten, his thirst drove him to fill his canteen with the water.

He did notice there were a couple of *dilly* bags floating in the billabong. He'd seen these before, these bags woven by Aboriginal people, but he didn't think much of it. When the first wave of cramps hit his guts it brought him to his knees, the second and third crippling him. Within an hour he was curled in the foetal position, vomiting and foaming at the mouth, sure he was dying. He saw movement from the corner of his eye, his listless gaze taking in solemn eyes set in a face as black as coal, before he lost consciousness.

He didn't know how many days later he finally awoke in a small tent made of sticks and paperbark. A thick, fragrant smoke drifted through the air around him, keeping away the flies and insects. He sat up quickly, his head spinning so dizzily he lay back down again. He groaned loudly, and the next thing he knew a face popped through the opening of the tent. Large eyes regarded him seriously. He vaguely recognised the face as the one he'd seen at the billabong. It belonged to a boy who looked to be in his late teens.

"Where am I?" he mumbled as the boy crawled inside and handed him a sack of water. Raf drank deeply.

"You another stupid whitefella, ay," the boy said in a broad Australian twang, his dark eyes twinkling mischievously. "Didn' you see them markings on the tree at the billabong?"

Raf groaned again and shook his head.

The boy sighed, but a smile hovered at the corners of his mouth. "It's the ironbark. It's poison, mate. We crush up the branches and leave the pulp in *dilly* bags in the water to stun the barra. Makes catching 'em easier. It poisons the water too, so we mark 'em trees so other blackfellas know not to drink it. Ya silly whitefellas got no business going walkabout up here on ya own." He turned and clamoured out the tent, but stuck his head back in. "I'm Jackie by the way. Ya lucky we find you. If it weren't for Jedda you woulda died. He saw where to find ya, told me t' bring ya t' him."

"Jedda?" Raf groaned, "Who's Jedda?"

But Jackie was gone.

Not for long though.

Over the next few days, through Jackie's frequent visits, Raf discovered he'd been taken to a Yolngu outstation, a remote community of Indigenous Australians. Its inhabitants lived traditionally with very limited outside influence which meant they were suspicious of strange whitefellas, especially peculiar foreign ones like him.

"What's ya name?" Jackie asked Raf the next time he came.

"Diego."

"Dee-go?"

"Dee-ay-go," Raf explained, suddenly aware of how thick his American accent must seem.

"Dingo?"

"Dee-AY-go."

"Dee-go?" Jackie scrunched his face up. "Dingo?"

This exchange was apparently relayed to every member of the community, and that was how Raf came to be known as Deego Dingo.

"Who's Jedda?" Raf asked Jackie the next time he came around.

"Jedda is *Ngangkari*. He got the vision, ya see. He knew ya was comin'. Told me where to find ya. Told me to bring ya here for healin'."

Jedda was the mob's cleverman, which was like a shaman or a witch doctor, a dimensional worker capable of great healing magic. Raf knew that under normal circumstances he wouldn't have been allowed to enter the community, that at best the Elders might deign to allow him to stay long enough to recuperate. He realised immediately that Jedda must be a deeply respected member of the mob for Raf to be allowed admission on his say so.

Raf, of course, was intrigued. He wanted to know more about Jedda, more about his healing, and more about the way of the mob. For the first time since he'd left Byron, Raf felt he was exactly where he was meant to be. Instead of running from something, he'd found something to run *towards*. He was desperate to meet Jedda. But the cleverman really made him work for it. It was weeks before he was escorted to Jedda's *humpy*, which is what the mob called their small tents made of sticks and paperbark. The two of them sat together outside, cross legged in the dirt, that fragrant smoke Raf had become accustomed to surrounding them. Jedda was a tiny man with skinny legs and a protruding belly. He was heavy-browed with a snowy white beard, his face deeply creviced.

Jedda was initially stand-offish, seemingly both bemused and amused by Raf. But when Raf asked Jedda how he knew Raf was coming, and how he knew how to heal him, he began to open up. He shared with Raf that he'd foreseen his arrival from that place in the centre of his forehead, that the two of them were meant to cross paths. He seemed to sense something within Raf that caused him to drop his guard.

Jedda was a *Ngangkari* who used his deep connection to the land, animals, the sky, and to the Dreaming, to heal others. He was a great protector of dimensional law, universal law and humanity. He sat and explained how he used plants, song, touch, his magic vision, and universal energy to see what others couldn't and to heal those others couldn't.

Raf told him of the traditional healers and medicine men he'd met on his travels, and by the end of their conversation, Jedda invited Raf to visit with him again the next day.

Days turned into weeks, then into months.

Living with the mob at one with the land, Raf had felt truly content. They had a kinship with the environment that resonated with him. He adored Jedda, who had simply taken Raf under his wing as though it were meant to be, teaching him about bush medicine and supernatural healing.

One day, Jedda stumbled upon Raf sitting in the shade of a gumtree, talking into his Dictaphone. Brow furrowed, Jedda asked what he was doing, having a conversation with a strange, lifeless contraption. When Raf explained he recorded his stories in this way because he'd always struggled with the written word, Jedda scoffed.

Such an affliction was easily fixed. He claimed that if Raf's brain and primitive reflexes were realigned, Raf would no longer struggle to read and write.

Jedda knew how to realign the human *Waug* or Spirit, which involved using his hands to move pain or blockages that were impinging on the free flow and wholeness of the person's *Waug*. He was a blood healer who could see inside of others, could see the sickness inside them and use his hands to pull it out. It reminded Raf somewhat of the Reiki he'd seen practiced in Indonesia. Over the course of several days, Jedda laid his magic hands on Raf. And, afterwards Raf could read and write with ease.

Jedda was a diviner, which meant he had the ability to communicate with Ancestral spirits through time, space, and other dimensions.

After Jedda realigned him, Raf's own innate ability to see through the veil between realms began to develop. He too, could see and hear the deceased, which Jedda informed him was a gift that would have come forth sooner or later. Initially, Raf was scared of the spirits popping up unexpectedly at all hours of the day and night. But Jedda soon made him see there was nothing to fear of the departed, that with the right know-how, the relationship between the dead and the living could be a synergistic one.

He showed Raf how to keep the deceased at bay when he needed peace, and how to help the lost ones who were stuck. A person's soul is their true essence, their true existence, he told Raf, so it was important to help them either move on to the in-between, or go home to family.

And when Raf's other powers started to emerge, Jedda helped him with those, too.

Raf also grew closer to Jackie, who usually sat in on these sessions, listening intently and assisting when necessary. Jackie had shown tendencies towards trances and visions from a young age, and was being trained by Jedda as a *Ngangkari.*

For five years, Raf lived with the Yolngu mob, his only contact with the outside world being when he ventured the two-days-travel into town to pick up basic supplies and mail.

Over time, Jedda helped Raf rid himself of his shadow, his darkness, holding a mirror up to all that he was, allowing him to see himself for what he truly was, all the good, all the bad, all the ugly, ugly, ugly, allowing him to choose what to keep, what to deal with and what to let go of. Jedda gave him the tools to release that which did not serve him, helping him grow stronger and brighter, more centred and grounded.

Raf grew up.

If it weren't for that broken heart that had driven him there, he wouldn't be the man he was today, outward looking, self-assured, self-responsible. "I get it," he said to Jedda one day. "Sometimes the worst things to ever happen to us lead us where we need to go."

He only ever asked Jedda once why he'd chosen to bring Raf to stay. Jedda had merely grinned his gap-toothed grin, tapped the centre of his forehead and said, "You and me, Deego Dingo *bunji,* together, one day we'll save the future of this time and place." He'd refused to elaborate further.

The day Raf received word his mother was unwell, he could read the message perfectly well. The crumpled letter was already months old. He had no idea if his mother was alive or dead, but he knew he had to go. With a heavy heart, he bade farewell to his newfound family, and he left Arnhem Land, left his mob, left Australia, and flew back home to California.

And as for the girl? He never saw or heard from her again, never got the chance to tell her he'd long-since forgiven her, to ask her if she'd found it in her big beautiful heart to forgive him. But he did still think of her constantly.

The only girl he'd ever loved.

Charley.

The girl who had his heart forever, '*Il mio cuore é il tuo per sempre*'.

Raf knew in his bones Indigo felt for Cordelia what he'd felt – still felt – for Charley. Which meant, no matter what, that girl would have Indigo's heart forever, be that a blessing or a curse.

chapter five

don't give up

harbord, new south wales

indigo

Dawn had called that morning to wish Indigo luck and drop some last minute pearls of wisdom on him. As a fellow empath and healer, she got him in ways most people never would. She'd taught him so much, made him into the healer he was today.

"Joshua couldn't be in better hands, hon," she'd told him. "I have complete faith in you… As long as you trust yourself and we don't have another crisis of faith like the infamous sea anemone incident of '94," she'd said with a giggle.

Indigo had burst out laughing. She was never gonna let him live that day down, well over a year ago, when he was just starting out and she allowed him to practice on her. She'd been lying face up on the table in her clinic, eyes shut, when all of a sudden he'd noticed something very strange protruding from her body. He knew right away he wasn't seeing it in the physical sense, but rather, clairvoyantly.

He'd crouched down for a closer look.

It was a funny looking thing, like a vortex or mini tornado spinning up out of her body, right above where he was working. It kind of reminded him of the sea anemones in the rockpools back home, tentacles open in full bloom. He'd bent closer, noticing the vortex-anemone-thing ran straight through her body, emerging from both the front and the back so that when he looked at Dawn side-on, he was able to see both sides of it simultaneously.

"Uh, Dawn?"

"Yes, honey?" She'd opened her eyes and propped herself up on her elbows.

"Don't freak out, but there's something really weird coming out of your body… Just *here*," he'd said, reaching to touch it with his fingertips. Whatever it was zapped him, and he snatched his hand back.

Dawn had sat up, blonde curls bouncing, as laughter pealed from her. She'd taken his hand in hers and guided it gently back to the vortex-anemone-thing. While it had zapped him again, she'd held his hand steady until he got used to the feeling, like warm, slow wind running and swirling between his fingers.

"What the hell is it?"

"Look closely," Dawn had said, laying back down. "Can you see any more?"

He'd peered down at her, concentrating really hard, and as he did, he'd seen more and more appear, until there were seven of the weird anemone-vortex-things spinning from her body: one from the crown of her head, one from her forehead, another from her throat, one from her upper chest, another from the centre of her pelvis, one from between her legs, and of course the one he'd originally seen, protruding from her solar plexus.

They were really quite beautiful, each a different swirl of colour.

"What the hell are they, Dawny?" he'd asked, mesmerised.

"They're chakras," she'd said with a knowing smile.

"*Chakras?*" He'd wrinkled his nose as he stared down at her. "But chakras aren't *real!* They're just woo-woo hippie shit."

Dawn had frowned. "I can assure you they're not. You're seeing them right now, aren't you?"

He'd needed a minute after that, so he left her there, lying on the table and beelined outside for some fresh air. The wind chimes on her front porch sung their haunting melody as he strode past them to stand amongst the wildflowers and angel and fairy statues that filled Dawn's garden. He'd lain down on the grass and stared up at the cobalt sky, trying to steady his spinning head.

He was living in a world where *chakras* were real? What the *actual* hell?

He'd stayed there, processing the reality that was now his life. Chakras and biofields and energy healing. What was next for him? Crystal collecting? *Angel card* readings? He'd scoffed out loud, because that was never, ever, gonna happen.

When he'd felt ready, he returned to Dawn's clinic to find her still lying on the table, patiently waiting for him.

"You alright, honey?" she'd asked.

He'd nodded, and she'd smiled to see he had his game face on. He sat back down beside her and, one by one, had placed his hands in her chakras, feeling how each one vibrated at its own specific frequency.

After that day, Indigo had begun to see these spinning vortexes – *chakras* – in all his patients. He'd found they projected a person's very essence, telling him everything he could possibly want to know about them before they could even open their mouths.

That still didn't stop his patients opening their mouths to voice their opinions. Especially the reluctant ones. Like Joshua.

"You know this is a waste of time, right?" he grumbled to Indigo now. He was lying face up on the massage table in the cosy little studio at the back of the Carlisle home; it was usually Scarlett's clinic. The room was ingrained with the scent of white sage, palo santo, and essential oils.

"It's not a waste of *my* time," Indigo responded lightly as he sat down in the chair at the head of the table and rubbed his hands together before laying them lightly on Joshua's shoulders.

He frowned deeply as raw panic began to rise inside of him and he struggled to keep his breathing even.

Joshua's body was so ravaged by disease, Indigo didn't know where to start. He recalled Dawn's advice, and took a deep inhale, centring himself, consciously clearing his own body of the black sickness that was empathically coiling to consume him. It was hard for him to separate himself from Joshua when he was so connected to him, so invested in the outcome. He had to get out of his own head. His aim was the deep meditative state in which he did his best work.

Joshua's biofield was streaked and globbed with black, just as it had been two days ago, the tell-tale sign of advanced cancer. Streams of white bubbled and flowed through the black indicating the cancer had metastasized. A lot of the diseases Indigo had helped heal in his short time working with Dawn had started in the patient's biofield, the blockages, imbalances and distortions slowly filtering down through the energetic layers to affect the physical body.

Indigo examined Joshua. There were hundreds of chakras located all over the human body, but Indigo was largely focused on the main seven.

In his short but intense career, Indigo had seen chakras that were wide open, chakras that were closed tight, some that were overactive, aggressive and loud, others that were slow, quiet and stunted. He'd seen chakras spin clockwise, he'd seen them spin counter-clockwise, and he'd seen some that didn't spin at all. He'd seen them close in response to outside stimuli, much like a sea anemone closes when poked with a finger. They were meant to reopen, although he'd seen some that had been permanently closed or open for so long that they affected a person's whole view of the world, not to mention their state of wellbeing.

It fascinated him how many illnesses, both physical and mental, could be healed where they began – in the chakras and biofield. How could you fix something with just medication or surgery when the disease wasn't even rooted in the physical and you were treating the entirely wrong aspect of the person?

Just as a person's heart beats without their conscious input or their kidneys filter blood without their awareness, their chakras, too, operate naturally. And much like their heart and kidneys, people seemed to take their chakras for granted, until they malfunctioned.

Every one of Joshua's chakras had problems – some were closed, others were spinning counter-clockwise, but the worst by far was his third chakra, his solar plexus, which was completely torn and exposed. A healthy adult chakra was supposed to have a protective film over it to keep out harmful forces and keep in nourishing energy.

Dawn had told him that, in her experience, most cancer patients she'd treated had at least one torn chakra correlating to the diseased organ. It often took years for the effects to filter down and culminate as cancer in the body.

Indigo's guardian, Sarita, usually turned up during his healing sessions to offer her assistance, and today was no different. Out of the corner of his eye, he could see her conversing with Joshua's guardian, a tall, blonde woman with dreadlocks who reminded Indigo of a Viking warrior. Sarita was buxom and regal, a vision in magenta and violet, a tumble of dark braids swinging down her back.

After a time, she came and stood behind him, placing her hand gently on his shoulder. The strong scent of geranium wafted over him as it always did when she was around.

"I'm sorry, my dear one, but his date of death is set," she told him in her delicate lilting manner. "And it is soon. You cannot prevent what is fated."

He shrugged her hand off, not wishing for her to break his concentration. "Don't care. Gonna try," he muttered through gritted teeth. He pressed his lips tightly together, his eyes intensely focused.

Some people came into this world with a set date of death written on their life map in permanent marker. If this were the case, it was said there was no way of saving them, no matter what, they would die at the exact moment they'd been born to.

But Indigo didn't believe in absolutes.

Day after day, he worked with Joshua, repairing his chakras, clearing his biofield, discussing every vision and memory and belief that arose. Joshua talked and talked, Indigo listened and listened, hour after hour, day after day. There was crying, there was laughter, there was anger, and there was everything else in between.

And then the day came when Indigo had finally cleared enough to tackle Joshua's solar plexus chakra. Dawn called this one the "power chakra" because it was the source of a person's personal power. He knew this wasn't going to be a simple fix, that this chakra was rife with deep-seated damage.

Indigo found he'd come to agree with Dawn that patients needed to be involved in their own healing when their disease was systemic. For a healing like this to have a solid foundation, for it to stick, the patient – *Joshua* – needed to talk, to understand, to accept, to let go. So, together, he and Joshua tackled Joshua's power chakra.

Joshua lay on the table, his lower body covered with a blanket, while Indigo sat beside him, chin in hand.

Indigo cleared his throat. "Tell me about Claire," he ventured gently, repeating the name that had been whispered to him by Joshua's guardian.

Joshua's breathing suddenly changed. The only movement in his face was a slight tremble of his lower lip. A moment or two later, he squeezed his eyes shut and turned his face away. Indigo sat quietly, giving Joshua the space of silence.

"I don't talk about her," Joshua finally whispered.

"I think you need to, Josh," Indigo said gently, placing his hand over Joshua's.

Joshua wrenched away and sat up, throwing the blanket off and swinging his legs over the side of the table, his back to Indigo. "*I said I don't talk about her!*" he snapped. Indigo put his hand on Joshua's arm but it was shrugged off aggressively.

"Josh…" he said in a low voice.

"Why are you making me do this?" Joshua moaned. He covered his face with his hands as his chest began to lightly convulse, and then his whole body began to shake, his shoulders rising and falling.

"It needs to come out, Josh. You need to talk about her."

Indigo had found the more his patients talked, the more the darkness seemed to ebb away. This allowed space for a little of the flame inside of them to be re-ignited.

He waited for Joshua to process, to ready himself to share the parts of himself he'd kept bottled up, hidden for so long. Indigo gazed out the window, watching the breeze rustling through the trees, the streaky clouds trailing lazily overhead.

Joshua took a deep shaky breath and finally spoke. "Claire," he began, swallowing hard, "Claire was… she was my big sister. Claire-Bear, I called her. There was quite an age gap between us, seven years, and because both my parents worked long hours in the family business, it was just the two of us. Claire was like a second mother to me." He gingerly lay back down, pulling the blanket to his chin.

"I was a bit of an awkward kid – skinny, nerdy – I got teased a lot. Those kids… they were absolute shits. I mean, I think that's why I've always been so protective of Robbie, because I know what it's like to struggle to make friends," he said softly. "Anyway, when Claire found out, she insisted on walking home with me every day so the bullies

76

wouldn't hassle me. Claire was popular. She was beautiful and bright and she hung around with the in crowd. When I got upset, she'd put her arm around me and say 'You know what, kiddo? Those kids? Mark my words that they'll amount to very little in life. Whereas you, baby brother, you will leave a mark on the world that they could never fathom. You dig me?'" He smiled so sadly at the memory, his eyes squeezed shut.

He took a deep breath and exhaled shakily. "When Claire was sixteen, she started seeing this guy named Darrell," he said, opening his eyes and turning to Indigo. "Darrell was older, I think he'd left school the year before, and while my parents didn't wholeheartedly approve of him, I liked him because he was always really nice to me and he didn't mind me hanging around with them. He used to pick us up after school and drive us home in his car." He cleared his throat.

"One afternoon..." He swallowed hard. "I was walking home alone because Claire had hockey practice. And Darrell pulls up alongside me and offers me a lift. Of course I accepted, and I remember being so excited because not only did all the kids at school see me climbing into his Datsun, but I also got to sit in the front like his buddy because Claire wasn't there. When Darrell offered to show me the tree fort he'd made with his mates when he was my age, I jumped at the chance. We were going on an adventure, just me and Darrell. So we drove down to the national park and we parked on one of the fire access tracks. And I remember turning to him, waiting for him to lead me to this magnificent fort he'd been bragging about the whole way there. But... but, um... well, instead he locked the doors and... and well, he... exposed himself to me and... he...he made me... do things to him. Things I didn't understand but I felt were wrong." He stopped talking and pressed his lips together so hard they disappeared.

Indigo felt bile surging in his throat; he had to close his eyes to compose himself, slipping his hand to Joshua's shoulder and holding on.

"Afterwards, he bought me an ice cream and drove me home. When he dropped me off, he told me not to tell my sister because she'd never forgive me for trying to steal him from her. I remember lying on my bed that night, staring at the ceiling, and my whole body felt so empty, so broken, like my guts had been torn out and left exposed for the world to see. Claire came in and asked me what was wrong, and I lied to her, told her I wasn't feeling well." He shrugged then, his eyes filling with tears. He blinked them away.

"Despite how hard I tried never to find myself alone with Darrell again, he had his ways and it happened a couple more times," he said flatly. "And then one weekend my parents decided to go away with friends of theirs. Claire convinced them we were old enough to be left alone, and you know, it was the sixties and no one thought anything back then of leaving a sixteen-year-old in charge of a nine-year-old so they agreed. After they'd left, Claire asked me if I could keep a secret. She was so excited, her eyes shining, a great big smile on her face. And then she told me that Darrell was going to come and stay with us for the weekend." He shook his head, words seemingly having escaped him for a moment.

He looked to Indigo, wide-eyed. "She saw right away, the look on my face, how my whole body had started shaking. She asked me what was wrong. And at first I lied. And oh God, Jesus Christ, how I wish she hadn't gotten it out of me, how I wish I'd kept Darrell's dirty secret for him! But she knew me better than anyone, she knew I hadn't been myself lately and she knew that right that very moment I was terrified to my very core. 'Come on, kiddo, lay it on me,' she said. And so I... I told her." He stopped talking and took a great shuddery breath as he scrunched his eyes shut.

"I just remember her going very still and very quiet, except for her chest which was heaving rapidly, her breath the only sound in the room. She was staring straight ahead, white-lipped and wide-eyed.

"And that was the moment Darrell chose to arrive, walking into the house without knocking as he always did when our parents weren't home. The minute she saw him, Claire charged at him like a bull, and this sound was coming out of her, like this raw, primal howl." He balled his hands to fists, clenching his jaw tightly. "She'd taken him by surprise and although she was about two thirds of the size of him, she managed to slam his body back into the wall. And she got some good blows in there, punching at him and scratching him with her nails, all the while screaming she'd kill him. It took him a moment or two for him to realise what was going on, but once he did it was all over so fast." He tucked his chin into his chest, tears seeping from his eyes.

"H-he grabbed her by the throat and pinned her against the wall and he started punching her in the face, over and over again. She was grasping at his hand and her feet were flailing in the air, and there was blood, so much blood. And I remember running over and hitting him in the back, trying to get him to let go, but he just turned and sent me flying across the room with one good backhand."

Indigo was frozen as he listened to Joshua speak. How could this wonderful man, this beautiful father, this loving, accepting, warm-hearted person be scarred by such horrors? He held tight to Joshua's shoulder as he continued to talk, his words spilling faster.

"I don't know if I was knocked out for a bit or just dazed, but when I picked myself up and turned to look at them, Claire wasn't grabbing at his hand around her throat anymore, and her legs weren't flailing about anymore, and she wasn't making a sound." He bit down on his lip.

"He released her and she slumped to the ground and he just stepped over her and walked out of the room, out of the house. He didn't even look back. I raced to Claire's side, trying to rouse her. I remember yelling, 'Claire-Bear, get up, open your eyes.' But… but she didn't. I was nine years old. I didn't know what to do. I didn't know how to help her, how to save her. I was completely overwhelmed by this… this sense of *powerlessness*." His whole body was trembling, his voice thick as tears coursed down his face.

"Eventually I came to my senses and ran to the neighbours for help, and they came, and called an ambulance. But it was too late. She was gone." His voice cracked. "And it was *my fault*. All my fault. If I hadn't gotten in the car with Darrell that day, if I had just done as he'd said and kept my mouth shut… He killed her because of me. She was trying to defend me!

"Even though Darrell's still in prison today, and he's paying for what he did, I'll never forgive him. But it's my fault she's dead, all my fault. And I couldn't help her, I couldn't fix it, I tried, but I didn't know what to do. It's my fault she's dead." He sobbed and sobbed, as all the memories, all the emotions he'd pushed down deep for so long bubbled to the surface. "It's all my fault," he kept repeating, over and over again, his body wracking violently.

Indigo wrapped his arms around Joshua, comforting him as best he could, knowing the dam had been broken, its contents unleashed, and those decades of grief, they all had to come out.

A long while later, the two of them sat quietly together outside in adjoining deckchairs, watching the sun dappling the grass through the trees.

"It wasn't your fault," Indigo said, finally speaking, finally breaking the silence.

Joshua shook his head. He was exhausted, spent, barely able to speak.

"It wasn't."

Joshua pressed his lips tightly together and looked away.

"If it were Matty," Indigo began, "or Robbie. If Darrell did to them what he did to you. Would you blame them? Would you want them to keep it quiet?"

Joshua stared into space, the expression on his face moving and changing so much Indigo found it impossible to read. Eventually his face began to crumple and he shook his head slowly. Indigo crouched down in front of him, taking Joshua's hands in his.

"You were a kid, Josh! You were nine years old. How was any of what happened your fault? This guilt that you've held onto for so long, it's toxic. Can't you see that it's literally killing you? You have to let it go. Your nine-year-old self, you need to forgive him, to nurture him, to love him. Look upon him as if he were Rob or Matty, a small boy who needs protecting, who needs your compassion, who needs your forgiveness.

"Your sister? She sounds like a really special person. I'm so very sorry you lost her, but she died defending the person she loved most, and if you ask me, that's a pretty honourable way to go."

Tears rained down Joshua's sunken cheeks. Indigo moved his hand to rest below Joshua's sternum, to his power chakra. "Forgive him, Josh," he whispered. "Forgive that little boy. Forgive *yourself.*"

And as Joshua shakily exhaled, his lips pursed, his brow furrowed, his power chakra grew stronger under Indigo's palm. It slowly began to vibrate, and then to spin, to straighten and to shine. Sometimes when Indigo worked on his patients, Sarita placed her hands inside of his, and this was one of those times.

The next day, when Indigo arrived at the Carlisle house, Scarlett was waiting for him in the kitchen. She burst into tears when she saw him. "I didn't know," she sobbed, pressing her hands tightly to her mouth.

"All these years we've been married, he never told me." Indigo wrapped her in his arms, soothing her gently.

"I mean, I knew he'd had a sister, that she'd been murdered by her boyfriend, but he never told me she was defending him... What that monster... d-did to him! How could he not tell me that, Inds? Something so *huge?*"

"He'd pushed it down so deep, Scar, built himself back up around it like a house of cards. If he'd acknowledged it again, his everything would have collapsed. It was too hard, the wound too deep."

"I'm so angry," she cried. "At that *bastard!* What sort of *monster* does that? To a nine-year-old kid? I'm glad he's rotting away in prison. I hope they *never* release him. Poor Josh... My poor, poor darling." Indigo held her until she stopped shaking, then sat her down and made her a cup of the fresh lemon and ginger tea he'd watched her make countless times before.

"How is he today?" he said as he handed her the mug.

She smiled vaguely in thanks, then wiped her eyes, tilted her head to one side. "Better than me. He's kind of quiet. Calm. At peace even. He's waiting for you in my clinic, so that's a breakthrough." Joshua had been an unwilling patient for the majority of the process. Indigo rested his cheek on the top of her head for a few moments before heading out back.

Joshua was standing at the floor-to-ceiling window, staring out at the backyard, his back to Indigo.

"Hey, Josh," Indigo said softly. Joshua turned and looked at him, and Indigo got a shock. He looked different somehow. Something in his demeanour, in his very being, had changed.

"How do you feel?" Indigo asked, gazing into Joshua's eyes.

"This may sound strange, but I feel... better. Quiet. Settled. Like I'm in possession of an inner strength I never knew I had."

Indigo leant on the massage table behind him. "And if I were to ask you how you feel about Claire? About her death?"

"I don't know. It feels... different somehow. More peaceful I guess. It will always hurt, but it doesn't feel so raw, like such a gaping black abyss in my life anymore."

Indigo nodded, placing a hand on Joshua's shoulder, gesturing for him lie on the table. Indigo covered his lower body with a blanket.

"I didn't know," Josh said, staring blankly at the ceiling.

"Know?" Indigo asked softly.

"That it's the things that are broken on the inside that break us on the outside."

Days passed. Together, they worked and worked. Joshua's chakras all began to spin beautifully in unison, his biofield grew bright and clean, and Joshua himself grew more and more peaceful, lighter, clearer... And Indigo grew more and more concerned. Because as beautiful as Joshua's energetic body was, his physical body remained the same – frail and broken and so entirely and completely ravaged by the cancer, that Indigo began to fear Sarita had been right – there was no coming back from this.

Indigo was sitting beside the massage table, his hands wreathed in golden green light. He held them out, palms down, a few inches above Joshua's torso, trying his hardest not to let his frustration, his panic, his terror show. Tears brimmed in his eyes as he continued to try with all his might, with everything he had, to fix Joshua's broken body. He couldn't give up. *Wouldn't* give up. He'd called Dawn almost every day for advice, for guidance, for support. He'd begged Sarita for help. He'd tried bargaining with Joshua's guardian, negotiating, offering anything and everything he could think of. But nobody would, *could*, help him. And now Robbie and Cordelia were due back tomorrow, and Joshua's cancer was advancing rapidly.

"It's ok, Indigo," Joshua said softly, breaking the silence. "It is what it is."

"No, Josh, I–"

"Indigo. Please listen to me. I want to tell you that I've been lying here, thinking how lucky I am." A slow smile lit his pale face. "Look at my life, my family. I've truly been blessed. I was lucky enough to find the love of my life, to have the time I did with her. I don't want to leave Scarlett... but I'm so very grateful I got to share my life with her. A thousand years with her would still never be enough. The day she agreed to go out with me, to let me into her world, that day changed everything. It was the best day of my life." He blew out a shaky breath.

"And my kids. I know now... that I won't get to see them grow up." He swallowed hard. "And I'm really struggling with that. *My God how I'm struggling with it...*" He inhaled deeply, squeezed his hand momentarily over his mouth. "But I'm so thankful to have had the privilege of being a part of their lives.

"My Matty, with his earnest little face, the way his enormous brown eyes bore so intently into mine when he's telling me his many, many complicated, fanciful stories about imaginary convicts and soldiers." He chuckled fondly. "That kid, Scar and I, we broke the mould when we made that one." He paused, seemingly lost in his thoughts.

"Robbie, with his amazing ability to be himself, so unapologetically. He has always brought me so much pride. He's incredibly sensitive, that boy of mine, easily hurt, but I know that he'll always have you and Cora to coax him back when he's run off to lick his wounds. And then there's my girl, my exquisite Cordelia." His chin quaked as he closed his eyes for a beat or two. "The first time Scar brought the kids to meet me, Cordelia looked up at me with those big aqua eyes, and I tell you, Inds, I was a goner. She's got the soul of an angel, my daughter. I'll miss her passion for life, how deeply she loves her family and friends ... how deeply she loves me.

"This body of mine? Where I'm going, I can't take this body with me. It is sick and it is broken and it is damaged beyond repair, but that's ok because I am leaving it behind. But, what I am taking with me, is my soul, and that soul... it is healed. And I thank you for that Indigo, because thanks to you, I am *healed.*"

Indigo had tears streaming down his face as Joshua delicately raised himself up onto his elbows to look at him. Joshua's face was serene, not an ounce of fear to be found in his eyes. "I am healed, Indigo," he repeated. "You can stop now." He nodded towards Indigo's hands, still held over his emaciated body, but now shaking uncontrollably. "Because you have succeeded. *I am healed.*"

Dawn's voice played in Indigo's head, advice she'd given him the very first time he'd visited her home: *In some cases, death is what heals.*

He hadn't truly understood her words, until now.

no more 'I love you's'

sydney airport, new south wales

cordelia

Cordelia's step faltered when she saw Indigo waiting at the baggage carousel.

She'd been expecting her dad, so was utterly thrown to see Indigo pacing the terminal in boardshorts and a white T-shirt, an Arizona Sun Devils baseball cap pulled low over his face. He was so tanned and tall and completely oblivious to every female in the vicinity blatantly scoping him out as they passed him by, checking out his powerful frame, his sharp jawline, his butt, which had always been worth a second glance. A third and fourth even.

But when she got up close and saw his face properly, she got a shock. He had bruise-like circles under his eyes and looked completely wrecked. He still managed a smile for her though. She returned it tentatively, because how could she not respond to something so heart-stopping?

Robbie was lagging behind her, green at the gills and fading fast. He wore dark sunnies and dragged his feet.

"Struggling a bit there, mate?" Indigo said as he strode towards them swinging his car keys in his hand. He embraced Robbie, then pulled away, wrinkling his nose. "You stink."

"I vomited on the plane," Robbie informed him, looking like he might hurl again at any moment.

"He claims air sickness, but the fact he was out drinking 'til five this morning, might have something to do with it," Cordelia said as Indigo leant to kiss her cheek. Her eyes fluttered closed as his lips lingered, warm and soft, and she inhaled his sandalwoody-sea-on-summer-breeze scent and all the memories it carried. She gathered herself as he pulled away, and when she looked at him, she was suddenly thankful that Robbie had stuffed their flights up and booked them home in the morning instead of in the afternoon with their friends. With Drew. She didn't know how he would have reacted to Indigo picking them up.

"Yeah, well, it was my last night with Gino," Robbie muttered.

Indigo raised an eyebrow.

"Rob's holiday romance," Cordelia explained.

"*Holiday romance?*" Robbie gasped. "I'll have you know Gino lives in Leichhardt and has agreed to accompany me to the formal!"

"That's awesome, Rob, I can't wait to meet him." Indigo smiled, but it was a wan version of his regular smile.

"You've already met," Robbie informed him. "At the Mardi Gras Afterparty back in '92."

"No way! *That* Gino?" Indigo gasped. "First kiss Gino?"

Robbie nodded smugly.

"Hot Wog Gino with the gay brother and the lesbian sister whose strict Catholic mother had no idea none of her kids was straight?"

"Do you *ever* forget *anything?*" Robbie chuckled, then winced, clutching his head.

"Memory of an elephant." Cordelia smiled up at Indigo.

"I need to go sit down," Robbie mumbled, staggering towards a bank of grey plastic chairs.

Cordelia watched him distractedly, then turned her attention back to Indigo. "Where's Dad?"

Indigo hesitated and she swore she saw his lip quiver before he bit down on it. He forced a grin, bright, big, completely incongruent with the look in his eye.

"Um," he said, running his hand over the back of his cap, "Josh couldn't make it. He asked me to come instead." He paused to regard her. "That's ok, isn't it? I mean, we're still mates, yeah?"

She nodded. "Is everything ok?" she asked, trying to catch his eye. He was scanning the information board pairing baggage carousels with flights.

"Nah, yeah," he murmured. "Ah, this one's yours." He moved purposefully towards the conveyer belt that had started sporadically spitting out luggage. He busied himself helping them find their bags – with a side of gallantly assisting a few damsels in distress extract their bags from the carousel – then picked up one of Robbie's and grabbed the handle of her wheelie bag. He glanced over at Robbie who was slumped in his seat. "Do I need to carry you, too, Rob?"

Robbie grimaced and lurched to his feet, trailing after them. When they reached Indigo's black Landcruiser, Robbie opened the back door and crawled inside, laying across the seats and closing his eyes. "AC please," he groaned. He was asleep before they'd left the carpark.

"So, Schoolies was good then?" Indigo asked Cordelia with a pointed glance at Robbie as he manoeuvred the car onto General Holmes Drive. Traffic was light. She tugged at a thread on the hem of the white denim cut-offs she was wearing with a white button-down shirt, the cuffs rolled to just above the elbow.

"Yeah, it was fun," she said, staring out the window at the billboards lining the road spruiking designer luggage and exotic destinations.

"C'mon, Cora, I need a little more than that! I didn't get to go to mine, remember? I'm living vicariously through you here." He shot her a tight smile. He was acting a bit weird, awkward even, although she wasn't surprised after what had transpired between them before she'd left.

She glanced down at his arm resting between them on the centre console, tanned and muscular, and had to resist the urge to reach out and run her fingertips along it, to lace her fingers through his. Instead, she turned her gaze out the window again and gave him the heavily edited highlights of their week away. After that, they made small talk until they pulled up in the driveway of her house. Small talk had never been part of their repertoire and it just felt *wrong*.

She went to open her door, but he continued to sit there, the car still running. He seemed hesitant to turn the motor off, to get out of the car.

She turned back to him. "Are you coming in?" she asked, chastising herself for hoping he was.

He looked at her and there was something in his eyes, something akin to broken devastation and that made her feel scared but she didn't know why. He turned off the ignition and nodded. "I promised Matty I'd take him to the beach." He leant over and shook Robbie's shoulder. Robbie didn't so much as stir. "Rob," he said, shaking him again. "Robbie, you're home." Nothing. Finally, he resorted to old tactics and held Robbie's nose until he gasped for breath and sat up with a start. He glared indignantly at Indigo who simply said, "You're home."

Robbie glanced at the house and nodded, opening the car door and slithering out. "I need my bed," he groaned.

Cordelia went to the boot to help Indigo with the bags. When they walked into the living room, her parents were sitting formally on the couch, hands clasped. A plaid blanket covered her dad's knees, and he looked even thinner than he had when they'd left. Robbie was slumped across the opposite couch, moaning he just wanted to go to bed.

"We need to talk to you and Cora first," Dad was saying. He saw Cordelia then and his face lit up. "My darling girl! Aren't you a sight for sore eyes!" But he didn't stand to greet her which was weird. Mum came to cuddle her tightly and she was smiling, but her face was tearstained and Cordelia's tummy flip-flopped.

"Come give us a hug?" Dad said, holding his arms out to her as Mum returned to his side, reaching for his hand again. Cordelia hesitated. She eyed them both suspiciously and walked tentatively towards them, leaning to hug Dad who felt like skin and bone. Indigo slipped wordlessly from the room and she could hear him chatting to Matty in the kitchen. The two of them emerged into the living room a moment later, Matty holding tight to Indigo's hand.

"We're going to the beach!" Matty announced. He was already in his swimmers. He saw Cordelia and Robbie then and his whole face lit up as he clapped his hands in pleasure. "You came back!" he cried, running to Cordelia and throwing himself into her arms. "Deadie promised me you'd come back so I knowed you would!"

Cordelia wrinkled her nose. Out of all Matty's imaginary friends, Deadie not only had the creepiest name, but he was also the only one Matty never drew. When questioned, Matty simply told them he wasn't allowed to draw Deadie.

"Yes, well," she murmured, cuddling him close and smoothing his fine blond curls from his face, "Deadie would know."

Matty scampered over to Robbie, who was sprawled on the couch, his eyes shut, one hand dramatically flung across his forehead. Matty screwed up his little nose. "Robbie, you smell *bad!*" he declared.

"That's just your breath blowing back in your face, munchkin," Robbie murmured, fumbling to blindly poke Matty in the tummy so he giggled.

"Let's hit it, Matty Moo!" Indigo called, holding his hand out again. Matty scampered back over to him and grabbed onto his fingers.

"Thanks, Indigo," her mother said softly, and Indigo's throat worked as he nodded and the two of them exchanged a look.

Cordelia stared after Matty and Indigo as they left, suddenly feeling light-headed. She looked back to her parents who were now gazing up at her.

"Come sit, darling," Dad said.

She planted her hands on her hips and narrowed her eyes. "What's going on?"

"We need to talk to you both," Mum said. "Robbie!" she said loudly, and he flinched.

"Wha?" he mumbled.

"Sit up please, sweetie."

"Don' wanna."

Cordelia moved to the couch and tapped him hard on the arm. "Rob." And something in the tone of her voice made him open his eyes. When he saw the look on her face he started, then jerked to a seated position, his bleary gaze suddenly trained on his family.

"What's wrong?" he said, looking from Cordelia to his parents.

Cordelia sat down beside him, wringing her hands in her lap. She gazed at her parents, wide-eyed. "You guys are freaking me out. Just say what you need to say. Please."

Mum and Dad exchanged glances.

"Stop doing that!" Cordelia demanded. "Just *tell* us."

Dad took a deep breath and she saw her mother squeeze his hand. "I-I thought I'd find the right words to tell you when the time came," he started, his now-protruding Adam's apple bobbing as he swallowed deeply. He looked awful and Cordelia's hands started shaking. Robbie reached out for her.

"You're sick," she blurted, trying to keep the accusation from her tone.

Dad caught her gaze and nodded. "Yes. I'm sick."

"But I asked you," Cordelia said, voice low, "all those times, and you told me you were fine, you told me not to worry, I don't understand–"

"How sick?" Robbie suddenly whispered from beside her. She glanced at her brother. He was so white he was almost translucent.

"I have stage four metastatic pancreatic cancer," Dad said quietly.

Cordelia felt the blood rushing in her ears. Her vision blurred, her breath coming faster, so fast she couldn't quite catch it. She moved her trembling hands to her mouth. "But... but they can make you better, right?" she said, blinking 'til her eyes focused.

Her father took a deep breath and looked her right in the eye. "I'm so sorry, my darling girl... But no."

Beside her, Robbie turned and vomited all over the rug. She barely noticed.

"What do you mean 'no,'" she whispered, her eyes locked on his. "You're a doctor. You know all the right people. Cancer is treatable, lots of people get it and... and... they don't... *die.*" She choked out that last word.

"We found it too late. It's... it's everywhere..." Dad broke off, looked away, tears rushing to his eyes. Mum slumped against him and Cordelia could see she was crying, too.

"But you're not going to die," Cordelia said and she heard a laugh emerge from her throat and it surprised her. "You're not going to die," she repeated, waiting for someone to agree with her. But no one did. Robbie was now sobbing beside her and she reached a hand out to rub his back. "You can't die!" she said, and she realised she was growing hysterical. "We need you, Daddy. You can't die!" She looked to her mother. "Mum? He can't die, right?" Mum just gazed at her wide-eyed.

Dad's whole face crumpled and he held his arms out. Cordelia rushed into them, laying her head against his bony chest which was now shaking erratically as he sobbed. Mum got up and went to Robbie, enfolding him in her arms as he wept. Cordelia was the only one who was dry-eyed. "You're not going to die," she said determinedly, taking his face between her palms and gazing deep into his eyes. "You're *not* leaving us."

"My beautiful Cordelia," he murmured. "Believe me when I tell you that leaving you is the last thing in this world that I ever want to do. But it *is* the last thing that I'll ever do. I'm so sorry, darling." His chin trembled. "I'm just so very bloody sorry." Tears flowed down his hollow cheeks and she reached to wipe them away.

The whole room jolted and her vision doubled as a rush of hot and cold terror washed over her. She stood abruptly and backed away from him, shaking her head. She couldn't breathe. She was so dizzy. She couldn't be here having this conversation. She turned on her heel and ran upstairs to her room, slamming the door and throwing herself face down on her bed. She squeezed her eyes shut, grabbing fistfuls of her pillow and trying to catch her breath. Her heart was thumping so fast, it was like she could feel each beat shuddering through her whole body, hammering in her ears. She curled into a ball on her side and tried to push it from her mind, tried to pretend she hadn't heard any of it, that *cancer* hadn't dared to invade her world and tear it apart.

After a period of time had passed she couldn't have measured if she'd tried, she heard a knock at her door. "Cora, honey?" It was Mum. The door opened a crack. "Can I come in?"

Cordelia didn't answer. She was lying on her side staring blankly out the window.

She felt the bed beside her compress and a hand on her back. "Sweetie?" Soft fingers moved to smooth her hair.

"How long?" Cordelia said, her voice like ice.

"What, darling?"

"How long have you known?" She couldn't hide the accusation burning in her throat.

Her mother's hand stilled on Cordelia's hair. "A... A couple of months," she admitted, her tone sheepish.

"*How could you keep this from us?*" Cordelia asked, turning to her in quiet fury.

"You had your final exams, we didn't want to distract you–"

"Exams? What do *exams* matter in the scheme of things? *We had a right to know!*" she cried, sitting up, glaring at her mother. "How could you keep this from us? What were you *thinking?* If we'd known we could have helped, we could have done… *something!* And we certainly wouldn't have gone away for a week when we could have spent it *with him!*" She paused and then asked in a low shaky voice. "How long does he have?"

Her mother looked away.

"Tell me."

She slowly raised her eyes to Cordelia's. "Not long." She swallowed.

"Months?"

Mum shook her head. "Weeks," she whispered.

"W… *weeks*?!" Cordelia gasped, and suddenly her whole body felt numb. "*Weeks*?! He has only *weeks* left and you let us just go off and *waste* one *away from him*?"

"Sweetie, I–"

"Get out," Cordelia said, a sob in her throat.

Her mother hesitated, went to hug her. Cordelia flinched away. "*Get out!*" she shrieked, burying her face in her pillow as a dark wave of desolation rushed up from the pit of her stomach to engulf her, smothering her, its weight annihilating. She clutched her chest as sharp talons of grief shredded at her broken heart. She was barely aware of the door closing softly in her mother's wake.

This wasn't real. It just couldn't be. Things like *cancer* didn't happen to her family. They were happy. They loved one another. They needed one another. She was so furious she could barely see straight. She jumped up and started pacing, raking her hands through her hair. Her father couldn't be sick. Surely this was some kind of mistake.

It wasn't real.

It wasn't real.

It wasn't real.

But she'd seen her mother's face. She'd looked into her Dad's honest eyes. She knew him. She knew how much he loved them, how he strove to protect them. He wouldn't hurt them in a million years, unless he had no choice.

And then mid stride, her knees turned to jelly and she sank down onto the bed, staring numbly at a spot on the carpet, wishing, wishing, wishing she could fade away to nothing, to a place where reality didn't exist.

chapter seven

make you feel my love

cordelia

Cordelia was still sitting there in a frozen daze an interminable time later, when there was another gentle rap on her door.

"Cordelia?"

Her stomach flip-flopped.

"Cora? Can I come in?"

She heard the door creak open, but she didn't turn around. Footsteps then, and he sank down beside her on the bed, close, but not touching her. He sat beside her in silence for a while, and his presence was calming, soothing. She felt herself emerging from her trance. She took a great shuddering breath in and exhaled. Wordlessly, she leaned into him, her head resting on his shoulder. He smelt like the beach.

"I'm so sorry, Cora," he whispered into the silence. He wrapped his arm around her, nestling her into the nook of his embrace where it was warm and safe, where she could believe everything would be ok.

"You knew," she said, drawing back so she could look into his hazel-flecked eyes.

"I did," he said, gazing at her intently. "But you needed to hear it from him."

"Is it real, Inds? Or is it just a bad dream?"

"With all that I am, I want to tell you it's not real. That we can go to sleep and when we wake up, all will be as it should." He closed his eyes for a long moment. "But it's real, Cora. I'm so sorry, because I know this is the worst thing in the world and I wish I could fix it for you, I wish I could take it all away and make him better." His voice cracked then and he looked away, shook his head almost imperceptibly.

"They kept it from us."

"Because they love you so much. If I've learnt one thing from Scar and Josh, it's the lengths parents will go to, to protect their children. They wanted so much to shield you from this for as long as possible. Because from this moment on, your life will be defined as Before, and After. And now you know, everything is different, everything has changed. They were protecting you from that."

"We had a right to know."

"You did," he agreed. "But it would have only meant feeling what you're feeling right now for longer. Maybe they were trying to give you the gift of time."

"He's going to die," she whispered, the reality too heavy to bear. "My dad is going to die."

"Yes," Indigo said, and she heard the wobble. "He's going to die." And he drew her back into his arms and rested his cheek against her head. "I'm so sorry, Cordelia. I-I couldn't save him." His voice was thick with unshed tears. "I tried so hard, I promise you, harder than I've ever tried at anything in my life. I wanted to make him well. For Scarlett. For Robbie. For Matty. For... for you. For me, too, because I love that man, he was the first man to truly accept me, to show me what it was to be a father, to be a man. I need you to know how hard I *tried*. But I couldn't fix it. And there's nothing that can be done."

When her tears came, they came with a ferocity she'd never known possible. Her body seemed to turn to liquid and she felt herself pouring off the bed towards the floor. Lightning fast he caught her up, and she held fast to him. He laid her gently on her queen bed and wrapped the warmth of his body around hers and she cried until her throat was sore and her eyes were swollen and his T-shirt was sodden. And he didn't speak and he didn't move and he didn't make a sound. He just lay there and held her, held her tight in every way with his quiet strength.

She must have fallen asleep because when she awoke, disoriented, knowing something was wrong, searching for it, and then remembering it all in a flurry of churning sorrow and pain and terror, he wasn't there anymore. She murmured his name, and she sensed movement and someone gripped her hand. She glanced up to see him sitting there beside her bed, having pulled the armchair from the corner of her room over so he could watch over her.

She gazed dully up at him, uncomprehending of how this could be real. He smiled a broken-hearted smile and touched her cheek. "You ok?" he whispered.

She shook her head.

"Here," he said, reaching for something on her bedside table. "Why don't you try to sit up, drink something?" She saw he had a glass of water in his hand. She nodded and dutifully sat, letting him bring the glass to her lips as though she were a child. She might as well replenish her tears because she couldn't imagine she'd ever stop crying. "Scarlett made dinner."

"I'm not hungry." Her voice sounded strange. Hoarse from crying.

"Either way. Maybe you should come downstairs, speak to Josh?"

"He hasn't been up? While I was sleeping? To see me?" It wasn't like him, to stay away when she was breaking apart.

"Cora..." Indigo said, glancing at the floor and then back at her. "He... Josh can't get up the stairs anymore."

"What?" she breathed. It was like all the air had been sucked from the room.

"He has a tumour on his lower spine. It's growing rapidly. It makes walking difficult."

"Oh my God," she moaned, covering her face with her hands as fresh tears started to flow. He moved to sit beside her on the bed, hugging her tight as she sobbed.

"So where... does he sleep?" she asked when she could talk again.

"We moved their bed down into the rumpus room. Your mum, she refuses to sleep a night apart from him," he said wistfully.

"Thank you. For being here for them. I can't believe how quickly this has happened." Her lips trembled.

"Sometimes it happens this fast. Especially with pancreatic cancer."

"How's Robbie?"

"He was asleep when Matty and I got home. Shock affects people in different ways."

"Ok," she said, biting her lip determinedly. "Let's go downstairs."

"Go wash your face. I'll wait for you, we'll go together."

She nodded dully, then she stood on shaky legs and wobbled her way to the bathroom across the hall. She gazed listlessly at her reflection in the bathroom mirror. She'd possibly never looked worse and she didn't even care. Her face was red and puffy, her eyes almost slits. Her hair was a tangled mess. She drew a brush robotically through it, more out of habit than anything else, and splashed cold water on her face, dabbing around her eyes in the hope the swelling might go down a bit. After a couple of minutes, she gave up.

Indigo was waiting for her at the top of the stairs. "Rob's still sleeping."

She nodded, and glanced down the stairs.

"You ready?" he asked.

She nodded again, and he grasped her hand briefly, helping her to go first.

When Cordelia appeared in the kitchen, Matty looked up at her, eyes shining. "Robbie vomited on the couch," he told her earnestly. "He vomited all over it and Mummy had to clean it up."

A vague wrinkle of the nose was the only response she could muster for her baby brother before her gaze travelled to her dad, sitting at the kitchen table, a bowl of clear broth in front of him. She immediately burst into tears and ran to him, burying herself in his arms.

"So Robbie hurled all over the couch, did he, Matty?" Indigo said as Matty turned to regard his sister curiously.

"Yeah, I show you," Matty said, jumping up from the table and leading Indigo into the living room, full of self-importance. "Mummy cleaned it all up though."

"I love you, Daddy," Cordelia choked, holding onto him for dear life.

"I love you too, darling girl," he whispered back, his voice shuddering.

"I'm scared. I'm so scared." She pulled back to look at him. "Are you scared?" And it felt like her heart was cleaving in two as she considered what he might feel about what was ahead of him.

"I'm not scared of death," he told her softly, and she could see in his eyes that he meant it. "The thing that terrifies me… is leaving my family. I'm scared of missing out on… on sharing the life we should have had together. I won't get to walk you down the aisle on your wedding day, or see you have kids of your own and hold my grandbabies in my arms." He swallowed hard as tears streamed down her face. "You, Cordelia," he said, cupping her cheek ever so gently. "You, I will miss every moment of my existence. I'll miss your face, your smile, that beautiful heart of yours. I'll miss solving the problems of the world during our witching hour chats…" he told her with a broken, faded smile. And she sobbed as she recalled all those nights she'd awoken from one nightmare or another, and wandered downstairs to find him home from a late shift at the hospital, watching TV because he found it hard to switch his brain off when he'd had a tough day at work. The two of them would sit and talk 'til all hours, discussing anything and everything, until she felt better and they both knew they'd be able to find the sleep that had been evading them.

He closed his eyes for a few moments, his chest softly rising and falling. He finally opened them, and they glistened with quiet strength. "It seems such a shame to leave a life I have loved so much, where I have been so blessed and so happy. I'll m-miss you all. So much I can barely stand it." He swallowed hard and paused to take a deep breath. "But I'm not scared of death itself. Not anymore, anyway."

manly hospital, new south wales

indigo

A week later, Indigo found himself sitting beside Joshua's hospital bed. His eyes burned with exhaustion and his heart ached with the acceptance of his defeat.

He laid his palm gently on the back of Joshua's hand where the skin surrounding the cannula was red and swollen, his fingers glowing as he alleviated the symptoms as best he could. That, at least, he *could* do.

Indigo squeezed his eyes shut and exhaled shakily, trying to push away the bewilderment that threatened to consume him. He was really struggling with this. What was the point of him having his higher senses, in working so hard to control them, to master them, if he couldn't use them to heal those he loved most?

The blackness was all through Joshua's organs, all through his bones. It was in his blood and in his brain. And there was nothing Indigo could do to heal it. Josh's pallor was a strange opalescent white and had a waxy sheen to it. Indigo could see his biofield breaking up, the energy coming away in globs and drifting into the ether. His chakras were wide open, great, yawning holes that were slowly starting to disintegrate, too.

Joshua drifted in and out of consciousness as his soul moved in and out of his body, gently exploring the membrane between life and death, teetering from one side to the other. His soul looked exactly as Joshua did in life, but had a certain shimmery translucence to it. It was connected to his physical body by a thin silvery cord much like a tendril of spider's web. Indigo watched as Joshua floated beside his unconscious body, tethered to it by that cord. As long as that cord was connected, he would remain earth-side.

In his last bout of consciousness, Joshua had weakly ordered his family out to get something to eat. They'd only gone because Indigo had promised to sit with him until they got back. They needed a break, they'd sat at his bedside day and night for days now. In fact, they'd barely let him out of their sight since Robbie and Cordelia had returned from Queensland.

Joshua floated back into his body and opened his eyes, meeting Indigo's. With great effort, he fumbled for Indigo's hand, his breathing shallow with the mere exertion.

"Inds?" His voice was so soft, a mere rasp.

"I'm here. What do you need?"

"I want to tell you… how grateful I am… to you. For all you've done for me. I'm grateful *for* you." He smiled gently and closed his eyes.

Indigo set his jaw and nodded. When he'd called Raf to tell him he'd failed, that he couldn't save Joshua from dying, Raf, of course, had shared words of comfort. "Remember, Indi, we are merely tourists travelling momentarily through the physical world. It is the discarnate world that is our one true home."

That phone call had contained more harsh truths than Indigo had cared to hear that day, just before the twins returned from Schoolies.

"Sarita was right when she said Josh's date of death was set," Indigo had murmured to Raf, gripping the phone hard, his eyes squeezed tight. "I've never wanted her to be wrong so much in all my life. But she was right."

"I'm so very sorry, bud," Raf had said, his voice low.

"Raf? Why do only some people come in with pre-determined dates of death?" Indigo had asked.

"It comes back to their learning, Indi," Raf had gently explained. "And the learning of those around them. Their death and the circumstances around it may be vital in teaching those around them a big lesson, so it has to happen at the pre-determined time." He'd paused for a moment, before continuing. "I had a patient a while back, a young mother. She had three children under the age of eight, and she was dying of a terminal illness. I hosted Micah for her, during which he revealed her date of death was set."

"You told her her date of death?" Indigo had asked incredulously.

Raf had gasped. "Micah would *never* be allowed to reveal anything that wasn't determined to be helpful. He didn't tell her her date of death, no, just that it was unchangeable. She needed to hear it. To make peace with it. Her death was bigger than her. She had to leave behind three small children and a bewildered husband. Her death had been written before she was even born because *their* lives had been written with her death as a major event from which to grow."

"Wow, that's so cold, man," Indigo had commented, frowning.

"It depends on how you view death," Raf had replied gently. "For me, death is not an ending, it is not final. It is merely a transition, a rebirth into the discarnate world, a gateway to the next phase. It was her physical body, her shell, that was dying, not *her*. But her physical absence from her children's and husband's lives, well, that was pivotal for them, for what they'd come in to experience and evolve from."

"What about her?"

"She was someone who very much liked to be in control, and she was a very involved mother. Her kids were her life, you see. For her to have to let go and know they would continue on without her to watch over and protect them, well, that was enormous for her. If we don't evolve, Indi, we stagnate. And I can tell you right now we learn nothing from stagnation. We need change in order to grow, and unfortunately it's negative change that forces us to make the biggest shifts."

"So, this woman," Indigo had asked. "She died?"

"Yes," Raf had said evenly. "She died."

"And the children?"

"They suffered greatly," he'd replied, his voice catching. "They endured a very dark, unimaginable time. But you know what? They survived it, and they are different people for it. The human spirit is incredibly strong when it needs to be, Indi, it always amazes me how deep we can dig when we're forced to."

"Her husband... How did he cope?"

"He didn't, at first. But eventually he got through it, because for the sake of his kids, he had to." Raf cleared his throat. "He went through some very bad days, very bad indeed. But, with time, things got better. And he was forced to reassess his life and his reality. He and his wife had married right out of college and had started a family straight away, so he'd been tied to a job he wasn't happy in. He quit his job and sold their house, and they moved out of the city back to his hometown, where his parents could help with the kids. He went back to school, and now he's a grief counsellor, a very successful one at that. He's helped more people than I can count get through what he'd been through."

Indigo had been silent for a time, processing. "So if that's how you feel about death," he'd finally said, "does that mean if someone you loved died, you wouldn't be sad?"

Raf had hesitated. "No, of course I would be devastated. But for their loved ones. For *myself*. For how *my* life would look without *them* in it. My sadness wouldn't extend to them. Because I know that they would merely be transitioning to the next phase of their existence and that they were perfectly well. We never die, Indi, we merely shed our physical bodies and ascend."

Sitting with Joshua now, Indigo shook his head, unable to stop his tears. He covered his face with his hands, trying to muffle his sobs so Joshua wouldn't hear. The thought of how his life – how the *world* – would look without Joshua in it, it hurt so fucking badly. He'd barely been able to look at Scarlett these past few days. She'd put her faith in him, hoping for a miracle, and he'd let her down. And she'd been so wonderful, so grateful to him for the time he'd spent with Joshua, that it somehow made him feel worse.

"Please, Indigo," Joshua said, eyes still closed. "I need you to... know that you should be... proud of what you've done for me these past... few weeks." His hand fluttered on the bed as he tried to reach for Indigo's again. Indigo grasped it, bending double as he wept. With the greatest of effort, Joshua placed his hand on Indigo's head in comfort. "The day you walked... through our... front door and into our lives was a blessing for... us all."

Indigo wiped his eyes on his T-shirt and straightened his spine, knowing he needed to be strong now.

"You don't have to share blood to be family, Indigo, my life is testament to that... You are family, Inds... You are one of us, and family comes first... second... and third. I know you won't... leave them again," Joshua murmured, his voice hoarse, fading. "I know you'll watch... over them for me. Especially Robbie and... Cordelia." Joshua squeezed Indigo's hand so weakly it was barely discernible. "She loves you, Inds, she always has. She's going to need you to be strong... I know you'll look after her." A solitary tear escaped and trickled slowly down Joshua's pale face. Just one lonely tear.

"Always," Indigo choked, standing to plant his lips on Joshua's forehead. It was cool and papery to the touch. Joshua walked so beautifully towards death, Indigo was in complete awe of his bravery.

Not long after, Scarlett entered the hospital room, her arm around Robbie. Cordelia carried Matty behind them. Matty squirmed to the ground and ran to Indigo, who carried him to a chair in the corner, pulling him into his lap and cuddling him close. Scarlett sat in the seat Indigo had just vacated, and Cordelia perched on the side of the bed; each of them took one of Joshua's hands. Robbie went to the furthest corner of the room, sliding down the wall to sit, his knees bent up as he plucked intently at a loose thread on the thigh of his jeans.

"Has he woken up again?" Scarlett asked.

"Just briefly," Indigo told her. "About half an hour ago."

Scarlett bent over and kissed Joshua gently above each eye, her lips lingering on his skin. "I'm here, sweetheart," she murmured, stroking his face. "I'm here."

Matty wriggled on Indigo's lap, kneeling up so he could cup his hands to Indigo's ear. "Inds, who is that?" he whispered, pointing directly at the tall blonde Viking woman standing next to Joshua's bed. Indigo baulked and pulled back, peering into Matty's earnest little face. "That lady," Matty reiterated, pointing again.

"That's your daddy's guardian," Indigo whispered back. "She's here to help look after him and get him where he needs to go."

Matty nodded thoughtfully. "He's gonna leave wiv her soon?"

"He is, matey," Indigo said, hugging him close. "But he's going somewhere beautiful and safe, somewhere he doesn't have to be in this body that's so sick and tired and full of pain."

"I don't want my daddy to go," he told Indigo, wide-eyed, sniffing. "Do you think he'll come back to visit me sometimes?"

"See that girl over there? In the corner?" Indigo whispered, pointing to the young dark-haired girl leaning against the wall by the head of the bed. She was dressed in a short shift dress and knee-high boots.

Matty nodded vigorously. "You mean Care Bear?" he asked, waving excitedly at her. She smiled and waved back.

"Care Bear?" Indigo asked, brows soaring.

"Yeah, Care Bear! She comes to visit *all* the time. She tells me things to tell Daddy, but when I tell them to him, he just looks at me funny or he makes that laugh that gwown-ups make when they don't think it's funny."

Indigo considered him for a moment or two. "Matty, do you mean *Claire*-Bear?"

Matty looked at him indignantly. "That's what I *said. Care* bear."

"Matty, that's your Aunty Claire, your daddy's big sister. She died when he was nine, and even though he didn't know it, she's always been there, watching over him. She'll be the first person he sees when he crosses over. And you know what? Just like she's waited for him, I have a feeling he'll hang around and wait for you. Which means he'll always be with you. So you'll still be able to talk to him, and maybe, just maybe, you'll see him from time to time."

Matty nodded thoughtfully. "Can I go give my daddy a cuddle?"

"I'm sure he'd love that, mate," Indigo said, coughing over the swell of emotion in his throat. Matty skipped across the room and clambered onto the hospital bed, snuggling into his unconscious father. Matty began whispering in Joshua's ear, glancing beside the bed to where Joshua's soul floated beside his body, attached to it still by that long silvery cord. Joshua had been conferring with his guardian, but stopped to give Matty his full attention. Earth-side, Joshua had the support of his family. Discarnate-side, he had his guardian and Claire. This close to death, he was being held on both sides.

Cordelia got up and came to sit next to Indigo, slumping down in the spare chair and rubbing her eyes. "I don't know how much longer he can hang on for," she said, her chin trembling. "I can't bear to see him like this, Inds, it's just so awful."

Joshua's mouth was slack, his breathing rough and intermittent, his lips chapped no matter how much pawpaw ointment Scarlett lathered on them. Just when they'd think he'd taken his last breath, he'd draw another, intense and laboured and raspy. Indigo knew he wouldn't go until his guardian finally broke the silver cord that bound him to his body.

"It's funny, so many times this week, I've heard his voice in my head," Cordelia continued. "Like right now, I swear I can hear him talking to Matty."

Indigo regarded her with interest before his gaze wandered over to the bed where Matty was staring intently at Joshua, head cocked to one side. Joshua hadn't woken up, so the conversation he and Matty were having was other-worldly.

"What's he saying?" Indigo asked casually.

"Right now? He's giving him the old 'don't sweat the small stuff' speech," she chuckled sadly. "It's always been his thing." She begun imitating her father, her tone and mannerisms spot on. "*Don't sweat the small stuff, darling, it may seem huge now, but I'll bet you a hundred bucks it won't even matter this time next year. And if it won't matter in a year, then it doesn't matter much now does it?*' It used to drive me insane!" The memory brightened her face just a little.

"Did you ever collect? On the hundred bucks?" Indigo asked.

She shook her head wistfully. "Not even once. I guess he had a point."

Matty laid his head on his father's chest, softly humming *You Are My Sunshine*. Indigo felt tears spring to his eyes. He'd heard Joshua sing that to Matty countless times when he was a baby, colicky and screaming.

Robbie, who'd been quiet since he'd entered the room, suddenly let out a guttural cry. "Can't they *do* something for him?" he choked, jumping to his feet. "This is fucking *barbaric!*" He paced around the room, his cheeks wet with tears. "He doesn't need to suffer like this."

Scarlett leapt up and pulled him into her arms, shushing him as his whole body shook with the force of his weeping.

Cordelia's hand crept into Indigo's, and he clung to it.

"Why can't they help him?" Robbie was moaning. "It shouldn't *be* like this."

"It won't be much longer," Indigo whispered to Cordelia. He could see Joshua's chakras and biofield were fast disintegrating. "And he's not in any pain, I promise you that. It's a lot worse for us than it is for him."

There was a brief knock on the door and Drew stuck his head in. "Hey, guys," he said softly. Indigo dropped Cordelia's hand. "I brought nourishment." Drew held up a bag emblazoned with the name of Scarlett's favourite little organic wholefood café.

"That was so thoughtful of you, sweetie, come in," Scarlett said in a low voice, turning and smiling sadly over Robbie's head tucked into her shoulder. Cordelia stood up and went to hug Drew.

Matty lifted his head from Joshua's chest and gave each of his father's cheeks one final kiss before slipping off the bed and scampering back to Indigo. It was getting far too raw for a three-year-old in there. "Do you wanna go for a walk, Matty?" he asked softly. Matty nodded vigorously.

"I'm gonna take Matty for some fresh air," Indigo told Scarlett, putting his palm on her shoulder as he passed her. She covered his hand with hers. Robbie was still crying in her arms.

"Hey, Pres," he said, holding out his hand to Drew as he passed him by.

"Wolfie," Drew nodded, clapping his hand and nodding at him. They'd seen each other a few times over the last week and, although things were awkward between them, they hadn't been best mates for so long for nothing.

Indigo turned to pick up Matty's backpack before he left the room. He glanced at Joshua, surrounded by his family, as well as his guardian and his sister, their celestial light warm and comforting. "You're in good hands, Josh," he murmured as he took Matty's hand and led him from the room. They bumped straight into Joshua's parents who gave Matty a tearful cuddle as they passed by.

"You had a good chat to Daddy then?" Indigo asked him as they walked down the sterile corridor.

"Yup." Matty nodded. "He told me, 'Matty, don't sweat the small stuff,' and *I* told *him* that Care Bear was there and that the lady who was waiting for him, the one he was talking to, was very, very beautiful and very, very *good*. I asked him if he was gonna go with her soon. He said it wasn't entiwewy up to him but he liked being here with us cos he loves us so much. Daddy said he would miss me so, so much. He told me his love will never ever ever go 'way, that it will stay with me forever and ever." He paused for a moment before adding, "I asked him to come and visit me sometimes, too. He promised to try, but I don't know if he can." He screwed up his face thoughtfully. "Deadie said Daddy might have to go and be a baby in someone else's tummy soon."

Indigo glanced away, too choked up to speak. He didn't think Josh would be moving on from the in-between for a long time.

"Hey, look!" Matty suddenly cried, letting go of Indigo's hand and breaking into a run, "It's Essie." He took off round the corner, Indigo hot on his heels.

"Matty, stop!" Indigo called. The kid was quick.

"It's Essie, Indigo, c'mon!"

"Who?" Indigo yelled, sprinting after him. Matty was pursuing a voluptuous woman with cropped platinum hair. He chased her into a room up ahead on the left. Indigo followed them to find Matty perched on the end of the bed, talking to the woman, who was now sitting in an armchair beside the window. Up close he could see she had a filmy luminosity to her. Indigo's head whipped to the hospital bed and saw that the body, hooked up to a myriad of machines and tubes, belonged to the woman in the chair. Peering at her, he could now see the super-fine silvery cord connecting her soul to her body. He wondered curiously how far those things could stretch.

"Matty?" Indigo said questioningly.

"Essie's my friend," Matty told him intently.

Indigo looked intently at Essie and smiled. "Hey, I've met you before," he mused, narrowing his eyes as he wracked his brain. He clicked his fingers as it came to him. "At that New Year's Eve party at the Carlisles', three years ago. You were the one making margaritas for all the doctors!" He remembered arriving to pick Robbie and Cordelia up to go to a house party and being impressed with the rager unfolding at their place. Those doctors and nurses sure knew how to let loose. Essie had been dancing on the table with Robbie while The Angels' *Am I Ever Gonna See Your Face* Again belted from Joshua's new surround-sound speakers. She'd had a jug of margaritas in her hand, liquid sploshing everywhere as she'd poured it into people's mouths.

Cordelia had been laughing, so carefree, the flippy skirt of her short, chocolate velvet dress twirling out as she'd playfully danced with Joshua, a shoe-string strap having fallen down one bronzed shoulder. Scarlett, pregnant and smiling, had squealed in delight when she'd seen Indigo walk into the party, grabbing his hand and pulling him into the fray to dance with them. He sure remembered Essie from that night though, because who wouldn't with that incandescent smile, that pealing laugh, that tight red sequined mini-dress... She'd been tanned then and her hair had been much longer, layered and bouncy, and she'd worn a tonne of make-up.

"You can see me, too?" Essie whispered now, her eyes filling with hope.

"I can see you," Indigo reassured her. "What happened to you?"

"I-I don't know," she faltered, looking away from him.

"Sure you do."

"You won't believe me." She raised her gaze to meet his.

"Try me. I think you'll find I'm pretty open-minded. I mean, do you think anyone would believe me if I told them we were having this conversation right now?"

"I suppose not," she grinned. Her smile was still beautiful, bright.

"Give us a minute, Matty, ok?" Indigo pulled Robbie's old Game Boy from Matty's bag and passed it to him. Matty's whole face lit up. He was only allowed it on special occasions, but right now Indigo needed him distracted. Matty scrambled over to the corner where he plopped down cross legged and switched the device on. Indigo heard the familiar bleep of *Mario Kart* starting up.

"Tell me what happened?" Indigo asked Essie again.

Her face fell, caught in the memory of what she was about to tell him. "It happened a while back. I've lost all sense of time so I can't tell you when exactly. I'd felt someone watching me for weeks, you see. But I never saw anyone, so in the end I brushed it off as paranoia. I'm a nurse and I work a lot of late nights, and I don't get much sleep, so I thought maybe I was just sleep-deprived, or I was overdoing the double espressos.

"Then, one night, I finished up my shift, and I was just about to walk to my car with one of the other nurses, when I found out one of my patients had taken a turn for the worse and wasn't going to last the night..."

Indigo sat and listened while Essie recounted a tale that made the hair on the back of his neck stand on end. As she told him about being kidnapped by a giant tattooed man with a forked tongue, of being taken deep into the bush, of a dark-haired maiden with a foreign accent, he realised the villains of her story were terrifyingly familiar. When she got to the bit about the arrival of their blonde high priestess who brought with her a feeling of black, empty nothingness, Indigo felt sick to his stomach.

Harper was not only ruthless, she was out of control! She wasn't just collecting from her victims, she was devouring all their *energy*, most of their life-force, in one fell swoop.

"I don't know what they did to me," Essie said, "but I've heard people saying I was found in the hospital carpark so they must have moved me once they were done with me. All I recall is waking up and wondering how I got here. I climbed out of bed, but when I glanced back I was still lying there like that," she said, sweeping her arm to indicate her frail body lying there. "No matter how hard I yelled or tried to get their attention, no one could see me or hear me, and I was outside of my body and I just didn't know what to do! It's been so awful," she sobbed, dropping her head into her hands.

"They've been telling my family there's little chance of me waking up now. They're talking about moving me to a care facility. What does that mean for me? That I'll have to sit here beside my body, day after day, year after year watching it slowly grow older until it finally dies of old age? I can't do that, I just can't! I'm stuck here in a living hell!"

"Fucking Harper," Indigo muttered under his breath. He sighed angrily, then explained as gently as he could what had happened to Essie, who had attacked her and what they'd done.

"But I don't understand," she said. "If these... warlocks... sucked out all my power, all my essence, how am I still sitting here talking to you?"

"The part of you sitting here with me is your soul. When they attacked you, the warlocks drained your energy, that's what they feed on. Your soul wasn't affected because the soul is everlasting. They can't touch that."

"Can you help me? Please?"

He stood, hands on hips, head tilted to one side, and regarded her physical body lying there.

"Her spinny-things aren't spinning fast enough," Matty announced, jerking Indigo from his reverie. Matty had pulled a chair over so he could stand on it next to Indigo, emulating him, hands on hips, head tilted to the side as he gazed at Essie's still body.

"Where did you come from, buddy?" Indigo asked, shooting him an exasperated smile.

Matty grinned cheekily and handed him the Game Boy. "It runned out of batteries."

"What did you say about Essie?"

"Her spinny-things. They're spinning slooow," he said, drawing a long slow circle in the air in front of him with his tiny finger. "And that one is broken," he added, pointing to her heart chakra, which Indigo could see was jagged and torn.

"Matty, could you see daddy's chakras – er, spinny-things?" Indigo questioned him.

Matty nodded vigorously. "Yeah, easy peasy lemon squeezy! He had one funny one, the one right here," he said, indicating his solar plexus. "It looked broken, too," he informed Indigo matter-of-factly. "I told him once that his spinny-thing was broken. But he just tickled me and laughed and said *my* spinny-thing was broken, too." He looked at Indigo thoughtfully. "*None* of my spinny-things are broken, Indigo, so I don't know why Daddy said that. Deadie said not to worry, that it wouldn't have maked a difference even if Daddy had listened anyways, whatever that means."

Indigo pulled Matty to him, kissing the top of his head. Indigo had never seen this mysterious Deadie, but Matty talked about him so much, he made a mental note to try and check him out properly sooner rather than later. When he'd previously tuned into Deadie, he'd gotten nothing but good vibes. He sensed in his gut that despite being in possession of a moniker that freaked the Carlisles out, Deadie only had Matty's best interests at heart. He had a feeling Deadie was Matty's guardian, as guardians only tended to show themselves on their own terms.

As for Matty's other "imaginary" friends, Chati and Roger, Indigo felt they might be overdue for a little assistance into the light. Indigo had met them both, and while Chati was only a child, a sweet Thai boy of around five, Roger he wasn't so sure about. Roger was a convict from the First Fleet – a largely harmless convict guilty of nothing more than stealing a few eggs to feed his family – but a convict nonetheless.

"What else do you see?" Indigo asked Matty, nodding back towards Essie.

"Her light-circle is very squashed," Matty informed him, tracing the outline of Essie's biofield with his finger, which was, in fact, very small and tight against her body. The coven had almost entirely drained her of energy and damaged her chakras so badly she could barely metabolise anything. No wonder she was stuck here in limbo, unable to regenerate.

"*Good*, Matty, that's right," Indigo praised him, holding up his palm for a high five. Matty clapped his little hand against Indigo's big one.

It was easy to see what the problem was. Indigo just wasn't sure how to fix it. He could repair her chakras and balance out her biofield right now, but he wasn't sure if he'd be able to reinstate the energy that was stolen from her. So how did he get Essie back into her body?

"You know there are others?" Essie suddenly asked him. "Like me. I hear the doctors and nurses talking. There are others who were found like this."

Ice trickled down Indigo's spine. "So this coven is out there, collecting from people all over Sydney, and leaving them for dead."

"Mummy says if someone takes something and it's yours," Matty piped up, "you need to say 'Excuse me please that's mine and you can't have it and give it back now.'" He wagged his finger for emphasis.

Indigo ruffled Matty's hair affectionately, "That's really good advice, Matty, but–" He stopped dead as he realised Matty was right. Without the pleasantries, of course. Harper and her coven had taken what wasn't theirs. And it was time to take it back. With whatever force necessary.

It was time to call for reinforcements.

chapter eight

love is

manly, new south wales

indigo

Indigo cuddled Matty close when he dropped him at Scarlett's parents' house that evening. He then returned to the hospital, where Scarlett, Cordelia, and Robbie were still sitting at Joshua's bedside. Joshua hadn't regained consciousness, and they'd been told he probably wouldn't again.

Indigo could see he was very close to passing over.

So they sat, as they had all week, by his bedside, beyond exhausted, on the verge of delirium, wondering if every intermittent, laboured exhale would be his last. Joshua's soul hadn't re-entered his body since Indigo had returned, and he'd spent the night in a huddle with his guardian, engrossed in conversation with her.

And then finally, as dawn broke, Indigo saw Joshua's guardian approach the silver cord that tethered him to his body, her hand raised gently, ready to break through the spiderweb tendrils. She turned and asked Joshua a question, and Indigo saw Joshua nod briefly and then re-enter his body.

Scarlett was dozing in the bed beside Joshua, her arms wrapped around his frail body, her head nestled into his shoulder. She sat bolt up when Cordelia cried out, "He's awake!" as she smoothed her father's hair from his forehead, peppering gentle kisses to his face. "I love you, Daddy," Cordelia whispered, her voice thick with tears. Joshua didn't reply, but his eyes remained locked on hers, telling her everything she needed to know.

"We love you so much," Scarlett sobbed, kissing his lips, soft and lingering, and looking deep into his eyes. "You are so, so loved." Indigo stayed in the background; he'd said his goodbyes yesterday. Robbie stumbled to Joshua and pressed his lips to his father's forehead, holding his face between his hands and gazing at him with raw adoration. Joshua looked at each of them, meaningfully, one last time, and then closed his eyes, one last time. A shuddery exhale left his body.

And just like that, the silver cord was broken. He was released from his earthly body; he was on his way back home.

The room immediately felt stark to Indigo. He'd gotten so used to Joshua's guardian and Claire hovering around, the space suddenly felt empty when they crossed over with him.

"He's gone," Indigo said softly, his voice catching.

Scarlett pressed her hand to her mouth, her body trembling, as Robbie laid his head on his father's chest; his body wracked with his sobs.

Cordelia continued to sit in the chair beside the bed, her breath coming harder and faster, her eyes growing wild as her hands clutched at her chest.

Indigo crossed the room quickly, crouching down in front of her, taking her hands in his.

"I... I can't breathe," she gasped, her chest palpitating shallowly, her cheeks flushing. "I can't breathe, Indigo... H-how can I breathe when he's g-gone forever and I'll n-never see him again and my heart is broken and it can't be r-real and I... I...I..."

"It's ok, it's ok," he soothed, squeezing her hands tightly in his to anchor her. "I've got you. You're just having a panic attack." Her eyes searched the room erratically as she spiralled further, her breath rapid and out of control. "Look at me, Cora," he said, his tone soft, soothing yet firm. Her eyes found his, locked on them, and he smiled at her reassuringly. "Breathe with me, ok?" She nodded obediently, her chest fitfully rising and falling as he took a deep breath in and she did her best to follow him. They exhaled long and slow together. Her breath was shaky but she managed to mirror it to his, over and over until it levelled out and her colour began to improve.

"Ok?" he murmured after a while, cupping her cheek in his palm. He focused all his attention on her, not wanting to look to the bed where Joshua's body lay so still and so white, where Robbie still cried as Scarlett mechanically stroked his back, gazing dumbly at the wall in front of her, a look of broken confusion on her face.

Joshua was gone. He was actually *gone*.

Cordelia continued to stare at him, her jaw wobbling, her eyes wide with bewilderment. And his heart broke for her. He wanted so badly to take her pain away, to bear this burden in her stead. If only he could hold his hands over the hurt and heal it like he did physical ailments, but his talents didn't extend to that. No one's did.

She reached out to wipe her thumbs gently across his cheeks and he realised then that he was crying. He pulled himself together and stood up, pulling her to her feet and wrapping his arms tightly around her, rocking her gently as she clung to him and cried.

How they would live without Joshua, they didn't even want to consider. It was too raw, too unimaginable, too surreal. They were about to venture into uncharted waters, embark on a life that would never be the same.

Indigo now understood what Raf had told him, because he was glad Joshua was finally at peace, and of course he knew that where he was going he would be taken care of. Joshua was exactly where he was meant to be. But despite knowing all this, his heart ached with a vast emptiness that echoed through his soul. Not for Joshua, but for them, for himself, for the family Joshua had left behind. The family who would now have to struggle to move on with their lives and find a new routine, a new way of living, that didn't involve their father, their husband, their anchor. And at this point, that was simply unfathomable.

Over the next few days, Cordelia and Indigo threw themselves into arranging the funeral, alongside a robotic Scarlett. Robbie hid away, refusing to leave his room, no matter how much Indigo tried to coax him to come out, to talk to him.

They busied themselves with what needed to be done so they didn't have to think or feel, or stop long enough to let the screaming pain barrel its way back in.

But then, after the funeral, there was suddenly nothing to do, nothing to keep busy with, nothing to hide behind, nothing to stop the agonising grief bubbling up and coursing through their bodies, seemingly tearing them limb from limb.

chapter nine

yesterday

sedona, arizona

raf

Raf sat out by the pool watching the weak winter sun come up, a black beanie pulled low on his forehead, a steaming mug of jasmine tea warming his hands. He stared up at the red cathedral of rock surrounding him, so magnificent that after all these years it still managed to take his breath away.

A couple of days ago, Indigo had called and asked them to come, so tomorrow he'd be making the journey to Sydney with Nash, Aurora and Sasha. He hadn't set foot on Australian soil since before his mother died. Fifteen years, it had been. Fifteen years since he'd lived in the Northern Territory in Arnhem Land with Jedda and his mob. Almost two decades since he'd lived in Byron Bay, back when he'd been so wildly idealistic, so blissfully in love. But that was back before it had all imploded.

It all seemed so long ago now.

He still had so many regrets about his mother's death, about not having gotten home in time to say goodbye. Because by the time he'd made his way back home to San Diego from Arnhem Land, he was too late.

Raf had arrived home the day of her funeral. He was devastated he'd missed the chance to see her one last time. He'd been just six days too late.

His father was inconsolable. The house was brimming with casseroles and lasagnes, delivered largely by the local widow contingent, each hoping to catch the attention of the now-eligible bachelor. Matias was only forty-nine and was still a very charismatic man, but it seemed his wife's death had caused him to grow a conscience, and he was determined to be loyal to her in death, if not in life.

Raf took up his old job at the diner, aiming to save up enough money to buy the dilapidated motorbike he'd spied for sale outside the local garage. It was old and broken down and needed work, but it was a classic and had good bones and he knew how to fix things.

He was back living in his old room at his parents' house. He had insisted he pay his father rent to help with food and groceries. Every week he'd leave money on the kitchen table for his pop, and every week his pop would try to return it to him. "I'm not living here if you won't let me contribute, Pops," Raf would say. His father would grumble and mumble under his breath, but he'd eventually give in and take the money.

Raf spent his days fixing up his bike and surfing, and his nights working at the diner. He was desperately unhappy. The house was so quiet, so empty without his mom pottering around, without his aunties holding court in the parlour. His aunties had never forgiven Matias for his roving eye and refused to come around now their beloved Sofia was no longer there.

As much as Raf loved his pop, home just wasn't home without his mom, and living without her, within the four walls he'd grown up in, just made him feel all the more empty. Living within four walls was now a foreign concept to him in itself, after so many years spent in a *humpy* in the Northern Territory.

He missed his mom, that went without saying. But he also missed Jedda and Jackie and his mob. He missed Arnhem Land in all its ethereal beauty. And there was also the other life he missed, the hypothetical life he could have had with her. With his Charley.

It haunted him. *She* haunted him. He could still picture her face, hear her laugh, feel her satiny skin beneath his fingertips. She'd been one-of-a-kind, that girl of his, and no one else had ever come close. There were so many days, nights, when he thought about calling her, writing to her, reaching out to her. She was older now. Maybe she was ready to settle down, to try again. Maybe she still loved him, too.

He realised now that he and Charley, they'd let their anger, their pride, get the better of them. He'd made a mistake in leaving. He should have stayed. He should have fought for her. After all, she was his night sky, his moon, all his stars. He cursed the arrogant misguided youth he'd been, so rigid, so close minded, so black-and-white.

He did try to call her. Once. But a strange man with a distinct Indian accent had answered the phone and told him the previous family had moved out about six years ago and he'd heard from the neighbours they'd abruptly left town, packed up and moved up north to Queensland, or was it out west to Perth? He wasn't sure which. In desperation, Raf had tried her father's store, but all that had awaited him there was a recorded message informing him that the number he was calling had been disconnected.

She'd vanished. Gone. And he took that as a sign.

It wasn't meant to be. And who was he to rewrite the stars?

It was time he moved on. Started living again, started doing what he loved again. It was time to chalk that whole experience up to the biggest mistake of his life, to learn from it, and to start trying to make something of himself.

One afternoon not long after, he was sitting on the beach in his wetsuit after a surf, watching the sun set. There wasn't another soul around, and he sat alone witnessing the fiery, fuchsia red meld into the stony grey of nightfall over the ocean.

Thanks to Jedda, dealing with spirits and ghosts was now second nature to Raf, so when he heard the sudden voice, it didn't startle him much. It brought with it a wave of calm and serenity which made him smile as he thought of the Ancestral spirits the Aboriginal Elders communicated with. Jedda had often scoffed that the whitefella was too quick to label those who hear voices as mentally ill. When Raf had lived in the Indigenous community, accepting guidance from those long passed had just been a normal part of everyday life.

"I have waited a long time to meet you in the here and now." It was a man's voice, rich and confident yet gentle and soothing. He heard it beside his ear, outside of himself. He turned to find its source, but no one was there. He was still alone, sitting on that beautiful beach, watching another day draw to a close on earth.

"Hello?" Raf had replied, glancing around.

"I am Micah."

"Where are you?" Raf had said, trying to locate the source of the voice. In Raf's experience, disembodied voices had a ghostly presence. But not this one, it seemed.

"I am nowhere and I am everywhere. I am not of your world, I am not of your plane."

"Are you a ghost?"

"I am not a ghost or an angel," Micah had replied. "Long ago I completed my incarnation cycle. I have no physical vessel. I am discarnate. I am teacher."

"What do you want with me?"

"Tonight, while you sleep, your body will be prepared," Micah had told him.

"Prepared for what?" Raf had baulked.

"For me. For your gift. For your greatest challenge yet. Tonight, while you sleep, I shall prepare your body to host discarnate. You will awaken tomorrow very sore and very displeased with me. But in time, you will see it is for the greater good."

"Do I have a say in this?" Raf had cried, fear creeping in.

"You always, always have a say. And you had your say and you agreed to this. It is your path, it was written long before you incarnated into the body you now inhabit. You chose this. You chose to be born to this hereditary line. You cannot change it now."

"What's going to happen to me?"

"Do not be afraid of your destiny," Micah had told him matter-of-factly. "You have the strength to endure whatever is put upon your path."

And just like that he was gone.

"Hello? Micah?"

Nothing.

He had so many questions, so many fears. He was spinning completely out of control, utterly confused with no idea what awaited him. But not once did he question his own sanity. If he knew nothing else, he knew this was real, that he was being guided from beyond.

That night, Raf didn't want to go to bed. He anxiously paced the house, afraid to go to sleep, trying to decide what to do. If only he could speak to Jedda. He'd know what to do. And what would he say?

He'd tell Raf to listen to his gut.

And when he closed his eyes and calmed his breath and tuned into that little voice inside him, Raf knew without a doubt that he could trust Micah. Micah was a part of his destiny.

So Raf went to bed. After much tossing and turning, he fell into a deep, dreamless sleep, comatose until early the next afternoon. He woke up groggy, as if he'd been drugged, and for a while he felt nothing, suspended in animation almost... And then, as he slowly regained consciousness and began to open his eyes, the pain came rushing, tumbling, shooting in.

He cried out in agony as he stumbled out of bed towards the bathroom, crashing into the walls in his delirious disorientation. He could barely see, try as he may he couldn't open his eyes very wide. Nausea was rising rapidly through his body with a cold and clammy rush. Just as he reached the bathroom door, vomit projected from his mouth, spraying the floor and wall in an uncontrollable arc. He staggered towards the toilet, hanging his head over the porcelain bowl, frantically retching over and over again. When he was done, he slumped back against the wall, trying to catch his breath, to still the spinning of the room.

When the dizziness finally subsided, he blundered to his feet. He was desperate for water. He wobbled his way to the sink and fumbled the tap on. As he bent his head down to lap at the water pouring from the faucet, he caught a glimpse of himself in the mirror.

He gasped.

His whole face was black and blue, his eyes swollen to slits. He looked down; his arms, torso, legs, were plum purple with bruises, his whole body burning as if on fire.

"What have you done to me?" he screamed, throwing his head back and gripping the sink in agony. He fell to the floor and curled into the foetal position, the coolness of the tiles providing desperate relief against his throbbing flesh.

When Matias came home that evening, he barely recognised his own son, so swollen and battered was the man lying on the bathroom floor in a pool of his own vomit.

"Diego!" he cried, falling to his knees, cradling his son's head in his lap. "Diego, who has done this to you?"

He wanted to call an ambulance, but Raf objected so violently he reluctantly agreed not to. He helped Raf into the shower and then back into bed, his son crying out at the slightest touch, and he sat by his side all through the night, giving him sips of water when Raf would allow it.

"Tell me who did this to you, Diego?" Matias demanded two days later when Raf seemed lucid enough for questions. But he received no answers. Raf merely groaned and turned away from him.

Matias kept vigil by Raf's bed for four days and four nights. He later told Raf he watched helplessly as Raf writhed and moaned and murmured to someone who wasn't there. He cooled his son's forehead with cold compresses and rubbed ice cubes on his parched lips.

On the fifth day Matias awoke, slumped in the armchair he'd dragged to Raf's bedside, to find his son sitting straight up in bed grinning down at him with an expression on his face that was not his own. His eyes were half-closed, but gazing in Matias's direction.

"Diego?" Matias whispered, confused and frightened.

"Do not be alarmed," Raf said. "This one," he continued, tapping his own leg beneath the bedsheets, "has sacrificed much to contribute to his purpose here on earth. And we owe you much gratitude for your commitment to him these past few days."

Matias sat bolt upright and drew back in fear. "Wh-who are you?" he stammered, eyes wide in terror, because this was not his Diego. "Where is my son?"

Raf continued to grin at him serenely, reaching his arms wide. "I am Micah. This one is right here still. He has just agreed to step aside momentarily to let me speak through him. It causes him no harm. He is here observing us, having merely retreated into a state of deep meditation."

"I-I don't understand," Matias whispered, glancing around the room. Had the devil himself possessed his son? "Who are you? *What* are you?"

"I am spirit, I am discarnate," Micah replied gently. "Many, many years ago I was just like you, with a body and a brain and thoughts and feelings, and I lived in the physical world, many times in fact. But not for a long time since."

"Are you a good spirit?" Matias asked fearfully.

"I certainly mean no harm to this one or anyone else. I am merely here to teach and guide those who seek it. This one committed to help me long ago."

"You're a spirit. A wise spirit?"

"Some might say." Micah smiled, his eyes never opening wider than halfway.

"If you claim to be a spirit, you must know things. Can I ask you a question?"

"Always, always."

"Uh, my-my wife. She… passed. Not long ago." Matias looked at Micah hopefully.

"Ah yes, of course. Let me look, let me look." He closed his eyes and placed his hands on his knees, still and silent for some time.

Finally, he spoke. "I see your wife fought very hard, but it was not on her map to beat that illness. Her accident made little difference to her circumstances. I know this one," he said, tapping his leg again, "wanted very much to get home to her before she passed. But your wife went when she was meant to go.

"Although, I can see she did not want to go," Micah mused, leaning back against the bedhead. "She gripped onto the branch of life until her knuckles were white. She did not want to leave. She would not have let go on her own. In the end, her guardian had to coax her fingers off that branch and help her go."

Matias's face was wet with tears. "A-and now? Where is she now? Is she safe? Is she happy?" He paused, hesitant. "Does… does she forgive me?" he whispered, his voice shaking.

"Know that after you die, even though you'll no longer have a body, you will still feel like you. People do not suddenly become pure angelic beings of light when they pass. They still have all the same thoughts and feelings and baggage they did on earth. If a person dies full of bitterness and negativity, they will merely transition into a bitter, negative soul.

"Your wife was very sick when she died," Micah continued. "And I can see she was met by her guardian and her birth mother who took her to rest and heal. She is surrounded by much love and the most beautiful white light. She is being very well cared for." Micah leant forward, crumpling his face as if deep in thought. "But I can see she does not wish to move on without seeing you and this one again. Yes, yes, I see she has decided to wait."

"To wait?" Matias asked.

"It is not uncommon, with mothers in particular. Most people, after they die, will eventually reincarnate. And although you do tend to keep the same core people in your lives over and over, life after life, it obviously will not always be the same relationship dynamic. So this lifetime, for example, you, her, and this one, were father, mother, and son. Next lifetime she may be your daughter and this one may be your mother or your best friend. So, you can see, you will all still be in each other's lives, but not in the same capacity."

"But Sofia and me… we may not be lovers in another life?"

"I did not say that. I can see you have been husband and wife many lifetimes before. You two have much karma together. Which means you may continue to come back in that capacity until you resolve it. But it will be up to you and your guardian, and your wife and hers how that can best be set up to happen. And please know, fate will always intervene if it's meant to, and by that I mean life will always put you in each other's paths if it is so destined."

"I always thought Sofia was my soulmate," Matias ventured. "The moment I laid eyes on her in that dancehall all those decades ago, I just knew in my bones she was the one."

"Well, yes, your soul would have recognised hers. Because, of course, you *knew* her. You two have been partners lifetime after lifetime. That is why you felt that jolt of recognition. It is why you felt so comfortable with each other, why you immediately 'hit it off,' as people tend to say.

"And it's not just that way for romantic relationships. It can happen with friendships, with parents and their children, with siblings. It is not uncommon to cross paths with a stranger and immediately click with them, becoming instant best friends. It's the same as when you hear of mothers holding their babies for the first time and saying, 'I know you', or of siblings being irreplaceably close.

"And, of course, alternatively there are some people you meet who you simply cannot stand upon sight. They, too, you know. How often have you heard someone say, 'I cannot *stand* that person but I don't know why'? Usually there will be big karma in that relationship. That person has wronged them in another lifetime. They may have stolen from them, betrayed them, raped them, injured them, possibly even murdered them or someone they loved. But they will continue to come together lifetime after lifetime until they resolve their karma.

"But you, your wife, and this one, you will never again be the exact same people you are in this lifetime. Your wife now understands this, and she has things she wishes to say to you and this one in the form you took this time around. So I have been informed she has decided to wait for you."

"Where is she waiting?"

"Between this lifetime and the next. It is the in-between, the equivalent of what you would call a waiting room. Time does not exist where she is, so it does not matter to her whether you join her tomorrow or in fifty years. She will wait for you, just as her mother waited for her."

"So when I die…?"

"She will be one of the souls who greet you."

Matias closed his eyes, a peaceful smile playing upon his lips. "Thank you," he whispered. "Thank you."

"Now," Micah concluded, "if you have no more questions, I shall step aside and allow this one to return."

Matias nodded, sitting up straight and leaning forward, anxious to see his son.

Micah leant back against the bedhead, his eyes closed, and was still and silent for some time, occasionally twitching or flinching. All of a sudden, he drew in a deep breath, and opened his eyes. He looked disoriented but peaceful.

He rubbed his eyes and smiled faintly when he saw Matias. Most of the bruising and swelling had gone down and he looked mostly back to normal.

"Hi, Pops," he breathed, reaching his hand out for his father's. Matias grasped his son's hand with deep affection, holding it tightly in his.

Raf was back.

When Matias asked him if he recalled the conversation he had had with Micah, Raf had admitted that he had been aware of it, but only as much as one is aware of a dream.

On his days off, Raf would usually surf, but once he'd finished fixing up his motorbike, he'd often jump on it and just *ride*. He could lose himself when he was riding, and one day, while losing himself, he was found.

The town was called Sedona. After he'd crossed state lines into Arizona, he'd been drawn to the small desert hamlet and, the moment he rode into its outskirts, he felt a resounding sense of serenity.

The sun was setting over the majestic red rocks that hemmed the town and Raf wasn't ready to leave, so he'd found a room at a B&B and stayed the night.

In that tiny yellow room, surrounded by a menagerie of beaten-metal alien sculptures and paintings of UFOs created at the hands of the sweet little old lady who owned the establishment, inspiration had struck. Raf had whipped out the notebook he carried with him always (which had replaced the Dictaphone of his youth), and started to write.

He'd soon filled the notebook and had had to raid the office of the B&B for more paper in the early hours of the morning. He'd eventually passed out on the bed, surrounded by pages of scribble, and when he'd awoken, not only was he in proud possession of the first five chapters of Sebastian Winters' debut novel, but he'd realised he never wanted to leave this town. Here, he found the peace he'd been searching for.

Sedona reminded him of his beloved Arnhem Land. He knew somewhere down in the depths of his belly that this was where he was meant to be.

So he left Sedona and rode back to San Diego, knowing he was merely going to pack up his things and tie up loose ends. He didn't know how to break the news to his father. The two had grown closer since his mother's death and he knew his pop would be devastated to learn he was moving on. But at least this time he wouldn't be living on the other side of the world.

His father seemed to have developed a lightness in his step since his unsolicited meeting with Micah. He'd relayed much of what was said, and it was clear to Raf that his dad's firsthand experience of Raf's hosting abilities had been very much premeditated by Micah. And for that, he was thankful. For his father had no doubt in his mind that Raf's gifts were genuine and meant to be shared.

Raf had felt sick to his stomach when he'd had to sit down with his father a couple of nights later to tell him he was leaving. "So, Pops… " he began, putting his knife and fork down and meeting his father's eye. They were sitting in the tiny kitchen having dinner at the formica table, the red-and-white-checked curtains flapping lazily behind them in the warm California breeze.

"When do you go, Diego?" his father asked gently, smiling earnestly at his son.

"You… you knew?"

"I had an inkling. We always knew you being here was only temporary, son. Although, if I could have it my way, you would stay here with me forever, but we both know that's not the natural order of things. I shall miss you dearly, but I will be happy with the fact you are out there living your life. You have been given a gift, Diego, and if you stay here it will be wasted."

"I'll miss you too, Pops," Raf murmured softly, placing his hand over his father's.

"Go out there, and live the life you were destined to live. And if it's not too much trouble, see if you can meet a nice girl and make me some grandbabies somewhere along the way," his father teased. Well, half-teased. Raf knew his pop was desperate for their family to expand beyond just the two of them.

Raf smiled sadly as he briefly opened the box he'd packed away in the recesses of his mind, that compartment that contained all memories of her, memories he tried not to look at too much. He shook his head and packed the memory back up tight again before it could escape. No good could come from dwelling on the past. He had to forget that part of his life and move forward.

"I'll see what I can do, Pops." He smiled weakly, knowing deep down that it wasn't likely. The exquisite pain that came with falling in love just wasn't for him.

A week later, he straddled his bike, all his worldly possessions in a pack on his back (his burgeoning manuscript tucked safely down one side) and bade his father farewell. He hugged him tight and breathed in his scent, Brylcream and mothballs, then revved up his bike ready to begin – to continue – his journey.

It wasn't until he stopped for lunch at a diner on the I-10 and opened his pack that he found it. An envelope stuffed down the back of his bag, nestled between two T-shirts and a spare pair of jeans. His name was scrawled on the front in his father's spidery handwriting.

The envelope was full of cash. Raf quickly counted it. It was every dollar he'd paid his father for his room and board since his mother's passing. Every single cent was accounted for. His pop had saved it all. For him.

Raf's eyes filled with tears. For all his dad's faults and mistakes over the years, there was one thing Raf knew to be true – his father's love for him was a beautiful thing.

Raf sat in his backyard, slowly sipping his tea, as he relived those memories that made him laugh and tear up and ache. It was stirring up a lot, this impending trip to Australia. A lot. It was going to be hard for him, going back. But he was willing to do it for Indigo.

He took a deep breath in, holding it for a beat or two before exhaling steadily, reminding himself nothing happened without reason. He obviously had unfinished business down there. He'd been around long enough to understand the divine timing of life. So maybe now was the time for him to deal with that part of his past, in whatever way he was supposed to.

He heard a twig crack in the forest behind him and his head snapped round, ears pricked, listening intently. He stared fixedly into the trees, looking for movement, a flash of colour, anything, but nothing seemed out of place. Frowning, he placed his mug on the ground and climbed to his feet, stalking slowly towards the back fence.

"Hello?" he called, squinting. "Is anyone out there?"

There was a vague disturbance in the silence… The breeze through the leaves maybe, or was it the inhale and exhale of someone breathing?

"Show yourself!"

Still nothing.

"I know you're there!"

Nada.

Raf shook his head. He was usually so composed. But here he was, yelling into the woods like a crazy person. It was probably just a javelina, as there were squadrons of them around at the moment.

But still…

He was reaching for the latch on the back gate when he heard the phone ringing inside. Thinking it might be Indigo, he hurried into the house, grabbing the receiver from its cradle on the kitchen wall.

"Hello?" He pulled his beanie off, ran a hand through his thick dark hair. He stared out the window, still preoccupied by the forest beyond.

"Diego?" The voice was feeble, shaky.

"Pops? What's wrong?" All else was forgotten as he shifted into high alert. His father sounded awful.

"Oh, Diego! You need to come home. You need to come. Please!"

"You're scaring me, Pops," he said, his gut churning. "What's happened? Are you sick? Are you hurt?"

"No, I'm not sick, I'm fine. The parlour flooded–"

"Do you need me to call a contractor, Pops?"

"No it's *fine*, Diego, *listen* to me," he wobbled out. He sounded close to tears. "I-I found something. Of your mother's... and I... I uh, I...." His voice cracked then and he went silent.

"Pops?" Raf asked, wishing he could reach through the phone and take his father's hands in his.

"I-I don't know how to..." His father broke off. "Please come, son. As soon as you can." He sounded wretched. Confused. Raf wondered if the old man's mind was starting to go.

"It's ok, Pops, I'll come tomorrow, ok? I'll call the airline now. I'll call you back with my flight details?"

"Ok, ok, good. That's good," Matias said, exhaling a gust of air.

They said goodbye and hung up and Diego immediately called United. He couldn't get on a flight until the next afternoon, but he had a lot to do between now and then anyway. He'd have to fly to San Diego, then head on to Sydney from LA. But he didn't know how long he'd be delayed. And Indigo needed him, too.

He squeezed his eyes shut tight, torn. He had to trust. Nash, Aurora, Sasha, they were going and he had complete faith in them. They were a family. They had Indigo's back. Maybe it was time for his little falcons to leave the nest, maybe they didn't need him as much as they used to. After all, the best teachers in the world were the ones who made themselves obsolete.

He finished packing, then went round to Nash and Sasha's place. As he strode up the front walk, he passed an attractive young lady slipping from the house, jacket balled up in her arms, hair tousled, stilettos in hand. She smiled sheepishly as Raf bade her good morning.

"Only me!" he called as pushed the front door open and walked into the white stucco, Spanish-style bungalow. He glanced upstairs as Nash's rumpled, auburn head appeared over the wrought-iron bannister.

"Oh, hey, Raf!" he said, flashing his trademark cheeky grin as he bounded down the stairs. Years living in the States had barely tempered his British accent. "Just one more sleep 'til we get to see Indi!" he declared, his excitement palpable. Indigo and Nash were soul mates in the most platonic way possible, and Raf knew Indigo had swiftly become one of Nash's favourite people in the world. Definitely top two, he'd say. Probably tied for first place with Aurora.

"I've just started packing."

"You've just started?" Raf said, raising his eyebrows. "But you're leaving first thing tomorrow."

Nash reached the bottom step and embraced Raf. "Yeah, it's been a hectic week at the ranch. I've gotta head back over there soon, actually. The lad Tommy hired to fill in for me while I'm gone? I've been attempting to show him the ropes. He's a monstrous prat... I have a feeling it's not gonna work out, but I refuse to even take a sneak peek," he said, referring to his pre-cog abilities. Thomas Blackrock owned the ranch Nash managed. A laidback, Native American man, Thomas was a dear friend of Raf's and it was Raf who had initially vouched for Nash. "I haven't taken a vacation day in three years. Never had anyone to visit before." He shrugged his broad shoulders as he continued to fill Raf in on his work dramas.

Nash could talk underwater with a mouthful of marbles. "...and it's not as though Tommy could say no to me taking the time off..." He sighed heavily, a frown shadowing his handsome face. "At least he'll appreciate me more when I get back. Anyway, this is the first chance I've had to pack. But it's all good, I don't need much. It's summer there right, so just a few T-shirts and some swim shorts and I'll be sweet. I'm not like Sash who finished packing yesterday." His laugh died on his lips when he noticed Raf's expression. "What's wrong?"

"Is Sash here?"

"Nope, he had to go finish up some paperwork at the dojo."

Raf thumbed his lip. "Listen, bud... I can't come with you guys tomorrow."

Nash's dark brown eyes bored into his for a moment or two, his brows knit, and Raf knew he was using his clairvoyance. "If Matias needs you, you gotta go to him."

Raf nodded. "He's not in a good way, buddy, he needs me to go down there. He doesn't have anyone else."

Nash squeezed his shoulder. "It's all good, Raf. Me, Sash and Rory, we got Indi, ok?"

"I know you guys do. I just feel terrible, letting him down when he's going through so much."

"Indi's tough, you know that. And hello-o-o? He has us and we're bloody brilliant! He'll be fine."

Raf couldn't help but smile because Nash tended to have that effect on people. They moved to the couch where Raf sunk down beside him. "Do you reckon you could take a look? At Pops? I'm worried he's sick or his mind is starting to go."

Nash nodded and closed his eyes, sitting still and quiet for a couple of minutes. "It's not his health," he murmured, his eyelids flickering. "And by the looks of him and his place, he's more than capable of looking after himself. He's distraught about something... He's crying. There's a letter–" He abruptly stopped talking and opened his eyes. "They've pulled the bloody curtains." He scowled.

Raf frowned. He knew exactly what Nash was talking about. The guardians had final say over any information transmitted psychically.

"You saw Pops with a letter, though?"

Nash nodded. "He had an envelope in his hand. He was clutching it to his chest and crying."

"Ok," Raf said, standing to draw Nash into a hug. "Thanks, bud. I'll let you get back to your packing. Have a good flight and I'll see you guys in sunny Sydney."

"You won't actually."

Raf shot him a look.

"You won't be coming, Raf. Not this time anyway."

"But I–" Raf broke off. He was ashamed to admit he'd felt a fleeting sense of relief. He kissed Nash on the forehead. "I'll go by the dojo and see Sash, tell him myself. Rory's at work?"

Nash nodded.

"I'll swing by the nursing home and see her, too."

Raf was so proud of them, Nash, Aurora, Sasha, his kids. He knew they weren't kids anymore, nor were they *his,* technically, but in his eyes, in his heart, they were and always would be. They were his family, the closest he would ever get to having children of his own and they were enough. More than enough.

The realisation he wouldn't get to see Indigo hit him hard. He missed Indigo a hell of a lot more than he'd thought he would. They'd become so close. Indigo, who'd been so broken when Raf had found him. Almost irreparably so. But so had most of the others, his family, his tribe. Life had come along and tried to break them all.

They'd been beaten down, tossed aside, chewed up and spit out by the world. They'd forgotten who they were, they'd lost their way. They'd lost their light. But together they'd healed each other, built one another back up, bit by bit, piece by piece, so that each of them was now confident and secure and whole. Well, not whole exactly. Those who are broken are never completely whole again, nor are they ever completely fixed. Because it was their brokenness that made them so beautiful and special and strong and worthy in the first place.

As they reached the door, he stopped to gaze at Nash, his heart swelling.

"What?" Nash asked, fingers groping at his chin. "Do I have something on my face?"

"No, I was just remembering when we first met."

Nash winced. "Wow, I haven't thought about that in a long time," he said, his hands automatically moving to finger the ropey scars that marred the insides of his elbows. Raf knew how hard it was for him to remember how he'd been back then.

"You've come so far." Raf smiled, looking at the fit, muscular man standing before him and thinking back to that frail, skin-and-bone boy lying in that London hospital bed, having been brought back from the brink of death. His arms had been covered in thick bandages that day, and they'd told him how hard it had been for them to find a vein that wasn't collapsed or blown through which to administer the antibiotics he so desperately needed. "Look at you now. I couldn't be prouder of the man you are today."

Nash swallowed hard and looked away.

"I love you, buddy, you know that right?" Raf said, pulling him into another hug. "We're so blessed to have you as a part of our family."

"Cheers, Raf. I love you, too," he whispered, giving Raf a heartfelt squeeze then releasing him. "I can't say I'm not disappointed you won't be joining us on our little adventure tomorrow."

"But you're so excited to see Indigo it overshadows everything, right?"

Nash shot Raf a sheepish grin. "Yep, as sorry as I am my brother-from-another-more-dysfunctional-mother is going through a shitty time and that there's a coven of murderous warlocks on the loose, I've missed Indi so bloody badly I'll take any excuse to go. Plus, I've always wanted to visit Australia. As an Englishman, it's a rite of passage to visit one's penal colonies and Australia's always been top of my list."

Raf cupped Nash's cheek and laughed.

Yep, his kids would be just fine.

don't cry

collaroy, new south wales

cordelia

"Do you wanna stay at my place tonight?" Drew asked, his hand stroking the length of her thigh as he cocked a suggestive eyebrow. At his insistence that a change of scene would do her good, the two of them had taken a drive down to Collaroy. They were parked in his grey Subaru at Fisherman's Beach, the ocean gently lapping at the boat ramp, the stars glimmering in the night sky.

"Hmmm, what?" she asked, shifting her vacant gaze from the inky black horizon. The car radio played so softly she could barely hear No Doubt singing *Don't Speak*.

"I said, do you wanna stay at mine tonight?" he said leaning in, his lips making their lazy way up her neck. "Let me try and take your mind off things?"

She shrugged him off. "Seriously?" she asked, staring at him incredulously.

"What?" He seemed genuinely confused.

"We cremated my father yesterday. Like, are you serious right now? Do you really think I'm in the mood?"

"It's what I'd want if I were in your shoes," he said, then paled when he saw her expression.

"Well, I guess that's the difference between men and women."

"Tell me how I can cheer you up, Cee? I'm sorry, ok? I love you so much, I don't like seeing you so sad all the time. I don't know what to do to help you. I mean, give me a clue, ok?"

"I –" she began. The truth was she didn't know what she needed either. She shrugged despondently.

"I'm sorry. About yesterday."

She looked at him questioningly.

"At the funeral. I just can't stop thinking about it. When you got up to speak, and you just started crying and you were standing there with your eulogy and your hands were shaking and you couldn't catch your breath and I just continued to sit there like a moron, watching you fall apart. I'm sorry for not knowing what to do. It seems to kinda be my thing lately, right? Not knowing what you need."

"It's ok," she murmured, feeling a stab of guilt, because she hadn't really given him the chance to help her. He hadn't been the one she'd looked to for help, the one she'd locked eyes with, begging for support.

"It should have been me that got up there with you, that took your eulogy and read it for you, so perfectly every single person there fell completely apart. Not *him*."

"It's not your fault," she said dully.

"It is. Sometimes I could kick myself for being such an emotionally retarded male. I'm an embarrassment to my gender."

"You're not," she said, smiling wistfully at him. "Look at how much you did, helping organise the wake. Dad would have loved it. The CD you burnt of all his favourite songs… It was perfect."

"When we were carrying the coffin out of the church," he suddenly blurted, "and Matty wanted so badly to help but he couldn't reach, it was Wolfie he ran to, to lift him up so he could grab the handle. Not Rob, not me, not either of your grandfathers. Wolfie."

Cordelia's mouth fell open. How long had he been waiting to get that one off his chest? And why was he bringing all this up? It had been hard enough at the time, watching the men who'd been a special part of her father's life lift his coffin and carry it from the church as her school choir sung *Will You Be There*. Matty had seen what was happening and had wanted to help, too. The memory caused something in her chest to swell, the ache consuming her.

"Wolfie's a big part of your family," Drew continued, oblivious to her pain. "He has some major history with you guys. I mean, no one knows that better than me, right? And it's fine. I don't begrudge that." He smiled tightly. "He and I… Well, hopefully we can get back to where we were one day. It's just hard right now… considering…" he trailed off, glanced at her.

"Considering?"

He flushed slightly, pursed his lips. "Your past with him. You were in love with him for so long, Cee, does that ever really go away?" His eyes bored into hers.

She felt sick to her stomach. Drew had always been a truth seeker and this was clearly no exception.

"I'm not blind, Cordelia, I know he's in love with you, he always has been. And now, now I can see it on his face every time he looks at you. I know things have been a bit rocky between us lately, that I haven't been in the best place. But I love you, Cee. You know how much I wanna make this work." He reached for her hand, kissed it. "You and I, we've built something pretty special, right?"

She nodded as she stared out into the darkness, her throat aching. She loved Drew, she truly did and the last thing in the world she wanted was for him to be feeling like this.

"Before we started dating, all I wanted was for Wolfie to come home. We were best mates for years. He saw me through so much. When Mum walked out on us, it was him who picked me up and put me back together." He swallowed hard, squeezed her hand. "But then, once you and me got together, if I'm honest, there was a big part of me that hoped he'd never come home. Or that if he did, it would be with some smoking hot, supermodel fiancé in tow."

She glanced up at him in shock. He'd never told her this before. "Why?"

"Because what's between you and him, how am I ever meant to compete with that?" The sadness in his eyes made her want to cry. "I guess what I'm saying is that I can't spend my life questioning your feelings for me, constantly wondering if you have doubts. The stress of that, I don't have the strength for it… I know it would make me into someone I don't want to be. I can't be second best. I deserve more than that. I know this is completely shit timing and for that I'm so sorry, but I need you to work out where you stand, what you want. If it's me, then I'll be the happiest guy in the world and we can get on with our lives." He tilted his head to one side, smiled at her, his eyes soft. But then they hardened up. "But, if it's him… Well, you need to admit it. To yourself and to me… I know how you felt about him once, I was there, remember?"

"Drew–" she began, a palpable weight crushing her chest so she could barely breathe. She stared down into her lap, blinking. She was so emotionally drained, tired to the very marrow of her bones.

"I guess for me the big question, the one I've tried my hardest to avoid, is how *do* you feel about him? Do you love him?" His throat worked, his breath wavering. "More than me?"

"Don't be ridiculous, Drew," she whispered. "You're my boyfriend, it's you I want to be with."

"It would mean more if you could look me in the eye," he replied dryly.

She raised her eyes slowly to meet his. He sighed heavily and rubbed his face with the heel of his hands. "Listen, Cee, I love you." And she could see in his eyes just how much, and it physically hurt her heart that he was hurting like this. "All I'll say is that I saw what his leaving did to you back then. Is it really worth risking it all on him again? When you have me, who will always love you, who would sooner die than hurt you? I know I've made mistakes, but I feel like I've learnt from them." He leant forward, brushed his lips softly against hers. She closed her eyes, tried to enjoy his kiss, but her whole body was jittering, her head light. "As much as I want to tell you I can be the bigger person and I'll be able to walk away from you with no hard feelings, the thought of not having you by my side, the thought of you with him… Well, it's eating me up inside."

She shook her head, because she was empty of words, empty of everything, really. Her hands were wringing in her lap, her stomach twisting in knots. He gathered her into his arms and kissed the top of her head, "I'm sorry, Cee, I'm so sorry. I didn't mean to pile on. I never wanna be the reason you're upset."

"Can you take me home?" she managed, her voice shaking.

When he dropped her off, he walked her to the door, wrapping his arms around her and gently pressing his lips against hers. "I love you," he told her again.

"I love you, too," she replied, because she did. But she didn't ask him in.

sydney airport, new south wales

indigo

The moment Indigo made eye contact with Nash at the Arrivals gate, Nash flung the luggage trolley at Sasha and start sprinting towards him.

"INDIIIIIIIIIIIIIIIIIIIIIIIIIIIII!!" He hollered loudly enough that half the airport turned to stare at the boisterous Brit. He launched at Indigo, scooping him up in a bear hug and spinning him around.

When Nash eventually put him back down, Indigo didn't let go. He couldn't. He clung hard to Nash, burying his face in his shoulder. He'd had to be so resilient for the Carlisles since Joshua's passing. In the days that had followed, at the funeral, at the wake, he'd had to be the infallible one, the stoic one, their steady place to fall.

But seeing Nash, Sasha and Aurora – his other family – arrive, allowed him to let go. He could stop being the strong one, finally. He felt his lip wobble, and the next thing he knew, his eyes had filled with tears.

"Ah, mate," Nash said, hugging him tighter. He cupped Indigo's face in his hands and pressed his forehead to his. "I'm so sorry."

Nash eventually stepped aside so Sasha could embrace him. Sasha palmed Indigo's cheek and stared into his eyes, his light brown gaze so full of compassion and understanding, a sob rose in Indigo's chest. "I've missed you guys so much," he said gruffly as Aurora tentatively reached to give him a quick, loose hug. "Thank you for coming."

"As if we wouldn't," Nash scoffed as he put on a dramatic voice and sung a verse of *That's What Friends Are For*, giving Dionne and Elton a pretty good run for their money.

Indigo laughed, swiping roughly at his eyes. "Ease up, I'm still getting over the last time you serenaded me, man," he said, thinking of the night before he'd left Sedona when Nash had gotten on stage at his farewell party and dedicated a song to him.

Nash just grinned and continued to sing loudly, jumping on top of the luggage trolley and clasping one hand across his heart, holding the other out wide. By now pretty much the whole airport was staring open-mouthed. But Nash clearly didn't give a shit. Indigo couldn't help but laugh as he dried his eyes on his T-shirt and grabbed Nash in a headlock, pulling him off the trolley. He hugged him before putting his arm around him and guiding him to his car, Sasha and Aurora following behind with the luggage.

"Fuck me, I missed you," Indigo said, looking at him sidelong and grinning.

"Missed you more," Nash quipped as they reached Indigo's black SUV and started piling their bags inside. "Shotgun!" he called over his shoulder to the other two. "How is your car so clean?" Nash glanced round the pristine interior as he climbed into the passenger seat.

"Not everyone lives in filth like you, Blaze," Aurora said, her lips quirking up, and Indigo knew she was thinking of Nash's dusty old pick up, a garbage tip of granola bar wrappers, banana peels, chip packets and half-empty bottles of water.

As they drove home from the airport, Indigo told them all about Joshua and the funeral, before he took a deep breath and turned the conversation to the topic of Harper, filling them in on the abysmal headway he'd made.

"She's completely vanished off the radar."

"We can't get a read on Harper herself either," Nash told him. "And it's not for lack of trying, right, Sash?" he said, glancing back at Sasha who nodded. "She's got herself a bloody accomplished shrouder, that's for sure. I'd love to meet him."

"Or her," Aurora said pointedly.

"It's definitely a dude," Nash said. "The energy coming off him reeks of testosterone." They crossed the Spit Bridge and continued up the hill towards Manly. It was a beautiful day, the sun glinting off the harbour below, and Indigo was proud Sydney was turning it on for his friends.

"Call me crazy," he ventured, "but I think we should go by her house."

"You're crazy," Aurora confirmed.

"You know where she *lives?*" Nash gave him some serious side-eye.

"Well, not exactly. I know where she used to live. It was her parents' house before they died and I know she inherited it."

"You think she's just gonna answer the door and invite you in for tea, brah?" Sasha asked, brows soaring.

"Definitely crazy," Aurora reiterated.

"Look, I just think we should cross it off the list, right?" Indigo turned the volume down on Nirvana mid *Something In The Way*. "She's just *out there*, guys, and she's attacking people and leaving them for dead, and she's getting more and more powerful with each attack, and what if she comes for Cordelia again? I mean, I'm there every day at the Carlisles', keeping an eye on her like a fucking stalker, but I can't be there all the time and I don't know what else to *do*."

"Ok, ok," Sasha said, placing a comforting hand on Indigo's shoulder. "We hear you, man. I get it. I'll come with you to Harper's."

Indigo flashed him a grateful smile. "That night on the beach, when she attacked Cora, when she revealed herself and asked me to join her fucked up coven... She told me she was gonna ask nicely once, that next time she wouldn't be mucking around. She honestly thought there was a real chance I'd change my mind. She's not going to be happy when she realises that's never gonna happen."

"If you're right and she *is* watching you, our arrival in town will make your decision pretty obvious," Aurora said.

"I know." Indigo set his jaw.

"On another note, have you spoken to Cordelia yet?" Nash asked. "About what happened at the hospital, and again at Josh's funeral? About your suspicions about her?"

Indigo shook his head tersely. He wished he'd never told Nash, who'd clearly blabbed to the others judging by their knowing looks. Bloody big mouth. There were no secrets with this lot. "I haven't found the right time."

"Christ, Indi! She *needs* to know, brother! If she has to get your attention in an emergency, it could be the difference between life and death."

"I *know*, Nash, believe me I know. It's not like I'm intentionally keeping it from her. Drew's always hanging around being all possessive and shit... And remember her dad just died, ok? It's hardly been the best time to drop *this* bomb on her!"

"I get that, Indi, but with Harper out there…"

"I wish Raf was here," Indigo blurted.

"Ouch! It's fine, Indi, they're only feelings, they'll grow back," Nash said tightly.

"That's not what I meant. You know how grateful I am that you guys are here. But… remember what Raf did to Skeet and his coven?"

"What, you mean that time you were stabbed and kidnapped by inbred warlocks?" Nash said archly.

"Skeet kidnapped Dawn's daughter, too," Indigo said defensively.

"Yeah… he didn't exactly *kidnap* Reggie, eh," Sasha interjected. "She was a willing captive, if I recall, and I do because I was there. That was the day you and I officially met, Indi." Indigo could hear the fondness in his voice.

"Dawn told me what Raf did to them after that," Indigo said. "How he wiped their memories. She said that although they will forever be warlocks, they'll no longer have any recollection of that or know how to access their powers. I was kinda hoping Raf might be able to, like, do that to Harper and her psycho coven." His knuckles whitened on the steering wheel.

"It wouldn't be enough," Aurora explained. "They're collectors. They're too powerful. Skeet and his coven are inbreds. Inbred power is murky. Unstable and easy to influence."

Disappointment rippled through Indigo's gut and he sighed deeply. "So what then?"

"Blaze and I will scout the hospitals and check out the victims, figure out how many of them are Harper's doing," Aurora said.

"I can take you," Indigo told her.

"We know your plate's pretty full, brother," Nash said as they turned into Indigo's driveway. "No babysitting required. We're pretty resourceful you know. You and Sash go check out Harper's potential viper's nest. Divide and conquer, mate."

"This is your house, eh?" Sasha asked in awe as Indigo reached for the remote attached to the sun visor. He pressed it and the black wrought iron gates began to open. They drove down the long driveway edged by rows of towering magnolia trees laden with creamy latte blooms, and then the Van Allen Estate appeared in all its glory. The Estate always made a good first impression, with its established gardens, expansive lawns and, of course, the enormous ivy-clad sandstone house that sat at the centre of it all.

"Whoa," Nash breathed. "I knew you were fully minted, but holy *hell*. Nice pile of bricks you've got here, mate. If it doesn't have a home theatre, a games room and a gym I'll be bitterly disappointed."

"Well then, lucky for you it does," Indigo said lightly as he parked at the top of the circular drive, under the shade of the ancient Moreton Bay Fig that took pride of place on the front lawn. Stalactite vines surrounded its majestic trunk and, just like the twin fig tree in the backyard, its canopy of branches would twinkle with fairy lights at dusk. Indigo never bothered to park in the underground garage, which was large enough to house Bernadette's luxury car collection, and Indigo's jetskis and motorbikes.

The big double doors at the front of the house flew open and Edita came hurrying out, her eagerness in meeting his friends showing in her wide smile. Short and stout, her pale brown hair pulled back in a severe bun, Edita wore a navy dress buttoned to the throat. Her husband Lukas was hot on her heels, craning his thick neck to see their houseguests as they emerged from the car, one by one.

"G'day, g'day," Lukas boomed with an enormous grin, holding out a giant, callused hand as introductions were made. Lukas was a mountain of a man, his healthy belly proof of someone who enjoyed a few beers at the end of a full day's work. He was loud and vibrant, always ready with a happy smile and a good yarn. Lukas didn't have a bad bone in his body. He and Edita met when he'd been hired to take care of the gardens at the Van Allen Estate when Indigo was only small.

Edita bustled everyone inside, Nash chatting a mile a minute, plying her with questions, Sasha gazing in wonder at his surroundings, as Aurora followed impassively behind. After showing each of them to their rooms, Edita ordered them to freshen up then come down to eat. She'd been cooking for days in anticipation of their arrival.

Once settled, they ate in the backyard, gathered around the long teak table Edita had set in the shade of the giant fig. It was agreed Indigo and Sasha would try Harper's parents' home later in the day when there was a greater chance of someone being home. Nash and Aurora would start checking out the hospitals during evening visiting hours. So now they had a few hours to kill.

"What do you guys wanna do ?" Indigo asked, leaning back in his chair and bending his knee into his chest. "We could go for a mountain bike at Manly Dam? Or a snorkel at Shelly Beach? The water's amazing at the moment. This time of year the bay's full of groupers, eagle rays, cuttlefish, Port Jackson sharks–"

"*Sharks?*" Nash baulked. "I'm far too jetlagged for sharks today. Or for riding up mountains." He glanced over at the twenty-five metre infinity pool, spotless blue and glistening in the sun. "Now that thing has my name all over it," he said, hooking his hands behind his head.

Aurora nodded in agreement. She'd already changed into a skimpy yellow bikini. "I don't do sharks," she said.

"Port Jacksons are the pussy cats of sharks," Indigo muttered under his breath.

"I'd love a surf, eh," Sasha said, admiring the ocean below the property. "Although obviously not there." It was a harbour beach and the waves were practically non-existent. Having grown up in Hawaii surfing every day, Indigo knew how much Sasha missed it, living in land-locked Sedona.

"That southerly's come through so Fairy Bower's going off. I'll take you down for a wave," Indigo said, excited to show Sasha his favourite break. Excited *someone* wanted to do *something* that would take their minds off the afternoon ahead.

"Right on," Sasha grinned, his hand curling into a shaka.

"Maybe I'll have a bit of a kip," Nash yawned.

"Don't do it, man," Indigo said. "Only way to beat jetlag is to push through."

Nash rubbed his eyes and groaned. "Fiiiiine. Would be good if you could jot down the names of every hospital we need to visit? Then at least I can figure out where I have to go."

Indigo nodded grimly. Harper was like a giant shadow looming over them all, and forgetting she was there was proving to be impossible.

Indigo stared up at the imposing property beyond the high hedge wall. He carefully scanned each sculpted bush and tree, each heavily-draped window, every shadowy corner and cranny. When he was satisfied all was quiet, he unlatched the gate. He held it open for Sasha.

"So this was Harper's parents' place, eh?" Sasha said. He was fixated on the enormous Federation mansion that seemed to go on forever. It was impeccably maintained, and with its stained glass windows and red brick façade, it screamed old money.

Indigo nodded.

"What happened to them?"

"There was a long history of domestic violence," Indigo said quietly, remembering the day he'd first met Harper's mum, Helene, how banged up she'd been. "Her dad, well, he drank a lot. They'd lost Harper's sisters in an accident years before, and I think he always struggled to come to terms with that. Anyway, the whole thing ended in a murder-suicide that dominated the local news for weeks."

"He finally went too far?"

"No, actually. It was Helene who finally snapped." Indigo exhaled steadily. "It was Harper who found them."

Sasha whistled low under his breath. "Wow. I know she's our mortal enemy and all, but man, that's super rough, eh."

Indigo set his jaw. Sasha was right, it *was* rough. But these days he found it difficult to muster much sympathy for his warlock ex.

The two of them followed the winding path that led to the dark green front door panelled with lead lights. When they reached the porch, Indigo hesitated.

"You good?" Sasha asked.

Indigo cocked a brow.

Sasha reached for his shoulder. "I got your back, ya."

Indigo flashed him a distracted smile, then raised his hand to knock on the heavy oak. He could hear the sound reverberating through the house. He waited a bit, then knocked again. No one came.

"I hate to say it, but I told you, man," Sasha said, pocketing his hands and leaning back on his heels.

But he'd barely finished his sentence when they heard a click and the door eased open a crack. A dark brown eye peered all the way up at Indigo. "Yes?"

"Uh, Fernanda?"

"Yes?"

"I don't know if you remember me–"

"I remember you, Master Indigo." A Brazilian accent clung to her words. Fernanda had run the Valentine household for years; Harper must have kept her on after her parents' passing.

The door opened a few more inches. Fernanda's eyes never left him. She'd aged since he'd last seen her, her shoulder-length curls now almost entirely usurped by grey, the lines on her face deeper.

"This is Sasha," he said, and her gaze darted briefly to the other man standing on her doorstep, then returned to Indigo. "So, how've you been, Fernanda?"

She continued to stare at him.

"Harper home?" he asked casually.

"I have not seen Miss Harper in months." Her eyes jerked momentarily to the left, then they were back on him. Indigo tried to peer past her, but she hastily pulled the door closer to block his view.

He narrowed his gaze at her. He knew he wasn't supposed to, that it was pretty damn rude, but considering the circumstances he really had no choice: he attempted to wander inside her mind.

He was met with an impenetrable wall of black shadow.

He glanced at Sasha. *'Her mind's been shrouded,'* he said telepathically.

'Yep, and it's not self-imposed.'

Indigo glanced around uneasily. *'From what sort of distance can they do that?'*

'With a shrouder as powerful as theirs?' Sasha rubbed his chin. *'It's infinite.'*

'So they're not necessarily here? Or nearby?'

'Well, no,' Sasha projected. *'But if they're going to the trouble to shroud her mind this hard, there's something in there they don't want us seeing.'*

"Fernanda," Indigo said, his voice low, "are you *sure* you haven't seen Harper?"

"That is what I said." Her tone was firm.

"Is everything ok? If it's not, if you need help…"

She scoffed loudly and slammed the door in his face.

"So what now?" Sasha asked.

"I guess that means we're done here, for now. Let's go." He shivered as they headed back up the pathway. "So I s'pose from that we can deduce Harper's around…"

"Yep, and she knows we were here."

every rose has its thorn

indigo

In the days following the funeral, Scarlett locked herself in her room for hours at a time. When she did emerge, she wandered the house listlessly, her gaze that of a deer in headlights as she went through the motions of gauging how her kids were doing and ensuring everyone ate.

Indigo was juggling his time between Nash, Aurora and Sasha and the Carlisles. To keep Matty occupied, he decided to teach him how to ride a skateboard. He took Matty to the skate park every day, smiling when the little dude determinedly tackled the ramps and half pipe, for which he was rewarded with one of Edita's brownies on the way home.

Matty, it seemed, was the only one of them who still had an appetite. None of them had been hungry in weeks, although the friends and neighbours who continued to kindly drop off meals on their doorstep didn't seem to realise that. Indigo had relayed this to Edita, but she still persisted in loading him up with food to deliver.

A few days after the funeral, Indigo was carrying a bleary-eyed Matty into the house, after he'd once again drifted off in the car. He took Matty upstairs and tucked him into the pillow fort they'd made the day before, then came back down to find Cordelia trying to shove the latest lot of sympathy food into the freezer. She was all long limbs and golden grace in a black mini skirt and a white T-shirt knotted at the waist, her feet bare, her nails painted a shimmery pearl.

"Why is it always lasagne?" she was muttering as she attempted to cram a foil baking dish into the already overly full freezer. "I'm sick of the sight of it. I'll never be able to look at it again without thinking of death." She cried out as a cascade of frozen goods tumbled out onto the floor. "*Fuck!*" she screamed, grabbing her left big toe which had been bludgeoned by a frozen chicken. "*Fuck this fucking shit!*"

"You ok?" he asked, grabbing her by the waist and effortlessly lifting her to sit on the kitchen table so he could get to work rearranging the freezer. He handed her a bag of frozen peas.

"I'm *fine!*" she said through clenched teeth, clutching the peas to her toe. "Everything's just fucking *perfect!*" She glanced up to see what he was doing. "It's no use, Indigo, it won't fit."

"I don't know about that," he murmured, deep in concentration. "I was *really* good at Tetris once upon a time…" He had the whole thing sorted in under ten minutes. "There," he said, standing back to admire his handiwork. "And there's space for more if you need it."

"Show off," she muttered under her breath.

"Do you want me to heat something up for you?" he asked, his eyes travelling over her, noting the prominent valleys edging her clavicles. "When was the last time you had a proper meal?" Grief showed in the thinness of her body, the dullness in her eyes.

"What are you saying?" she asked defensively. "That I look like shit?"

"You couldn't look like shit if you tried," he said, which was true, although she didn't look as healthy as he would have liked. "But I'm gonna find you something to eat anyway. I know I'm hungry." He opened the fridge and poked through a few casserole dishes until he found something that wasn't lasagne. He turned the oven on and popped it in.

"How's your toe?" he asked, lifting the peas off so he could examine it. "It's not broken, but you're going to have a nasty bruise. Do you want me to–"

"No," she said abruptly, sliding off the table and hobbling to the fridge. She opened the door and begun transferring dishes to the newly freed-up freezer. "It's fine. Everything's fine."

"No, it's not," Indigo said gently. He tossed the bag of peas back and forth between his hands, then reached around her to shove them back in the freezer. "Cora, can we talk?" He'd been trying to pull her aside for a quiet chat for days now. He needed to talk to her about what had happened at the hospital, then again at the funeral. Nash had been on his arse for days now about his failure to do so.

Her shoulders slumped and she exhaled wearily. She continued to stand there for a moment or two, then shut the fridge before following him into the rumpus room. He slid the big double doors closed behind them. Someone had left the radio on and Poison were crooning about roses and thorns, about melancholy cowboys, the scars of love and darkness and dawn.

Indigo sat down on the brown suede couch and Cordelia settled herself at the opposite end, picking up a cushion and hugging it to her. Her hair was pulled casually back with a tortoiseshell claw clip, loose tendrils falling free to frame her face. She gingerly pulled her feet up under her, favouring her damaged toe, and looked at him expectantly.

"I hate to see you so miserable," he began. He examined her so closely she shifted and looked away. "It's not just Josh, is it?"

"I don't know," she replied flatly. "It's... it's everything."

"What's going on?"

She sighed deeply and closed her eyes. "Inds..." she finally whispered when she opened them, and the pain in those aqua depths made his heart squeeze. "I can't talk about this with you."

"What do you mean?" he asked, brows pinched. "You always said you could tell me anything."

"Not this. Not anymore." She shook her head sadly and began to stand up.

"Wait. Please don't go. I hate the way things are between us."

She sat back down, staring at the floor. "I don't know how else to be around you," she finally replied, finally meeting his eyes. "Drew and me... Things are... messy," she said so softly he barely heard her, but his heart was leaping so he must have.

"Messy?" he repeated evenly, hating that he felt hopeful and guilty at the same time. "Messy how?"

"I told you how he wrecked his knee last year?"

He nodded. He'd noticed Drew's limp when he'd seen him and he'd reflexively taken a good look at his knee, able to see the damaged cartilage, the scar tissue and the mangled nerves. He'd also been able to see the leylines of energy that had been cut during surgery, mucking up the flow to his whole leg. A vision of how it had happened had come to him then too, the sickening accident on the football field, the skiing injury soon after. As much as he wanted to offer his help, he got the feeling Drew didn't want much to do with him.

"Well, he's been in a tonne of pain ever since. It's been terrible. He can't sleep, he's struggling to study. It hurts him all the time. And it seems the only way he can manage his pain is with drugs. And I'm not talking pharmaceuticals." She paused, pressing her lips together, before adding, "Weed to sleep, speed to study."

Indigo didn't say anything. He'd been able to tell from Drew's biofield that he'd been regularly using. Frequent drug use generated an etheric mucus that hung around the head like a greyish green cloud.

"I don't think it's good for him, Inds. He's not himself. I mean, a little bit here and there for fun is one thing, I can handle that, but taking this shit all the time? And now, he's stressing out about you being back. About you and me, about our… history." She shrugged sadly, tears blooming in her eyes. "He said I have to choose. Him or you."

"I thought you had chosen," Indigo replied, trying to keep his tone light despite his quickening pulse. "That day on the beach. You chose him."

She shrugged again, absentmindedly twisting the ring that was a permanent fixture on her right hand, the ring Scarlett had given to her on her thirteenth birthday. "I thought I had, too. But Drew seems to think I'm not being… honest with myself. And you know, half the stuff that's going on in his head, he doesn't say it, you know how he is, but…" She stopped, clamped her jaw.

"But what?" Indigo said, leaning forward, holding his breath in anticipation.

"Look, this is going to sound crazy… but it's like – it's like I can hear it anyway," she admitted softly. "I just know what he's thinking *all the time*. I guess we've been together for a while now. I suppose that's just what happens with couples."

Indigo exhaled sharply. Because just like that she'd made it really easy for him. He had his way in. "I know this isn't the ideal time, Cora, but I've actually been wanting to talk to you about that."

"About what?" she asked, eyeing him wearily.

"About some of the things you've said to me lately. About hearing people's thoughts."

She screwed up her nose. "What are you talking about?"

He drummed his fingertips to his mouth as he regarded her. "Listen, ever since you told me word-for-word what Josh was saying to Matty at the hospital when he was unconscious, I've had my suspicions. And then, at his funeral…"

He hesitated. He needed to tell her. With Harper out there somewhere, she *needed* to know. "You know you asked me for help, right? With your eulogy?"

"*What?* No… I looked to you because I couldn't do it on my own. It was a glance, nothing more."

"No, Cora. I *heard* your words. In my head. And now, what you've just said about hearing Drew's thoughts…"

She narrowed her eyes at him.

He'd discussed this at length with Nash, but now, sitting here with her, it wasn't the easiest topic to broach. He just had to say it.

He took a deep breath. "Well, to be blunt, I suspect you might be… different… like, in the way that *I'm* different." He stared at her boldly. "I think you have higher senses, too, Cordelia."

She flinched and paled.

"I reckon you're telepathic."

"I'm not," she whispered, shaking her head emphatically.

'*I would argue that you are,*' he said, but not out loud.

She reeled back, staring at him in fear. "Don't do that," she whimpered. "I don't like it, it freaks me out."

"You have a gift, Cora," Indigo told her out loud, then, '*You just need to learn how to manage it*'.

"I never had this gift before! I don't think I ever had it until… until…" Her eyes went wide. "Until the night I was attacked on Queenscliff Beach! The night you saved me, and you… you *did* something to me! What did you *do* to me, Indigo?" she demanded. That was the night Harper and her coven ambushed Cordelia, immobilising her before slitting her throat. Indigo had had to heal her, had saved her life.

"Are you *serious?* You think I'd ever harm a hair on your head?" Her thinking that, it stung like hell.

She continued to stare at him. He could hear the chaos erupting inside her mind, a mishmash of competing thoughts so confusing that they apparently rendered her unable to articulate a single one of them.

"You *know* I wouldn't," he said, gazing at her with complete sincerity. "That night... " He swallowed hard, closing his eyes briefly as he relived the horror of it all. "I... I had to do something... Your neck wound, it was pretty bad. So I healed it, yes."

"And?" she prompted, gaze boring deep into his.

"And uh, I *may* have had to realign the flow of your body, repair a couple of chakras, clean out your biofield–"

"Oh, is *that* all?" she said, brows soaring.

"Think back to when you were a child," he said, gaze now locked on hers. "You told me you used to have all those bad dreams? How you used to wake up and sense something was there, that you used to hear whispering voices?"

She nodded tersely.

"I reckon you've always had a connection to other worlds... to other... lives. It's only as you've gotten older that you've closed yourself off, shut down your higher senses because you started to believe people when they told you that you were just imagining things and that hearing voices wasn't normal."

Her mouth dropped open.

He knew this revelation was a lot.

"And when I I healed you that night," he continued evenly, "it must have opened up your senses again, realigned what you've always been. Once I got everything flowing the way it's meant to, it allowed your higher senses to come to the forefront, to start working the way they're meant to. You still have a ways to go, but it's a start. You didn't actually think I'd ever do anything to hurt you?" he asked softly, feeling wounded she could say such a thing.

She continued to stare at him in shock for a moment or two before softening. "I'm sorry. I *do* know that, Inds, in my heart I do. I'm just emotional is all, it's been a... big week. A *bad* week." She set her jaw, her eyes fluttering shut. "I don't even know what to say." She sighed with the weight of the world, hugging the couch cushion tight. She

shook her head and shot him a look of complete overwhelm. "I just…
I can't deal with this right now, Indigo. Not on top of everything else."

He nodded, because he got it, he really did. The hollow in his chest
ached for her and all she'd had to endure of late.

"Ok, I'm sorry, I know it's a lot. But just so you know, t's a pretty
cool club to be a part of." He opened his palm, playfully emitting a lazy
stream of bioplasma that writhed effervescently a few inches above his
hand.

She cocked her head in thoughtful observation. "What *is* that stuff?
It's what you used against those warlocks that attacked me, right?"

She could *see* it.

And that very fact confirmed so much.

"Bioplasma," he replied wiggling his fingers so it undulated in
waves. "It's just a projection from my biofield."

"Can I touch it?"

He nodded and she poked a finger into it, watching it react to her
touch.

"I can feel it," she said, a look of surprise on her face. "What exactly
is it?"

"Charged particles that exist in a state somewhere between energy
and matter," he explained as she prodded it again and it moved around
her finger.

"You're right, it *is* pretty cool."

"Yup, once you get used to them, having higher senses is actually
kinda awesome. Like telepathy," he said pointedly.

She made a face.

"Ok, ok, we can talk about it another time. When you're feeling up
to it. I'll just say one more thing and then I'll drop it." This was the most
important part, but he was trying his damnedest to be nonchalant.

She opened her mouth to protest, but he held his hand up before
she could say anything.

"No, Cora, this is important. I want you to listen really carefully,
ok?" And just like that, nonchalance was out the window. "If ever you
need me – for *anything* at all – I need for you to just focus really hard
and talk to me as though I'm next to you. I'll hear you."

Just like he'd heard her at the funeral when she'd asked him for help with the eulogy she couldn't get through.

He reached out and took her hand, squeezing it firmly, yet gently, in his. He wanted nothing more than to take her in his arms and reassure her everything was going to be ok, but he felt like he'd be crossing some invisible line by doing so.

"Got it?"

"Got it." She suddenly looked so exhausted. She wasn't up to delving anymore into what he was saying.

"So, you were telling me about Drew?" he said knowing it was time for a subject change.

"He loves me, Inds," she said, pulling her hand from his. "And he's been so amazing, so supportive, so loyal. He's such a good guy. If it wasn't for him, I don't know where I'd be now. I owe him so much."

It hurt him to hear this, but he managed to keep his face neutral.

"I know he's a good guy, Cora, in fact, he's a *great* guy. If he wasn't, I'd have a lot more to say on the matter. But this isn't about who's a good guy and who's not. It's about what *you* want."

"I-I'm just so confused… I don't know what to do," she whispered, her voice catching.

He exhaled heavily through his teeth. "Look, I'm far from impartial on this subject matter, and I don't want to put any more pressure on you… But the thing is, *I* know what I want. *Drew* knows what he wants. And as you're well aware, it's really fucking unfortunate that we want the same thing. You."

She covered her face with her hands, a ragged sigh escaping her lips. "We can't go on like this. It's breaking his heart, Indigo. I hate myself for it." She dropped her hands and met his eyes. "And I hate you a little bit for it, too."

He held her gaze, trying to stop the hurt flooding his eyes. He failed and she saw it. He reached out and gently wiped away the tear that had escaped her eye and was trickling slowly down over her cheekbone.

"You hate me?" he repeated, his hand dropping to hers, his fingertips tracing hers.

"I need to try to right now," she whispered. "Because I certainly can't love you, not when it would destroy the person who's meant the most to me this past year."

Indigo's fingers slid from hers. He knew she was right. It took every ounce of his strength to keep his hands to himself when he was with her. It was almost impossible not to pull her to him and kiss her, not to scoop her up in his arms and carry her upstairs to her bedroom so he could show her just how damn much he loved her. He pushed away the inundating need to fight for her because right now, her heart was such a delicate, fragile thing and in all this he knew it would end up as collateral damage.

"Listen, I'll back off, I'll give you all the time and space you need," he told her instead. "Just so you know, I promised Scarlett and Matty I'd spend Christmas with you guys…"

"I know."

"But after that I'm heading back to the States."

He felt the mood change as though all the air had been sucked from the room. She visibly stiffened. "H-hang on… You're *what?*" What little colour that was left in her face had drained away and her mouth had dropped open.

"I'm flying back to the US after Christmas." He frowned.

"Oh I *heard* you," she choked. "I just can't *believe* it. How can you do this to me again, Indigo? You come back here, create absolute *chaos*, make a *million* heartfelt declarations and promises, you essentially throw a *grenade* into my life… And then you decide to just up and *leave* again?" She swiped roughly at her eyes with tremoring hands. "Well, all I can say is *thank you*. *Thank you* for making it so easy for me to *hate* you." Her tone dripped icicles.

"Whoa, whoa, *whoa*," he interjected holding his hands up. "Hang on a minute, I *am* back for good." He leant forward and cupped her face between his palms. "I'm just flying back to the States for a few weeks, and then I'll be right back here in Sydney, ok? This is my life now, Cordelia, I have two families, two homes: here with you, and in Sedona. I'll spend most of my time here, but every two or three months, I'll be over there for a couple of weeks." He dropped his hands to hers, giving them a quick squeeze.

"So that's where you're going in January?"

"Uh… eventually," he said, wondering how to backpedal, because this conversation was about to go where he really didn't want it to.

"Eventually?"

"I need to go visit Luis in New York and see how he's doing first."

"Luis? Your old roommate from hospital? The one you cured of triplegia?"

He nodded. "And then I… I uh, I promised Wilson I'd spend New Year's with him in Aspen."

"*Wilson?*" Cordelia asked, eyes wide. "Since when do you spend the holidays with your *dad?*" She looked genuinely shocked and a little worried.

Indigo shrugged. "Since he and I reconnected before I left the US to come back here. I went to see him in New York, when I was living in Sedona. He had my passport, all my things. Plus he'd, um, he'd helped me with something–"

"With what?"

"Do you have to know *everything?*" He shot her a smile of mock frustration.

"You know I do." She winced as she shifted, upsetting her toe.

He raised an eyebrow in exasperation, "Cora," he said, beckoning her to let him look at it. "I mean, come on…"

She sighed and obliged him. He cradled her dainty foot in his lap, rubbing his hands together then placing one on either side. She watched in fascination and he suspected she could see the warm golden-green light swirling to encase her toe.

He continued to speak as he worked on her. "You see, my father, well, I asked him to hook me up with his plastic surgeon–"

"Your face *does* need work," she deadpanned.

"Ha ha, you know how I feel about that stuff. Have you seen Wilson lately?" He put his hands either side of his face and pulled the skin upwards briefly, then rolled his eyes. "But he obviously knows a lot of really great plastic surgeons, and I needed a recommendation for Luis." He moved his hands back to her foot.

"For *Luis?* From what you've told me about Luis, he wouldn't be able to afford a plastic surgeon, particularly not one your dad would use."

"No, he wouldn't," he said, and he felt his cheeks warm as he added. "But *I* could. Look, Cora, Luis played a big part in saving me, and I know I got him up walking again and all that, but his face... I couldn't fix that." He cleared his throat. "And no one should have to walk around looking like that. I have this huge trust fund, years of guilt money from both my parents. I mean, the income alone is enough for me to live on very comfortably, you know that. So why not spend some of it on something meaningful, on something that will change someone's whole life?"

She was staring at him, eyes narrowed.

"What now?" he sighed.

She shook her head at him. "Just you."

"Just me what?"

"If you hadn't noticed, I'm trying my hardest to keep you at arm's length, and then you go and tell me shit like this and you make it impossible for me to hate you! You're determined to worm your way back in, aren't you?" Her lips held the ghost of a smile, her gaze soft. "So what happened with Luis?"

He gave her foot an affectionate squeeze. "How's that feeling now?"

She wiggled her toe, an expression of surprise coming over her face. "It's better. Thank you." He gave her a playful wink. "You were saying? About Luis?" she prompted, tucking her legs back beneath her.

"Wilson's doctor, he met with Luis and felt confident he could help him. Not only that, but Wilson convinced him to do his part pro bono, so that was one less medical bill," he grimaced. "American hospitals are *expensive*. Anyway, Luis is just about to have his final surgery and I promised I'd go see him. I need to do a little bit more work with him, you see. All that healing I did on him back in New York, it was done without his conscious input. If he wants to really get better, fully better in every sense of the word, I need to go back and delve a little deeper. We started when I was last in New York, but we're not quite done yet."

"And your dad? You ok having to spend New Year's with him? Because you're of legal age now, they can't make you go." She looked really concerned and he knew she was thinking about how badly he'd spiralled last time he'd been forced to be with Wilson. "What's going on there?"

Indigo frowned. "Yeah, no. Can we talk about that another day?"

"Nope. Complete honesty remember, Inds? Tell me now."

"Listen, Cora, I mean, I don't know if this is the right time…"

Her face clouded with fear. "Can you just tell me, please?"

"*Shit*, Cordelia…" He glanced away, then met her eye. He *really* hadn't wanted to go here with her just yet. "When I went to see Wilson a few months back, I found out that he… that he had cancer."

She looked stricken. "Oh my God. Is he ok?"

"Yes. He is." He closed his eyes, trying to figure out how much to tell her. Everything. He had to tell her everything. "When I found out how sick he was, and I realised I could help him, well…"

"You offered to heal him," she said flatly.

He nodded.

"And it worked," she said, a statement, not a question. "So it worked for your dad, but not for mine." She was staring into space.

"Cora, I'm so sorry, Wilson wasn't as far along as Josh was, he'd already had the largest couple of tumours in his lung removed and it hadn't spread very far–"

"So your dad, who's spent his life being a shitty father and a shitty human being is able to be healed, whereas my dad, who spent his life as a devoted father, helping others and making the world a better place, *wasn't*?" She wasn't angry, just completely confused, dumbstruck. "I don't understand. How is that fair?" She raised her eyes, so bewildered, to meet his. He could see they were sequined with tears. "How is that fair, Indigo? It's not fair." She began to sob. "It's not *fair!*"

He moved across the couch and pulled her into his arms, rubbing her back as she cried. "I know, I know, it's not fair, it's not." He'd struggled with it, too, more than she could ever imagine. But the fact of the matter was, life wasn't fair. It was never meant to be.

"I'm so sorry," she suddenly breathed, pulling back to look at him. "I don't mean that I'm not glad your dad's not sick anymore, of course I'm happy he's well, it's just… I miss my dad so much. And I just don't understand why he had to die? Why did *my* dad have to die, Inds?" She broke down again, sobbing on his shoulder. "He was so young, he had so much life left to live! We need him so much. It hurts so much, it… it just hurts *so damned much*, some days I don't think I can bear it!"

Indigo held her tight as she cried, tracing soft patterns down her back. He didn't know what to say. Did she really want the truth right now? That Joshua had designed his own life before he was born, that he was always going to die that day, no matter what anyone did? That because their lives were entwined with his, his death was inevitably written in their destiny, too?

As for Indigo's father, it was only ever one possibility that the cancer would kill him, depending on which fork in the road he chose. It was always meant to make him stop and examine his life, to reassess, to question what was important. It was always meant as a possible turning point in his life, not necessarily as a full stop. And it seemed to have worked, because the man was slowly but surely starting to change. Wilson had realised it wasn't his money or his possessions that would warm him in his later years, but his children, his grandchildren, his family.

He had a lot of ground to make up, a hell of a lot, but he was trying as best he knew how. He'd gone to each of his sons and begged their forgiveness, begged to try and repair their relationship, and he'd invited them all to his house in Aspen for New Year's. He really seemed to want to make amends. His brush with death appeared to have had the desired effect.

"Oh God, I'm s-so sorry, Inds," she bawled into his chest, shoulders shaking, "I'm a m-mess! All I seem to do these days is cry."

"I don't ever want to hear you apologising for that. You cry as much as you need." He could feel it, the unbearable weight of her grief, the crushing burden of its heaviness. A weight that heavy needed to be released or it would consume her, and the only way to release the energy of that grief was through those tears, through those sobs, through the wracking of her body.

Cordelia's tears eventually stopped, but he continued to hold her, her head nestled into his shoulder. She felt so good in his arms that he never wanted to let her go. He closed his eyes tight, breathed her in. After a while, she pulled back, her red-rimmed eyes travelling over his face. "Tell me? Tell me what happened when you went to New York."

Indigo smiled sadly. "Here's the deal. I'm gonna go get that food I heated up and we're gonna eat it together while I tell you, ok?"

She raised her eyes to the ceiling in exasperation but she nodded. "Deal."

So he went to the kitchen and made up a couple of plates then returned to the couch, handing her one. She baulked. "I can't eat all that!"

"Try," he said firmly.

She tentatively took the utensils he offered her and forked off a small hunk of tender lamb shank, raising it to her mouth.

He nodded in approval, and began to speak…

chapter twelve

the living years

six months ago...

manhattan, new york, june 1995

indigo

"Oh, Mr Indi, thank goodness you're here," Ana Maria said. She'd been waiting for him when he got off the elevator in the foyer of Wilson's Fifth Avenue penthouse. The large gap between her two front teeth seemed to stretch even wider as she smiled at him.

"Hey, Ana Maria." Indigo nodded at her formally. Ana Maria had been Wilson's housekeeper since before Indigo was born, but Indigo had never quite warmed to her. She was his father's lap dog and gate keeper and she seemed to hold Wilson to deity status. He guessed at the end of the day, Wilson was all she had. He was the man she'd dedicated her life to. She'd stood back and watched the way Wilson had treated Indigo for years and never intervened, never thrown a word of kindness or support Indigo's way.

He dropped his duffle bag on the floor and looked around the apartment, just as austere as he remembered, all soaring ceilings and marble and damask in shades of blue and gold. "Where is he then?" he asked, desperate to get this over and done with. He wanted to get to Lenox Hill Hospital to see Luis. When he'd rung from Sedona to say he was coming by to pick up his stuff, Wilson had told him they needed to talk. When Indigo had hesitated, Wilson had asked him again in a tone

Indigo would have described as akin to begging if he'd thought Wilson capable. They'd had a few stilted phone conversations over the past months regarding Wilson's plastic surgeon, but had never ventured into anything personal.

Indigo didn't have much to say to the man who'd neglected him his whole life and treated him like shit when he'd lived with him. But there was an overriding part of him, his inner child he assumed, who reared its traitorous head on the rare occasion one of his parents showed him any interest.

"He's resting in his room, Mr Indi," Ana Maria said in her melodic Jamaican lilt, hands repeatedly smoothing the skirts of her dress, eyes darting nervously around the room. She wore her hair in a short-cropped afro and her heavy-set figure was clad in the maid's uniform Indigo believed she insisted on more than Wilson.

"What's going on?" he asked, surprised to see the usually efficient, business-like housekeeper rattled.

"Come," she said, beckoning him towards Wilson's bedroom. Indigo shrugged and led the way through the sprawling apartment, Ana Maria waddling behind him.

The door to Wilson's room was open. Indigo hesitated, gripping the doorframe to steady himself, reminding himself that he was strong now, that the man in there could no longer hurt him. He emptied the air from his lungs, then reached to rap abruptly on the heavy mahogany.

"Enter," came the feeble voice from inside. Ana Maria turned and bustled off.

The room was vast, and Indigo almost had to squint to see his father way down the other end. Wilson was sitting up in his enormous, gilded, four-poster bed in a pair of sapphire silk pyjamas. His room was decorated in shades of velvet navy and garish gold. Indigo walked across the opulent space, approaching the bed tentatively. His father had aged considerably since he'd last seen him. He'd let the blond dye grow out from his hair so it was now snowy white, and his skin looked papery. He appeared pale, sickly.

"Wilson?" Indigo said, coming to stand over him.

"Indigo," Wilson said, and he smiled at him. Indigo reflexively jerked back. His father had never smiled at him in his life. It was a smile he'd only ever seen in photographs or on the big screen.

Indigo narrowed his eyes. He could tell straight away his father had recently had surgery on his right lung; the anaesthetic was still visible in his system and he could see where Wilson's chest had been sewn back together. Globs of black streaked his biofield. Indigo knew straight away what that meant.

"Lung cancer?" he asked, and Wilson looked taken aback.

"How did you know? I instructed my team to keep it out of the media." His voice was soft and wheezy.

"I can see it," Indigo said boldly, no longer afraid of hiding who he was from his father. "That's what I do now, Wilson. I'm a healer. I can see the sickness inside of people." He described the tumours his father had had removed. A green-brown mucus clouded Wilson's biofield, a tell-tale sign of extensive chemotherapy.

"The chemo's not working," he ventured.

"No, It's not."

Indigo cleared his throat, broke eye contact. He couldn't believe he was feeling sympathy for the narcissistic tyrant who'd made his life a living hell, the man who'd made him feel so unloved and worthless it had tipped him to the brink of suicide. But now, Wilson just looked like a scared, frail old man, small beneath the bed covers.

"My treatment's not working, Indi. I–I asked you here to say..." He coughed nervously. Indigo perched warily on the foot of the bed, as far from his father as he could get.

Wilson gazed at his hands folded in his lap, seemingly gathering himself. Indigo fought the urge to look away. "I've always thought I was invincible," Wilson finally said. "So I've never thought much about my mortality. But this... well, this *disease*, it's forced me to acknowledge the fact that one day I *am* going to die. And when I die, what will they say about me?"

"Whatever you instruct your PR team to tell them to say, I guess," Indigo said.

"No. Not my public. I'm talking about my family." He cleared his throat. "My boys, their children – *you*. What will you say about me when I'm gone, Indigo?"

Indigo averted his eyes to a spot on the gaudy Persian rug. "Honestly? I guess I'll say that I was your son but you never bothered to get to know me." A lump formed in his throat. "That you never wanted me, and that my very existence was a huge disappointment to you." He raised his eyes to defiantly meet his father's.

Wilson looked unsurprised, but sad. He nodded curtly. "I... I'm sorry," he whispered.

"What?" Indigo said, brow furrowed.

"I'm sorry," Wilson said again, louder this time. "I've spent the past few months fighting off demons I've spent my life running from. Lying in bed, being forced to stay put with only your thoughts and memories for company, well, all the shitty stuff starts to creep in." He reached for Indigo's hand. Indigo instinctively snatched it away. Wilson coughed and awkwardly returned his hand to his lap. "I'd like to try to... make amends with you." Indigo's stomach lurched. "I'd like to try to get to know you, Indigo. I know it's a big ask. But... please?" Indigo swore he saw tears glazing his father's eyes.

Indigo shook his head. It was too much. A rush of emotion tumbled over him so he didn't know what to think, what to say. He stood up abruptly and backed towards the door.

"Indi?"

"I-I can't."

"Please?"

"Let me think about it. I'll... let you know."

He grabbed his bag from the foyer and took the elevator back down to the lobby where the doorman hailed him a cab. He focused as hard as he could on not thinking of his father while he dropped his stuff off at his hotel, showered, and walked the block to the hospital to see Luis.

When he stuck his head into Luis' room, Luis was sitting up in bed swearing ripely, his dark head bent intently over a Game Boy. "Fuck's sake! You call yourself a Mighty Morphin Power Ranger? Punch attack my butt! Quit draggin' ass, Billy!" When Indigo first met Luis, he had only half a face. Now, after several surgeries, he almost looked like a regular guy, despite the fact he had only one eye.

Indigo slouched against the doorframe, his smile turning into a grin. "Hey hey, roomie."

"Indigo Wolfe from 'Straya!" Luis cried, jumping out of bed and slapping his hand before pulling him into an embrace. He was slight-framed, his head only reaching Indigo's shoulder. "Quick, lock the doors before he does another runner!" Luis quipped, grabbing tight to Indigo's arms. "You can't keep this boy in no hospital."

Indigo rolled his eyes and shook his head good-naturedly. "How you doing?" He pulled back so he could stare into Luis' reconstructed face. "Wow," he said, nodding approvingly, "looking good, man." The surgeon was excellent.

"Yup, apparently I got good genes." Luis laughed. "My skin responds well to treatment." Luis was half-Afghan and half-Puerto Rican, and what he was saying appeared to be true, as Indigo had to look really hard to see his scars.

"How many more surgeries to go?"

"Two, they think." Luis' smile lit his whole face. Indigo was used to Luis only being able to half-smile so was thrilled to see the grin that raised both cheeks up high. "Round four's tomorrow."

"I can't get used to you walking," Indigo said wistfully, as Luis crossed back to the bed. He walked with a wide-gaited shuffle and Indigo tilted his head and frowned as he examined him, calculating how it could possibly be improved upon.

"I'll never run no marathons, but why would you wanna anyway?" Luis plonked onto the bed and indicated the chair beside it. "Come, sit, take a load off. I'm gettin' a crick in my neck lookin' all the way up at your tall ass." Indigo sat down, propping his feet up on the bed. "They say me walking, it's a miracle. But you and me, we know different, right?" He looked Indigo dead on, his eyes knowing, then leant forward. "I got your note, Indi. The way you healed me... what you did for me. I have no words. Thanks, man."

Indigo ducked his head, chuffed, yet still unsure he'd done enough. "I'd like to try again. I reckon I can do better. Get you running that marathon."

Luis grinned. "Sure dude, I ain't gonna say no to that. To the healin', I mean. It's a hard no on the marathon. Far as I'm concerned, you should only be runnin' from clowns and murderers. Never did understand your fascination with runnin'. Every damn mornin' while it was still dark, you were up and runnin' those trails. And they call me loco!"

Indigo laughed.

"You wanna drink?" Luis offered.

"Sure," he said, intently rummaging through his satchel for the gift he'd brought. He wasn't paying attention when Luis handed him the glass of water and he'd already taken a big swig before he spied the eyeball sitting in the bottom of the glass. Water spurted from his mouth in an arc.

Luis guffawed, slapping his thigh in mirth.

"Dude!" Indigo gasped, wiping his mouth.

"It's my new party trick, man." Luis laughed, reaching for the glass. He fished his fingers in, grasping the eyeball, then shook it off and popped it into his empty socket. He blinked and looked at Indigo. "Whaddaya think? It's a pretty good match, no?"

Indigo put his hands on Luis' shoulders, looking from his fake eye to his real one. "It's extraordinary. You can barely tell." The glass one didn't move like the real one, but it just looked like Luis had a lazy eye. Luis offered him the drink back. He pulled a face and shook his head, pretending to gag, "I'm good, thanks." He dove back into his bag, pulling out the Game Boy games he'd bought Luis and handing them to him. "Merry Birthday."

"Wow, thanks, man!" Luis exclaimed, sorting through *Mortal Kombat, Smash Bros,* and *Zelda.* "So what's been goin' on with you?" Luis eased himself back into the nest of pillows he'd obviously sweet-talked a nurse into procuring for him.

Indigo frowned.

"What's wrong?" Luis asked.

"My father," Indigo said, because if anyone understood estranged fathers it was Luis.

"What's the bastard gone 'n done now?"

"Gotten cancer."

Luis widened his eyes and Indigo told him about his encounter with Wilson. "Watcha gonna do?" he asked when Indigo finished.

He shrugged. "I don't know what to do, Luis. Like, I think of all the awful things he said to me when I was obviously mentally unwell. Not only did he not offer me any help, but he treated me like shit. He made things a thousand times worse. How am I meant to forgive him for that?" He blew out a big gust of air.

"I dunno, dude," Luis said, gazing at him sympathetically. "I know I couldn't. But you've always been a bigger person than me." He winged his arms up behind his head. "I guess at the enda the day, it comes down to this: if he dies and you haven't made amends, how will you feel? Because how you feel about him, if it's so bad you won' give a shit, then there's your answer. But if it's gonna play on you the resta your life… Well, then you know what you gotta do."

Indigo nodded. He knew Luis was right. He just had to decide which camp he was in.

Indigo tossed and turned most of that night, a battle raging between his head and his heart. His head was loud and unforgetting and unrelenting, reminding him of the monster his father had been, of how much he'd hurt him over the past nineteen years. Fool me once, shame on you; fool me twice, shame on me.

But then his heart would chime in, compassionate and aching, telling him his father was only human, that he'd made mistakes like anyone, that someone asking for another chance at least deserved the opportunity to be heard.

Indigo had tried to stop listening to his head a long time ago.

The next morning he called Raf, who helped him realise he was always going to give Wilson a chance. He'd just really needed to think he had the power of a choice.

And then he went to see his father.

Wilson pushed back his sheets and struggled to a seated position when Indigo entered his bedroom. His face broke into a hopeful smile befitting the movie star he was.

"I thought I'd seen the last of you, boy," he said gruffly as Indigo sat on the foot of his bed.

"You really thought I wouldn't come back?"

Wilson frowned. "Your brothers didn't. Just you and Denny."

Of Wilson's five sons, Denny was the second youngest, although he had a decade on Indigo. He lived in Santa Monica and had just welcomed a baby girl with his wife.

"The others want nothing to do with me," he said with a bitter grin that twisted his mouth. "'Too little too late' were Cobie's words, if I recall correctly." Indigo didn't blame his half-brothers.

"So what do you expect from me, Wilson?" Indigo asked bluntly.

"Oh," his father said, looking taken aback. "I... I guess just... time. Time with you. I want to hear about your life, Indigo."

Indigo stared at Wilson, trying his best to ignore his father's guardian who had materialised on the other side of his bed, a well-muscled Latino man with kind eyes and flowing dark hair. 'Help him,' the guardian said to him. 'You can choose to save him'. Indigo pursed his lips and pretended not to hear.

"What do you want to know?" he asked instead.

"Everything," Wilson said, reaching for the glass of water on his bedside table with shaking hands. Indigo moved without thinking, scooting forwards and picking up the glass, holding it to his father's lips. After he set it back down, he didn't move to the far end of the bed again.

"Tell me, how is your health?" Wilson asked. "Because one of my biggest regrets is not getting you the help you needed when you were..." he frowned, seemingly searching for the right word. "... ill," he finally said.

"You can say it. When I was suffering *depression*."

Wilson looked away and shook his head. "No," he finally said, so softly Indigo had to strain his ears to hear him. "I can't say it. Because then I'd have to address my role in it."

"So address it. If you want a relationship with me, you need to own all your mistakes, just as I have." He stared boldly at Wilson who cowered into his pillow, turning his head away. "When you stop denying your mistakes, you might actually learn something from them."

Wilson licked his lips, squeezed his eyes shut tight. "When I think of the... the things I *said* to you," he said, voice wobbling. "Of how I treated you... I-I'm not proud of how I've acted towards you, Indigo. I definitely could have been... warmer. More present. More attentive. I can see that now." As an empath, Indigo could feel what his father was feeling, and he could feel that where once had lived a cold-hearted brute now dwelled a scared, old man faced with the fragility of his mortality.

"You have to understand, Indigo, that I'm from the generation of 'stiffen up that upper lip and get on with it'. If ever I was feeling down, I was expected just to dust myself off and carry on. I truly am sorry," Wilson said, meeting Indigo's eye. And he meant it. His whole life Indigo had waited for one of his parents to admit they'd been neglectful, to beg for his forgiveness and want to make amends. But now that it was actually happening, he didn't know how to feel about it.

"I hear you," Indigo said, because he didn't yet feel ready to accept the apology.

'*Please help him,*' Wilson's guardian asked again.

This time Indigo acknowledged him. '*He can be saved?*'

'*His date of death is not set,*' the guardian replied.

Indigo sighed heavily. He knew this meant that depending on Wilson's choices, on the forks in the road of his life he chose, he had the power to decide his own fate. It meant that if Indigo stepped in now, he could very well survive.

'*If you do not help him he* will *die,*' the guardian said.

The last thing Indigo felt like doing was spending the amount of time – the quality of time – with his father required to heal him. He'd told Raf and the others he was only going to New York for a week. This was going to take a lot longer than that. He had clients back in Sedona he'd have to reschedule, too.

At least being here now didn't hurt the same way it did back when he was seventeen. He was strong enough now to shield himself from the city of feeling that resided here, that had crushed down upon him so brutally back then.

"I'm willing to help you, Wilson," he finally said.

"You… you're what?" Wilson said, staring at him in disbelief.

"I want to help you. To beat this thing, to get well."

Wilson pressed his trembling lips tightly together. "I-I don't know what to say," he whispered, gazing up at Indigo in disbelief. "After everything I…" He broke off and stared intently at his hands curled in his lap.

"But we have to do things my way and you have to agree to my rules."

"Like what?"

"Well, for one, you have to promise me no more smoking. And I'm talking ciggies *and* cigars."

"My cigars?" Wilson gasped. "But I only have one every now and then–"

"Fine then," Indigo said, standing up. "Forget it."

"No!" Wilson said, reaching his arm out. "Ok, ok, no more cigarettes, no more cigars."

"We can only work together if you follow my diet and lifestyle recommendations." Indigo knew from experience a lot of these recommendations would be coming from his father's guardian. "If you're serious about your health, about getting well, you'll do it."

Wilson nodded curtly. He wasn't a man who liked being told what to do.

"You need to be involved in your own healing. You can't just lie back and expect me to do everything, it doesn't work that way. You need to make a commitment to your health, put the effort in, show me you're genuine." He leant back, arms crossed and stared his father down. He swallowed a smile then as Wilson's guardian whispered to him. "And you need to go vegan," Indigo relayed, trying not to let the satisfaction show on his face.

"*Vegan?*" Wilson spluttered as if it were a dirty word. The man lived on fillet steak, Wagyu burgers, French cheese, and lobster.

"For a little while, not forever. Your body's far too acidic. Cancer loves an acidic environment," he said, repeating what the guardian was telling him. "We need to get you to an alkaline state. That means no alcohol either. And as for that fridge full of diet soda you've got out there..."

"Don't say it."

"It's all gotta go, Wilson."

"You might as well just kill me now," Wilson grumbled, staring at him incredulously.

Indigo shrugged. "Well, that, of course, is the alternative."

"Are *you* a-a *vegan?*" he asked, his lip curling in distaste.

"No. I was for a while, but it didn't work for me long term. Diet is a very personal, very individual thing. It took some time, but I found what works for me."

"Which is?"

"It's more what it's not," Indigo explained. "I can't really handle junk food and processed food or heaps of sugar anymore; it just makes me feel like shit. I feel better on a wholefood diet, and yes, it is largely plant-based, but I do eat meat."

"So you expect me to do what you can't? I can't live on plants! I'm not a rabbit. I've seen those vegan types, all puny and weak." He screwed his nose up.

"One of my very dearest friends is a strict vegan," Indigo said, thinking of Raf. "And he's a hell of a lot stronger and healthier than *you*." He sighed heavily. "You should view this as something empowering, Wilson. Diet is such an important piece of the puzzle here. When you're conscious of what you eat, you start to take back control of your health. And look, this isn't forever. It's just for now."

Wilson's guardian leant in and informed Indigo that his father was intolerant to wheat and was to go permanently off gluten. Indigo bit his lip to keep from laughing. He decided he'd scared his father enough for one day and he'd save that little tidbit for later.

Wilson sighed deeply. "Fine," he finally agreed, and Indigo could hear his mind ticking over, hear him thinking that this was a load of baloney, but it was the sacrifice he was willing to make to spend time with Indigo. And that made Indigo feel not quite happy, but something akin to happy.

As he gazed intently at his father, he could see the man's heart chakra was completely torn and twisted, the protective coating ripped from it. It no longer spun, just wobbled erratically in place like a wheel on a broken axle. He was in no way surprised that a man like Wilson was living with a non-functioning heart chakra. It explained his cruelty, his inability to love, his inability to connect to others.

Indigo furrowed his brow and leant in as he observed something in his father he'd only seen a couple of times before in his healing practice: thin cords of bioplasma protruding from the heart chakra like vines. He'd begun to see these only very recently as his clairvoyance grew and strengthened.

He'd asked Dawn about them when he'd first seen them. She'd initially been in awe, telling him she'd never been able to see them herself. But she knew of healers who could. She'd explained that every time a new relationship was formed between two people, whether it was romantic, platonic, or familial, these cords grew between their chakras. They were a means of connection and energy exchange. In a healthy relationship, these cords were bright and shiny and pulsating. But in an unhealthy relationship, they were dark and dirty and stagnant.

As he observed the fine cords of brittle bioplasma dangling from his father's damaged heart chakra, he saw their ends were ragged and frayed like old ropes. He'd never seen cords like these before, just dangling out there in space, not connected to anything.

He sighed heavily, knowing he was going to have to wade through a mountain of shit to help his father heal from this. He knew nothing of his father's life or childhood, but he had a feeling he was about to find out more than he ever wanted to know.

Indigo was aware he'd come in and completely upended his father's life. He'd made Ana Maria throw out all Wilson's soda and junk food, and hire a chef that specialised in gluten-free vegan food. He'd gotten rid of all his father's cigarettes and cigars, and flushed his stashes of weed and coke. They'd packed up his bar, and Indigo had a water filter installed in the kitchen.

He'd offended Ana Maria when he'd gone through all her cleaning products and Wilson's toiletries and chucked anything containing chemicals. He'd given her a list of products to buy to replace them. She'd grumbled and muttered under her breath, but Indigo had given her a pointed look and she'd merely grabbed her purse and headed to the local health food store.

She'd also been instructed that she was to bundle Wilson into his wheelchair every day and take him out for a walk in Central Park for some fresh air and sunshine. This upset Wilson more than anything. He was beside himself that someone might recognise him, and insisted on wearing a wig, a cap and enormous sunglasses.

As expected, Wilson was a challenging bastard to work with. He was incredibly closed and completely out of touch with his emotions. He'd spent the past 72 years presenting a certain façade to the world, and it was extremely hard to break through. Indigo only worked with him every second day, needing time to rest and regroup in between.

The days he wasn't with Wilson, he was with Luis, who provided much needed light relief.

After three weeks of chipping away, gearing both himself and his father up to tackle the core issue he'd identified on day one, Indigo woke up one morning knowing that today was the day. He'd checked out of his hotel a week ago and moved into his father's penthouse. But living there this time was different to the last time. As his father had grown stronger, the two of them ate dinner together most nights, and even Wilson reluctantly admitted the "bunny food" prepared by his new chef was so delicious he barely missed his meat and his cheese and his wheat. Barely.

They'd talk over dinner, and Wilson grew to know Indigo better than he ever had. Indigo knew they would never be close, but their relationship would at least be existent.

So that day, as Wilson lay face-up on the massage table he'd had delivered an hour after Indigo said he needed it, Indigo took a deep breath and asked the question whispered by Wilson's guardian: "Tell me about your father."

Wilson coughed, then cleared his throat and stared intently at the ceiling. "My father was a brilliant man," he finally said, his tone gruff. "Brilliant and inspiring and incredibly successful."

Indigo sat quietly for a minute or two, then repeated, "Tell me about your father."

"He was a trailblazer. A stockbroker. He worked on Wall Street in the twenties, he was exceptional at what he did, his wealth was testament to that."

Once again Indigo waited until the silence grew uncomfortable then asked again.

"He ..." Wilson faltered then cleared his throat again. "He was highly respected and well regarded in New York society–"

"Tell me about your father." He'd mastered the tone of firm yet nurturing.

"He.... He..." Wilson closed his eyes, his lids fluttering. His shoulders slumped as he let go and all the walls suddenly fell away. "I barely knew him," he whispered. "He was never around, and even when he was, he considered me a nuisance. I was an only child and as much as I adored my mother, she was weak and sickly and spent most of her time in her rooms. My earliest memories are of me wandering from room to room on my own in our big old mansion. I was alone most of the time."

"What happened when you were six?"

Wilson's eyes shot open and he stared up at Indigo. "I turned six in October of 1929. The day before Black Friday."

"The Wall Street Crash?"

"Yes. My father... he lost everything." He swallowed hard. "He put a pistol in his mouth the next day."

Indigo closed his eyes, reeling. He'd never known anything about his grandfather, not even that.

"My mother... She didn't cope. We lost the house, the cars, all our staff, all our money, everything. The day we were evicted from our home, my mother told me we were going for a walk. I was too young to question the suitcase in her hand, too young to understand what was happening when we arrived on the doorstep of St Joseph's Home for Boys. She promised me it was only for a little while, that she'd come back for me when she was back on her feet. But I... ah, I never saw her again." A muscle in his jaw quivered but he remained stoic.

Indigo swallowed fast over the lump in his throat, glancing at the broken cords of bioplasma floating from Wilson's heart chakra. He'd called Dawn and asked about their significance and she'd confirmed what he'd guessed: that these cords were once connected to someone else's heart chakra and had been torn out at the decimation of that relationship. Usually, the person doing the abandoning was the one to rip these cords to break the connection. That's why the loss of a loved one was often felt as a physical pain, because the tearing of these cords was felt at a very deep level, a palpable ache, a broken heart.

Indigo could immediately see which cord had once connected Wilson to his mother; it was positioned slightly to the left and went deep into the centre of his heart chakra. The maternal connection, the first and deepest connection Wilson had ever made.

The end of this cord was constantly in motion as if looking for someone else to connect to. Another cord protruded to the right of this one – the paternal cord – and he could see it had been torn off by Wilson. The end of this one lay stagnant, motionless. There were a number of finer cords on the left side of the chakra, broken like frayed string, some of them belonging to ex-wives and girlfriends. Five others sat to the right, connecting to Wilson's sons. He looked down in interest at the one joining his heart chakra to Wilson's. The cord was weak, but was the strongest of them all. Indigo would have to figure out how to repair or remove the damaged cords if he wanted to repair the chakra. He would be relying on Sarita and Wilson's guardian to guide him through that one.

"I don't think you need to hear about what it was like growing up in an orphanage during the Great Depression," Wilson continued. "But I'm sure you can imagine those nuns were tasked with housing an overwhelming number of needy children with very few resources. You complain about your childhood, claim that you were neglected, but excuse me if I disagree. You never went to bed in an overcrowded dormitory with an empty stomach, scratching your skin raw from lice bites, untouched by another human for weeks at a time. You were warm and you were clothed and you were fed. I always made sure you were very well provided for. No matter what had happened between myself and your mother, I sent your child support cheque religiously and made sure all the right people were managing your trust fund. Bernadette's always been useless with money and I wanted you to be financially secure."

He sighed heavily. "Yes, I was an absentee father. I admit that. I could have done better, so much better. But... I never knew what it was to *be* a father. I barely knew my own. The last time I saw him he was slumped over his desk in his study, his brains splattered over the window behind." He said it so matter-of-factly.

"You found him?" Indigo breathed.

Wilson stared fixedly at the ceiling. "I heard the shot, I went to investigate." He clasped his hand absently across his chest, seemingly lost in another time and place. He eventually levelled his gaze to meet Indigo's. "I've recently started seeing a therapist, and I've realised that a child needs love in order to grow into a fully functioning human being. And I'm sorry, Indi, I am, because if I'd realised that sooner..." He cleared his throat. "I believed that by making sure my kids had all the physical comforts of life that I was doing the right thing by them. That's why I always considered you so ungrateful. You had *so much*, Indigo, you were so spoilt, yet you were still so unhappy, lying around the apartment all day, drunk or high, always so surly and defiant and disrespectful. When I was your age, I was on Broadway doing eight shows a week."

Indigo had to swallow a retort. This wasn't about him.

Wilson sighed deeply and continued. "I never considered the emotional needs of my children, because, well, I never considered my own. I don't think I've ever experienced *real* love my whole life. I suppose that's why I went from woman to woman, from marriage to marriage. I was always looking for someone *to* love, for someone to love *me*."

It was on the tip of Indigo's tongue to suggest to Wilson that if he'd taken the time to care for his children, he would have found that love he'd been looking for his whole life. In his experience, kids were the biggest givers of unconditional love in the universe.

"I remember lying awake at night in that rat-infested orphanage, thinking that I'd show them all one day... I'd make something of myself and I'd make everyone love me and then I'd never have to be alone again. That's why I got into acting. The first time I got up on stage, and everyone was watching me in captivated silence, and then at the end of my performance, when they all jumped to their feet and cheered, well, I'd never felt anything like it in my life. The warm glow of being in the spotlight was addictive."

He closed his eyes, his whole face alight as a soft smile played upon his lips. "It made me feel seen, and it made me feel special. And then I started getting movie roles and suddenly I was famous, revered by everyone. People would rush me on the streets and scream they loved me, and they would write to me by the sackful telling me I was perfection. And the *women!*" He grinned at Indigo. "How the women would throw themselves at my feet, jump into my bed, beg to marry me... I know you think of me as just an old man, but I was young once, Indi, young and devilishly handsome, so they said. You've seen pictures of me in my twenties, I looked a lot like you do now."

He gazed up at Indigo, a wave of sadness suddenly washing across his face. "I should have just picked one and stuck with her. But I was never happy, never satisfied. I always wanted the next one, because there was always one more beautiful or more experienced or more willing. And it was easier to move on than to let someone in, to have to share that dreaded pillow talk dames come to expect, probing you about your childhood, trying their hardest to release your demons, to make you weak and vulnerable so they can try to save you. But I'd decided never to be weak and vulnerable again, to never rely on anyone but myself. Because look what happened when I was six and I relied upon my parents?"

Indigo flinched. The sins of his grandparents, filtering down to affect generations. He knew in his case, it would stop with him, but his brothers? He couldn't say how they'd been affected by the parenting that had defined their father's parenting, that defined how they parented their children.

"So I-I closed my heart to love, because love only ever results in rejection and pain," Wilson whispered, and with those words the implication of this seemed to dawn upon him. "Oh my God," he breathed, and Indigo could see the grief sitting over his heart like a plate of armour.

"You can let that belief go," Indigo said softly, placing a hand over his father's chest. "Once you've seen the lesson that needs to be taken from these experiences, your life starts to make sense."

Over the next couple of days Indigo worked to clear the dark, stagnant energy from Wilson's heart chakra so it began to spin once more. With the help of Sarita and Wilson's guardian, he tackled the cords of bioplasma, cleaning and strengthening them. He didn't know what to do with the dangling ends of the torn ones, but he eventually just turned them back towards Wilson's chest and connected the loose ends to Wilson's heart chakra, believing self love was what was needed for him to heal. Not the egotistical arrogance Wilson had displayed his whole life, but gentle, nurturing self love.

A month after they'd first started, he was finally finished with Wilson and the man was strong and healthy and cancer free.

He'd also spent more time with Luis, visiting him in hospital and then, once he was released, in the basement studio in Brooklyn he shared with his cousin. Luis was moving a lot better the longer he and Indigo worked together. By the time Indigo flew back to Sedona, Luis was excited that he might be able to take the job out at La Guardia Airport his cousin had offered to help him get.

"I'm so sorry, Indi," Wilson said one night after dinner as they were saying good night in the hallway outside Wilson's room. "For what I did to you, for forcing you to move here to live with me when you were seventeen. When that exposé was published and my public turned on me, I panicked. I can see now that my whole self worth was based on the love of my fans. I was desperate... I couldn't not have them adore me anymore, I had to fix that, whatever it took. And when I acknowledge now what bringing you here did to you..." He took a deep, ragged breath and looked at the floor, shaking his head slowly. He eventually raised his gaze to Indigo, and his eyes were actually glistening. "How can you ever forgive me?"

And Indigo felt his father's pain, his remorse, so acutely he could barely breathe. "It's ok, Wilson," he said with a hard swallow. "I do forgive you."

His father stared at him in disbelief. "You... forgive me?"

Indigo nodded, because he did. "Part of my healing has been accepting we're always exactly where we're meant to be, even if it feels like the end of the world. Me moving here, it was a turning point in my life. It changed everything. That spiral into darkness, I needed to go way, way down in order to come out the other side. It forced me to look at myself, to make me *choose* to get well, and it led me to discover who I truly was."

Wilson continued to stare at him. He slowly reached his hand out to Indigo's, grasping it tightly in his. Eyes locked on his son's, he said gruffly, "You're an extraordinary young man, Indigo, and it's been a privilege getting to know you these past weeks. I'm so very proud to call you my son."

Indigo exhaled sharply, his gut tightening. He nodded curtly and briefly squeezed his father's hand, then dropped it, turning quickly and walking away.

A few days later, as Indigo was leaving for the airport, Wilson asked him to spend New Year's with him at his house in Aspen. He'd had grand plans of it being a big family reunion, he and his boys all together for the first time, but he hadn't had many takers, just Denny and his family. Indigo only hesitated for a moment before agreeing to go. A proper family ski trip! How exquisitely surreal in the most wonderful way possible.

harbord, new south wales, december 1995

indigo

"Inds! That's huge! I'm so happy for you," Cordelia said, a gentle smile lighting her whole face as she gazed at him. "So, you're going then? To Aspen? To see your dad?"

They were still sitting together on the couch in the rumpus room of the Carlisle home. He'd had to coax and cajole her a bit, but she'd eaten all of her lamb shank and most of the mashed potato and slow-cooked carrots while he'd told her about New York and his father.

He shrugged and nodded. "If I don't at least try to continue to build a relationship with him, I'll always wonder. Besides, it kinda feels good, to actually be wanted by one of my parents for once. God knows my mother never wanted me. She still doesn't." He smiled to lighten the load of his words, but Cordelia obviously saw the pain etched in his eyes and reached out to softly trace the plane of his cheek.

"She doesn't know what she's missing," she told him tenderly. "Just ask Mum and Dad." She winced. "Dad loved you like a son, Inds, you know that."

He nodded and looked up at the ceiling, blinking hard.

"He adored you. Mum always will. I hope things work out with Wilson, I truly do. But if they don't, you know we'll always be here for you, right? We'll always be your family, no matter what."

"I don't know," he murmured. "It sure hasn't felt that way lately…" Gazing deep into her coral-sea eyes, he leant his arm along the back of the couch, his fingertips resting lightly on her shoulder. His thumb dropped to the ridge of her collarbone, softly caressing, and he could feel the sparks of electricity trailing where he touched. She was his moon and he the sea, drawn to her, powerless to resist the urge to touch her. It took every bit of strength he had to stop himself pulling her into his arms, from kissing her the way he'd kissed her in his car the other day, because that, that had been some kiss. "I *miss* you Cordelia. I mean, before any of this, we were friends, we were *best* friends. And I miss that."

"I know," she whispered with a shaky exhale, closing her eyes. "I know things between us haven't been great since you got back. And I... I miss you, too. You know I'd do anything in the world for you, Indigo." She opened her eyes and met his gaze, a gaze that was filled with so much, that blazed with such intensity.

"Anything?" he asked suggestively.

"What? Like let you rearrange my freezer?" she laughed, lightening the mood. "Or allowing you to force-feed me when my stomach is twisted into knots? Yeah I'd say I've proven I'd do anything for you."

"Touché," he smiled, inclining his head slightly, lifting his hand from her body. "By the way, if you and Rob wanted to come to Aspen after Christmas, there's plenty of room at Wilson's." Where he could keep a close eye on her and keep her safe.

"So none of your brothers are going?"

"Just me and Denny. The others just can't see any way of mending fences. And you know what? I get it. If he'd asked me a year ago, I reckon I would have said no, too." He smiled brightly then. "So how's about it? January in Aspen? A bit of skiing, a bit of shopping, après drinks at the Jerome, lunch at Bonnie's, truffle fries at Ajax Tavern?"

Shadows gathered in her eyes. "I don't see how we can leave Mum right now. Besides, how would that look to Drew, me running off to the other side of the world with you..." She trailed off. "My life is complicated right now."

"Fair enough. Pres is welcome to come, too, of course." Although as the words left his lips, he realised he didn't really mean them, and he felt like an arsehole.

"With his knee?"

Indigo shrugged. "His knee's fixable. I've been wanting to talk to him about letting me have a go at it. And if I can help him heal it, then he'll be back skiing in no time."

"Let me think about it, ok?"

"Ok, no pressure," he assured her. "No matter what you decide, I'll be back by February. For good."

To seal the promise he put his hand over his heart, a heart that was hers and only hers and would be forever.

chapter thirteen

it must have been love

cordelia

"Peyton said Sandy can't *believe* we're not going to the formal tomorrow night," Cordelia said. "He's ordered her to talk us into going, because apparently we'll regret it for the rest of our lives if we don't." They were lazing around the living room, her mum stretched out on one couch with Matty snuggled in the crook of her arm, Cordelia and Robbie on the other, her feet propped up on a pillow in her brother's lap.

"It's your Year Twelve formal," Mum said. "Sandy's right. I think you *should* go." The twins looked at her as though she'd suggested they fly to the moon.

"Urgh, it's way too peopley out there," Robbie yawned, glancing in the general direction of the street, neighbourhood, world that lay beyond their house. They'd barely ventured out since the funeral. Even Robbie, whose spirit animal was the social butterfly, hadn't wanted to see anyone.

"I'd need to find my eyes first, to apply the necessary makeup," Cordelia informed her mother, pointing to her puffy face, the bruise-like bags beneath her eyes. She thought she'd have been dry by now, but somehow the tears just kept on coming. It seemed she had an endless well inside of her.

"She's right, Mum," Robbie agreed. "She's got enough luggage under those eyes for a two-week trip to Paris."

"It's your Year Twelve formal. You only get one of those," Mum said, pasting on her brightest smile as she smoothed Matty's curls from his face. "Besides, it would do you good to get out of the house. We can't all sit around like this forever. It's getting depressing." She got a faraway look in her eyes as she added, "Your father would have liked you both to go."

"Really, Mum?" Robbie sniped. "Is that the card you're gonna pull from now on every time you want us to do something?"

"Take the rubbish out, Rob," Cordelia imitated her mother. "Your father would have wanted it." A smile teased at the corners of her mouth.

"Stack the dishwasher, Cora," Rob joined in with a chuckle. "Your father would have wanted it."

"Wash the car, Rob." Cordelia giggled. "Your father would have wanted it."

"*Stop peeing on the toilet seat, Matty!*" Matty cried, sitting bolt upright and holding a finger out, trying so hard to join in, but not quite getting the gist of the game. None of them could keep a straight face after that.

"Clean your room, Cordelia," Robbie laughed. "It was your father's dying wish!"

"It actually was," Mum quipped deadpan. They all went silent for a moment before bursting into fits of giggles. Once they started laughing, they found it hard to stop. Maybe they were delirious with grief, but it felt *good* to laugh. It seemed they hadn't in so long.

They were still rolling around in guffaws of laughter, tears of glee running down their faces, when Drew turned up.

He stood at the entrance to the room, staring at them open-mouthed. Cordelia was aware they'd all been so melancholy for weeks, he was likely utterly confused at the paradox of the scene before him now. She smiled up at him standing there so baffled, his broad frame clad in khaki shorts and one of his well-loved Nirvana T-shirts.

"Come, sit," she urged, beckoning him to the spot beside her on the couch.

Robbie moved to a beanbag on the floor, stretching out his long legs and crossing them at the ankles. "Mum's been trying to convince us to go to the formal tomorrow," he told Drew, winging his arms behind his head.

Drew's face lit up. "Really?" he said, looking hopefully at Cordelia. "Do you want to go? I'd love to take you." He sat down so close to her he was practically in her lap and she wiggled away a bit.

"Ummm… I dunno," she mused, exchanging looks with Robbie. Were they ready to go out and face the world yet? It seemed disrespectful to their dad somehow.

Robbie shrugged glumly. "I've been stood up anyway," he admitted quietly.

Cordelia sat bolt upright. "*What*? What happened to Gino?"

"Well, it turns out that despite all his bold post-coital promises up in Surfers, Gino just couldn't commit in the end," Robbie said, his voice dripping in disdain.

"That's what you get for inviting a good Catholic school boy," Drew said. "His mama was never going to approve of him going to a formal with another dude."

"Yeah, that and the fact he was a total scrub. Turns out he had two other guys on the go," Robbie said.

"What a f–" Cordelia glanced at Matty. "What an effing a-hole."

"You're better off without the douchebag," Drew added.

Robbie smiled wanly, "Yep. He's a cheat and a pathological liar to boot. I'm unsure at this point if Gino was even his real name. Whatever. His loss and all that. But the fact still remains, I'm a loser with no date."

"No date for what?" Indigo asked. They glanced up at his sudden arrival. He was barefoot in navy striped boardshorts and a pale pink T-shirt, its deep vee showing off both his spectacular tan and the wolf's fang that hung low from his neck from a strand of fine black leather. His hair was damp and tousled and she assumed he'd just come in from a morning in the surf.

"Indigo!" Matty cried, wriggling out of Mum's embrace and throwing himself into Indigo's. Indigo caught him easily, settling Matty on his hip. He smiled around the room, nodding awkwardly at Drew.

"What's up, Pres?"

"Hey, Wolfie."

Things between them were still uncomfortable. Drew wasn't used to Indigo being back. And Cordelia realised it must be strange for Indigo, seeing Drew with his arm around her, sitting on that couch with her, the couch Indigo had sat on with her countless times before.

Drew's arm suddenly felt incredibly heavy around her shoulders.

"So tell me," Indigo asked, focusing on Robbie. "No date to what?"

"To the formal tomorrow," Robbie sighed, examining his cuticles. "Mum thinks we should go, but Gino bailed on me."

Indigo's brows shot up. "I thought that was way off the cards?" He frowned, hoisting Matty higher on his hip.

"Apparently not." Robbie shrugged.

"So I'll go with you?"

"Yeah, because that's what I need right now, a *pity date*." Robbie rolled his eyes.

"It's not a pity date." Indigo rolled his eyes back at him. "It's just two best mates hanging out." Robbie's eyes involuntarily wandered over to Drew, Indigo's former best mate. *Awkward.* Indigo cleared his throat. "Besides, I missed my Year Twelve formal. If you let me take you, you'd be giving me the chance to make it up." Cordelia stared at a spot on the couch, trying to swallow the feelings of jealousy rising up inside of her. She wasn't allowed to feel this way, wishing it was her Indigo was asking.

Robbie waved a hand in submission. "Why the hell not? It was always my dream to arrive at the formal with the most popular boy in school on my arm."

"Yeah, except last I checked it's no longer 1992," Indigo quipped, flashing him a crooked grin. "So you're shit outta luck, Rob."

"Shit," Matty chirped. Mum and Indigo both shot him a look. He grinned his cheeky, baby-toothed grin.

"*Sorry, Scar,*" Indigo mouthed.

She winked at him and then clapped her hands in excitement. "Good, so it's settled, you're all going." She smiled slyly and added, "Your father would have wanted it." Drew and Indigo looked on in confusion as the Carlisles dissolved into fits of giggles.

Later that night, Cordelia walked Drew out to his car.

"It's meant to be stinking hot tomorrow," he said.

"Yeah, apparently there's a heat wave coming," she replied vaguely.

The weather. They'd been reduced to talking about the weather. Things had been stilted between them all evening. Well, not just all evening, ever since she'd found out her dad was sick really, if she was being honest.

He reached for her hand and she casually dodged him. Every time he'd touched her lately, it'd just felt wrong and she'd had to actively stop herself from stiffening. The rush of love she used to feel when she looked at him seemed to have ebbed away, and now she felt empty when she was with him. And she'd never been good at pretending. He was such a beautiful human and the guilt she felt for feeling the way she did weighed heavily.

They arrived at the curb, and he forcefully grasped her hand, raising it to his lips so he could kiss the back of it. He sighed heavily. "You've already gone, haven't you?" he said gently, his eyes searching hers.

"Pardon?" she said, her stomach lurching.

"I can see it in your eyes, Cee. Those beautiful expressive eyes, you can't hide anything in those things." His stare was so intent she averted her gaze. "You've already checked out. Of us. Of this relationship."

The sudden ache in her throat was suffocating and she could barely breathe. All she could do was stare dumbly at the ground.

He blew out a sharp breath, leant back against his Subaru and thrust his hands deep in his pockets as he gazed up at the clear night sky. "So this is how it ends," he muttered.

"I'm sorry," she said softly, clearing her throat. She moved towards him, resting her forehead on his chest. She squeezed her eyes shut. "I'm so sorry, Drew." Because she truly was. She didn't understand how love could just go away, but somehow it had. For her at least. He didn't wrap his arms around her. His hands remained in his pockets.

She stepped back, gave him the space she could feel he needed.

A bitter laugh burst from him. "I guess it was too good to be true, you and me. You know, Cee, when I first realised I'd fallen for you, I tried to talk myself out of it. I felt bad, you know? Wolfie was my mate, and I felt like I was crossing a line by pursuing you. I knew it was dangerous, to give my heart to someone I knew had been so desperately in love with someone else for so long. But in the end, I couldn't help it. The heart wants what it wants, right? But now I see how dumb I was to listen to it. Because my heart, it's fucking stupid. Obviously. And now it's gotten what it deserves. Because it's broken."

"I truly am so sorry," she said, her voice catching. She reached for him but he side-stepped her, opened the car door. She blinked rapidly, exhaled a shuddery breath.

"I don't wanna hear it, Cee," he said coldly. "It's probably best we jump from this wreck of a relationship now though, because there's no point in going down with a sinking ship. And let's be honest, in the cold light of day we aren't what we used to be, right?"

"Don't say that. What we had was good. I'll always remember it as being so, so good."

"Just not good enough, obviously," he snapped, climbing into his car.

"I'm so sorry," she choked again, because what else could she say?

"*So you should be.* I asked you to be honest with me, to be honest with *yourself*, Cordelia. That's not too much to ask, is it? I'm not an idiot. I know you can't make your heart feel something it doesn't. And I know it's time to give up the fight. I'm *done.* I can't make you love me the way I want you to and the longer I try, the more it hurts." His voice cracked and she could see he was close to tears. She reached for him and he recoiled. "I'm gonna go now before I say something I can't take back."

He closed the door firmly, started the engine, then opened the window. He sighed heavily, gazing out at her for so long she almost squirmed. His expression was unreadable. And then his eyes softened. "Listen, I'll still take you to your formal tomorrow night. You shouldn't have to go alone, not after the month you've had. And you came with me to mine, right?"

Tears welled as she remembered his formal last year, the night he'd kissed her for the first time. How different her life had been back then.

She nodded, because he was right, she really didn't want to go out there and face the world alone tomorrow night.

"Do me a favour though, yeah?" he said. "Don't tell anyone we've broken up 'til afterwards. I can't deal with a night of woeful looks and patronising questions."

"Ok," she said softly.

And then he screeched out from the curb and was gone. She sat down in the gutter fighting back the tears, tears for everything they'd had and everything they'd been and everything they'd shared over the past year. She *had* loved him, she *had*. Because how could she not have? He was so gorgeous and kind and unique.

And in another life, he could have been the one.

But not in this life, not when it had Indigo in it.

She roughly wiped her eyes. There was something else swelling inside of her, and she realised it was a sense of relief. And for that she felt like a piece of shit.

So now both she and Rob had pity dates to their Year Twelve formal. It was a sad time for the Carlisle twins, in more ways than one.

better

indigo

Indigo stepped outside the formalwear shop, wiping the sweat from his brow. It had taken most of the day, but Robbie had *finally* picked out a tuxedo he'd deemed worthy. Robbie was a super high maintenance date. No surprises there.

With the last minute change of plans, they'd all been in a mad rush that morning trying to find something to wear to the big event. It was a desert-hot day and the only place Indigo had wanted to be was the beach, even though the only place he was meant to be was visiting hospitals with Nash. Formal prep seemed frivolous by comparison, but Nash had insisted he was a big boy and more than capable of going alone. In the end, Sasha had volunteered to go with him, reassuring Indigo they totally had his back.

Robbie had had his heart set on a black, slim-cut, velvet tuxedo like the ones he'd seen featured in the Versace fall Ready-to-Wear line, so Indigo had been dragged all over Sydney until Robbie found something that fit the bill.

When Indigo had walked into the Carlisles' yesterday and overheard Robbie and Cordelia discussing going to the formal, he'd had had to dig deep to hide the wave of panic rising in his chest. They'd previously been so adamant they weren't going, and quite frankly it had been a weight off. He couldn't believe they'd done a complete one-eighty. This wasn't a scenario he'd planned for.

It made him feel… uneasy. There were just too many unknowns.

They'd hardly left the house since the funeral, which, with Harper lurking around God-only-knew where, had made his life easier. But the formal? There'd be a massive crowd there, which made it chaotic to start with. Chuck in copious amounts of alcohol and the emotion of it being their final school event ever, and they had the makings of a messy night.

Thankfully, Gino turning out to be an arsehole had given Indigo the perfect opportunity to tag along and keep an eye on things. As much as he felt bad for Robbie, he was grateful the universe had delivered.

Robbie jumped out of Indigo's car that afternoon, leaving him with strict instructions to source vegetable corsages for them to wear that evening, just like the ones the gang from *Beverly Hills, 90210* had worn to their Spring Dance in Season One. Indigo had given him hell about his *90210* obsession for years, even though back in the day Indigo himself had never missed a Sunday night dinner at the Carlisles' for reasons other than the fact it was roast lamb night. It had become their routine; he and Cordelia would sit with Robbie while he watched his favourite show, Indigo outwardly making fun of the characters and storyline, doing his best to hide the truth that he was in fact desperate to know if Dylan would choose Brenda or Kelly (he was firmly Team Brenda), and if Donna would ever give David her virginity.

Times had certainly changed since then. Brenda had been booted off the show, Donna was no longer saving herself for marriage, and Cordelia was in love with somebody else. But Robbie still had his Jason Priestly haircut, so some things remained the same.

After dropping Robbie off, he returned home. Edita was sitting at the kitchen table, humming while she peeled carrots. She was never happier than when she had a house full of people to fuss over.

"Hey, Edie," Indigo said, tossing the garment bag containing his tuxedo over the back of a chair.

"How was your day, Indi?" she asked, smiling up at him.

"Long." He grinned, grabbing a carrot on his way past and taking a healthy bite. "The others home?"

"Nash and Sasha are still out, but Aurora is by the pool." She stood up and went to the sink, rinsing off her vegetable peeler. "Do you have everything you need for tonight?"

"Almost. You don't happen to know where I can get a vegetable corsage, do you?"

She looked at him questioningly as her fingers moved to the outline of the pendant she always wore hidden beneath her dress. "Give me a picture of what you want, and leave it with me," she said, reaching up to adjust the wolf's tooth around his neck. The fang was studded with two small crystals, one obsidian, the other amber.

"Thanks, Edie, I need to get in the ocean before I have to put that monkey suit on," he said, nodding to the garment bag. "I'll see if Rory wants to come."

Aurora was lying topless by the pool reading a book. Indigo stuck his head outside and called, "Wanna hit the beach?" She nodded as she rose gracefully to her feet and strolled brazenly towards him in her miniscule, gold g-string. "Rory, this isn't Ipanema, Manly's a family beach you know. I mean, it's up to you, but you might wanna cover the gals up," he said, nodding towards her chest while being mindful to keep his eyes locked on hers. Indigo had spent a lot of time swimming with her in the creeks and rivers of Sedona and was used to her bathing attire, or lack thereof. Aurora didn't possess the body hang ups of mere mortals and to he and Sasha (but maybe not Nash), the sight of her bare pert breasts had become as familiar to them as the nose on her face. She rolled her eyes and went back to grab her bikini top, slipping it on and tying it. The two teeny-tiny triangles left nothing to the imagination.

"Happy?" she huffed as she followed him out to his car, pulling a scrap of fabric over her head that turned out to be a dress. "I didn't realise Australians were so damned uptight about nudity. They're breasts, for fuck's sake. They're a natural part of the human form. What's the big deal?" She climbed into the passenger seat and clipped her belt on.

"I'm not having this discussion again," he said as he turned the key in the ignition and headed down the long driveway. "You know I don't give a shit if you parade down Manly Corso stark naked, but you need to be aware of your effect on other people. You go out in public topless, you're likely to give some old codger a heart attack. Or worse, give some poor pimply juvenile delinquent a raging hard on his mates will never let him live down," he chuckled. She rolled her eyes, but he could see she was trying to swallow a smirk. Aurora couldn't care less whose feathers she ruffled, and often had to be reminded of acceptable social behaviour.

"So Nash and Sasha have been gone awhile?" he ventured, changing the subject.

"Yeah, after those last couple of hospitals, they wanted to visit the sites of some of the attacks, see if they could pick up on anything. Then they were planning on popping in at the venue your prom–"

"Formal," he corrected.

"–ok, *formal*, is being held at tonight to make sure it's secure."

"I know I freaked out a bit at first, but I think it'll be ok. Fun even. And I'll be there to keep an eye on things."

"Yeah but you can't be everywhere."

"If Sash taught me to bilocate, I could be in two places at once." He grinned broadly.

She shot him a withering look. "Anyway, Blaze can get a better read of it when he's on the premises. He can't get to Harper or her coven, they're still shrouded, but he can take a look at what's going to happen on the grounds and ensure it's all smooth sailing."

"As much as I have a bit of a bad vibe about tonight, it's not exactly Harper's style to storm into her old school on formal night and start attacking students," he said, as he found a park on the South Steyne beachfront and reversed smoothly into it. "She's operated under a cloak of darkness so far. She's always valued stealth over theatrics." As he got out the car, a prickle down his spine had him glancing around furtively. He hated how constantly looking over his shoulder had become second nature to him.

"I agree," Aurora said, climbing out the car and walking beside him towards the sand. They laid their towels out and stripped down to their swimmers.

"You agree?" Indigo said, turning to her and widening his eyes in mock-shock. "*You* agree with *me*?"

She shrugged as they strolled towards the water's edge. "Even a stopped clock is right twice a day."

"That's probably the nicest thing you've ever said to me, Rory," he joked, putting his arm around her and making a big show of smooching her cheek.

"Yeah well, don't get used to it." She eyed the clear, aqua sea lapping the sandy shore. To their right, the rocks wrapped around the headland towards Shelly Beach. "It looks cold. Is it cold?"

"Hmmm let's see," he replied mischievously, scooping his hand through the water and spraying her with icy droplets.

She recoiled and smacked him in the chest. "Asshole!" she admonished, but her cheek twitched as it did when she was trying not to laugh.

"It's nice though, right?' He chuckled, splashing her again.

"Fuck off!" she cried, backing away from him. "Here's a tip, Indi. There is not one person in the history of the world who has *ever* enjoyed being splashed."

"What if they were on fire?" he asked as they waded in, diving through a big wave in unison.

She surfaced and glanced around to see if anyone was watching, then narrowed her eyes in his direction. A wall of water rose from the sea and flattened him. When he popped back up, spluttering, she gave him a pointed look, then draped her hair over her shoulder and swum away from him.

After their swim, they dried off and lay in the sun, enjoying the feel of the rays tingling their skin. "We'd better go," he murmured drowsily after a while. "I feel guilty Nash and Sash have been doing all this legwork while I've been stuffing around all day."

"Blaze likes a mission. You know he can't sit still. He's not big on relaxation. And as if Sash minds – as long as he gets to surf every day, he's happy."

When they got home, the boys were hanging by the pool, cold drinks in hand.

"Tough day there, Indi?" Nash called, when he spied Indigo sauntering out of the house, shirtless in his boardshorts, a towel slung around his shoulders. "You're not overexerting yourself too much there, are you, mate?"

Aurora poured herself onto a chaise longue, immediately reaching around to untie her bikini top.

"Spare a thought for me," Indigo grinned, pushing his Ray Bans on top of his head. "I'm about to don a tuxedo and, for the sake of my diva date, I'll have to put on a brave face and pretend I'm not gonna melt into a puddle of sweat." The weather bureau had promised a southerly change was coming through to break the thirty-eight degree heat, but not for a few hours yet. "How did you guys go today?"

"Same old, same old. It was definitely Harper's warlocks who attacked all those people, brah," Sasha said. He was lying on his back on a chaise longue in a pair of navy and green boardies, shading his eyes with the crook of his elbow.

"Yeah, ok," Indigo mused. "So what do we do? We can't keep letting Harper put people into fucking comas. We need to figure out how to restore them, how to get back what was taken from them."

"I totally agree. Unfortunately this isn't my domain, sorry, brah," Sasha said.

"Rory and I may have a couple of ideas. We'll toss them around tonight, see what we come up with," Nash said, standing up and approaching the deep end of the infinity pool. He dove in and swam a lap under water before surfacing where Indigo now sat on the ledge, legs dangling in the water. Nash rested his chin on his forearms on the edge of the pool and squinted up at him.

"And everything looks cool on campus?" Indigo asked.

Nash nodded. "I had a bit of a gander. There'll be no warlocks storming the formal tonight."

"Good. Although if Harper doesn't show herself soon, I reckon we're gonna have to consider baiting her out of hiding," Indigo said, leaning back on his hands.

"Yep, I know, mate. Sash and I were just saying that today. Right now, she's got the upper hand," Nash said.

"I'm so done with that," Indigo sighed.

"I'm resigned to the fact she's simply impossible to find," Nash said.

"It's not for lack of trying, ya," Sasha interjected

"I know," Indigo said. "And I'm so grateful you guys are here; I'd be lost without you. But I'm getting tired of constantly looking over my shoulder, second-guessing every bad feeling, worrying she's going to try and hurt Cora again." His hands clenched into fists. "I know she's coming for me, so where *is* she?"

"It's a pretty simple solution then," Aurora said lazily from her sun lounger, eyes closed. "We all know who Harper's weakness is. *You*, Indigo. The same way Cordelia is yours. We use that against her."

"Seriously?" Indigo muttered under his breath, glowering at her.

"Harsh but true," Nash agreed. "Indi, you know you are."

"Exactly. So we work with that," Aurora said.

Indigo reached for Nash's wrist, tilting his watch so he could see the face. "Shit." He climbed to his feet, dusting his hands off on his boardies. "I'm gonna be late." He glanced at Sasha. "You'll still be popping in tonight, right?"

Sasha gave him the thumbs up.

"Have fun, guys," Indigo said as he headed towards the house.

"Ok, we'll be here, just hanging around on high alert in case we're needed," Nash joked, "hopefully getting spoilt with another one of Edita's gourmet creations. And if this heat doesn't let up, we'll be submerging ourselves in the pool the rest of the night. I tell ya, Indi, I could get used to living like this." He glanced towards the kitchen where Edita was pottering around. "Private chef, freshly laundered towels... I'm barely out of bed in the morning before it's made..."

Aurora snorted. "Ha! Make the most of it while you can, Blaze. Talk about champagne tastes on a beer income."

"By the way, if you're looking for your electric razor, it's in my bathroom," Nash called after Indigo.

Indigo turned and gave him a withering look.

"Sorry..." Nash apologised with a cheeky smile.

"Whatever's mine is yours," Indigo said. "Apparently."

"I forgot to pack mine!"

"It's cool, man. I have no issues with you borrowing my razor. Now my *toothbrush* on the other hand..."

"I already apologised for that," Nash said with a sheepish grin. "I forgot to bring mine and Rory wouldn't let me use hers!"

"You're fucking disgusting," Aurora said with exasperation, but Indigo could see she was biting back a smile. "And you have the packing skills of a five-year-old."

"That toothbrush belongs to you now, mate," Indigo called over his shoulder as he headed inside. He'd already bought a new one.

He retrieved his razor from Nash's room, then cranked up the AC before jumping in a cold shower. He grumbled to himself as he buttoned his shirt. The top button was stiff and impossible to fasten, and he felt like he was being strangled. He ended up having to remove the wolf's tooth necklace from around his neck, leaving it on his bedside table. He finally managed to manoeuvre the top button through the hole.

He slicked his hair back and grabbed his jacket before taking the stairs two at a time to the waiting limo. Nash came out, waving two vegetable corsages which were ridiculously perfect.

"Courtesy of Edie," he said, thrusting them at Indigo.

"Thanks, mate. Tell her she's a legend." Indigo smiled.

"Look at you all suave and fancy-pants in your tuxedo," Nash said, looking him up and down. "I guess it's hard for anyone to look like a minger in formalwear though."

Indigo laughed, shoulder-checking him as he ducked into the limo.

Nash rested his arm on the car roof and leaned inside. "I really am sorry about your toothbrush."

"No, you're not." Indigo grinned.

"No, I'm not." Nash chuckled. "And I'm not sorry about your razor either."

The grin froze on Indigo's face. "Why would you be sorry about my razor?"

"Let's just say that face of yours is looking smooth as my–" he clicked his tongue and pointed to his crotch and winked.

Indigo felt himself pale. "You didn't?" he whispered.

Nash guffawed, his eyes twinkling.

"*Not* cool, bro! I used that on my *face!*"

"Well, I used it on my... *everything,*" Nash said as he closed the limo door and sauntered back inside, his shoulders shaking with laughter.

That razor belonged to Nash now, too.

chapter fifteen

alone

reinenoir

Tick tock tick tock tick tock...

Enjoy your fun while you can, Indigo.

Enjoy your fun while it lasts.

It was so easy for her to watch his every move from under the veil of Artax's shroud. She could walk right up to him and stand in front of him and still he wouldn't see her there, draped in shadow. Like this afternoon, when she'd followed him to the beach and watched him swimming with that haughty walk-in. Reinenoir suspected she would actually like the cold bitch if she wasn't one of the obstacles in the way of her plans. Indigo had been laughing and mucking around with her like he didn't have a care in the world, completely oblivious to the fact his world was about to come crashing down around him.

Yes, tick tock, Indigo, tick tock. She'd given him the time she'd promised to think about her offer, to change his mind. The fact he'd called for reinforcements, well, aside from being incredibly flattering, it unfortunately gave her the feeling her offer would be rejected. And that wouldn't do at all.

But all hope was not lost. Reinenoir could be incredibly persuasive when she wanted to be, especially when she really wanted something.

And one way or another, she wanted Indigo Wolfe.

Tick tock, Indigo, tick tock...

chapter sixteen

lay all your love on me

cordelia

"Oww!" Cordelia cried, swatting her hand in the direction of the teasing comb Robbie was using to attack her hair.

"Oh my God, calm your farm, Cora! What's up your arse, anyway? You've been in a bad mood all arvo."

"Did you know?" she asked, as he removed the cucumber slices he'd placed over her eyes to reduce the swelling caused by yet another afternoon of crying. She was surprised her tear ducts hadn't simply washed away at this point. "That Indigo has a new girlfriend? You guys just spent most of the day together."

"He does not?" Robbie gasped, wide-eyed.

She nodded solemnly. That afternoon Cordelia had driven into Manly to pick up some dessert for her mum. She'd parked on the beachfront and headed over to their favourite little organic café where she'd ordered some raw Snickers balls and some double-fudge, sweet-potato brownies. Afterwards, she'd wandered over to the beach, wanting to sit awhile by the ocean.

Tonight would be the first night she and Robbie were leaving Mum and Matty home alone since Dad had died. Every time she remembered her dad was gone, it was like a jolt to her nervous system, and then the spider legs would begin their steady scamper in her gut again.

She'd been walking along the pathway above the beach, about to sit down on the wide concrete steps above the sand, when a familiar figure had caught her eye, tall, ripped and golden brown. And he wasn't alone. She'd taken a few steps back until she was hidden behind the trunk of a Norfolk Pine, her heart hammering as she'd peered out to watch him.

Indigo had been walking down the beach with arguably the most striking girl Cordelia had ever seen. She was tiny beside Indigo's six-foot-three frame, her kick-ass body clad in the teeniest gold bikini. Her long ebony hair fell sleekly to her waist, and her flawless skin was the colour of coffee grounds.

Cordelia had watched as he'd put his arm around the girl, drawing her to him and heartily kissing her cheek, before reaching down to playfully splash her, a big grin on his face. She'd seen the affection in his eyes.

Cordelia had turned abruptly away. She'd felt sick as she'd walked robotically towards her car, numb with disbelief. It had been mere weeks since Indigo had claimed she was the only one for him, that he would love her and only her all his life.

But he'd apparently been full of shit.

It wasn't as though Indigo had ever struggled with a lack of prospects. Maybe there were only so many times he could hear no from her before he gave up and moved on with his life.

But surely he couldn't be that in love with her if he could move on so quickly, so easily. And that girl had been so bloody hot Cordelia would have had trouble turning her down. Maybe it was for the best. She'd only just broken up with Drew; general consensus would probably say that she needed a bit of time on her own.

But the truth was, if her love for Drew had been like swimming in a backyard pool, what she felt for Indigo was like diving headfirst into the ocean – deep and vast and infinitely endless.

"So he hasn't told you he's seeing anyone?" she asked Robbie as he opened her make-up drawer.

He shook his head, then began to apply her foundation. "I just can't see it," he mused. "I mean, he's only been home a few weeks and most of that time he's been ensconced here at Casa Carlisle. When would he have had time to meet this gold-bikini-wearing hussy?"

"This is Indigo we're talking about. He just has to breathe and chicks flock to him."

"This is true," Robbie agreed, deciding on a shimmery pearl shadow and artfully dusting her eyelids. "But the question begging to be asked, is why do you care? You're with Drew, right?" He moved to stand behind her. She met his eyes in the mirror. "It shouldn't matter if Indigo's dating, like, Claudia Schiffer." He bent forward and kissed the top of her head. "Unless you're having second thoughts?" He raised his brows challengingly.

She averted her eyes, her promise to Drew to keep their break-up quiet at the forefront of her mind. Robbie had a really big mouth.

"Indigo's been through a lot. He deserves to be happy." Robbie said, leaning his chin on her shoulder, gazing at her reflection. "You can't call dibs on all the boys, Cora. You can't tell Inds you've chosen Drew, but then expect him to just sit on the shelf and wait. It doesn't work that way."

"I know that. But it's just… the things he said to me the other day. I don't know how he could say those things and then simply move onto someone else."

"You think he wasn't hurt?" Robbie asked gently. "By your rejection? You totally palmed him. Imagine laying yourself bare and telling someone they were the love of your life, and them saying, 'ew no thanks'. Inds has a right to make his own choices too."

"First of all, as if I said 'ew'. Inds could never be ew. Second, quit being logical. It's your *job* in life to support your twin and her feelings, dammit!"

He squeezed her shoulders. "You know I'm always Team Cora. I get that you're hurt, but you can't blame him for moving on. He doesn't belong to you."

She nodded, but as she did, she couldn't help feeling that to the contrary, she and Indigo were tied together by some inexplicable force that made her feel that he did belong to her, because for the life of her she couldn't fathom him ever belonging to anyone else.

Once Robbie had helped her with her hair and makeup, he left her to finish getting dressed so he could "make himself pretty". She was fastening the ankle strap of her stiletto when her mum poked her head into her room.

"Oh, sweetie," she gushed, the tears that never seemed to be far from reach these days gathering in her eyes. "Look at you. You're a *vision.*" Cordelia stood and wrapped her mother in a hug.

"Thanks, Mum," she whispered.

"Come sit a minute," she said, taking Cordelia's hand and leading her to the bed. They sat side by side. "Is everything ok, darling? I mean, besides the obvious," she added with a sad smile.

Cordelia stared at a spot on the carpet and exhaled wearily. She *had* to tell someone. "Drew and I…" she said, pressing her lips together and raising her eyes to Mum's. "We broke up last night."

"Oh, sweetie, I'm so sorry to hear it." She put her arm around her daughter and cuddled her close.

"But I can't tell anyone, not even Rob, because I promised Drew I'd keep it quiet until after tonight."

Mum frowned, nodding in understanding. "Break ups are rough, darling. Do I even need to ask what happened?" Her eyes travelled to a photo collage on Cordelia's wall, Indigo front and centre.

Cordelia felt her lip waver. "I tried to make it work, Mum, I really did. But it wasn't fair on him, to continue to be with him when my whole heart and soul belong so completely to someone else." A tear escaped her eye and trickled down her cheek. "Oh God, my makeup. Rob will kill me." She half laughed, grabbing a tissue and dabbing her cheek, then balling it in her fist, leaning her head on her mother's shoulder.

"I feel like an absolute piece of shit," she said, her voice wobbling. "Drew was there for me when I needed him. He's such a beautiful guy and it honestly killed me, hurting him like that. The worst part is, I do love him. A part of me always will. But…"

"But just not the way you love Indigo," her mother finished for her, giving her a big squeeze. "Blind Freddy can see that."

"I don't think I'll ever love anyone the way I love Indigo." She smiled weakly. "I tried to do the right thing and stick by Drew. I mean, I thought we were happy… Until Indigo came back. And then I spent all that time feeling guilty for feeling what I did for him, feeling disloyal to Drew." As she spoke she twisted the ring she always wore. "There are times that I hate how I feel for Indigo, I hate that for me there isn't anyone else, how I can't see how there ever can be."

Mum stared down at Cordelia's right hand, suddenly distracted. She picked it up and gave the fine band a spin. "Why is this so loose?" she asked, her eyes raking over Cordelia. Her eyes filled with tears as she realised. "You're not eating properly. And I hadn't even noticed how much weight you've lost. I've been so caught up in my own grief... Oh God, sweetie, I'm so sorry I didn't see it."

"It's fine, Mum, really it is. It's not like last time, I promise," she said, referring to the period after Indigo's suicide attempt when she'd stopped eating altogether. "I just haven't had much of an appetite these days. But I'm eating, I swear. In fact I stuffed a whole brownie in my face this afternoon whilst sitting in the car crying. That's why you and Matty have to make do with only one to share tonight..." She smiled faintly.

Her mother regarded her through narrowed eyes. "Ok, I believe you, but just so you know, I'm gonna be all over this from now on." She reached out and gently ran her finger over the ring. "Remember to take care of this, ok?" she said softly, her throat working.

"It's ok, Mum. I'll guard it with my life, I always have."

"I have an idea," Mum said, jumping up and disappearing from the room. She returned a minute later, something clutched in her palm. She opened her hand and Cordelia saw another ring there, a slender white-gold band set with a large oval amethyst. "Put it on," she said, handing it to Cordelia. "On the same finger. It's smaller, it will stop the other one from falling off."

Cordelia smiled and slipped the ring on. It fit perfectly. Mum reached over and hugged her. "Please don't say you hate how you feel for Indigo."

"What?" Cordelia said, brow creased.

"You said before, that sometimes you hate how you feel for Indigo. But, honey, the kind of love you have for him, well, it's something to be honoured, cherished, never hated." She leant her cheek on Cordelia's head.

"When Dad... died," Cordelia stumbled over the word, "I realised that Indigo was the only one I wanted there, to support me, to hold me. He was my rock, my safe place to fall. It's funny how going through the shittest of shit times can bring about the most intense clarity. For better or for worse, it's him, Mum."

She felt her mother nod. "Did I ever tell you about the very first time I ever laid eyes on Josh?" she asked, pulling back, the side of her mouth quirking up in the saddest of half-smiles. "You and Robbie were toddlers, babies really, and as much as I adored you both, I wasn't in the greatest place. I was so young and had so much responsibility on my shoulders. I was completely overwhelmed. And I truly believed I was damaged goods, that no one would ever want me ever again." Her eyes fluttered shut for a beat.

"As you know, Dad had been studying Medicine in London and he'd come home to Sydney to spend Christmas with his parents as he did every year. This was when we'd just moved in next door to them with Granny and Pa. Anyway, I'd had a particularly bad night the night before with the two of you rascals, and I felt like death warmed up. For some reason that's beyond me now, probably out of delirium, I'd trudged out in my pyjamas to get the mail.

"I don't think I'd brushed my hair in days. I was pale, I was puffy, I smelt of sour breastmilk vomit... Anyway, I'm peering into the letterbox and a taxi pulls up at the kerb, and this very handsome stranger emerges, so sophisticated in his tan slacks and navy blazer. He must have felt me staring at him because all of a sudden he looked up, and we made eye contact. I've never wanted the earth to open up and swallow me more!" She laughed and shook her head.

"So, he's looking at me, and his face breaks out in the biggest smile – you know the one – and he says, 'Rough night?' And I just burst into tears, turned on my heel and ran into the house, slamming the door behind me. Josh being Josh, an hour later the doorbell goes, and I hear Mum talking to someone. He'd come to apologise for upsetting me. You two were asleep, so I'd had time for a shower and a change of clothes. I'd even washed my hair," she said, running her hand through her tresses. "So I came downstairs, and he had this huge bunch of freesias in his arms, which he handed to me while saying sorry on repeat. Mum subtly brought in some tea and Christmas cake and we ended up chatting and laughing for a couple of hours, until one of you woke up and I had to go feed you."

"Wait, he brought you freesias?" Cordelia asked. "Even back then?" She knew her father had always brought freesias for her mother, that it was their flower, but she hadn't realised it went back that far.

Mum nodded, melancholy in her eyes. "He did. Anyway, as you know, we became friends after that and he wrote to me constantly after he went back to London. And you also know he asked me to go out with him, but I said no." She stared into space, her gaze wistful. "At first because I wasn't over the... the death of your... your biological father. I'd loved him so much and losing him like that, it had almost killed me. I didn't think I'd ever be able to open my heart up to something like that ever again." Her voice wobbled and she pressed her hands tight to her mouth for a moment. "Loving someone the way I loved him is the most beautiful, most raw, most vulnerable thing we can ever do, and unfortunately, grief is sometimes the price we have to pay for that." She wiped at her eyes, smiling suddenly through her tears.

"But, well, Josh, he was so amazing. We connected. And over time, I realized I'd somehow let go and fallen desperately in love with him. Unbeknownst to me, he'd apparently fallen in love with me the moment he laid eyes on me by the mail box – barfy pyjamas, birds nest hair and all.

"So when he finished his studies in London and moved back to Sydney, he asked me again to go on a date with him, and the rest, as they say, is history. He brought me freesias again that night, they'd kind of become our thing by then, and we kissed for the first time, and from that moment we were inseparable. He got a residency here in Manly, and we began our life together."

She exhaled shakily. "When he... when he got sick, when he was dying, I had the time to reflect upon our life together, and I can tell you right now, that the journey with him – that wonderful, beautiful, amazing journey – it was worth the bone-jarring, agonising crash of finality that brought it all to a screaming halt. I wouldn't swap the time we had together for anything in the world. I think even if we'd both lived 'til we were a hundred, I'd still think it wasn't enough time with him, so I keep telling myself I need to just be grateful for the time we did have, for the wondrous gift that gorgeous man was to me, to us all." She paused, her voice thick with tears, to gaze into her daughter's eyes. Cordelia glanced up at the ceiling, willing the tears not to fall and smear her mascara.

"True love is a gift, Cora, a very rare, very precious gift. Something to be cherished and nurtured, something that must be acknowledged for the treasure it is. And when you find that person, every moment with them is so precious because you don't know what the future holds, you don't know how many moments you have, how many grains of sand you have left to slip through the hourglass of your life. So you need to make each one count, you need to take life and live it like you mean it."

Cordelia held the tissue under her eyes to absorb the tears leaking out. "I screwed up, Mum," she choked. "Indigo… he doesn't want me anymore, he's met someone else."

"Are you sure? Because I find that very hard to believe. I've watched that poor boy for weeks, torn between doing the honourable thing and respecting you and Drew, and struggling with the guilt of following the intensity of his own heart. He's put himself out there for you time and time again."

"I saw him at the beach. With another girl."

Mum went quiet. "So you do the mature thing and you talk to him," she finally said. "Because he's the only one who can give you the answers you need." She stood up and went to Cordelia's dresser, opened her makeup drawer. "Now let me touch that face up before Robbie sees what we've done to his handiwork." She cupped Cordelia's cheek in her hand and smiled.

chapter seventeen

i still haven't found
what i'm looking for

san diego, california

raf

Raf pulled a tan suede jacket over his t-shirt and jeans, then threw his canvas duffle bag over his shoulder. He strode out of the airport, slipping on his sunnies as he hailed a passing yellow taxi cab. Once he gave the driver his father's address, he rested his head against the back of the cracked vinyl seat and closed his eyes tightly.

He had a bad feeling about this.

A bad feeling.

He was worried about his pop. The old man had been on his own for so long now, with his mom gone almost fourteen years now. His father had dated a bit here and there, but he hadn't seemed to find anyone to settle down with again. In fact, it seemed to Raf that his father had dated more women before his mother had died than he had afterwards. It was the guilt, maybe. His father had loved his mother madly, but he just hadn't been able to keep it in his pants. And she'd known that. She'd known he wasn't faithful, and while she wasn't happy about the fact, in some twisted way she found it almost flattering that all those women wanted the man who always came home to her.

His mother, she'd had the face of an angel, but the temper of a devil.

Raf always regretted not being there when she died. He'd been selfish back then, he knew that, selfish and self-absorbed as he'd attempted to heal a broken heart, which was ironic considering to this day he had yet to succeed in doing so. It amazed him when he looked back now, he recognised how playing the victim could shape your attitude, colour your memories and perceptions.

He'd been given a chance at love and he'd thrown it away, so now his life was his to live alone. Coming back home always brought it all up for him.

Raf must have dozed off because he jumped when the cab driver shook his shoulder and informed him they'd arrived. He thanked him and handed over the cash before climbing out, grabbing his worn bag, and making his way up the front walk of his childhood home. He caught sight of his reflection in the window and sagged a little. He looked tired.

Raf was tall like his father, but his whole life people had commented how lucky he was he'd gotten his looks from his mother. He ran a hand through his hair, dark and tousled where it was longer on top, but he'd noticed lately it was streaked more and more with salt and pepper where it was cropped shorter around the temples. He'd observed a few greys coming through recently in the neatly trimmed stubble that shadowed his face, too.

Raf had been so worried about his father since that phone call, the way he'd been stumbling over his words, clearly distressed. He'd sounded so confused, so... old.

His whole life, his pop had exhibited behaviour befitting of the fiery Latino he was, bold and passionate. It scared Raf, watching his father age, seeing that part of him ebbing, tempering, flickering out. His parents had loved one another desperately, but their passion for one another often exploded into physical violence. His mom had tended to express her displeasure with his pop by throwing plates and other tableware at him, to the extent they quite often had nothing to eat off in the evenings.

Raf was twelve when he learned that love and loyalty were not one and the same. His father adored his mother, but he was not faithful to her. When Raf caught his pop in the school's janitor closet with his sixth grade teacher, Miss Santos, the broken crockery that had littered his childhood suddenly made sense.

One day, after another heated plate-throwing incident, Raf had asked his mom why she stayed. She'd seemed shocked by the question, and then finally replied, a small smile of superiority playing upon her lips, "He may sleep with all those women, but it's *me* he comes home to at night." Aside from his twelve aunties, Sofia didn't much like other women. "What goes around comes around," she'd say to Raf. "They'll get what's coming to them."

And Raf found more often than not, they did. Not long after her tryst with Matias, Miss Santos fell down the stairs at school and broke her leg in two places. Mrs Cooper, the widow who lived down the street with whom Matias had been having an affair in Raf's thirteenth year, developed breast cancer soon after and had to have a double mastectomy. Then there was Bella Cancio, who'd had a fling with Matias the summer she came home from college. She'd been in a terrible car wreck on her way back to school and, although she'd survived, she'd been horribly disfigured. As far as Raf could tell, his mother never felt any pity for these women, in fact she seemed almost smug whenever news came their way of another accident or illness befalling one of Matias' mistresses.

"My family is my world," Sofia told Raf often. "May the Moon Goddess help any women who dare try to take either of my men away from me."

Raf walked into the house, peeling off his dusty combat boots and leaving them by the front door as he'd always done. "Hey, Pops, you home?" he called out as he dropped his bag in the hallway and made his way towards the living room. He noticed the door to the parlour was ajar and frowned. He recalled Pops saying it had flooded. The parlour had been his mother's room and, after she'd died, his father had all but sealed it off, refusing ever to go in there.

His mom had held court in that room with her friends – his aunties – almost every afternoon of her life. "Secret women's business," his pop would say when Raf asked what was going on behind that closed door. Of all different ages, shapes and colours, his aunties would arrive almost every weekday afternoon, sweeping into the house and ensconcing themselves in the parlour, closing the door firmly behind them. When Raf was little, he would try to peep in, desperate to be privy to this infamous secret women's business.

As far as Raf could tell, all they seemed to do was sit around and drink tea and do arts and crafts. Strong aromas would emanate from the room, lavender, rosemary, bergamot and cedar from the lotions and oils and creams his mom and aunties would make. They'd sell them to the neighbourhood women who came knocking on the door and were ushered into the parlour under a cloak of secrecy. One day, Raf saw his mother and aunties making scary looking dolls out of wax. He never saw them sell those though, although that didn't surprise him – they were gruesome.

Raf inhaled the familiar scent of his parents' house, garlic and washing powder, yet today seemingly overpowered by the smell of damp. "Pops?" he called again as he ventured into the living room. His father was slumped in his favourite armchair by the window. His eyes were closed, his mouth slack. The newspaper he'd been reading was lying in a heap on the floor. His chest moved up and down rhythmically in deep slumber.

People had always said that what Matias lacked in looks, he more than made up for in charm. Rail-thin with floppy hair, he had a face his wife had declared to be an acquired taste for a sophisticated palette, and a smile that altered his whole appearance.

Raf smiled fondly at his father and draped a quilt over his lap. He picked up the crumpled newspaper and folded it neatly, laying it on the coffee table before quietly exiting the room.

Pops being asleep, well, it felt almost like a bit of a reprieve, a stay of execution. Raf scooped up his bag and climbed the stairs to his old bedroom. His surfboard and wetsuit were exactly where he'd left them, and he quickly changed. He left a note on the kitchen table for Pops, then borrowed his keys, loading up his board and taking his father's car down to La Jolla.

He loved living in Sedona, with its soaring red rocks, its tranquil forests and magical vortexes, but the one thing he really missed was the beach. Raf had always been a mad keen surfer and it had taken a lot of adjustment for him to live away from the waves. He made his way to Windansea, where he spent a couple of hours out on his favourite break before paddling back in.

Raf always found the ocean so settling and soothing, but as he waded out of the water that day, his stomach was a seething mass of nerves. He quickly changed back into jeans and a T-shirt before climbing into his father's Cadillac. The closer he got to his childhood home, the worse the pain in his gut grew. He tried to breathe deeply, to calm himself, to no avail. His body was warning him that something big was about to go down, *that* he knew, but he had no idea what.

"Pops? I'm back!" he called as he strode into the house.

His father emerged into the hall, wiping his hands on his apron. "My boy, my boy," he cried as he engulfed his son tightly in his arms. "It is so good to see you, Diego."

"I missed you too, old man," Raf said, squeezing his pop tightly and kissing him on the cheek. The sick feeling in his stomach, the twisting, churning mess of scrambling spider legs and beating butterfly wings, increased at his father's touch.

"What's going on, Pops?" he asked, pulling back from his father's embrace and peering into his face. Pops held his gaze steadily before abruptly breaking it. He lowered his eyes, his whole body sagging as he sighed.

"Can we at least eat first?" he said, seemingly hesitant now to tell Raf why he'd asked him to come.

"I couldn't eat right now even if I wanted to," Raf replied, patting his abdomen.

His father's shoulders slumped. "Yes, yes, you're probably right. Come and sit, my boy." He led Raf into the living room where he took up position in his favourite chair again. Raf sat on the couch beside him, looking expectantly into his eyes.

Pops sighed again, shakily this time, and dropped his head into his hands, scrubbing at his face before finally raising his chin. "The night... the night of your mother's accident... Have I ever told you about that night?"

Raf shook his head. "Not in detail, no." The old man had never wanted to discuss it.

"You see, by that point your mother was very, very ill. She'd refused treatment, she didn't want to lose her hair, and well, it wouldn't have made much difference anyway. She wanted to stay at home for as long as possible – we both wanted that – so I was caring for her. With the help of your aunties, of course," he added bitterly. His pop had never gotten along with Sofia's friends. His dalliances were the worst-kept secret in the neighbourhood, and Sofia's friends were never able to forgive him the way she could.

"That night, I'd tried to feed her a little apple sauce but she'd refused. She was almost past eating by then. So I sat in the chair by her bed and read to her as she so loved. *Flowers in the Attic*, we were reading, you know how she adored her romance novels." He smiled wistfully. "Afterwards, I'd given her her medicine, then tucked her in for the night and retired to your bedroom where I'd taken up residence towards the end of her illness. I vaguely heard the phone ringing in our room, but not enough to register it. I didn't even hear her leave. You know I've always been a heavy sleeper," he explained.

"I was awoken about three am by banging on the front door. It was the police, come to tell me about the accident. Your Aunt Henny had picked her up, God knows where they were going. Henny died on impact, so I was never able to ask her. I rushed to your mother's bedside, and I sat with her, and I held her hand, for three days and nights. It was on the third night that she passed. She never regained consciousness." He twisted the wedding ring he still wore, his gaze vacant as he relived the memory. He shook himself off after a moment or two and continued.

"The hospital staff, they gave me her personal effects, things she'd had on her when she was brought in by ambulance – it wasn't much really. A torn, bloody nightdress, her slippers, and her purse. It was all in a big manila envelope. And I never could bring myself to open it. In my grief, I stashed it in the cabinet in the parlour when I got home and never thought of it again. Until last week, that is."

He stared at Raf, his eyes glazing. "That room... I never go in there. I wasn't allowed in when she was alive; it felt wrong somehow to go in there after her death. But there was a leak in the bathroom above, and water was pouring down through the ceiling light, flooding the whole room... And, well, after the plumber fixed the problem, I was left to clean up the mess. I had to pull up all the carpets, open all the windows, and when I went to move the cabinet, the manila envelope fell out. And her purse caught my eye, because there was a smaller envelope hanging out of it, so... so I opened it." A tic in his cheek began to shudder as he looked Raf straight in the eye. "It-it was, well, it was an old letter you see, son. I don't know if it was in her purse when she left the house that night or if it came from Henny, but there it was." His voice cracked and he dropped his head into his hand, his shoulders slumping.

"It's alright, Pops," Raf said, placing his hands on his father's arms. "Whatever it is, it's alright."

Pops reeled up and shook his head violently. "It's *not* ok, though, son, you see, it's really not." He laughed bitterly. "I loved your mother, Diego. Some days, when she was particularly nasty, I had no idea why. I know it might be hard for you to believe that, considering my... uh, past indiscretions. But that being said, I knew her for what she was. She was an incredibly selfish, self-centred woman who always put herself first. And she would do anything to keep you and me for herself.

"When you left us to go see the world, it broke her heart. You know she severed all ties with her adoptive family back when they tried to stop our marriage. You and I, we were her only family, we were everything to her. When you left, she was devastated. She cried for weeks, did you know that?"

Raf shook his head, guilt tossing his gut.

"But she always said to me, 'He'll be back. His ties are to America, his family is here, he will always come back to us.' And I suppose if I'm looking for a reason as to why she... she did it, that's the only one I can come up with."

"Did what, Pops?" Raf's stomach was a plethora of agonising knots.

He grabbed Raf's face between his hands and touched his forehead to his son's. "Please know I never knew, Diego, I promise you, I never knew." His voice cracked then and Raf could feel the tears trickling down his father's craggy face.

He took the old man's hands in his, squeezing them hard. "You're really scaring me, Pops."

His father reached down the side of his chair and pulled out a small, yellowing envelope, the neat scrawl on the front unfamiliar. Raf could see it was water damaged. "Read this, my boy," Matias said, pushing the envelope into his hands. "The water has made a lot of it illegible, but... You need to read what you can".

Raf had to swallow hard to hold down the bile that was rising in his throat. He knew in his bones that his whole world was about to come tumbling, crashing down upon him, he just didn't know in what capacity, or just how severely, or how he would feel about his mother in the aftermath.

"I'll give you some privacy," Pops said, climbing stiffly to his feet, kissing his son on the top of the head before walking slowly from the room. "I'm out here when you need me."

Raf sat with the envelope in his lap for some time, just staring at it, working up the nerve to open it. Eventually he took a deep breath and, with trembling hands, he slid it open, easing out its contents, smoothing the water-pocked pages so he could read them more easily.

It took ages to decipher, so much of it illegible, the words faded or forever washed away, but with each word he managed to decode, he felt sicker and sicker.

He managed to make it through the whole letter before the bile disgorged itself from his stomach, tumbling and swirling from his gut so fast he had to drop his head between his knees and breathe deeply to prevent himself from letting loose all over the living room floor. And then came a howling sound, so forlorn and primal he barely recognised it was coming from him.

His father came rushing back into the room then, straight over to the couch where he gathered his son in his arms and held him and rocked him while he wept and railed and broke into a million little pieces.

They both knew Raf's life would never be the same.

chapter eighteen

like the way i do

manly, new south wales

indigo

Indigo tugged at his bowtie as the stretch limo pulled up outside the Carlisles'. This was going to be a fun ride to the formal, what with Drew all cold and aloof and cuddled up to Cordelia. It had naturally worked out that the four of them would go to together tonight, and he knew Drew was less than thrilled about it. Fair enough. It was *awkward*.

He climbed out of the ridiculous black limousine that seemed to take up half the block, and strode to the door, a ridiculous boutonniere of radishes and parsley pinned to his chest, another clutched in his hand. He'd gone the traditional route with his tuxedo, black trousers, crisp white shirt, black jacket with satin lapels, black bowtie.

He almost walked straight into the house as he always had, but paused and changed his mind. This was a formal event; he should pick his date up in a formal manner. He rang the doorbell and stepped back to wait.

"Who is it?" he heard Cordelia call out, her voice accompanied by the click of her heels on the stairs.

"It's only me."

"Since when do you ring the bell?" she asked, and he could hear the smile in her voice as she flung the door open.

His jaw fell and he exhaled sharply, rendered speechless as his gaze caressed her head to toe, inch by glorious inch.

Under his intense survey, a blush bloomed on her cheeks.

"You're a knockout," he finally breathed.

A shy smile tugged her dusky-pink lips and she twirled slowly on the spot so he could admire her from all angles. She wore a long white satin sheath with a high slit up one thigh, a deep vee at the front, hugging her in all the right places, held up by two wide straps that crossed over her bare back. Her hair, parted on the side and swept back into a low textured bun, a loose tendril left free to frame her face, her skin bronzed and dewy, her feet slippered in high silver heels, her makeup perfect, hiding all the anguish he knew she'd been living with these past weeks. Her jewellery was minimal, small diamond studs in her ears and a large amethyst ring on her right ring finger stacked above the band she always wore.

She was preternaturally stunning, so beautiful his heart physically ached.

Maybe this had been a mistake.

She reached up to straighten his bowtie, and the very nearness of her caused his vision to blur, stirring those damned butterflies in his stomach that seemed to exist only for her. She smelled like heaven, like ylang ylang and jasmine and sunshine. She smelled like home. As her fingers grazed the flesh of his throat, a jolt rocked his entire body. She lifted her gaze, slowly, slowly to meet his, that voluptuous lower lip of hers caught between her teeth. He knew she felt it, too.

"Listen, Inds," she said, clearing her throat, her wide aquamarine eyes suddenly serious. "I wanted to ask you about–"

"Is that my hot date?" Robbie called, bounding down the stairs in his black velvet tuxedo, and Cordelia immediately clammed up. "Well, well, well, don't you scrub up alright?" he said, looking Indigo up and down, nodding in approval at his clean-shaven face and slicked back hair. "Guess you'll do alright," he joked, adjusting Indigo's lapels. "Just think how ah-maaa-zing our photos will look, which is the main thing, right?"

"You're not looking too shabby there yourself there, Rob." Indigo grinned. He handed him his corsage and Robbie practically squealed in delight. "Courtesy of Edie. Who knew she was the MacGyver of crudités?"

"It's perfect!" Robbie gushed. "Just like the ones Brandon and Dylan wore! Pin it on me, Cora." He thrust it at his sister.

"You do realise these things are like, *so* five years ago?" she teased as she attached it to his lapel.

"Do I even look as if I care?" Robbie purred, admiring himself in the hallway mirror. "I love it and I fully intend to bring the trend back. I think between me and Inds, we have the power to influence fashion. Look at what we did for karaoke parties five years ago."

Just then Drew arrived, looking suave in his black tuxedo, his hair neatly combed and parted on the side, his face neatly shaven, and, Indigo realised with a frown, his white bowtie neatly matching Cordelia's dress.

"Hey, guys," Drew said, glancing around in what seemed to be discomfort. He sidled over to Cordelia and stiffly planted a kiss on her cheek. "You look really beautiful," he said softly, squeezing her arm as he handed her a white wrist corsage. She slipped it on, then pinned the boutonnière she'd chosen for him to his jacket.

"Thanks," she whispered. "So do you."

Robbie cleared his throat theatrically.

Drew glanced over at him. "Looking good, Robster," he told him graciously. "Wolfie." He smiled tightly at Indigo and shook his hand. "Why do you have, like, garnish hanging off you?" he asked, looking from Indigo to Robbie, his nose wrinkling.

"I'll have you *know*," Robbie stated dramatically, "that tonight, we are bringing vegetable corsages back in." Robbie's eyes moved down to the white rose Cordelia had pinned to Drew's lapel. He wrinkled his nose. "Not that you'd understand, what with that boring old cliché attached to you." He glanced at Cordelia's wrist corsage and gasped.

"What?" Drew asked defensively.

"Oh, nothing," Robbie murmured, turning his back on Drew and mouthing, '*Baby's breath*', to Indigo, his eyes wide, his face contorted in horror. Indigo suppressed a smile and shook his head in amusement. Robbie had always declared baby's breath to be almost as big a crime to the flower industry as the carnation.

Scarlett hurried to the bottom of the stairs where they were congregated, casual in a pair of denim cut-offs and a floral peasant blouse, barefoot as always. Her eyes glittered with tears as she surveyed them all. She waved a camera, her silver bangles jangling. "You all look so divine, there's no way I'm letting you leave without taking some photos first." Everyone groaned except for Robbie, who jumped into action, flapping around organising everyone, deciding on the perfect location and perfect lighting.

They ended up in the backyard under the frangipani tree that had started to bloom, its fragrant white and yellow flowers providing the perfect backdrop for their photos.

"We have to have a toast before you go!" Scarlett exclaimed, running into the house to retrieve the bottle of champagne she'd had chilling in the fridge.

"Mu-um!" Robbie complained. "We have to get going or we're going to miss the pre-drinks." Pre-formal drinks were a big tradition, with everyone heading to Sian's house this year for the warm-up to the main event.

Cordelia shot him a death stare and quickly added, "But of course, we can have just one." She reprimanded Robbie under her breath, "Everyone else's parents are coming to pre-drinks but she doesn't want to go without Dad. Just let her have a champers with us."

Robbie looked stricken.

Scarlett returned with six glasses on a silver tray and a bottle of Moët. Indigo went to the back door to meet her, taking the bottle from her. He popped the cork and quickly began to pour as the champagne came frothing out. He filled the fifth glass then hesitated as she went to pass him the sixth.

"What?" she asked, the line between her brows deepening.

"Oh, Scar," he breathed, tilting his head, his heart lurching. "There are only five of us." He glanced over to where the others were chatting in the far corner of the yard.

"Oh God," she choked, the colour draining from her face with the realisation. "I-I just... I-I still count him, you know?" she whispered, her big blue eyes filling with tears again as the sixth glass slipped from her fingers, its fall cushioned by the grass below. Indigo took the tray from her and placed it on the table behind them, then wrapped his arms around her in an enveloping hug, rubbing her back. "I know, I know, we all miss him. He should be here for this, he should".

"I just don't understand, Indigo, he had such an amazing life force, and it's just... just *gone*. Just like that. All that vibrancy, all that knowledge and experience, all that energy, all that love... and it's just *gone*. Where does it all *go*? How can he just not *be* here anymore?"

Indigo just held her tighter.

"Goodness," she said, pulling away from him and wiping her eyes as she plastered on a big smile. "That's enough of that! Ignore me please, I'm just an old sad sack." He picked up the tray and they headed towards the others, handing out the champagne flutes.

"Tonight is all about you four," Scarlett said. She held her glass up. "I could go on all night but I'll keep it short and sweet. Here's to you all, and to my babies, celebrating the end of an era tonight. It's been a privilege watching you all grow into such beautiful, bright, shining souls. I couldn't be prouder of any of you. Cheers!"

"Cheers!" they parroted, taking big swigs from their glasses.

"Now go!" she ordered. "Take the rest of the champagne in the limo with you."

"You don't have to tell me twice," Robbie said, swiping the bottle and kissing his mum on the cheek.

She gave each of them a warm hug, covering them in kisses as she sent them on their way. "Stick together, take care of each other, and I'll see you when I see you."

The four of them piled into the limo, Robbie enthusiastically refilling everyone's glass. Indigo subtly tipped his champagne into the gutter before he shut the car door. He hadn't drunk since that night on the bridge two-and-a-half years ago, and the few polite sips he'd just taken had gone straight to his head.

Drew quickly drained his glass and then pulled out a hip flask, taking a big gulp of what smelt like bourbon. He winced and smiled lazily, offering the flask to Cordelia. She shook her head, indicating the champagne she was still sipping. Robbie, on the other hand, grabbed the flask off Drew and gulped down most of its contents before putting the champagne bottle to his lips and draining that, too.

"Woooo!" he yelled, pumping his fist in the air.

"Slow down a bit, Rob," Indigo said lightly. "I don't think either of us want this night to end with me holding your hair back while you boot into a public toilet."

"It wouldn't be the first time," Cordelia murmured.

"Yeah, like that's gonna happen... Not!" Robbie shook his head at Indigo, then leaned forward to the driver and slurred, "Oh. My. GOD! Can you turn this up, please? *I love this song!*"

The driver muttered under his breath, but did as asked, and the beat of Melissa Etheridge singing *Like The Way I Do* filled the car. Robbie sang along with ear-piercing passion, word perfect, gesticulating with wild aggression as he did.

And suddenly it was super uncomfortable. Indigo, Cordelia and Drew each sat stiffly, their gazes on the floor, out the window, anywhere but on each other. Indigo eventually couldn't help but steal a quick glance at Cordelia, only to catch her glaring at him with stormy eyes. He flinched, and she reddened and quickly looked away. His gaze fell on Drew, who was staring sullenly from Indigo to Cordelia, jaw set stiffly, arms crossed, but he also looked away when he noticed Indigo watching him.

Why were those two pissed off at *him*?

He could feel the anger and resentment... and... and... sadness rolling off them in waves. He had to actively stop himself from delving into their minds to read their thoughts; he'd made that vow to Raf long ago never to telepathically intrude on anyone for personal gain.

"Fuck you, Gino!" Robbie yelled, oblivious to the inappropriateness of the song and the fact the tension in the limo was thick enough to cut with a katana. "Hope you're having fun cowering in the closet with your man-skanks while we have the best night *ever!*"

"If you open that sunroof and stand up, I'm outta here," Cordelia commented dryly.

"*That's a great idea!*" Robbie exclaimed, fumbling for the button.

"Don't even think about it, mate, or I'll break your fingers off," the driver interjected brusquely. Robbie snatched his hand back, eyes darting forwards over what little he could see of the man: a thick neck melding into a meaty head topped with a severe buzzcut. He was ex-SAS and Indigo had hired him tonight as a precaution – for his combat skills – not his ability to tolerate drunk teenagers.

"We're here," Cordelia said.

"Thank God for that," Indigo muttered under his breath, desperate to escape the weird vibes. He climbed out the car first, carefully surveying the landscape through narrowed eyes, checking for anything untoward.

"Relax, Inds," Cordelia said as she ducked out the limo, squeezing his arm as she swept past him. "You're gonna give yourself an aneurysm."

Pre-drinks were in full swing at Sian's, their school friends milling around her manicured backyard, some elegantly sipping champagne, others tossing it back like cheap beer. A group of parents stood off to one side under the sculpted crepe myrtles, proudly eyeing the little darlings they'd gotten to eighteen and were about to send out into the big wide world. A waiter in full monkey suit was passing tiny canapés around while strains of operatic music wafted over the yard. Tealight candles floated in the spotless pool even though it was still light out.

"*Oh my God*, Shi," Robbie screeched loudly as he stumbled up to Sian and flung an arm around her. "Is this a party for eighty-year-olds?"

"*Gee thanks*, Rob," Sian replied, shrugging him off her. "Drunk much?"

"Hey, Shi," Indigo said, stooping to kiss her cheek as he swept in to rescue his date from himself. "Great party. Really. He doesn't know what he's talking about." He gave her an apologetic smile as he hooked his arm around Robbie's neck and wrapped his hand over his mouth.

Robbie's tongue darted out to lick Indigo's palm, so he quickly let go. Robbie wriggled out of his grasp. "It's a totally *shit* party!" he announced. "I mean seriously, what the actual fuck is this music? Am I *in* an elevator?"

The whole party stopped to look at Robbie, some of the parents in the corner shaking their heads and muttering their disapproval.

"Take it down a notch or two, Rob," Indigo murmured, wiping his palm down the thigh of his pants to remove Robbie's slobber whilst smiling his most responsible smile in the direction of the parents.

"Level three, Ladies' Lingerie," Robbie called in a posh English accent. "Going up."

"Stop!" Indigo hissed at him.

"Dad says today's music glorifies sex and drugs and won't allow it in our house," Sian said in a small voice, eyes downcast, cheeks flaming. Indigo's heart went out to her.

Not Robbie's though, apparently. "Oh my God!" he guffawed. "Your house is that town from *Footloose!*"

Sian's father was now coming towards them, a disapproving scowl on his bulbous face. Mr Roberts was a tall man trapped in a small man's body, short and nuggety like a bulldog. He was a total dick and the last person Indigo felt like dealing with right now.

"Rob, Bruce Roberts is headed our way," Indigo said through clenched teeth and a fake smile. Robbie immediately stopped laughing and stood up straight, wavering a little on his feet. Indigo put an arm around Robbie to steady him.

"Mr Carlisle." Mr Roberts nodded. "Mr Wolfe, I'd heard rumours you were back in town, still spreading disrepute everywhere you go, I see." He puffed up to his full five feet five and glared way up at Indigo.

"Da-ad!" Sian cried, looking around in embarrassment. "Everything's fine, honestly."

"You boys been drinking?" Mr Roberts demanded, eyeing Robbie suspiciously as he rocked back and forth on the spot. The fact he himself was serving alcohol at his party seemed to have escaped him.

"We *are* over eighteen," Robbie informed him, smiling clumsily. "And I'm sure you're well aware that eighteen is the legal age for alcohol consumption in Australia. I mean, look, eeeverybody's drinking!" he slurred, spreading his arms wide.

Mr Roberts' eyes landed on Indigo's arm wrapped securely around Robbie. "Where are your *dates*, boys?" he asked accusingly, screwing up his wide nose.

"This *is* my date," Robbie told him, hugging Indigo closer to him and placing a hand proudly on Indigo's chest. "Isn't he *dreamy*? Don't we make *the cutest* couple?"

Mr Roberts recoiled, his lip curling. "*He's* your date?" he spat, looking from Robbie to Indigo. "Exhausted Sydney's supply of women have you, Wolfe? Moved onto the menfolk now, have we? Not that I'm surprised, growing up with those Hollywood types, where anything goes. *Bloody disgusting*, I tell you! Taking another bloke to your Year Twelve formal, it's *unnatural* I tell you!" He shook his head at them and muttered under his breath, "Wouldn't have flown back in my day, bloody poofters, thinking you have the right to behave like what you do is *normal*. It's anything *but* normal! It's *sick* and it's *wrong*."

All the colour had drained from Robbie's face. Sian was beet-red with embarrassment. Anger seethed in Indigo's belly, and he had to clench his hands into fists to extinguish the bioplasma writhing to be unleashed.

He could see Cordelia sweeping across the lawn towards them from where she'd been talking to Peyton and Sandy, her beautiful face marred with concern. He pasted on a large, fake smile and, as Mr Roberts glared venom at them, Indigo dipped Robbie, and kissed him full on the lips.

"Actually, we're *very* happy together, thank you, Bruce," he announced, taking Robbie confidently by the hand. "And for your information, our love is a very beautiful, very natural thing, despite the fact we still aren't afforded the rights we should be. Like the fact it's 1995 and we still don't have the right to *marry* the person we *love.*" He made to walk off, pulling a stunned Robbie with him, but stopped, leaning down to whisper in Mr Roberts' bristling ear. "Nobody knows the male body like another man. I highly recommend test-driving a bit of man-love, if you ever get the chance. It might actually loosen you up and put a smile on that miserable old dial of yours. Have a good night, sir." He winked and strode off, leaving Mr Roberts open-mouthed, speechless, spluttering behind them.

time after time

manly, new south wales

indigo

Cordelia caught up with them as they reached the side gate, grabbing Indigo's arm. "What the hell just happened?" she demanded, glancing back towards the party where everyone was standing stock still, staring after them.

"We're leaving," Indigo told her through clenched teeth. "The man's a close-minded bigot."

"He said I was unnatural, Cora," Robbie interjected softly, his face contorted with hurt, shame, embarrassment. "He called us poofters."

"He said *what?*" Cordelia cried, turning on her heel to storm off towards Mr Roberts, presumably to give him a piece of her mind.

Indigo grabbed her hand. "Stop, Cora. I think we've made our point. Let's just go."

She paused and looked to Robbie, who nodded, his eyes pleading. "I just wanna leave."

She pursed her lips, hesitating, before nodding tersely in agreement. "Ok. I just need to go get my purse and my… Drew. And I should tell Shi we're leaving. It's not her fault her dad's a prick."

She stalked off, meeting them a few minutes later at the limo, Drew in tow. It looked as though Drew had snuck off to punch a few cones with some of the boys during the short time they'd been at the party. His eyes were red-rimmed and he had a big dopey grin on his face.

"You promised me you were only doing it at night, to help you sleep," Cordelia was chastising him under her breath.

"Well, I don't really think that matters anymore, does it?" Drew was saying, his lips sticky on his teeth. "Broken promises and broken dreams, right, Cee?"

Indigo narrowed his eyes at the two of them.

"And why are we leaving? Is it over already?" Drew glanced around. He seemed surprised to find himself sitting in the limo again.

Robbie was just sitting, staring into space, pale and quiet. He seemed very sober all of a sudden.

"You ok, man?" Indigo asked, leaning forward and squeezing his knee.

"You never get used to it," Robbie murmured, eyes still staring, unfocused.

"To what?" Indigo asked.

"To how nasty people can be," Robbie replied softly. "You tell yourself it's only words, that it doesn't matter what anyone else thinks. But you know what?" he asked, raising his eyes to meet theirs. "It *does.* It *does* matter what they think. I mean, it *must*, because their words hurt. When they're that sharp and vicious and hateful, it cuts to your very soul."

"The bloke's a dipshit. It doesn't matter what an ignorant, narrow-minded prick like that–" Indigo began.

"*Yes, it does*," Robbie snapped. "When someone looks at you with so much disgust, with so much hate, it makes you feel like a big, fat *zero*."

"You're not a big fat zero," Cordelia cried, moving to put her arms around her brother. "*He's* a zero. He's *less than* zero. You? You're my other half, so you're at least a hard fifty."

"You know the worst part? I struggle *so hard* to accept that men like Bruce Roberts are out there in the world, alive and well and thriving, when Dad *isn't* anymore," Robbie said sadly, a faraway look in his eye. "Remember what he said when I came out to him and Mum?"

Cordelia nodded, her eyes glistening. She gripped Robbie's hand tight.

"I was so scared to tell them. I don't know why, I mean, of course they were always going to be cool about it, but I was fifteen and bloody terrified of what I was. Anyway, Mum, well, she just smiled and hugged me so tight and whispered she loved me, but Dad, I'll never forget his reaction," he said, tears beading on his lashes. "He walked up to me really slowly, and he placed a hand on either side of my face and he looked me dead in the eye and he said 'You, my son, are glorious just as you are. Don't ever let anyone tell you otherwise.' And he kissed me on the forehead, and gave me one of his famous hugs, and he whispered, 'Never ever try to be what you're not, I love you so much.' And at that moment I felt as though I could face anything, do anything, *be* anything. I truly believed I'd never have to hide away, or be ashamed. I thought I'd always be able to be me, to be loved just as I am."

"Josh was an incredibly wise man," Indigo said gently, as Cordelia squeezed Robbie tighter, rocking him in her arms.

"He was a fucking sensational man," Robbie said, his lip trembling. "And not a day went by that I didn't know what a blessing he was and how bloody lucky we were to have him in our lives. He didn't have to die for me to realise that. I always knew."

Cordelia nodded, clearly too choked up to speak.

"He and Mum just accepted us for what we were. They raised us to find our place in the world, and to never, ever apologise for what we were. Dad would tell me, 'The world deserves to see you, so go out there and be seen.' When I didn't want to go to school because I wasn't like the other kids, he'd say 'Why would you want to be like everyone else? It's those who are different that will make a difference to this world.' And when I'd come home in tears, yet again, because someone else had called me a nasty word or made fun of me or excluded me, Dad would just sit me down and he'd say, 'The people who are mean to you, *they're not your people,*' and then he'd tell me that one day I'd look back and realise that being different was a gift. That I was special, and that only those who were strong enough to handle it were given the privilege of not being like everyone else."

"We're never given more than we can handle," Cordelia said. "He always used to say that. But you know what else he used to say? That it's up to us *how* we handle it... and that we're never meant to handle it *alone*," she added pointedly. "That everyone has a tribe, whether they've found it yet or not, it's out there, a tribe of kindred spirits who will feel like home."

Robbie wiped his eyes with the back of his hand.

"You alright?" Cordelia asked him, peering into his face. He nodded and flashed her a small, wobbly smile. She squeezed his arm and went to sit back beside Drew. "What happened back there anyway?" she asked, looking from Robbie to Indigo.

Indigo quickly filled her in on the exchange that had occurred, word for word.

"No," she breathed, her eyes wide. "You actually *said that* to Mr Roberts? He'll be *furious*! He'll never forget this, Inds."

Indigo shrugged. "I don't give a shit," he smirked, leaning back in his seat and stretching his arm casually around Robbie's shoulder.

Drew started laughing and couldn't stop, doubled over, unable to catch his breath. He managed to hold up his hand for a high five. Indigo slapped his palm and started laughing, too. Robbie, whose face was dark as thunder, looked from Drew to Indigo, and then to Cordelia who was trying to keep a straight face. Drew was now crying with laughter. Cordelia's hand covered her mouth, her mirthful eyes betraying her. She eventually gave up the fight and began to giggle, too. The corner of Robbie's mouth twitched as he looked from one to the next.

"*Man-love*," Drew gasped, wiping tears from his eyes, setting the others off even more.

"I can't believe you guys *kissed* in front of him!" Cordelia laughed uncontrollably, bent double. She laughed so hard an enormous snort erupted from her nose.

Indigo's sides ached as he pointed at her and gasped, "Oh my God!" She flipped him off, blushing furiously. He winked and she smiled widely at him. Fuck. He'd missed that snort, that killer grin, her wild laughter. He'd missed *all* of her.

"Test driving a bit of *man-love*," Drew guffawed again, seemingly unable to move past that particular part of the exchange.

"You should have seen his face!" Indigo said, slapping his leg and hugging Robbie to him.

Their laughter was infectious. What were friends for, if not to defend you to the death and then make you see the lighter side of it? Robbie began to smile, then chuckle, and before long he, too, was rolling around laughing uncontrollably with the rest of them.

"Oh my God, I love you guys," he panted. "And fuck me, I've missed you, Inds." He smiled, nudging him with his shoulder. "Pass me those CDs would you, Cora?" He held out his hand for the CD case that had been left out for their perusal. "Let's breathe some life back into this party!" He thumbed through the discs before settling on one, passing it over to the driver.

"Are we still going to the formal?" Cordelia asked.

"Shit yeah, we are!" Robbie replied as the Violent Femmes began to question their inability to get just one kiss.

"You know what this song reminds me of?" Cordelia asked.

"The summer of '92!" the others cried in unison.

"This is seriously the theme song of my tortured youth," Robbie declared, smiling at the memory of their 1992 summer holidays when they'd listened to the Violent Femmes CD over and over again, blaring it out over the pool speakers at the Van Allen Estate until Edita had threatened to disconnect the stereo system.

"Indeeego," Robbie imitated Edita, covering his ears with his hands as she used to. "I cannot listen to zis terrible muzeec a minute longer!"

"And zee language!" Indigo added. "It is zimply atrocious!"

They stopped at a service station for snacks, then instructed the driver to take the scenic route to the formal so they could make a fashionably late entrance, anticipating that by the time they wound their way up the hill towards the school, the party would be in full swing. And hopefully the incident at Sian's had been forgotten.

The formal was being held in the school's enormous auditorium. North Head Grammar was known to locals as the castle on the hill, and its auditorium was unlike most other schools'. Back in the 1800s, before it was North Head Grammar, the campus was a seminary, a fact which was reflected in its blended neo-Gothic Romanesque design. With its ornate vaulted ceiling and black-and-white checkerboard floor, the auditorium was perfect for a formal event. A sprawling, arcade-like veranda spilled out onto rolling lawns edged by towering palm trees and Norfolk pines. At the centre of the grounds sat the sandstone fountain at which Indigo and Robbie had spent their lunchtimes as school boys. Far below, the twinkling lights of Manly stretched out in a horseshoe towards the inky blue ocean.

The forecasted southerly change hadn't yet hit and the thick heat lingered, hot as a Sedona summer day. The slight summery breeze that rustled the surrounding trees barely touched the humidity.

Robbie had been head of the Formal Committee, and even after Joshua's illness had forced him to resign his position so close to the finish line, his influence was apparent, with simple black tablecloths and white floral arrangements adorning the tables – not a carnation nor a sprig of baby's-breath was to be seen. The high ceiling was smothered in black and white helium balloons, their monochrome ribbons dangling just out of reach like satiny vines.

"I'm personally offended by the sheer volume of paisley vests and elbow length gloves in this room," Robbie whispered into Cordelia's ear as they walked into the auditorium.

She giggled. "There's an obscene amount of black velvet chokers and satin cummerbunds, too."

"My God, does *anyone* we go to school with have taste?"

"Just us, clearly," Cordelia replied playfully, tucking her arm through his.

"Yeah but only because you have *me* to style you," he shot back. "Remember that terribly dark period where you stopped letting me dress you? You even succumbed to that hideous hypercolour T-shirt craze," he said, referring to the T-shirts made of a fabric that magically changed colour in patches where heat was applied.

"Yeah, like, six years ago!" Cordelia squeaked. "And watch you don't fall off that fashion high-horse there, baby bro. Your past ain't exactly fashion-disaster-free."

Indigo coughed. "MC Hammer parachute pants. 1990," then coughed again as he slung an arm around his date.

Robbie elbowed him in the ribs. "Shut up. We all experimented in our youth, alright."

"Yeah, some more than others," Indigo quipped.

"Hang on, Rob," Cordelia suddenly said. "I just remembered that *you* had hypercolour *undies!*"

"Did not!" he snapped, the blush rising up his cheeks giving him away.

"Ha ha, yeah right, you did too!" Cordelia giggled, "You're paying me out about a hypercolour *T-shirt* when all along you had hypercolour *underpants*! I bet those things changed colours in all the wrong places!" She bent double trying to catch her breath, as Robbie blushed even more furiously. She laughed until she snorted.

"Aaaand there it is," Robbie said.

Indigo burst out laughing. That was her second snort for the night and it would never not be funny. "You two are both as bad as each other. It's an absolute disgrace."

They made their way towards their table just as the waiters started serving dinner. Their classmates stared at their little group of four as they passed, some because word had spread about what had happened at Sian's, others because they hadn't seen Indigo Wolfe in the flesh in years.

People whispered behind their hands as they passed:

"Did you hear what he said to Sian's *dad*?"... "So he's *gay* now?"... "I always thought he'd end up with Cordelia."... "But she's with *Drew*..."... "Wait, so he's with *Robbie*?"... "Why are all the hot ones gay?"... "Where's he *been* all this time?"... "Why does he have radishes pinned to his chest?"... "It's a vegetable corsage, idiot, it looks fucking *awesome*..."

They found their table and sat down, eyeing the four empty seats as alternate plates of chicken and steak were placed in front of them. Sian, Will, Peyton and Sandy were meant to be joining them but were yet to appear.

"What if Sian never speaks to us again?" Cordelia asked, glancing around in dismay. As the words left her mouth, they saw Sian pushing her way through the crowd towards them, her jet-black hair piled on top of her head in an elaborate up-do, a look of utter distress marring her porcelain features.

When she reached their table, she rushed to throw her arms around Robbie and Indigo, her expression frantic. "I'm just *mortified*! I cannot *believe* my father, like, said those dreadful things to you, I'll *never* speak to him again!" she said vehemently, her eyes flashing. "*Ever*! I'm totally going to ask him to *un*-adopt me and I'll finally go find my *real* parents. I mean, we all know it's not possible for my *real* dad to be the biggest arsehole in the world because that title's already gone to *Bruce*. If I ever get the chance, I swear I'll push him into oncoming traffic."

"Don't do that, babe," Robbie said. "He'd probably survive in a vegetative state and you'll be stuck pushing his wheelchair and changing his nappies the rest of your life."

She grabbed Indigo's hand, then Robbie's, looking from one to the other. "You know I like, totally do not agree with a *word* of what he said, don't you? You *know* how much I love you both. Please forgive me? I'll totally die if you hate me for this."

"Sian Marigold Roberts, you have *nothing* to apologise for," Robbie told her. "Of course we don't hate you. We've been mates for years, and you know I vehemently believe we cannot be held accountable for the sins of our fathers. Sure, your dad's a small-minded, arrogant dickhead with, I highly suspect, a micro penis and closeted homosexual tendencies, but is that your fault? No. Of course it's not."

She looked confused.

"It's all good, Shi," Indigo clarified, squeezing her hand warmly. He could feel how sick she felt about the whole thing; her stomach was in knots. "We're just sorry we ruined your party."

"You didn't ruin it," she insisted, forcing a smile. "In fact I think you've ensured it will go down in infamy."

"Come sit with us, Shi," Cordelia said warmly. "Where's Will?" Everyone knew that when it came to Will and Sian, one rarely went anywhere without the other. They'd even applied to all the same universities.

"Oh, he's like, over there with his footy mates somewhere," she replied, waving her hand in the direction of the veranda as she gathered up the long, velvet skirt of her red strapless dress so she could sit down next to Indigo. "I'm sure he'll come as soon as he smells the food." Will had never turned down a meal in his life.

Peyton came rushing over, acres of ice-blue taffeta flying in her wake, plonking herself down and eyeing the others with concern. "What's going on? What's happening? Have we all kissed and made up?" She'd tried to tame her wild red locks into a neat chignon, but had failed dismally. Wisps and curls stuck out at all angles, many hanging like corkscrews to brush her pale, freckled shoulders.

"There's been no more kissing," Robbie informed her. "But a lot of making up."

"Oh, thank *God*! I thought I'd be stuck refereeing twelve rounds in the ring." She grinned wickedly and leant forwards. "Did you really tell Mr Roberts he should try anal?" she asked Indigo, who burst out laughing, spraying the mouthful of water he'd just swigged back.

"Indigo Alexander Wolfe!" Robbie complained, wiping water off the sleeve of his tux. "I'll have you know I only date guys who swallow."

Peyton threw back her head and guffawed, slapping her knee.

"Wolfie told Mr Roberts he should test drive a bit of man-love ," Drew told Peyton, starting to laugh again. He clearly still found the term very amusing. "Man-love," he repeated lazily.

"Oh my *god*!" Peyton cried. "What did Mr Roberts do? Did he like, totally *die*?"

Robbie gave her a theatrical blow-by-blow, complete with actions and voices. Everyone laughed along, Sian more out of embarrassment than anything else. She shifted in her seat in discomfort. Indigo quickly changed the subject.

"So where's the after-party?" he asked, glancing around the table. Will had arrived and was wolfing down his steak and most of Sian's dry chicken. He even ate the questionable sauce, a white congealed mess rapidly forming a skin on top.

"Well, it was meant to be at Sandy's house," Peyton told him. "But his mum, like, totally found the massive bag of pills he'd stashed in his room this arvo and cancelled the *whole* thing!" After Sandy and Peyton had hooked up at Schoolies, they'd quickly become an item.

They glanced over to Sandy who was on the stage next to the DJ, his pale-yellow shirt untucked and unbuttoned to reveal his milk bottle torso, his mousey hair unruly, his eyes covered by yellow-lensed sunglasses, a glowstick in his hand, dancing frantically as Faithless chanted about their inability to sleep.

"I guess his mother didn't find *all* his pingers," Robbie commented dryly.

"Let's go dance with him!" Peyton urged, her eyes shining enthusiastically.

"I don't think I could keep up," Indigo replied lightly, glancing up at Sandy who was now doing the worm while his classmates dancing below cheered him on.

"Yeah and I've got this knee thing..." Drew murmured.

Everyone else at the table mumbled their excuses.

"Whatever," Peyton shrugged. "You're all a big bunch of party poopers." She kicked her shoes off and tore off to join her boyfriend on stage, gyrating her hips against his in time with the music, then falling in step beside him to perform the running man in perfect synchronicity. The DJ now had The Real McCoy singing *Another Night*.

Indigo leant over to Sian who was sitting, staring into space, as she tore a coaster into pieces. "You ok?" he asked softly.

Her head snapped up and when she met his eye, she pasted on a bright smile. "Yeah, totally."

But he could feel she wasn't.

"I'm sorry about what happened with your dad. Don't worry too much about it," he reassured her. "Everyone will forget about it pretty quickly."

She shrugged forlornly, her shoulders slumping. "He's... he's not a good person, Inds," she said in a small voice. "How am I supposed to deal with that? I mean, he's always been a decent *dad,* but as a person? He's, like, *so* narrow-minded, and he can be *such* an arsehole." She smiled wanly, then reached for her champagne glass, draining it in one hit. "I can't count how many times I've quietly thanked my lucky stars I'm not actually related to him by blood," she admitted, plopping the empty glass back on the table.

"Have you ever thought about looking for them? Your birth family?"

"Of course I have! Wouldn't you be curious where you came from if you were me?"

He nodded.

"I know my parents love me, but I just don't, like... *see* myself in them. I have nothing in common with my sisters either, and I wonder, I do, if there are people out there who *are* like me." Will was sitting on her other side, engrossed in conversation with Robbie and Cordelia, and she reached for his champagne glass, sculling that, too.

"It must be difficult," Indigo said, taking the empty glass from her hand and replacing it with his water. She took a tiny sip, then handed it back to him. He was momentarily distracted as he saw Sasha bilocate in. Indigo glanced at the clock on the wall. Right on schedule, Sasha was nothing if not punctual.

"You have no idea! I mean, I don't even know *why* they gave me up for adoption." Eyes glistening, she glanced away. "Like, why didn't they *want* me?"

"I'm sure it had everything to do with them and nothing to do with you," he said, giving her arm a gentle squeeze.

"I don't even know what I *am*, Indigo," she said, meeting his gaze. "Or what I want to do with my life. I've never found my passion. I have no idea what I'm good at, or what I want to be. I applied to UTS to study Business, and Sydney Uni to study Commerce because that's what Will was doing and we wanted to be together. But is that the best reason for making life decisions? How co-dependent do I wanna be? I love Will so much–"

Will turned at the sound of his name. "Yes, honey bunny?" The moment he saw how distressed she was, he gasped, gathering her into his arms. "What's wrong, pooks?"

"Nothing," she murmured. "*Everything!*" She looked like she was about to cry.

"Oh, baby-cakes, it's ok, it's ok," Will crooned, as he stood, her hand wrapped tightly in his, pulling her up. She wobbled on her feet. "Let's go outside and get some air." Indigo passed Will his water to take with him, and Will smiled in thanks as he ushered Sian towards the exit.

Indigo had spent his childhood wishing he was adopted, that his real parents would one day swoop in and save him. But listening to Sian now, he realised it was more complicated than that.

He'd been trying not to stare at Cordelia all night, but was failing miserably. He watched her now, engrossed in conversation with Robbie, her face bright for the first time in weeks, a lock of hair falling over one eye as she threw her head back in laughter. His gaze fell on Drew, sitting beside Cordelia, glancing sideways at her while fishing casually in his pockets for something. Indigo saw him pull out a baggie and subtly scoop out a small pill which he placed on his tongue, washing it down with a swig of beer. Drew glanced up right then and saw Indigo watching him. He had the decency to freeze and redden a little, but he held Indigo's eye defiantly. Indigo raised an eyebrow at him. Drew gave him a dirty look and pushed his chair back, shrugging his jacket off as he stalked off.

Sandy wasn't the only one up on stage now dancing wildly as the DJ spun his decks. The room was dark, the only light emanating from the strobes that pulsated over the dancefloor, making the bodies moving to the music look as though they were playing in slow motion, rising and falling as Haddaway questioned what love was.

Cordelia touched his arm. "Inds? Did you see where Drew went?"

He hesitated.

"Indigo? Do you know where he is? I'm a bit worried, he's not himself tonight."

"Outside."

She nodded in thanks, flashing him a small smile before standing up and wandering off in search of her missing date.

"Don't leave school grounds," he called after her. She raised a hand up over her shoulder. Indigo made eye contact with Sasha and jerked his chin towards Cordelia. Sasha nodded, then subtly slipped outside after her.

Indigo could feel someone trying to catch his eye and glanced up to see Robbie, now on the dancefloor with a group of friends, waving madly for him to join them. The last thing he felt like doing was dancing, but he needed to shake that off. He was Robbie's date, after all, and tonight was meant to be all about Robbie, not his sister or her boyfriend.

He pasted a large grin on his face and slipped through the sweaty, gyrating crowd to Robbie's side.

"Where's Cordelia?" Sandy asked, glancing around. "She didn't leave, did she?" His pupils were massive.

"Nope, she's outside with Drew."

"C'mon, Inds, show us your famous moves then!" Peyton cried. "I'm sure we can request Vanilla Ice if that's what it's gonna take."

Indigo threw his head back and laughed. "My moves are pretty rusty," he yelled over the music. "I can't remember the last time I had any use for them."

"What would Bernadette say? All those years of hip-hop lessons she made you take?" Robbie asked.

"You mean the ones I did in the hope of winning her love?" Indigo joked. Because he could laugh about it now.

"Come dance with us and you might just win *my* love," Robbie said, spinning on the spot. "And you know it's worth its weight."

Indigo chuckled. The DJ changed tracks and Robbie squealed in excitement as Young MC instructed them to bust it.

"Indigo, you big stud! Dance with me now or lose me forever!" Robbie yelled, holding out a hand to him. Indigo shrugged in defeat and took the proffered hand, allowing Robbie to drag him deep onto the packed floor. If you can't beat 'em and all that…

Almost an hour later, they relinquished their positions to Sandy who was still motoring on like a little Energiser bunny, and went outside for some fresh air, detouring past the bar.

"Where in the hell did Cora get to?" Robbie panted, taking a big sip of his Midori and lemonade.

"Dunno," Indigo replied. "I think she may have her hands full with Pres."

"Yeah, you don't have to be a genius to figure out those two are heading towards splitsville," Robbie said, then quickly clamped his mouth shut.

Indigo swore his heart skipped a beat. "Hey?" he managed.

Robbie gave him a withering look. "Oh *come on*, Inds, you're kidding me, right? I mean, you've gotta feel sorry for the guy. Drew's a top bloke and he's to die for, but he's got one insurmountable flaw: he's not you."

Indigo stared at him. Robbie had never gotten involved in the situation between he and Cordelia, preferring to play Switzerland. The alcohol had loosened his tongue.

"I told Cora I'd back off," Indigo replied cautiously. It was a shithouse situation. He and Drew had so much history and Indigo had so much affection for him still.

Robbie rolled his eyes so far back in his head he could probably see his own arse. "This is *me* you're talking to, Indigo. Like seriously, there's some invisible force between the two of you that us mere mortals will never comprehend. You were Cora's first love, and she's never fully gotten over you. Believe me, she's tried, but I think it's obvious she hasn't succeeded and that Drew's gonna end up as collateral damage. The poor guy's imploding before my eyes. He's not an idiot, you know, he's just flown through his first year of Medicine, for God's sake!"

"I still can't believe he's gonna be a doctor," Indigo said, smiling proudly. "Pres, who failed Year Eight science."

"Yeah, after you left, he completely changed. Stopped wagging, stopped rocking up to class stoned, and he started actually doing the work. It turns out he's a closet big brain."

"Well, I'll be," Indigo murmured. Indigo, like Drew, had been far from a model student, but school had always come easy to him, whilst Drew had barely scraped by. "So, you're saying I really was a bad influence, then?"

"On the contrary! Indigo Alexander Wolfe, *you* were a *fabulous* influence!" Robbie laughed. "You made life *fun*. I mean, I'm surprised we're all still *alive*, but we always had a shitload of fun." He grinned widely then drained the rest of his drink noisily through his straw. "Hey, Inds?"

"Yeah?"

"You seeing somebody?"

Indigo furrowed his brow. "No," he said slowly. "Why?"

"Oh nothing..." Robbie said, glancing away. "But you'd tell me if you were, right?"

"What's going on, Rob?"

"Cora saw you at the beach today all over some gold-bikini-wearing little tart."

"Gold-bikini-wearing little tart?" Indigo mumbled as it suddenly dawned on him. "Oh, you mean *Aurora*!" he said, sliding his hands into his pockets. "Yeah, we're totally just mates."

'*Incoming*,' he heard Sasha project into his head, and he looked up as Cordelia rounded the side of the building, tugging Drew by the hand.

'*You good?*' Sasha asked.

'*Yep, thanks, mate, you can head off.*'

"Yoo hoo! Cora!" Robbie called, waving at her.

"You did not just say yoo hoo," Indigo muttered.

Robbie shot him a withering stare before turning his attention to Drew. He crossed his arms and looked him up and down. "Geez, Drew Lincoln Prescott, what have you taken, and can I have some? You're not half off your chops, are you?"

Drew just grinned and stared at him intently. Cordelia threw her hands up in exasperation. "Let's just say he loves me, he loves you guys, he loves everybody, *including* Mr Landry, who he just hugged and thanked for being the best teacher *ever*."

"You hugged Mr *Landry*?" Robbie asked, screwing his nose up.

"Totally," Drew replied enthusiastically. "He was, like, the best maths teacher ever."

"Most anally retentive you mean?" Robbie said, widening his eyes at Cordelia and grimacing. "What did he say?"

"He said, 'Lucky for you, you don't go here anymore, Mr Prescott,'" Cordelia said, "'or else I'd have a lot of questions for you.' I think he was ok about it though, he's always had a soft spot for Drew since he came top of his three unit maths class." Drew was now rhythmically caressing the soft velvet of Robbie's sleeve. Cordelia grabbed his hand away. "That being said, Drew, I think I'm done with this for tonight." She glanced towards the auditorium where everyone was dancing. "It's my Year Twelve formal. I'm meant to be having fun with my friends."

Drew stared at her sullenly. He was rocking slightly on his feet. "Fine. Go be with your friends. I can take care of myself." He turned on his heel and started walking away. "Have a good night, all."

"Drew…" Cordelia called, taking a step to follow him.

Robbie grabbed her arm. "Let him go. He chose to write himself off. You're his girlfriend, not his babysitter."

She bit her lip, her eyes following Drew as he slowly melded into the shadows and vanished.

Indigo touched her arm lightly. "You go back in. I'll make sure he gets a cab."

Her shoulders slumped in relief; she smiled her thanks at him before allowing Robbie to lead her back towards the auditorium. Indigo watched until they were safe inside, then took off after Drew. He caught up with him wandering aimlessly down the driveway, trailing his palm through the bushes. His shirt was untucked and his sleeves were rolled to the elbow.

"Pres!" Drew turned slowly, blinking a few times as he tried to focus on Indigo. "Let's get you a cab, mate." Out on the street, there were a number of taxis waiting for the formal to let out. He stuck his hand out and hailed one, giving the cabbie Drew's address and depositing him on the back seat. He then headed back towards the auditorium.

As he stepped through the big double doors onto the chequerboard floor, he saw Cordelia hurrying in his direction, an angelic vision in white. Head down, silver clutch tucked under one arm, a tuxedo jacket he assumed was Drew's draped over the other, she strode for the exit, moving impressively fast for someone in such high stilettos.

She was *leaving*.

Eyes fixed to the floor, she hadn't seen him standing there. As she passed him by, he caught her hand, stopping her dead, swinging her to face him.

chapter twenty

suddenly

cordelia

His large hand wrapped around hers, her pulse quickening at his very touch. "You're not bailing?" he asked, head tilted to one side, his eyes searching hers.

As soon as she'd gotten back inside with the thumping music and the jittering strobe lights, Cordelia had realised she didn't want to be there. It was hectic and chaotic and still hot as hell, and the masses of guys dancing in tuxes meant the whole room stunk of wet wool and sweat.

Knowing she'd get hell from Robbie for leaving, she'd made the excuse she was heading to the bar, then slipped over to their table to collect her purse. She'd seen the tux jacket Drew had forgotten hanging there on the back of his chair and grabbed that, too.

Her eyes had travelled slowly around the room, coming to rest on her friends, all dancing, laughing, having the evening of their lives. And she'd never felt more alone. She was drained, a hollowness pressing on her chest. Suddenly the sadness felt overwhelming.

So she left, chin to chest, eyes trained on the ground, avoiding everyone, invisible like a phantom in the night. Hopefully no one would even notice she'd gone.

Cordelia was almost at the exit when a warm hand caught hers. Indigo. She knew it was him before she even looked up, the electricity

241

pounding through her veins as it always did when he was near. He tilted his head to one side, his chiselled face folding into a frown, as he asked if she was leaving.

"I'm tired, Inds," she whispered. "I'm just over it, you know? It's been a pretty average night... not exactly how I pictured my Year Twelve formal. I probably shouldn't have agreed to come in the first place." He was so close she could see the swirls of jade and gold in his irises. In that moment, she realised she'd never tire of staring into the depths of those eyes.

But they weren't hers to stare at.

She pulled her hand from his and crossed her arms.

"How *did* you picture it?" he asked.

With you, she wanted to say. But she didn't.

"I-I don't know," she said instead. "Having a date who's not totally baked might have been a start. Someone who might actually want to dance with me." She smiled wryly.

Indigo ran a hand through the back of his hair and glanced away. "I'm sorry it's not the night you imagined," he said, looking back at her. "But I wish you wouldn't leave."

"Will you dance with me?" The words had passed her lips before she'd even realised they were coming.

He bit the corner of his lip, regarding her intently. "You want to dance with me?"

Dancing with him sounded like heaven. Especially since the DJ had decided to bring the party down a notch or two and was spinning into a ballad. The room was dim, blanketed in a smoky haze. She'd danced with Indigo plenty of times before, but never to a song like this, a slow song that would require them to get all close.

One last dance. A dance to say goodbye to everything they could have been.

His eyes moved around the room before resting upon hers. "*Do you?*" he asked again, and he looked almost... vulnerable. "Want to dance with me?"

Oh hell, yes, she wanted to. So much she could barely breathe. But all she could manage was a nod. Then her pride rose up to take over. "One dance. Just so I can say I danced at my formal."

His expression shuttered slightly, his shoulders tense, but then he inclined his chin and held his hand out to her. She reached for him, her fingertips inches from his, when a sudden shyness gripped her. "You sure?"

"Abso-fucking-lutely." His mouth kicked up at the corners and, as the auditorium filled with Bon Jovi singing *This Ain't A Love Song*, he hitched one brow and murmured, "I'm game if you are." His hand was right there, extended expectantly toward her. "Don't leave me hangin' here."

Indigo had always had one of those smiles you couldn't help but smile back at and she was powerless to fight it. She closed the gap between them, her fingers grazing his tentatively, and then his hand filled hers, warm and electric. It crossed her mind how right it felt, holding hands with him, as he led her to the edge of the dancefloor. He took her clutch and Drew's jacket and chucked them onto the nearest table, then stepped forward, folding her into his arms.

The minute her cheek touched his chest, her eyes fluttered closed. She inhaled deeply, her breath a shaky staccato. She was completely engulfed by him, by his sandalwoody-sea-on-summer-breeze scent, by the steady metronome of his heart. And she knew in that moment that this was where she belonged. There was only Indigo, and she never wanted to let him go.

Being in his arms was everything, his thumb tenderly tracing the ridge of her bare shoulder blade, the warmth of his breath in her ear. She could feel every sculpted muscle in his torso straining against the fabric of his shirt as he gently swayed with her, and she allowed herself to melt into him, to lose herself in all that he was.

Time seemed to disappear altogether, so she didn't know how long they'd been locked together like that, her in his embrace, he in hers, when she suddenly felt him tense up. And then his arms were sliding from her body and he was stepping away from her.

Her eyes sprung open and she saw what had made Indigo release her. Drew was standing in the doorway, his face crushed with disbelief and hurt, confusion flaring in his bleary eyes.

"Forgot my jacket," he mumbled.

Indigo opened his mouth to say something, but Drew just shook his head and turned and stumbled out the door.

"Shit," Indigo swore under his breath.

"It's ok," she said.

"No. It's not. I'll go talk to him." And before she could grab his arm and explain that it really was ok, that they hadn't done anything wrong, he was gone.

Cordelia caught up with Indigo on the sidewalk, having followed him by instinct and now hesitant to find herself standing there before him, lost for words, his gaze deep on hers.

"You shouldn't be out here on your own," he chastised, glancing around. Drew was nowhere to be seen.

"I'm not on my own. You're here."

"I'll walk you back in," he told her, glancing towards the gates emblazoned with the school's crest. While a lot of her classmates were congregated outside, it seemed the majority were still inside, probably slow-dancing on the darkened floor they'd just vacated.

"I've just spoken to the limo driver. He'll be right here waiting for you at eleven, ok?"

"What, you're leaving?" Her heart sank.

"I'll be back by eleven to take you home, but right now I'm gonna go after Pres. He's totally wasted and he's upset…" He peered out onto the darkened street. "Make sure you and Rob stick together, ok?"

"It's fine, Indigo," she said impatiently. "Stop being so overprotective."

"Seriously, Cora? You of all people know it's justified." He slid his hands into his pockets. "Of course I'd rather stay, I'm doing this so you can go back inside and enjoy your night with your friends."

"Oh, don't put yourself out on account of me," she said coolly. "You clearly have more important things to worry about these days." She hated herself for the petty shit she could hear spewing forth from her lips, but she couldn't rein it in. She was just filled with so *much*. So much grief and hurt and guilt and jealousy, so much that seemed to have nowhere to go but out of her mouth in the form of childish passive-aggressiveness.

He took her gently by the elbow and lead her into the shadows cast by the mottled sandstone wall that ringed the campus. "Rob told me what you saw this arvo. Listen, Cordelia… it's not what you think." He stared at the ground then, and shook his head. "But even if it was, why does it matter?" His whole body seemed to sag.

"I can't do this anymore. This isn't who I am," he told her, his voice lowering an octave. "I wanted this so bad for us, Cordelia… But I'm not the guy who goes after someone else's girl. I don't want other people to get hurt here. I *love* you, Cora. So much. Always have, always will. But Drew and I, we've been mates for years and I promised I'd back off, for his sake and yours." He smiled dejectedly.

She stared at him, swallowing the dryness in her mouth.

"You've made your choice, Cordelia, and I'm trying to respect that. But you *have* to let me go. I'm running for my life here. Call it self-preservation. I'm strong, I can probably find a way to get over you, to live without you, but I can't do that when you keep giving me mixed signals." He closed his eyes for a beat or two and when he opened them, he just looked defeated. "So let me go. If Drew's your choice, then please… *Just let me go.*"

He turned on his heel.

"Indigo!' she cried. "Don't you walk away from me! Come back, *please.*"

He swung back around and gave a kind of half-laugh, eyes flashing. "Don't you *ever* say I just walked away. You know how I feel about you. But it shouldn't be this *hard*, Cordelia! If you loved me, if you wanted to be with me, you'd know. You'd know the way *I've* always known. I thought this, this *thing* between us, that it was undeniable. But I was wrong." He stared down at her. "Clearly." He turned to walk off again.

"Drew and I broke up."

Indigo halted, his back still to her. "What?" He swung to face her. "When?"

"Last night. He asked me not to tell anyone until after the formal. But it's over, Inds. We're done."

"Fucking hell," he muttered, pinching the bridge of his nose. "Are you ok?" His expression darkened. "He's clearly not."

She shrugged helplessly, staring at the ground. What a mess. "It wasn't fair to him, continuing to be with him when all I can think about is… is you." Lips trembling, she raised her eyes slowly to meet his, scared of what she'd find there. He just looked stunned. So she kept talking, unable to keep it in a moment longer.

"For weeks now, I've tried to make sense of all this, and when I added everything up logically, I always arrived back at Drew. But the thing is," she swallowed hard, "it's *not* logical, is it? When it comes to love, there's absolutely no sense to it. Because… because you're the one I want, Inds," she blurted. "It's you that I love. And no amount of logic or reasoning makes an ounce of difference to that. Because how I feel for you… it transcends it all. It transcends everything."

He stepped tentatively towards her, and her exhale caught with a shudder as he reached out, his fingers brushing hers.

"You… you *love* me?" he whispered. His hazel-flecked gaze enveloped her and time seemed to stand still as she stared into his eyes. She could live and die inside those eyes.

She tilted her head and stared up at him, a sad smile playing upon her lips. "I do. I'm in love with you, Inds. So badly. But this time, I guess it's my timing that's atrocious."

"If you mean what you saw–"

"It's alright," she reassured him wistfully, crossing her arms. "I know you, Indigo. I know the story of your life by heart. I'm under no illusion about your history, I'm fully aware it hasn't exactly been devoid of girls… of women. I know you're seeing someone now, and it's ok… it just… it just *hurts* though, you know?" Indigo being with someone else felt like a raw, seeping wound inside of her, a pain so deep and physical she could barely stand it. Is this how he'd felt, coming home to find her with Drew?

"Cora–"

"But maybe you're right," she reasoned. "Maybe things *shouldn't* be this hard. I mean, first you tell me you love me, then you shut me out for two-and-a-half years – and it took me years to get over that Indigo, *years* – then you come back home, you tell me I'm the only one… and then swiftly move onto someone else."

"Is that really what you think of me?" he breathed, his eyes so wounded.

"I'm a one-guy-kinda-gal, Inds, I can't give away little pieces of myself here and there. For me, it's all or nothing. I can't be yet another notch on your bedpost, Indigo. I can't be just another word on your page."

He stared at her, his eyes widening. "Another word on my page? Are you fucking kidding me? I've been head over heels for you since we were kids, Cora. From the beginning, it's been you. I'm yours. I've *always* been yours." His voice was so raw, so laced with emotion, his eyes bright with unshed tears. "You're not another word on my page, Cordelia, how could you even think that? You, you're everything. You're the whole fucking library."

All the air left her lungs. Her hands trembled, her gaze fixed on his, her heart exploding. "But-but that girl today? At the beach?"

"That was Aurora. I don't know what you think you saw, but we were just mucking around. She's a mate, nothing more. A disapproving big sister, if nothing else." He shrugged. "You're all I think about, Cora. I know what makes me happy, I know what I want in life. And that's you. *Only* you." His voice cracked.

His eyes were so etched with longing and as they travelled over her, it was like she'd forgotten how to breathe. Afterwards, when she looked back at that moment, it all happened so fast she couldn't recall if they'd thought before they'd merged. All she remembered was she hadn't been able to hold back a moment longer.

Without a thought in her head she grabbed him by the shirtfront, and his arms were suddenly around her as his lips collided with hers in a kiss that told her everything she needed to know.

That kiss.

The kiss.

His kiss.

Her heart pounded as his kiss filled up all the dark spaces inside of her 'til she was brimming with warmth and light and him, him, *him*.

His tongue was sliding skilfully over hers, and she couldn't touch enough of him at once, her fingers tangling softly in his hair, skimming the curve of his neck, trailing his broad shoulders. She pulled the hem of his shirt from his pants so she could slip her hands beneath the fabric, running them up and down the length of his muscular back, his skin pebbling in her wake. "It was never difficult," she whispered in between frantic kisses, "knowing how I felt about you. It was always the most obvious thing in the world, to you, to me, to everyone. It was always you, Inds, always."

He pulled back, his eyes serious as he stared into hers. "We're written in the stars, Cordelia," he said huskily. "You were born to be mine." And in that moment, it was just him and her. The rest of the world had faded away to nothing. He nuzzled her nose with his and kissed her again. And as he did, he took her hand gently in his and placed it over his heart, a heart he whispered was hers and only hers and would be forever.

He kissed her forehead, long and lingering, then drew back to smile at her. She returned it, reaching to tuck a wayward strand of hair behind his ear, to tenderly trace the powerful line of his jaw, their chests rising and falling erratically in unison. Her eyes locked on his, begging him to kiss her again, for her mouth felt utterly bare when it wasn't covered with his.

His smile faded then, his lip curling, the look in his eye dangerously primal as he edged her deeper into the shadows thrown by the wall, pushing her up against the sandstone, caging her body with his. His lips were millimetres from hers, his breath heavy as he slowly threaded his fingers through hers, manoeuvring her hands up over her head, pinning them against the wall, his body melding into hers so there was barely any trace that one was once two. Only then did he finally lower his mouth to hers again.

"So many years, Cora," he murmured between long, slow, dizzying, kisses. "So many trips around the sun all by my lonesome, thinking only of you. All those too-hot-to-sleep summers, all those no-one-to-warm-me winters, it's been you, only you." His lips lingered on her cheeks, her throat, the dip of her shoulder, flames smouldering where they touched, the weight of his body so deliciously heavy against hers.

He released her hands, his palms sliding down her arms to cup her face. "Beautiful girl, I've dreamed of this, of you," he murmured, gazing at her through lowered lashes. "Thought of nothing but this, but you..." His voice caught. "I've never wanted anything more in all my life, than I want you." He was pressed so tight against her she could feel exactly how much.

"Oh God, Inds," she breathed. "I want you, too. So much." She clung to his neck, kissed him with all the exquisite fire burning in her belly. His hand skated down the curve of her body to the thigh-high split in her slinky dress, lingering to stroke the skin there, his lips never leaving hers. In one smooth movement he hooked her legs round his waist and picked her up, her back braced against the warm sandstone. She gasped as she sank her hips into his, his tongue strong yet gentle yet relentless against hers. Threading her fingers tightly through his hair, she moved steadily against him, her mouth absorbing the moan that slipped from his throat.

There was nothing but *them*, the universe stopped and ended right here with them and only them. Yet somewhere outside the bubble of *them*, she was vaguely aware of an exaggerated clearing of the throat, then someone said, "Uh, sorry to interrupt, brah…"

She and Indigo jerked, breaking apart. A dark-haired guy was standing there beside them, eyes ducked, cheeks flaming. He had a kind face, and while his presence was unwelcome, it was also calming.

"Seriously, Sash?" Indigo chastised with a groan. "Perv much?" His grip on Cordelia slackened, and she slid slowly through his palms 'til her feet touched the ground.

"You know this person?" Cordelia whispered, eyes wide with mortification as she stared at the guy who'd just obliterated the very private moment she'd waited five years for.

"Yeah, unfortunately I do," Indigo grumbled, shooting the guy a dirty look. "Cora, this is Sasha. Sash, this is Cordelia."

"So nice to finally meet you eh, Cordelia," Sasha said with a distracted smile. He turned to Indigo. "I'm really sorry, Indi, but that little mission you just sent me on? There's been a… development. Can I have a word?"

Indigo straightened his shirt, raking his hands through his hair. "Give me a minute, ok?" he murmured to Cordelia. He smoothed down her dress then pressed his forehead to hers, before allowing Sasha to drag him away. Harried whispering ensued, then Indigo returned looking frazzled.

"I hate to do this, beautiful, but I gotta go."

"You're *leaving? Now?*" She pouted at up him. Was he seriously gonna pash and dash on her? "Everything ok?"

"Not really, but it's nothing I can't handle," he said elusively, tilting her face to his. He lowered his mouth to hers in a kiss she felt he'd intended to be quick, but had immediately began to heat. "You fucking undo me, Cora," he growled against her lips.

The sound of Sasha pointedly clearing his throat again had them reluctantly pulling apart. "Kind of in a hurry here, Indi," he said, arms crossed, tapping his foot.

"Ok, ok, I'm coming, man," Indigo said over his shoulder. He stepped away but she pulled him back to her, encircling his waist and laying her head against his chest. "I *really* gotta go," he said.

"I guess we should say goodnight then," she said hollowly. That was the last thing in the world she wanted right now. She wanted more of him, all of him, every single bit. She could hear the steady thrum of his heartbeat. "I wish you could stay," she whispered. He was so warm and vibrant, his scent dizzying. She never wanted to say goodnight to him ever again.

"Fucking *hell*, I wish I could stay." He glanced at Sasha again. "But I really can't. It's your Year Twelve formal, go have fun with Rob and the girls. But *please*, Cora, don't forget: the driver will meet you out here at eleven sharp. If I'm not here, get in that limo and go. Make sure you and Robbie leave together."

"I *know*," she said, widening her eyes at him. He'd only told her a million times.

He twined his fingers through hers and pulled her towards the school, where he brushed his lips quickly to hers, then squeezed her hand and pushed her gently through the gates.

"Come *on*, Indi," she heard Sasha urge.

She could feel Indigo's eyes on her retreating figure, making sure she was safely inside. "I'll call you," he called softly after her, and she turned, raised a hand, and blew him a kiss.

indigo

"Seriously, dude?" Sasha chastised. "You send me on an urgent mission after your super messed up friend, and now we've just lost a good five minutes because you can't stop making out with your new girlfriend?"

"Cora's been through enough recently, I didn't want to worry her," Indigo said as he followed Sasha quickly out onto the street. "If I'd just taken off, she would have stressed out the rest of the night. So, where is he?"

"On the cliffs, up there," Sasha pointed in the direction of North Head. Indigo had telepathically asked Sasha to look in on Drew after his abrupt exit from the formal. He was incredibly grateful that Sasha's ability to bilocate meant that while one Sasha was here with Indigo, another Sasha was at this moment simultaneously with Drew. "He's not looking good, man, he's totally wasted, teetering way too close to the edge for comfort. Won't listen to a word of reason from me, eh," Sasha said as they briskly walked the two blocks to Indigo's house. They needed his car.

Indigo's stomach lurched. He and Drew had been mates for years, and Indigo had never known him to have depressive or suicidal tendencies, but Drew probably would have said the same thing about him a couple of years ago. One thing Indigo now understood, was that it was impossible to know what sort of demons someone was struggling with internally. And the sad fact was, Indigo didn't really know Drew anymore.

They approached the enormous wrought iron gates that guarded the entrance to the Van Allen Estate. Indigo reached for the pad concealed by the bushes where he punched in the code that would allow them entry. His worry now increasing at a rapid rate, he slipped through the gates and began to jog down the driveway, Sasha hot on his heels.

"Thanks Sash," he said as they reached his car, "I know where he is."

"You sure?"

"Yep. Just stay with him 'til I get there, ok? And listen, I know I've left Cora and Robbie in good hands," he said, thinking of the limo driver, "but I'll love you forever if you could pop back in on the formal after that?" He jumped in his Landcruiser and floored it, making his way to Darley Road, then up under the sandstone arch that guarded the entrance to the national park at North Head.

Indigo drove as far as he could down the dark road edged by bushland, abandoning his car near a familiar trail that cut deep into the scrub. North Head had played an integral role in Sydney's coastal defence against enemy ships during World War II, and the whole area was still dotted with old forts, buildings, and relics. He knew exactly where Drew would be.

The light of the full moon guiding him, Indigo ran down the dusty track, emerging onto the sheer cliffs that rimmed the northernmost entry to Sydney Harbour. His eyes widened when he saw Drew standing on the crumbling concrete ledge of the ruins of an old gun pit, staring down at the sea far below. His back was to Indigo. Sasha stood off to one side, watching him silently, close enough to grab him if need be. When Indigo appeared Sasha nodded, and disappeared.

"Hey, Pres," Indigo said in a low voice, approaching him slowly. His heart was beating a mile a minute and he took a couple of slow, deep breaths to calm it. Indigo knew how it felt to stand on the edge of a precipice, tottering between this life and the next. After his experience on that bridge that night over two years ago now, seeing someone standing too close to a ledge, like Drew was now, triggered a visceral raw panic streaming through his body.

He tuned into his friend, feeling into his emotions and mental state. Drew was rolling hard, out of his mind high. It was the 'out of his mind' bit that concerned Indigo. He glanced down and saw Drew's toes were teetering off the edge into fresh air. Indigo's eyes widened.

"Pres... Can you step back a bit for me, mate?"

Drew turned absently, pinning Indigo with a penetrative stare. The blue of his irises were all-consumed by pupil. Indigo could hear the crashing of the waves below, the rustle of an unseen animal in the underbrush. "Go away," Drew eventually said, jaw working.

"Yeah, nah, I'm not gonna do that."

"This used to be our place, Wolfie."

"I know, man." Indigo reached slowly for Drew's arm, relief coursing through him as his hand closed firmly around Drew's bicep. Drew allowed him to guide him back onto solid cement. This spot had played a supporting role in the evolution of the phenomenon that had been Indigo and Drew. As kids, the two of them had played pretend wargames here, and as teens, they'd come to drink and smoke weed. "In fact..." Indigo said, pulling Drew with him as he bent to dislodge a large stone wedged under the corner of the pit. He rummaged gingerly behind it, emerging with a beat-up bong made from an old plastic Coke bottle and a piece of garden hose. He held it up triumphantly.

Drew burst into hysterical laughter, doubling over and clutching his knees. As quickly as his laughter started, it stopped and he stood up, regarding Indigo intently, his eyes wide, flickering. "Everything's changed, Wolfie. And it will never be the same." He sat down heavily on the ledge.

Indigo put the bong back where he found it, replaced the stone, then sat down beside Drew. He dusted his hands off on his tux pants and turned to his old mate.

"You abandoned her, man," Drew said, running his tongue over his teeth. "She was fucking devastated when you left."

"I know," Indigo said, guilt plunging through his guts.

"You *don't* know," Drew insisted, leg jittering up and down. "You weren't here. It was fucking brutal. She didn't go out, she didn't smile, she just went through the motions. I didn't think it could get any worse, but then she came back from that trip to New York, and she was completely messed up. She stopped eating, I don't think she slept at all, she was just a nervous wreck."

Indigo hung his head. His chest ached to hear what he'd put Cordelia through. But now, he thought determinedly, now he could spend the rest of his life making it up to her.

"You just left! You left her. But you know what? You left... me. You left me, too!" Drew's eyes bored into his. "You were my best mate, Wolfie. We did everything together. You were the one who propped me up after my family fell apart. You were always just *there*. And then, all of a sudden, you weren't. Did you ever stop to wonder how that made me feel?"

Indigo felt like a piece of shit. Of course he'd missed Drew, too, but he'd never stopped to consider the impact his absence had had on him.

"You see, *I* got how she was feeling," Drew continued. "Don't forget she was my friend, too. We'd spent a lot of time together over the years. And you know, after you left, we just... clicked. We had fun together. She made me laugh. I like to think I made her happy. How could I help but fall in love with her?" Drew laughed morosely then, throwing his head back to stare up at the moon above them. "And then you came home. And you just being here.... How could you *not* get in the way?"

"I'm sorry, mate."

"You sit there and judge me. You judge me for drinking, for smoking weed with the boys. I saw your face when I took that E-"

"Look, Pres-"

"Why do you think I needed to get loose tonight?"

Indigo looked at him. Of course he knew why, and it made him feel like crap.

"Because of *you*, Wolfie," Drew said softly, closing his eyes, rocking gently back and forth where he sat. "Because now, now I have to sit there and see the way your eyes never leave her. I have to sit there and see how you can anticipate her needs more clearly than I ever could. And that's not even the worst part. The worst part is that although I know that she truly cares about me," he choked, "I've seen the way Cordelia looks at you when she thinks no one's watching."

Indigo didn't know what to say.

"Cee's a good person, a beautiful person, and she felt she had to be loyal to me because *I* was the one who was here, *I* was the one who supported her, who never left her, never hurt her..." Drew said, grinding his teeth. "I did almost everything right. Unlike you, who left, who hurt her, who broke her heart. And, yet, *still* she loves you more."

Indigo put his hand on Drew's arm. "Listen, Pres-"

"*Fuck* you, Wolfie!" he snapped, shrugging Indigo off. "Seeing her there, dancing in your arms tonight, I wanted to fucking smash your face in, I wanted... " He trailed off, his mouth twisting into a grimace. He shook himself off. "And obviously it's pretty shit timing, with Josh and everything..." He frowned sadly. Joshua had meant a lot to him, too. "And how do I know I can trust you? Not to leave? Not to break her again?"

"I won't ever leave again," Indigo vowed.

"Whatever. It's not my problem anymore. Me and Cordelia, we're done."

"I'm sorry, mate," Indigo said, because he *was* sorry that Drew had been collateral damage in all this, that he was hurting so badly.

Drew scoffed. "Sure you are." He stared fixedly at Indigo, chewing on the insides of his cheeks, and something in his eyes suddenly changed and he grinned, slow and wide. "But you know what? Despite everything, even when I'm so pissed at you I want to punch your lights out, I love you, man, I really do. I missed the shit out of you, Wolfie."

He threw his arm around Indigo and hugged him crushingly tight. "I love you so much and I missed you and I love you… and that love, mate, it's alllll that matters, you know?" He was so fucking high.

"Yeah, I missed you too, Pres." Indigo chuckled. He had, and he hoped one day they could be mates again. But right now he wanted Drew away from here, safe, where he could keep an eye on him. "Let's get outta here, ok?" He stood and offered his hand to Drew, pulling him to his feet. "You know I can't take you home like this, right? You're staying at mine tonight. The bed in the pool house is made up, so you can sleep there."

Drew didn't object, he simply allowed Indigo to sling his arm around him and lead him silently back through the bush to his car.

robbie

Robbie had been dancing for about half an hour when the first wave of nausea overtook him. The hazy tendrils coiling from the DJ's smoke machine were furling their way down his throat, choking him so he couldn't catch his breath. His stomach heaved again and he made a run for it, lurching through the crowd into the fresh night air, emptying the contents of his stomach into the bushes below the veranda.

"*THAT* is revolting! You are the most disgusting human in the world, Robbie Carlisle."

He turned his head to see Miss-Goody-Two-Shoes-head-prefect, Delaney Jones, standing there with her frumpy friends, their snooty little noses wrinkled as they backed carefully away from him.

"The most disgusting human *in the world*, you say? Oh my God, I don't know what to say… I don't even have a speech prepared or anything!" He wiped clumsily at his mouth with the back of his hand. "What time is it anyway? My limo awaits!"

Robbie retched again, causing Delaney and her friends to squeal, hitch their dresses up and run. "Oh, because you're all so bloody perfect…" he slurred, trying his hardest to prise his eyes wider than slits. He'd had way too much to drink, but it was the cigarette that had done him in. It was always the cigarettes that pushed him over the edge, yet when he was drunk he craved them. When Sandy had slipped a ciggy into his mouth, he'd accepted it enthusiastically.

He stumbled down the sandstone steps onto the grass. The stars in the sky above him were swirling and he couldn't quite find his balance, shoulder-charging the wall several times as he made his way up the driveway and through the school gates.

He got as far as the street before his knees gave way. He sank onto the curb and dropped his head into his hands in an attempt to stop the spinning. Damn that Sandy! Robbie was beginning to suspect that ciggie had been laced with a little something extra.

He groaned loudly, clutching his stomach which felt like it had a thousand knives twisting inside of it. He barely registered the sound of rhythmic footsteps growing louder until a concerned voice suddenly asked if he was ok.

He tried to raise his head, to look up, but he could only see a pair of strong, tanned legs clad in shorts and pale blue Nike running shoes. The owner of the voice crouched in front of him and tried to lift Robbie's chin.

"You don't look so good. Can I call someone for you?" the voice was asking.

"Yeah, if you could call my date, that'd be great," Robbie slurred, not even caring that he was sitting in the gutter like a bum. "I already got stood up once tonight by Gino, who told me he'd come to the formal with me, but then decided that not only is he a player, but he's only gay between the sheets and not on the streets... So I got a new date, but he left to go find my sister's boyfriend, and I don't remember whether he's coming back for me or how I'm meant to find our limo with the scary driver who wants to break my fingers..." He was trying to focus on the face swimming before his, which in his expert opinion was super-hot, in a blurry kind of way.

"Heyyyyy... congratulations on the face," he said, reaching a hand out to clumsily squeeze a pair of cheekbones that put Johnny Depp's to shame. He paused then and grimaced as a wave of nausea swelled to overtake him. His cheeks puffed as he dry-retched. "Excuse me, please." Robbie held up one finger as he turned and vomited in the gutter. "Ugh, that didn't even taste good on the way in." He hurled again.

When he was done, he spat a wayward chunk out of his mouth before continuing, barely able to open his eyes. "What's your name?"

"I'm–"

"And I mean your *real* name. Not some made-up pseudonym you give out willy-nilly, depending on your mood and how many numbers you have on your booty call rotation."

The stranger chuckled. "My real name's Hisashi."

"Robbie," he said, pointing a thumb at his chest. "Right, so, Hisashi, if you could call Indigo Alexander Wolfe," he said, punctuating each word with a clumsy shake of his finger, "and tell him he needs to come and pick me up, that'd be really... really... great... thanks." His head lolled and he lost all sense of balance as road flipped to sky. A hand caught his head right before it hit the pavement. The last thing he remembered was being lifted by strong arms before the soothing darkness took him.

cordelia

"Woooooo!"

The opening strains of Frankie Valli and the Four Seasons singing about a particularly special night in December of 1963 was guaranteed to be met with a collective roar of delight, followed by a stampede of people streaming towards the dancefloor. The song had become an iconic anthem for the class of '95 and Cordelia knew it would be the final one of the night.

As the song came to a close and the auditorium lights came up, she glanced around for Robbie, whom she realised she hadn't seen for some time. Cordelia had been accosted by Peyton and Sian and forced onto the dancefloor the minute she'd walked back into the auditorium after her encounter with Indigo, and had been ensconced there ever since.

Brow furrowed, she distractedly hugged the girls goodbye and went to collect her clutch, all the while looking for Robbie in the now-thinning crowd. He definitely wasn't inside. Spying Drew's jacket, she picked it up, hooking it over her forearm, then headed outside, craning her neck for any sign of her brother. "Have you seen Rob?" she asked a group of girls milling around by the fountain.

"I haven't seen your feral brother since he hurled his guts out in those bushes," said Delaney, the head prefect, her eyes flashing with judgement. "And that was about an hour ago."

"Did you see where he went after that?"

"I think he left. He disappeared down the drive muttering something about a limo. He was practically paralytic, you know."

"Shit!" Cordelia hurried down the driveway as fast as she could in her stilettos. She burst out through the school gates onto the street, looking up and down the hill. There were groups of students climbing into cars and limos, but she couldn't see Robbie amongst them.

It was eleven o'clock and there was no sign of their limo either. She quickly concluded that Robbie had taken it and gone home, leaving her there alone. She knew all sense of reason went out of his head when he was hammered. Was the driver coming back for her?

Seething, she went to the payphone outside the school and picked up the receiver. It was dead. She hung it up, and tried again. Still no dial tone. She slammed it down, then headed back inside to find her friends.

As she traipsed back through the gates, she spotted Peyton and Sandy hurrying towards her, his skinny arm wrapped around her waist as he dragged her along. He seemed on edge, his gaze searching. "What's the big rush?" Peyton was saying. Sandy's face broke into a grin as his eyes settled on Cordelia, his shoulders dropping. "Hey, babe! Did you find Rob?" Peyton asked.

"Nope," Cordelia said crossly. "He left without me."

"That doesn't sound like him."

"Yeah, well, when Rob's smashed, he's a different person. Are Sian and Will still inside?" Sian lived closer to her than Peyton and could drop her on the way.

"Nup," Sandy said. "They left already."

Peyton glanced at him in surprise. "I didn't see them leave?"

He raised an eyebrow at her. "That's because you were too busy kissing me." He smooshed his mouth to hers and she giggled.

"Can I grab a lift with you guys?" Cordelia asked.

Peyton and Sandy exchanged glances. "Uh, we're not going home, sorry. Sandy booked us a hotel room in the city."

"My mum's majorly pissed about the pills she found," Sandy explained. "And I got the guy I bought them off looking for me, too. I can't go home tonight." He scowled.

"Oh," Cordelia said, glancing around, biting her lip. "That's cool. I'll be fine."

"We're not just gonna leave you, Cee," Peyton said.

"We'll help you find a cab before we go," Sandy told her.

"Oh, thank God," Cordelia said, smiling in relief.

The three of them wandered out onto the street, looking around. All the taxis that had been lined up earlier had gone. But as luck would have it, the moment they stepped off the curb, a taxi pulled out from its parking space down the road and flicked its lights on. Sandy raised his hand to flag it down, smiling when its indicator went on.

"That was easy." Peyton grinned. "It was obviously meant to be."

Sandy opened the back door for her, then leant over and spoke to the driver. The driver continued to stare straight ahead, but nodded when Sandy told him he'd made a note of his ID number and to take care of her. She hugged Peyton and kissed Sandy on the cheek, then climbed in, looking over her shoulder for Robbie one last time as she gave the driver her address. She waved to Peyton and Sandy, who were now looking for a taxi of their own, then closed her eyes and rested her head back on the seat, suddenly exhausted. She was glad the after-party had been cancelled. Her feet were killing her and she just wanted to go home and go to bed so it would be morning already and she could see Indigo.

Indigo. She smiled to herself as she raised her fingers to her lips, reliving the feeling of his mouth on hers, his strong hands on her body. Her stomach flip-flopped and a tingle of warmth spread through her. Tomorrow, she'd be able to see him again. To kiss him again, to hold him close and lose herself in those pretty eyes of his.

Her reverie was shattered when she caught the faint whiff of a familiar scent, a scent that caused the hairs on her arms to stand on end. Her eyes snapped open and she glanced out the window. Her heart rate sped up when she saw where they were.

"Excuse me!" she called to the taxi driver. "I need to go to Harbord, you're going the wrong way."

The driver didn't respond. She wondered if maybe his English wasn't great, if he'd misunderstood her.

"Excuse me!" she said again. Fear gripped her belly. "Can you hear me? We need to turn around." She tapped the driver on the shoulder, but he ignored her. She stared in shock at the back of his enormous body. His face was obscured by the black hooded sweatshirt he wore. A feeling of dread washed over her.

"Pull over!" she cried, kicking the back of his seat and yanking at the door handle, which wouldn't budge. "Stop the car! My friend has your ID number, he'll report you!"

Relief coursed through her veins as he began to slow and pull onto the shoulder of the road. It was short-lived. The moment the car stopped, he turned, and she recoiled as the pungent stench of his breath hit her with full force.

"Not my ID, not my cab," he hissed with a cruel grin.

She opened her mouth to scream at the sight of his tattooed face and his forked tongue, but a giant fist came screaming towards her, chunky silver rings glinting in the moonlight. He punched her once in the temple, then passed his hand in front of her face, muttering under his breath. And then, nothingness.

chapter twenty-one

dumb things

robbie

Robbie could smell vomit.

Vomit and cigarettes and stale champagne and Midori.

He wrinkled his nose and rolled onto his side, groaning as he slowly came to. He tried to wet his lips with the tip of his tongue, but his mouth was gummed together, dry as sandpaper.

Water. He needed water.

He forced open his lids, and it felt like glass was smashing in his head. He was lying on a couch in a darkened room. The drapes were open and the light of the full moon streamed in, illuminating all it touched with its silvery glow.

He knew this room.

With great effort, he sat up, groaning. Someone had left a bottle of water on the coffee table in front of him. He grabbed it and drank thirstily. He glanced up at the enormous framed photograph of Bernadette Van Allen hanging over the fireplace in front of him. She was wearing a gold, one-shouldered swimsuit, her ruby lips pouting, her blonde mane teased and curled to defy gravity. It was the poster from one of her most famous movies, *The Reef*, the movie that had made her an international sensation and rocketed her to stardom in the seventies. It was the poster that had hung above the fireplace in Indigo's lounge room forever.

261

How the hell had he gotten to Indigo's?

He stood gingerly and looked around. He could hear music. It was Metallica singing *Nothing Else Matters*, and he made his way towards it. Bernadette Van Allen's palatial home had always felt a bit to Robbie like a gallery or a museum. Everything was exquisite and perfect and opulent, but you were scared to touch anything. The house was decorated in shades of white, ivory, and cream. From the high, ornate ceilings to the pearly, marble floors in the foyer, to the grand, sweeping, alabaster staircase, to the thick, creamy, embossed wallpaper, to the vases of hydrangeas and snowberries and roses in shades of vanilla that Bernadette insisted fill the house, even in her absence. That said, Robbie always felt as though Edita wove some kind of magic over the cold mausoleum, because in spite of all its stiff grandeur, it always felt safe inside.

As he walked through the house, Robbie noticed more and more signs that Indigo had come home and started claiming the house as his own – neat stacks of books and surfing magazines here and there, CDs piled beside the stereo, and a lot of the large professional photos and paintings of Bernadette that had adorned the walls had been removed.

There were signs of life in the kitchen: the juicer left out, a large bowl overflowing with fruit on the marble countertop, a stack of unopened mail in the corner beside two surfboards which leant against the large bi-fold doors. The faint aroma of white sage hung in the air.

Robbie quickly figured out the strains of soft music were coming from the pool area and as he got closer he heard the murmur of voices.

"Hello?" he called out as he approached.

"Oh hey! You're awake." The voice was male with an American accent that had a relaxed oceanic intonation to it. "Come join us."

Robbie walked tentatively across the lush, green lawn and into the sandstone-paved pool area where four people sat, casually sprawled on deck chairs and chaise longues, drinks in hand. The only one he knew was Indigo, who flashed him a sympathetic grin. Indigo was still wearing his tux pants, his shirt unbuttoned to the waist to reveal his smooth, tanned chest.

"Uh… How am I here?" Robbie asked, flushing with embarrassment. As the words left his mouth, his gaze fell on the utterly gorgeous creature sitting beside Indigo, his striking features lit by a warm grin. His glossy jet-black hair was parted casually on the side and hung past his shoulders. He was shirtless, his hot-as-hell body clad only in jogging shorts. And runners. Very familiar, pale-blue, Nike runners.

"You!" Robbie gasped, staring at the man, his face burning hotter as he frantically tried to recall the full horrors of what he'd said and done in front of him earlier. "H…Hisashi, right?"

Indigo chuckled. "Gosh, we *are* being formal, aren't we? I don't think I've ever heard anyone call you by your proper name, Sash." He grinned and turned to Robbie. "Robert Carlisle, aka Robbie, this is Hisashi Banyen, aka Sasha." Sasha's light brown eyes sparkled warmly. "He just happened to come across you sprawled in the gutter on his run tonight."

"Hey, Robbie," Sasha replied with an easy nod, his gaze bright and direct. This was a man comfortable and confident in his body. *As he should be*, Robbie thought, unable to take his eyes off him. Sasha had a tattoo on his inner forearm, eight asymmetrical shapes that looked like a map of some kind. "How are you feeling, eh?"

"I'm ok," Robbie mumbled. He felt himself flushing to the tips of his ears. He was suddenly very aware that he was a complete mess and he stank of puke. Mortified, he glanced from Indigo to his friends. It was like a bloody supermodel convention round here, and he realised in dismay that he was the only non-hot person in the vicinity. He ran his hand through his hair, trying to smooth it down.

"Hey, I'm Nash." Robbie turned to see a delectable redhead bouncing up out of his chaise longue. He had a jawline that could cut glass, and wore boardshorts and a tank top, his skin pale as moonlight.

"Oh, please *do* pardon my manners," Indigo said, with a roll of his eyes. "Nathaniel Willoughby the Third, meet Robert Carlisle the… First." Indigo barely flinched at the playful jab Nathaniel – Nash – gave his ribs as he strode towards Robbie, his dark eyes glinting with mischief.

"Cheers, Indi." Nash grinned an infectious grin. "Pleasure to finally meet you, Robbie," he said, holding out his hand. Robbie shook it. Nash's sexy British accent reminded Robbie of James Bond; it somehow seemed incongruent with the elaborate skull tattooed onto his large bicep with its weird empty iridescent-blue eye sockets and its creepy bat-like wings.

"And this is Rory," Indigo said, indicating the petite girl lounging barefoot on a chaise longue, her slim legs crossed at the ankle.

"Aurora." She corrected Indigo, her peevish tone suggesting she corrected him a lot. She nodded at Robbie. "Charmed," she said, with a smile that didn't quite reach her eyes.

Robbie couldn't help but gape at her. *This* was the girl Cordelia had seen Indigo with that afternoon. She was stunning, her long, ebony hair caught up on one side with a clasp adorned dramatically with a peacock feather, her eyes highlighted with shimmery, cobalt shadow. She was clad in a long, sheer, black skirt with thigh-high slits and a black satin bikini top, her wrists adorned in studded, black leather cuffs.

But as he looked Aurora up and down, he realised Cordelia had nothing to worry about. As breathtaking as she was, this chick could have been president of the Itty Bitty Titty Committee, and Indigo had always been a boob man.

"Robster!"

Robbie pivoted to see Drew emerging from the pool house in a plush white bathrobe. He was swaying on his feet, staring intently, unblinkingly at Robbie. Beaming, Drew rushed towards him with his arms out, pulling Robbie into a tight embrace, rocking him gently in his arms. "I love you, man. I love you *so* much. I *missed* you. Even though Cee doesn't love me anymore, we'll always be mates, right?"

Robbie baulked. Exsqueeze me?

"I thought I put you to bed?" Indigo sighed, standing to take Drew by the arm.

"Couldn't sleep," Drew replied. "I just keep having all these *ideas*! All these *thoughts*! So, check it: what if *UFOs* are people from the *future* travelling back in time to observe our primitive way of life? Right? *Right*?" He eyed the pool then and declared, "I wanna swim!"

"You've already had a swim," Indigo told him patiently.

"I *need* another," Drew insisted, shaking Indigo off, shedding his bathrobe and jumping into the pool in his boxers.

"Twat," Nash muttered under his breath, shaking his head. Aurora was watching Drew, eyes narrowed. Sasha was trying not to laugh.

"He's gotta come down *soon*, right?" Indigo asked the others helplessly.

"Where's Cora?" Robbie asked.

"I left her the limo, remember?" Indigo said. "The driver had strict instructions when and where to pick her up."

"Well, I hope she wasn't late. That guy was terrifying as fuck for a limo driver," Robbie said.

Indigo flashed him a sheepish grin. "That's because he's not *technically* a limo driver. He's the guy who was hired to protect Bernadette a few years ago when she had that stalker."

Robbie furrowed his brow. "O-kayyyy..."

"It's all good. He called about twenty minutes ago to let me know Cora was home safe."

"Join us for a drink, ya?" Sasha patted the spot beside him on the plush beige-and-cream-striped chaise longue. He handed Robbie a sparkling water, smiling warmly. "This'll help with your future headache."

Robbie perched awkwardly beside him, holding his breath, dismally aware it probably smelt like a filthy pub floor the day after St Patrick's Day. Sasha put his hand lightly on Robbie's arm and Robbie shyly met his gaze.

"Thank you," Robbie murmured softly as he returned Sasha's smile. "For being my knight in shining armour tonight."

"Right on," Sasha winked. "The pleasure was all mine."

cordelia

Cordelia groaned faintly and drew her knees up into her chest. She was lying on her side on something rigid and cool. Not her bed. Where was she? Was she dreaming? She urged herself to wake up, trying to force her eyes open, but they were so heavy and she was so sleepy. Her temple throbbed with blinding pain, making her want to throw up. There was something trickling down the side of her face and she raised her fingers to it. It was warm and sticky. Blood. The wound was tender to the touch and she whimpered.

Her teeth were chattering. The promised southerly had finally reared its head, the wind whipping through to chill the air. Whatever she was resting upon was unforgiving against her flesh. She rolled over and cracked her eyes open just a slit, bright pain pressing on her skull with the sheer effort.

Above her, the moon beamed through the twisted tree canopy in all its glorious fullness, casting an eerie silvery light on all it touched. Eucalypts, their tall trunks ghostly, stood all around her, her nostrils filling with the familiar scent of their leaves mingled with damp earth and rotting leaves. She didn't know where she was or how she'd gotten there. She squeezed her eyes shut, trying to remember, but at the same time, not wanting to.

With a sudden rush, it all came flooding back to her. Not being able to find Robbie. Sandy hailing her a taxi. The warlock from the beach, Artax... Artax! He'd taken her! But where was he now? She sat bolt upright, ignoring the searing pain that threatened to take the top of her head off, and glanced around, trying to get her bearings.

She was in the bush, in the centre of a natural clearing arched with branches. She glanced down, noting she'd been laid on a circular platform draped in a deep plum cloth. Four large, white candles were placed around her, at her head, feet, to her left and her right. Tealight candles edged the rim of the clearing, their flames gently flickering. She looked down at the cloth she'd been laid upon and saw a symbol embroidered there in silver thread, a five-pointed star inside a circle. What the hell was this? It reminded her of the altar at the front of the school chapel. Had she been brought to the middle of the bush and placed on an altar like some sacrificial offering?

Woozy and disoriented, she slid clumsily off, landing unsteadily on her feet, swaying slightly as she found her balance. The heels of her stilettos sunk deep into the leaf litter. She quickly bent down to unfasten the ankle straps, kicking them off, then straightened up and glanced around.

Move it! Go! Run! Run now! With every fibre of her being screaming at her to get the hell out of there, she started moving towards a narrow opening in the trees, blindly choosing the first path out of this fresh hell. She pulled up sharply when she heard voices in front of her, one of them serpent-like and undeniably Artax's. He must have only left her alone for a moment. And now they were returning, obviously expecting her to still be lying unconscious upon their creepy altar.

Ok, so definitely not that way. She spun quickly and stumbled back across the clearing, her heart pounding in her ears as she managed to make it to the tree line. Only then did she pause to glance over her shoulder. Artax had emerged into the clearing, a great, towering lump now cloaked in his dark-purple robes. He was so busy talking to a smaller, similarly attired warlock that he hadn't noticed her missing.

"The limo driver, you took care of him?" Artax was saying.

"We did. Lady Reinenoir put a glamour on Margot – you should have seen her; she looked identical to the Carlisle girl, right down to the dress. The driver didn't suspect a thing."

"Good. The Maiden would like to begin ssshortly," Artax said.

"But the High Priestess is yet to arrive."

Their exchange was interrupted as a sound rung out, a deep melodic chant of one voice harmoniously joined by others. Many others. Cordelia glanced behind Artax and saw a line of candles bobbing and wending their way through the bush, carried by the owners of the voices. Waves of ice swept through her body, crippling her guts and she bent double. A fog of fear began to descend upon her, muffling her thoughts, numbing her senses. If ever there was a cue to leave, this was it.

Cordelia forced herself to stand up, to pull herself tall, taking a deep breath and centring herself. She had to take back control. She needed to *run*. With a steady exhale, she took off into the bush, ignoring her knotted stomach, holding her arms up in front of her face as she crashed blindly through the scrub, dodging tree trunks and jumping fallen logs and branches, stumbling on the hem of her long gown more than once.

"*Where isss the girl?*" Artax's bellow carried through the trees. "The sssleep ssspell I cassst should have been imposssible for a mere mortal like her to break!"

She ran until her dress was torn and streaked with dirt. When she felt as though she'd put a good bit of distance behind her, she stopped to catch her breath and gather her wits. Her feet were cut and bloody, but she barely noticed. She crouched down, listening. She could hear footfalls crashing through the underbrush, coming closer and closer. Her heart was hammering in her chest. They were right behind her. Knowing her dress was holding her back from outrunning them, she grabbed it by its tattered hem and ripped the bottom off to mid-thigh.

The full moon was a blessing and a curse, providing the light she needed to see where she was going, yet stealing any cover of darkness.

She noticed the bush up ahead thinned out a bit and took off again, bursting from the trees and skidding to a halt at what seemed like the ends of the earth. She was standing on the jagged edge of a sheer, rocky cliff, the wild sea crashing untamed at its base a hundred metres below. She could see the lights of the Sydney skyline twinkling far away across the ocean on the opposite headland, Centrepoint tower standing proud and tall, the harbour stretched endlessly before her. North Head. They'd brought her up to North Head. She was still in Manly. Not far from home at all. She doubled over, clutching her knees, panting, relief coursing through her now that she knew where she was.

She stood, wrapping her arms around herself. What appeared starkly beautiful by day, was infinitely creepy at night. There was an old maritime quarantine station nearby built in the 1830s to process contagious passengers on ships arriving in Sydney. There were three cemeteries surrounding the station as well as a mass grave, those inside anonymous, nameless, forever lost. The buildings were said by locals to be haunted. Very haunted. But right now, she'd rather take her chances with the ghosts than with the warlocks.

She strained her ears to listen.

Silence.

Deadly silence.

She needed a plan. She could easily walk to Indigo's from here. Or she could get to Manly Hospital just outside the national park and call him to come and pick her up.

Her thoughts were shattered by a sound. A shuffling, crunching sound. She turned slowly towards the tree line from where she'd emerged, gaze wide, her chest rising and falling rapidly in horror. Before her eyes, a large figure broke through onto the clifftop, charging for her like a wild animal.

Artax. He'd found her.

"I've got you, you little bitch!" he screamed. His face was still obscured by his hood, but she could feel his eyes burning into her. Something in his hand glinted in the moonlight – a strange dagger, its blade sharp and golden.

'She's here! I've got her!' he called to the others. Although this time she heard it inside her head. She backed away from him, fear flooding her veins. Her hands were shaking uncontrollably and she made

herself curl them into tight fists. She would not freeze. Not again. Not like last time.

And then through the sheer terror, something wended its way into her consciousness, something Indigo had said to her a few days ago: *"If ever you need me – for anything at all – I need for you to just focus really hard and talk to me as though I'm next to you. I'll hear you."* She could see his face so clearly in her mind, that face she knew by heart. She felt his name bubbling up inside her and, when she opened her mouth, it came tearing out. "INDIGO!" she screamed at the top of her lungs, before turning on her heel and running for her life. *'INDIGO!'* she screamed a second time, but this time it was inside her head, the syllables projecting from her consciousness like radio waves.

indigo

Indigo sat bolt upright in bed, his bare chest heaving. He was drenched in sweat, his sheets twisted from some unrecalled nocturnal struggle. He'd been dreaming. Of altars and pentagrams and candles. Of a large tattoo-faced man with a golden athame. Of being chased. Chased through the bush, his arms and legs scratched, his feet bleeding, an anvil of terror sitting on his chest. He clutched the right side of his head as pain shot through it, sharp and woozy.

And then he heard his name being screamed and he realised it wasn't the first time and that that was what had woken him in the first place. In a cluttered tumble, he understood it wasn't him being chased through the bush by a tattoo-faced-man, his legs scratched and bleeding. Not him, but *her*.

He threw back the covers and sprang from his bed, grabbing a discarded pair of black jeans from the back of a chair and tugging them on, fumbling in a drawer for a black T-shirt and pulling that over his head as he threw his door open, running down the hallway, banging on doors to rouse the others.

"Cordelia," he gasped, as lights flickered on and doors opened all over the house.

chapter twenty-two

stay

cordelia

Cordelia veered off the clifftop path and ran through prickly scrub, the bush growing thicker and denser as she went. It was darker in here, the shimmering moonlight struggling to penetrate the shadows. Branches reached out to snag her dress and snatch the pins from her hair. Twigs and bark snapped underfoot as she ran, broadcasting her whereabouts. She'd lost all sense of direction. But she could feel him, feel them, feel them coming, feel them around her, beside her... even *below* her? They were closing in on her.

Her legs were badly scratched, her feet torn to shreds, but she barely felt it. All she could feel was them. And she could hear them. Hear their thoughts, hear their words. She knew how badly they wanted her and it terrified her.

They must be close now, because she was so cold, the pain in her abdomen excruciating. She stopped for a moment, needing to gather her thoughts, and she knew instinctively that she had to try to block theirs out. And when she did, she could hear it, the ocean to her left, the waves, crashing onto the rocks below, guiding her like a beacon, telling her she was going the right way. *Keep going*, she told herself, *just keep going*. She took off running again, but now she felt like she was running through water, her legs leaden, her mind growing foggier.

They'd found her. They were so close now.

271

They must have fanned out to encircle her. Their darkness smothered her. She cried out and doubled over with the pain. There were so many of them. Too many of them.

She stumbled forward; she had to keep moving. But then all of a sudden the trees were gone and with them her cover, and she found herself blinking, out in the open. She'd emerged onto the grounds of North Fort. It was an old army base, and she stopped dead at the sight of the low buildings linked by lawns and rust-hued gravelled pathways, at the squat stone wall encircling it all. She couldn't just feel them now, she could see them. They were coming from all directions, some seemingly emerging from the bowels of the earth to surround her in a perfect circle, just like last time, but more. All cloaked in deep purple, all with hoods obscuring their faces, just like last time, but more. So many more than last time. She turned in a circle, counting twelve. Twelve warlocks surrounding her.

She flinched as one stepped forward and drew a sword from a sheath at his waist. But he didn't approach her. Instead, he drew a perfect circle with its point on the ground around her. The others came to stand inside the circle, shoulder to shoulder.

Cordelia fell to her knees as a warlock stepped forward. She looked up, her breath coming faster as she recognised the straight, black hair and the strong jaw. It was the Maiden.

"Indigo," she moaned desperately, fighting the wooziness in her head.

Cordelia shrank back, holding up a shaking hand in a pathetic attempt to ward the Maiden off, but she stalked closer still. The next thing she knew, someone had grabbed her roughly from behind, forcing her to her feet. "You're proving to be quite the pain in the arssse," Artax hissed into her ear. "That's twiccce you've escaped us, there won't be a third." She recoiled from his putrid breath, ducking her nose into her shoulder.

"Isss the High Priestesss ready?" Artax asked the Maiden.

"Her arrival is imminent," the Maiden replied in her staccato singsong as she stepped forward and grasped Cordelia's chin between bony fingers. "You won't run again," she said in a manner that suggested she expected to be obeyed. Her eyes were hard and black as coal.

Cordelia tore her face from the Maiden's grip, glaring at her defiantly. She was aware her lip was wobbling from the force of the adrenaline coursing through her veins, and she set her jaw. "What do you want with me?"

The Maiden smiled, a gruesome twisted smile. "Oh, honey, what makes you think this is about you?" she scoffed. "Your energy is very bright and lovely and will be a nice snack for us, yes. But you're merely the bait tonight, a lure for a much bigger prize."

"No," Cordelia whispered, dread growing in the pit of her stomach.

"Last time we took you was a test, to make sure he would come. We did not understand quite how powerful he had grown and needed to see for ourselves. But ever since, we've been watching. *She's* been watching *him*. She has her sights set on him, and I can assure you there's no point fighting it."

"Please, no," Cordelia gasped. "Take me, leave him out of it."

"You're the one who called for him." The Maiden grinned widely. "As we knew you would."

Cordelia felt a sob rising in her throat. This was all her fault.

"Ah, sssshe's arrived," Artax interrupted.

Cordelia followed his gaze to where a cloaked figure was approaching, gliding towards them in robes of a brighter amethyst than the rest of the coven, chin held high, face obscured, long, buttery hair falling past her shoulders, dead straight and sleek. Their High Priestess.

The High Priestess was still a good distance away, but just like last time, Cordelia could feel her as though she were right beside her. The darkness emanating from her was deep and bottomless, vast and wide, as though she were an abyss, a black hole sucking all happiness and light from around her. Her power was immense, and she radiated a terrifying strength, commanding all eyes to her.

Artax released Cordelia and stepped back into formation, taking his place in the circle. "Blessed be the evening, High Priestess," the coven said in unison, bowing to her as she approached.

Although Cordelia couldn't see the High Priestess' eyes, she felt them lock on hers. A flood of rage swamped her, and right there and then, she hated this woman with an intensity that burnt so deep and dark, it was like nothing she'd ever known. In that moment, she felt capable of tearing her limb from limb with her bare hands. She'd do anything to stop her laying a finger on Indigo. "If you touch him,"

Cordelia snarled through clenched teeth, "I will come for you. And if you hurt him, I will keep coming for you until I've destroyed you."

She could feel the High Priestess' gaze boring into her, cold and hard and intrusive. She was silent for so long that Cordelia began to wonder if she'd heard her.

But then she spoke, her voice an icy monotone. "You are no match for him, and you are certainly no match for me. The fact *you* think you can take *me*, just proves how pathetically naïve you truly are." She turned to her coven. "Begin!" she cried.

Cordelia's stomach dropped as her rage morphed to dread.

They began to chant again, their voices rising and falling and blending as one in their enigmatic wordless song. They began to circle Cordelia in a clockwise direction, their bodies twisting and moving as they raised their hands to their goddess moon in the sky and then to her. Even though she was expecting it this time, the terror rendering her immobile, she still struggled to fight it.

But this time something was different.

Her breath came sharp and shallow as they stopped suddenly. She watched as what looked like swirling vortexes opened up over their chests, great writhing hooks unfurling from within in long black streams, coming at her from all directions. They were made of a substance that looked similar to what she'd seen Indigo project from his palms – bioplasma, he'd called it – but darker and a lot more *vicious*. Her instinct was to repel them, and with that realisation, she could suddenly move again. She bent and twisted and dodged, hitting out with her hands to deflect them over and over and over again, until she was panting and overwhelmed.

But they just kept coming and coming.

And then it happened.

One got by her, its aim true, firing like an arrow to lodge firmly into her chest. She cried out, her back arching as a second hit her square in the sternum.

A dark cloud immediately began to descend upon her, fuzzing out the world, the woozy dizziness coming fast and furiously. With two hooks in her, their frenzied attack seemed to halt. She thought of Indigo. She thought of Robbie. Was this the end for her? Would she ever see them again?

"*Cora!*" she heard her name then, garbled and far away, and she swore she could see Robbie there with her, flickering in and out like a TV screen with a dodgy aerial, but there all the same…

And then he wasn't.

She looked and looked, her eyes searching, but now she couldn't see him at all and she felt so sad, so alone.

"Come back," she whispered hoarsely. *Come back, come back, come back!*

She blinked then, long and slow, and when her eyes opened, Sasha was suddenly standing there beside her, his thick, raven hair swept back off his face into a knot on the top of his head.

"You alright, babe?" he asked her.

"Sasha?" she mumbled, trying to focus on his face. "Are you really here?"

"I'm here. I've got you."

She nodded dumbly as if it were completely normal for someone to materialise beside her, while Sasha closed ranks around her, drawing her protectively into his arms. But the hooks pumping and sucking at her, it was too much and her legs gave way and she could feel herself fading fast. Sasha caught her, one hand under her knees, the other against her back, holding her tight against his chest. His presence was comforting, and somehow seemed to keep the warlocks at bay.

He wrapped a hand around the cords protruding from her chest and his touch instantly steadied them, stopped them from pumping anything further from her.

"Get them out of me," she muttered. "Please."

"I'll do more harm than good if I try, sorry, babe. Help's on the way."

Her eyes flickered closed; she had no strength left to hold them open.

"Open your eyes, Cordelia. Look at me, *look at me!*" She drowsily forced her lids open, her eyes locked on Sasha's, so full of light they seemed to be pulsating. "I won't let them come any closer. The others are coming I promise, he'll be here soon but you have to be strong, you have to fight this, ya."

"No… he can't…Tell him… not to come…" she mumbled. Her head lolled to the side and she saw the coven closing in around them, edging nearer and nearer, their chanting growing louder and more urgent.

"Back off," Sasha snarled, holding her tight. He was short, but he held himself as if he were ten feet tall. She could feel his muscles strung tight, ready to move if need be. They didn't come any nearer.

Her mind was swimming and she didn't know what was real and what wasn't, and then she swore she heard the sound of a motorbike, maybe two, coming closer, and she opened her eyes again to see the warlocks behind them scattering, and the next thing she knew a bike had skidded to a violent halt behind her. Indigo jumped off; his face turned to thunder when he saw the two great bioplasmic hooks protruding from her chest.

He reeled to face the warlocks. "You take from her, I take from you!" he roared. Sasha let go of the cords and held Cordelia steady in his arms. Indigo grabbed one bioplasmic stream in each hand, holding tight, a look of deep concentration upon on his face. She glanced down to see the flow had reversed, so instead of pumping away from her, it now streamed towards her, the colour changing from black to white as it passed through his palms. She was immediately energised with a burst of overwhelming power as two warlocks cried out and crumpled to the ground.

Indigo swept his arm through the hooks, tearing them in half with a ferocious scowl. He then carefully plucked the remnants from her sternum, holding his hand briefly over the area, a soft glow wreathing his hands. And she felt strong and whole again.

And then Sasha was transferring her to him, and she was safe in his arms. He placed her onto the back of his bike, and she tightened her arms around him as he revved the throttle, heading straight for the wall of warlocks. Most dived out the way when he showed no signs of slowing down, but two came charging at the bike at full speed. Quick as a flash, Indigo let go of the handlebars and cocked his palms. Cordelia saw the bioplasma streaming from his hands, like wind and light and heat, not gentle and playful like when he'd shown her on the couch that day, but a bio-blast with a force akin to nuclear. The next thing she knew, both warlocks had fallen to the ground.

A second bike pulled up, and an auburn-haired boy and the girl from the beach – Aurora? – jumped off and moved towards Sasha, who looked relieved to see them. The three of them stood shoulder-to-shoulder, unwavering. The coven had formed a semi-circle now, trying to close ranks behind them.

"Who're they?" she asked Indigo.

"Nash and Rory," he told her as he turned the bike towards the stone arch that would lead them back to the road.

Cordelia glanced over her shoulder. Aurora lazily flicked one finger and two warlocks were knocked violently off their feet. Nash held his palms out threateningly, slowly turning his head and narrowing his eyes as though trying to select a target.

"I need to get you out of here," Indigo said as he revved the bike and accelerated. She glanced over her shoulder and saw a fresh swarm of warlocks in purple robes streaming from the surrounding darkness towards them. How many was that now? Too many to count.

She was glad to get away.

Indigo accelerated hard.

They almost made it, too.

They were a couple metres from the stone arch when the Maiden stepped out right in front of them. He swerved to go around her, but she thrust her hand out, palm facing them and the bike came to a sudden dead halt, as if it had hit a brick wall.

Cordelia and Indigo were launched high into the night sky. As if in slow motion, she felt him grab for her in mid-air, grasping her arm and pulling her to him, putting his body between hers and the impending gravel, and she braced herself for impact as they plunged down, the ground screaming towards them. But then she heard someone yell, "I've got you!" and she realised it was Aurora, and she felt herself, still in Indigo's arms, rise up, up, up into the air.

She glanced down in confusion and saw Aurora standing below them, her hand thrust out, her eyes narrowed. "It's ok," Indigo whispered, scooping an arm under her knees as she held on tight to his neck. Aurora slowly lowered them so he landed firmly on his feet, still holding her. He placed her gently on the ground and pressed his forehead to hers. "Are you alright?" he murmured.

She nodded, her breath erratic. They'd landed beside Nash, Aurora and Sasha but she was barely aware of them.

"You shouldn't have come," she moaned. "It's a trap, Indigo–"

"Indi!" Nash cried, as something streamed by them, hot and fast and unknown. A bio-blast, she realised with a jolt. From *them*. Indigo pushed her behind him, hands raised, and she gasped as the warlocks closed in around them, the Maiden front and centre.

Indigo cocked his hands, his palms writhing, bristling, crackling. His eyes never leaving the warlocks, he murmured in a low voice, "You need to leave. Now."

"I'm not leaving you." She grabbed onto his waist, pressing her cheek to his back.

"My car's just outside the gates. We brought Robbie and Pres to take you home."

She glanced up and saw his black SUV pulling up. The passenger door opened and Sasha jumped out and started jogging towards them. She blinked and turned to Sasha already standing beside her, then looked back to see him running towards them from the road. Two of him. "Bilocation," she murmured.

The driver's door opened and Robbie slipped out as Drew climbed out the back. They both started beckoning her. She shook her head and clung to Indigo. She was terrified to let go of him, to let him out of her sight. The thought of anything happening to him was unfathomable.

"Cora, please," Indigo groaned. "I need to know you're safe."

Sasha reached them. "All good?" Indigo nodded tersely. "This is what you've been training for, ya," Sasha told him, grasping his shoulder.

Everyone was still, silent. Nobody moved on either side. All Cordelia could hear was the sound of her breath, the sound of Indigo's heart pumping, her ear still pressed up tight against his back.

"Bring him to me." The voice was slow and strong and commanding. Cordelia peeked around Indigo to see the High Priestess standing behind her coven, her robes fluttering in the slight breeze that had kicked up, her arms raised, palms up. "*NOW!*"

The warlocks charged at them from all directions like a rolling purple wall.

"Cora, please! You being here, it's only gonna make it harder! I can't concentrate unless I know you're safe. We can handle this, I swear!" Indigo turned to grip her shoulders. She looked from him to the warlocks bearing down on them.

"Promise you'll come back to me." Cordelia cupped his cheek. "Promise you won't die, Indigo Wolfe." Indigo raised his hand back over his shoulder and bio-blasted a warlock dead-on, his eyes never leaving Cordelia's. "Promise me."

"I promise," he said, taking her palm and pressing his lips to it, then pushing her towards the road.

"So, we shooting to kill or what?" she heard Nash ask as she began to walk away. Pain shot through her feet with every step, and she sucked in a sharp breath as she glanced down to assess the damage. They were shredded to ribbons from her run through the bush.

"No," Indigo replied sternly. "We maim, we disarm, we neutralise. But nobody dies here tonight."

She was halfway to Robbie when she heard yelling behind her. She skidded to a stop and turned. Indigo leaned to the right as a stream of bioplasma flew by, followed by a large boulder and a log. Bodies were scattered on the ground – motionless, crumpled purple heaps – but the warlocks kept coming, attacking from all sides.

Indigo smashed his fist into a warlock's face, ducking and pivoting to kick another's legs out from under it. From there he shot a sharp burst of bioplasma into the warlock's chest, rendering it unconscious. Sasha delivered a roundhouse kick towards an opponent, hitting it square in the ribcage and knocking it momentarily to the ground. He spun and weaved, as another warlock threw a punch toward him, responding with a fast jab to its jaw.

"Cordelia!" Robbie yelled. "Don't stop now! Move your arse!" He ran towards her, his face white as he grabbed her wrist.

Cordelia took one step then yanked her arm away. She looked at Indigo, then back to Robbie. "I'm sorry, Rob. This is all my fault. I can't leave him."

"Cordelia!" Robbie cried. "NO!"

But she turned away and ran – limped – back towards North Fort, back towards Indigo, back towards the battle.

robbie

"Fuck!" Robbie yelled, kicking the stone arch and exhaling heavily, hands on hips. He turned back to Drew who was loping up behind him.

"She didn't just... ?" Drew asked, staring into the darkness after Cordelia.

"Yup," Robbie snapped.

"Come with me," Drew said, running back towards the road. Robbie reluctantly sprinted after him. Drew opened the boot of Indigo's car and pushed the surfboards aside, rummaging around and triumphantly pulling out a skateboard.

"What the hell are we gonna do with that?" Robbie asked, screwing up his nose.

"Have you seen what's going on up there?" Drew asked, eyes shining with excitement. It dawned on Robbie that all of Drew's conspiracy theory dreams were unfolding right before his eyes. Drew hooked the skateboard under his arm. "We can't go in there completely unarmed. You've clearly never gotten one of these to the back of the head."

"What bare-knuckled hell did you grow up in?" Robbie asked incredulously.

"In a house of boys, you learn bloody quick that pretty much anything can be used as a weapon." Drew grabbed Indigo's denim jacket out the car. "For Cee. It's getting cold now that southerly's coming through." Robbie nodded. He'd seen her tattered formal dress, now torn to mid-thigh. It certainly wasn't appropriate attire for a battle.

As they crept quietly towards the chaos, Drew reached into his pocket and pulled out a small plastic baggie. He sprinkled a pile of white powder onto the back of his hand in the valley between his thumb and index finger, then quickly snorted it.

"You're fucking *kidding* me, right?" Robbie snapped. "You and your fucking nose candy."

"If you knew how hard I was coming down, you'd be grateful I've got something to fire me back up again."

"I dunno, man," Robbie said, glancing at him sideways. "There's a time and a place. If we get outta this alive, we need to get you some serious help."

"I'm fine," Drew grinned, wide and lazy, as he rubbed the excess on his gums. "You wanna partake?"

"I'm good." The wind had picked up a bit, and grit and debris were swirling in the air. The branches around them swayed and rustled.

"There!" Robbie said, pointing to Cordelia standing in the shadows of the bushes, watching the battle like a deer in headlights. He grabbed her elbow. She jumped and whirled around, softening when she realised it was him. "What the *hell*, Cordelia? Are you *crazy*?!" He'd never wanted to kill her more.

"Holy shit," Drew breathed, his eyes wide as he took in the scene unfolding before them. A seething roil of purple-cloaked bodies engulfed Nash and Aurora, as Sasha took on two warlocks that dwarfed him. Drew tilted his head, watching with interest as a second version of Sasha suddenly appeared behind the two warlocks, then disappeared as they turned and swung at him, only to reappear elsewhere, taunting them as they came at him again.

"Sasha... is he?"

"Yup," Cordelia replied. "That right there is bilocation in action."

"I *knew* it! I knew it was real." Drew turned to Robbie with a smug smile, pointing a finger in his face. "I told you, man! I *told* you! And you said I was crazy!"

"Ok, ok," Robbie said, stepping back a bit. "You were right, I was wrong." He put a protective arm around Cordelia. She shrugged him off, shooting him a death stare.

"What the hell happened to you tonight?" she snapped. "How could you just ditch me like that?"

His stomach dropped to his feet. "It wasn't a conscious choice, I swear, Cora. I passed out in the gutter outside of the formal. Sasha rescued me and took me to Indigo's. We thought you'd gotten home safe in the limo, I'm so sorry."

She regarded him coolly. "Ok, lots to unpack there, but now is not the time." She glanced back into the fray. "Where's Indigo?" she said, her voice edged in panic. "I'm going to go find him." She pointed to the side of the fort.

"Absolutely fucking not." Robbie grabbed her arm and dragged her back.

Cordelia struggled, trying to pull her arm free. "Let me go right now, Robbie. This is not the time for your bossy bullshit."

"As if I'm going to let you go traipsing off into the night alone, shivering in the scraps of your dress." He glared at Cordelia, shaking his head dismally as his eyes travelled over her. "RIP gown, you were taken far too soon."

"Here." Drew suddenly appeared at Cordelia's side, holding up Indigo's jacket for her to shrug into. She threaded her arms through the sleeves and smiled softly at him in thanks as he rolled the cuffs up for her.

Frowning, Robbie gently touched his fingers to the wound on her head where Artax had punched her, then looked down at her feet and gasped. "Has Jaws been snacking on your tootsies? My *God*, Cora, you're definitely not going anywhere on those!"

"I'm *fine*," she said through clenched teeth. But she wasn't. Her feet were hurting worse every minute.

"Please stay here, Cora. I'll go look for Indigo. It's my duty as your brother and the sober male in this situation," Robbie said. She opened her mouth to respond but he held his hand up. "Do not even think about questioning my masculinity here. Besides, with Dad gone..." He trailed off, his voice hoarse when he spoke again. "It's my job to protect you. Please let me do this, Cordelia. I couldn't stand it if something happened to you."

"I don't need protecting."

"Call it what you will. I'm going. You're staying." He looked at Drew. "Guard her with your life."

Drew glanced at Cordelia. "Always," he murmured.

Robbie hugged his sister tightly then took off into the night, sticking to the bushes that lined the wall ringing the fort. It was dark there in the shadows. His heart hammered in his chest as he gazed transfixed at all that was unfolding. He blinked in disbelief as Sasha simply appeared behind the giant hulking warlock encroaching on Nash, and tapped him on the shoulder, only to disappear when he turned.

He was so busy watching, that by the time he heard the footsteps behind him it was too late. A hand closed over his mouth and he was grabbed roughly and shoved into the moonlit yard.

chapter twenty-three

breathe

indigo

Under a full moon, the wind lashing the trees, North Fort had become a different sort of warzone. Scowling, Indigo slicked his hair back into a short ponytail and ran at the warlock attacking Sasha. He front flipped into the air, landing in a crouch before Sasha, springing up to kick the warlock in the face. He sneered at its lank purple hair and bloody nose, thrusting his hand out and firing bioplasma into its chest. The warlock crumpled to the ground.

Sasha nodded proudly at his protégé, then spun to confront the warlock sneaking up behind him. "Go help Nash and Rory."

Indigo raced towards Nash, punching a warlock and kicking another's knees out from under it along the way. He sped up when he saw Nash facing off with the tattooed monstrosity, Artax, flexing his fingers, his jaw set. "So you're the grand shrouder," Nash snarled, cricking his neck, hands poised. "I'd say it's a pleasure, but your ugly mug's enough to scare small children." In a blink, Nash flicked his wrist, shooting a stream of iridescent energy straight at Artax. Nash's confident stare faltered when his bio-blast simply bounced off the behemoth, evaporating in a puff.

What the fuck.

Artax shook himself off, his lip curling in a grimace as he advanced towards Nash. The force of the impact had knocked his hood off, and

Indigo was momentarily distracted by Artax in all his glory: the tats, the horns, those inky black eyes!

Nash flicked both his wrists this time, firing bioplasma in quick succession, one stream hitting Artax in the forehead, the second in his chest again. Artax stumbled back a few steps, then charged at Nash like an angry bull.

Approaching stealthily from behind, Aurora's eyes moved from Artax to Nash, her expression lethal. She swiped her fingers at Artax, and the behemoth came crashing down on his back. Nash stood over him, palms down, drilling a steady stream into him so forcefully his hands shook violently. When Artax didn't get up, Nash pivoted to shoot bio-blasts at the attacking coven. For every one he took down, another snuck past his defence. Where a warlock got close enough to reach Nash, Aurora was there, flicking it off its feet.

Indigo ducked and smashed his elbow into the warlock running at him. He flung bioplasma into its chest, making sure it stayed down.

Sasha was fighting two warlocks, appearing and disappearing like a frenzied warrior. Aurora telekinetically hurled an enormous log, pinning a warlock beneath it. Braced against Nash, she kept slinging warlocks into the path of his destruction, a sheen of perspiration on her forehead.

Not a good sign, Aurora breaking a sweat.

Indigo battled towards his mates, flipping a warlock over his shoulder and glancing to his left at a sharp cry. He pivoted, his stomach plunging when he saw Robbie kneeling on the ground in the shadow of a building. Two warlocks had their hooks lodged in him, feasting greedily.

Robbie wasn't meant to be there!

He was meant to be with Cordelia!

Indigo swung around, perusing the battle ground, his heart strangled in his throat. He couldn't see her anywhere. She *had* to be safe. Drew had clear instructions to take her home; *surely* he would have stepped up.

Indigo changed course. Robbie was in deep shit, and Indigo needed to get to him. A war between the coven and his friends lay between him and Robbie. Indigo decided it was easier to go *up* than through. He leapt onto the wall of the nearest building, scrambling up the drainpipe onto its roof, bolting to the far end, then jumping onto the low wall below. He ran its perimeter, ducking the streams of bio-blast that came flying at him and firing back just as fiercely. He somersaulted off the wall and landed behind Robbie. He was fucking *pissed*, his gaze dark as he stalked towards the warlocks.

Frightened, the cowardly bastards yanked their cords from Robbie. He crumpled to the ground as they fled. Indigo fired twin streams of bioplasma, nailing the first warlock in the head and the other in the back, satisfied when they went down hard.

"Shit!" he swore, skidding to his knees in front of his friend. He felt Robbie's pulse and quickly scanned his body. He was out cold and would be until Indigo could heal him, but he'd be ok. Indigo hoisted Robbie over his shoulder and kicked in the rickety wooden door to an adjacent building, laying him gently inside the maintenance cupboard. Indigo pulled the door shut behind him.

Panting, he started for his friends, spying Sasha and Nash standing triumphantly over a pile of warlocks. But then the largest of the crumpled purple heaps began to twitch, and they both stepped back, visibly paling, as Artax rose slowly to his feet, his face a mask of unbridled fury.

On the opposite side of the fort, Aurora faced the Maiden, gazes locked, their power bristling around them.

Forced to make a split second decision, Indigo raced for Sasha and Nash, trusting Aurora could hold her own until they could get to her. When a stream of swirling red bioplasma came hurtling at him, he managed to dive out the way just in time. He hit the ground, hard. Quick as lightning, he rolled as another came at him. Growling, he crouched, scanning for the source of the attack.

And then he saw her.

A lone warlock, standing apart from the rest, behind the battle lines. She was wearing a satiny cloak of purple more vibrant than the rest, the hood obscuring her face. Her slender frame was almost regal, her blonde hair trailing in the breeze like a flaxen curtain.

Harper.

As he watched, she held out a dainty palm, the air in front of her distorting as a cyclonic stream of red flew from her hand, travelling towards Aurora.

Aurora was now on her knees, the Maiden standing over her, palms held out towards Aurora, trapping her in place. Nash suddenly appeared, hands cocked, firing at the Maiden, who dove out the way, releasing Aurora who hit the deck. Harper's bio-blast shot over her head, missing her by a breath.

That was too close. Enough was fucking well enough.

Indigo had to stop Harper. Now.

He stealthily circled around the back of the buildings, approaching her from the rear. He rounded the wall and she came into view; he had her in his sights. He crept up quickly behind her, pulling his biofield in to make himself as small as possible, drawing deep on his power. His fingers twitched as it writhed and buzzed in his palm, itching to be released.

He raised his hand and blasted at her just as she spun to face him.

Quick as a flash, she threw her hand out, releasing a flood of bioplasma at the exact same time, hers roaring to meet his, clashing in mid-air, his hand trembling with the effort of holding hers back. He threw one final burst at her, then cut it off and weaved as her stream flew over his head. He fired at her again, but she ducked it.

Before he could even register what was happening, she threw her other hand out towards him, cocking her head to the side, and just like that, he couldn't move. She'd frozen him on his knees. Try as he might, he couldn't move a muscle.

A slow smile spread upon her full crimson lips, and she reached her free hand up and drew back her hood.

"Hello again, Indi," she purred. "Long time no see." She waved her hand casually and he could move his mouth, his head, but try as he might, nothing else, the rest of him still frozen in the grip of her power.

"Harper," he breathed. "Let me go." She looked the same, a little more mature maybe, her face a bit more angular. She would be twenty now. She'd been widely regarded as the hottest girl in school, and her ice-cold magnificence was certainly unwavering.

"I've told you, my name is *Reinenoir*. Don't make me correct you again," she said, seemingly staring into his soul, and it was like he could feel her caressing the insides of his mind with her long, blood-red nails. "Indigo Wolfe," she said, her tone seductive, "the boy who thinks he's better than me. So *good*. So pure. So pathetically righteous." She looked him up and down, almost hungrily.

"What do you want?" Indigo asked, immobile on his knees before her.

"You know what I want, *mon cherie*," she drawled, narrowing her eyes at him. "You."

He laughed, short and sharp. "Never gonna happen."

"I hoped you'd change your mind."

"Not in a billion years."

"And this is the hill you want to die on?"

He glowered, matching her silent stare. She pressed her lips hard together. "Such a shame, really. You and I, we used to be great together." She cocked her head to one side. "Perhaps you need a reminder?"

She approached him slowly, her eyes never leaving his. She was so tiny, she was only a head taller than him standing when he was on his knees. She bent down, slowly reaching her hands up underneath his T-shirt, caressing his pecs, then raking her nails down his back. "Mmmm… Someone's been working out."

He couldn't stop her from touching him, couldn't shake her claws off his body, her touch like poisonous icicles down his spine. She smiled a vicious, little smile. And then she leant in, pressing her mouth forcefully to his in a kiss that made him sick to his stomach.

Her lips moved against his, cold and hard, her venomous tongue forcefully prising his mouth open. Unable to push her away, he clamped his lips shut and tried to turn his head, but she grabbed his face and wrenched it back around so she could kiss him again.

"Stop it, Harper!" He gagged, but her kiss only became more violent. He bit down on her lip, hard enough to draw blood. Her head jerked back, but she maintained her vice-like grip on him. He was sickened to see she was smiling, blood dripping from her teeth.

"Bad boy," she murmured. "Trying to hurt me. I think you've forgotten how much I like that."

She wrapped herself around him, dug her nails deeper into his back, and he gritted his teeth; he could feel the scratches seeping. "Scream my name, Indi," she whispered into his ear. "I'll hurt you 'til you do. Just like old times."

He turned his face to hers, his lip curling in disgust. He drew his head back, then lurched forward, cracking his forehead into hers in a headbutt that doubled his vision and sent her reeling. One thing he knew she abhorred was any damage to her precious face. She quickly regained her balance and stood tall, touching her fingertips to her forehead, pressing at the blood that now trickled from her split skin, her expression lethal.

She smiled then, but it was frosty and it didn't reach her eyes. "We could have been great together, *mon cherie*. I suppose, though, that if I have to, I can rule the world quite easily on my own. Especially once I've devoured what's yours, collected it for myself. Your light shines brighter than most. What you have, well, it's really quite special, one-of-a-kind even. By adding your powers to mine, I'll finally be ready to challenge *the Witch Queen*."

"*Witch* Queen? Who or what, the fuck, is the Witch Queen?" he demanded, still choking on the taste of her vile lips.

"Don't play dumb with me, Indi."

"Harper, I–"

"Shush, now," she said, immobilising his mouth with the flick of her finger. "My sources tell me you're a quadruple threat?" She looked at him questioningly. He didn't answer because he couldn't, so she continued. "An empath, a clairvoyant, and I've seen you're telepathic and psychokinetic." She narrowed her eyes at him. "I can't say I'm surprised, considering you're the last of your line. Consuming your powers would make me unstoppable."

'It doesn't have to be this way, Harps.' She could freeze his body but she couldn't freeze his mind. *'Release me and we can talk about this.'*

She scoffed, shaking her head in disbelief. "*Release* you? That's not going to happen, mon cherie. If you won't join me, I'll make sure you never see another sunrise. You do realise you're not even supposed to be here?"

'What?'

"You shouldn't *be* here, you shouldn't be *alive*," she hissed. She laughed then, at him, cold and nasty. "Why you had to switch things up on my watch is beyond me. Things were going so well, with you set to… *remove yourself* from the situation so beautifully that night on Bear Mountain Bridge." Her mouth twisted into a cruel grin. "It was a sight to behold, Indigo, in the months and weeks prior, watching your slow descent into darkness. And we may have had a bit of a play, too, adding to your burdens, so to speak. It's such fun, messing with the Akasha who don't yet *know* they're Akasha, whose higher senses are out of control. And yours! Yours were like nothing I'd ever seen." She stared deep into his eyes then and chanted:

"You are nothing."

"You are worthless."

"You are toxic."

"You are unlovable."

She flicked her hand again, releasing his face from her hold, allowing him to speak.

Indigo stared at her, feeling so sick he could barely breathe. "Tha-that was *you*? *You* were the one who projected those thoughts into my head?" He recalled lying in his bed in his father's penthouse all those days and nights, in the very depths of his depression, staring listlessly at the ceiling and repeating those sentences over and over until they became his thoughts, his reality, until they became *him*.

She threw her head back and laughed. "And you were such a quick study! We had you repeating it, believing it, in no time at all. And that wasn't my only appearance. You recall those final moments on the bridge that night?" She leant in close to his ear and whispered *"Do it! Do it! Do it!"*

He squeezed his eyes shut, nausea rising in waves from his belly.

"H-how could you *do* that?" he breathed, opening his eyes to see her grinning like a Cheshire cat. "What is *wrong* with you? You were always a bitch, Harper, but this… You're *sick*. Sick and twisted."

"You say the sweetest things," she crooned, stroking his cheek. Then, just as fast, she slapped him, her wrath bubbling up. *"All you had to do was die and stay dead!* With you out the way, the path was clear. We were *ready*. And then your little band of heroes went and fished you out of the river and ruined everything. One measly moment, and they set a whole new timeline in motion!" She was seething, her face twisted in fury. "You were never *meant* to be saved. You're meant to be dead!"

"Sorry to disappoint you, *Harper*," he spat. "But maybe, *just maybe*, you're not as all-knowing as you *think* you are?" He knew his date of death was never set in stone. That night, the option of him being saved, it was always there. A trickle of cold sweat ran slowly down his back. How could she have known about the timeline, what surviving that night on the bridge would mean? Raf had only told Indigo the night before he'd left Sedona. He'd sat him down with Nash, Aurora, Sasha and Dawn and hosted Micah, then sworn them to secrecy.

"You think I don't know what Diego Rafael knows? Are you really that naïve, Indigo?" she gloated and he realised she'd wandered into his head. He pushed her out, shut her out.

"Tonight I will set things right." She looked him up and down, her pupils dilating. "I'd forgotten how exquisite you are. The world won't be the same without you around to decorate it. But that's the whole point. When you're around, the darkness can't prevail. And my friends here and I, we like it dark. It makes it much easier for us to control the close-minded, the downtrodden, the miserable!

"That's the way things were meant to go. But when you survived, when your little *pals*," she glanced over her shoulder to where Aurora and Nash and Sasha were still battling her warlocks, "intervened and saved you, well, the world as it was supposed to be veered off course. A world with you in it is a world of peace. It's a world where twin buildings won't fall, where bombs won't annihilate tourists on tropical islands, where princesses won't perish in tunnels, where future presidents won't fall from the sky! Because of you, the timeline looks very different now. When you survived, the human race entered the golden age."

He glared up at her, standing over him, her seeing things so differently than how he did. She was wrong! Nash had shown him events from the timeline Harper was fixated on. He'd seen it, and he knew it was full of darkness and sadness and misery.

One of the worst things he'd seen in that timeline was two planes crashing in New York in six years time that would begin a war on terror that would change the world and kill millions. On that timeline, twenty-five years from now, a pandemic would sweep the globe, closing borders and shutting down the world and forcing people to hide away in their homes. Nash had shown him other things, too, things that scared him shitless. But that was the future of an alternate 1995, a 1995 in which he'd died, not this one, not the one where he survived.

"You're the catalyst, Indigo. That night on the bridge was a turning point for the human race." She paused to consider him, still trapped inside his frozen body, yet his eyes bored into hers with such defiance. "But I can see you know that already."

He set his jaw and fixed his gaze straight ahead.

"Lucky for us you're still such a newb! It was so easy to lure you here. I remember the meek, insipid, little thing that Carlisle bitch used to be, but even back then, the way you looked at her... You *never* looked at me that way. But who's laughing now? She's your downfall, your weakness. We've been watching you, we've been watching *all* of you. We know everything about each and every one of you and can pre-empt everything you think you can throw at us. You've lost, Indigo."

He knew his friends were exhausted, and he didn't know how much longer they could fight. They'd managed to take out a good number, but Harper seemed to have an endless cache of reserves. Was their Akashic hereditary power any match for all Harper's warlocks had collected?

At least as long as he was occupying Harper, she wasn't hurling bioplasma at them.

"They won't fight without you. I know you think they will, but they won't. They may even surrender to me, join my coven."

Indigo wanted to laugh in her face. He knew his friends would never turn warlock.

"They won't have much choice, really. So let's finish this, shall we? It might actually be fun, extinguishing your bloodline." She paused for a second, smiling at him. "How about I give you one more chance to come over to my side? Maybe this will help you see things my way."

Before he could reply she raised her arm towards him and twisted her hand, squeezing her fingers together. He reared back as agonising pain seared through him from head to toe. It was as though every single bone in his body was being snapped at once. All air was pressed from his lungs so he was left gasping. It was unbearable, unfathomable, all-consuming torture.

"I'm going to enjoy this." She smiled viciously, twisting her fingers harder, the pain shooting through him harder, every nerve, every cell, every organ screaming in agony. He heard a sound, a dreadful bloodcurdling sound, and he realised it was coming from him. He was no longer frozen. She'd released him, obviously preferring to watch him writhe and howl on the ground.

"Just give me a sign, Indigo. Say you'll join me and I'll stop right now!"

He was vaguely aware of his friends bolting towards him, Nash leading the charge, screaming his name. Aurora's eyes widened in horror as Nash disappeared under a fresh wall of purple, inundated. Without hesitation, she turned and threw herself after him. Sasha was swiftly dragged into the fray, the three of them now fighting for their own lives.

They couldn't help him. He was on his own. And he could see no way out. Harper's strength was immense, immeasurable. She'd stolen the strength and power of so many.

And with horror, he realised she was undefeatable.

She balled her hand into a tight fist, and he felt like every organ in his body was being crushed and twisted, exploding, as though she'd set fire to him and his whole body was burning, melting. He couldn't get air into his lungs. Wave upon wave of agony coursed through him, unrelenting, blinding, leaving him delirious. This must be what it felt like to be choked, crushed, beaten and burnt alive.

He was dying. He knew that now.

She was going to kill him.

As painfully as possible.

chapter twenty-four

never tear us apart

fifteen minutes ago...

cordelia

Cordelia crouched next to Drew, hidden behind a boulder, eyes wide and heart thudding as they watched the carnage unfolding around them. She looked everywhere at once, trying to spot Indigo.

She'd seen him only moments ago, fighting so hard and capably alongside his friends. She was in awe of his agility and strength. Searching frantically, she sighed in relief when she saw him appear through the swirling dust, then pivot suddenly and take off in the opposite direction, ducking and weaving behind buildings and around and over walls. The way he moved so effortlessly, with such grace, he was poetry in motion.

Where was he going now?

Her stomach dropped like a stone when she saw *her*. The High Priestess, standing apart from the others. Cordelia recoiled. That's who Indigo was stalking.

Indigo fired at the High Priestess just as she turned, her ruby stream slamming into his in a shower of bioplasmic sparks. Cordelia gripped Drew's arm, willing Indigo to take the bitch down, even as the force of her power drove him to his knees. The High Priestess sauntered closer, her amethyst robes swishing silently across the ground.

With one hand thrust at Indigo, she lowered her hood, blood red nails gleaming against moonlight hair.

Cordelia gasped, collapsing against the boulder.

Harper. The High Priestess was Harper Valentine.

"Holy *shit*," Drew murmured.

Cordelia pressed her hands to her mouth as Harper continued to stand opposite Indigo, who strangely, wasn't reacting, wasn't moving. She couldn't look away as she watched Harper grip Indigo's face between her talons and kiss him. And he *let* her. A barbell was suddenly crushing her chest and her breath turned choppy.

"Why is he letting her kiss him? Why isn't he fighting back?" She felt Drew lean into her, propping her up and she realised she was trembling with rage. She wanted to strangle the moll!

Cordelia grasped the boulder, her body vibrating with the desperate need to smack Harper back to where she came from. Why was Indigo just taking this? Her bloody feet shifted in the dirt, her teeth bared in a snarl, when Indigo suddenly headbutted Harper hard enough to make her stumble backwards.

"Yeah, mate!" Drew exclaimed, as Cordelia sagged with relief.

On the periphery of her vision, Cordelia could see the fight on the other side of the Fort unravelling. Nash was battling Artax, his power clashing against the tattooed ox's brutish strength. Aurora's hands were a blur, her fingers darting and weaving as she combated the encroaching Maiden. Sasha was everywhere at once, holding the line as he took on multiple warlocks. But Harper seemed to have an endless supply, with more and more warlocks entering the fight all the time.

Cordelia's gaze slid from the battle that dug craters into the ground and ripped age old trees from their roots, to Indigo's friends fighting so hard, to Indigo, who suddenly seemed completely immobile, lifeless almost, eyes open, staring blankly.

She peered at him, heart pounding. She knew in her bones something was wrong. Really wrong. She needed to do something. She shrugged Drew off and stood, taking a step beyond the shadows, her bare feet stumbling down a rocky incline. She cried out immediately, swearing at her wrecked feet as Drew lurched forward and dragged her back to safety.

"Let me go." She tried to yank free. "They need our help."

Drew pushed her back against the boulder, forcing her to sit. She hated that she faltered when she went to stand. Her feet were even more ripped up than she'd realised.

Drew crouched before her. "No way, Cee, I promised I'd keep you safe. You're *not* going out there. You can barely walk. Like seriously, what can you possibly do to help? What's going on out there... Well, I don't even know what's going on out there, but I do know that it's next level."

"I don't know either! But I can't just sit here and do nothing! I can't just watch..." A lump filled her throat and she struggled to her feet.

"You think it's not killing me, to just sit here and watch my oldest friend in the world get his arse handed to him?" He stood and gripped her shoulders. She glared up at him, her jaw set, her eyes fierce. His shoulders slumped in defeat. He'd always known when there was no point fighting her. "Ok, Cee. You win. Here's the plan. I'll go round this way, and you go that way," he said, pointing around the perimeter of the Fort in two different directions. "The aim is to get as close to Wolfie as possible."

"And then what?"

He shrugged and forced a goofy grin. "We're both intelligent people. I'm sure we'll think of a way for one of us to distract Harper long enough for the other to get Wolfie away. Rob's round there watching, see if you can scoop him up along the way, then at least it will be three against one."

He snatched up Indigo's skateboard, took a deep breath, squared his shoulders, and made to step out. She grabbed his elbow. "Drew. Be careful."

"Don't worry about me, Cee. As the youngest of three boys, I've copped a few hidings in my time, you know I can hold my own. They may have magick, but they're flesh and blood and I'm more than capable of a bit of bodily harm. Stay out of sight, and I'll see you on the other side." And with that he slipped into the shadows and was gone.

Wincing, she began to hobble her way around the outside of the wall, clinging to the bushes, her gaze fixed on Indigo. He was still kneeling stiffly, unnatural, strange somehow, Harper's hand stretched towards him as she murmured to him. But he gave no reaction, no response. Something wasn't right.

There was an abrupt cry to her left and she pivoted just as Aurora fell to her knees in front of the Maiden, clutching her stomach. Nash cried out her name, fighting with all his might to get to her. Cordelia choked a scream, her breath hitching when she suddenly spotted Drew charging headlong into the fray, skateboard held aloft, roaring a battle cry. *No*, Drew! He whacked a couple of warlocks square in the head with the skateboard as he ran to help Aurora. *Stupid impulsive idiot!*

Chin trembling, Cordelia took a step forward so she was standing on the precipice of the bushes, of the shadows. Feet screaming in protest, she slid another step forward, and with that step was instantaneously immersed in complete pandemonium. Her senses were immediately overloaded, and she stiffened in fear.

"Stop," Cordelia whispered, reaching a hand out. There was a yell to her right, and she turned, uncomprehendingly, to see Sasha and Drew, back-to-back, four warlocks rapidly advancing on them.

"Please stop," she breathed meekly, her eyes wide with dread, as she looked from Nash to Aurora to Drew to Sasha. "I-I don't know what to do," she whispered, a lone tear escaping her eye and streaking slowly down her grimy cheek.

A sound came then, shattering the night air, so loud and terrible that everyone stopped dead in their tracks and turned towards the source. It was a screaming, primal howl of agony sickening enough to halt a battle.

She saw Artax and the Maiden smile triumphantly, because it was Indigo, writhing on the ground. Harper stood over him, her mouth twisted into a cruel grin, her hand twisted into a grotesque shape. Ice coated Cordelia's bones. It was the worst thing she'd ever seen, the worst thing she'd ever *heard*.

Sheer terror in his eyes, Nash shoved past the grinning Artax and started sprinting for Indigo, shouting his name, Aurora and Sasha right behind him. They tried to get to him, they really tried, but they were quickly swallowed by a seething mass of warlocks.

And all she could hear was Indigo screaming, and Harper laughing, and there was no one left to help him... No one but her.

Her hands were shaking, her stomach roiling, her legs leaden as she watched in horror. "No," she croaked, her lungs failing her, her voice hoarse, snatched by terror. "Stop..."

indigo

'Awww you look like you could use a break, mon cherie.'

He could hear Harper's voice in his head. All of a sudden he could breathe again, and the residual burning eased from his tired body.

He couldn't just lie there. He *had* to get up. He curled slowly into a ball, drawing his legs up so he could get his feet beneath him. His muscles immediately gave way and he tumbled to his knees. His breath was heavy, and everything was pain. His head lolled but he fought it, raising his eyes to defiantly meet hers.

"Join me. And this will all be over."

He spat blood at her feet, glaring at her with a hatred as intense as his agony.

With the flick of two fingers, her telekinetic power connected with his face, the blow smashing into his temple so his head reeled back. Again and again she struck, each punch striking his face, his body, with a force comparable to that thrown by a heavyweight boxer.

"That's your final answer?" she asked, as blood seeped and ran down his face in rivulets.

"I will *never* join you," he snarled.

"You've always been too honourable for your own good," she sneered. "The sheer stupidity of choosing *death* over joining me? Maybe I overestimated you. I guess I'll just have to cheer myself up by collecting what's yours. Let's get on with it then, shall we?"

She threw her head back and opened her arms out wide.

Indigo could see her heart chakra, a swirling, black hole, growing wider and wider, opening up like an abyss, bioplasmic streams beginning to unfurl from within like great writhing snakes. He knew eventually they'd hook into his chakras, prise them open, as hard as he'd try to pull them closed. The slight breeze that moved about them suddenly escalated, whipping up around them to blow through Harper's robes, lifting her hair and twirling dead leaves across the gravel.

He couldn't resist anymore.

After everything, it was all going to end right here, like this.

His heart was heavy with the devastating realisation he was going to leave this earth when he had so much yet to do, right when Cordelia was finally his again. A couple of years ago he'd wanted so much to die, had tried to die and failed. It seemed almost wasteful that now, after he'd worked so hard to not want to die anymore, it was actually going to happen.

Death didn't scare him, but letting go did. Letting go of this life he'd grown to love, of those he loved in the here and now as they were in this lifetime.

"It feels so good righting the wrongs of the world!" Harper cried.

As her hooks streamed closer, moving pictures danced before Indigo's eyes, scenes from his life, faces, so many faces: Robbie, Scarlett and Joshua. Matty. Drew. Luis. Edita and Lukas. Nash, Raf, Sasha, Dawn and Aurora. They gripped his heart, his soul, but just like on the bridge that night, that final face he saw was hers.

Cordelia.

Always Cordelia.

He was spent, broken, panting in agony, blood dripping from the corner of his mouth, but he managed to whisper her name one last time, the syllables dancing on his lips and bringing peace to his heart.

He could see her, and he clung to that. So beautiful, even with her face dusty and tear-stained, her white dress torn, her long, tangled hair flickering in the wind behind her. Her expression was fierce, strong, determined.

Confusion clouded his brain as he tried to decipher what was real and what was not – because he saw her coming closer and closer; she was behind Harper now. But Harper hadn't noticed her, too occupied with him. She was there, right there, he could swear it, walking barefoot and bloodied across the battlefield towards him. She was murmuring something, her lips forming the same word over and over again, the wind catching her voice and carrying it away. He felt the corners of his mouth turn up at the very sight of her. But then he shuddered, realising she truly *was* there, that she *shouldn't* be there, that she *couldn't* be there, not so close to Harper, Harper who was psychotic and heartless and remorseless and would eliminate her without a second thought if she saw her.

She was nearer now, so close he could hear her as she raised her arms out in front of her, her palms facing Harper, facing him, he could hear her as she fell to her knees and closed her eyes tight and screamed it, the word he realised she'd been saying over and over on her approach:

"STOPPPPPPPPPPP!"

And as she screamed it, commanded it, demanded it, everything did. It all stopped. And then, blackness.

chapter twenty-five

(everything i do) i do it for you

five minutes ago...

cordelia

"Stop," Cordelia murmured again, cheeks damp as she moved toward Indigo flailing on the ground. It felt as though she were floating in a dream.

Harper opened her hand with a flourish and Indigo slowly, shakily pushed himself to his knees. His eyes were half closed and there was blood trickling from the corner of his mouth, but he was still trying to stand to face Harper. But Harper struck again, sending his head reeling with a mere flick of her fingers, over and over until he was bloody and swollen.

"S-stop," Cordelia whimpered again, voice shaking, limping closer still, her sights set purely on him.

When Harper reached her arms out and threw her head back, Cordelia knew what was about to happen.

"No, please no," she breathed, her heart pounding in her chest, her blood rushing in her ears.

And just like that, anger rose to challenge her fear, fury swirling with terror, an oscillation of emotion twisting through her like a tornado. *Enough* was *enough*. She'd sat back and watched while Harper and her warlocks attacked Indigo's friends. They'd ambushed her, *taken* her –

twice. They wanted Indigo. And they'd used her, used his love for her, to get to him.

As Harper arched her back, Indigo began to sway on his knees. Cordelia saw the toxic hooks unfurling from Harper's chest, and she knew they'd suck out all his power, energy, *life.* And then Harper would finish him off. He was going to die.

Cordelia couldn't take anymore. And then something came over her, something inherent, something instinctual, something born from her very soul. All that anger and fear and hopelessness ignited a flame inside of her, unleashing something deep from within.

Stillness descended, a silence that was almost deafening and everything faded away except for Harper and Indigo, they were all she could see, all she could hear, all she could *feel.*

"Stop," she whispered with vehemence.

Narrowing her eyes, she pulled herself tall and started moving with purpose, still walking, but walking tall and strong and powerful, her shredded feet, her pain, forgotten. "Stop," she murmured, her eyes hardening, rage rising up inside of her. "Stop … Stop …. *Stop.*"

Indigo saw her then, and he whispered her name, a delirious smile tugging at the corners of his mouth. She had no idea what she was going to do when she got there, all she knew was that it was all too much, and it needed to stop, *right now.* She couldn't do nothing. She couldn't lose him now, not when they'd finally found each other again.

A world without him in it was unfathomable.

Harper's hooks landed, hitting him hard. And as Cordelia moved toward him, the life leaving his body as fast as she could move, all she knew at that moment was that she couldn't live without him. She just couldn't.

Right before her eyes, the light was rapidly fading from his. She was laser-focused. She had to stop it. She would save him or die trying. It had to stop, it had to stop, all she knew was that it all just had to–

"*STOPPPPPPPP!*"

She screamed it, roared it, falling to her knees behind Harper, holding her arms out in front of her and squeezing her eyes shut as she awaited the retaliation that she knew would be swiftly coming.

Only it didn't.

The dead silence remained; all she could hear was her own breath, rapid and ragged.

But nothing else.

Just… nothing.

the sound of silence

cordelia

Cordelia slowly opened her eyes, gasping, falling back onto her hands in confusion as she surveyed the scene before her.

It was like she'd stepped into a photograph, a moment caught in time.

Harper was standing over Cordelia, her mouth open in a silent scream of fury, her hand drawn back as though ready to strike.

But it was a strike that never came.

Indigo was on his knees, his eyes locked on her, but vacant and blank, so unlike she'd ever seen them. Both were frozen in time. Like the wax dummies she'd seen at Madame Tussaud's in London. She glanced around her. Everyone else was frozen, too. All was deathly silent and still. Even the wind had vanished. She climbed shakily to her feet, her body a jumble of jittering nerves, her heart hammering, and looked listlessly around her. It was like standing in the middle of a graveyard.

Fear gripping her gut, she stepped towards Indigo and reached her hand out to him, slowly, tentatively, timidly. With a gasp of relief, she felt he was warm to the touch.

She turned and wandered, bewildered, through the ghostly landscape, past Sasha stuck in mid-air halfway through a jump kick, past Nash firing a bio-blast at Artax, past a scowling, determined Drew who'd just brought the skateboard down on the head of the Maiden, who was attacking Aurora.

Everyone was *frozen*. Almost as if… when she'd screamed for everything to stop, it… *had*?

Had she done this?

She'd wanted it all to stop, wanted more than anything for Indigo's friends to be safe, for the warlocks to back off, for Indigo not to be dying. *Indigo.* She wound her way back to him. Harper's hooks protruded from his chest like thick black snakes, but they, too, were frozen. She shook his arm. "Wake up, Inds," she pleaded, shaking harder, grabbing him by the shoulders and rattling him. He remained unchanged.

"*Please*, Indigo. I need you." She fell to her knees, drawing his hands to her chest, but they were heavy, a dead weight. They slipped through her fingers, settling back at his sides. "If you can hear me, please wake up."

Nothing.

She sat down heavily, knees to chest, head in hands. The other day Indigo had tried to tell her she had higher senses, that she was telepathic. But this… this was more than that. She hadn't listened, hadn't wanted to hear it, and now look what she'd done!

Because she *had* done this to them, to everyone, to *him*, she knew it. But she didn't know how or how to *undo* it. She tried to replay it in her head, but it had all been so chaotic, so confusing…

She remembered how badly she'd wanted it all to stop. Wanted it with all her heart and soul, her very being. She remembered raising her hands and yelling for it all to stop. She jumped to her feet and went and stood in front of Indigo again, absentmindedly twisting her ring around her finger as she gazed down at him. Rubbing her hands together like she'd seen him do, she whispered to the heavens above to help her make this work.

But her hands were shaking so violently, her breath so erratic she was dizzy. Eyes narrowed with the effort of her concentration, she calmed herself, breathing in and out, slowly, deeply like she did in yoga. Operating more by her gut than anything else, she drew herself tall and exhaled steadily. She closed her eyes and repeated to herself over and over '*Wake up, Inds, please wake up, please wake up, please wake up…*'. Everything else disappeared until it was just her and that thought, razor sharp in her head. She forced it from her head down into her hands, which she raised and threw towards Indigo, wishing, hoping, praying with everything she had for it to work.

Indigo wavered on his knees and fell forward, face down in the grass.

"Indigo!" she cried, rushing to his side, turning him over and bending close. She glanced over her shoulder to Harper and the others. No movement. She turned her attention back to Indigo.

His eyes were closed, and his face was black and blue and ghostly white.

"Inds," she whispered, stroking his face and grasping his limp hands. "Can you hear me?" She kissed his forehead, his bruised cheeks, and then his cut lips, pressing hers to his in the wild hope that she could 'Sleeping Beauty' him awake.

She felt his lips move ever so slightly beneath hers and she pulled back to see his eyes were open, the left one almost swollen shut but open just enough, and gazing up at her.

"Cordelia," he whispered, reaching up to touch her cheek. Relief surged through her veins to see him restored and she threw herself upon him, kissing him deeply. "What the hell happened?" he asked when they broke apart. Wincing, he raised his hand to his face, grimacing as he cautiously assessed the damage.

It all seemed to flood back to him with a jolt because he sat up quickly, flinching and hunching to clutch his ribs. He looked around slowly, taking in the frozen scene surrounding them. Even the trees and wind remained still, the leaves and debris halted in suspended animation.

"What the..." he murmured, his gaze coming back to rest on her. "What is this?"

"I don't know. I-I just wanted it to stop, and then... it did."

"*You* did this?" he asked, wide-eyed, clasping her hand in his. "Holy shit, Cora! I know I said I suspected you had higher senses, but... I mean... I never dreamed... Nothing like *this*!" He was staring at her with something akin to pride. "How?"

"I honestly have no idea," she admitted, and that made him frown.

He gave her hand a squeeze, then clambered slowly to his feet, grimacing with the effort. He glanced down at the bioplasmic hooks still attached to his chest. His jaw tightened as he reached for them, one after the other, reversing their flow then tearing them out.

He limped over to Harper, circling her. He tentatively reached out and poked her. He turned back to Cordelia. "Was I like this?"

She nodded.

"She's a fucking psychopath," he muttered, glowering at Harper. He then pinned that glower on Cordelia. "She could have *killed* you, Cora! I *told* you to leave. Why didn't you listen to me? I don't know *what* you were thinking."

She glared back at him, hands clenched. "Maybe I was thinking I didn't want you to *die*, Indigo? Maybe I was willing to risk *everything* to prevent that? When I say I would die for you, I'm not fucking around!"

He closed his eyes and exhaled steadily. When he opened them, she could see in those gold-flecked hazel depths that she was forgiven. "I *love* you, Cora," he whispered, throat bobbing. "More than anything."

"I love you, too," she said, softening. She glanced around. "What are we going to do about the others?"

He staggered over to his mates. "Man, I wish I had a camera. Check Sasha out!"

"Indigo." He didn't seem to hear her, as he moved around his friends, poking Sasha in the ribs, lightly slapping Nash's cheek, waving a hand in front of Aurora's face. He gaped at skateboard-wielding-Drew, then chuckled quietly to himself, shaking his head affectionately.

"Indigo!" she called, louder this time.

"Yeah?" he glanced over his shoulder at her.

"We can't leave them this way."

"Of course not," he replied distractedly as he hobbled over to one of the buildings, his arm held protectively across his ribs. He yanked at a wooden door and leant to drag something out from inside, dropping to his knees beside it with the greatest of efforts.

"Inds!" Cordelia said impatiently. But she suddenly spotted what he was so intently focused on: her brother lying in there small and limp, eyes closed. She rushed over. "What happened? Oh my God, is he ok?"

"It's ok, it's ok," he reassured her, reaching for her hand. "Not only is he frozen like everyone else around here, but there was a bit of an incident with a couple of warlocks. Don't worry though, I'll have him back to his old self in no time." He began checking Robbie's pulse and temperature.

She felt like she was going to be sick. "The warlocks got him?" she asked, kneeling down to touch her brother's face.

"Yes, but he'll be fine, I promise." Indigo quickly filled her in on what had happened then went back to examining Robbie.

"Indigo?" She stood up and walked back out onto the grounds of the fort, surveying her handiwork. "Indigo?" she repeated when he didn't answer.

"Geez, babe, I hear you, I'm coming." He grinned as he climbed stiffly to his feet. The force of his smile reopened the wound on his lip and blood begin to trickle from the corner of his mouth. "Who knew my girl was such a badass? This is incredible, Cora. *You're* incredible."

"Yeah, easy for you to say. You don't have to figure out how to *un*freeze them all," she said, reaching up to gently wipe the blood from his chin with her thumb. "So, Harper Valentine, hey?"

"Mmm." He averted his gaze.

"You *knew*?" she whispered, staring at him incredulously.

He nodded slowly. "But only since that night on the beach, when they attacked you."

Her hands flew to her hips. "*Seriously*, Inds? You didn't think that might have been information worth mentioning?"

"It took a while for me to get my head around it, and I didn't want to frighten you. Then you went to Queensland. And then… Josh."

She pressed her lips together and closed her eyes for a beat or two. "Please don't keep stuff like that from me again. You don't get to decide what I do and don't know."

"I'm sorry, beautiful." He took her in his arms, his lips caressing her forehead so warmth spread down her temples, down her cheeks, down to her lips which quickly found their way to his. He kissed her, slow and lingering, protesting when she suddenly pulled away.

She cupped his cheek. "We need to focus on undoing all of this," she said, surveying the scene.

He nodded reluctantly. "Well, how did you bring *me* back? Actually, go back to the beginning. Tell me how you did this in the first place?"

"I dunno. It was like…" She stopped then and furrowed her brow. "The only other time I've felt like that, was at Rob's and my thirteenth birthday party, with Harper."

"With *Harper*? What are you talking about?"

"It was after Robbie first got on stage with that stupid karaoke machine. Harper and her friends were standing behind me being judgy bitches, and I… I just got so *angry*, and I wanted her to shut up, and I wanted to wipe that smug look off her face, and Peyton said something about her nose job, and I remember wishing something bad would happen to her nose… Then like tonight, everything just went still and quiet. And I was just completely focused on her, like so completely intensely, and I swear I could hear every nasty thought in her head. The next thing I knew, her nose was bleeding."

"I remember that. She came to me hysterical because she thought she might have to get her nose re-done." He raised an eyebrow. "*You* did that to her?"

"I… I didn't know it at the time. But now, after tonight… I think so, yes."

He gave a half laugh. "Nothing she didn't deserve."

"And tonight was the same, with the stillness and the silence, and me, wanting it all to stop like I've never wanted anything." She was speaking so fast, rambling, and she had a feeling she'd ceased blinking some time ago. She continued to explain to him exactly what had happened, in great detail.

"Afterwards, I was so scared, Inds… All I wanted was for you to wake up, and I held that thought in my mind, and I let that thought, like, flow down into my hands and then, this sounds weird, but it's like I… I *threw* it at you."

"You *threw* the thought at me?" he mused, rubbing his chin.

She shrugged. "That's the only way I know how to explain it."

He grinned, the wound on his lip opening up again. "So, you just do that five more times," he said, his tongue moving to the cut. He wiped his mouth with the back of his hand.

"What about Harper and the others? We can't just leave them here like this. Imagine the fallout when they're found?"

"You may have a point." He screwed his nose up as he looked from Harper to her warlocks. "Let's just focus on unfreezing Rob, Nash,

Rory, Sash, and Drew and then we can figure out a way to deal with the coven." He knelt slowly back down beside Robbie. He was putting on a brave face, but she could see him wincing with every jolt.

"Are you sure you're ok?" She knelt in front of him and peered up into his face. She frowned. He looked terrible. She reached out tentatively to touch his swollen eye. He grimaced and pulled away, holding his forearm protectively over his chest.

She gently moved his arm aside and slowly, slowly, lifted his T-shirt. He had a faint scar on his lower left side she'd never seen before. She bent to inspect it, touching it ever-so-softly. She glanced up to gauge his reaction, because the last thing in the world she wanted was to add to his pain. An expression of calm smoothed his face. She ran her fingertips lightly over his chiselled pecs, his ribs, the peaks and valleys of his abdominals, all mottled black and blue and plum. He inhaled sharply and she snatched away her hands.

"Did I hurt you?"

"No," he whispered, eyes closed, breath shallow.

"What then?"

"The opposite. You, touching me like that, it feels... good. Unbelievably... good."

Reaching towards him again, she tenderly traced the line of his ribs. She bent closer, pressing her mouth to his warm body, her lips caressing the worst of his bruises, kissing them better, wishing she could take his pain away, that she could heal him the way he could heal her.

He groaned deeply. "You're playing with fire there."

"Look what she's done to you." He was a mess.

"I'm tough, remember? I'll be fine," he murmured, his voice catching, his fingers moving through her hair.

She pressed her lips tight as tears filled her eyes.

He looked down at her. "But *you're* not, are you?"

The tears spilt over, hot and searing. "Hey, hey, hey, beautiful, come here," he whispered. He drew her to him, gently gently, his arms around her waist, pressing himself to her as much as his battered body would allow. He touched his forehead to hers. "It's ok, it's ok."

He was so warm – he was always warm – and she felt so safe in his arms. His lips were on her cheeks, her eyelids and then on her mouth.

He tasted of her tears, of his blood. She kissed him back, kissed him with all the relief and all the gratitude and with the realisation she'd be thankful for him every minute of every day of her life, knowing she'd never ever take him for granted.

"She was going to kill you," she said between kisses.

"But she didn't. Thanks to you." He pulled back to look at her with those extraordinary eyes of his, his hands cupping the sides of her face. "You *saved* me, Cordelia. You saved my life." He smiled at her so proudly, pressed his lips to her forehead. "All this time I thought I was meant to come back here and save you, but in the end it was you who saved me. In every way."

"When I thought you were going to die," she whispered, "that I might lose you forever…" Her hands were trembling and he took them in his and held them steady. The moment she'd realised it was him she'd die to defend, was the moment she'd realised they were irrevocably connected in a way she never could be with anyone else. She swallowed hard over the lump in her throat. "I don't know what I'd do if anything happened to you."

"You, Cordelia, are so strong and so brave. You can survive anything."

She looked at the ground and shook her head slowly. She couldn't live without him, not now, and that scared her senseless.

"You just stopped the most notorious coven of warlocks in the world right now. Single-handedly!" he said with a chuckle. "There's nothing you can't do."

"What does it mean? What I did… What I can do? What *am* I, Indigo?"

"I don't know exactly. But one thing I do know, is that you're in good company." He looked to his friends. "We can sit down and figure this all out when it's over. But it's not over yet. You need to bring the others back. I'll be with you every step of the way." She went to turn away but he reeled her back around. "But first…" He raised his hand to the oozing welt on the side of her head where Artax had punched her. She felt a warm glow and then the pain was gone. He shifted his attention to the deep cuts on her feet and legs, and when she looked down all that was left were a few smears of blood. She smiled gratefully at him and brushed her lips to his.

She knelt down beside Robbie and smoothed the hair from his forehead. "He's kind of nice when he's peaceful like this," she said, smiling fondly at her brother. "He was really brave tonight, Inds."

"Of course he was. There's nothing Robbie wouldn't do to keep you safe." She shot him a glance and he added, "When he's sober. Now you need to bring him back. Although... Just give me a minute first." He cradled Robbie's head on his lap as light began to swirl from his palms, a gilded emerald, flowing like liquid gold to completely encase her brother. After a few minutes, Indigo shook his head, then gently disentangled himself from Robbie before limping purposefully away.

"I need to find the warlocks who attacked him," he muttered, walking through purple-cloaked bodies until he reached two apart from the rest. He turned to Cordelia. "This one!" he called, and nearby he pointed to another, "And this one!"

He stood between the two warlocks, arms crossed, staring back and forth from one to the other.

Cordelia placed her hand briefly in the centre of Robbie's chest, then went to join Indigo. "Whatcha doing?" She rested her head on his shoulder, running her fingers under his shirt to stroke the small of his back. Now she was allowed to touch him whenever she wanted, she couldn't *not* touch him. He pulled her close and kissed the top of her head, his eyes never leaving the warlocks.

"This one attacked Rob. I don't know if you can see it, but if you look at his biofield – " he traced the outline with his finger "– it's different, just here." He indicated an area above the warlock's head.

"I can't see what you see. What's different?"

"Well because it's frozen like the rest of him, I can see the top layer of his biofield is made of energy that's not his. It's Robbie's. I can tell from the consistency and colour. It's like a layer of oil sitting on water."

"But how do you get it back? Can you separate it?"

He grinned down at her. "Dunno. How about I have a play and hope for the best? Not like he's going anywhere." He kissed her palm, his lips lingering, before he stepped towards the warlock.

Cordelia watched him for a while, poking and prodding and moving his hands this way and that, sighing in frustration every now and then. She pulled a face and took a step back when he started having a conversation with someone she couldn't see.

"Uh, Inds?"

"Mmm?' he said, turning to regard her distractedly.

"Who you talking to?"

"Sarita. And Robbie's guardian."

"Who's Robbie's guardian?"

"I don't know his name," Indigo said, glancing over his shoulder. "But let's just say Rob would approve: he's tall, dark and angelic, with a killer smile."

She opened her mouth to ask another question, but could see he wanted to get back to it, so she returned to Robbie. She lay down beside him and stared at the full moon up there in that black sheet of sky sequined by endless stars.

She didn't realise she'd dozed off, her arms wrapped around Robbie, her head on his chest, until she felt soft fingers in her hair, heard her name being whispered. She opened her eyes and gasped when she saw Indigo's face, black and blue, crusted with blood, one eye swollen shut. She sat up with a start. "Holy shit, your face!" she cried, gently feeling for that incredible bone structure she knew was under there somewhere.

"Judging by your expression, I'm glad there are no mirrors around here," he said, raising his fingers gingerly to his jaw. "Is it getting worse?"

She winced and nodded.

"So tell me, Cora, do you still want me? When I look this heinous?"

"I will want you always. Whether this face is bruised or scarred or bloody, or lined with years. It changes nothing." She took his face gently between her hands and laid soft kisses on his forehead, his cheeks, his lips. "On a completely unrelated topic, did you happen to keep the number for your dad's plastic surgeon?"

He laughed. "The irony is I need someone like me to fix me."

"You can't heal yourself?"

"Dunno, I've never tried. But that's not my concern right now." His eyes were shining. "I figured out how to fix Rob."

"I had no doubt you would."

"Thanks to you, actually. I drew Robbie's energy out of the warlocks' biofields into my hands, then focused on sending it back to him. Look how you inspire me." He kissed her cheek and nodded at Robbie. "Your turn now. Close your eyes, and take a deep breath in, hold it, hold it, now release. That's the way. Now twice more," he said, and she did as instructed. She began to feel calmer.

Her eyes still closed, she focused on Robbie, her hands held out before her, palms up, her fingers slightly curled. With '*wake up, wake up, wake up…*' running on repeat in her head, she moved the thought down her arms and into her hands. She then flicked her hands towards Robbie.

Robbie gasped, his back arching, his arms stiff by his sides. His eyes sprung open, wild and searching. Cordelia threw herself at him, hugging him tight.

"What happened?" he muttered, eyes glazed. "Is it all over?" He saw Indigo and gasped. "Christ, Inds, did you go twelve rounds in the ring with Mike Tyson? It's a sad state of affairs when I'm the better looking one."

He slowly sat up, taking in his surroundings. He tilted his head to one side, narrowing his eyes. "Hang on. Did you chuck me in a *cupboard?*"

Indigo laughed. "It was for your own good, mate."

"What if I'd *died*, Indigo?" he gasped, clasping his chest. "Imagine the irony of me going to all the trouble of coming out of the closet, only for my body to be found concealed in that dreadful dark and dingy little thing!"

"You weren't going to *die*." Indigo rolled his eyes in exasperation.

"So what happened? Did we win? Where is everyone?"

Indigo and Cordelia quickly brought him up to speed.

"So wait," Robbie said, staring at Cordelia. "Now you've got magical superpowers, too?"

Cordelia shrugged nonchalantly.

"So I'm officially the dud twin then? You got the brains and the beauty and now you get the magical superpowers, too? Am I just made of all the junk left lying around Mum's uterus after you were created?" But he was grinning as he hugged her to him.

"Unfreeze the others," he said as Indigo pulled him to his feet. Indigo helped Cordelia up, wrapping his arm around her shoulders, his lips moving over the top of her head. "I need to see this for myself–" Robbie stopped dead when he turned and saw them.

"Waaaait," he whispered in slow awe, eyes like saucers as he pointed from Indigo to Cordelia. "What's happeninggg? I mean, I had my suspicions earlier tonight, obviously, but are you guys... I mean, is this *finally* happening?"

Indigo and Cordelia exchanged shy smiles then nodded.

"*Oh my fucking God!*" Robbie cried, bounding forward and throwing his arms around them.

"Ow!" Indigo complained, grasping his ribs.

Robbie was grinning from ear to ear. "I'm *so* happy!" But then his expression fell. "Hang on. What about Drew?"

"We broke up yesterday." Or was it the day before? What time was it?

"*What?*" he cried, hands on hips. "And you neglected to tell *me*, your confidante, your *womb*-mate, your better *half*?" He was starting to get really high-pitched.

Indigo quickly intervened. "Let's park it for now, Rob? Cora needs to get on with this."

She nodded and started towards his frozen friends.

"Do Sasha last," Indigo said, admiring Sasha levitating in the air, his leg stuck straight out before him mid-jump kick. "The others have to see how freakin' awesome he looks!" He laughed.

Cordelia shook her head. "You're such a juvenile," she admonished with an affectionate roll of her eyes.

"Forever young, beautiful," he replied. "Forever young."

"Frozen-jump-kick-Sash will forever be superior to all other Sashas," Nash declared, walking slowly through the frozen purple statues, stopping occasionally to nudge one with his toe or poke another in the chest.

"I wouldn't know, ya," Sasha grumbled. "I'm the only one who didn't get to see."

"Hold still," Indigo chastised, hovering a glowing hand over two of Sasha's fingers, each black and blue and bent at different angles. A moment later he'd mended the broken bones and Sasha's fingers were good as new.

Cordelia could feel the weight of eyes on her, and turned to realise the full brunt of Aurora's suspicious gaze. "*You* did all this?" Aurora asked incredulously, regarding the frozen warlocks. Cordelia shrugged nonchalantly, then flicked her a shy smile, unsure how to behave around this intimidating supermodel-superhero hybrid.

"So... what now?" Nash asked, slinging an arm around Aurora's shoulders. She allowed him the grace of all of five seconds before shrugging him off and striding over to frozen Harper.

"She's the one we need to worry about," she commented.

"We need to neutralise them as best we can," Indigo said, thumbing his lip. "They've stolen higher senses from a lot of powerful witches. Plus, there are a lot of people out there they've drained who need their energy back in order to heal."

"And how exactly do we do that?" Robbie yawned.

"Probably similar to the way I fixed you up," Indigo mused. "I assume if I separate the stolen energy from their biofields it will return to its rightful owners. Although it's a bit harder when I don't know who the owners are." He beckoned Nash over and held his hand to Nash's face. Light flared from his palm, and Nash's black eye and split lip mended.

Aurora scoffed loudly. "You do realise that this is what I do right? That I can move energy from any*one* to any*where*?" She turned to Nash. "Blaze? You've been to see all the victims, yeah?"

"Right you are."

"So he can show me where it needs to go," she said to Indigo. "You separate it, Nash gives me the picture of its owner and I move it out."

Indigo nodded. "That's definitely the quicker way to do it." He looked Aurora up and down then quickly repaired a deep gash in her leg, then carefully lifted her shirt to heal the nasty looking haematoma on her stomach.

"So you guys are *witches*?" Drew breathed, looking at each of them in turn. "Like *real* honest-to-God *witches*?"

"We don't like that term," Nash informed him irritably.

"Sorry, my bad. But… you kind of *are*, right?"

Nash sighed. "*Technically*, we're a subset of the broader witch group. We're Akasha. We have highly-evolved higher senses."

Drew swung around to look at Sasha. "You can bilocate."

Sasha grinned and nodded, "I can, ya."

"What's that like?"

"Listen," Nash interrupted, "the sun's going to be coming up soon, so whatever Indi's gonna do to these warlocks, he needs to do it faster."

"And by warlocks," Drew said, looking around at the robe-clad figures, "you mean them. And they have powers too?"

"*Mate!*" Nash said in exasperation.

"We can talk later, Pres," Indigo said.

"Yeah," Drew said. "Because I got a lotta questions for you about this double life of yours, Wolfie." He wandered over to sit on the sandstone wall.

Sasha smiled at Indigo. "I'll go fill him in. It's the least I can do after he jumped in blind tonight, eh." He went and joined Drew on the wall.

"Clock's ticking, Indi," Nash said. "If we don't do something soon, we're going to have the crack-of-dawn joggers and cyclists to deal with."

"I promised Essie I'd help her," he murmured, standing in front of the Maiden, who'd been on the receiving end of Drew's skateboard when Cordelia had frozen her. Her mouth was twisted in fury, the large rock she'd been telekinetically hurling hovering mid-air before her outstretched hand. Indigo plucked the rock from suspended animation and casually tossed it over his shoulder. He tilted his head to examine her, his expression pensive.

"So the people they attacked, they were all witches?" Cordelia asked softly.

"Mostly," Indigo said. "Although not all were aware of their true power."

"But the ones who were? Are they in hospital, too?"

"Doubtful," Aurora said. "I think Harper only got greedy recently. Up until then, they've just been collecting higher senses, not decimating their victims' energy and leaving them comatose."

"The witches they stole from, where are they now?"

"Laying low I'd say," Aurora said, flicking her ponytail over her shoulder. "Hiding out from Harper. I would imagine they'd feel pretty vulnerable without their powers."

"So if they weren't amongst the victims in the hospital, how is it possible for Nash to find them?" Cordelia asked. "To return their powers?"

"Seriously?" Aurora sneered, shooting Cordelia a dirty look.

"N-no," Cordelia stammered, holding up her hands. "I didn't mean to imply that he couldn't...". Aurora was scary, and by appearing to question Nash's ability, Cordelia was now firmly on her bad side.

"I have my ways, doll," Nash grinned, winking and tapping the centre of his forehead.

Indigo was sweeping his hands quickly around the Maiden, not touching her body.

"What the hell are you doing?" Robbie asked, rubbing his bleary eyes.

"Separating the Maiden's energy from that she's collected. Anything that's not hers, I've moved to one side for Rory to deal with."

Indigo worked fast, moving onto the next, then the next, then the next. Aurora and Nash followed quickly behind him. Cordelia watched in fascination as Aurora paused briefly beside each warlock and placed her hands on Nash's forearms, closing her eyes for a moment or two. She'd then nod decisively, flick her finger, then they'd move onto the next warlock.

Occasionally they'd switch things up, and Nash would put his hand on the warlock's head, a look of intense concentration on his face. He'd then nod to Aurora and she'd grab hold of his forearms and continue the process from there.

"What about the demonic she-bitch?" Robbie asked, glancing over at Harper, his lip curling.

Indigo sighed heavily. "I don't know. I have massive reservations about reanimating her, but we're running out of time and options. We're just going to have to return what she stole and leave it at that for now. At least that will remove a lot of her power."

Robbie cleared his throat. "Umm, so to play devil's advocate, may I be the one to raise something no one else has? Why not take her out... permanently?"

Indigo's head snapped up as he stared at Robbie in shock. "Because I'm a healer, Rob," he said softly. "I don't get to decide who lives or dies, nor would I want to."

"But she tried to kill you," Robbie said, eyebrows arched.

"He makes a valid point," Aurora agreed flatly.

"I'm not a killer," Indigo said adamantly, frowning at them both. "That would make me no better than Harper and her coven. And we *are* better than them."

"Speak for yourself," Aurora muttered under her breath, exchanging a look with Nash.

Robbie shrugged, still glaring at Harper. "Well you're definitely a better bloke than me, Inds, but I guess you always have been. She's hurt a lot of people, nearly killed you and my *sister.* Have you considered that by letting her go, you're allowing her to harm more people?"

Indigo shook his head again. "This isn't up for discussion. We don't kill people."

"Fine," Robbie huffed. "Can we at least shave her head and burn her eyebrows off?"

"Robbie!" Indigo and Cordelia said at the same time.

He held his hands up, miming zipping his mouth, although he swapped a smirk with Nash.

Indigo moved closer to Harper, studying her intently. "Her energy field is massive."

"I've never seen anything like it," Nash said, hands on hips as he craned his neck up to take in her whole biofield. "She's collected from a lot of witches over the years. No wonder she's practically unstoppable." He grinned at Cordelia. "Thankfully, we had our secret weapon here."

"Yeah," Indigo agreed. "So secret, not even we knew we had her."

He began to sweep his hands around Harper; he spent a lot longer on her than he had on her coven. When he was done, Nash and Aurora moved in. It took them ages.

"My God," Nash groaned. "There are so many! She certainly kept the lion's share for herself. I wonder if her coven knows she cherry-picked their victims? This is gonna take forever."

"Less whining, more pre-cogging," Aurora said.

"So you guys are just winging it here then?" Robbie asked. "You've never done this before right?"

"Nope." Indigo shrugged.

Robbie grabbed Indigo's chin in his fingers and moved it back and forth, his eyes clouding with concern. "Urgh, your face looks horrific, Inds. It's criminal what she's done to you, it's the equivalent of someone defacing Michelangelo's David."

Indigo pulled gently from his grip. "It's no big deal."

"I mean," Robbie continued, "you kinda look like Sloth from *The Goonies.*" A smile teased the corners of his mouth and he bit down to stop it spreading.

Nash burst out laughing behind them. "He's not wrong!" he cackled.

Robbie looked at Nash and cracked up, the two of them laughing wildly as if releasing all the pent up adrenaline accumulated these past few hours. "Right?" Robbie panted, doubling over. "*Right?*" He wiped his eyes, trying to catch his breath.

Indigo grinned, flipping them off.

"He does not look like Sloth!" Cordelia cried, slapping Robbie's shoulder.

"Yeah you're right," Nash shot back. "Sloth's better looking."

She wrapped her arms around Indigo, shooting the boys the evil eye. Arseholes! Sure, they were funny arseholes, but they were arseholes all the same. She gazed up at Indigo's poor, beaten-up face. "You're still gorgeous," she said, stroking his cheek and smiling. Because he was.

"She's lying." Robbie chuckled.

"I'm not. Leave him alone."

"Yeah," Indigo smirked. "Leave me alone or I'll sic my girl on you. If she can take down a whole coven without even trying, she can totally kick both your puny arses."

"True dat," Nash nodded, nudging Indigo affectionately on his way back to Aurora, who was tapping her foot impatiently, hands on hips.

When Nash and Aurora finally finished with Harper, Indigo said, "What do we do with her now?"

Nash closed his eyes, concentrating hard. "Good news, lads and ladies, now her hideous henchman isn't shrouding her, I can see everything. She's going to be pretty powerless when she comes to." He opened his eyes and grimaced. "And pretty bloody furious. Her coven will be relieved we've stripped her of her collection. I suspect she'd incinerate them otherwise.

"Hang on, hang on, there's another vision pressing in over the top..." He held his finger up, eyes snapping shut again. "We've got about fifteen minutes to move our arses before we're met with a bunch of nosy cyclists who are, at the minute, heading our way."

"Ok then," Indigo said, clapping his hands together. "We'd better get going."

Drew and Sasha climbed down from the wall and came to inspect their progress. Sasha walked over to Robbie and Drew beelined for Indigo.

"Hey, Wolfie," Drew said, brow furrowed, "how come I can't see... the things I could see last night anymore?"

"Whaddaya mean?" Indigo asked, cocking his head to one side.

Cordelia took a step towards them, frowning as she watched the exchange from a distance.

"Last night, I could see what was coming out of your hands, I could see the... the energy moving through the air like lightning. But I've been sitting here watching you now, and as far as I'm concerned you could be a street mime. I can't see it anymore. Any of it."

"You were high last night," Indigo murmured, more to himself than to Drew.

"Huh?"

"You were high last night," he repeated louder. "It was the drugs. Sometimes they can open up your mind, prising open the gates of order and reason so you see things you wouldn't otherwise."

Drew grinned then. "Cool! So they're not all bad then." He reached into his pocket and pulled out a little baggie filled with white powder.

Quick as a flash Indigo reached out and snatched it, tearing it open and tipping it onto the ground.

"Hey!" Drew protested, staring down, crestfallen.

"It's not something you wanna fuck around with, mate. You open too many gates in your mind at once, you end up with psychosis or schizophrenia or something." Indigo ground the powder into the dirt with the toe of his biker boot.

"Gates?" Drew asked. "What the hell are gates?"

"The way I've seen it, the human mind is compartmentalised and we only have access to certain parts of it at certain times, if at all. Some of these compartments are conscious and others are subconscious, but either way, each compartment is secured with a gate. People like me and Sasha and Rory and Nash, we have more gates open, which is partly why we have higher intuition than most, as well as psychic abilities, but we've had to learn to live with that as it's definitely not easy. For most people, having the gates closed is how they stay sane."

"How so?"

"Well, I recently treated someone diagnosed as schizophrenic, and they had a lot of their subconscious gates open and were therefore accessing previous lives simultaneously to this one, seeing them and living them in the now, not knowing what's now and what's then."

"Whoa, that's trippy," Drew breathed.

"And if you've ever seen a bipolar person have a psychotic episode, you'll know they can become incredibly strong and psychic and dangerous even. This usually happens because their anxiety rises to such an intense level that it opens all the gates in their mind and they lose complete control. That's why I need you need to quit this shit, because taking too many drugs, it can fuck with the gates in your mind, it can wedge them open, sometimes irreparably. It's just not worth it because it can literally drive you insane." Indigo exhaled sharply and shook his head, glancing thoughtfully over his shoulder to where Harper still stood frozen. "Look, I gotta get back to the others, but you and I need to have a proper chat when this is all over. I want to take a look at that knee, too."

They stared each other down. Drew finally broke eye contact. "It's cool if I take your car, right?"

Indigo nodded. "Course it is."

"I'll drop it back later."

"No rush."

Drew kissed Cordelia on the cheek. "Who would have thought tonight would end up being one of the best nights of my life? Win some, lose some, eh?"

She pulled him into a hug, resting her cheek on his chest. "I truly am sorry, Drew," she murmured, hating that she'd hurt him. He'd always mean something to her.

"Far be it for me to fuck with destiny, right?"

He gave her a final squeeze and shot her a wobbly grin before loping off towards Indigo's car, swinging the skateboard over his shoulder. She gazed after him fondly. He'd been so brave tonight. Stupid. But brave.

"Night all," he said with a wave of his hand. "It's been utterly surreal."

"Night," they chorused.

"Hey, Pres!" Indigo called after him. Drew stopped and turned. "Um, thanks, man. We couldn't have done it without you."

Drew grinned and threw him a thumbs up before turning and sauntering off. Cordelia noticed Aurora gazing after him with a strange look in her eye. Nash, who was staring intently from Aurora to Drew, lip curled, shook his head slightly, then grabbed her hand and led her to his bike.

Indigo put his arm around Cordelia and walked her to his motorcycle. "Ok," he told her, taking both her hands in his, "once we're far enough away, unfreeze them all."

"What if I can't do it?" she asked nervously. "There're so many of them."

He wrapped his fingers into the collar of her jacket – *his* jacket – popping it up, using it to draw her near. He bent his forehead to touch hers. "You can do it." She closed her eyes, relishing the feeling of his skin on hers. "I have complete faith in you. You blow my mind, Cora, there's nothing you can't do."

"Ahem," Robbie coughed pointedly. "We don't have all day here."

"It's fine," Indigo reassured him. "She can handle this. Just go."

Sasha cleared his throat. "Fancy a walk?" he asked Robbie, flashing him a crooked smile.

"Why not?" Robbie replied with a shy grin. "I've had a power nap, I'm fresh as a daisy, I could walk to Timbuktu and back right now." And with that, he and Sasha turned and headed out the gates of the fort, their heads bent together in conversation.

Nash revved his bike, glancing back at Indigo. "Ok?" he shouted.

Indigo nodded, starting up his bike, too. Cordelia climbed onto the back as Nash and Aurora took off, spraying rust-hued gravel in their wake. The sun would soon rise, but right now the grey before the dawn touched the deathly still landscape behind them in all its strangeness. Indigo turned to Cordelia. "You ready?"

She took a deep breath and nodded, moving her arms gently around his waist, careful not to squeeze his battered ribs too hard. As they sped under the sandstone arch that would lead them back onto the main road to Manly, Cordelia crossed her fingers, and took a deep breath, steadying herself. She said a small prayer, then focused all her energy on what she needed to happen.

With one arm still wrapped around Indigo, his hand securely on hers lending her strength, she flung her hand in the direction of the coven. They glanced back over their shoulders to see the movement of limbs as the warlocks began to awaken behind them.

"That's my girl!" He squeezed her hand affectionately before gunning the bike hard.

"Are you sure the powers they stole won't go back to them?"

"I'm, like, ninety-eight percent confident," he quipped, caressing the back of her knuckles with his.

She closed her weary eyes and leant her cheek against his shoulder, inhaling his essence deep into her lungs. All was right with the world when she was in his orbit.

Four cyclists, their middle-aged bodies stuffed in lycra, shook their heads in disapproval as the two motorbikes streaked past them down the hill, going way over the speed limit. "Slow down you hooligans!" one yelled, before turning to his mates and commenting that kids these day were reckless, disrespectful, and incapable of contributing anything of any worth to the world.

manly hospital

essie

Light flickered and danced before Essie's eyes. She squeezed her lids shut again and groaned. The brightness made it feel like her eyes might explode in their sockets.

"Essie?" a voice was saying. She felt a cool hand on her forehead, fingers brushing the inside of her wrist. "Essie? It's Dr Hamstead. Can you hear me?"

She tried to answer, but something was blocking her throat, choking her.

"Don't try to answer, Essie, you're still intubated, just squeeze my hand if you can hear me."

She felt a hand in hers then and she pumped it weakly.

"Yup, we've got another one!" she heard a female voice cry from somewhere else in the room. "She's awake, too!" Then the clatter of heels fading into the distance.

Essie tried to open her eyes again, her lids flickering rapidly against the sunlight streaming in through the window.

"What the hell is going on around here this morning?" Dr Hamstead muttered. "She's the third one today." Then louder, "I'm going to remove the tube from your throat now, Essie, this will only be uncomfortable for a minute." She felt him peeling tape from around her mouth. "Try and take a deep breath in for me if you can, Essie," and the next thing she knew she was gagging, vomiting up the endotracheal tube, her throat red raw from its longevity.

Her eyes began to focus and she gazed up at Dr Hamstead, and then to the nurse who was tenderly dabbing the edges of her mouth, his familiar, brown eyes brimming with concern. Derek. She remembered Derek, alright. She'd been smitten with him from the day he'd moved from Mississippi to Manly and taken a position at the hospital alongside of her.

"It's good to have you back, Nurse Mathews," Derek said softly, his dimples deepening as he laid a large palm on her forehead and smiled at her. "You had us really worried there for a while."

She tried to answer him, but was unable to muster more than a rasp.

"Do you know why you're here?"

She suddenly felt frightened. Eyes wide, she shook her head.

"You don't remember anything that happened, sugar?"

Another shake. Blank darkness was all that was there. And fear. A nagging, niggling fear.

"It's ok," he reassured her. His southern accent was warm as treacle, his tone so soothing she started to relax. He sat down beside her and took her hand in his, and she felt anchored, protected. "You're safe now, Essie, and you're gonna be just fine. You hear me? You're gonna be fine."

chapter twenty-seven

falling

indigo

As they rode home, Indigo relished the weight of Cordelia's chin on his shoulder, her fingers creeping beneath his T-shirt to caress his abdomen. He leant back into her. With her torn dress and her bare legs pressed against his, he could barely concentrate on the road.

They pulled up at a red light and he lowered his hand to her thigh, stroking the satiny skin so goose bumps scattered across her flesh. She pressed up to him, layering slow, lingering kisses up the plane of his cheek, her breath soft and warm. He whispered that he loved her, and she whispered back that she would die for him.

But he already knew that.

The moment they parked outside the Carlisle home, he half-turned in his seat, planted his hands on her waist, and in one smooth movement picked her up and swung her onto his lap so she was straddling him, her back to the handlebars.

"Oh," she gasped, her eyes widening in surprise to suddenly find herself nose-to-nose with him. She smiled as she wrapped her long legs around him. "Why, hello there." He gazed at her in the half-light. Her face was grimy, her hair tangled, her dress torn and dirty, and yet she was the most overwhelmingly beautiful thing he'd ever seen, sitting there in his denim jacket which he didn't know when or how she'd acquired.

What they'd been through together tonight, the strength she'd displayed, it only made her more beautiful.

He closed his eyes and pressed his forehead to hers, his breath heavy. He reached for her hands, his fingertips fluttering over hers. The electricity between them was all-encompassing, his head spinning so he couldn't think straight.

"Indigo…" she murmured breathily, and it was a plea and a promise all in one.

Heady with longing, his lips found hers then, and he was kissing her, slowly, slowly, his tongue moving against hers as he kissed her deeper, deeper.

Her lips trailed up the line of his jaw to his ear and gently over his lobe as she whispered, "Do you wanna come in?" And then her mouth was back, drawing a searing kiss from his.

"Do I wanna come in?" he growled, his lips never leaving hers. "Cordelia, I wanna come inside with you like I've never wanted anything in all my life."

Every cell of his body ached with need, ached for her.

He pulled back reluctantly, glancing towards the house. "But the sun's almost up. Which means Matty's almost up. Which means your mum's almost up. And I can't come in looking like this," he said, his hand moving to his face, battered and bloody.

She stroked his cheek, her feather-light touch moving to his brow. She frowned because clearly he looked awful. "We can sneak in?" she suggested, her ethereal eyes locked deep on his. "We don't have to see anyone." She leant in and brushed her full lips against his, her tongue sweeping into his mouth. Her arms snaked around his neck, as she pressed herself tight against him so all he could feel were the insane curves of her body straining against that thin slip of a dress. She wasn't wearing a bra, for fuck's sake. He groaned deep in his throat.

"I know for a fact your bedroom door doesn't lock, and since when has Matty ever knocked?"

"Never," she sighed, those killer lips now wandering over his throat, her hands roving under his T-shirt, touching, touching, touching. Her fingers dipped shallowly inside the waistband of his jeans and he felt like he was going to explode. He was fast coming apart at the seams under her palms.

"*Fuck,* Cora," he rasped. "You're *killing* me."

"Am I?" She blinked innocently, which did nothing to hide her knowing smile.

He bit his lip – hard – then grabbed the collar of her jacket, yanking it down to expose her shoulders. He ran his palm down the centre of her chest, and she arched into it. Gathering her closer, her hips sunk to his as he kissed her freely while the grey sky edged to a hazy pink around them. His ribs screamed in protest, but he didn't care.

The heavy slap of feet broke them from their tryst, and Indigo whipped around, suddenly on high alert. But it was just an early morning jogger pounding past. "By all means, don't let me stop you," the man said, laughing.

"A neighbour of yours?" Indigo murmured in her ear.

"I don't know," she squeaked, her face buried in his chest. "I'm too mortified to look."

"He's gone, it's safe to come out now," he chuckled as she disentangled herself from his embrace. "Bu-ut that's probably my cue to head." The sky had lightened and the kookaburras were laughing their morning song.

"Nooooo..." she objected, burying her face back in his chest. "Stay, Inds, stay forever." His sentiments exactly. He never wanted to be out of reach of her ever again. He kissed the top of her head and reached for her hands, interlacing his fingers through hers. The appearance of the jogger had put him a little on edge. Logically, he knew Harper and her coven were probably still trying to figure out what the hell had just happened and were in no state for another attack, but his amygdala was yet to catch up. He gazed down at the one person that had the ability to take his mind off anything.

"When am I gonna see you again?" she asked, tilting her face to his, his thumb caressing the back of her hand as he closed the distance between their lips once more.

"Tonight," he said between long dawdling kisses. "My place."

She skimmed the tip of her nose against his. "Promise?" Her voice was breathy.

"Cross my heart," he said, squeezing her hand then placing it over the left side of his chest. He reluctantly helped her off the bike, climbing off after her, her hand still clasped in his, drawing her into his arms, holding her tight against him. "I'll walk you to the door," he murmured into her hair, reaching beneath her jacket, his thumb gliding back and forth over the bare curve of her lower back. This time he'd make damn sure she got home safely.

"You're *such* a gentleman," she said playfully, her arms twining around his neck.

"I can tell you that's the last thing I wanna be right now," he growled, kissing her hard, thunder rising in his blood as his hand slid to the silky curve of her backside. He could feel the faint outline of what had to be the most miniscule g-string in existence, and he swore under his breath.

It was taking everything he had not to tear what was left of that dress from her beautiful body, so strong was his ragged desperation to feel all of her against all of him. His head was light with his all-encompassing need for her, all his senses overloaded with her, her, her. He'd never known it was possible for another person to have such an effect on him until now; she could bring him to his knees with a single touch.

He was fast losing control. He momentarily contemplated slipping up the side of the house with her where the bushes provided complete cover and secrecy, where he could finally give in to everything he'd ever wanted...

But that wasn't how he wanted their first time to be, her thrown up against a wall amongst the banana palms and agaves. He wanted to take his time leisurely exploring her, to enjoy every golden inch of her with complete freedom and abandon. So he shook the notion from his head and managed to compose himself enough to walk her to her door.

After another prolonged goodbye on her front porch, he finally managed to let her go. Although it was one of the hardest things he'd ever had to do, with her hands electric all over his body and her dusky-pink lips soft on his, her breath warm against his ear as she begged him over and over to come in as heat soared through his veins.

Indigo rode back home, antsy and distracted. He knew he should be tired, but he was so wired he didn't know how he'd sleep. Slipping quietly inside, he went straight up to his room, beelining for his ensuite where he turned the shower on hot and stripped off.

The scalding water stung his cuts and he winced. He examined his aching ribs. He'd never healed himself before, always relying on Dawn, but Dawn wasn't here now. Holding his hand over his torso, he concentrated really hard. He could see two ribs were cracked and he focused on knitting the bones back together.

He eventually climbed out of the shower, wiping off the mirror so he could study his face. It looked terrible, his cheeks cut and bruised, his lip split, but having washed the dried blood off was an improvement, and the swelling in his eyelid had gone down slightly. He cupped his hands over his face, holding them a few inches out and repairing the superficial gashes, moving the stagnant energy to get fresh blood to his bruises. A smile touched his lips. If he could heal himself, that was a game changer.

He turned slightly so he could see the deep scratch marks, jagged down his back. He scowled as he healed them over. Fucking Harper.

Afterwards he went into his room and found a pair of pyjama bottoms, tugging them on, then lay down in his cool, crisp sheets. He rolled onto his side and caught sight of his wolf's tooth necklace, sitting there on his bedside table. He'd forgotten to put it back on after the formal last night. He reached for it, his hand closing around its familiar outline. Exhaling heavily, he closed his eyes, just for a moment, the necklace clutched in his hand. Before he knew it, he was out.

chapter twenty-eight

one

indigo

Someone was leaning over him, their breath hot in his face.

"Indi?"

Indigo was lying on his side curled into a ball, a pillow hugged into his chest.

"Indi?" Louder this time.

Indigo groaned. As consciousness reared its head, so, too, did the pain. He was stiff and sore and everything hurt. He winced and tried to open his eyes. Only one cooperated, the other still slightly swollen.

"What?' he grunted, glaring up at Nash who was perched on the edge of his bed, happily munching on a bowl of muesli and berries topped with what smelled like coconut yoghurt.

"It's half two, man, you've slept all day," Nash said, peering at him. "Geez, you look like shit, brother! You don't think we should maybe take you to the A&E? Get you checked out?"

"No," Indigo said, turning onto his stomach and closing his eyes. "No hospital, I'll be fine. I did a quick healing last night. I'll do another one when I get up."

Nash rolled him onto his back, bending in close to examine Indigo's bare chest. "Your ribs, mate, they could be broken?" They were still quite bruised, although the large splotches covering his torso were more a greenish goldish brown than their former black. "You don't have Dawn at your disposal down here."

"They're not broken. They were cracked, but I fixed them. I don't know what Harper did to me last night, but I think it felt worse at the time than it actually was… I'm damn sore today though." He sighed heavily as he manoeuvred himself to a sitting position. Last night had been a bloody nightmare. "Have you looked in on Harper and her coven?"

"Course I have. They are *not* happy with us." Nash chuckled. "But the good news is, they don't know what hit them – literally."

Relief coursed through Indigo's body "So they don't know it was Cora who stopped them?"

Nash shook his head. "They're trying to piece it together as we speak. I reckon it will only be a matter of time though, Indi."

Indigo raked his hands over his face. "So what do we do?"

"Nothing we can do right now. They're mostly neutralised – they've all been stripped back to their original powers, which isn't exactly nothing." He pursed his lips. "Look, mate, I know when Robbie brought it up last night, you shut it down ridiculously fast, but she's as weak as she'll ever be right now. I think we need to consider– "

"No."

"The others are just followers. Without Harper to lead them, they'll disband. They probably won't even collect anymore."

"No."

"What's the plan then, brother?"

"I… I don't know." He literally had no plan. He was in way over his head with this.

"They're fucking pissed, man, and that Harper's a spiteful bitch. I reckon we need to think about keeping Cordelia close."

Indigo nodded tersely. He'd already decided that.

"Edie made you this," Nash said, offering him the half-eaten bowl of muesli. Indigo took it and dug in. He was suddenly ravenous.

"She's asking questions," Nash said. "She was about to come and wake you up so I very gallantly intervened."

"Where's everyone else?"

"Rory's gone to the beach, and Sash and Robbie are asleep by the pool."

"Rob didn't go home?" He finished eating and placed the empty bowl on his nightstand.

"Nope." Nash grinned then, a mischievous glint in his eye. He elbowed Indigo to move over and climbed onto the bed, leaning against the charcoal linen headboard then turning to look at him. "Sooo, you and Cordelia, huh?"

Indigo regarded him through narrowed eyes. "No one likes a cocky pre-cog. Did you know?"

Nash cocked an eyebrow. "Mate! Like I need my powers to see what's clear as day! You know I try not to look at my friends' futures unless I'm forced to. It tends to complicate matters." He nudged Indigo with his shoulder. "That girl was made for you, brother. She's well fit and one of the good ones. I like her, and I like her for you."

Indigo grinned. "So do I, mate, so do I."

"A vast improvement on your ex-girlfriend, that's for sure, not that that would be hard." He grimaced. "That Harper, she's a real prize. I can't believe you ever fancied her?"

Indigo shrugged. "I was fourteen and she was super-hot... and really adventurous in the sack – that was pretty much the criteria in those days. What can I say, I was about as deep as a puddle back then. It wasn't until I met Cora that I understood how much more I wanted, how much more I deserved. Besides, Harper wasn't that bad back in the day." He paused, swallowed hard. "I've been thinking, Nashie, about Harper, about how... *warped*... she's become. Like, I don't even think she's sane anymore. And something keeps coming back to me; a conversation I had with Drew, of all people, triggered it actually."

Nash made a face at the mention of Drew's name.

"I think when Harper stole all those powers, that it fucked with the gates of her mind," Indigo said, gazing intently at Nash. "Look at how drugs affect the human mind, and what is power if not a drug? It's gotta have a similar effect, right? The higher senses she stole, she was never born to handle those, to command so many. Harper was always cruel, but I never pegged her as a ruthless killer. It's like she's no longer governed by the rules of sanity."

Nash nodded thoughtfully. "So each time she stole a higher sense, another gate in her mind was wedged open, opening parts of her mind she was never going to be capable of handling." He tilted his head back, gazing at the ceiling as he mulled the idea over. "That makes a lot of sense actually. She's next-level crazy."

Nash sat, scratching his finger back and forth across the band of his wristwatch, eyes lowered. He cleared his throat. "What she did to you last night, Indi... the walloping she gave you... I-I thought you were going to die... and... and I couldn't get to you." His voice cracked and he cleared his throat again. "And I've never been so scared in all my life." He leant his head lightly on Indigo's shoulder. "What would I do without you, Indi?" he whispered.

Indigo shifted slightly to put his arm around Nash, wincing as his ribs twisted.

"Sure you're ok?" Nash lifted his head to peer from Indigo's ribs to the bruises on his face.

"It's gone down a lot," he said, touching his eye. "I'll be right." He leant his head back against the headboard and closed his eyes. "She *knew*, man. About the timeline."

Nash exhaled sharply. "I had a feeling that might have been the case."

Indigo shot him a look. "Gee, thanks for the heads up."

"Well, *we* knew. Why wouldn't they?"

Indigo frowned thoughtfully. "I still find it hard to believe, that one person could make such a difference to the world."

"Well, it's true. I was there, I heard it with my own ears. And I'll never forget that night," Nash said with a mock pout, "because that was the night you broke my heart and deserted me..."

six weeks ago...
sedona, arizona, october 1995

indigo

"It's not like you'll never see me again," Indigo said patiently, as he and Nash drove to the bar where Nash was throwing him a farewell party. It was the bar Nash and his band regularly played at and it had become their local hang. It was the bar Indigo had played at when he'd filled in for Nash's lead guitarist who'd had a motorcycle accident earlier in the year.

"Yeah, but it won't be the same though, will it?" Nash complained as he parked his Chevy on the street and they climbed out. He opened the back door and extracted his guitar case. "You're my best mate, Indi, my brother. What am I gonna do without you?" He pressed his lips together and looked away.

Indigo pulled him into a bear hug and kissed the side of his face. "I'll miss you, too, man. But I'll be back before you know it. I agreed with Dawn that I'd come every two months or so to work with her." He squeezed Nash hard, then slung his arm around him as they walked into the bar. "You of all people know why I have to go now, that I need to be there when they come for Cordelia." He paused then. "And you're *sure* I can't just warn her beforehand? Stop the whole thing happening?"

"We've been through this, Indi. If you don't let it happen, they'll only keep coming, and next time we might not know when or where. This way, we have some control."

Everyone had wanted a piece of Indigo that night, so he and Nash hadn't had a chance to talk much after that, especially since Nash was up onstage for a lot of it, performing with his band. When Nash had grabbed the microphone and announced, "Appearing by popular demand, for the last time for quite some time because he's abandoning us for greener pastures, Indigo Wolfe!" Indigo had wanted to kill him. He hadn't played with the band in months.

He'd bowed his head and tried to refuse, but Nash had started everyone chanting his name, so he'd reluctantly climbed up on that stage and perched on the stool beside Nash's. Holding the guitar Nash's bandmate Nelson had pushed into his arms, he'd performed one last time, a duet with Nash, a mash up of *Baby, I Love Your Way* and

Freebird, a tune they'd practiced for fun, mucking around in Nash's living room.

"He's going to be impossible once you're gone," Aurora told Indigo later that night, as they sat at a table with Sasha, Dawn and Raf. "I don't know how we're even going to begin to console him." Her eyes were soft as she gazed over at Nash, standing at the bar chatting up a pretty girl who was clearly a big fan, if the scrap of paper she was slipping into his pocket was anything to go by. Aurora narrowed her eyes at the girl. Nash collected phone numbers like Dawn collected crystals.

"I'll only be gone a couple of months," Indigo said, taking a sip of his mineral water.

"And you're already fully booked the two weeks you're here, honey," Dawn said, placing her hand over his.

"Who am I gonna spar with when you're not here, eh?" Sasha said, swirling the ice in his whiskey. "No one can keep me on my toes the way you can."

"Come on, guys," Indigo groaned. "This is hard enough as it is." Raf's mouth quirked into a sad smile as he reached to cup the back of Indigo's neck with his palm.

Raf leant towards him. "Let me know when you're ready to head out. I need to talk to you before you go."

"Sounds ominous," Indigo said but was drowned out by Nash, who'd climbed back on stage and had the microphone in his hand again.

"I wanna thank you all for coming out here tonight to say so long, farewell, *sayonara, auf wiedersehen* and good bye to our dear friend, Indi. This last song tonight, I dedicate to you, brother." He smiled and winked, before beginning a rendition of Billy Joel's *Vienna*, which he'd tailored to Indigo, changing the chorus to, *"I've come to realise, that Sydney waits for you."*

Indigo took the song as it was meant: Nash understood he had to go and wished him well, no hard feelings. But it had the intended result of bringing a tear to his eye.

Later that night, they all gathered in Raf's living room, sprawled on the couches, chatting and sharing late night snacks. When Raf grew serious they fell quiet, turning to look at him expectantly.

"I want to host Micah for Indigo tonight. But I want you all here for this."

The five of them exchanged glances. They'd never had a group hosting session like this before.

"What are–" Nash began, but Raf held his hand up.

"No preamble tonight, buddy," he said gently. "Let's begin, shall we?" He looked at Indigo. "Come sit." He indicated the end of the couch closest to him, then closed his eyes and sat back in his chair, his hands gripping the armrests. He was still and silent for some time before jerking abruptly, his arms stiffening and lifting into the air before coming down to rest gently on his knees.

"Ah yes, it is always, always nice to see you," Micah smiled, his eyes opening to mere slits. Although they were all in the room, it was clear he was addressing only Indigo. "We shall begin. I would like to tell you the story of a young man studying to be a doctor. He'd always had a special talent and interest in healing, you see, and wished to formalise it. We are looking back to England right before the First World War, and when war broke out, he put his studies on hold and enlisted as a medic in the Royal Army Medical Corps. He was sent to the Western Front where the horrors he saw plagued him day and night. Gas burns, blistered skin, shredded bodies, torn limb from limb."

Indigo shifted in his seat, leaning closer to Micah.

"One day, a hospital ship docked off the coast in the North Sea and he was charged with transporting the dead and wounded aboard. And that was when he met her. She was a nurse, and the moment he laid eyes on her, her loveliness reminded him that there were still things in the world that were good and pure and true."

As always, when Micah spoke to him of his past lives, Indigo could close his eyes and see the characters at play as they were then and as they were today. It was like Micah spoke in pictures as well as words. He could see himself back then in his medic's uniform, his hands callused, his nails dirty, his hair dark and cropped short. And her, he saw, too, strawberry-blonde and fair-skinned, although it was hard to picture her face as anyone other than Cordelia because he knew the two shared the same soul. It was just the same when Micah had told him of his life as a Minoan beekeeper; he'd known then that Cordelia had been the love of his life in that lifetime, as she was in every lifetime.

"She, too, was surprised," Micah continued, "that her heart could still be stirred when she'd believed it cold and dead after her recent experiences: charred flesh and septic wounds and frightened, desperate men calling for their mothers as they bled out, waiting futilely for medical attention they were deemed too far gone to qualify for. So much meaningless loss of life. But he'd smiled at her, and she'd felt peace." Micah smiled serenely then.

"What is it you humans say? That when you know, you know? Well the two of them knew instantly. Their romance was swift and true. They fell in love, there on that battlefront, a glimmer of happiness amongst all that fear and horror and sadness. He wanted to marry her. She agreed only if he promised to wait until after the war. Married women were not allowed to serve as nurses and would be shipped home immediately, and despite the lack of equipment and supplies and the sights and sounds and smells that haunted her dreams, she wanted to be there, she wanted to do her bit to help. He promised they could wait, because for her he would wait forever." The room was silent except for the sound of Nash's leg jiggling up and down. Aurora reached out and pressed down on his knee, shooting him a pointed look.

"But then an accidental pregnancy forced their hands," Micah continued. "It was 1916, and there was nothing more scandalous than a woman pregnant and unmarried, so just as she was beginning to show, the two of them hastily wed, knowing it meant she would be sent home. He was terrified by how much he would miss her, the thought of being separated was a physical ache in his chest. But he was also relieved in many ways that this had happened, because knowing she was going home, that she would be safe, was of great comfort to him." Indigo exhaled steadily. He had a bad feeling about where this story was going; a sense of foreboding had him clenching his hands to fists.

"She was to leave on a hospital ship bound for England, and he saw her off, both of them crying as he bade her farewell, her still in the uniform one of her fellow nurses had let out around the midline to accommodate her growing bump. He kissed her deeply and promised her he would see her back home in London." Micah paused there, seemingly gathering his thoughts. When he spoke again, his tone was changed.

"But that was a promise he was not able to keep. News of the devastating fate of her ship spread through the Royal Army Medical Corps like wildfire, until someone finally found the courage to pull him aside, look him in the eye and break it to him." Micah shook his head sadly, his face folding into a wistful frown. "A stray torpedo they said, not meant for the hospital ship, but obliterating it just the same. It had gone down with all hands on deck. The young man was completely broken, inconsolable. Knowing she was gone, he lost all will to live."

Indigo clenched his teeth, digging his fingers into his thighs. The others were all staring at him with such solemn sadness in their eyes, he couldn't look at them. He focused all his attention on Micah who continued to speak.

"A couple of days later, when a medical officer asked for volunteers to go into the trenches as stretcher-bearers, the young man was sitting slumped on the floor in the corner, staring vacantly into space as had become his way. He vaguely heard the request and, as it took shape in his mind, he realised that this could be his way out. He didn't want to live anymore, not without her and the baby, so why not go out valiantly? But by the time he volunteered, all spots had been filled. He approached a young Australian medic he'd come to know well and begged him for his spot, cajoling and convincing until at last his friend reluctantly gave in, asking if he knew it was akin to a suicide mission." Micah bent forward from the waist.

"And so he climbed aboard the field ambulance, heading towards the rat-infested trenches filled with rotting corpses and thick, deep mud. He worked hard that day; he was so single-minded he barely noticed the shells exploding around him, the bullets whizzing by. It was hard work carrying the wounded on those stretchers, sometimes having to use the dead as stepping stones to get traction in the mud."

"Bloody hell," Nash muttered, and Aurora threw him another look.

"And then, having filled the last ambulance load, he climbed aboard with his colleagues, delivering first aid to his patients by rote as they bumped across the battle field towards the hospital tent," Micah said. He hesitated there, his fingers flexing on his knees while the others sat in deathly silence, waiting.

"It was said that the shell came out of nowhere," he continued after a time. "But it was a direct hit and the ambulance didn't stand a chance." Micah cleared his throat. "He died there in the wreckage amongst the flames and twisted metal, holding in his mind the image of her face. 'I'm coming, my love,' he murmured. 'Wait for me, I am coming.' And with that, he closed his eyes and left his body, travelling to where she waited so patiently to greet him, travelling to a place of peace, a place where he believed he and she would continue their journey together forever. And as he left, he vowed to never, never let her go again, to love and hold her there in his arms for all of eternity."

They all sat in morose stillness, the energy in the room thick with sorrow. But Micah wasn't finished with his story.

"Back at the field tent, news arrived of what had befallen the stretcher bearers that day. One man was particularly broken up by the news, a young Australian medic by the name of Howard Florey. You see, Howard was the friend the young man had begged to switch places with. Howard knew that if he had gone, he would have been in that ambulance, and that it would be he who was dead rather than the young man. He pondered his life that night, the role of fate and what was meant to be, as he lay awake on his camp bed. Why was he spared when so many had fallen?" Indigo furrowed his brow. He knew who Howard Florey was. Where was Micah going with this?

"Now, I am not sure if you are aware of a scientist from Adelaide by the name of Howard Florey, but I can tell you here and now that because our young man switched places with him, Howard survived the war, he returned to Australia and eventually, in 1945, received the Nobel Prize for his role in the discovery of penicillin. It is believed two hundred million lives have been saved by his breakthrough."

Indigo stared at him in stunned silence. "But... but what does that mean?"

"It means that throughout the timeline of the world, there have always been certain turning points. At these turning points, things can go one way or another, and the way in which they go alters the timeline in a colossal way. When that girl died in 1916, devastating the young man, it set in motion events that would change the trajectory of the human race. For if Howard Florey had gone to the trenches that day instead of the young man, the world would not have penicillin, and penicillin has affected the human race in enormous ways."

Micah paused then, seemingly thoughtful. If he'd been human, Indigo might have thought he was trying to find an easy way to tell him something.

"Just as your death then altered the trajectory of the world," he finally said, "so does your life now. That night, on that bridge in New York, when you failed to commit suicide... I am going to tell you now, that your survival altered everything. It set a whole new timeline in motion."

Indigo drew back in shock, his whole body tingling as numbness rose to encase him. His gaze shifted from Aurora's direct stare, to Dawn and Nash's sympathetic smiles, and he could see that they already knew. He locked eyes with Sasha who he vaguely recalled having mentioned something about the ripple effect of his death to him the night he was kidnapped by Skeet. He'd been so preoccupied with other things at the time he'd forgotten all about it.

He turned his attention back to Micah. "I don't understand."

"When you were pulled from the water that night and brought back to life, a new timeline was set in motion, the old one left behind."

"Is that a good thing or a bad thing?"

"The old timeline," Micah said, folding forward stiffly from the waist, "was one of terror and war and sickness and darkness. But now, now it is all different. It is much lighter now. The human race has entered into an era of peace and awakening, and your survival that night, it was the catalyst."

"But *how*?" Indigo asked, raking his hands through his hair.

"In ways you will not even be aware of. Because your reality is the only one you know," was all Micah would tell him.

And that was the burden Indigo was left with that night, the burden of knowing he'd somehow singlehandedly changed the world, and no matter which way he turned it as he contemplated it and discussed it with Raf and Nash and Aurora and Sasha and Dawn 'til the sun rose in the sky, the only conclusion he could arrive at was that the responsibility of it all was so great he had no choice but to set it aside and carry on with his life, because to live any other way, it would drive him insane.

manly, new south wales, december 1995

indigo

Indigo stretched his arms gingerly over his head, his ribs aching in protest. "I guess I'd better get up," he groaned. "See if I can't clean my face up a bit more before Edie sees it."

"Want me to get you some ice?" Nash asked.

"Yeah, nah, thanks, mate," Indigo replied.

There was a crash outside, and his head whipped towards the window. "What was that?"

Nash furrowed his brow at him. "That's the lads setting up for the party."

"*Party*?" Indigo said, wrinkling his nose. "What party?"

"You don't know? Bro, your mum's home, and apparently she's throwing some big bash tonight."

"She's *what*?" Indigo gasped, rushing to the window. The backyard was full of workmen setting up an enormous marquee. Others were carrying in white rattan sofas and chairs and he could see a wooden dancefloor being installed under the Moreton Bay Fig. "Kill me now," he muttered under his breath. The last thing he felt like dealing with today was Bernadette, and the only thing worse than Bernadette was Bernadette and all her hangers on. "Dammit! I've invited Cordelia over. We were counting on a nice, quiet night, just the two of us." He scowled in the direction of the backyard. "Fuck me!"

Nash grinned cheekily. "Apparently not anymore."

Indigo gave him a withering look. "Is she here?" he asked, pacing the room. "Bernadette?"

"She was. But Edie said she went into Paddington to do some shopping."

Indigo stormed towards the door.

"Ah, mate? You might want to fix your face a bit first? Edie's gonna have a lot of questions if she sees you looking like that."

Indigo threw his hands up and changed direction, heading for his ensuite instead.

Nash's head popped round the bathroom door where Indigo was examining his bruises in the mirror. "I might leave you to it then, brother. Unless you need anything?" Indigo shook his head and Nash started backing out. "Ok, considering your grand plans for this evening just went to shit, I'm gonna get out of here and give you some privacy."

Indigo shot him a questioning look in the mirror.

"Remember, masturbation still counts as sex with someone you love."

Indigo rolled his eyes. "Charming as always, my dude." He found himself laughing, despite how pissed he was at Bernadette.

Nash cracked a wicked grin, cackling as he left.

Indigo turned the shower up as hot as he could stand it and stood there, one palm braced on the white marble wall, letting the water pour over him. He climbed out and wrapped a towel around his waist, then sat and meditated for fifteen minutes. When he felt considerably calmer, he threw on a pair of gym shorts, then did another healing on his face and ribs. It was apparently more difficult to heal yourself than others, because while his ribs no longer hurt and his face had gone down and his eye was no longer swollen, when he checked the mirror he was still visibly bruised, although they'd faded to a splotchy, yellowy green.

He pulled on a singlet and went downstairs, calling for Edita.

"What is wrong, Indigo?" she said, rushing into the kitchen where he was staring into the backyard, scowling. She stopped short when she saw his face, her hand moving to clasp her pendant through her dress.

She grabbed his chin in her fingers, examining him from all angles. "My God! What have you done to yourself?"

"Don't worry about it," he said, pulling away. "I'm fine."

"But, Indi, you are hurt! Let me help–"

"I said I'm fine," he said shortly. He jerked his head towards the back yard. "What's going on out there, Edie? Since when is Bernadette back?"

"She arrived home unannounced this morning and said she was throwing a party tonight. What is she going to say when she sees your face?"

Indigo laughed bitterly. "As if she'll give a shit!"

"I don't think–" Edita abruptly stopped talking, narrowing her eyes and grabbing the neck of his singlet, yanking it down abruptly. She gasped. "Where is your wolf's tooth?"

"Oh, I took it off before the formal last night," he said with a wave of his hand. "I couldn't do the top button of my shirt up over it. I haven't lost it, it's upstairs in my room."

Her lips had morphed to a thin white line. She squeezed her eyes shut for a beat or two. "Go and get it," she ordered, teeth clenched. "*Now.*"

He was about to protest, but he saw the expression in her eyes. He'd learnt at a young age there was no point arguing with her when she had that look in her eyes.

"*Now!*" she repeated, pointing to the stairs.

"Ok, ok," he grumbled, shoulders slumped. "I'm going." What was the big fucking deal? His grandmother was an artist and the necklace was one of her creations, so yes, it was precious, but it wasn't as though he'd lost it or anything.

"I'll fix you something to eat," she called after him.

"*Thank* you."

He stomped upstairs and retrieved the necklace and put it back on, then came back down to get the loaded plate of eggplant parmigiana and salad she'd prepared for him. He took it up to his room, then sat down on the edge of the bed and picked up the phone, punching in the number he knew by heart.

cordelia

"Was that him?" Mum asked when Cordelia returned to the kitchen, unable to wipe the grin from her face. She'd only woken up half an hour ago. The phone had rung as she'd been telling Mum all about the formal and what had happened with Indigo, being careful not to make any mention of being kidnapped by warlocks. She'd wrapped the remnants of her formal dress in a plastic bag and put it in the neighbour's bin early that morning. The last thing her mother needed right now was any more stress.

She nodded. "Apparently Bernadette's in town," she said, picking up the toasted chicken focaccia Mum had made her and taking another bite.

Mum made a face. She was protective of Indigo, and Bernadette and Wilson were top of her burn list.

"She's throwing a big party tonight. He wants me to come." She yawned.

"You're going, right? I mean, I know it's probably the last thing you feel like doing after such a late night last night, but now you and Inds are... What do you kids call it these days? Dating? Going out? Seeing each other? Boyfriend-girlfriend?"

Cordelia stifled a giggle. "You forgot 'going steady'. Isn't that what you called it back in your day?"

Mum laughed. "Surely if there's a big party on there tonight, we can expect Robbie home any minute? He'll need at least an hour to primp and preen, right?"

"I don't know," Cordelia mused, tearing off a corner of sandwich. "I think there's someone at Indigo's who's captured his... er... interest."

Her mother looked at her questioningly. "So we're over the whole Gino thing then?"

"Watch this space." Cordelia yawned again and stood. "I guess I'd better go have a shower and start getting ready," she said, tossing her crusts in the bin and stacking her plate in the dishwasher. She kissed her mother on the way past.

She was humming to herself, foraging through her wardrobe, trying to decide what to wear, when a sudden scritching noise sounded behind her. She jumped, wheeling around. Heart pounding, hands trembling, her gaze travelled jerkily over her bedroom. The scritching came again, from the window. Her shoulders sagged. It was just a branch scraping across the pane. She strode across the room and yanked the curtains closed.

Breath shaky, hand pressed to her heart, she started inhaling and exhaling slowly, methodically, in an attempt to steady her nerves. After last night, she didn't know if she'd ever not be jumpy again. All she knew was that she felt a lot safer when she was with Indigo. The sooner she could get to his place, the better.

By the time she emerged from the shower, hair dripping wet, skin flushed pink, she felt a lot calmer. And thankfully, Robbie had returned home, very much across the theme of the party and with very definite opinions about what she should wear.

you give me something

indigo

Indigo sat in dismay, surveying the chaos that had descended upon his sanctuary. His mother was having problems with her most recent toy-boy husband, and apparently breezing back into town and throwing herself a lavish party was her chosen solution.

Hundreds of people were milling around the lawn, drinks in hands, chatting and laughing. Indigo was by the pool with his friends, whilst a bevy of actresses and models strutted across the lawn, attempting to catch the eye of one of the producers or directors holding court in the enormous marquee it had taken a small army of men all day to erect.

All these strangers in his home. Indigo was carefully studying every single face that passed by. There were a few familiar ones at least; he watched as Peyton and Sandy clinked their glasses against Sian's and Will's, the four of them laughing and chatting. How nice it must be to live the oblivious life of a normie, he thought wistfully. Sandy glanced over at Indigo and grinned, raising his glass to him.

An epic reggae band was killing it beside a crowded dancefloor overhung with garlands of glowing festoon lights. Bernadette had flown the band in from Jamaica especially, which meant the shirtless Lenny-Kravitz-esque-looking lead singer, which the majority of the party's female population were currently eye-fucking, had apparently known about the party long before Indigo.

Bernadette loved a themed party, and this one was something along the lines of 'tropicana extravaganza'. An abundance of palm fronds, frangipanis, orchids and birds of paradise spilled from vases, and mountains of coconuts and pineapples covered every available surface. Rattan lanterns glowed in the trees and tiki torches edged the lawn, whilst waitstaff clad in grass skirts toted trays of colourful cocktails and canapes. There was even a whole row of pigs turning on spits way down the back of the yard. Bernadette never did anything by halves.

Right now, she was swanning around in a bralette and matching slinky, pink, paradise-print skirt, thigh-high splits up both sides, an elaborate crown of flowers and vines adorning her head. She was working the crowd, greeting her guests with double-cheeked kisses and the kind of enthusiasm she seemed to reserve for anyone that wasn't him. He could feel himself glowering at her when Nash elbowed him in the ribs.

"Mate," Nash reprimanded. "You've got to loosen up and have some fun." Indigo glanced at him sidelong. "Despite the jeans," Nash added with a smirk.

Bernadette had been horrified when Indigo had emerged in a pair of old, worn jeans earlier that evening, and had immediately sent out for a designer pair to be procured from a high-end boutique which bent over backwards to reopen just for her. Ridiculously expensive, stiff, dark, and so not him, Indigo's new jeans had been the butt of his friends' jokes all night. He was this close to storming upstairs and changing, but he'd already had to listen to a dramatic monologue about his uncouth hair and what her friends would think when they saw his face, and he wasn't ready to endure another regarding a pair of pants. The more he could fly under her radar, the better.

"I mean, look at me," Nash said. "Rory's over there talking to some gym-junkie pretty boy with what I assume must be a dire hair-gel addiction, and I'm still totally chilled out and having fun."

"Sure you are, dude," Sasha laughed with a wink. "She's only been caught in your tractor-beam stare all night."

Nash shot him a look. "Who is he, anyway?" he asked nonchalantly.

Indigo glanced over. "I think that's Summer Bay's latest recruit."

"Hold up. He's on *Home and Away*?"

"You know it?"

"Uh *yeah*," Nash said, eyes round. "I'm English, remember? We're brought up on a steady diet of Australian soaps, living vicariously through your never-ending summers. Do you know how many guys from the boarding house would give their left nut to be at a party with *Home and Away* stars?"

He suddenly stopped talking, and Indigo turned to see what had caught his eye. A striking, rail-thin girl with wavy blonde hair was making her way towards them. "Indi Wolfe?" she cried, tugging the sleeves of her red hibiscus-print dress down off her shoulders. "Is that you?"

Indigo stood up and smiled at her, allowing her to kiss him on both cheeks and throw her arms around his neck.

"I almost didn't, like, recognise you," she said, the staccato rise and fall of her intonation revealing she was Beverly Hills born and bred. She pulled back to touch the longish ends of his hair and regard his bruised cheeks. "Like, what happened to your face?"

He shrugged non-commitally and was saved by a kick to the shin from Nash. "Introduce me," Nash said from the corner of his mouth as he stood.

"Brooklyn, this is my mate, Nash Willoughby, Nash, this is Brooklyn Ford." Indigo had known Brooklyn for years. She, too, had a very famous mother, actress Silvie Ford, currently in Australia filming her latest blockbuster. Unlike him, Brooklyn was following in her mother's footsteps, here from LA to tackle a supporting role in Silvie's film.

Nash grinned impishly at Brooklyn. "What are you drinking?" he asked smoothly as he took her hand and led her towards the bar. Indigo sat back down next to Sasha.

"Ah, how quickly he finds the methadone he needs to temper his Rory addiction," Sasha said with a laugh.

"Maybe this one will be the cure." Indigo's train of thought suddenly stuttered and vanished. He glanced around. He couldn't see her, but the lurch in his stomach that only she had the ability to set in motion told him she was there somewhere.

Then the crowd shuffled and parted and there she stood, long-limbed in a tiny, white mini dress printed with emerald palm fronds, a dress so sexy he wanted it on his bedroom floor – now. Her hair hung loose down her back in glossy waves, and she wore sky-high, suede stilettos of the palest green. Her brow furrowed, her eyes searching,

searching. And then they landed on him. She cocked her head to one side, a smile immediately tilting up the corners of those plump lips.

His eyes locked onto hers, hazel brown on azure blue, and in that azure he saw a flame of intensity he was sure was reflected in his. She held his gaze, unwavering, and that gaze held so much, said so much. He couldn't feel his body. All the air pressed from his lungs so he could barely breathe. Sasha waved a hand in front of his face, but he hardly saw it, and he knew he was grinning like an idiot. Wordlessly he stood, drawn magnetically towards her by an inexplicable force.

Robbie sauntered up, Midori splice cocktail in hand, arms held wide, wearing the only tasteful Hawaiian shirt Indigo had seen tonight. "Finally, I am amongst my people! Look at me, rubbing shoulders with all these celebrities." He slapped Indigo's butt as he passed him by. "Aloha, Inds. Got yourself some new jeans there, mate?" But Indigo merely flashed him an absent smile, his gaze quickly dragged back to her.

"You're stunning," he said when he reached her. He plucked a white orchid from a flower arrangement and slid it behind her ear, then drew her into his arms and lowered his mouth to hers. It may have been a mistake to kiss her, because now he'd started, he never wanted to stop, his body still so raw, still aching from their encounter outside her house that morning.

"I *missed* you," she whispered against his lips, running her hand up under his shirt and lightly down his side.

"Me, too," he whispered back. His heart pounded as he sank into the kiss. She was pressing herself against him, palming his cheek, the nape of his neck. She pulled back then, her eyes intent on his.

"Your face," she smiled, touching the mottled greenish-yellow. "It looks so much better. It doesn't hurt anymore?"

"Nah-uh." Her fingers tenderly explored his ribs, her eyes glued on his to gauge any change in his expression. "I reckon I'm like, ninety percent healed," he said, his lips millimetres from hers.

"I'm glad." She pressed upwards to close the gap between them, kissing him ever-so-slowly.

A group of drunken party goers stumbled past them, screeching with laughter. All of a sudden, he was very aware that they were in the middle of a crowded party when all he wanted was to be far away from prying eyes, to be alone with her, to have her all to himself. "I don't wanna be here," he murmured. "Come with me." Surely they could find a quiet corner somewhere in which to hide away.

He took her hand and led her towards the edge of the yard where the workmen had been setting up couches and chairs earlier that day. The party was in full swing and the effects of the freely flowing booze were apparent, if the pool full of scantily clad bodies was anything to go by.

"Hey, Inds?"

"Mmmm?" He turned to smile at her.

"What's with the jeans?" she asked, covering her mouth to suppress a giggle.

"Not you, too?" he groaned. "That's it, I'm burning them."

They pushed through the crowd and, just when he thought he'd found a secluded spot, they were confronted with Bernadette reigning supreme on a rattan couch, a group of wanky-looking men fawning all over her, the collective stench of their cologne eye-watering. She was bent over a low table, and as they approached, she straightened up and dabbed her nostrils, then handed a rolled up bill to the dickhead next to her.

"Indi, my little ray of sunshine!" she tittered as she spotted him glowering at her. "Are you enjoying my little soirée?" She stood and sashayed towards them, her long skirt swishing around her miniscule frame. Her blonde hair was stylishly cut into a layered shag she'd publicly accused one of the stars of that new show, *Friends*, of copying and taking credit for, and her pouty lips were stained a deep shade of fuchsia.

"Hi, Bernadette," Cordelia said, leaning to kiss her cheek.

"Cordelia!" Bernadette gushed. "I haven't seen you in ages. Look how grown up and divine you are. What's been happening, darling?" Bernadette ran her tongue over her teeth, her blue eyes swallowed by pupil. "Your dad still single-handedly running Manly Hospital?"

All the colour drained from Cordelia's face, her fingers clutching tight to Indigo's like a lifeline.

"For fuck's sake, Bernadette," Indigo said in a low voice, stepping protectively in front of Cordelia. "You truly are just the most tactless person ever to walk the earth." He towered over her, staring her down.

He'd sent a copy of the Order of Service from Joshua's funeral to Bernadette's PA, along with a note letting her know what had happened.

"That's my boy! Always *so* respectful of his mother. What have I done wrong now?" She reached to adjust the collar of the Hawaiian shirt he wore open at the neck. It was black with pale pink and mocha flowers and she'd made him wear it, because what was he if not her own personal Ken doll. He pulled away.

"My dad passed away last month," Cordelia said softly, her voice nearly lost against the background noise of the party.

The scowl froze on Bernadette's face. "Oh. Oh, I see. Well, that's terribly sad, kitten, I'm sorry to hear it, he was a real sweetheart." She smiled then and clapped her hands together. "But this is a party, and there's no room for sad faces at a party, is there?" She leant in and smiled at Cordelia. "Would you like a line? It looks like you and Mr Grumpypants here–" she grabbed Indigo's chin and waggled it "–could use a bit of cheering up."

Indigo twisted his face from her grip and shook his head at her as he grabbed Cordelia by the waist, guiding her away ahead of him. "I hope you have your plastic surgeon on speed dial for when your nose disintegrates from inhaling all that coke and bullshit! Great parenting as always, Bernadette," he said over his shoulder.

"You *are* over eighteen!" she called after him. He glanced back as she turned to her adoring admirers. "My son, everyone!" she announced, holding her arms wide and smirking. "Head of my fan club and a walking advertisement for birth control!" Indigo didn't even flinch; she'd referred to him that way his whole life. Luckily Cordelia was far enough ahead of him that she didn't hear, because he knew she wouldn't let that one slide.

As they wended their way through the crowd, Nash bounded up to them, Brooklyn now attached to his hand. He gave Cordelia a big hug and introduced the girls.

"What's all the commotion?" he asked.

"Just Bernadette being Bernadette," Indigo replied.

Brooklyn grinned sympathetically and beckoned over a waiter carrying a tray of vibrant cocktails, passing them each a concoction topped with a hunk of pineapple skewered with a little umbrella. "Oh my God, your mom is like, even more of a diva than mine, Indi! You guys look like you could use a drink."

Nash grabbed Brooklyn round the hips. "Let's go dance, you sexy minx," he said with a wink, pulling her towards the dancefloor.

"Sure you're ok?" Indigo asked Cordelia, peering into her eyes.

"I'm ok," she assured him with a small smile.

cordelia

His gorgeous face was heavy with concern. "Are you really? Because Bernadette... I'm so embarrassed. She's just the *worst.*"

"Inds," she said, fighting to keep the waver from her voice, "it's fine, honestly." Bernadette's question had shaken her, but tonight she was determined not to spiral, determined to wall up the grief threatening to devour her. She took a small sip of the fruity pink cocktail in her hand, then shook her head, wrinkling her nose. The bartender had gotten a bit overexcited with the rum. "Nope. Can't do it." She'd slept most of the day, but was still feeling a bit seedy after last night.

Indigo took her glass and placed it with his on the table behind them. He pressed his lips to her forehead, then cupped her face in his hands and she was immediately possessed by the intensity of the light, the heat, pulsating from the depths of his eyes. "I just want to make it all better for you," he whispered, closing his lids for a beat or two. He bent to ghost his lips over hers, his kiss deepening as she responded. "Come dance with me," he said softly, and she knew he was trying to take her mind off things.

If only he knew he didn't have to try, that when she was with him, he consumed her.

He led her to the darkened dancefloor lit only by the moon and the dewy flicker of the twinkling lights strung overhead. The reggae band was tearing it up, packing out the steamy dancefloor with a rendition of UB40's *(I Can't Help) Falling In Love With You,* as a smoke machine somewhere emitted a steady stream of hazy mist to blanket the ground ethereally. The yard was crammed with people, talking, laughing, drinking, but they all faded to grey as he steered her through the throng to where they could join the other bodies moving anonymously in the shadows.

"Come here, beautiful." He tilted his head to one side as he crooked a finger at her, beckoning her in close. His eyes smouldered on hers, and she could see nothing but him, him, *him* in the crowd as he spun her once then enfolded her tightly in his embrace, swaying with her in time with the music. She inhaled deeply as that scent of his permeated her senses, so familiar and heady and all-encompassing. Her arms wound around his neck as her lips found their way back home to his. His fingers tangled through the lengths of her hair, moving beneath to caress the bare skin between her shoulder-blades.

And then he was kissing her senseless, his hands moving skilfully over her body, powerful and electric on her flesh as he ran one up the back of her thigh. She slid her palms over the rear of his jeans, tracing the sculpted line of his backside, pulling him closer, closer, closer. She felt close to imploding. Her senses were already so heightened from this morning outside her house when she'd dizzily pleaded with him to come in again and again.

She arched back as his lips burnt embers down the curve of her neck. "Indigo," she exhaled, her voice wavering, and he caught her up, melding his body to hers. The top of his shirt was already buttoned low but she reached to undo a couple more, skimming her thumb up and down the centre of his muscular chest as she gazed up at him. "I love you," she breathed. But it wasn't enough – the way she felt about him, it was way past anything words could express.

He leant in close. "I know." She felt his lips on the shell of her ear, his breath heavy as he uttered, "Show me."

The world seemed to ebb away as she squeezed her eyes shut and nodded once, the restraint in that nod a complete paradox to all that was roaring inside of her.

She slipped her hand into his, following as he expertly ducked and weaved through the crowd, past gyrating bodies and scantily clad, lip-locked couples, leading her away from the dancefloor, past the bar and across the lawn into the house.

They stumbled into the dark, deserted games room, and he was suddenly wrapping his arms around her from behind, pressing himself against her back, as his lips found the place where her neck curved into her shoulder. Heat flared through her belly and she gripped the edge of the pool table. She tilted her face over her shoulder to his... and then he was kissing her breathless. He palmed the front of her dress, hitching up the hem, and she gasped as his fingertips softly skimmed the skin at the tops of her thighs.

"You're a fucking goddess," he panted. "Do you have any idea what you do to me?" If it was half as much as what he did to her, she wondered whether they'd actually make it upstairs. But then he was steering her through the maze of rooms. As they reached the grand arching staircase, he twined his fingers through hers again, pulling her swiftly behind him as they ran up the steps, up, up, up, away from the party, away from all the people, beelining for the sanctuary of his bedroom.

rush rush

cordelia

The music faded as he led her down a familiar empty corridor and then he was opening the door to his bedroom, drawing her inside and slamming it shut, so he could back her up against it, ravaging her mouth with his. In the décor of his enormous room, she could see him, smell him, feel him so completely in the whitewashed floorboards, pale-grey walls, king bed dressed in charcoal linens, sheer, white curtains moving gently in the breeze drifting through the half-open windows. It was neat and tidy, so unlike hers.

He pulled back to look at her, the green and yellow of his eyes radiant, his chest swiftly rising and falling. He breathed her name then, exhaled it, as he leant in to kiss her, gently parting her lips with his tongue. His hands slid around her waist, then slowly, slowly up the teeth of her zipper 'til he reached the top, pulling it down, drawing her dress from her shoulders, letting it fall to the floor.

His swallow was audible as his eyes raked over her body, unbridled desire etched all over his face.

He ran his fingertips over the dip of her shoulder and under the delicate strap of her bra, easing it down her arm, his lips meandering in its wake. And then his mouth was back on hers, his palm caressing the side of her breast through scant ivory lace, sliding smoothly across to knead it, and as he did a sound emerged from somewhere deep inside him, a cross between a growl and a moan. It was a sound that weakened her knees, turned her insides over.

She pulled at his clothes, fumbling at the remaining buttons of his shirt, tearing it off and pouring herself against him, flesh finally on flesh, his body hard and bronzed, her skin throbbing deliciously against his. The only light in the room emanated from a salt rock lamp burning in the corner, casting shadows on the walls, faintly illuminating the silhouette of their intertwined forms.

His tongue sought hers as she wrenched his jeans open. "I don't like these," she murmured against his lips.

He chuckled as he pulled them off, but instead of adding them to the growing pile of clothes on his bedroom floor, he kicked them up, caught them, and tossed them out the window. "Consider them gone."

She kissed him, laughing, laughing and kissing, as she stepped out of her heels. She pushed up on her toes so she could rub her nose to his. He wore nothing now but a pair of snug, grey, Calvin Klein boxer-briefs, which he wore so very, very well. He picked her up and it seemed as though she weighed nothing in his arms. She locked her legs around his waist as he backed towards the bed, his mouth never leaving hers, inhaling and exhaling as one.

Her body was overflowing with a tingling warmth, an ever-rising warmth she never wanted to stop feeling.

He hit the bed and sat, wrapped in her limbs, pulling back to stare at her as he ran his thumb over her lower lip. "You're incredible." His voice caught. She ducked her head, her cheeks flushing as she smiled shyly. He leant in, grazing his lips up her cheek to her earlobe, whisper-soft. "You *smell* incredible," he murmured, the stir of his breath in her hair.

"Now this," he whispered into her ear, tracing the sheer scalloped edge of her push-up bra, "this I really... *really*... like." He pulled back and cocked an eyebrow at her, smirking his sexy, little smile. "Too bad it has to go." In one smooth move he flicked the clasp, letting it drop to the floor.

His palms glided down to her hips, and he blew out a shuddery breath as his hazel gaze caressed her breasts, taking in every gentle curve and soft swell. He shook his head ever so slightly. "Holy fucking shit." Suddenly self-conscious under his intense stare, she made to cover herself, but he grabbed her hands and held them in his.

"Cordelia," he breathed. "Cordelia, you, are so very, *very* beautiful. And I could stare at these for the rest of my life." He grinned a dreamy grin. "In fact, I think I just might." Cupping the nape of her neck, he ran his tongue along the seam of her lips. His hand trailed down to her chest, thumbing the hardened peak of her nipple so fireworks exploded through every nerve she had. She heard a moan emerge from somewhere inside of her. And then his mouth was on her body, hard and soft and gentle and fierce and everything all at once.

She tilted her head back, weaving her fingers through his hair, murmuring erratically that she never wanted him to stop. She was aching for him, had done for so long. She could barely grasp that finally, after all this time, it was going to happen.

Sitting there astride him, she could feel every single inch of him so deliciously hard against her. His face buried in her neck, she rocked against him, and he made that low, growling sound deep in his throat again that made her tremble with want.

In one smooth movement he scooped her up and laid her on the bed, his pupils flaring as he settled beside her, drawing her into his arms so they were nose-to-nose, their breath mingling. Her heart was already racing, but as he stared deep into her eyes, it sped up tenfold.

"Hi…" she whispered, her fingers unfurling on his cheek, and he smiled tenderly and mouthed it back. Tracing the curve of her body, his lips found hers once more. He drew her hard against him and his hands were in her hair as their kiss intensified. And then he was touching her everywhere all at once, kissing her so hard, his tongue moving endlessly, exquisitely, against hers. The molten heat pooling deep in her belly spilt over, spreading to encompass her so she didn't know which way was up. She'd never wanted anything as badly as she wanted him.

She ran her hands over his shoulder-blades and down his back, the muscles rippling beneath her palms, her fingertips beelining for the waistband of the Calvins that stood between her and him. "Take these off," she told him, easing them down, and he moved to help her. She pressed her lips to his forehead, his eyelids, his lips, as she reached down to finally touch him, *finally* explore him. A shaky exhale escaped her lungs. He was so beautiful, every bit of him pure perfection. He quivered as she continued to stroke him, his breath broken, his eyes half-closed.

She wove her legs through his, and his hand was moving over her knee, lingering on her thigh, running up, up until his thumb was hooking into the side of her g-string. "Now this," he panted, toying with the fabric, kissing a trail of sparks down her throat, "this is one of the sexiest fucking things I've ever seen." His fingertips were caressing her gently through the lace, skilfully circling her so she whimpered. She was so ready for him it wasn't funny. "But holy shit, it definitely has to go. Like, right *now*."

She was suddenly very aware she was wearing an ivory lace thong… nothing but a tiny ivory lace thong. Just a very brief, very silky, ivory lace thong…

Until she wasn't.

Afterwards, she lay the length of his back, draped over him like a silk sheet, her chin resting on his shoulder-blade as she sleepily caressed him, unable to keep her hands off him for even a moment. His skin was slick on hers, so warm, so smooth, electric beneath her fingertips. He had the body of a Greek god, so toned and strong and tanned. He was beauty personified, and she was determined to explore him.

She coaxed him over, brushing his mouth with hers to rouse him. His eyes half-opened and the edges of his mouth turned up into a sleepy smile. "Hey, beautiful," he murmured. She kissed him deeply, and he sighed contentedly as her lips moved down the curve of his neck towards his clavicle, then wandered lazily over his chest, straying lower and lower. She was resolved to kiss every flawless inch of him.

She'd known him for so long, but there were parts of him that she'd never seen, never known, that had been secret until now. And now she was free to wander his body, to see it all, feel it all, touch it all. Now his secrets were hers too, as hers were his, theirs to share always. The mole on his inner thigh, the small, mocha birth mark shaped like a trident on his little toe, none of him went unexamined. She was ravenous to know him, to know all of him, to know him in his entirety.

He reached for her then, manoeuvring her gently onto her back and climbing on top of her so all she could feel was the exquisiteness of his weight pressing down on her, his lips warm velvet on her flesh as they trailed from the hollow of her throat past her shoulder to her breast.

His tongue flickered expertly over the bud of her nipple and she arched back gasping, pressing her hips to his as he gently bit down, drawing her into his mouth. He seemed to know exactly what she wanted without her having to say so. But of course he did, when the two of them could communicate without speaking. When she was with him, she didn't want for anything, it was pure perfection, nothing existed but the two of them. "I love you," he told her, smiling up at her so tenderly, but she knew he meant so much more.

He made love to her again, slower this time, taking his time, whispering softly to her, and just like before, he brought her to the brink, holding her there, suspended in time and space before tumbling over the edge with her.

Later, when they could breathe again, they lay on their sides, their bodies slippery with sweat, his pressed snugly to hers, their heads on one pillow, as he gazed soulfully into her eyes. "It's never been like this for me before," he confessed, his voice catching, his fingertips tracing lazy feather-light patterns across her shoulder, down her arm. "I didn't know it could be like this."

"Me neither."

"Promise me, Cora... that it will be this way forever," he said vulnerably, "that we'll always be together."

She reached to touch the scar on his forehead, frowning wistfully. "I promise," she told him, reaching up to brush her lips over his scar, his cheeks, his eyelids. "I can barely breathe when I'm not with you." There was only him, no one else, and she knew that this was the way it would always be, the way it always had been.

"I will love you always, Cordelia, in this and every timeless now, 'til my last breath and beyond." He sealed his vow with a kiss, a kiss so deep she swore her heart skipped a beat.

She could have lain there in that bed with him forever and let the world keep on turning out there without them. All she wanted was him. The things he made her feel! Things she never wanted to stop feeling, things that made words like forever and always and eternity seem inadequate.

He gazed at her with those eyes she so loved, smiling softly as he tenderly touched her cheek. His face. That face. She would never, could never, get tired of staring at that face.

"Can I ask you something?" His voice was low.

"Anything."

"About Drew…" he said tentatively, his eyes never leaving hers.

"Mmm?" she said, brow creased, thinking that was the last topic she wanted to discuss right now.

"I… I didn't steal you from him, did I?"

She could see it had been plaguing him. She smiled at him, so gently, and shook her head, so slowly. "I don't think you can steal something that was always meant to be yours."

indigo

They lay in his twisted bedsheets, limbs intertwined, noses almost touching. They talked and laughed, laughed and talked. God, how she'd always made him laugh. They'd never run out of things to talk about, and he found it hard to imagine they ever would. The salt lamp cast a gentle luminosity over the weave of their bodies, dappled, ever moving between shadow and light.

As the moon rose higher in the sky, they lay in drowsy silence, curled into one another, somewhere between sleeping and waking. "What's going on in that beautiful mind of yours?"

"You're welcome to take a look and see," she murmured, lids closed, pressing her forehead to his, inviting him to read her thoughts.

He pulled back after a moment or two, his mouth falling open. "Seriously? *That's* what you're thinking?" He burst out laughing, folding into her.

"Don't tell me it didn't cross your mind at some point," she said, more awake now, eyes twinkling. "You could have been a dud root and then where would we be?"

"You really do have a way with words, angel face," he said, drawing her back to him and giving her a playful tap on the backside before dropping a kiss to the hollow of her cheek. "But come on, you and me, we were always gonna be great together."

"Yeah, yeah, everyone knows you're *amazing* at everything, Inds."

"So you've always told me," he said with a grin.

He couldn't dream of life being more perfect. To have fallen so completely in love... And to have her love him back? He couldn't imagine ever wanting for anything else as long as he lived. She was all he needed in life, him and her together; they could handle anything, they could take on the world.

When she looked at him that way with those soulful aquamarine eyes, it killed him a thousand times over. He traced the ridge of her hip, her skin like gossamer beneath his fingertips. He couldn't keep his hands off her. He gazed at her, taking in her gentle curves, the soft swell of those utterly perfect breasts, the concave sweep of her stomach, her limbs so long and lean from hours spent between a surfboard and a yoga mat.

She was fucking breathtaking.

And she was *his.*

The truth was, he'd never made love to anyone before.

Sure, he'd had plenty of sex, but it had always been such a primal thing for him, a physical need, not a means of expressing himself, of showing someone what he felt for them. But now, with her, when words could never be enough, connecting his body to hers, using it to show her he loved her, he knew it was the only way he could convey the infinite depth of what lay within his heart. Making love to her was the rawest, most soul-baring thing he'd ever done.

He brushed her hair from her face, ensnaring his fingers in the lengths to draw her head back so the silky skin of her throat was exposed. He couldn't resist that part of her, and he lowered his mouth to it, savouring her, roving, roving until his lips met hers in a kiss so intense he momentarily forgot where, who, what he was. Every breath she took was his, as his was hers. He pulled back to hold her gaze, his hands exploring, caressing. She reached for him and he rolled on top of her, the softness of her beneath him utopic as he murmured she was beautiful and he loved her so.

Her fingers were kneading his back, his hips, his backside, pulling him close as close could be. All he could do was *feel.* Her chest domed as he moved lower, plying her body with breathy-soft kisses. He'd never known anything as divine as her.

She smiled playfully as she pushed him onto his back and climbed on top so she was kneeling over him, her hair cascading past her shoulder blades, treacle and blonde, tangled and wild. He stretched his arm out, fumbling in his bedside drawer, but she grabbed his hand, stopped him. "Don't," she whispered, leaning to kiss him. "I already told you, I'm on the pill. We don't need that."

"But… are you sure? I mean, I don't know, babe…" At this point, with her sitting there on top of him, all that heavenly, bare, golden skin gloriously glistening, there was no blood left in his brain. He couldn't think straight, could barely process what she was saying.

"I'm sure." She gently sucked on his lower lip. "I hate those things."

He hated them, too, who didn't? Christ, she was so fucking hot and he loved her so much and he wanted to be inside her so fucking badly he could barely see straight. But… but…

"I want to feel *you*," she breathed. "All of you. You and me, no barriers, just *us*." And that was his undoing.

"Yes," he rasped. "*God*, yes."

She reached between them, angling him upward, sliding slickly onto him until he was buried to the hilt. Skin to skin. No barriers. Just them. His lungs emptied as a moan tumbled from her lips, and she arched backwards, her eyes flickering closed as she single-handedly rocked his world.

"Cordelia," he breathed, "Cordelia, Cordelia." She felt so damn good, he was barely hanging on. He ran his palms down over her breasts, skimming the curve of her waist until her hips were in his hands, and he was guiding her slowly, slowly back and forth on top of him as she exhaled shakily to the ceiling. She bit her lower lip and gazed down at him, her eyes locked deeply on his as he continued to move in her.

"How will I ever get enough of you?" she whispered breathily as he burned for her and wondered himself how he would ever, in a million years, get enough of her.

They barely slept that night, dozing dreamily here and there, before the intoxicating cocktail of adrenalin and oxytocin coursing through their veins roused them again.

"I think I need food," she said early the next morning, as they lay wrapped in the warmth of one another. Dawn light broke softly through the fluttering curtains. They hadn't had dinner last night and he was famished, too, but he was so content he didn't want to move, never wanted to move ever again, in fact.

"But that would mean having to get up," he murmured, burying his face in her sweet-smelling tresses, "leaving here... Having to go out there and re-join the real world." He'd decided being in his bed with her was his favourite thing in the world.

She rolled to face him, resting her chin on his chest as she gazed softly into his eyes.

"You don't really wanna go out there, do you?" he asked, running his thumb over her bottom lip. "I mean, for a start, there are other people out there."

"Mmmhmm I know." She wrinkled her nose. "We'd have to put clothes on." She lightly kissed his pecs. "And really, to cover up a body like this is an absolute travesty." Her tummy rumbled then and he laughed as her cheeks bloomed pink and she ducked her head.

"Ok, ok, I get it." He chuckled. "I need to feed you."

He sat up, frowning as something small and hard dug into the back of his thigh. He reached under the sheets, fumbling for whatever was hidden in the tangled folds.

"Lose something?" he asked, holding the object up between his finger and thumb.

"My ring!"

He took her hand and gently slid it back on, then held her hand up and spun the ring which pivoted easily around her finger, giving her a pointed look.

She lowered her eyes and sighed shakily. "You know that... with... everything.... I just haven't had much of an appetite lately. But I didn't think it would just fall off like that. You know I can't lose it, Inds." She slipped the ring off and clutched it in her fist.

"Give it here then," he said, holding out his hand. She placed it in his palm and he slid it onto his pinkie where it sat firmly, securely. He held his hand up to show her. "Ok?"

She nodded. "Ok."

"I'll keep it safe until you start to feel better. And I know it doesn't seem like it now, but you know one day you will, right?" He drew her back into his arms, kissed the top of her head. "Josh being gone... it's always gonna hurt. But I think maybe, with time, the grief stops being so... raw, and like, gets a bit easier to live with, you know?" She nodded, and he lowered his mouth to hers.

She pulled back. "Inds?"

"Mmm?"

"Did you like me better before? When there was… *more* of me to love?" And although her tone was light, he could tell she was unsure, vulnerable.

He took her face in his hands. "You, Cordelia are the most beautiful girl in the world, no matter what." And it was true, she would always be beautiful to him because he couldn't see a way to separate how she looked from who she was, it was one and the same. Her inner glow burnt so intensely, it overrode anything physical. Although the way she looked… it was a lot.

"I have loved you and that gorgeous body of yours through every iteration, every phase, every version."

"Even the puppy fat phase back when I was thirteen?" she giggled.

"Yeah, baby." He grinned wickedly, thinking back to that sweet, soft girl who'd nurtured and cared for him in ways he never even knew he needed. "I've always been totally fucking infatuated with you, even back then."

"You're such a liar!" she cried, climbing to her knees to swat him, trying not to laugh.

"Uh-uh," he shook his head as he knelt up against her, grabbing her tightly around the waist, drawing her in for a kiss. "I swear it's true. I think that you, Cordelia Carlisle, are pure perfection. Then, now, and always," he declared, tilting her chin so he could stare into her eyes. He cupped her backside and gave it a good squeeze as he growled playfully into her ear.

"Now, I fully intend to get you some food, and you know Edie will make you whatever your heart desires. But right now, all my heart desires is you." He kissed her neck. "With me." He kissed her shoulder. "In my shower." His lips found hers again. She draped her legs around him and he scooped her up, carrying her into his ensuite where they proceeded to steam up every single surface, all thoughts of breakfast forgotten.

chapter thirty-one

more than words

cordelia

The next evening, they sat around the outdoor fireplace near the pool. Cordelia snuggled into the crook of Indigo's arm, her cheek upon his chest, the steady thump of his heart beat almost lulling her to sleep as Nash strummed on his guitar. Aurora and Sasha sat on the opposite couch beside Nash, whilst Robbie sat beside Cordelia, his long legs sprawled out in front of him.

Indigo had upped Nash's education on Australian music since he'd arrived in Sydney, giving him a couple of new CDs to study every day. Today's lesson plan had involved Cold Chisel, and Nash was showing off the day's accomplishments with *Flame Trees*. Cordelia loved listening to him play. He had a really edgy, soulful voice.

It was a little cooler tonight so she wore a cardigan of Indigo's over her black floral mini dress, the long sleeves pushed up to her elbows. She'd found it in the back of his closet, the tags still on it and she'd giggled to see it was Gucci, so not his style, black and chunky-knit. Clearly something his mother had bought him that he'd never worn.

She absentmindedly raised her fingers to her lips, plump and bruised from his endless kisses the night before. They'd barely slept and she knew she was running purely on adrenaline. But she'd never felt so content in all her life.

She'd learnt last night that Indigo was insatiable.

And for him, so was she. Her craving for him was a constant, never ending thing.

Her body was paying the price now though, she was raw and tingly and tender, but in the best way possible.

Last night had changed something between them, expanding and growing so she felt a physical attachment to him, almost like they were two parts of the same person, as if he was the other half of her and she was achingly incomplete if at least some small part of her body wasn't touching his.

She burrowed in tighter against him, a blissful sigh escaping her lips. He smiled as he glanced down at her, taking her hand, pressing the back of it softly to his mouth. He pulled her closer, his fingers stroking the lengths of her hair as his lips moved over the top of her head.

Bernadette had apparently hooked up with the lead singer of the reggae band from her party, and was now spontaneously winging her way to Jamaica with him. When Edita had told Indigo, he'd merely rolled his eyes and said, "So lovely of Mummy dearest to stop by," as he'd surveyed the mess she'd left for them to clean up. Edita and Lukas had been stuck doing the lion's share, and had both hit the hay early, clearly exhausted.

Nash finished playing and thrust his guitar at Indigo. "Your turn, brother."

Indigo protested, tried to hand it back, but Nash refused to take it. "Come on, mate," Nash cajoled, picking up his Crown Lager and taking a big swig. "We all know you're not shy. Play that Bon Jovi song you were faffing around with before you left Sedona."

"Oh yeah," Sasha said. "That was sounding great, eh."

Cordelia reluctantly disentangled herself to give him room, sliding closer to Robbie. Indigo positioned the guitar, moving his fingertips fondly down the neck and over the strings, closing his eyes for a quiet moment before he began to play. It was *Born To Be My Baby*, but like she'd never heard it, slowed way down and so husky and emotional she felt it to her core, his eyes clinging to her as he sung every word just for her. He was so fucking sexy with that guitar, she wanted to rip his clothes off right there and then.

When he finished, he leant to kiss her oh-so-tenderly, wiping his thumb across her cheek to capture the tear she hadn't even realised was there.

"Wow," she said, her voice low.

Robbie leaned in close to her ear. "Holy shit, Cora, if you don't take your panties off right now and throw them at him, I'll chuck mine," he stage-whispered.

She elbowed him in the ribs. "Ew, don't say panties," she said, screwing up her nose, but she was smiling.

"By all means, keep your panties, mate," Indigo said as Robbie bemoaned the fact no one had ever serenaded him so romantically. Nash took his guitar back and began to strum a laidback rendition of Silverchair's *Tomorrow*, as Cordelia slid back to Indigo. His arm settled around her shoulders, warm and heavy.

She found herself yawning. "If you're tired we can go to bed," he murmured.

"To bed or to sleep?" she asked quietly, pulling back to look at him, her eyes teasing.

He shot her a suggestive smile and leant to whisper in her ear so she blushed.

"Ew," Robbie said, screwing up his face as he stared at them in disgust. "You know I can hear you right?" He narrowed his eyes at Indigo. "That's my *sister*, dude."

"Awww, leave 'em alone," Nash said, looking up from his guitar. "Our dear young lovers here, finally getting their shit together." He looked at them and winked and Cordelia felt herself redden further.

"Speaking of young lovers," Robbie said to Nash. "What happened between you and Brooklyn Ford last night? She was running round the party telling everyone you were an English stud muffin. I *love* her mum, she's, like, iconic."

"She used me for my body," Nash declared dramatically. "She got me totally trollied, had her way with me and, when I awoke this morning, she was gone. No note, no morning encore, no spooning, no snuggles, nothing."

"Maybe she only slept with you because she wanted to know whether the carpet matched the drapes… But then she found out there *was* no carpet?" Indigo chuckled.

"I'll have you know she very much appreciated my hardwood floors," Nash smirked.

"I hear she'll be in Aspen for New Year's," Indigo told him. "And it's a pretty small town."

Aurora exhaled sharply through her teeth. "As fascinating as this conversation is, does no one think it's important we figure out a plan of attack going forward here? I mean, we didn't come here purely to work on our tans you know."

Cordelia squeezed her eyes shut as Indigo pulled her tight against him. That afternoon, Nash had burst into Indigo's room and announced he could no longer see Harper, her Maiden or Artax. Which meant they'd regrouped and shrouded.

Aurora leant forward, eyes flashing. "Am I the only one who thinks we can't afford to be complacent here? I thought *you* of all people would be taking this more seriously," she said, looking her nose down at Indigo. "Or are you too wrapped up in your sickening little love bubble there to give a damn?"

"Rory, that's not fair. Do you think I've forgotten for one second that she's out there? But Harper's gone to ground, and clearly Artax's power to shroud was hereditary, not collected."

"For fuck's sake, Indi. What's to stop them collecting again? And the fact he can shroud again already only proves they're a continued threat. You know we haven't seen the last of them. They almost got the better of us the other night. In fact, they would have if it wasn't for *her*," she said, nodding tersely towards Cordelia.

"*Manners*, Rory," Indigo said sharply.

Aurora took a sip of her beer and rolled her eyes in exasperation. "*Sorry.* If it wasn't for *Cordelia.* You're all so *sensitive.* Indigo, if it weren't for the duchess here, you'd be dead." She didn't even blink and Cordelia's stomach lurched. "And we don't even really know how Cordelia did what she did. I mean, what the fuck *was* that? Some kind of psychokinesis? I've never seen anything like it." She made eye contact with Cordelia for the first time. "She needs training. Being in possession of a power like that without knowing how to use it..." She exhaled through her teeth again and shook her head. "Look what your higher senses did to you, before you learnt to manage them."

"Come on, Rory," Indigo said, his voice low. "Now's not the time–"

"We're only here until Christmas! You need to take advantage of us while we're around." She glanced at Robbie then and added, "For *both* of them."

"*Aurora!*" Indigo snapped, fire in his eyes.

Robbie was sitting stock still, staring at him. "What's she talking about, Inds?" His gaze slid from Indigo to Aurora.

"Nothing," Indigo said, scowling. "We can talk about it later."

"Just tell him," Aurora said, throwing her hands up in frustration.

"Yeah, Indigo," Robbie goaded. "Just tell me."

Cordelia could feel the tension in Indigo's body. She slipped her hand into his and squeezed it. He met her eye and she could see he was torn as he raised his free hand to rub his forehead.

Aurora scoffed at Indigo. "Between what you've told me and what I've seen for myself, they're obviously both Akasha, right? Think about it, that's why you've always been so drawn to them."

"What does that mean?" Cordelia asked, her heart hammering in her chest. She glanced up at Indigo, who looked stricken. His grip on her hand was now vice-like.

"We always incarnate together," Aurora said matter-of-factly. "Life after life, this little Akasha family of ours, our soul family, always comes back together, even in those lives we didn't know what we were, we were still as one. There is such a deep soul recognition that exists between us, it's why you three gravitated towards one another," she said, looking from Indigo to Cordelia to Robbie.

Cordelia's mouth fell open. '*Is that true?*' she asked Indigo telepathically. He looked down at her and nodded, then fixed Aurora with a glare.

"Inds?" Robbie said, looking decidedly pale.

"Thanks a *lot*, Rory." Indigo raked his hand over his face and sighed heavily. "I never fully understood why Raf kept the whole Akasha thing from me for so long until right now. I mean, sometimes ignorance is bliss, right? What you don't know can't hurt you."

"Indigo!" Robbie said. "Stop spouting cheesy cliches and tell me what Aurora's talking about. I don't have any of these magical powers you super freaks are blessed with, how can I be… Akasha?"

"I'm serious!" Indigo said. "They can't steal something from your mind that you don't know."

"Just tell him, brah," Sasha said firmly.

Indigo's eyes travelled around the group, landing on Robbie. His shoulders slumped in defeat. *"Fine.* So listen, Rob, do you recall that night Cora was attacked? Not the other night up at North Fort. I mean the first time? At Queenscliff?" He hugged Cordelia protectively as she stiffened against him.

"Is that a trick question?" Robbie said.

"I don't mean what we've told you, I mean, do you recall any of it… firsthand?"

Robbie was clearly about to make another smart-arse comeback but stopped short. The colour drained from his face. "What do you mean, *firsthand?"*

"I mean, if I ask you to think, *really think,* can you see it all unfolding like you were there?"

Robbie's lip quivered. He was silent for a time. Finally, he whispered, "I thought it was a dream."

"You see, afterwards, when we spoke about it, Cora was adamant you were there."

Cordelia nodded at Robbie, smiling wanly. She still recalled that night so clearly, outnumbered by the coven, begging for Robbie to help her. And then he'd suddenly appeared, reaching for her hand. He hadn't said a word, but he'd been there, she swore it.

"But… I don't understand," Robbie breathed, his eyes bright. "How could I have been there when I was home the whole time? I was asleep! Do you know how many sleepless nights I've had wishing I'd *only* been there so Cora never would have been attacked?"

"It's ok," Sasha told him, leaning forward to lock eyes with him. "Just breathe, ya."

Robbie bent double, his hands on his knees, and gulped in big breaths of air. "I don't understand," he kept saying, over and over.

Sasha went to the bar fridge and grabbed a bottle of water, returning and handing it to Robbie. He knelt down in front of him, hand on his shoulder, murmuring, "It's ok, it's ok." Robbie took a few big swallows of the water as he composed himself. Sasha sat on the couch next to him, rubbing his back. "Just tell us what you remember."

"I-I don't know. I'd dropped Cora at yoga and gone to the video shop. I'd wanted to grab a copy of *Speed* before they all went. Two hours of Keanu on a bus, you know?" He forced a lame smile. "I'd promised to pick her up after her class, but... I fell asleep." He dropped his head into his hands, clearly still wracked with guilt. Sasha continued rubbing his back in big circles.

"I remember hearing Cora calling for me. And I knew she needed me, it's a twin thing. Sometimes we have a kind of sixth sense about one another's wellbeing. And now, looking back, I can't for the life of me recall if I was awake or asleep. But I knew with everything I had that I needed to get to her. And I remember now it was the strangest thing ever, because I was lying on the couch at home, and my movie was still playing. I could hear Dennis Hopper's voice: '*Pop quiz hotshot, There's a bomb on a bus...*' But at the same time I could *smell* the ocean, I could *hear* the waves, I could *feel* the breeze on my face... and I could *see* Cordelia, her hand reaching out for mine, her eyes, so full of terror, begging me to help her, and just as I turned to see these figures dressed in dark cloaks, I heard someone yelling her name. And for some reason, when I heard that voice, I just knew she was going to be ok, that she didn't need me anymore... And the next thing I knew, I was back on the couch waking up. It was super weird," he mused, and something in his face changed. "It was almost like I was–"

"–in two places at once," Sasha finished for him.

"Yeah." Robbie frowned. "That's exactly how it felt, like I was in two places at once."

"You saw what Sasha could do the other night, right?" Indigo asked. "How he could project a second version of himself?"

Robbie nodded. "Bilocation, right?" And Cordelia knew he was thinking of how he'd made fun of Drew for believing in it.

Sasha nodded, and as he did, a second version of him appeared in front of Robbie. Robbie did a double take, looking from one to the other. "And we have our suspicions you can do it, too." The second Sasha disappeared.

"Yeah, right!" Robbie scoffed. "I think if I was able to be in more than one place at a time, I'd know."

"Not necessarily," Indigo interjected. "The night Cora was attacked, the night she says she saw you on the beach, *I* saw you, too. Only briefly. You disappeared pretty much as soon as I arrived, but you were definitely there, because I remember wondering why you were just standing there like a lump. But then you vanished and I questioned whether I'd imagined it all, until I had time to think about it afterwards.

I called Cordelia's name, and you seemed relieved to see me and then you disappeared. I've tried to test you a couple of times since, without luck, obviously."

"Like when?" Robbie demanded.

"Like the very next day, when Cora wanted to go for a surf, I told you that she was in danger of another vamp attack and that she needed looking out for. But you didn't show up."

"When else?"

"Umm, yeah..." Indigo started to laugh. "When we were tux shopping a couple days ago? I *may* have fudged the truth when I told you that shop in Double Bay had the last one in your size in all of Sydney and that they wouldn't hold it for us."

Robbie turned to Indigo, open-mouthed. "Are you *totally* kidding me?" he gaped. "Messing around with couture, of all things!"

Indigo only laughed harder.

"I can't *believe* you, Indigo Wolfe!" Robbie snapped, but he was trying not to smile.

"You think you've got problems." Indigo chuckled. "I'm the one who had to drive you all the way across to the other side of Sydney in traffic when it backfired on me!"

"I think they call that karma," Robbie retorted.

"Touché, Rob." Indigo grinned. "Anyway, I have high hopes that Sash will be able to succeed where I have failed, so I am officially putting you in his capable hands."

Robbie glanced at Sasha then and smiled shyly, the tips of his ears reddening. "Really?

"If you'll allow me, I'd love to take you under my wing, eh," Sasha said, flashing him a big grin.

Robbie nodded happily, kneading his hands in his lap.

Something was right there on the edge of Cordelia's memory, something now slowly taking shape. "H-hang on. The other night, up at North Fort... I swear you were there then, too."

"Uh, *yeah*? I *was* there, Cora. I mean, I may have spent most of the night passed out in some dingy closet–" he shot Indigo a dirty look "–but I was there."

"No, not *then*. I mean *before*. Before anyone else came, you were there, I swear it. You were kind of flickery and transparent, but you appeared briefly, just before Sasha bilocated in."

Robbie frowned.

"It's something you need to explore," Aurora told Robbie. She then looked coolly at Cordelia. "As for you, duchess, it looks like we'll be spending some quality time together while we figure out your *gifts*."

Cordelia baulked and looked at Indigo. "Can't *you* just teach me?" she whispered, her eyes pleading.

"Rory's better, babe," he said, and she pursed her lips, her shoulders slumping. The last person she wanted to spend one-on-one time with was Aurora.

glory box

cordelia

He was standing in the moonlight, framed by the open bedroom window, his back to her. He was still wearing his jeans, but he was shirtless, his muscular torso luminescent in the glow. His hair was almost long enough now to touch his shoulders; she loved it like this, tousled, the part uneven and messy, the warm, honey hue she remembered from their childhood now melding blonder towards the ends. He was so indecently gorgeous, she still couldn't believe he was hers to touch whenever – however – she wanted.

Portishead played from the stereo system in the corner, and clusters of flickering candles dotted the room.

As she came up behind him, she noticed his shoulders were bunched up, his hands clenched to fists by his sides. He was staring out over the backyard towards the water, and he seemed lost in his thoughts, preoccupied. She wrapped him in her arms and pressed a kiss between his shoulders, resting her cheek there. "Inds… Are you ok?"

His hands covered hers. "Better now you're here."

"You can tell me anything, you know."

"I know, beautiful." He brushed his thumb over hers. "I'm fine."

Cordelia didn't believe him, but she knew not to push. Indigo would talk to her when he was ready. And, in the meantime, she knew exactly how to distract him – distract both of them – from high stakes destinies and looming danger.

Trailing her hand down to his jeans, she unfastened the top button with a clear snap. She felt his inhale as she slipped her fingertips inside the waistband of his boxer-briefs, his shudder deep as he sunk into her.

She moved her fingers slowly over his body, teasing, enticing, then ran the flat of her palms firmly up his stomach, stroking his pecs with a feather-light touch. She smirked a little at his shiver, enjoying his heartfelt groan when she pinched his nipples, loving how he leaned into her, head thrown back.

She pressed her lips to the warmth of his back, unable to stop kissing him, touching him, inhaling him. His flesh still carried a hint of salt from their surf that afternoon.

She took her time circling round to his front. Standing on tip-toe, she brushed her lips to his, meandering down, down until she was on her knees, moving her mouth over the ridges of his abdomen, dowsing it in slow, lazy kisses, sinking into the heady power she commanded over him while kneeling before him.

She reached for his fly, leisurely dragging it down, then lowered his Calvins inch by inch, until he was free. He was ready to go; he was always ready to go. She gazed up to catch his eye, tilting her head playfully to one side. He blew out a rough breath as a sultry smile curled his lip.

His fingers kneaded through her hair as her mouth continued its languid tour of his body, and she could hear his breath turn shallow. She feathered soft, deliberate kisses all over his lower abdomen, tempting, teasing, her lips trailing across his taut flesh, up, down, and around, exploring everywhere except the one place she knew he really wanted them.

"Cora," he rasped. "You're killing me."

"At least you'll be smiling when you go," she murmured huskily.

She slid his pants down further and he gripped her hair in a loose ponytail, tightening his hold when she moaned softly. She grasped him in her hand, hot and rock hard, then pressed up on her knees, her breath sliding over his warm skin. He groaned deep in his throat as she lowered her mouth towards the tip, her tongue flickering lightly over it, circling him with the gentlest of pressure.

His whole body went rigid as he arched into her. "*Fuck*, baby." He was watching her intently with hooded eyes.

"You like this?" She blew gently where her tongue had just been and he shuddered as warm air met wet skin.

"Yes." He swore roughly. "*God* yes."

"You want more?"

"Yes. So much more." He could barely speak.

She angled him towards her, and in one smooth movement took him deep into the back of her throat and he rumbled a groan, jerking forwards as he gasped her name.

Her hands skated down the sides of his waist, over his backside, then to his hips so she could guide him in and out of her mouth. His large palm loosely cupped the back of her head, the other braced against the window frame.

Just as she felt him starting to lose control, she pulled back, and with one final, long, deep, lingering draw, she rose to her feet.

"Are you kidding me, babe?" he growled. "Please don't stop."

She shot him a playful grin, then pulled his face down to hers, her lips meeting his in a frenzy as he kissed her with all the ferociousness of a man on the brink, a man who needed more, who needed her, right here, right now.

"I want you, Cora." His breath was ragged as he pushed her dress up, his fingers slipping expertly inside her silky black g-string so she quaked. "I can feel how much you want me."

He wasn't wrong.

His tongue was urgent against hers as he started tugging down her underwear. She grabbed his hands in hers.

"Wait," she murmured against his lips, a girl, a woman, in control. She pulled back, stretching up on her toes to rub her nose against his. "Let's both slow down a little. We've got all night." She drew his pants up but left them undone. He blew out a long, low, steady breath, pressing his forehead to hers as he gathered himself. She felt him nod.

She slid her hand into his, then led him slowly across the room, glancing back to throw him a suggestive smile. She came to a halt at the foot of the bed. He swept aside the lengths of her hair and kissed the back of her neck, slipping the cardigan from her shoulders, letting it fall to the floor. He skimmed his palms down the sides of her arms, lacing his fingers through hers, bringing her hands up over her head so he could peel off her dress, then her underwear, whispering his wicked intentions for her as he stripped her bare. He cupped her backside, his fingers feather-light as he ran its curvature before he spun her to face him.

Her skin taut, she closed her eyes and parted her lips in anticipation as he leant in, his mouth almost touching hers, almost but not quite so she could feel his quickened breath, so she could almost taste him but not quite. He paused there, so close yet so far and she could feel herself trembling. *Freaking tease.* She whispered his name, just his name, but she was begging with every fibre of her being for him to kiss her, the anticipation the most exquisite form of torture.

He whispered hers back, and she was acutely aware of the steady rise and fall of his chest, his body surging closer and closer to hers with each inflation. He reached for her then, and her stomach dipped and swirled as his long fingers wandered skilfully over her nakedness, touching her in a way no one ever had.

And then when she could take it no more, he finally, finally closed the gap between them, his parted lips meeting hers, drawing the very breath from her body and, for seconds, *eons*, the world seemed to stop. He lingered there as if he wouldn't be able to savour the sensation of all that burned and flickered between them, should he dare move a muscle. She quivered and he finally stirred, taking her lower lip between his teeth and biting down ever-so-gently before kissing her so intensely her knees gave way.

He was still more clothed than she'd like and she swiftly remedied that, not wanting anything between them another moment, and then he was gloriously naked before her. He hooked his arm around her waist, lifting her effortlessly onto the bed, climbing on top of her, gazing raptly into her eyes as he brushed a lock of hair from her face, the side of his hand gently trailing her cheek. He kissed her then, and she could feel that kiss in every cell, every strand, of her being.

He then proceeded to have his way with her in every way, all through the night, leaving her breathless and more in love with him, if that was even possible. They were connected now in a way that was infinite. Precious. Wholly theirs.

As dawn was breaking, she lay awake in his arms, her back pressed to his stomach, his body curled around hers, his hand cupping her breast as though it had always belonged there. She could tell from his breathing he'd dozed off, but she couldn't sleep. Now she was all orgasmed out, her brain had woken up and was analysing the things Aurora had said last night, what she and Indigo had revealed. Was that what he'd been worrying about when Cordelia came into the bedroom earlier on?

She rolled over to observe him, transfixed by how beautiful he was in the vulnerability of slumber. The sheet had slipped down, and her eyes were drawn to the faint scar on his lower left side. She ran her fingers along it, the scar he'd told her he'd gotten the day he'd met Sasha and Dawn. It amazed her how the scar on her neck that he'd healed after Harper slit her throat had vanished, yet his body still held this scar. He'd told her it was because he and Dawn had different healing techniques. Nash had said Dawn had told him it was because Indigo was a better healer.

She reached to caress his cheekbone, to smooth the hair from his forehead, squeezing her eyes shut as she pressed her lips tenderly to his temple. Her stomach fluttered as a wave of feeling crushed down over her and she wondered how it was possible to love someone so damned much. She'd come so close to losing him, to having him taken away from her before they'd even really begun.

Her chest *ached* at the very thought. Because Harper was still out there. She'd nearly killed Indigo, what was to stop her trying again? The others kept saying she wasn't as powerful now, as though her being less magical made her less of a threat. But she was pissed off and she was certifiably crazy and that was enough to make her a real threat in Cordelia's eyes. There were plenty of non-magical ways to hurt someone.

Something swelled inside of her, and she knew in that moment, that she would do anything to protect him, anything. Because this love of theirs, it was so very endless and vast and bigger than the two of them in the here and now. She would kill for him. She would die for him. And that thought jogged free a memory of something Aurora had said last night, something Cordelia hadn't one hundred percent understood.

She leant forward, her lips whispering over his, and she felt him respond, the movement almost imperceptible.

"Inds?" She was kissing his face, stroking his smooth chest.

"Mmm?" But he didn't open his eyes.

"Inds?" she whispered, nibbling his earlobe so his hands gravitated to her hips, dragging her on top of him.

She pulled away a bit, sat up, and he opened one eye. "Hey there, my beautiful girl," he drawled sleepily. "Where do you think you're going?"

"I need to ask you something," she said, drawing the sheet to modestly cover herself.

He rolled onto his side, bending up his elbow and propping his head in his hand. "Well, why don't you come here and ask me?" he said, cocking an eyebrow at her suggestively. With his spare hand he reached to pull the sheet from her body, grinning at what he saw beneath.

She couldn't help but smile as she swatted him away and pulled it back up. "No," she said, pointing a bossy finger at him. "I require your full attention, Indigo Wolfe."

He groaned then and turned onto his back, folding his arm behind his head. "Fine," he grumbled, closing his eyes.

She hit him lightly on the arm. "Don't you dare go back to sleep!"

He groaned again and prised his eyes open. "What, angel face? I'm so tired. If you don't recall, someone kept me up all night again with their insatiability for my body." He grinned wickedly then as she hit him again. "Ok," he said, holding up his hands in defeat and sitting up. "What is it that's suddenly so important?"

"What Aurora was saying last night... All that stuff about soul recognition and reincarnation and Akasha..."

"Yeah." His tone was evasive, his expression oddly closed off.

"What did she mean, Inds? Because it sounded like she was saying that you and I know each other from... other lives?" She searched his eyes.

He didn't look away. His eyes held hers, his fingers laced through hers, when he finally spoke. "Cordelia. This isn't our first lifetime together. Not by a longshot. We've been lovers before. You and me... we've been forever for eons."

Cordelia tried to speak and couldn't. Tried to think and couldn't. She stared at Indigo, her heart a thick drumbeat.

"It's funny," he said, "because when I look back now, to the first time I saw you sitting there in the quadrangle at school, I couldn't tell you the day of the week or what class I was heading to, but I remember laying eyes on you and thinking, I *know* her. I guess that's the soul recognition Aurora mentioned last night. My soul saw yours and it instantly knew you." He traced her fingertips lazily with his as he spoke.

"Why didn't you tell me?"

He grinned, long and slow. "I've been playing it cool, babe." She raised an eyebrow at him and his smirk flipped to a frown. He sighed with the weight of the world. "Well... I guess I felt that saying to you, 'I've followed you from lifetime to lifetime, always seeking you out, even when I didn't know that it was you I was looking for...' Well, it sounds a little... *stalkerish*, don't you think?"

"Maybe," she said, narrowing her eyes at him. "Although did you ever consider *I* might have been the one following *you*?" She walked her fingers up his chest and poked the tip of his nose, leaning over to kiss it.

"Maybe we've just been following each other," he said quietly as she nestled into him, resting her cheek in her favourite spot, the place where she could hear his heavenly heart beating away. "Raf always says that the people we're meant to have in our lives, that we always come back together one way or another, that we'll always find them."

"How?"

"Fate. If it's meant to be it will be. If someone is meant to be in our lives, the universe will conspire to make sure they are."

"And you and me, you *know* we've been together... before?"

He didn't reply so she glanced up at him. His eyes were closed and he was seemingly lost in a thought, or maybe in a memory. She slid down 'til her head was resting in his lap. She gazed up at him. His hands moved through her hair as he opened his eyes to contemplate her with such softness.

"When Micah told me of a past life I had in the time of the Minoans, when he spoke of the girl I fell in love with, the girl who became my wife, I could see her so clearly in my mind's eye, and I recognised immediately that you and she shared the same soul." His fingers travelled the plane of her cheekbone. He smiled wistfully. "I was a beekeeper. And I healed animals. We met when you came to see if I could do anything about a disease that had wiped out your family's sheep." She closed her eyes as he spoke so she could try and picture the story he wove as he described their life together four thousand years ago on the island of Crete. There was something so familiar about his story, something just out there on the periphery that she focused hard upon, trying to grasp the memory.

"And tell me," she said cautiously, opening her eyes when he finished telling her his tale, "did we live happily ever after?" Lying there in his lap, she reached her hand up to stroke his face. She knew the answer, it was all coming back, hazy and dream-like. But she needed to know.

"We lived happily, yes," he said, a strange expression on his face. She moved to smooth his creased brow. "But that life, it wasn't a long one."

"Tell me?"

"We were expecting our first child. You stepped on a bee. You were allergic," he said tightly. "I couldn't save you."

His words were like a stab to the heart. Her hand froze on his face and her eyes widened. Her dream. She'd dreamt that life – *that death* – recurrently her whole life. She inhaled sharply as the familiar images tumbled through her now: the sudden sharp pain to her foot, the rapid swelling of her throat, her lungs burning for oxygen so she'd awaken drenched in sweat, gasping for air.

She told herself it was just a story, that it wasn't their life now, but the emotion flooding her body, it sure as hell felt real.

"My dreams," she whispered.

"Yes," he replied, "But they were never dreams. They were memories of your past lives."

"Past deaths, you mean." She waited for the shock and disbelief to come. But they didn't. It was like he'd just confirmed something she'd always known deep down. She felt validated, like everything was falling into place. But she'd always woken up at the moment of her passing, had never known what came after. And she needed to know. "So what happened next? After I died?"

"You were my everything. I couldn't live without you. So I carried your body to the ocean and swam out to sea, swimming and swimming until I couldn't swim anymore."

"You... you *killed* yourself," she breathed.

He nodded tersely. "Let's just say that night on the bridge in New York, that's not the first time I've chosen to go out that way."

A wave of nausea crashed over her. She sat up abruptly and dropped her head between her knees, gasping for air. He pulled her tight against him, murmuring for her to just breathe.

"You've done it a lot?" she finally gasped, raising her eyes to his.

"Often, souls who commit suicide, it's not their first time. It becomes a hurtful pattern, an instinctual habit, a cycle that needs to be broken. It can take lifetimes of repeated patterns to learn what we must. And lessons that aren't learnt are only repeated, the consequences growing harsher each time."

Cordelia's voice broke as she asked the question that sat heaviest on her. "So, if we've been together life after life, does that mean... that I was there? All those other times? That I just let it happen? Just like this time?"

"Cora, no." Indigo leaned into her, grasping her face between his palms as he lay his forehead against hers. "What I did on that bridge... It wasn't your fault. Not ever. You didn't *let it* happen, ok? It was my decision at the time."

All the guilt and grief was rising to the surface like flood waters. "I should have been there. I knew in my gut something wasn't right, I knew I needed to fly over there, that you needed me. But I didn't."

"Cordelia," he said, gently kissing her cheeks, "none of it is your fault. *None of it!* Depression is a very inward disease, all I could see was *my* pain, *my* grief, *my* darkness. What happened, it's all on me. *My* life is *my* responsibility. My grief, my sadness, the dark thoughts that played on a loop in my head until they became my reality... I was the only one who could break that cycle."

She glanced up, willing the tears not to fall but she mustn't have succeeded because he wiped a thumb under each of her eyes. "I wasn't strong back then, angel face. My higher senses were out of control, and that allowed other people, other entities – Harper even – to get inside my head and affect my thoughts, to get inside my body and affect my emotions. That will *never* happen again."

"But if I'd been there," she sobbed, the tears falling faster, "it might have been different. I want you to bring me into your darkest hours, Indigo. I just want to make it better for you. I just wanna make it all better, all the time."

"You do, my love, you do. You make it all perfect." She curled herself into a ball, laying her head back in his lap as he stroked her hair, her shoulder, her back. She was suddenly so very tired, and his touch was so soothing, his hands so large and warm. "You've always taken care of me. Even when we were kids. Remember those parties we used to go to at the Prescotts', the ones you used to call a front row seat to Darwinism?"

She smiled drowsily at the memory.

"I remember once, standing on the roof of Pres's house, skateboard cocked ready to launch off into the pool. And then I heard your voice." He chuckled softly and put on a high-pitched voice. "'Indigo Wolfe! Don't you even think about it! You get your butt down here at once before you smash your head in!'"

"I don't sound like that!" She giggled at his poor imitation. He leant to kiss her forehead.

"And I remember peering over the edge, and there you stood, so pissed off and so worried, hands on hips, eyes flashing, and so very, *very* lovely. And it was more than clear my life wouldn't be worth living if I didn't do as I was told, even though there's no way the boys would ever let me live it down. And in that moment, I knew."

"Knew?"

"That it was you." His voice hitched. "You, Cordelia, are why I breathe, why I dream, why I smile. You are why I wake up every morning." Her heart felt like it could burst with happiness. She smiled softly and reached for his hand, interlaced her fingers through his, so content. As her breathing evened out, her eyes flickered and begin to close. "When I have you, I have everything," he told her.

"This time will be different," she murmured as she began to drift off. "This time we're gonna be together forever, 'til we're old and grey. I'm never letting you go, Inds, ever again. Never... ever... again."

"I'll never let go either," he whispered. "I never have, and I never will. Real love stories never end, and ours, babe, ours is epic."

Through her drowsiness, she was aware of a sudden tension in his body, a tension so incongruent with his beautiful words that her eyes sprung open. He was staring fixedly into space, his face folded into a frown so intense her stomach turned over.

There was something he wasn't telling her, she knew it. He had a secret he wasn't willing to share. As long as they'd known each other, the two of them had always told each other everything. Except when he was being overprotective.

She shut her eyes before he could see she wasn't asleep. It took all her effort to keep her breathing even, to feign slumber, so he wouldn't know that she'd seen. Because right now, if there was something he felt he couldn't tell her? She was terrified of what that might be.

chapter thirty-three

all my life

robbie

"Are you *crazy*?! What the fuck is *wrong* with you?" Cordelia's shrieks brought Robbie and Sasha bolting out into Indigo's backyard. So much for quiet meditation time.

Cordelia was running around like a mad woman, head tipped upside down while she furiously batted at her hair.

Aurora stood off to one side, arms crossed, a calculated smile on her lips. "Calm down, duchess, it's only a spider."

Robbie grabbed Sasha's arm, both of them collapsing into laughter as they watched Cordelia totally freaking out. She dragged her hand frantically through her hair, eyes widening as she located the arachnid and untangled in from her locks. She flung it at Aurora. Aurora casually dodged it, rolling her eyes. Cordelia stalked towards her, fury rolling off her in waves. "I'll have you *know*," she seethed through clenched teeth, "that Australia is home to some of the world's deadliest spiders, you *psycho*! Ever heard of a funnel web? Or a red back? Are you an arachnologist? Can you tell the difference?"

Aurora pinned her with an indifferent stare. "So I guess you can't telekinetically stop a spider being thrown at you, then?"

"Don't think I'm not telling Indigo when he and Nash get home, that you threw a *spider*. In my *hair*. With your *mind*. We're *through*, Aurora." Cordelia stormed off towards the house. "And fuck you very much, to the both of you, too," she snapped as she swept past Robbie and Sasha who were crying with laughter.

"Oh my God," Robbie gasped, "Forget Harper, *those* two are gonna kill each other."

Sasha wiped his eyes and shook his head. "On that note, let's take five, eh?" The two of them sauntered across the lawn to the outdoor kitchen where Sasha snatched a couple of small bottles of San Pellegrino from the bar fridge, passing one to Robbie with a gentle smile. They sat down on opposite couches, Sasha drawing a knee up into his chest.

"Your sister's hilarious, dude."

"Excuse me, I'll have you know *I've* got the monopoly on funny. Cora pretty much got everything else. Don't take funny away from me, Sash."

"Cora got everything else? I don't know about that..." Sasha murmured, his light brown eyes sweeping over Robbie so deeply, so intensely, Robbie felt himself blush.

"Cora's always been the beautiful one, the smart one, the kind one, the one with all the friends."

"Looks like you've got some pretty great friends to me?"

"Yeah, I do, *now*. But not always. I wasn't always great at reading the room. Like, officially, I came out when I was fifteen, but Cora always says I unofficially came out in Year Five when I did a dance in front of the whole school to *I Should Be So Lucky.*"

Sasha's brow furrowed. "Don't think I know that one."

Robbie gasped, clutching his chest. "You don't know *I Should Be So Lucky*? It's only Queen Kylie Minogue's first and greatest hit! I'd play it for you right now, but Kylie's been banned from this house ever since she challenged Bernadette for her toga as Goddess of the Gays."

Sasha chuckled. "I have a lot to learn about Australia."

"Lucky you've got me to teach you," Robbie said, propping his feet up on the coffee table.

"Ok, so the other day when Lukas asked me to help him out with the barbie in the arvy? Then told me he was off to get some snags?"

"He was asking you to grill meat with him in the afternoon. And he was going to buy sausages."

Sasha pulled a face. "Yeah. Makes total sense. And right now Indi and Nash have gone to the servo to get petrol for the jetskis?"

"They're at the service station – the gas station – buying, well, gas."

"A formal is a prom, that I now know very well. But answer me this: why, when you Aussies are so laid back and chilled out, do you have this crazy, intense need to save time by shortening everything?" He shot Robbie a baffled grin.

"What can I say? We are a complex race of people."

"I really love it down here, Rob," Sasha said wistfully, "the beaches, the climate, the locals, and of course, the epic surf... But I do feel like I need a translator half the time, eh."

"Just wait till you hear about bottle-O's, brekky, and chucking sickies." Robbie grinned.

Sasha took a sip of his drink then bent forward. "So did you say you came out at *fifteen*? That's super brave."

Robbie shrugged. "Yeah and I've been surviving out here on my lonesome in this homosexual desertscape ever since." Before he could stop it, the question he'd been wanting to ask Sasha forever was out: "So, what's your story?"

Sasha leant back in his seat, his expression unreadable. Robbie picked at the label on his bottle, wondering if he'd crossed a line. "My story?" Sasha finally said. "There's not much to tell, really, eh. I mean, I guess I've dated a lot, but never that successfully, and never with much passion or fervour or intention. I've never been in love, if that's what you're asking, and I've never gotten attached to anyone. But that's cool, ya. I've always known that when the time was right, I'd find my destination, so I made the decision to just sit back and enjoy the journey. You know, experiment, have a bit of fun, because that's what it's all about, right?"

"You've *never* been in love?"

"Nope. You?"

"Definitely! First there was Keanu, then Luke Perry, Jason Priestly, Brad Pitt..." He forced a laugh.

Sasha cocked a brow at him, and Robbie's shoulders slumped.

"I thought... I *thought* I might have loved Gino, but I know now whatever that toxic shit show was, it definitely wasn't love. I guess I don't know what love – I mean, honest to goodness *real* love – is meant to feel like."

Sasha shot him a sympathetic smile. "I hear ya. In high school, all my friends were dating girls, so when one of my surf buddies, Alicia, who I'd known forever, made a move on me at a party one night, I totally just went with it. But she didn't really do it for me in a massive, colossal way, nor did any of the chicks who came after her. So after graduation, I opened up the dating pool a little, dipping my toe here and there into the realm of boys, starting with Billy Travers, a frustrated college quarterback intent on hiding his gay from everyone but me. And that was pretty fun for awhile, but Billy, well, I guess he didn't set my heart on fire. So I threw the net wider, opening myself up to anyone and everyone – men, women, men who were once women, women who were once men, people who were neither, people who were both, whoever caught my eye, really, never fully knowing what I liked, just putting myself out there in an attempt to see if anyone would stick. But no one ever has."

His eyes locked with Robbie's, something unspoken hanging there just out of reach, something that made Robbie's palms dampen and his heart speed up. But then Sasha looked away, busying himself with collecting their empty bottles and rearranging couch cushions, muttering they needed to get back to their training. Because while Robbie didn't know what love was meant to feel like, what he felt when he was with Sasha, well if that wasn't love he didn't know what was. With that to-die-for face and that seriously sculpted bod, Sasha was sex on legs. And he was so sophisticated, so worldly. Robbie wanted to hit himself for being so stupid, for thinking he'd felt some kind of reciprocal spark between them.

Because Sasha was a shooting star, a shooting star that belonged in someone else's sky.

It was probably for the best that Robbie's dreams were where he remained. Like, did Robbie really want to be in one of those couples that strangers looked at and assumed Robbie must be loaded, because what else would someone who looked like Sasha see in someone who looked like him?

Sasha was, quite simply, amazing. Over the past week, Robbie had come into his own under his tutelage. Indigo had given Robbie a couple of healing sessions to "get his energetic bodies aligned and working in unison" whatever that meant, (a lot of what Indigo said to him these days sounded like gobbledegook), but it worked so what did he care?

Once Indigo was finished with him, he'd been turned over to Sasha, who'd been so patient and gentle. He just had this *way* about him. This way of explaining things. This way of not judging. This way of living and breathing and simply existing that Robbie couldn't get enough of.

"You coming?" Sasha said, stopping under the giant fig tree to wait for Robbie.

"Yep," was all he could manage as he jumped up to follow.

"For crying out loud, bro, I'm with Cora and Indi on this one. Knock it off already," Nash groaned as he chucked his cap and sunnies onto the nearest deck chair. The afternoon was hot and humid, the air abuzz with cicada song. Indigo's infinity pool was a glistening inky-blue and had never looked more inviting.

Robbie felt his cheeks warm. "Was I doing it again?" he asked sheepishly.

"*Yes.* And it's not the constant singing under your breath that's driving us all insane, it's the fact it's the *same song*, over and over! You've *got* to give Whitney a break, dude. It's getting dangerously contagious; you've got everyone singing it. I heard Cordelia humming it last night while she was making dinner, and this morning I caught Indi giving it a crack while he was hosing down the jetskis… which wouldn't have been so bad if he hadn't just caught it from me, so I couldn't even give him shit about it!"

Robbie had had *How Will I Know* stuck in his head for days now, mindlessly singing it softly on repeat without realising it.

"You know, if there's a certain… uh… *muse* inspiring these lyrics on a loop, maybe you should serenade him instead of the rest of us," Nash said with a wink and an impish grin.

Robbie felt the heat in his cheeks spread to the tips of his ears. So he deflected. "Pot, kettle, *black*, much?" he smirked, planting his hands on his hips.

Nash squinted at him, screwing his nose up.

"Oh come *on*, mate, every night you sit there, strumming away on that sexy little guitar of yours, gazing longingly at Rory with stars in your eyes while you croon your sad love songs."

"That's bollocks."

"*Mate.* Come on. How long have you been in love with her?"

Nash opened his mouth then closed it. His lips twisted into a resigned smile. "Since before I met her," he confessed.

"*Before* you met her?"

"You're talking to a pre-cog here, bro. I met these guys in my dreams long before I ever laid eyes on them in the flesh. And I can tell you, the first time I laid eyes on Rory in the flesh, it was very *much* in the flesh. Sasha took me under his wing soon after Raf brought me to Sedona, and one stinking hot day he suggested we head to Slide Rock for a swim. He hadn't warned me Aurora would be there, so I wasn't prepared for this stunning creature lounging half-naked on a sunbaked stone like some mystical mermaid."

"So, Rory's never, *ever* met a bikini top she liked then?"

"She has not." Nash chuckled. "Anyway, Sasha introduced us, and I was just completely tongue-tied."

"*You?* Tongue-tied?"

"Believe me, mate, it hasn't happened before or since. But that flawless face of hers, that iridescent cocoa skin, that insane *body*, so impeccable it's like it's the original blueprint from which all lesser female forms were derived... And as we've established, in my defence, she *was* topless. So she sat up, and she gave me the once-over, and I guessed by the wrinkle of her nose she wasn't at all impressed by what she saw."

"I find that hard to believe."

"To be fair, I wasn't much to write home about back then. I was in... recovery, so I was pretty scrawny and sickly," he said in a small voice, absently fingering the wicked-arse scars on the insides of his elbows. "So she looks me over, from my feet to my sweaty pit-stained T-shirt, past my flushed cheeks, to the tips of my red hair, and then she just flicks her hair over her shoulder and says, 'Fancy a dip, sport? You look like you're about to catch ablaze.' Unfortunately, first impressions stick, and she's referred to me as Blaze ever since."

Robbie laughed as he rubbed suncream on his nose. "I won't hear a word against that chick."

"She's definitely something. I'm only human, man. How could I not immediately fall in love with her blunt, take-no-prisoners attitude. And then I got to know her, and I saw her kick-arse strength. Rory's so independent and self-assured, and you've seen firsthand she doesn't waste time with anyone's shit. She's the polar opposite of the delicate, well-bred girls I grew up around." He had a distant look in his eyes as he poured his heart out. "I didn't know then that Raf had already asked her to train me, but I owe her so much. She was the one who taught me how to manage and access my higher senses without needing to constantly relive... stuff... to trigger them."

A sudden yell had both boys glancing across the yard to where Aurora and Cordelia were in the throes of a heated argument.

"No love lost between those two," Robbie commented as Cordelia stormed across the lawn, hands thrown in the air, snapping angrily over her shoulder at Aurora, who was smiling smugly. "Geez, man!" he exclaimed as Nash stripped down to his boardies. "I thought you were wearing a white rashie! That's your *skin*?"

Nash flipped him off and Robbie burst out laughing. "You homegrown Aussies with your mandatory golden-brown tans. Just remember you were all migrants once, a lot of you descendants of us pale ginger Brits. Anyway, I'm not *that* white."

"Can you even *get* a tan?" Robbie asked, wrinkling his nose as he stared at Nash in fascination. He was eye candy incarnate with his racy British accent and his super-cut body, but he needed to spend some serious hours in the tanning bed Bernadette had had installed in the gym downstairs. It wasn't as though anyone else ever used it.

"Well, it's more of a sickly yellow than a tan *per se*... But yeah, yeah, I'm not always *this* pale. I *have* just arrived here from winter, you numpty."

"Yeah, but so have Aurora, Sasha and Inds."

"*Excuse* me! That's monstrously unjust, you can hardly count Rory and Sash, they've both already got a pretty good head start in that department – and yes, I'm sickeningly green with envy. And as for Indi, that boy's a freak of nature. Look at his genes, for Christ's sake! He's what you get when two movie stars procreate. You can't compare me to *him*."

Robbie laughed as they cannonballed into the pool, breaking through the surface to splash and dunk one another.

"Uh oh, incoming," Nash suddenly murmured out the corner of his mouth. Robbie looked up and sighed. Cordelia had spotted them and was headed their way, her pink-and-navy floral maxi skirt swishing ferociously around her ankles.

"Is it too late to hide?" Robbie joked. He and Nash had been stuck in the middle of the two girls all week.

"Depends," Nash replied. "How long can you hold your breath for?"

"Oh, you'd be surprised…"

"I *CANNOT* cope with that… that *person,* a minute longer!" Cordelia fumed as she approached the pool, shooting another dirty look over her shoulder. She flopped down into the nearest deck chair and dropped her head into her hands.

Robbie rolled his eyes at Nash and mouthed, "Mamma Mia, here we go with this shit again."

"Indi and Sash still not back?" Nash asked, in an attempt to diffuse the situation.

Cordelia shook her head. The surf was pumping so Indigo and Sasha had headed over to Queensie for a wave. "And Aurora said that if I went with them, it meant I wasn't taking my training seriously," she said through clenched teeth, twisting the knotted hem of her pale pink baby tee.

"She may have a point, doll," Nash said lightly. "We're leaving soon, so you need to take advantage of Rory while she's here." He drew back, wincing in anticipation of her response.

Sure enough she pouted then groaned, "I've *tried*, Nash, but we're just never gonna be friends. It would be a lot easier if she had more emotions than a freaking potato. It's like trying to reason with a robot! I've been trying to be civil and listen to her, but all she does is bark at me and point out everything I'm doing wrong." She frowned and looked at the ground before whispering, "And she's really mean."

"She's not *that* bad," Nash said weakly. "Once you get to know her."

"Didn't she break your *arm. On purpose?*" Cordelia asked, arching a brow at him. Indigo had told the twins about the day he'd met Aurora, how she'd broken Nash's arm to see if he could heal it.

"Yup," Nash replied. "Ok, I'm out, it's all you, bro," he said to Robbie as he hoisted himself out the pool, grabbing his towel and heading for the house. "You girls are driving me barmy!"

Robbie folded his forearms on the edge of the pool, resting his chin on them. "Cora, this is getting really old. You two *have* to find a way to get along."

"She's a total fembot, Rob."

"She's not *that* bad." Personally, he didn't mind Aurora. He loved her blunt honesty and lack of filter. "Still no luck with the freezing thing?"

She shook her head. She hadn't been able to summon the ability to do it again, much to Aurora's blatant frustration. He knew Cordelia was concerned what Aurora might stoop to, to motivate her, after what she'd done to Indigo with Nash's arm. They were all well aware of what Cordelia's motivation to freeze had been last time. But Indigo had assured them he was confident Aurora wasn't planning on trying to kill him.

"And yes, she *is* that bad," she said, winding a finger through the lengths of the loose braid that hung over one shoulder. "You saw what she did this morning. She threw a *spider* in my *hair*. With her *mind!*"

Robbie fought to keep a straight face. "Y-yeah I saw. What type of spider was it by the way? Are we talking a daddy-long-legs or a funnel web here?"

"It was a *huntsman*. A *massive* huntsman!"

Robbie had to duck under the water for a moment or two to compose himself. When he broke through the surface again, Cordelia immediately continued her tirade. "But she's *American*, right? She doesn't know the first thing about *Australian* spiders! For all she knew, it could have been a *super* venomous face-eating spider that was gonna lay *eggs* under my skin and hatch *millions* of baby spiders into my *brain!* So on some level, she's totally trying to kill me."

Robbie widened his eyes at her. "Cordelia Carlisle, you need to dial the drama down a notch or two. And that's coming from *me!*"

"It was *seriously* traumatising."

"Yes, it sounds positively dreadful," he deadpanned. "A real tale of survival. Who do you think they'll cast as you in the movie?"

She shot him a death-stare, but he could see her mouth twitching at the corners.

"Look," he sighed, "maybe you need to up those meditation sessions with Sasha?"

"Yeah, maybe," she mused, a faraway expression in her eyes and suddenly all the anger faded away. She covered her face with her hands, her shoulders drooping, a ragged breath causing her whole body to shudder. "It-it's been such a shit time, Rob. I miss Dad, I miss him so much, it's like an actual physical piece of me is missing."

Robbie's stomach plummeted. The very mention of Dad still hit him like a tonne of bricks. "I miss him, too," he murmured, as tears rushed to his eyes. It was hard to believe he was really gone. Just... *gone*. And that he was never coming back. It was so final, so, *so* final, and they just hadn't been prepared for that finality. Robbie still expected him to be sitting at the dinner table, waiting to ask him about his day when he got home at night; he still expected him to answer the phone when he called. He thought of things he wanted to tell Dad, a joke, an anecdote, a little bit of gossip that would make him smile, questions only he would know the answer to, and then he would remember he just wasn't *there* anymore. Dad was gone forever. His light extinguished just like that. And the void he had left was simply unbearable.

"And you know, the thing is, sometimes I just feel *so* guilty, you know?" Cordelia said.

"Whatever for?"

"Because when I'm with Indigo, it's like he makes me forget it all and in those moments that it's just me and him, I feel... happiness. Like, real, true unadulterated *happiness*. And then when I remember about Dad, when we go home and I see how broken Mum is, well, I feel so guilty for those snatched moments of joy."

Robbie climbed out of the pool and put his arms around her.

"Ew you're all wet," she moaned, but she didn't pull away. In fact she held him tighter.

"You have nothing to feel guilty for," he murmured into her hair. "You deserve to be happy. If I had my way, you'd be happy every minute of every day, Cora."

"Thanks, Rob," she sighed, squeezing him and stepping back to grab a towel. "I just don't have the emotional capacity to spend my days having to deal with someone who hates my guts."

"She can't be all bad. Nash is pretty great, and you know he's totally in love with her, right?"

"Thanks, Captain Obvious," she snorted. "I mean, she's absolutely stunning, but aside from that, I don't know what he sees in her."

"The heart wants what it wants," Robbie pontificated. "There's no rhyme or reason to who we fall in love with. It's impossible to understand from the outside. Chemistry is a funny thing. I mean, did you have a choice? With Indigo?"

A smile spread across her face and she shook her head. "I didn't have a hope in hell." Her expression changed suddenly as she gritted her teeth. "Ok so I'd better get back, the Ice Queen awaits." She sighed heavily as she turned to leave.

"Are you making any progress at all?"

"Yup, how else do you think I know she's waiting for me?"

"She's projecting orders into your head?"

Cordelia nodded, "Mmmhmm, I cannot escape, no matter how far I go. But telepathy isn't enough, now she wants to see if I can do the telekinesis thing, too. Hence the spider." She shuddered at the memory, then headed off to join Aurora.

"Hey, Cora?" Robbie called after her. "This telepathy thing… Can you read *anyone's* thoughts, or just thoughts that are projected at you?"

She glanced over her shoulder and gave him a sly smile. "Wouldn't *you* like to know?" She winked. "Have fun with *Sasha* this arvo."

Robbie felt himself redden as she started pointedly singing *How Will I Know* as she strolled away.

Robbie's eyes opened, and he blinked slowly. Where the hell was he? Was he dreaming? His head swivelled to take in his surroundings. He was slumped on a little cream sofa in the corner of a room. It was so still and dark, it must still be night. He sat up. He recognised this room, with its whitewashed floorboards and its ivory, embossed, papered walls and its sheer, white curtains. All the bedrooms in the Van Allen Estate followed a similar theme.

He heard the gentle sound of someone breathing, and his gaze swung to the bed, travelling slowly over the heavenly form of Sasha lying there in the moonlight, deep in slumber. Robbie watched the rhythmic rise and fall of his smooth, caramel chest, in awe of the tranquillity that relaxed his faultless features as he slept.

And then he jolted as reality set in. Hold up! He was in *Sasha's* room? Perving on him sleeping like some creepy stalker! Oh my *God*. Oh. My. God! How did he get here? In the midst of his panic, his surroundings suddenly shifted, and the next thing he knew he was back in his own bed, wondering if it had all been a dream.

Bilo-fucking-cation. If this is what *this* was, it was going to get him into deep shit.

He told no one what had happened and pushed it out of his mind the next day. But when the same thing happened the next night, Robbie realised he was definitely bilocating. In his sleep. And once it started, it was on. Oh yeah, it was on like Donkey Kong! Robbie couldn't have stopped if he'd wanted to. Drawn to Sasha, his visits became more and more frequent. He was completely torn about what to do, because if he told Sasha about it, he might put two and two together, and how insanely embarrassing would that be? Sasha was so far out of his league they were barely the same species.

And if he told Cordelia or Indigo, well, it wouldn't take long for those two to figure out he had a bit of a crush – a bit? – well, a *lot*. And he couldn't deal with their shit right now.

So that day, he hopped into the silver Jeep he shared with Cordelia, and he drove over to Indigo's ready to start his day with Sasha, as he had every day that week. And he said nothing to no one.

Robbie was in complete turmoil. He wanted so badly to please Sasha and tell him he'd managed to bilocate on his very own, but the thought of the questions that little tidbit of information would generate had him quaking with humiliation.

Robbie had never met anyone like Sasha. He was so confident within himself, it was hard to believe he was only twenty-two. Yes, he was brutally hot, but it was more than that. Sasha *knew* himself, he lived as himself with no excuses and no apologies, he never hid his differences or dimmed the light inside of him, and Robbie found that incredibly, *incredibly* attractive.

"What's wrong, Robbie?"

Robbie tore his gaze from the content little turtle he'd been watching sunbaking on a stone, and made himself focus on Sasha. The two of them were sitting by the pond in Indigo's front yard, apparently meditating. But he couldn't concentrate.

"I don't know. All of this, I mean, it's a *lot*, right? I've been an outsider my whole life, Sash. And now? If I can do what you say I can do, well, it makes me even more of a freak, right?"

"We're all freaks, eh, Robbie," Sasha said, flashing that irresistible grin of his. "It's just that some of us fight it and try to hide it, while others let their freak flag fly. You should try it, it's super liberating." He hitched an eyebrow. "And you know what? Not only does it scare off all the sketchy lemmings you didn't want in your life in the first place, but embracing your inner weirdo means you find your people. Your fellow freaks, the ones who totally get you, who make life interesting and most importantly *fun*, eh." He winked.

"But people generally don't like weird. Like, at school. I was different so I was excluded, bullied, beat up, even." Robbie cleared his throat. "Until Inds, the other kids... they didn't exactly, um... like me." He lowered his eyes, his cheeks heating.

"But Indigo *saw* you," Sasha said pointedly, sweeping his raven hair over his shoulder. "And he liked you. Because our boy Indi's a total freak, too. Right? Hand on heart, it's never really bothered me when someone hasn't liked me. Because I know they just don't get me. Let's face it, I'm not for everyone – who is? There's like, what? Almost six billion people on this planet? I always had faith in the odds of the existence of at least one or two who'd make me feel loved and understood and included, who'd make me feel good about myself, eh. And look at me now – those people in there?" he said, glancing towards the house. "They're fucking sensational, and they're *mine*."

"I can't imagine someone like *you* knows what it feels like to be bullied." Sasha was just so *cool*. Who'd bully him?

"Never assume anything about anyone, Rob. There was this dude in my class, sophomore year. Hank Jones. Army brat, meathead, not the sharpest tool in the shed. Anyway, Hank took it super-personal that I had the audacity to live in Hawaii after Pearl Harbour. The irony was, he didn't even know I was half-Japanese, the fact I was Asian was enough for him to hate me, eh." He glanced down at the tattoo on his inner forearm, which Robbie now knew was a map of the Hawaiian islands. "I'd walk into the classroom and he'd shush everyone, ordering them not to talk because the filthy nip spy was in their midst. He'd chuck paper planes emblazoned with 'gook' at my head in class, and tape pictures of the sunken wreck of the USS Arizona to my locker."

"Why are people such arseholes?" Robbie said, chest heaving. He picked up a pebble and pegged it hard into the pond.

"Right?" But then Sasha shrugged. "It actually didn't bum me out that much. He was an ignorant idiot and he was *wrong*. Blaming me for invading Pearl Harbour made about as much sense as blaming him for invading Vietnam."

"What did you do?"

"You see, Rob, I figured out pretty fast, that if you own who you are, no one can ever use it against you, ya? Because if it truly doesn't bother you, then all their ammunition is gone, just like that." He snapped his fingers. "Hank thought he could shame me for being Asian, but I'm actually super-dooper proud of my family and where I came from. So when we had this cultural day thing, I stood up in front of the whole school and did my presentation on my Japanese heritage. I talked about my grandparents and all they'd taught me, about all the time I'd spent in Japan, the senseis I'd studied under over there, and how I had multiple black belts in martial arts. I even talked about Pearl Harbour.

"Now, whether it was the realisation that I was proud of my culture and he hadn't succeeded in shaming me, or him finding out I could totally kick his ass five ways to Sunday, I'll never know." Sasha laughed. "But Hank never messed with me again."

Robbie could sit and listen to Sasha for hours. He could sit and *look* at Sasha for hours. No one had ever made him feel the way Sasha made him feel. In fact, he hadn't known it *was* possible to feel this way about other human being. When Sasha was mentoring him and their hands accidentally touched, Robbie felt those elusive sparks fly, the ones he'd read about or heard about in love songs but had always rolled his eyes over and discounted as fantasy, as romantic mumbo jumbo.

Robbie had always thought love at first sight was a myth perpetuated by Hollywood. Until the very moment he'd laid eyes on Sasha the night of the formal, because if that wasn't love at first sight, he didn't know what was. And there had been times since then, many moments in fact, when Robbie dared to let himself fantasise that maybe, possibly, Sasha felt it, too. There were times when he turned quickly and swore he'd caught Sasha staring at him. Times when he convinced himself the excuses Sasha had made to extend their sessions seemed flimsy...

Yep, Robbie was torn and confused and all over the shop. And it wasn't just the Sasha thing. Memories were beginning to resurface for him, memories from his childhood. He vaguely recalled being six or seven and closing his eyes at night, only to open them and find himself no longer in his bedroom. He'd always freaked out, squeezing his eyes shut, repeating to himself over and over that it wasn't real. And when he'd open them again, he'd be safely back in his bed in the little room he and Cordelia had once shared at their grandparents' house. Looking back now, he began to question what had been real and what hadn't. That was back in the day when Cordelia would have those terrible nightmares from which she'd so often awakened, thrashing and crying. And that was something he'd begun to question lately, too.

That night Robbie bilocated again.

But this time, he didn't wake up until the next morning.

And this time he hadn't bilocated to the sofa in the corner of Sasha's room.

He awoke to find himself curled beside Sasha on his bed, his hands tucked peacefully under his cheek. He groggily opened his eyes to see Sasha sitting beside him, bare-chested, smiling softly, the white sheets draped over his lower body.

"Morning." Sasha winked.

Robbie blanched, his embarrassment so intense he could die. He just wanted to disappear. And the next thing he knew, he did. He instantaneously found himself back in his own bed at home, sweat upon his brow, his breath heavy.

A moment later, the phone on his bedside table began to ring. He picked it up.

"That was totally awesome!" Sasha said. "You're really starting to get the hang of it."

"Thanks, Sash," Robbie whispered, mortified. *He was starting to get the hang of it?* Did that mean Sasha knew he'd been there before, on other nights? It was in that moment Robbie knew it was all real. His gifts, his powers, the reality of what he could do, and Sasha... Sasha was so real.

"Come back?"

Robbie almost dropped the phone. Sasha was asking him to come back. But back where? To the house? To his bedroom? To his bed?

Robbie hesitated, unsure of the invitation he was accepting, but then he realised he'd accept any old invitation from Sasha, anywhere, anytime. With bells on. He'd walk over cut glass for Sasha, over burning coals, over cheap polyester wearing a suit adorned with carnations and baby's breath.

"I'm on my way," he purred, hanging up the phone and leaping out of bed, heading for the shower.

sasha

When Indigo had told Sasha he was going to the formal with his mate, Robbie, the other night, Sasha had been more worried about a Harper attack than anything else. So he'd done as asked, bilocating in now and then over the course of the evening. And there from the shadows, he'd seen the boy Indigo had been talking to on the edge of the dancefloor. At that moment, the world around him ground to a halt, time stood still, the air squeezing from his lungs. Long-legged, dark-haired, and maybe not exactly traditionally handsome, but fuck, he was righteously *gorgeous* – attractive as all hell, especially when he smiled.

Robbie.

Sasha knew his name was Robbie. Indigo's 'date'. Cordelia's brother. And he knew he was single, because Indigo had explained the situation, how Robbie's boyfriend had ditched out on him at the last minute, providing Indigo with the opportunity to go instead.

And Sasha had known he was something special.

That Robbie was going to be something special to him.

Not because anyone had told him. But because he'd just known it, deep in his heart, in his gut, the minute he'd laid eyes on Robbie, like a lightning bolt.

It was totally a moment of intense soul recognition, of remembering that this person had been put here on this earth just for him, that he was meant to find him.

And now, finally, he had.

Robbie had come along, and Sasha suddenly felt he no longer had to bother trying to label himself and what he liked, because now he knew: *Robbie* was what he liked. It was as simple as that.

In the days since they'd met, Sasha had totally questioned himself, wondering if he could mentor Robbie properly as Indigo had asked him to if he was romantically involved with him. And the truth was, he didn't know if he could. Look what had happened the night of the formal, when he'd allowed himself to be distracted by Robbie, and he'd totally dropped the ball with Cordelia.

Sasha liked to be in control of himself, of his emotions, and the way he felt about Robbie, well, that challenged everything. Harper and her coven were a continued threat, and Robbie needed to be ready for them, just in case, just as much of the rest of them.

He'd reluctantly come to the conclusion that now wasn't the right time to put himself out there, to potentially start anything up. Quite frankly, how he felt for Robbie wobbled him out a little. He'd known him for days, yet it felt like years. In reality, he knew it had been lifetimes.

It was a lot. And so he'd kept it professional, kept his platonic distance, only gazing longingly at Robbie when he wasn't looking, pretending the brush of their hands was accidental, coming up with totally lame excuses to extend their mentoring sessions so he could soak up every last possible moment with him.

Over the past week, he'd been vaguely aware of an inkling of Robbie's presence in his room in the small hours of the night, but it was dreamlike and hazy, nothing ever concrete enough to be sure of. But then that morning, when he'd woken up to find Robbie had bilocated into his bed, his heart had totally leapt. If Robbie was visiting him in his sleep, clearly Sasha was on his mind, playing on his subconscious, occupying his thoughts and dreams. He'd had to draw so deep, cos it had taken every ounce of self-control not to snatch Robbie up into his arms, confess his love and prove it.

Robbie had woken up and Sasha could see he was totally mortified for having put himself out there without meaning to, but then he'd disappeared before Sasha had had the chance to tell him that he wasn't dangling out there solo in his feelings. He couldn't stand the thought of leaving Robbie hanging. So, he'd rung him before he lost his nerve, asking him to come back, and it was only after he hung up that he began to think maybe he'd been a little bit ambiguous about why he wanted Robbie to return.

Of course, he was super-dooper thrilled his protégé had bilocated so awesomely, and he knew they totally had to build on that and get Robbie consciously doing it while he was awake. But that's not why he wanted him back. Professionalism be damned, there was no way he'd be able to concentrate another day with Robbie while he was holding back so much. He'd never experienced anything like this and, if he was honest, it scared him a bit: the unknown, what these intense feelings might do to him, to his easy, ordered life.

But he showered, and he dressed in red, white and navy shorts and a pale-blue polo, and he waited for Robbie to return. Barefoot, pacing the room nervously, a million random thoughts tumbled through his head. His heart jumped in his chest when he finally heard a gentle rap at his door. He had to take a deep breath to compose himself before he moved to answer it.

He pulled the door open to see Robbie standing there, his dark hair damp yet perfectly coifed, the faint scent of his aftershave overwhelmingly tantalising.

Their eyes locked. Both were breathing heavily as they stood and faced one another, feeling each other out, the intensity between them totally electric.

Without a word, Sasha reached to slowly, tentatively, coil his fingertips through Robbie's. Robbie stared down at their intertwined hands for a moment or two, then deliberately raised his eyes to meet Sasha's, the column of his throat working. His pupils flared.

Sasha smiled then, and Robbie's face broke into a beautiful grin as Sasha drew him close. He raised Robbie's hand to his mouth, pressed his lips to his palm, laying soft kisses down the inside of his wrist.

Robbie's eyes fluttered shut, and Sasha leant up to cup his cheek, his hand sliding to the nape of his neck as he pressed up on his toes to brush his lips lightly across Robbie's, fireworks exploding through his belly.

This, this, this. He'd never felt anything like *this*. This was totally what he'd been waiting for.

Robbie pulled back. "Are... are you sure?" he murmured, eyes downcast.

"Hell, yeah, I'm sure," Sasha growled, trying to capture his gaze.

"But you're so..." Robbie exhaled steadily. "And I'm... this," he said, indicating his face. He finally met Sasha's eye.

Sasha stared at him incredulously. Was he *kidding*? "Robbie..." He exhaled through his teeth. "Don't you see? You're the complete package. You, you're everything I've ever wanted. You're everything I've been waiting for. The journey is over, Rob, because you, *you* are my destination."

He gazed up at Robbie, so tall and thin, his face not quite symmetrical but so unique, and there was just something about him, an X factor, a certain *je ne sais quoi*, that Sasha found totally impossible to resist. He was unlike anyone he'd ever met. A vibrant, quirky, force-of-nature, Robbie was so smart and quick-witted and so funny and dramatic, he made Sasha laugh until his sides ached. Robbie was like a magical door to a whole new world, a world of wonder and possibility and beauty. And Sasha wanted so badly to walk through that door.

He pushed up to claim Robbie's lips once more, and Robbie responded, their kiss deepening, the teasing strokes of his tongue against Sasha's causing heat to pool low in his abdomen, driving him totally, insanely wild. He pulled him into the room, Robbie kicking the door closed behind him as he willingly allowed Sasha to drag him into his bed...

chapter thirty-four

that's the way love goes

cordelia

"Our minds are incredibly busy and insanely loud, ya," Sasha explained. It was Cordelia's first session with him post spider-throwing-incident, and to be frank she was still low-key pissed at Aurora. They were sitting cross-legged on a rug in a shady corner of the backyard overlooking Little Manly Beach below.

"We're always thinking and worrying and listening to our own internal dialogue. Living inside our minds is totally like living inside a busy airport terminal; it's crowded, it's loud, we're surrounded by snippets of other people's conversations and drama, announcements are blaring over the loudspeaker, children are yelling, babies are crying…" He chuckled. "If you wanna be heard over all that, you'll have to speak very loudly and clearly, ya? And if your travel companion is speaking super-quietly, there's no way you'll hear what they're saying." He grinned. Sasha was honestly the smiliest person she'd ever met. Hanging out with him was so easy.

"Now, imagine you and your friend board an empty plane," he continued, leaning forward, his eyes shining passionately. "There's no one else on the aircraft and it's completely silent. You could sit and whisper to one another and hear every single syllable as clear as day. Your mind needs to be like that empty plane, not that busy airport terminal, if you want to be able to telepathically communicate with someone."

"That seems impossible," Cordelia argued. "How can you have *no* thoughts in your mind?" Even when she was deep in meditation and she believed her mind was clear of thoughts, she realised she was thinking, *hey cool, I'm not thinking,* which seemed to defeat the purpose.

"Like anything, it takes commitment and practice, eh. It's not so much about not thinking as it is about just quietly noticing your thoughts and letting them go. It *is* possible, trust me. Just ask Indi, ya, he totally argued about this with me until he was blue in the face. But he quickly managed to nail it."

Cordelia smiled, rolling her eyes affectionately. Of course he had.

"Nash will tell you the same thing. For his clairvoyance to work accurately, his mind needs to be super-clear and quiet and empty, a blank screen if you will. Meditation has helped him learn how to empty and focus his mind on command, which allows room for whatever needs to come in. I totally promise you, meditation is the key to managing your higher senses." He winked.

"And if that's not motivation enough, let me put it this way, babe: for someone with your gifts, with such a strong ability of telepathy, it's totally going to happen whether you like it or not, ya," he said bluntly, and her stomach lurched. "You're going to hear other people's thoughts, you're going to hear voices and whispers – whether they're coming from this realm or the next – so I'd strongly advise that you learn to control your gifts. Otherwise, you'll end up gravely ill, or highly medicated, or in the loony bin as countless souls have before you. Admitting you're hearing voices is totally *not* socially acceptable... Although for me, it was the fastest way to make the right kinda friends, let me tell you." He laughed, his eyes crinkling, then leant back on his palms and regarded her closely.

"So listen... You need to let Aurora help you, babe. Her methods may be a little sketchy, she may not do things the way the rest of us do, but I promise you, she means well, and she *will* help you master your abilities. But you need to do the work, too," he told her with the stern look of a teacher lecturing a student. "This is bigger than you, Cordelia, you've been given a gift, eh, and with it comes responsibility. So, sort your shit out with Aurora–"

"But–"

Sasha held his hand up to silence her. "I've spoken to her as well. She's going to try harder to get along with you, too. So, *please*, promise me you'll at least *try* to make peace and get on with it?"

Cordelia bit her lip as she regarded him. "Fine," she eventually sighed. "I promise I'll *try* to get on with her".

"Right on," Sasha grinned putting his arm around her and pulling her into a big hug, "That's all I ask. And believe me, babe, we've all totally been there with Rory, ya, so I'm speaking from experience when I tell you it *is* possible to get along with her. No one is all good or all bad, Cordelia. We can choose what we see in others."

She scrunched her nose, the very thought of Aurora annoying her.

"You need to understand that Aurora's a walk-in, which means she's fast-tracked her way here because she needs to get stuff done quickly," he said as he squeezed her hard and released her. "She's not super-dooper fussed with trivialities such as feelings and thoughts or with being liked. She sees what needs to be done and she just does it. So, when she offends you, she doesn't do it to be nasty or to hurt you. She does what she does because she believes it will totally get the fastest results. It may help to keep that in mind when you're with her."

"Why *is* she here?" Cordelia asked, because Indigo had told her about Aurora, but she still didn't fully understand why she'd returned to Earth in this way. It was pretty freaky that she'd just taken over someone else's body like that.

Sasha shrugged. "Not even she knows why exactly. She says she knows she's here for a specific purpose, ya, for a set mission, and that she'll know what that is when it presents itself." And that was the end of that.

That afternoon, Cordelia was sneaking off to yoga when Sasha pointedly asked her to hang out with him and Aurora. He informed her Aurora was an incredibly accomplished yoga teacher and invited her to practice with them instead.

"I thought Aurora worked in an old people's home," Cordelia grumbled.

"She does. But she teaches yoga in the mornings before work."

Corelia went to protest, but Sasha held a hand up. "Trust me, Cora. Indi used to do her classes a couple of mornings a week when he was living in Sedona, and you know he's totally pedantic about needing a good work out."

So she'd reluctantly given in. And she'd reluctantly had to admit that Aurora was the best yoga teacher she'd ever practiced under.

Afterwards, the three of them lay towels out on the back lawn, ice clinking against the sides of their drinks, the sun beating down on their swimwear-clad bodies. Aurora seemed to spend half her life lying in the sun; she couldn't get enough of it. She reached around to untie the top of her little black and silver bikini, dropping it on the grass and leaning back on her palms, face tilted to the sky. She closed her eyes, the bejewelled stud in her bellybutton glinting in the sunlight.

Cordelia rolled onto her stomach, sliding her sunnies off and resting her face in the crook of her elbow. In her ivory strapless one piece, she felt positively dull next to Aurora. Aurora was such a closed book, a fortress, impossible to penetrate in any way. Cordelia had spent so much time with her, yet all she pretty much knew about Aurora was that she was a telepathic, telekinetic walk-in who worked in an old folks' home and taught yoga in her spare time. And that she seemed to get off on being mean. As Cordelia lay there next to her, her curiosity got the better of her, and her mind wandered towards Aurora's.

"It's considered extremely uncool to just barge into someone's head and start reading their mind without their permission," Aurora said, her words dripping with boredom. Sasha pointedly raised an eyebrow at Aurora, and she added, "Yeah, yeah. It's probably wise to do as I say, not as I do.

"It's one thing, Cordelia," she continued, "if someone's projecting their thoughts at you so loudly that you have no choice but to read them, but to invade someone's head, to delve into it and prise out their most private thoughts is akin to reading their diary and considered completely fucking taboo."

Cordelia felt the heat rise up her cheeks. "Sorry," she muttered. She knew the rules, of course she did. And she knew it had been driving Robbie crazy lately, not knowing whether she could read his mind on a whim. She'd decided it was a sister's right to mess with her brother a bit and had failed to tell him her abilities were guided by strict parameters. It was more fun this way.

"Rory's right, Cora," Sasha said, rubbing sunscreen on his muscular shoulders. "We're held to a higher standard than others, because our abilities are stronger than others'. I mean, everyone's totally telepathic to a degree, even if it's just on a subliminal level. Like when you suddenly start thinking about someone and the next minute they call? Or when friends finish each other's sentences, or you just know what someone is about to say, right before they say it."

Cordelia nodded peevishly. It wasn't liked she'd *asked* for all this pressure and responsibility, for this to be her life now.

"You're joining me and Rob again tomorrow, ya?" he asked. The past couple of days she'd crashed Sasha and Robbie's daily meditation practice, although she'd been feeling like a bit of a third wheel, what with all the longing glances and subtle touching when they thought she wasn't looking.

They were all acutely aware that Robbie and Sasha had started something up, yet the boys were yet to officially announce it. She got it. Sometimes, with something so precious and personal, you needed to be ready before you shared it with the world.

Cordelia was determined to persevere with the meditation sessions because they'd helped her deal with her grief and her guilt. They'd also allowed her to cope better with Aurora. As Cordelia's ability to re-centre herself grew, Aurora's ability to rile her up decreased. And here she was now, sunbaking with Aurora's tits in her face yet again, trying her best to form some kind of civil relationship with her, for the sake of the others, if nothing else. Due to Sasha's intervention, things between Aurora and Cordelia had thawed a little. Not much, but enough.

It killed Cordelia to admit it, but Aurora was an excellent teacher. Under her guidance, Cordelia had managed to hone her telepathy skills to a fine art, mastering both projection and reception. But try as she might, she wasn't able to move things with her mind. Stop them, yes, although that seemed to only be a one-time thing, never to be repeated, because she hadn't been able to do it again since that night.

"You coming to see Mum and Matty this arvo?" Cordelia asked, gazing at Robbie, sitting beside her at the long, teak table in Indigo's backyard. She fished an ice cube out of her drink and crunched down on it while she waited for him to respond. "Rob?"

"Huh?"

"Mum and Matty? Inds and I are meeting them at the beach again this arvo?"

"Look how utterly divine my boyfriend is," Robbie murmured. He was watching Sasha through lowered lashes. Sasha and Indigo were sparring with katanas on the back lawn, both barefoot and shirtless, their bronzed bodies dripping with sweat. Indigo had tied his hair back, which Cordelia had come to learn was a sign he meant business. "Don't you just love the smell of testosterone in the morning?" Robbie said admiringly.

"Boyfriend, hey?" She nudged his shoulder with hers.

He shot her a look. "As if you didn't know."

She laughed. "Of course I know. *Everyone* knows!"

He looked aghast. "Everyone?"

She put her arm around him then and leant her head against his. "Even Edie mentioned it to me before she and Lukas left for Thailand. You guys aren't as subtle as you think. I'm happy for you, Rob. Sasha's a keeper."

She looked up at the sound of clanging metal. "Ugh, I hate it when they do this," she said, drawing a finger through the condensation on her glass. "It makes me nervous."

"You know those swords aren't sharp, right?" Robbie's eyes were glued to Sasha.

"I still wouldn't want to be on the business end of one of them. Besides, the sound of metal on metal just sets my teeth on edge."

"It's an artform, Cora. Sasha's been studying the ways of the samurai most of his life. And of course, Indigo's just naturally good at it. He's only been training with Sasha for like, eighteen months and look at him go." They watched as Indigo completed a perfect backwards somersault, landing effortlessly on the garden bench behind him, sword still in hand, a triumphant grin on his face.

Sasha laughed and flipped forwards, twisting mid-flight to land on the other end of the bench, their swords clanging loudly as they continued their duel, leaping over the back of the bench in unison.

"Sasha's amazing. Who taught him?"

"So, the story is, Sash's dad used to be a Buddhist monk. His mum was visiting Thailand with her father on some philanthropic trip, and the two of them somehow crossed paths and fell in love, which was completely forbidden. And so, his dad, like, gave up his monkhood for her, and had to leave Thailand. Then Sash's granddad, who was apparently a total legend, helped them relocate to Hawaii, under the condition that any kids they had, be sent to Japan every school holidays to learn about Japanese culture and the way of the samurai."

"What a cool grandpa!" Cordelia said.

"Right? Sash's granddad arranged for him to train under some of the best senseis in Japan and, when he wasn't doing that, his grandma was teaching him how to cook. That's why he's so good at making all those Japanese dishes." With Edita away, it had fallen on them to cook for themselves, and Sasha and Cordelia had been the ones to step up. When Sasha was at the helm, it was either Japanese comfort food on the menu or crazy fusion that somehow always worked.

"His brother, though," Robbie continued, "well, apparently he hated their trips to Japan, and once he reached the age of, like, twelve, he refused to go anymore."

Robbie focused his attention on the boys, ducking and weaving and flipping in a blur of rippling muscle. "Oh, to be so coordinated," he commented dreamily.

Sasha had continued Indigo's martial arts training when he'd arrived in Australia, the two of them sparring in one form or another every day. This constant preparation for battle made Cordelia a little uneasy. She'd noticed Robbie sat and watched them every day without fail, whether they were practicing Aikido, Hapkido, Tae Kwon do, or Iaido, or toying with swords or staffs.

"He offered to teach me, too, you know?" Robbie said.

Cordelia glanced at him sidelong.

"I refused, of course."

Of course he had. He'd offered to teach her, too, and she was seriously considering it. Not the swordplay, the self-defence. "Don't you think that with a coven of warlocks hanging around, it might help, knowing how to defend yourself?"

"I know only too well where my strengths and weaknesses lie, Cordelia, and having feet, hands and swords flying at me from all directions would not bode well for me. I'm not sure if it would be possible for Sasha to continue to find me attractive if he saw me in all my uncoordinated glory, cowering in the corner, my hands clasped protectively over my precious face."

Cordelia snorted.

"What am I gonna do, Cora?" he murmured, suddenly serious as he stared transfixed at Sasha. "He's leaving soon. It's not fair. I've finally met someone I can see a real future with, who I'm completely obsessed with, and he lives on the other side of the world. Long-distance relationships are the pits."

She leant her head on his shoulder. "I know. It sucks. But you do remember you're both in possession of a little ability called bilocation, right? Surely that means you can be together on some level whenever you want? I mean, really neither distance, time nor space should matter much to you two?"

"But still," Robbie bemoaned, "it won't be the *same*. You don't understand, I'm not as good at it as he is, so when I bilocate, half my attention is in one place and the other half is in another, so he'll only be getting half of me."

"Well, it's better than nothing. Most people in your situation would be stuck with only the phone for contact."

"Someone should invent video phones," Robbie suggested. "So you can see the person you're talking to instead of just hearing them. Like on *Back to the Future Part 2*."

Cordelia giggled. "Yeah, I can't wait for the day I can call someone on the phone and see them while I talk to them, all while riding my hoverboard. Seems like *way* too much pressure, imagine having to get dressed and do your hair just to talk on the phone? Gone will be the days of racing for the phone from the shower in nothing but a towel."

"Just you wait, it'll happen one day and you'll have to eat your words. By 2015 if the movie's right."

"I'm not overly excited about that future. I wouldn't want to live in a world where Biff Tannen rules Hill Valley."

Robbie rolled his eyes. "You have no idea what you're talking about. Marty McFly and Doc Brown totally fixed the space-time continuum. Biff only ruled in an alternative timeline, an alternate reality, which was reversed when Marty burnt the Sports Almanac."

She frowned at him. "Does that mean that only one timeline can exist at once, or that both timelines exist in alternate planes of reality?"

Robbie shrugged. "Do I look like a quantum physicist to you?" They watched as Sasha threw his head back and laughed at something Indigo said before chucking him a bottle of water. "Things with Inds are good?"

The boys were now strolling towards the pool. Cordelia made eye contact with Indigo. "Wanna swim, beautiful?" he called, flashing her that heart-stopping grin of his.

She smiled back and shook her head. He shot her a mock pout, then turned to continue his conversation with Sasha. She frowned after him. "Yeah, great, things are great. Really great."

"One more great and I might believe you." Robbie squinted at her. "This is me you're talking to, womb-mate. What's wrong?"

"Nothing! It's just… I mean, I dunno… Everything's so incredible, it truly is…"

"But?"

She bit the corner of her lip, then sighed heavily. "I think he's keeping something from me, Rob."

"*Inds?* Doubtful. Why do you say that?"

"I don't even know why. Just a feeling, I guess. When we're together, he's so present and loving and, you know, just his amazing, perfect self. But a couple of times now, when he thought I wasn't watching, he's let his guard down and I can tell he's stressed about something."

"Ummm… hello? Maybe it's about the fact his psycho ex-girlfriend's out there trying to kill us all?"

"It's not that."

"How do you know?"

"Because it's something he doesn't want to worry me with."

"Why don't you ask him?"

She stared at him, hands wringing through the skirt of her pastel-striped sundress. "Because I'm scared to hear the answer, Rob. What if he's having doubts about us? What if I'm not…" She cleared her throat. "What if I'm not what he thought I'd be?"

Robbie guffawed. "Bullshit, Cora. I've known Inds for years, and I've never seen him smitten like this. To steal from Meg Ryan in *Top*

Gun, 'there are hearts breaking wide open all over the world tonight... *because unless you are a fool, that boy is off the market. He is one* *hundred percent, prime-time, in love with you'."* His impersonation was perfection, and she couldn't help but smile as he put his arm around her and hugged her close. "Now, stop stressing, ok?"

She nodded. But her stomach was still fluttering. Because how she felt about him? She knew without a doubt that if he broke her heart, that was something she'd never recover from.

Most evenings, they had dinner together at the weathered teak table under the big Moreton Bay fig in the backyard. Sometimes after dinner, they'd play pool or swim. But they'd always end up sitting around the outdoor couches, drinking, chatting, laughing, and listening to CDs, unless Nash was strumming away at his guitar, regaling them with acoustic versions of their favourite songs.

Sometimes Sian and Will or Peyton and Sandy dropped by to hang, and tonight it was the latter. Cordelia had never known Sandy to be in a bad mood, but the last couple of times she'd seen him, he'd been quiet and irritable, a permanent scowl fixed to his face. Tonight was no exception.

"What's with Sandy?" she asked Peyton when she was finally alone with her in the kitchen. Sasha had cooked them a sensational meal of several small courses he'd branded an "izakaya experience", so they'd offered to clean up.

Peyton's brow bunched as she handed Cordelia the plate she'd just rinsed. "Things are... things aren't good, Cee," she said softly.

Cordelia paused in stacking the dishwasher the minute she heard Peyton's tone. "What's wrong?"

"He's got a lot going on at the moment. And he's so distracted and angry all the time. I'm so scared I'm losing him, Cordelia." Her voice wavered. "I love him, you know? We've been friends for so long... Even before we got together, we've always gotten on like a house on fire. But things just aren't the way they used to be between us. I can feel him slipping away."

"Oh, Peyts," Cordelia said, reaching for her hand, squeezing it. "I didn't know. But if there's other stuff going on for him, maybe it's not about you? Do you know what's bothering him?"

"I'm not s'posed to tell anyone…" Peyton glanced around, then lowered her voice. "The thing is, Cee, well, he owes a lot of money to a lot of people. And some of them are *really* bad," she confessed, shoving her corkscrew curls back off her face.

Cordelia felt her eyes widen. Bloody Sandy. He never failed to disappoint. "Since when?"

"Since ages. And then after his mum found all that ecstasy in his room on the night of the formal and flushed it, well, things have gotten pretty dire."

"Shit, Peyts, what does that mean?"

Peyton's eyes filled with tears as she threw her hands up in the air, shrugging. Cordelia swept her into her arms, hugging her tight. Anger swelled inside of her. Sandy had never been her favourite person, and now, seeing Peyton so upset, it turned her off him even more.

"These guys are seriously bad dudes." Peyton sniffled, pulling away and swiping at her eyes. "Like, if he doesn't pay up, they could hurt him real bad, Cee. They've even threatened to kill him!"

"What? Oh my God." Cordelia handed her a tissue. She clamped her lips together to stop the words bubbling up inside of her from escaping, but it was too late. "Listen, Peyts, I say this with love, because you know how much I love you right?" she blurted.

Peyton's eyes narrowed.

"Please don't be mad, but I don't think you should be hanging around with Sandy right now. I mean, what if you get caught in the middle of all this? I don't want you to get hurt. Maybe you should stay away from him for a while? At least until he sorts his shit out." Or forever, if Cordelia had her way.

Peyton stared at her in deathly silence. "Wow," she finally managed, and her hands were shaking. She shot Cordelia a toxic smirk and reached for her wine glass, draining it in one hit. "Not exactly the supportive response I was looking for. Tell me what you *really* think, won't you, Cee?" Her words dripped with sarcasm.

"Always have, always will," Cordelia said lightly.

"He's my *boyfriend*, Cordelia! I can't just abandon him when things get rough! He needs me right now, more than ever. Would you do that to Indigo if he was going through a crappy time?"

"I'm just worried about you."

"I know you are. And I know you like to fix people's problems, Cee, but I can take care of myself, ok?"

Cordelia frowned, then nodded slowly.

"You can't tell anyone what's going on with Sandy, ok? And couples rules don't apply here, so not even Inds."

She saw Cordelia hesitate and pointed a finger at her. "I'm serious, Cee, you can't tell him, ok? This is in the vault. Swear to me?"

Cordelia sighed heavily. "Fine, I swear," she said, hooking her pinkie around Peyton's. "What's Sandy doing about it all?"

"I don't know," she said, turning to pick up another plate, turning the tap on. "But at this stage he's so desperate, I'm scared of what he'll do. I just wanna help him, you know? I wanna make it all better for him. Oh, Cee, I'd do anything to make it better for him!"

Cordelia realised then just how much Peyton loved Sandy. She pulled her friend into her embrace again. "I know you would, Peyts, I know. Just be careful, ok?"

It was early summer and the days were growing longer, the nights warmer. Nash, Sasha and Aurora would be going home soon. Later that night, as they sat together, knowing the end was drawing close, they were a lot quieter than usual, reflective, nostalgic. Nash's fascination with Australian music had become almost obsessive and he was playing them his most recent favourite, Augie March's *One Crowded Hour*, his voice rich and wistful.

Indigo had been inside making a phone call and Cordelia looked up as he emerged from the house. He leant against the doorframe, arms crossed, as he watched his friends, a pensive smile upon his face. She got up and went to him, circling up behind him and wrapping her arms around his waist, leaning her cheek against his back. The heat of his body haloed her. He turned and drew her into his arms, leaning to kiss her.

"Don't worry," she murmured, knowing how sad he was his friends were leaving. "You'll still have me."

"Then I'll have everything," he told her, rocking her gently.

Robbie was lounging on one of the couches, his hand resting on Sasha's thigh, both having thrown away any pretences now they only had a couple of days left together.

Nash looked up then and saw Indigo watching them all. "Sure you don't wanna come home with us, Indi? I know you can't bear to part with me again."

Indigo laughed. "Lucky I'll be seeing you in Aspen for New Year's then, isn't it, Nathaniel?" Nash had been first in line when Indigo had invited them. Robbie had been a quick yes once he realised Sasha was going, despite the prospect of a lengthy flight over the Pacific. Cordelia had agreed once Mum had convinced her she'd be fine without the twins for a couple of weeks. Cordelia hadn't been planning on mentioning it to her at all, but her mother had been over with Matty the other day, and Nash had let it slip, and Mum had insisted it was too good an opportunity to pass up.

Nash put his guitar down gently and picked up his beer bottle. "I know this is a shitty thing to say, Indi, but your dad's big Aspen family reunion crashing and burning, well, it kinda worked out well for us, right?"

"Nice, Blaze, real nice," Aurora chastised, pegging a bottle cap at him and shooting him a tight, exasperated smile.

"You could still come?" he said to her, his gaze laced with hope.

She shook her head, her eyes softening. "I'm not built for the cold. And I don't see the point in riding all the way up a mountain just to slide back down it over and over again."

"You're all going to Aspen?" Sandy asked. He got nods all round. "Nice for some," he muttered under his breath, pulling out a pack of Winnie Blues and lighting up. Peyton reached for his hand, but he snatched it away and crossed his arms over his narrow chest.

"Did you manage to get a hold of Raf, brah?" Sasha asked Indigo.

"Still no answer at his dad's place. But I spoke to Dawn. Apparently, he called yesterday to ask her to water his plants. He said he was taking some time, going on a bit of a road trip."

"He ok?" Sasha asked.

Indigo shrugged. "According to Dawny, he said he just needs to be alone right now and he'll be in touch."

"So he's a no to Aspen then?" Nash quipped.

"I was looking forward to meeting this famous Raf," Robbie said, draining the Baileys from his glass and putting it on the coffee table with a clink of ice. He reached for Sasha's hand.

"So come to Sedona afterwards?" Nash suggested, picking up his guitar and plucking at it. "See our little corner of the world. Cora's coming, right?" Cordelia and Indigo nodded.

Robbie and Sasha exchanged glances.

"What was that?" Nash asked.

"What?" Sasha asked, reddening slightly.

"That look," Nash said, staring them down.

"Oh, uh, we're going to head over to Hawaii after Aspen," Sasha explained. "I haven't seen my folks in a while and I thought it might be nice to show Robbie the local sights of my hometown, eh."

"He's promised me I won't have to trek up Diamond Head this time," Robbie announced. He tore his adoring gaze from Sasha to meet Cordelia's eye.

She swallowed over a lump in her throat. Last time they'd been in Honolulu, Dad had bribed them to climb Diamond Head with promises of the traditional Hawaiian dessert, *shave ice* at the end. Robbie had complained the whole way up. She knew they'd both climb Diamond Head fifty times over now if it meant doing it with their dad again.

"Well, well, well," Nash drawled. "Meeting the parents already, are we? You guys have certainly gone from zero to a hundred in two seconds flat."

Sasha shrugged. "When you know, you know, right?" Robbie just grinned and ducked his head into Sasha's shoulder. "And so what? I've met Scarlett plenty of times."

"And she *loves* you." Robbie beamed as he refilled his glass with Baileys then reached for Sasha's, topping his off with Macallan. "Maybe not as much as Matty does, but she's a close second."

"We need to spend a night at my place soon," Cordelia said quietly to Indigo. They were still standing apart from the others. "I feel like a bad daughter, especially since Rob and I are taking off overseas after Christmas."

"You're not a bad daughter. Not one day has passed without us seeing Scar and Matty." Every afternoon that week they'd seen her mum and baby brother. Some days, Mum brought Matty over to Indigo's for a swim. Other days they went home to her house, or met them at the beach for a sunset walk and rockpool forage. "We'll be able to spend more time at your place once these guys go, I promise."

"I know, but Matty told me today that Robbie and I don't love him anymore. Apparently you don't either," she said and Indigo frowned.

"We're still taking him to the beach tomorrow morning, right?"

"Yes, but he's told me we have to invite Rosie."

"Ah yes, Matty's girlfriend." Indigo grinned. He turned to Peyton. "That ok, Peyts? If Rosie comes to the beach with us tomorrow?" Rosie was Peyton's niece and she and Matty adored each other.

"Yep. I was babysitting for my sister anyway, so I was looking for ways to occupy Rosie." Sweet little Rosie had Down syndrome and Peyton often helped take care of her.

"Which beach are you going to?" Sandy asked.

"Manly, I think," Peyton told him.

"Who's going?"

"Inds, Cora, me, Matty and Rosie, I guess."

"What time?"

"I don't *know*, babe," she said, her tone tinged with exasperation. "I s'pose around ten-ish. What's with all the questions?"

"Were you going to invite me?"

"I didn't think taking the kids to the beach was your scene. But of course you're more than welcome to come."

He scowled deeply and looked away.

manly beach
cordelia

Matty ran through the lapping tide, laughing uncontrollably as Indigo chased him. Rosie, red-haired and giggling, brought up the rear. Indigo swooped down on Matty, picking him up and throwing him over his shoulder. He then turned and scooped Rosie over his other shoulder and ran into the ocean. It was pretty flat out there today, the swell almost non-existent: shit for surfing, perfect for the kiddos.

"This is great," Peyton said, leaning back on her hands and grinning. "Let's bring Indigo every time we take the kids out, he's the best babysitter ever." She turned in Sandy's direction with a surly frown. "Unlike *some* people."

"Lay off, alright, Peyton? You know I don't like kids. They're loud and whiney and their fingers are always shoved knuckles-deep up their nostrils, and for some reason their hands are always sticky... Probably due to all the nose picking."

"You're the one who insisted on coming today!"

"Wish I hadn't." He pushed himself to his feet and stalked off up the white sand towards the wide concrete steps that would lead him to the Corso.

Cordelia sighed and adjusted the leopard print bandeau bikini top she was wearing with skimpy red bottoms as she turned onto her front. All those two had done all day was bicker. This recent new side of Sandy was incredibly unpleasant. For all his faults, Sandy had always been light-hearted and fun. But now, he was like a giant black raincloud consuming everyone around him with his misery.

"Don't start, Cee," Peyton said.

"I didn't say anything!"

"Just keep your sighs to yourself, ok? Sandy's really stressed out right now, give him a break."

"As long as you're happy."

"I am," Peyton said firmly.

"It's all good then." But it wasn't really. She lay flat, chin resting on her forearms. Indigo was now throwing the kids high into the air, both of them shrieking with laughter as they landed with giant splashes into the clear, aqua water. It was a perfect summer's day, the sun high in the cobalt sky, its rays tingling Cordelia's skin, the sound of the tide lapping the shore lulling her into a state of deep relaxation.

"Lucky they're wearing floaties," Peyton said, standing up and tying a sarong over her lime green bikini. "I'd better go tap him out, right?" She strolled to the water's edge and called, "Who wants ice cream?"

Matty and Rosie practically walked on water, they moved so fast towards Peyton. Indigo shot her a grateful look before striding up the beach towards Cordelia. When he reached her, he threw himself on top of her, laying the length of her back.

"Argh! You're all cold and wet!" But she was laughing as he shook his hair over her and kissed her bare shoulder. "There's a perfectly good spot here next to me," she said, indicating the towel laid out beside hers he'd vacated earlier to play with the kids.

"Nope," he murmured into her ear. "Too far away." She was glad when he stayed exactly where he was. His lips moved over the curve of her neck and she closed her eyes, wishing they were alone so she could roll over and surrender to him, so they could do all the things he was now whispering he wanted to do to her.

"Excuse me, you two, there are children present," Peyton said as she returned with Matty and Rosie who were slurping Paddle Pop ice creams off sticks in a race against the heat. They were clearly losing the battle if the sticky rivers of chocolate running down their arms were any indication.

Indigo groaned and discreetly shuffled sideways off Cordelia to lie face down on his towel.

"You two better get straight into the ocean when you're finished with those," Cordelia said, staring at their chocolate-coated faces in amusement. "Come here, Matty Moo." She sat up and pulled him to sit between her knees, as he shoved his ice cream towards her mouth in generous offering. She took an enthusiastic lick of the bottom to try to stop it dripping, then laughed and kissed his chocolate-covered cheeks. Rosie came and sat with them, holding her melted mess towards Cordelia.

"Want some of mine, Cee?" she asked, smiling widely as she gazed intently at Cordelia with her hooded eyes. "It's good. Chocolate Paddle Pops are my favourites."

"But you've got hardly any left!" Cordelia said.

"That's ok, you can have some."

"Oh, Rosie that's so kind." She smiled, leaning forward and taking a small lick. Rosie's gorgeous little face beamed.

Rosie leant in conspiratorially and whispered, "I think Indigo's asleep!"

Cordelia glanced at him, lying face down, his T-shirt draped over his head, and nodded. "I think you two wore him out." She touched her finger to Rosie's flat little nose.

"Indigo!" Rosie called. "Are you sleeping? Want some ice cream?"

He rolled onto his side, pulling the T-shirt from his face and flashing Rosie a lazy grin. "How can I sleep with all the racket you lot are making?" He reached out to tickle her tummy so she squirmed and giggled.

He shifted his focus to Cordelia, looking her up and down thoughtfully. "Now you haven't been in the water yet, have you, beautiful?"

"I'm just warming up to it."

"It's so nice in. Come swim with me?" he asked, climbing to his knees, lifting an eyebrow at her.

"Maybe in a minute," she said shuffling slowly away from him. He had that look in his eye as he inched towards her.

"I think now is better," he murmured, a smile teasing the corners of his mouth.

"Don't you dare," she said as he lunged at her, grabbing her around the waist. He picked her up and carried her to the ocean, stopping briefly to kiss her before charging headlong into the water as she shrieked and laughed.

After their swim, they flopped back down onto their towels to bake in the sun. Indigo reached for her hand, kissed it, then held it in his as he stared into her eyes, smiling tenderly at her.

"There you are!" Robbie's voice tore her gaze from Indigo's. "This place is a bloody mob scene. It took us forever to find you." Robbie was standing beside Sasha, his nose wrinkled as he surveyed the packed beach. Almost every inch of sand was covered in a rainbow of towels, beach umbrellas, blow-up toys and eskies.

"Robbie!" Matty cried, launching himself into his brother's arms and burying his face in his chest. He peeked out to stare at Sasha.

"Hey, cutie," Sasha grinned, touching his cheek.

"Hi, Sasha." Matty beamed, his face flushing as he stared at him, mesmerised. Matty was in awe of Sasha.

"You ready to race me in the pool again?" Sasha asked.

Matty nodded emphatically, reaching for him. Robbie transferred him into Sasha's arms, and Matty snuggled into him, his eyes closing in contentment. Robbie bent down to Rosie's height. "You coming too, Miss Rosie-pants?"

She looked up at Peyton, eyes shining. "Can I?"

Peyton looked at Robbie. "Is that ok?"

"Course it is. The more the merrier. We need someone who can beat Matty in a pool pony race. He kicked my and Sash's butts yesterday! You up to the challenge, missy?"

"Yes! Yes! Yes!" she said, jumping up and down.

Cordelia and Peyton packed up all the kids' stuff and handed it to the boys. Robbie hoisted Rosie up to sit on his shoulders.

"Bye, Indigo!" Rosie called, waving at him.

"See ya, Rosie! Thanks for hanging out with me today."

Rosie blushed, grinning wildly.

Matty was almost asleep in Sasha's arms. Cordelia bent to smother his small face in kisses. "Inds and I will come soon, ok, Matty Moo?" His nod was almost imperceptible.

"They probably need more suncream," she told Robbie.

After the four of them headed off, laden with towels and beach toys, Peyton sighed heavily. "I guess I better go find my grumpy boyfriend." She trudged off up the beach, hand tented over her eyes.

Cordelia lay down beside Indigo, curling her body into his, trailing her fingertips lazily over his bicep.

The first few times Indigo stirred, shifted, and glanced over his shoulder, she barely noticed, but the third time, when he pushed himself to his knees and turned around, scanning the sand and the paved area beyond, it was impossible to ignore.

"What's wrong, baby?" she asked, sitting up.

"I... I dunno," he mused, standing up and shielding his eyes as he stared around the beach. He bent to pick up his cap, pulling it low on his head. "I just had a strange feeling..." he said softly. "Like we're being... watched."

Cordelia glanced around, tummy plunging. "What do you mean? By who? You don't mean..."

"I don't know," he said as she slipped her sunnies on and pushed to her feet. He put his arm around her and absently kissed the side of her face. He was still scanning the crowd, which was crazy thick.

All of a sudden he went white. "Stay here," he ordered, squeezing her arm, and then he was pushing his way through throngs of people, his gaze set on something – someone?

Cordelia craned her neck to watch him, but she eventually lost sight of him amongst the other beachgoers. She sat stiffly on her towel, eyes constantly searching the beach around her. A few minutes later, Peyton appeared, flushed and breathless. "Indigo said we had to take you home."

"Huh?" she said distractedly. She was still looking for him.

"Indigo said we need to leave. Now." She met Peyton's eye. She was dead serious.

"I'm not just gonna go and leave him here, Peyts."

"Look, I have no idea what's going on, but he said it's not *safe* here, Cee. He said to tell you that 'she's here', whatever that means." Cordelia gasped, her hands moving to her mouth. "Inds said he needs to know you're safe. We need to go."

She frowned, torn.

"Quickly," Peyton said, reaching for her elbow. "Sandy's waiting in the car. We need to leave. *Now.*" Cordelia barely had time to grab her white mini-dress and pull it on before Peyton was dragging her up off the beach and into Sandy's car.

chapter thirty-five

you oughta know

reinenoir

She ducked and weaved through the crowd, scowling.

It made her sick, it truly did, the sight of *him* with *her*.

Reinenoir threw her enormous sunhat onto the passenger seat of her dark-plum Jaguar in disgust. Jaw clenched, she gathered the skirt of her grey linen dress in one hand and climbed into the car, adjusting her Chanel sunglasses, then smoothing the flyaways that had escaped her slick bun. She turned the ignition, glaring back towards the beach as she peeled away from the curb.

Reinenoir had always had masochist tendencies, and clearly still did, as she would have liked to have watched them for longer. But of course, he'd sensed her pretty quickly, as she knew he would. When he'd stood up on the beach and shaded his eyes and started searching, she'd turned nonchalantly and strolled slowly away. But not before deliberately pulling off her hat and sunglasses, just long enough for him to see her. And of course, he'd come after her.

Just like they'd planned.

She still hadn't gotten used to Artax's weakened shrouding abilities. It was a real inconvenience no longer having that complete protection. Now, the further she got from Artax, the less hidden she was. Especially around someone as inherently powerful as Indigo.

Reinenoir pulled up at a red light, scowling at her reflection in the rear-view mirror as she turned the air conditioning up and reapplied her lipstick in her favourite shade of femme-fatale red. She reached for her concealer, dabbing some on the small pink mark in the centre of her forehead where Indigo had headbutted her the other night. She pursed her lips.

He'd been insanely handsome today in his pale-pink, floral boardshorts, that gorgeous physique of his dripping wet, his rumpled blond hair damp and salty. If he were hers, she'd make him cut that hair.

She frowned, balling her hands to fists so her long nails dug into her palms. She breathed deeply as she focused on the pain. It soothed her somewhat, soothed the intense anger burning inside of her, rage that she still found him so irresistibly attractive. She abhorred weakness, and he was her weakness, a weakness she couldn't seem to shake.

It cut her, it truly did, seeing him with that Carlisle bitch, all sickeningly beautiful and lithe and long-legged in her little bikini. She'd been all over him, too, the little whore, smiling her smug smile. Of course she was smiling – she was being fucked by Indigo Wolfe, which meant she was being fucked *well*. And the way he looked at her, like she was the only girl he'd ever seen, the only thing he *could* see… Reinenoir could see he was madly in love with her, and it nauseated her.

The girl, she was a complication.

A big one.

A complication none of them had counted on, least of all her.

She was the reason he'd rejected her the other night. And his pig-headed rejection of her – yet again! – had pushed her over the edge. In her fury, she'd gotten carried away. She'd almost killed him.

She'd never admit it to anyone, but part of her was glad he'd survived.

Part of her?

All of her.

Because he was meant for her.

And really, there was only one person standing in the way of her winning him back.

But not forever. Not for much longer now at all.

Yes, that girl, she was a relatively easy problem to solve.

The decimation of Reinenoir's collected powers, on the other hand, now that was a much bigger issue. Knuckles white on the steering wheel, she drove over the Spit Bridge, heading back to the Eastern Suburbs where she was holed up in a waterfront estate in Vaucluse. It wasn't as if she could stay at her parents' old place in Mosman. He'd come looking for her there. With that bi-lo ninja-freak friend of his. She and Artax had had to hide when he came to the door, ordering her housekeeper Fernanda to tell him she hadn't seen Reinenoir, shrouding Fernanda's mind so he couldn't see inside of it. He'd bought it and left, but who knew if he'd return. He wasn't stupid. Far from it.

So, for now, she was in exile. She'd gone to ground, telling no one where she was other than her Maiden Orwen, and Artax, of course, who she needed. Not like she could glamour anymore! That cocky, ginger, prick friend of Indigo's was proving a constant nuisance, relentlessly using his pre-cog abilities to try to find her. She could feel him on the edges of her boundaries, trying to force his way in.

He was powerful.

But Artax was on it.

She'd disbanded her coven for now, informing them she'd make contact when she had the time and energy to lead them again. It was up to them to regain their powers, to prove their worth to her. They were all pretty useless at the moment, after what had happened up at North Fort. They'd all been pretty useless that night, too, when she thought about it, so she'd really let them have it.

What Indigo and his little pals had done that night, to her, to her coven – she still couldn't believe that they'd gotten the better of her. No one had ever gotten the better of her! She still hadn't figured out how they'd done it. At first she'd thought Diego Rafael must have slunk into town under her radar, because what had been unleashed that evening, it was something only he, or an Akasha of his breeding, was capable of.

She gripped the steering wheel tightly, heart pounding with fury.

All those precious powers she'd spent years collecting!

All gone in one fell swoop!

So now she was left only with what was inherently hers, which wasn't nothing, but not enough to fulfill all her dreams, all her plans.

Witch Queen.

She wanted the title and all that came with it so badly.

And she *deserved* it.

She'd been so close to challenging the reigning queen for the throne, too... It was about time the crown reverted to *her* side. Back to the warlocks. Indigo and his friends, they'd set her back years! Isadora still wasn't speaking to her. She blamed her granddaughter for the whole thing, said her feelings had clouded her judgment.

But Reinenoir disagreed. And she was determined. She'd never been one to back down. She knew what she wanted and as she drove, she began to flesh out a plan as to exactly how she could get it.

Because right now, Reinenoir had nothing.

Less than nothing.

Nothing but her obsession, which grew and grew every day to the point of insatiability.

For him.

Always for him.

Only for him...

Luckily, she'd thought ahead. Because at least she had a failsafe in place. Someone on the inside. Someone who was letting her know exactly where Indigo and his little whore were at all times.

Someone they thought they could trust...

They were so naïve, those two. Too trusting to realise everyone had their price, be it money, power, desire, or love.

And she'd found someone in their circle willing to trade.

Then she'd lured him away from his tart.

Her bit was done.

Now all she had to do was wait, because soon, her biggest problem would be no more...

chapter thirty-six

creep

sedona, arizona

dawn

Dawn pulled up at Raf's, parking crookedly in the driveway. She had just enough time to water his plants before her next client.

She leant over and popped open the glovebox, extracting the angel-wing keychain from inside. She jumped out of the car, flipping through the keys, moving past Aurora's, past Nash and Sasha's, 'til she came to Raf's.

She reached the front door and placed her palm flat against it. She smiled. Good-O. She could feel the ward was still in place. Raf always had some ward or another protecting his house. Whenever he was out of town, he cast one that only allowed soul family to enter.

She was about to slide the key into the lock when she felt the hair on her arms stand on end. She froze, gripping the key tightly, ears perked. She peeked furtively over her shoulder, but nothing seemed amiss. But then a wave of feeling crashed over her. She shuddered. Someone was nearby, someone with a sore head and anger issues. Someone who felt just awful.

The joys of being an empath.

Breathing heavily, she shoved the key into the lock, pushing the door open and dashing inside. She slammed it shut and leant against it, panting. Inside, with the ward protecting her, she felt nothing.

She kicked her pale-pink tennis shoes off, then bent to scoop up the letters scattered beneath the mail slot, stacking them neatly on the rustic rosewood console. The house was neat as a pin, as always, the space so reflective of Raf with its warm, earthy palette. The terracotta-coloured curtains were drawn tightly over the floor-to-ceiling windows.

She checked her reflection in the hallway mirror, retying the emerald bow around her curly blonde ponytail and smoothing her bangs. Dawn gazed at her mint-green turtleneck and frowned. She'd only bought it last week and hadn't had a chance to set to it with her bedazzler yet. It would be a good project for her and her baby girl Phoebe over the weekend. Phoebe was fifteen now, but she'd always be Dawn's baby.

Phoebe was awkward as all get out and so painfully shy she wouldn't say boo to a mouse. She couldn't be more different to her big sister, Reggie, who'd just turned eighteen and had a chip on her shoulder the size of Texas. None of the girls' four big brothers had ever given Dawn as much trouble as Reggie. Reggie had never forgiven Dawn for intervening when she ran off with that warlock, Skeet, last year, and had barely spoken to her since. In Reggie's eyes, Dawn was not only the most embarrassing, interfering mom in the world, but also public enemy number one: killer of teenage hopes and dreams.

Dawn loved Reggie with all her heart and soul, but couldn't help but hope Phoebe would turn out different. Reggie had always been rebellious and opinionated. She was pig-headed as hell, too, to the point of stupidity. Dawn hoped the house never caught on fire, because if she said she smelled smoke and Reggie disagreed, the girl would dig her heels in and stay put. She'd rather burn to death than admit Dawn was right.

It didn't help that Reggie's genetic higher senses were coming in hot, much to the girl's dismay. The last thing she wanted was to be like her mom. She wasn't scared of her abilities – she'd grown up around Dawn and her friends so she saw higher senses as "normal" – but she didn't particularly want any herself. This new generation of Akasha were proving to be more powerful than the one before and, from the little she'd deigned to share with Dawn, Reggie's fledgling empath abilities were astounding. With a bit of training, she could grow into a phenomenal healer.

Dawn padded to the laundry in her pink scrunchie-socks. Raf's watering can was under the sink in its usual spot. She filled it up and set about the task of ensuring each plant got a nice long drink. Raf's house was easy as pie. He only had a few houseplants. Nash and Sasha's on the other hand... she grimaced. Sasha had an addiction to plants and candles.

When she was done, she returned the watering can to its home and headed for the front door. She checked her rainbow Swatch. She had fifteen minutes before her next client. She needed to move her caboose.

But when she reached the front door, she hesitated. Taking a deep breath, she opened it a crack and peered out. It was quiet as a graveyard out there.

She pushed the door and stepped out. She was immediately bombarded with a whole lotta yuck. She shivered. It was confusion and fear and anger... Her eyes darted around the perimeter, but no one appeared.

She pulled the door closed, giving the handle a good yank to ensure it was locked, then locomoted her backside to her car. She pulled the door open and dove in, quickly hitting the central lock button behind her.

As she peeled out of the driveway, she made a note in her mental rolodex to mention to Raf she had a feeling someone was watching the house when he next called, whenever the dickens that would be. She hadn't heard from him in a while now, but she wasn't too worried. Raf could take care of himself. At least the house was secure, the ward would see to that.

that ain't bad

manly beach

cordelia

Sandy accelerated out of his parking space, cutting off a ute. He flipped them off when they hit the brakes, honking their horn angrily, yelling expletives.

"Woah, slow down, Sandy." Cordelia waved an apologetic hand at the pissed off driver. When she turned back, she noticed they weren't driving towards Indigo's. "Hang on, where are we going?"

Sandy put his foot down hard. His shoulders were bunched up around his ears.

"Sandy? This isn't the way to Indigo's. Where are we going?"

"Inds asked us to take you to Sandy's place," Peyton said, turning to smile at Cordelia in the backseat.

"To Sandy's place?" She furrowed her brow. "But everyone else is at Indigo's."

Peyton shrugged and reached for the radio, fiddling with the dial and turning it up so *Gangsta's Paradise* blared through the car. Cordelia could barely hear herself think.

"Sandy?" Cordelia yelled over Coolio.

"We're just following instructions, Cordelia. Wolfie was really antsy. Don't shoot the messenger."

She leant back in her seat, squeezing her eyes shut. Indigo had told her they were being watched. And then, before he'd disappeared, he'd seen something or someone that had freaked him out. Had it been Harper? Had she really been there? What had happened that he hadn't had time to find Cordelia himself?

Ten minutes later, they pulled into the driveway of Sandy's family home, a modern glass-and-steel abode that had clearly been some architect's wet dream. It was right on the beach in Clontarf, casting its imposing presence over every other house in the vicinity.

"Are your parents home?" Cordelia asked as they climbed out the car.

"Nope. My whole family's on holiday in Whistler. I got disinvited because of the pill incident." He approached the keypad next to the front door, punched in a code, and the enormous steel door swung open.

"Maybe we should go to Indigo's?" Cordelia said, taking a step back.

"Don't be silly, Cee, just come in," Peyton said, dragging her inside.

Sandy disappeared, muttering something about needing to make a phone call, and Peyton guided Cordelia into a giant living area that resembled a glass box overlooking the water. The furniture was dark and minimalist, the floors grey, polished concrete, the view stunning, but Cordelia felt uneasy.

"I should call Robbie. Check in and see how Matty and Rosie are doing."

"Sandy's on the phone. You'll have to wait 'til he's off. Wanna drink?" Peyton said, wandering over to the black marble bar in the corner and pulling open the fridge behind it. "Coke, Diet Coke, Sprite, Fanta? Or we could crack open a bottle of vino? Settle in for the arvo?" Her smile was hopeful.

"Uh, no, water's fine," Cordelia said, glancing around for the phone. There was one on the wall beside the bar.

"You're just a barrel of laughs today, aren't you, Cee?"

"Can we close the curtains or something?" she asked distractedly. There was just so much glass, she felt exposed standing there. Anyone could be looking in at them. *Artax* could be out there, watching her. Or that awful Maiden. She hugged herself tightly. The AC was blasting on high; it was arctic in there.

Peyton opened a bottle of Evian and poured two glasses. "Sandy's mum thinks curtains ruin the aesthetics of the room. There aren't any." She pulled a sharp knife from the knife block on the counter and grabbed a lime from the bowl in front of her, slicing it neatly and plopping a wedge in each drink. "But don't worry, it's one-way glass. No one can see in here." She returned to where Cordelia was now perched gingerly on a sleek sable leather couch and handed her a drink. "Gotta go pee. I'll be back in a minute."

Cordelia sipped her water, eyes darting round the room. Her heart was hammering, her palms clammy. Something felt off. Her gut radar was going nuts. She placed her drink on the stainless steel coffee table and shook her head. All this talk of Harper and her coven was clearly making her crazy. She was safe here with Sandy and Peyton. Indigo wouldn't have told them to bring her here if she wasn't. Sandy's house had a state-of-the-art security system to rival Fort Knox's.

"Everything ok?"

She startled, and her head snapped up. Sandy was standing in the doorway, staring at her. He was red-cheeked, eyes flicking wildly over her. He ran his hands through his mousey-brown hair and shot her a bright grin.

She climbed shakily to her feet. "I think I'm g-gonna get going."

"Wolfie said you need to stay here," he said evenly. He leant an elbow casually on the bar.

"When, Sandy? *When* did you see Indigo?"

"Before. At the beach."

She jumped when she suddenly heard Indigo's voice in her head. *'Where are you?!'* He sounded frantic.

'Inds! Thank God! Is everything ok?'

'No, Cora, it's not ok. WHERE ARE YOU?'

'At Sandy's. He said you told him to bring me here.'

'At Sandy's? *I never said you should go to Sandy's!'* Her stomach dropped. *'Cora! What's going on?'*

'But they said…' Her breath was coming fast and heavy. Why would they lie to her about something like this? Peyton would never lie to her! She bit her lip. Sandy, on the other hand…

'I don't know what's going on. I'm sure it's just a misunderstanding. Sit tight, Cora, I'm on my way. Make sure Sandy locks the door and turns the alarm on.'

'Ok. But hurry!' She squeezed her hands in her lap. She was light-headed, spinning with confusion.

"Is the front door locked?" she asked Sandy.

He nodded. She stared at him. He shifted under her gaze and looked away.

"So before, when you saw Inds at the beach, he definitely said to bring me here?"

Sandy cleared his throat. "He said it wasn't safe there, that Reinenoir was there."

Cordelia felt what little blood was left in her face drain away. "What did you just say?"

"He said Reinenoir was there. That we had to get you somewhere safe."

"How do you know that name?" she whispered.

"Oh. Um. Wolfie said it."

Her heart plummeted to her feet. Indigo would *never* use that name.

Oh shit. Oh fuck. Oh fuck, fuck, fuck. She tried to stay calm, to keep her breathing even. She couldn't let him know she knew he was lying. But why was he lying to her? And where was Peyton? How long did it take to pee?

She glanced out the window, trying to calm her breathing. "I might call Robbie. See how Matty's doing." She started edging towards the phone. He stood unmoving, watching her nonchalantly. Eyes locked on his, she reached for the receiver.

But before she could grab it, he stepped in front of it.

"Sorry, Cee. I can't let you do that."

Her mouth went dry.

"Give me the phone, Sandy." She reached around him, her hand closing round the receiver.

Lightning fast, he lunged. Next thing she knew, he had the knife Peyton had used to cut the lime in his hand. In one swift movement, he sliced through the coiled phone cord, rendering the receiver she held useless.

"I'm sorry, Cee."

"I'm leaving."

"No, you're not." He thrust the knife at her, his hands shaking. She squeezed her eyes shut tight. If there was ever a time to freeze someone, it was now. Come on, come on, come on. Freeze, Sandy, *freeze*! But when she opened her eyes, he was still moving towards her. Crap.

"You're not going to stab me, Sandy," she said, swallowing hard.

She'd known him forever. This was just a momentary lapse of judgement. She could talk him around, make him see sense. Sandy was a lot of things, but he wasn't violent, and he wasn't a killer. Why would he want to hurt her, anyway?

He stepped closer to her, inching forward until the point of the blade was touching her chest. "Don't presume to know what I will and won't do, Cordelia. This isn't personal. It's just a means of solving all my fucking problems."

"What do you mean?"

"I mean, they promised me that if I… got rid of you, they'd pay my debts."

"Who?" But of course, she already knew.

"Reinenoir. At first, she only wanted me to keep an eye on you, to keep tabs on you and Wolfie and let her know where you were. She offered to pay me, and I really needed the money. I even followed you up to Surfers." He rubbed his chin thoughtfully. "Then she wanted me to get you to the formal. I was tasked with distracting Wolfie by drugging Robbie, then getting you into that cab at the end of the night – and did she pay a pretty penny for that! Of course, Drew writing himself off took care of the Wolfie issue, so that worked out better than I ever could have imagined."

Bile rose in her throat. All this time, she'd *trusted* him. She hadn't particularly *liked* him, but she'd trusted him.

"And now, well, she's offered to take care of everything – and more – if I do this one thing for her." He raked a hand through his hair. "I don't have a *choice*, Cee. I… I don't want to hurt you. I don't want to hurt anyone! But you have to understand, this is the only way out for me."

So this wasn't a threat. He fully intended on killing her. "You *do* have a choice, Sandy." Her voice wobbled. "You're not a murderer. Please don't do this."

He pushed her hard in the chest so she stumbled backwards. He brandished the knife at her.

"Stop it, Sandy!" She threw her hands at him, trying with all her might to freeze him. But it wasn't working. She didn't get it. Aurora had said it was tied to her emotions. She was scared shitless right now… Did that not count? "I know you, Sandy, you're not a bad guy. You won't be able to live with yourself if you do this."

"Just sit the fuck down and shut up! Let me think!"

She hung her head and turned slowly as if to head back to the couch. As he lowered the knife, she spun quickly and smashed him across the face with the severed phone receiver. Then, just like Sasha had taught her, she swept her leg under his and shoved him so he landed hard on his back. Winded, he loosened his grip on the knife and she snatched it up, bending down to hold the blade to his throat.

Shock froze his features. She raised an eyebrow at him and smirked.

"Not quite the pathetic, weak, little pushover you were expecting, hey?"

Just as she was congratulating herself on her spectacular display of self-defence, Cordelia was body-slammed from behind. She hadn't seen it coming and she went flying. The knife tumbled from her hand. When she opened her eyes, she was lying in a heap on the ground, gasping for breath. Peyton was standing over her, chest rising and falling rapidly, eyes filled with fire. Peyton bent down and snatched up the knife, holding it towards her.

indigo

Indigo pulled his Landcruiser onto Sydney Road and floored it. Sandy's wasn't far, he'd be there in a matter of minutes. Sandy's father's business dealings were just as shady as Sandy's, and Indigo had seen their house with its bullet-proof windows and back-to-base alarms. The security system at the Whitcomb's was top-notch. He just hoped Sandy had enough brains to use it.

He didn't know why Sandy and Peyton had lied to Cordelia to get her to Clontarf. It made no sense. All he knew was that Cordelia had sounded uneasy and that he had a bad feeling.

Cordelia had proven she could handle herself in a sticky situation, but that didn't dampen the innate compulsion inside of him, his dire, primal need to protect her at all costs.

He'd seen Harper at the beach before. It had only been a split second, but he'd seen her alright. But then she'd vanished into the crowd and he'd lost track of her.

She was around.

Somewhere.

And that very fact meant none of them were safe.

cordelia

Peyton thrust the knife towards Cordelia again, jaw set like stone as her gaze flicked to Sandy. "Get up," she told him. He staggered to his feet beside her. "Are you alright?" She palmed his cheek and stared deep into his eyes. One was swollen shut where Cordelia had whacked him with the phone.

"Peyts–" Cordelia began.

"Shut *up*, Cee."

"Why are you doing this?" Cordelia said, a sob in her throat.

"*Why am I doing this?* I just walked in to find you standing over my boyfriend, holding a knife to his throat! Have you lost the plot? You've made it clear how you feel about poor Sandy, but to lock me in the bathroom and attack him? *Why?*"

"Lock you in the bathroom?" She frowned, sitting up. "I didn't…" Her gaze swung to Sandy who was delicately fingering his eye and glaring at her.

And then something shifted and he pasted on a bright smile. "You've got it all wrong, babe," he interjected, his tone light-hearted. "Cee and I were just mucking around and it got out of hand."

"Mucking around?" Peyton's brow furrowed.

"Yeah, you know, she was showing me some of the moves Wolfie's new mates taught her and she went too far."

"Why lock me in the bathroom?"

"Oh, that door's been dodgy for ages," he said with a wave of his hand. "We've been meaning to get it fixed."

"Look at me, Peyts," Cordelia said, holding her hands up and climbing slowly to her feet. "Sandy's trying to kill me. He cut the phone, and held a knife to me. He's the one who–"

"Is this some kind of joke?" Peyton said. "Because it's not funny."

"It's not a joke, Peyts. I swear, he attacked me."

"Shut up, Cordelia!" Sandy snapped. "You *liar*. She's trying to set me up!"

"Peyton. He's going to kill me."

"Yeah, right, why would I do that?" Sandy turned to Peyton, then sighed heavily and sagged. "Ok, ok, look, babe, I didn't want to do this because I knew it would hurt you, but here's the truth: Cordelia tried to convince me to break up with you while you were in the bathroom. She said I wasn't good enough for you, that I was a bad influence. When I told her I loved you and I'd never leave you, she got really mad and said she'd make me look so bad you'd have no choice but to dump me. And then she went mental and attacked me!"

Peyton reeled to Cordelia, her face a mask of fury. "*What*?" she screeched, knuckles white on the knife handle. "You know how I feel about him! How *could* you, Cee? I asked you not to interfere. I told you I could take care of myself!" Hysteria was clearly clouding Peyton's brain.

"I *didn't.*"

"Don't lie, Cordelia!" Sandy yelled. The problem was, Peyton trusted Sandy.

"I'm *not* lying. You know I wouldn't do that, Peyts. I swear to you on our friendship, I'm telling the truth."

Peyton glanced from Sandy to Cordelia. Cordelia could see the wheels churning in her head.

"Why did you tell me Indigo wanted me to come here with you?" Cordelia asked Peyton. "Why did you lie to me?"

Peyton's brow crumpled. "What do you mean? Sandy saw him on the beach. Indigo told him we needed to bring you here." She turned to Sandy. "Right?"

"You weren't there?" Cordelia breathed. "You didn't actually see Inds yourself?"

Peyton shook her head. "But that's what he said, right, babe?"

"Course it is," he said.

"Ok then, Sandy," Cordelia said evenly. "If I'm causing trouble between you and Peyton, I guess I've outstayed my welcome. You won't mind if I leave then." She turned on her heel and started for the front door.

She'd made it two steps when Sandy lashed out and grabbed her by the hair, yanking her to him, holding her between him and Peyton. He was grinning his ugly, gummy grin as he pulled her hair harder, twisting her into him. She cried out as her eyes began to water.

"Let go of her, Sandy." Peyton frowned. "You're hurting her."

Peyton jumped as the doorbell started to ring. Over and over. And then someone was pounding at the door. Sandy pushed a button on the panel on the wall. A tiny image of the front steps came up. "Wolfie," he muttered under his breath. "Shit."

"Sandy!" they heard Indigo yelling. "Let me in! Cora? Are you in there?" He continued to hammer at the door. "Open up now!"

"He's going to kick the door down," Peyton said.

"Let him in, Peyton," Cordelia said.

"Don't you dare," Sandy told her.

"What the *hell* is going on around here?" Peyton cried, throwing her hands up in the air.

"Indigo! Help!" Cordelia screamed. In a burst of anger, she slammed her head back hard into Sandy's face. She heard a crack, and he released her to grasp his nose. She started to run, but he grabbed her elbow, yanking her back, and as he did, he snatched the knife from Peyton.

Cordelia saw a flash of metal and felt true fear as she grappled with him, fighting desperately for her life. She managed to knee him between the legs and yank herself free, but suddenly there was pressure and then a pain like nothing she'd ever felt before. She looked down in shock at the knife protruding from her stomach. She staggered back.

Peyton screamed. "Oh my fucking *God*, Sandy! What did you do?"

Cordelia fell to her knees. She reached for the knife hilt protruding from her abdomen, blood blooming out around it like a mandala. The pounding on the front door was getting louder, and she could vaguely hear Indigo yelling at Sandy to let him in.

"I had to do it! If I kill her, they'll take care of all my debts."

"*Debts*? You just stabbed my best friend for *money*?"

"You don't understand. If I *don't* kill her, my life is over. I'm a dead man, Peyton. They'll kill me!" His eye was black and blue and blood was pouring from his nose. "I'm sorry it has to be this way, but it's me or her, babe."

Peyton was crying now. "So it's true then? You *are* trying to kill her?"

The banging on the front door stopped, and then a rhythmic slamming started.

"I'm sorry, babe, I know she's your best friend, but this is the only way out for me. You know that right? I love you, babe," Sandy said gently. He held out his arms and Peyton staggered into them.

"I love you, too," she sobbed. "I love you so much."

"We need to finish her," he said. "Then it's a clean slate. Pass me another knife, babe, and I'll slit her throat. You don't have to watch, I'll make it quick, she won't suffer, I promise."

Peyton's eyes travelled to Cordelia. They were so full of pain. "I'm sorry, I'm so sorry," she mouthed. It was all so surreal. Cordelia could hardly believe it was her Sandy was talking about. The blade in her stomach hurt so bad she couldn't move, couldn't stand, couldn't run. She watched numbly as Peyton fumbled at the knife block behind the bar and held a knife out to him. It was the biggest one in the block. Cordelia felt a tear trickle down her cheek. She was vaguely aware of a series of mini explosions coming from the direction of the front door.

Peyton placed her palm on Sandy's shoulder, squeezing it tenderly as he reached for the blade in her other hand. But before he could grasp it, she pulled her arm back and drove it forward, hard.

Sandy went rigid. He stumbled back, staring in shock at the knife handle jutting from his chest. "What the fuck, babe?" he slurred.

"I d-do love you," Peyton told him, tears dripping from her chin. "But I love her more."

Sandy collapsed onto the floor, and Peyton fell down beside him. "I'm sorry, I'm so sorry." She was waxen-white, shaking, teeth chattering... And her eyes, they were just blank.

There was a giant explosion and the next thing, Indigo was in the room.

indigo

It was absolute carnage in there.

A metallic scent hung in the air.

Sandy was lying on his back in a sea of blood, a knife handle sticking from his bony chest. Peyton lay still and silent beside him, curled around him, her head on his shoulder. Her face was smeared red, her clothes spattered and soaked.

Cordelia was kneeling behind them, wavering, her face ashen, her hands cupped over her stomach. Crimson billowed out around them to stain her white dress. Terror plunged through his guts and he cried out. He vaulted over Sandy, skidding to his knees, grasping her face between his hands. Her eyes were glassy. "Shit, baby, oh shit, what's happened, are you hurt?" He scooped her up and laid her gently on the couch. "I'm here now, I'm here." He smoothed the hair from her face, then turned his attention to her belly, carefully moving her hands out the way. She winced and hissed in pain.

His heart plummeted to his feet when he saw the knife. "Oh fuck. Oh fuck, oh fuck, oh fuck." He clasped her cheek, pressing his lips to her clammy brow. "It's ok, beautiful, I'm here now, I'm gonna make it all better. Just hold on, ok?"

She stared listlessly up at him.

Quick as a flash he grabbed the blade and slid it out. She screamed.

"I know, baby, I know." He clamped his hand over the wound, then focused all his might on healing it. Golden light swirled with emerald coiled to surround his hands as he repaired the damaged organs, knitting the tissue and muscle and skin back together. When he was done, there was nothing but a fine silver line.

He slid his hand to the nape of her neck, pressed his forehead to hers. He was close to tears. "Talk to me, angel face. Tell me you're ok."

"You came." Her voice was hoarse.

"Did you ever doubt I would?" He pulled back to look at her.

"Not for one second." Her eyelids flickered, then fluttered open.

"Oh God, you scared me so much today. I love you, baby," His voice cracked. "I love you so much."

"I love you, too," she whispered, as he brushed his lips to hers.

"Indigo!" He jerked at the sound of Peyton's voice. "Please help, Inds."

He looked down at Cordelia. "Who did this to you?"

"Sandy."

"*Sandy*?" he cried. What the *actual* fuck?

She took a shuddery breath and nodded.

Fury barrelled up inside him and he had to clench his fists to stop bioplasma exploding everywhere. He helped Cordelia sit up, handed her a glass of water from the coffee table, then stood and stalked over to where Peyton now sat next to Sandy. The pool of blood around him was so vast, so thick, Indigo had to be careful not to slip on it. Peyton was covered in it.

Sandy was very still and very white.

"I... I think he's dead, Inds," Peyton said, eyes huge. "I killed him. I killed him." Her chin wobbled. She was in shock. He leant over and put his fingers to Sandy's neck. There was a pulse, but it was very faint, intermittent.

"Go sit with Cora," he told Peyton. She stood robotically and shuffled to the couch.

Indigo knelt down over Sandy and put his hands over the wound. He'd never felt so unenthusiastic about healing anyone in his life. He took a deep breath, but before he could begin, Sandy shimmered and rose up out of his body.

Sandy stood over his corpse, staring down at himself in horror. Indigo's hands dropped to his sides. There was no silver cord attaching Sandy to his body. The damage was irreversible.

"What's happening?" Sandy said.

Indigo exhaled heavily and stood. "I'm sorry, Sandy. You're dead." He watched as Sandy's guardian appeared behind him, a wild-haired woman with a deeply lined face.

"Dead? I'm not dead. I can't be dead!" Sandy cried, growing more and more hysterical. "How can I be dead when I'm right here talking to you?"

"I can assure you, you're dead," he said flatly. He watched stoically as Sandy went into panic mode, going through the motions of trying to lie back down inside his body. When that didn't work, he started pacing the room, muttering to himself.

"Sandy!" Indigo said, and his head snapped up. He stopped pacing. "Why did you try to kill Cora?"

Sandy's face crumpled. "I'm so sorry. I had no choice."

"You *always* have a choice."

"She said she'd take care of all my debts if I did it. That she'd fix everything."

"*Who?*"

"Reinenoir."

Indigo started shaking. He felt like he was going to explode with rage. "How long?"

Sandy shrugged. "Her henchman, Artax, approached me in early November. Said they'd seen me with Cordelia on the beach at Queenscliff one night – she'd been walking alone in the dark and I pulled over, offered her a lift… She turned me down, though, said she was happy to walk."

Indigo clenched his jaw. That was the night they'd attacked Cordelia, the night Harper had slit her throat.

"They said they knew I could get to her, to you, that they knew I was in debt, and they'd pay me to keep tabs on the both of you, to keep them informed of your whereabouts." Sandy glanced away. "And I guess it all just escalated from there."

"We trusted you!" Indigo cried. "You were our friend." If Sandy still had a body, Indigo would be pummelling it black and blue right about now.

"You don't understand, Wolfie! They were gonna kill me if I didn't pay up."

"How's that working out for you now, Whitcomb?"

Indigo pushed his hands through his hair. Maybe he did trust too much, believe too much in those who didn't deserve it. Harper had used that against him. He was a fool! The scent of geranium filled the air and Sarita appeared behind him, put her hand gently on his shoulder. "Calm down, my dear one. Your anger will not serve you here today. He has already paid the price. Help him move on and be done with him." Indigo exhaled long and slow, trying to steady himself.

"I'm sorry," Sandy said. "I really am, Wolfie." He glanced around the room, lost, confused, scared. "What am I meant to do now?" he asked in a small voice.

Indigo nodded to Sandy's guardian. "You're gonna be fine, Sandy. I promise. Go with her. She'll take good care of you." Sandy whipped round to look at the woman, who smiled tenderly at him. The minute they locked eyes, Sandy visibly relaxed. She reached out and took his hand in hers. Sandy looked back to Indigo for reassurance. Indigo set his jaw and nodded.

Sandy allowed her to gently lead him away, into the swirling light vortex that had appeared, the doorway that would take them into the in-between.

"Hey, Sandy!" Indigo called after him.

Sandy turned to look at him.

"Make better choices next time, ok?"

Sandy shrugged before continuing on his way, disappearing into the light. Sarita placed her hand on Indigo's shoulder, then left.

Indigo closed his eyes and focused on Nash, Aurora and Sasha. '*I need you guys. Now.*' If he'd known what Sandy was planning, he would have called them sooner. He'd never imagined him capable of violence. They responded immediately, and he filled them in, gave them the address and directions, then turned his attention to the girls.

They were sitting on the couch, staring straight ahead, pale and wide-eyed. Cordelia had her arms around Peyton, cuddling her close. He perched on the coffee table in front of them. Cordelia's gaze slid to him. "How is he?" she mouthed.

He shook his head and she squeezed her eyes shut, pressed her hand to her mouth.

"Peyton?" Indigo said. She continued to stare ahead into space. "Peyts?" She was somewhere else. Somewhere she couldn't see or hear him.

"What the *hell* happened here?"

Cordelia told him everything. "She had to make a choice. She stabbed him to save me, Inds," she finished in a low voice.

"She made the right fucking choice," he growled, glancing at Sandy's body.

"What are we going to do?" Cordelia said, gaze flicking to the dead body, all that blood. He could see the panic mounting in her eyes as her hand went to her abdomen. "I mean, he's dead, and I'm fine. How do we explain that to the police, to his family? Peyton stabbed him, surely she can't get in trouble for that? If she hadn't, it'd be me lying there instead of him."

Indigo leant forward, enveloped her hands in his. "Help's on the way, babe. When they get here, I want you and Peyton to leave. Take her back to my place, get the both of you cleaned up. We'll deal with all this."

"But how?"

"It wasn't a secret what Sandy did for a living. There were a lot of rumours going round that he owed a lot of money to a lot of people." Cordelia glanced away guiltily. "You *knew*?"

"Peyton confided in me. Swore me to secrecy. He was getting death threats."

Indigo rubbed his eyes wearily. "We can use that. Peyton's been through enough."

"Hello? Indi?" Nash called. "How much bioplasma did you use on that fucking door?"

Indigo sagged in relief. "In here."

Nash appeared in the doorway, Aurora and Sasha hot on his heels. They stopped dead. "Holy hell," Nash breathed, surveying the scene.

Indigo gestured to Aurora who strode over and settled beside him on the coffee table. She reached for Peyton's hands, holding them tight in hers, then glanced at Indigo. "Are you sure?'

"Do it," he ordered.

"Peyton," she said, and Peyton immediately looked up, met her gaze. Aurora's eyes began to glow, iridescent gold. Peyton stared into them, mesmerised. Her eyes began to glow, too. "Peyton, you and Sandy had an argument at the beach today and he left. You haven't seen him since."

"Me and Sandy had an argument at the beach today and he left. I haven't seen him since." Peyton repeated in a monotone.

"You've been at Indigo's with Cordelia, looking after Matty and Rosie. You were there the whole afternoon."

"I was at Indigo's with Cordelia, looking after Matty and Rosie. I was there the whole afternoon."

"What is she doing to her?" Cordelia gasped.

"She's doing what needs to be done," he said gruffly.

"What the hell is this? Some sort of fucked up Jedi mind trick? *'These are not the droids you're looking for.'* You never told me she could do this. What the hell, Inds, am I next?"

He pulled her to her feet, guided her into the corner. "Deep breaths," he told her, squeezing her hands in his. He inhaled slow and steady, nodding at her so she mirrored her breath to his, in and out, in and out, until she was calm. "Ok?' He smiled at her, reaching to tuck a strand of hair behind her ear.

"Ok," she nodded, leaning heavily into his chest. He wrapped his arms around her, his face buried in her hair as he held her.

"Why didn't you tell me Aurora could do that?" Her voice was muffled.

"It's not exactly a skill she likes to broadcast. She only uses it on very rare occasions."

"Has she ever used it on me?" She pulled back to look at him.

"Of course not, Cora."

"Is she going to? Am I next? After Peyton?"

"Do you want to be?"

She hesitated for a split second, and he knew she was actually considering it. But then she was shaking her head. "No. I don't want her to do that to me, ever."

"In that case, she never will. She couldn't anyway, it only works on normies. But do you understand why we need to do this to Peyton? It's for her own good. She just killed her boyfriend. No matter what we think of Sandy, Peyton, she was in love with him. She shouldn't have to live with that."

Cordelia nodded.

He gripped her shoulders, leant forward to kiss her, and then he was pressing his keys into her hands. "Take Peyton, go to my place. Robbie was taking the kids home, but he should be back by now. The two of you get her cleaned up. Don't mention Sandy or anything that went down here today. You were never here. Got it?"

"Got it. What about you guys?"

"Don't worry about us. We'll do what needs to be done, then we'll come home. I love you."

"I love you, too." She kissed him one last time, then went to the couch to retrieve Peyton, taking her hand, pulling her gently to her feet, and bundling her quickly from the room.

chapter thirty-eight

cryin'

indigo

"I still can't believe Sandy's dead," Drew said, rubbing his chin. "I mean, I never thought something like that would go down right here in Manly. This isn't South Central LA. This isn't *Boyz N The Hood*. Like, they just… broke into his house and murdered him in cold blood?" He blinked rapidly, tears beading on his lashes. He was lying on the table in the room Indigo had converted into a makeshift clinic.

Indigo squeezed his shoulder. "I know, man, it's rough."

"We'd all heard the rumours, that he was in deep shit, but if I'd known it was that bad, I'd have tried to help him somehow. I know Sandy wasn't perfect, but he was always a good mate to me. He got me through some tough times."

Indigo made a face.

"Maybe not in ways you approve of, Wolfie, but it was what I needed at the time." He exhaled sharply through his teeth. "Play stupid games, win stupid prizes, I guess. How's Peyton coping?"

"Not well." The girl was a mess, and rightly so. He'd never forget how brokenly she'd wailed when the police had come by his place looking for her that night and she'd heard Sandy was dead.

"What are the cops saying?"

"After Peyton and Sandy had words at the beach that day, he left and drove home. Shortly after, the dealers he owed money to showed up.

459

Used explosives to blow the front door down. When they discovered Sandy still didn't have their money and wasn't likely to, ever, they stabbed him in the heart and left him to bleed out. They were evidently pros, because they left no fingerprints, no evidence, nothing."

Everyone in Manly knew what had apparently happened to Sandy Whitcomb that night last week. Only six people knew what had really happened. And those six would take it to the grave.

"Life's so fragile, isn't it?" Drew said as he slid off Indigo's table, shuffling his feet back into his thongs. "It blows me away how it only takes a split second, one bad decision, for everything to change. I mean, look at me. If you'd been here last year to help when I wrecked my knee, the pain wouldn't have gotten the better of me, I wouldn't have started using so much, and well... things might have turned out differently."

Indigo shrugged. What could he say?

"Although Cee and I, apparently we were never meant to last," he said glumly, sliding his hands into his pockets.

Indigo shot him a questioning look.

Drew sighed heavily, chewing on his thumb nail as he seemed to consider whether or not to tell Indigo something. "Last year, when I was looking for a solution, Scarlett recommended this psychic healer in the Blue Mountains. She's a bit like you, actually, an energy healer. She was the only person I got really remarkable results from."

"So why didn't you continue seeing her?"

"Ah." He smiled tightly. "We didn't exactly see eye to eye."

"How so?"

"She read my future," he confessed, frowning. "She told me the girl I was in love with, that she wasn't my destiny." He screwed up his nose. "I couldn't hack it, you know, hearing that? So I called her a scam artist and told her she was full of shit and I walked out and after that I couldn't exactly go back, could I?"

Indigo rubbed his forehead.

"I guess even she could see Cordelia wasn't meant to be mine. I think I was the only one who couldn't." He smiled sadly. "You and Cee, you guys were inevitable. I know that now."

Indigo wanted to apologise again, but he'd said sorry to Drew so much that the word was losing its meaning. He did occasionally wonder what would have happened if he'd died that night on the bridge, if Cordelia and Drew might have lived happily ever after. He assumed, if your soul mate died, it was still possible to fall in love with someone you didn't have as deep a connection with and make a life with them.

"I think one more session should do it," he said, changing the subject, and Drew nodded tightly.

"Thanks, Wolfie. For this. You don't understand what it's like, after all this time, to suddenly have no pain." His voice cracked. "To be able to sleep through the night." He quickly looked away, blinking rapidly, then swallowed hard, before adding, "I might even start playing rugby again."

Indigo smiled. "I reckon you should." Drew was incredibly talented.

"Anyway, I just wanted to say… thanks, mate." He held his hand out and Indigo reached to shake it. He noticed Drew's eyes drawn to Cordelia's ring sitting there on Indigo's pinkie. Drew pressed his lips together, but he didn't say anything.

"Do you wanna… get a drink sometime or something?" Indigo asked.

"I thought you didn't drink anymore?"

Indigo smiled. "Do you wanna grab a water or something sometime?"

"I think," Drew said, glancing out the window, "that it might be too soon for me just yet. For things to go back to normal for you and me… considering…"

He didn't need to finish his sentence. Indigo had noticed a broken bioplasmic cord dangling from Drew's heart chakra when he'd been working on him, and he'd instantly understood it had once been connected to Cordelia. He'd been able to see that Drew had actually been the one to tear it, breaking the connection between the two of them. Indigo hadn't been able to bring himself to mention it to Drew, which wasn't his usual style. He'd just quietly cleaned it and turned the frayed end back to Drew, reconnecting it into his chest, hoping it might somehow help to heal his broken heart.

Indigo nodded. "It's cool, I get it. I just… I do miss you, man," he confessed, because he did. They'd been friends for most of their lives, and Indigo felt really sad about how things had turned out.

Drew nodded, but he didn't make eye contact. Fair enough, he had every right to be pissed off. Indigo knew he could never make it up to Drew, what his coming home had done to him, but these healings had been his way of trying.

"Let me walk you out," Indigo said, opening the door and leading Drew down the corridor. He noticed Drew's limp had all but vanished.

Drew paused to glance out the window, down to where Aurora was practicing yoga on a mat on the back lawn. She wore nothing but a metallic blue g-string, and as she reversed her warrior, Drew whistled low under his breath. "Not a bad view, eh?" He grinned.

Indigo elbowed him, but couldn't stop the smile growing on his face, because it seemed Drew *would* get over Cordelia.

"You all set for uni next year?" Indigo asked, as they continued down the hallway.

"Yeah, maybe. I, uh, I've actually applied to study overseas, in the US, so we'll see how that goes. I mean, there's nothing keeping me here now, right? Maybe if my leg goes back to the way it was, it might help my chances of getting a footy scholarship or something. After everything that's happened, and, well, after that night up at North Fort… the world seems kind of *bigger* now. It seems a waste to just stay here in Sydney when there's so much more out there to see and do and experience."

When they reached the front door, Drew thanked him again.

"It's all good, mate, just wait 'til you get my bill," Indigo joked.

"Yeah, yeah, cheque's in the mail." And he smiled then, a real smile because Indigo had seen his dimple. And that smile gave him hope that their friendship might one day be repaired.

chapter thirty-nine

zombie

sedona, arizona

dawn

The sun set fast this time of year, and it was already dark by the time Dawn pulled up in the driveway of her pale-pink bungalow.

Her husband, Earl, was away at a book fair in New York, so it was just her and the two girls home for supper tonight. Maybe she'd order pizza. Phoebe was at her afterschool job at the library. Reggie was probably home, but Dawn knew it wouldn't have crossed her eldest daughter's mind to lift a finger to start on dinner.

Dawn picked a loose bead from the peace sign that emblazoned the thigh of her jeans and reached for her purse. She was glad it was Friday night. What was it the kids said? TGIF? She smiled to herself. See? No matter what Reggie said, she wasn't *that* embarrassing. She could be down with the hip lingo.

But honestly, TGIF. With Earl away, and Raf, Nash, Aurora and Sasha out of town, it had been a busy week. Not only was Dawn running her clinic and single-parenting, but she'd somehow found herself as chief house-plant-waterer-and-mail-collector for her friends. Not only that, but Christmas was coming up real fast, and she had a mountain of wrapping to attend to. She was, quite frankly, more than ready for the weekend.

She opened the car door and climbed out. The chill hit her hard, and she pulled her fuchsia puffer jacket tightly around her. Humming absently to herself, she rummaged through her purse for her keys. Just as her fingers closed around the fluffy pom-pom keychain, a flash of movement caught the corner of her eye.

Heart in her mouth, she swung around, surveying the yard.

For the first time in her life, she cursed her obsession with angel and fairy statues, particularly the life-sized ones which seemed intent on messing with her tonight.

"Hello?" she called feebly. "Anyone there?" She rolled her eyes at herself. What was she expecting? Someone to call back, *'Yes hi, only me, put the kettle on, I'm here to murder you?'* Nothing moved. It was probably just Catthew, the neighbour's cat, who seemed to prefer her yard to his own. She continued up the path to her front door where the porch lights glowed.

And then a wave of *feeling* crashed over her. She gasped. A pounding headache. A churning of fear and confusion and blinding, seething, anger. She recognised this emotion. It was exactly what she'd felt at Raf's the other day.

She was fumbling for the lock when she distinctly heard the shuffling of footsteps behind her. She whirled around, peering out at the yard. The shadows were closing in around her. A sudden panic swelled through her belly.

She squinted hard at one of the statues. She swore it moved. "Hello?" she called, voice shaking. "Show yourself!"

Before her eyes, the statue unfurled, rising up tall and lean and distinctly man-shaped. A scream caught in her throat.

He stalked towards her.

She stared at him as she stumbled clumsily backwards into the door. She wasn't like Nash and Indigo and the others, she only had the power to heal, not harm. He was coming closer and closer. Her hands were shaking, and she dropped her keys with a metallic splat. She fell to her knees, feeling around for them in the gloom.

The anger and fear and confusion were all encompassing now. She didn't want to feel that, so she shoved him out, blocked him out. The shadows draped heavier over her and she glanced up, cowering because he was standing right over her. He smelled of sour body odour and cigarettes. A shard of light hit his face then, and she gasped.

Holy bananas! It couldn't be!

How could he be back?

Had he returned for Reggie?

"You know me?" he demanded, shoving a strand of long greasy hair off his face. His dark eyes seemed cloudy.

She fell back on her hands and scrambled away.

"Who am I?" he roared. "Tell me who I am! Because for some reason, I ain't got a clue!" He raked his hands over his face. "I been wandering for months now, and then I got t' this town and it looked real familiar so I decided t' stick around some. And then one day I saw *him* on the street—"

"Who?" she whispered.

"I don't know his *name*," he thundered, eyes wild. "A *man*. The man with the dark hair. Drives a navy Mustang!"

Raf. He meant Raf.

"I followed him home t' his house. Watched him for a while. But then he just up 'n disappeared. Didn't know what t' do 'til the day you showed up. And you looked kinda familiar, too. So I followed you back here. Been watchin' ya ever since." He casually pulled a gun from the waistband of his filthy jeans.

Dawn gasped. "Please, Skeet!"

His face went still, quiet. And then he smiled, baring stained teeth. "Skeet," he murmured, as though trying the name out to see how it felt in his mouth. "Of course. That's m' name. Skeet. I gots a feelin' you knows exactly why I can't recall who I am or where I comes from. And you gonna tell me." He loomed over her, pointing the gun at her.

She shook her head. Raf hadn't made the decision to wipe the memories of Skeet and his warlock family lightly. They were dangerous. Loose cannons. If Skeet got his memories back, he might come for Reggie again.

"Tell me!"

Dawn squeezed her eyes shut, shaking her head.

"Tell me or I'll beat it outta ya!"

The front door was suddenly wrenched open. "What's all the noise out here, Mom?" Reggie complained. "I can barely hear *Melrose Place*—" She stopped dead when she saw her mother cowering on the ground, Skeet standing menacingly over her.

"Skeet?" she breathed, gazing up at him, her blue eyes wide. She ran her fingers through her shaggy blonde hair and pulled at the hem of the black daisy-print mini dress that was trying and failing to contain her generous figure.

"You know me?" Skeet asked, subtly tucking the gun back into his pants, his cloudy gaze trained on her.

"Of course I do, bubby. It's me. Reggie." Ignoring Dawn, she stepped closer to him. "You've been gone for so long. What've they done to you, bubby?"

"I dunno. But I have a feeling you the one I been looking for."

Reggie glared down at Dawn. "I *knew* you had your friends do something to him! That he didn't just up and leave me by *choice*. How could you do this to me, Mom? I *hate* you," she spat venomously. She reached her hands towards Skeet, laying a gentle palm flat on either side of his face. A soft orange glow began to emanate from her hands.

"Reggie?" Dawn said, her fear escalating. "What are you doing? Stop that *right now*."

Skeet's eyes snapped shut for a moment or two, and when they opened, they were clear and lucid. "Reggie?"

She nodded.

"Oh Reggie, bubs, I done missed you so damned much!" He drew her into his arms and lowered his mouth to hers, kissing her in a way that turned Dawn's stomach.

Reggie had no idea what she'd just done. Dawn's blood thundered in her veins so her hands shook. She clambered clumsily to her feet. "Reggie! Stop that *at once*, young lady!" She reached for Reggie's arm, tried to pull her away.

Skeet broke the kiss off, turning his attention to Dawn. His gaze flamed with fury.

"This is *your* fault. You the one who sicced Raf on me and my kin!"

"Reggie! Come here *right now*!" Dawn shrieked.

Reggie locked eyes with Dawn, then reached for Skeet's hand, deliberately threading her fingers through his. She set her jaw, her gaze cold as granite.

"I remember *everything*!" Skeet bellowed. "Diego Rafael confounded me, but now thanks to Reggie here, it been reversed, ain't it? For

months now, I ain't known who I was, what I was, where I was from!"
He looked at Reggie. "They been tryin' t' keep us apart, Reggie bubby!
I think they forgettin' you belongs t' me. Let's get outta here."

"*No!*" Dawn yelled, stumbling forward, smacking him across the
face with all her might so his head snapped back.

He grinned a slow grin, then snatched the keys from her grasp,
handing them to Reggie. "Go wait in the car, bubs, I needs to have a
word with your momma 'ere." Throwing Dawn one final arctic glare,
Reggie leant up to press her lips tenderly across Skeet's, then turned on
her heel and headed for Dawn's car.

"Reggie!" Dawn screamed after her. "Don't you even think about
it!" Her chest heaved and she began to sob.

Reggie didn't even look back.

Skeet's lip curled into a smirk as he stepped menacingly towards
Dawn. He reached into the waistband of his jeans for the gun. "You
gonna pay, bitch."

Even though Dawn was expecting it, when the first blow came, a
swift pistol whip across her cheek, it sent her reeling.

chapter forty

don't dream it's over

manly, new south wales

indigo

On Nash, Aurora and Sasha's last morning in Sydney, Indigo and Robbie took them to the cliffs at Jump Rock near the Van Allen Estate. The view from the top was spectacular, the sun sparkling off the clear, turquoise water below where a flotilla of boats bobbed on their anchors. To their left, the white sand of Collins Flat Beach melded into the bushland behind.

They climbed to the highest rocky outcrop and Indigo declared the jump to be a rite of passage for all Manly locals – honorary or otherwise – before swiftly backflipping over the edge into the ocean far below.

Never ones to back down from a challenge, they'd all followed him quickly over the ledge, whilst Robbie sat glued to the rock platform, legs dangling over the side.

"Come on, Robbie!" Nash called up from where he was bobbing in the ocean below. "It's not that high!"

"The jump's not my problem," Robbie yelled down. "It's the climb back up!" He pointed to the slippery rocks at the base of the cliff they'd have to scramble over to get back to the top. They were covered in slimy weed and razor-sharp oysters. Indigo had been there when Robbie had sliced his foot open down there a few years back. Robbie had never forgotten the trauma of Joshua digging oyster shell from the arch of his foot and sewing him back up. No matter how many times they'd come here over the years, he'd never jumped again.

The others found the route back up to be but a minor inconvenience. It certainly didn't deter them from spending the morning jumping and climbing, their flips growing more and more daring every time.

"Cora ok?" Indigo asked Sasha as they swam towards the cliffs after a synchronised, double back somersault.

Sasha grinned and nodded. "We've had a great morning together." Cordelia had insisted on staying back at the house to prepare a farewell lunch. She'd headed off to the farmer's markets that morning, which was one of her favourite places to spend time. She loved perusing the fresh produce and chatting to the vendors selling their wares. Bi-lo Sasha was playing bodyguard, grocery-lugger and kitchen hand.

"I'm out," Aurora said after her tenth or eleventh jump. She sat down beside Robbie, towelling her hair dry. "The testosterone level around here is outta control," she said as Nash and Sasha sailed over their heads, somersaulting over and over before hitting the water feet first.

"I'm hungry," Robbie complained to Indigo, who was standing behind them at the top of the cliff. "Can we wrap this up and head home?" Robbie got super-grumpy when he needed to be fed.

"I'm fucking starving, too," Aurora said, leaning back on her hands, swinging her legs gently back and forth over the side. "And as much as it pains me to admit it, I'm gonna miss your little duchess' cooking."

"Cora's always shown love through food. It's her way of nurturing people," Robbie said.

"She's an amazing cook," Indigo said, jumping down to the ledge beside them. "And I reckon lunch is probably ready by now so we should head back." He shook water over Robbie. "Come on, Rob, just one jump? I'll boost you over the oysters."

Robbie crossed his arms and shook his head.

Indigo shrugged. "We gotta go," he told Nash and Sasha when they reappeared a couple of minutes later. "Last jump."

Sasha crouched down next to Robbie. "You gonna jump with me, babes?" he asked, holding out his hand. Robbie stared at Sasha's palm, chewing on his bottom lip. No one was more shocked than Indigo when Robbie sighed in resignation and entwined his fingers through Sasha's, allowing him to pull him to his feet.

"Ok," he sighed. "Just *once*. But no flippety flips or any of that fancy bullshit. We go straight down."

Sasha kissed the back of his hand. "Right on. Anything for you, *ko'u aloha*." He grinned, and Robbie returned it as the two of them approached the edge and stepped off. Indigo stared open-mouthed. For years he'd tried to cajole Robbie to jump with him, and all Sasha had to do was ask once. It was officially official: Robbie was head over heels.

Nash came up to Indigo and held his hand out, fluttering his eyelashes at him. Indigo burst out laughing and nudged him with his shoulder. "Get outta here."

Nash turned his attention to Aurora, bowing deeply and offering her his hand. She glanced up at him, shooting him a withering look. "What he said," she replied, nodding towards Indigo. But a small smile tugged at her lips.

"Is that so?" Nash said, stepping closer to her, a cheeky glint in his eye. Lightning fast, he bent to scoop her up, chucking her over his shoulder. "Geronimo!" he yelled as he stepped off the cliff with her.

"I'll fucking kill you, Blaze!" she yelled as they went over the edge.

Indigo peered down into the water below where Robbie was now freaking out about climbing out over the oysters. "Rob!" he called down. "You're gonna cut yourself if you don't calm down!"

"Shut up, Indigo!" Robbie shrieked. "I hate you all right now! Don't just stand there like a big useless lug! Come and help me!"

"You'll be the death of me, Robbie Carlisle," Indigo muttered, as he front-flipped off the ledge.

With all his flailing and panicking, Robbie of course managed to slice the front of his shin open.

"Christ, Rob, everyone else has done this like, fifteen times today," Indigo said as he sat dripping wet on the rocks, Robbie's leg in his hands. "You do it once and you deadset manage to destroy yourself."

Sasha sat with his arm around Robbie, who was gritting his teeth and writhing and glaring at Indigo. "Just hurry up and fix it before I bleed to death!" he wailed, madly flapping his hands back and forth so vigorously Indigo feared he might take flight.

"Jesus Christ, it's just a flesh wound," Indigo muttered before glancing around to make sure no randoms were watching, then laying his hands on Robbie's shin. Fragments of oyster shell popped out and the skin began to seal up. Wounds that fresh were always easy to heal and Robbie was good as new in no time at all.

"You're all good, Rob," Indigo said, holding out his hand and pulling him to his feet. "No blood transfusion necessary."

Robbie bent down to examine his leg, looking up at Indigo then looking back down to his leg where all that remained was a pale silver line. "Ok, so that's fucking cool," he said, running his hand over it.

"I aim to please," Indigo said lightly. "That scar should fade in a couple of days."

"I'm hungryyyyyy!" Robbie complained, moving swiftly on to his next problem. "Can we *go*?"

Indigo rolled his eyes. "Sure, mate."

They climbed back up the cliff and walked home to his house where the table was beautifully laid with platters of lemon-and-rosemary barbequed chicken, pumpkin and quinoa salad with toasted almonds, roasted veggies with lentils and tahini pesto, and crispy roast potatoes, all adorned with fresh herbs, all organic and locally raised and grown.

Indigo made a beeline for Cordelia, sliding his arms around her waist and kissing her gently. He pulled back to peer into her face. "You feeling ok?" His hand automatically gravitated to her stomach which still bore the scar from the Sandy ordeal. It was fading more and more every day, but the memory of how she'd gotten it certainly wasn't and probably never would.

She pulled a face. "Inds, I'm *fine*. Just like I've been fine the other million times you've asked." She pressed up on her toes to kiss his nose, then pushed him gently away. "Can you please make sure everyone has a drink? Lunch is getting cold."

Nash sidled up. "Cheers, doll, this looks amazing," he said, putting his arm around her and kissing the side of her face.

"I might have made a little something special for you for dessert," she whispered conspiratorially.

He clutched his hand over his heart. "Not pavlova?" His eyes grew large. It was his favourite and he'd not-so-subtly hinted at the fact since he'd arrived in Australia.

She winked. "With passionfruit curd, vanilla custard, cream and fresh raspberries."

He whooped and hugged her tighter. "This girl of yours, Indi, is the raddest of rad chicks. When she eventually gets sick of your ugly mug, I'll gladly take her off your hands."

"When I said 'what's mine is yours', it didn't extend to my girlfriend," Indigo said, shooting Nash a mock-scowl. He grabbed Cordelia by the hand and drew her into his lap where he wrapped her in his arms and kissed her deeply.

She was his and only his, and always would be.

The phone started ringing inside. "I'll get it!" Robbie announced, disappearing into the house.

He returned a moment later, frowning. "We have a gentleman by the name of Earl on the phone. Sounded *super* stressed out, wants to talk to one of you?"

"Who's Earl?" Cordelia asked.

"Dawn's husband," Indigo said. "I wonder what he wants?"

"I'll go find out," Nash said, turning on his heel and striding inside.

The next morning, Indigo and Robbie took Nash and Sasha to the airport. The mood in the car was pensive.

"It's Cora's first Christmas without her dad," Indigo said as they pulled up at Departures. "And with Harper out there, I need to know she's settled, that she's safe… I can't bail on her now. But I'm flying out Christmas night so I won't be too far behind you."

"Indi!" Nash chastised, leaning over from the passenger seat to cup his neck. "You've told us a million times. We totally get it. It's cool, bro. Dawn would understand."

Indigo hung his head, kneading his hands in his lap. He was worried sick about Dawn. Her daughter, Phoebe, had come home from work to find Dawn beaten to within an inch of her life on the front porch, her sister Reggie missing, along with Dawn's car. Dawn was currently in hospital with broken bones, and she'd undergone several surgeries to repair internal damage. Although she was yet to regain consciousness, she was stable now and would recover in time.

Indigo wanted to get over there and help speed that recovery along. Sasha and Nash were rushing home to join in the search for Reggie. They'd decided Aurora would stay to watch over Cordelia. No one knew where Raf was to even let him know what was going on, and his mind was still shrouded so they couldn't reach out to him.

Nash hugged Indigo tight outside Departures and whispered, "I'll think of you every time I brush my teeth."

Indigo pulled back, staring at him, unsure whether to laugh or gag. "You've still got my old toothbrush?"

"*Mate*," Nash scoffed. "It's one of those fancy electric ones. My teeth have never been so white and shiny. I'm never giving that thing up! Oh, and thanks for the razor, too."

"You're rank, man but I love you." Despite everything going on, Indigo laughed, pulling him in for another hug.

"Love you more, brother," Nash said, squeezing him tight, then scooping up his bag and heading into the terminal, waving over his shoulder. Indigo shook his head affectionately before moving to hug Sasha, who managed to disentangle himself from Robbie long enough to say goodbye. Even though he'd be seeing them in a couple of days, it hurt deep in his guts to let them go. He hadn't realised how it would feel, saying goodbye to them, how much it sucked, them living on the other side of the world.

Afterwards, he dropped Robbie off, then drove home feeling a little deflated and nostalgic. He'd gotten used to having them around. To Sasha's quiet calm presence and experimental fusion cooking. To Nash sprawled on the couch strumming his guitar when he wasn't constantly pilfering Indigo's stuff like a magpie. At least Aurora would still be there, as would her clothes and hair products, littering the house as they had these past few weeks.

Tomorrow was Christmas Eve. Two Christmases ago he'd been in a mental health facility. He'd spent last Christmas in Sedona at Dawn's place, where they'd all sat down to turkey and Tofurky, which was their tradition. His heart lurched. Dawn wouldn't be home in time for Christmas this year. Neither would Raf. Indigo made a mental note to try him at his dad's place again when he got home. He hadn't spoken to Raf in so long, and he felt his absence acutely.

Indigo's life had been so different a couple years back. He'd hated it then, and he knew now that if you hated your life, it became unliveable. If only he'd known then how important it was for him to find something to love about his existence, and that only he had the power to do so.

His thoughts turned to Cordelia, the thing he loved most about his existence. Edita and Lukas weren't due back 'til tomorrow, and he'd invited her on a real date tonight, offering to take her to his favourite little bistro in the city. But she'd looked up at him with those big expressive eyes of hers as she'd gently reached up under his shirt to stroke the small of his back whilst suggesting they stay in instead. And his body had responded in all sorts of ways.

Aurora had a date of her own tonight. She'd told them not to expect her home, which Indigo had actually been happy about. He and Cordelia had been surrounded by other people for weeks now, and the prospect of having the house to themselves, just the two of them, of not having to worry about being quiet or discreet or considerate for a whole night, well, it was a novelty he couldn't wait to take advantage of.

He put his foot down hard on the accelerator.

Aurora must have been waiting at the window, because the moment he pulled up, she strolled out the front door, dressed to kill in a vinyl minidress and towering ankle boots. She clearly couldn't wait to get out of there.

"Need a lift?" he asked, climbing out of his SUV.

She shook her head as she strutted past him. "Don't wait up."

"Hey, Ror?" he called after her.

She paused, turned. "Yeah?"

"Who's the mystery guy?"

She patted her slicked-back hair and winked. "Wouldn't you like to know?" She spun and sauntered off.

He watched her for a moment or two, then hurried towards the house. "Hey, you," he called, as he walked through the front door.

"In here," Cordelia called back. She was in the kitchen, chopping pumpkin and potatoes. She was delectably barefoot in a long, black dress, an olive-green apron tied around her tiny waist, her hair twisted up in a knot on top of her head. He came straight at her, spinning her round and pulling her into his arms, crushing his lips hungrily to hers. After everything that had happened, with everything that was looming over them, they needed a night of normalcy together, just the two of them. He needed to forget. And she had the power to make him.

"Why, hello," she murmured as she hooked her arms around his neck and kissed him back.

"You're cooking?" he said, glancing at the pile of snow peas and broccoli beside the chopping board, the bunches of mint and the sprigs of rosemary.

"Roast lamb. Your favourite." She brushed her lips to his again.

"You spoil me," he said, his mouth now wandering the place behind her ear. "Christ, you smell amazing," he groaned. She was utterly intoxicating.

"I like spoiling you."

"I'm totally digging this whole domestic bliss thing," he murmured, untying her apron and chucking it over his shoulder onto the floor. He lifted her smoothly onto the white marble countertop, pushing her dress up and sliding his hands beneath so he could grasp her thighs.

"Here?" She giggled as he nibbled the hollow of her throat, but she was reaching to pull his T-shirt off, wrapping her legs around his waist.

"Here, there, and everywhere, baby," he whispered into her ear, as he pulled her underwear off. "Every single room, every position we can think of…" He eased the top of her dress down and ran his thumb down the centre of her breast, and she bit down hard on her lower lip. "Every beautiful, sexy, smoking-hot inch of you is mine tonight."

"But there's like… forty or fifty rooms in this house," she breathed, her neck arching as his lips roved over her collarbone, down her chest, towards that taut, pink nipple that was just begging for his mouth.

"I do like a challenge," he said as he drew it in. Breathy moans fell from her lips as she reached for the waistband of his shorts. She slipped her hand inside, their dinner prep all but forgotten.

Hours later, he held her as she slept, content in the fact she was safe in his arms, knowing that he would protect her now and always, 'til his dying breath and beyond.

He closed his eyes, listening to the rhythmic rise and fall of her breath. But sleep wouldn't come. He was worried about Dawn. He was worried about Harper. And he was worried about the secret he was keeping from Cordelia.

The two of them weren't meant to have any secrets, he knew that, and it was eating him up inside that he was keeping this from her. But he couldn't tell her, not now. She'd been through enough this year, with Josh, and Harper, and Sandy… At least she was oblivious to the fact he was holding back, that he was hiding something, because if she knew, it would hurt her, and that's the last thing he wanted.

He'd vowed to protect her at all costs, to keep her safe, to love her for all eternity. And he'd figured it out. Worked out how to do that. How to hack the universe. How to cheat the fates and defy the odds and keep her with him always.

There was only one way it could happen.

And she wasn't gonna like it.

So for now, he was keeping it to himself. He had no choice.

The next morning, Edita and Lukas arrived home from their holiday in Thailand. They'd booked it at the beginning of the year, before they knew Indigo was coming home, and he'd only found out about it when he'd overheard them trying to cancel it.

He'd insisted they go, that he and his mates were more than capable of looking after themselves (although Nash had jokingly complained about the lack of fresh towels and turn-down service after she'd left). Edita never did anything for herself, other than the weekly book club meetings she'd attended religiously for as long as Indigo could remember.

She'd been adamant she wouldn't go away and leave him, but then suddenly, a week after Bernadette's big party, she'd relented out of the blue and agreed to go. She'd simply told Indigo he was in good hands with his friends and agreed to take the time off.

Indigo and Cordelia were still asleep in his bed, a tangle of limbs and hair and breath, when they were awakened by the clunk of car doors slamming and the chatter of voices.

"What time is it?" she groaned into his chest.

He glanced at the clock on his bedside table. "It's after ten," he mumbled, dragging her sleepily towards him so he could brush his lips to hers. She lay her bare body on his, relaxing into him. He smoothed the hair from her face and squeezed her backside, kissing her deeply.

"We should get up," she said, smiling against his lips, her tresses cascading in a sweet-smelling waterfall to cover their faces.

"Soon," he promised, stroking the small of her back. He loved having her in his bed, her hair tousled, her lips plump and raw, her eyes glistening brightly with all that she felt for him.

An hour later they showered and wandered downstairs.

"Ah, Indi!" Edita exclaimed. She clutched him to her ample bosom, fussing over his too-long hair, grabbing his face between her hands and exclaiming that the bruising that had marred his face when she'd left had all but gone. She then embraced Cordelia tightly, declaring her too thin, before purposefully striding into the kitchen to start cooking for them.

He glanced out the window. Aurora was in her favourite spot, sunbathing half-naked on a chaise longue.

"Where's Lukey?" Indigo asked.

"Gone to get a tree," Edita said pointedly, as though the fact Indigo hadn't thought to put up a Christmas tree was sacrilegious. He made a face. He'd already had to take charge of putting up the Carlisle Christmas tree last week, with Robbie hindering more than helping; he hadn't particularly wanted to repeat that exercise.

After a late breakfast of avocado on freshly baked sourdough with fetta, toasted sunflower seeds, basil and roasted cherry tomatoes, they watched as Edita moved through the house from room to room. She shook her head and muttered under her breath in Lithuanian, before rolling up her sleeves and hauling the vacuum cleaner out of the cupboard with a giant sigh. The house was clean. It just wasn't *Edita* clean. Any help offered was flatly refused. She liked things done her way.

Lukas returned home and Indigo helped him erect an enormous tree in the foyer (which admittedly was a lot easier without Robbie barking bossy orders and fussing and flapping about pine needles and sap). The four of them decorated it so that it twinkled and glowed as though dowsed in icicles, whilst Aurora continued to lounge like a lizard by the pool.

Indigo had tried to ask her about her date the night before, but she'd just smiled secretively and buried her face deeper in the book she'd been reading. He and Cordelia had discussed it and decided Aurora was seeing the actor she'd met at Bernadette's party, the one from *Home and Away* she'd spent half the night talking to. Who else could it be?

Later that afternoon, Aurora sauntered into the lounge room, fully dressed for the first time that day, her hair swinging down her back. "You heading home soon?" she asked Cordelia.

Cordelia glanced up from the movie she was watching with Indigo and nodded.

"Cool. Let me know when you're leaving, I'll come with."

Cordelia grabbed the remote and hit pause on *Die Hard*. "You're coming?" Her cute little nose scrunched way up.

"You know you can't go on your own," Aurora said matter-of-factly. "Besides, Scarlett was gonna show me that book on Indigenous herbal medicine." As she left the room, she called back, "By the way, *Die Hard*? *Not* a Christmas movie."

"Um… seriously? '*Now I have a machine gun, ho-ho-ho*,'" Indigo quipped, but she was already gone.

Cordelia clenched her jaw, glaring after her. "Funny how she can't stand me, yet she and Mum have hit it off like nobody's business."

"Aurora likes you just fine, angel face," Indigo said, smoothing her hair behind her ear and smooching her cheek.

She shot him the most withering look he'd ever been on the receiving end of. "I can't believe you're going away and *leaving* her here with me!"

"Babe…" He scrubbed his hands wearily over his face. He knew it wasn't ideal, but he really had no choice.

Her shoulders dropped. "I'm sorry. I'm just venting. I don't want you to worry about me."

"I'll always worry about you."

"Well, don't. You just get over there and focus on Dawn and Reggie. I'll be fine. I know if I were Harper, I'd think twice about messing with Aurora." She smiled and pulled his face to hers. "I'm just grumpy because I'm really, *really* gonna miss you." She pouted.

"I can't even think about not being with you," he murmured, closing his eyes and pressing his forehead to hers. They hadn't spent a night apart since Bernadette's party. He couldn't imagine sleeping without her now. He tilted her chin up and stared into her eyes.

She looked like she was about to cry. "I'll miss you more than anything," he whispered as he bent to kiss her. His hands were in her hair as she pressed her body to his. Oh God, how was he going to drag himself away from her tomorrow night? He laid soft kisses on her cheeks, her eyelids, her jaw, returning to her lips in between.

Her arms slid around his neck and he pulled her onto his lap. She rested her head in the nook between his chin and his shoulder and exhaled heavily, sinking into him as he tightened his arms around her, holding her like his life depended on it.

Later, he kissed her goodbye beside her car, knowing he'd see her again in a few hours.

Being Lithuanian, Edita had always put a lot more importance on Christmas Eve than Christmas Day, and this year she'd invited the Carlisles to join them.

Cordelia glanced coolly at Aurora, already buckled into the passenger seat, and gave him a tight smile as she climbed in. He leant into the car. "Be nice," he said, pointing from one to the other. "Both of you." Aurora rolled her eyes at him.

After they'd left, he went for a surf, then showered and dressed in navy shorts and a baby-blue-check, button-down shirt. He headed downstairs, his feet bare. Rolling his cuffs up, he approached the kitchen, pricking his ears up as he overheard an exchange of urgent whispers.

Two voices.

Both female.

Frowning, he stepped through the doorway. Edita was standing in the walk-in pantry, face flushed, speaking heatedly with a tall woman with regal posture whose back was to Indigo. The woman was clad in wide-legged, cream slacks and matching camisole, a sheer, ivory scarf looped elegantly around her neck. Her thick, lustrous hair – the most magnificent shade of silvery white – was pulled back into a stylish chignon.

Edita's mouth snapped shut when she locked eyes with him, and the other woman swung around.

"Grandmother?" Indigo breathed, wide-eyed. He hadn't seen his mother's mother in years. Serena didn't approve of Bernadette's life choices and was adamant her relationship to her famous daughter never be made public. Widowed by her second husband years back, she lived in a small beachside hamlet on the Central Coast of New South Wales with her dogs and her cat, where she kept largely to herself. She was an artist – an accomplished painter and sculptor – with a severe case of wanderlust. She was always travelling, always interstate or overseas at some exotic location or another.

"Indigo, darling," Serena said in her charming manner, gliding towards him with that graceful confidence she'd always exuded. She was in her mid-sixties, and still a very attractive woman. She put a hand on each of his shoulders and looked him up and down, scrutinising him so closely he squirmed. Her palm slid to his cheek, and she frowned at the scar on his forehead, at the faint, yellowish stain of bruises, then trailed her fingers down to rest upon the wolf's tooth that hung from his neck, glancing briefly at Edita, then back to him.

She tilted her head thoughtfully to one side, then nodded decisively, her face breaking into a smile. "Merry Christmas, dear," she said, smoothing his hair back. "It's wonderful to see you."

"You, too, Grandmother. What brings you down here?"

"Is it a crime for a grandmother to want to see her only grandson at Christmas?"

She'd missed the last nineteen. Why now?

"Your grandmother will be joining us for dinner," Edita told him with a tight smile. She looked a little shaken. It was on the tip of Indigo's tongue to ask her what they'd been whispering about so heatedly, but Serena linked her arm through his and led him to the lounge room, sitting straight-backed beside him on the couch, bending her knees and neatly crossing her ankles. She proceeded to grill him about every aspect of his life to the point of exhaustion.

Indigo audibly sighed in relief an hour later when he heard a car in the drive. A minute later, Matty came tearing in and threw himself into Indigo's lap. Matty stared up at Serena, regarding her curiously, his little eyes travelling over her large diamond necklace and matching earrings, down past her stacked, bejewelled bangles, to the rings she wore on every finger dripping with rubies, emeralds and sapphires and, of course, more diamonds.

"Are you a queen?" he finally asked, wide-eyed.

Serena's face broke into a large smile, her green eyes twinkling.

"I'm Serena," she said, holding her hand out to him. "It's lovely to meet you."

"I'm Matty," he said, shaking her hand in his small one and grinning at her. "You're very beautiful. And *very* sparkly!"

"Why, thank you," she said, bowing her chin to him.

"Hey, Inds, is Matty with you–" Cordelia hurried into the room and stopped short when she saw Serena. "Oh, I'm sorry, I didn't realise you had company," she said, her gaze curious. She was a vision of dewy gorgeousness in a flowing teal dress, her hair caught up in a low side-bun.

Indigo stood, hoisted Matty onto his hip and went to kiss her, murmuring in her ear that she looked stunning, before taking her hand and leading her to the couch. "This is my grandmother, Serena Wildes. Grandmother, this is Cordelia."

Serena stood, staring intently at Cordelia for some time, before smiling warmly and reaching her hands out to grasp Cordelia's. "I've so been looking forward to meeting you, my dear."

"It's lovely to meet you," Cordelia said, leaning to kiss her cheek as Scarlett and Robbie came in search of Matty. Aurora drifted in behind them, her gaze intent as she looked Serena up and down with interest.

Over a meal of roasted duck with all the trimmings, Lukas and Edita regaled their guests with tales of their adventures in Bangkok, Chiang Mai and Koh Samui, recounting how they'd haggled at markets, ridden elephants and swum at idyllic, deserted beaches. They spoke of the tropical storms that had rolled through each afternoon, and of all the interesting characters they'd met. They were both tanned and happy and so content with their lot in life, it made Indigo smile to see it. They'd been so hesitant to proceed with this holiday, umming and aahing for days before they finally agreed to it; he was glad they'd been able to relax and enjoy themselves.

Indigo's eyes travelled around the table, coming to rest on Cordelia sitting beside him, and he almost had to pinch himself. Sometimes he couldn't quite believe that this was real and she was his. He was so fucking in love with her that he could barely see straight. He reached for her hand and kissed it and, when he caught her eye, she smiled that smile that instantly stopped his heart. She glanced down at his hand and stroked his pinkie. "Where's my ring?' she whispered.

He followed her gaze, his stomach lurching in panic. Then he remembered. "It's upstairs in my bathroom," he told her so the others couldn't hear. "I don't like to wear it in the shower in case it falls off and sometimes I forget to put it back on."

"As long as you haven't lost it," she said lightly.

"Never," he said, draping his arm over the back of her chair, running his thumb over her bare shoulder blade.

Serena managed to charm everyone over dinner, even though she didn't share much about herself, preferring to listen than to talk. Indigo remained cautious to draw any conclusions about this mysterious woman he barely knew; she was incredibly closed and he found it near impossible to get a read on her. He remembered when he was younger, how she used to drive down to sit by his bedside when he had one of his episodes – when he felt too much and heard too much and it was all just too much and the darkness came – how she'd hold his hand and stroke his forehead, how she'd always come with a gift for him (the last gift had been the beaded bracelet he'd given Cordelia the first time he'd kissed her, until Serena had sent the wolf's tooth necklace he now wore).

But he hadn't had an episode in years. And he hadn't seen her in years.

After dinner, they lit the candles on the Christmas tree, and then the Carlisles took Matty home to set cookies out for Santa. It was way past his bedtime.

Cordelia gave Indigo a lingering kiss goodbye and whispered that she'd leave the back door open for him. He whispered back that he'd follow in a couple of hours. He wanted to be there when they awoke on Christmas morning. He knew how tough the first one without Joshua would be for them all. But then again, wouldn't every Christmas forever more? Christmas had always been a massive deal in the Carlisle home, with Joshua front and centre of it all, stipulating they all wear the silly paper hats that fell from the Christmas crackers while blasting his cheesy carols all day.

Indigo made eye contact with Aurora as she climbed in the car. She nodded tersely. Aurora was a night owl and was happy to hold vigil on the couch 'til he got there.

Indigo detoured past the Christmas tree to blow the candles out on his way back inside. Edita insisted on real candles because that's what she'd had as a child. She scoffed at the suggestion the whole lot could go up in flames. Lukas was in the dining room, stacking the dishes Edita had earlier insisted no one was to help clear, and Serena and Edita were having an intent conversation on the couch. Serena looked up when he walked in. "Walk me out, Indigo dear," she said, leaning to squeeze Edita's hands in hers before standing. She linked her arm through his and they walked in silence to her car. When they arrived at her white two-door Mercedes, she kissed Indigo's cheeks and he bent to open the driver's door for her, holding it open as she climbed in.

"It really was lovely to see you, darling," she said. "Bring that divine girlfriend of yours and come visit me sometime. Stay for the weekend if you like, my cottage is right on the beach."

"Merry Christmas, Grandmother."

He smiled as he closed the door, but as she took off down the driveway, it faded fast. He was thoroughly confused. He'd had almost nothing to do with her his whole life. Why had she suddenly turned up now?

He headed back inside and approached Edita, who was at the sink washing up. "Everything ok?" he asked, peering deeply into her eyes.

"Of course it is," she said stiffly, averting her gaze and plunging her hands back into the sudsy water. "Why wouldn't it be?"

"I just thought... You and my grandmother..."

"Everything is fine, Indigo," she said, although she wouldn't meet his eye. Wordlessly, he picked up a tea towel and began to dry the dishes she'd left draining on the sink while Lukas pottered in and out carrying glasses and plates.

When the kitchen was clean, the three of them returned to the Christmas tree to exchange gifts. Edita frowned at the extinguished candles but didn't say anything. Lukas was almost shaking with excitement as Indigo opened his present and smiled expectantly as Indigo tore the paper back to reveal an enormous stack of counterfeit DVDs, their covers distorted and faded, their titles emblazoned in large Thai symbols. "Oh w-wow, thanks, Lukey," Indigo stammered, forcing a big grin onto his face and making a point of sifting through the stack.

"I know how much you used to love those movies your mum's PA would send from America when you were just a young lad. Check this one out, Indi mate," Lukas said, leaning forward excitedly and pulling a copy of *Braveheart* from the pile. "It's still in the cinemas, it won't be coming to the video shop for at least a year! That's a bit of alright, yeah?" He grinned enthusiastically and pointed at *Se7en* and *The Usual Suspects* adding, "These, too."

"Wow, that's awesome, I've been hanging to see all of these. Especially this one," he said, holding up a copy of *Twelve Monkeys*. He made a mental note to hide the latest box of DVDs Bernadette's PA had sent from LA the other day, although he suspected Nash had probably magpied half of those.

"Lukas spent hours bargaining with the vendors at Patpong Markets in Bangkok for those movies," Edita told him with a roll of her eyes. "He assures me he got a very good deal."

"I'm sure he did," Indigo replied, eyeing Lukas with affection.

"Let's chuck one on now, eh, mate?" Lukas suggested, his blue eyes shining, "All of us together?" He looked so hopeful, Indigo didn't have the heart to tell him they would all be seasick after sitting through a pirated movie filmed in the cinema on a hand-held video camera.

"Great idea," he agreed instead. "You choose." He thrust the stack into Lukas's hands as Edita picked up wrapping paper.

Halfway through a super dodgy forgery of *Dangerous Minds*, the picture shaky and the audio tinny and interspersed with the sound of movie-goers munching popcorn and rustling candy wrappers, Lukas and Edita claimed jetlag, and retired to their room on the ground floor of the house.

Indigo had assured Edita he'd lock up before he left, so he wandered from room to room, switching off lights and making sure all the doors were secure. The house creaked around him, its emptiness palpable. A nostalgic sadness washed over him.

He knew how lucky he was, that his life was brimming with people who loved him, who cared about him, who he loved and cared about… The family he was born into? It wasn't much to speak of. But the family he'd made for himself, the family he'd constructed out of the broken pieces of his life? Those people were his whole world – Edita and

Lukas; Raf, Sasha, Aurora, Nash and Dawn; and of course, Scarlett, Matty, Robbie and Cordelia.

Cordelia. The very thought of her brought a smile to his lips as he made his way upstairs to finish packing. God, he was going to miss her. He was flying out tomorrow night. He'd originally planned on going straight through to New York to see Luis, but now he was going to Sedona instead. Healing Dawn was his priority. Cordelia was flying over with Aurora and Robbie for New Year's; he was meeting her in Aspen. Right now, the thought of being apart from her for a week sent a clawing ache through his chest.

She was all that was bright and pure and true, and he never wanted to be without her.

He opened his wardrobe and threw a couple of extra sweaters into the large duffle that lay open on his bedroom floor. He'd tried calling Raf's dad's house in San Diego again that afternoon, but there'd been no answer. The other day, Dawn had assured him everything with Raf was ok. But he still couldn't shake the feeling that it wasn't. For now though, he had to trust it was because he had so much on his plate, and Raf, Raf was so strong and so together, Indigo had to assume he would always be fine.

He sighed deeply as he rummaged in his bedside drawer for his passport, stuffing it down the side of his carry-on bag along with his plane ticket. Remembering Cordelia's ring, he hurried into the bathroom and retrieved it from the vanity, sliding it back onto his finger. He returned to his room and flopped back onto his bed, folding his arms behind his head, staring up at the small char mark on the ceiling, the result of he and Drew mucking around with an aerosol can and a cigarette lighter when they were really stoned one day years ago.

His mind wandered to the conversation he and Cordelia had had in this very bed the other morning. It had been bugging him because he hadn't told her the complete truth. He hated that he was keeping something from her. But it was only because he was trying to protect her, protect her in a way he'd failed to in so many other lifetimes. As far as he could see, there really was no point in telling her, for the brutal truth would do nothing but upset her, cause the untold stress upon her that had plagued him, an ever-niggling presence just there in the back of his mind.

She'd been so distraught when he'd told her of their lifetime in Crete, how her demise had led to his. And she'd asked him outright about the other times. He'd avoided the question, because how could he tell her that there had indeed been others – so many others – and that their union, lifetime after lifetime, always ended the same way?

He squeezed his eyes shut as images danced through his head.

Stacked stone houses on a beautiful island. Beehives. Her, clasping at her throat as she gasped for air, one hand on her rounded stomach.

A muddy battlefield, a medic's uniform. A nurse. Her, boarding that ill-fated hospital ship home, her dress let out around the waist. Debris in the water.

Herbs and potions. A dark forest. Accusations and pointed fingers. Her, burning at the stake, flames licking her swollen belly.

Always with the baby.

Their baby.

A baby that was never to be born.

But this time, he knew it would be different.

Because he was aware and he was prepared. He knew the mistakes he'd made in the past and he'd learned from them. It always went the same way: them, euphoric happiness, the pregnancy, then death. Always death.

In his mind, he could see only one way to break the cycle: the pregnancy. He could never let it happen. He was happy for it just to be the two of them, together forever. They didn't need anything else.

He'd always wanted kids, to be a father, but if he had to choose, it was a no-brainer, it was hands down her, always her. She was more than enough. And he hoped he was, too. Because right now, that was the only way he could think to keep her with him. It was the way it was going to be this time if they were going to be together, and the way he felt about her, he knew they *had* to be together.

It was fine for now. She was on the pill and he knew she took it fastidiously at the same time every day so there was no chance of any slip-ups.

He knew this wasn't something he could keep from her much longer, but for now, when she'd already been through so much this year, it had to be.

i dreamed a dream

vaucluse, new south wales

reinenoir

Reinenoir stormed to the window and yanked the drapes closed against the blink of coloured Christmas lights. Fucking neighbours and their cheery holiday spirit! She was in no mood for carols and lights and laughter. It was Christmas Eve yet she had nothing to celebrate.

She swept across the room and settled herself back at the dining table, picking up her pencil and gazing down at her list. Her collection on paper. Everything she'd lost that night up at North Fort. Everything she needed to regain to continue her quest for the crown.

Indigo and his little pals had set her back *years*, and her patience didn't stretch to years. She needed her powers back, and she needed them *now*.

She had to devise a plan she and her inner circle could complete without outside help, because Sandy had proven relying on normies was a futile exercise. Bloody Sandy Whitcomb! She squeezed her pencil so hard it snapped. Shrieking, she hurled the broken pieces against the wall, followed by a wine glass, burgundy liquid splattering the paintwork. How hard was it to get rid of one weak, defenceless girl? Reinenoir had cleared the path by separating her from Indigo, and *still* he'd failed. Useless waste of space. At least Sandy had gotten what he deserved, although she suspected the story the media was reporting wasn't the true tale of his demise. She knew firsthand how easy it was to deceive the authorities when it came to murder.

She dragged her hand wearily over her face and down her mauve shift dress, trailing lipstick fingerprints in femme-fatale red down the front. She hadn't slept much since the night Indigo stripped her of her collection. But she'd been watching him. Him and his *whore*. And watching them at the beach the other day, playing with those kids – the little blond brat and that plain little Down syndrome girl – it had planted a seed of an idea. They were so light, so open, those children. And she could see what they meant to that Carlisle bitch, to Indigo.

The expression about taking candy from a baby hadn't come about without merit.

'*Orwen!*' she called telepathically to her Maiden. '*I need you, now.*' Thankfully Reinenoir still had the powers she was born with. Indigo had taken everything else, but he didn't know how to take those.

Her Maiden was nothing if not efficient, hurrying immediately from the other end of the house to join Reinenoir at the table. Her eyes grew round as she sat down and took in the appearance of her High Priestess. "When was the last time you slept, my lady?"

Reinenoir turned slowly to the mirror on the wall beside her. Her hair was dishevelled, her lipstick smeared, and mascara was smudged beneath her eyes in flaky black half-moons. She stared at the faint blemish in the middle of her forehead, given to her by *him*, and grinned manically. "Rest is for the weak," she said, shifting her gaze from her reflection to the bearded dragon draped across her Maiden's shoulder. She scowled at the horrid little thing. "I asked you not to bring Mortimer near me! How much longer are you lizard-sitting for anyway?"

"Just until Madame DuPont recovers from cleaning up your... er, *our* mess." Reinenoir could have sworn judgement flashed briefly through the Maiden's eyes.

"*Careful*, Orwen," she said coolly. "Has Artax located the traitors?"

After North Fort, there had been rumblings of an uprising in the coven she'd temporarily disbanded. But, as she always had, Reinenoir knew when there was unrest in the group, when an uprising was coming and it was time to cull. It was guaranteed that if it was thought about enough, Reinenoir would hear it.

Her Grandmother, Isadora, had had to step in to protect her in a display of power that showed them *all* that the DuPont line was not to be messed with. And now Artax was dealing with the instigators.

"He'll be home with the first batch soon," the Maiden said.

A thrill of delight shivered through Reinenoir. She was more than ready to collect from those traitors, to cross a few items off her list.

She'd collect from them.

Then she'd put her plan into action and take some candy from some babies.

And somewhere along the way she'd do her own dirty work and get rid of that Carlisle bitch herself.

When she was restored to her former glory, and Indigo was unencumbered and broken down and desperate, she would be there to build him back up, to give his life worth again, to make him see how foolish he'd been. And then he'd see that she had been his destiny all along.

Together, they would rule the world.

throw your arms around me

cordelia

It was really late when Indigo slipped into her bed that Christmas Eve. She'd dozed off waiting for him, and she came to when she felt his arms slide around her waist, his warm body coiling around hers, moulding tight against her as he kissed the nape of her neck. He murmured softly that he'd missed her and her beautiful body, that he loved her desperately and that she was the best Christmas present he ever could have asked for, a present he was going to unwrap right that very minute.

He did just that, and she lay in half-waking bliss as he caressed her all over, his magic hands moving expertly over every bit of her, lingering where she most wanted them until her blood roiled in her veins and she could no longer remain submissive. She tilted her face over her shoulder to his, their lips meeting in a frenzy of feeling and breath and ecstasy as he claimed what was his and always would be.

When she awoke the next morning, she remembered it was Christmas.

And as she lay there with her eyes closed in the land between dreaming and waking, for a brief moment she believed her father was still alive and well, downstairs in their kitchen making his traditional Christmas morning waffles that he would indulgently serve with ice cream and home-made vanilla custard.

"Cora? Indigo?" a little voice said as a small finger poked her shoulder. "Cora!" Poke, poke. "Indigo!

"Whaaaaaaat?" she mumbled, and she felt Indigo stir behind her, his muscles stretching and tightening against her.

"Santa came!" She opened her eyes just a crack to see Matty's small face millimetres from hers.

"Morning, cutie-pie." She smiled sleepily as Indigo reached past her to pull Matty's tiny, warm body into bed with them.

"Indigo?" Matty said.

"Mmm?"

"Can you have a sleep-over in *my* room one day?"

"A sleep-over? In *your* room?" Indigo asked, rolling onto his side to face him, head propped in his hand.

"Yeah, in *my* room. Deadie told me you used to sleep-over in Robbie's room, and now you sleep-over in Cora's. So when is it *my* turn?"

Indigo laughed his deep, belly laugh, tickling Matty and cuddling him close. "You'll have to ask your sister, little man, see if she's willing to part with me for a night." He looked over Matty's head at Cordelia, who narrowed her eyes at him. He winked as Matty squirmed free and jumped from the bed, grabbing their hands, tugging as hard as he could.

"Get *UP*, guys! It's present time! Mummy said we can't open the ones under the tree until you come down." His soft blond curls were tousled to afro proportions.

"What about your Santa sack?" Cordelia yawned. The deal was that Matty was allowed to open all the presents Santa left for him in the sack he'd excitedly laid out on the end of his bed the night before, but he had to wait for the rest of the family before he touched any of the gifts under the Christmas tree.

"I *already* opened all those ones up," Matty said, holding up a blue Power Ranger figurine and a Beanie Baby monkey, his eyes shining in delight. "Look!" he said, thrusting them in his sister's face.

"Wow!" Cordelia exclaimed, sitting up in bed and taking the toys he was proffering. She examined each one carefully, knowing she was expected to.

"You must have been top of Santa's Nice List this year, Matty Moo!" Indigo exclaimed as he took the Power Ranger from Cordelia. "*So cool, I've always wanted one of these.*"

"You can have a go whenever you want?" Matty offered.

"Thanks, little dude," Indigo grinned.

"Well, I like the monkey best," Cordelia said.

"He's Chati's favourite too," Matty told her. Cordelia nodded, knowing that meant she was considered to be in good company. If Matty's drawings were anything to go by, Chati was his only age-appropriate imaginary friend.

"What's his name?" Cordelia asked, holding up the monkey.

Matty scrunched up his face deep in thought before deciding. "Bananas," he told her assuredly.

"Bananas is just gorgeous, you lucky boy," she said, kissing the monkey on its nose. "You must have been so so good this year for Santa to bring you two of the things you wanted most."

Matty nodded enthusiastically. "You know I was. Although he didn't bring me a Woody." Behind her, Indigo snorted a laugh, then covered it with a cough. Scarlett had taken Matty to see a movie called *Toy Story* at the cinema a week ago and it was all he'd talked about since. "Now get *UP!*" he demanded bossily, pulling them by the hands again.

"Ok, ok, Matty, you win," Cordelia grumbled. "At least let me brush my teeth. We'll be down in a minute, ok?"

"Ok, but ONE minute," he told her, pointing at them in warning. She drew a cross across her heart and he turned and scampered out the room.

"Merry Christmas, beautiful," Indigo smiled, enfolding her in his arms and snuggling her back down under the covers.

"Merry Christmas," she whispered as he rolled on top of her and kissed her deeply. She lightly stroked his shoulder blades, his back flexing beneath her palms as he settled between her thighs.

"How you feeling?" he asked, pulling back so he could see her face. "About today?" She swallowed hard and he pressed his forehead to hers, closing his eyes and whispering, "I know, I know. I'll be here by your side all day, ok?"

"Until you go to the airport." Her stomach lurched. "I don't want you to go." The ache in her heart was palpable. She could barely cope with being away from him for a few hours, let alone a whole week.

"I never want to be apart from you." He started kissing her passionately again, his hands inching lower.

"We can't," she groaned as things began to escalate.

"But I've got something special for you," he murmured.

"Is it the thing Santa didn't give Matty?" She giggled.

"Yep." He grinned cheekily.

She burst out laughing. "We've gotta get up or Matty will be back to see why we're not."

He blew out a steady breath, grumbling good-naturedly into her shoulder as he rolled off her so she could stand. She pulled a matching midnight-blue kimono on over her silk cami-and-shorts-set, then leant over to feather her lips over his, pinning him to the bed by his wrists so he couldn't grab her and pull her back in.

She went into the bathroom to clean her teeth and brush her hair. A few minutes later, he came in behind her, kissing her cheek and opening the vanity to grab the toothbrush he kept there, smiling at her as he squeezed toothpaste onto it. He'd pulled a white singlet on over his light-blue-and-white striped pyjama bottoms. When he was done brushing his teeth, he held his hand out to her and she took it, and together they went downstairs to join her family under the Christmas tree.

"Merry Christmas, my darlings!" Mum cried, jumping up to embrace them. She smiled brightly, but her eyes were red and puffy and it was obvious she'd been crying.

"Merry Christmas, Mum," Cordelia whispered, tears rushing to her own eyes. She drew in a deep, ragged breath to try and compose herself as her mother stroked her hair. Dad's absence was the loudest thing in the room.

"Happy merry turkey day, Cora." Robbie said, striding over with a squirmy Matty in his arms and kissing her on the cheek. Matty won the battle and was released.

"Merry Christmas, Rob," she smiled sadly, as Indigo clapped him on the back and lunged after Matty, throwing him over his shoulder so he squealed with glee.

"Presents!" Matty yelled, wriggling to the floor and dancing around them excitedly in his Buzz Lightyear pyjamas. "Presents and waffles! Waffles and ice cream!"

"Oh…" Cordelia breathed, stricken. Presents, yes. But waffles, no. Who was going to break it to Matty? "Mum?" she asked, turning to her mother, panic on her face. Who was going to tell Matty that there would be no waffles this year? All she wanted was for her baby brother to have a happy Christmas.

"It's ok, Cora," Mum assured her, squeezing her arm. "It's under control." She glanced at Indigo.

"Well, somewhat under control." Indigo laughed as he headed into the kitchen.

"Apparently Dad entrusted his secret waffle recipe to Inds before he died and made him promise he'd keep the tradition alive," Mum explained.

"Although I'm beginning to fear his faith in me was misguided," Indigo called from the kitchen.

"Do you want some help, babe?" Cordelia asked.

"No," came the hesitant reply. "I should be fine. How hard can it be, right?"

She looked at Robbie and shrugged. Robbie went to the stereo system and selected a disc from the CD tower, and *(Christmas) Baby Please Come Home* began to play. They sat and chatted while Matty poked and prodded and shook the presents under the Christmas tree, before curiosity got the better of Robbie and he casually meandered over to the kitchen and peeked in. He baulked, his gaze widening. Biting his lip, his eyes shining with excitement, he strode casually to Cordelia's side, plopping down beside her, grabbing her arm and murmuring, "Oh my God, oh my God!"

"What? Why are we whispering?"

"It's finally happened!" Robbie cried under his breath, squeezing her arm tighter. "After all these years, it's *finally happened!*"

"*What's* happened?"

"We've found it, the one thing Indigo's not good at, we've *finally* found it!" She looked confused so he nodded towards the kitchen. She sauntered over and stuck her head in, her hand moving to her mouth to stifle a giggle. Every surface was covered in flour and spilt milk and broken eggs. The floor was dusted in sugar and big gobs of what looked like sour cream. Not even the ceiling remained unscathed.

"Oh my God!" Cordelia laughed. Robbie was bent double laughing beside her. "You can't cook!" He'd always stood back and let her take charge in the kitchen, but she'd never given it much thought.

"Yeah, well, feel free to come and lend a hand," he grinned, his cheeks flushing as he ran a hand through the back of his hair.

Cordelia shook her head. "Oh no, Dad entrusted his beloved waffle recipe to you. It's all yours."

"Rob?" Indigo asked.

"Ew, no, thanks," Robbie shot back, glancing at the flour on Indigo's hands and PJs. "Fruit salad and cereal are about as far as my culinary talents extend. Everyone knows I can't cook for shit."

"Robbie said the 'S' word," Matty sang.

Mum widened her eyes at Robbie in admonishment. "Do you need me to come and help, sweetie?" Mum asked Indigo, surveying her kitchen with unusual calmness, considering her usually pristine domain had been somewhat decimated.

"Nah, yeah, I wouldn't say no…" Indigo grimaced. "Unless you're all keen on blackened Cajun waffles?"

"Ew," Robbie said, wrinkling his nose.

"Um, no, honey." Mum giggled. "I'll help."

"Thanks, Scar. The recipe says I have to beat the eggs. What exactly am I meant to beat them with? And why?"

"And what in God's name have those poor eggs done to deserve said beating?" Robbie laughed.

"My God," Cordelia muttered, her eyes widening. "You weren't joking that you need help."

"But presents first!" Indigo replied, narrowing his eyes playfully at Cordelia. "Right, Matty?"

"Right!" Matty yelled, grabbing Indigo's hand and dashing towards the tree. "I'll give them out!" He snatched up a large one and tilted it up so Indigo could read the card, gazing at him intently for direction. "That one's for Mummy," Indigo whispered to him. "From Robbie."

"For you, Mummy," Matty said, rushing over to the couch where his mother was sitting, her arm draped around Cordelia's shoulders. He held out the gift to her.

"For me?" she exclaimed.

Matty nodded. "Open it! Open it!"

When all the presents were opened and the living room was a sea of crumpled wrapping paper and discarded packaging, her mum went into the kitchen with Indigo to help finish making the waffles and put the turkey in the oven.

"Thank God she's helping him with breakfast," Robbie said quietly to Cordelia. "It was an absolute shit show in there." Matty was running around the living room with Woody under one arm and Buzz Lightyear under the other, Indigo having pulled some strings to have them sent from the US earlier that week.

"Well, I guess he's never needed to learn how to cook," Cordelia replied as she stuffed torn paper into a large, green garbage bag.

"I must admit I'm quite chuffed with my Christmas present," Robbie said, holding up the plane ticket Indigo had given him. "*Business* Class. Haven't you always wanted to get on a plane and turn *left*?" He was clearly thrilled Indigo had insisted on using his travel agent to organise their flights to Aspen and that it would never cross his mind to book a seat in Economy. "Although it does concern me that he actually thinks he's sticking it to the establishment by refusing to fly First…"

"The establishment?"

"You know, like he's trying to prove a point to his parents? I think he thinks he's slumming it in Business, like I don't think he actually realises the plane goes as far back as cattle class."

"Don't be mean!" she said, hitting him lightly on the shoulder. "You know he grew up differently to us. Does this mean your air sickness phobia won't be rearing its ugly head?"

Robbie just pulled a face then grinned goofily. "Anyway, just one more week and I get to see Sash. *Properly.*"

Cordelia's heart leapt to see her brother so happy. She put her arm around him and laid a big kiss on his cheek. "You're not seeing some version of him today?"

"We have a bilo date tonight. But obviously, that's top secret," he said, glancing towards the kitchen where Mum was laughing at something Indigo had just said.

"Say hi to him for me," she said with a smile. "I'm gonna go take a shower."

"Yeah I was gonna say...." he said, wrinkling his nose at her. She punched his arm on her way past.

She returned to her room after her shower to find someone had left a plate on her desk piled high with golden brown waffles, vanilla ice cream and smooth glossy custard. They looked exactly like Dad's. She smiled sadly as she stared at them, throat suddenly constricting. She sank down on the end of her bed, a wet towel wrapped around her, and burst into tears. The next thing she knew she was being pulled into a warm embrace and Indigo was cuddling her and whispering to her and holding her tight while she sobbed.

Later, after she'd calmed down and they'd eaten the waffles, he went to shower and Cordelia got dressed. By the time she came downstairs in a long, white, strapless sundress, her hair loose, silver bangles pushed high up her arm, both sets of grandparents had arrived. Much to Matty's delight, this meant yet more present opening. When Edita, Lukas and Aurora showed up a while later, lunch was almost ready and Cordelia was worried her mother might develop a cheek ache from the enormous fake smile she'd had plastered over her face all morning.

Indigo was extremely busy all day regaling her grandmothers with scandalous tales of his mother, helping her mum serve and wash up, and playing cricket with Matty. They'd even roped Cordelia into playing. While they played, they chatted away. Riveting stuff. "Hey, Matty," Indigo asked out of the blue. "What's your third favourite shark?" Thus began a lively discussion on hammerheads versus tiger sharks, because obviously great whites were number one. She was thrilled when Robbie wandered into the backyard and she could pass the cricket ball off to him after her dismal attempt at bowling.

She smiled to herself as she headed back inside. She loved watching Indigo with Matty; he was so good with him. The thought crossed her mind what a great father he'd be one day, and even though she knew she was getting *way* ahead of herself, it made her excited for all that lay ahead of them.

She'd never been one to plan for the future in great detail, but being a mother was something she wanted so badly, she'd always known that. And Indigo? She knew without a doubt she wanted to build a life with him, because she could see no future without him in it. One day, they'd have a family of their very own, she was sure of it.

As she walked inside, she heard the doorbell ring. Edita and Lukas's jetlag had gotten the better of them and they hadn't left that long ago; she wondered if they'd forgotten something. "I'll get it!" she called to no one in particular and strode to throw open the front door. Her eyes widened in shock. She covered her mouth with her hands as those damned tears rushed to her eyes again. She shook her head, completely overcome.

"Hi, you gorgeous thing! How about a hug?" Essie stepped forward and wrapped her arms around Cordelia, squeezing her tightly and raining kisses on her face.

"It's so good to see you out and about," Cordelia said, pulling back so she could peer into Essie's face, then look her up and down. "You look so good!" Her pixie cut had grown out a bit, but was still just as blonde, and although she'd lost a little bit of weight during her hospital stint, her voluptuous curves were still present and accounted for.

"So do you, Corsy..." She trailed off, her eyes glistening. "How've you all been? How are you coping?" she asked softly, her voice catching. Her face suddenly crumpled, all pretence falling away. "I-I just can't believe he's *gone*... That I *missed* it all. I wasn't there for him, for *any* of you." Her eyes overflowed and she doubled over, wrapping her arms around herself tightly in grief. "I didn't even get to say goodbye," she sobbed.

Cordelia led her to the bottom of the staircase and sat her down, taking both her hands and holding them tightly as tears fell from her own eyes.

"Oh, I'm sorry, I'm so sorry," Essie gushed. "This isn't about me, I'm making it all about me and it isn't. But they only just told me you see, when they discharged me from the rehab place. Do you know I was actually pissed off at Josh, wondering why he hadn't been to see me, why none of you had–"

"Your sister asked us not to. They didn't think you were strong enough to hear about Dad when you first regained consciousness, so they asked us to give you space until you were ready. I'm so sorry,

Essie. We did visit you in the hospital when it first happened, but then you regained consciousness, and they moved you... And they *have* been keeping us up to date with your progress. We were so, so happy when you woke up! It-it's just been a really shit time..."

"Oh, babe I know," Essie said, kissing the back of Cordelia's hand. "I completely understand... I'm just so... *so heartbroken*. And *shocked*. And I'm *angry*," she railed. "Because I didn't get a chance to say goodbye to one of the best friends I've ever had!" She clenched her teeth, her eyes flashing through the tears. "How can he just be *gone*, Cora? Just like that? I deal with death every day at work, but when it's someone you love..." She covered her face with her hands, her shoulders shaking as she sobbed. Cordelia wrapped her arms around her, holding her tight and whispering gently to her.

"Who are you talking to, sweetie?" Mum asked, suddenly emerging from the kitchen, beautiful in a short, black, ruffled dress. She gasped when she saw Essie.

"Oh, Ess..." she murmured as she hurried to her side, lip wobbling, eyes filling. Cordelia stood up as her mother took Essie in her arms, rocking her back and forth as they both cried.

"They've only just told her about Dad..." Cordelia began.

Her mother glanced up at her and nodded, then whispered, "I've got this, honey, you go join the others."

When Mum and Essie walked arm and arm into the living room half an hour later, they were met with one giant group hug as Robbie and Cordelia descended upon them.

"Have you met my parents?" Mum asked Essie, leading her over to where Cordelia's grandparents were ensconced in armchairs by the window, both nursing food comas. Essie greeted them warmly, leaning to kiss each of them on the cheek. "This is Cora's friend, Aurora," she said. Aurora was carrying an armful of glasses to the kitchen, but paused to smile. "And of course, you know Kaye and Mike," Mum said softly, as Dad's parents wandered in from outside to see what all the commotion was about. Essie started crying again as they engulfed her in a giant bear hug.

"You guys are being very loud and noisy in here!" Matty announced, charging into the room with a cricket ball held tightly in his hand, Indigo sauntering in behind him. "Essie!" Matty squealed as he spotted her, tearing over and throwing himself into her arms.

"Hey, bugalugs!" She caught him, swinging him around, then bending down to kiss his cheeks and nuzzle him in the neck, right in the spot she knew would make him squirm and giggle.

"Have you met Indigo, Essie?" Mum asked. Essie glanced up from Matty and did a double-take when she saw Indigo. She narrowed her eyes and cocked her head to one side, staring at him in bewilderment.

"Hey, Essie." Indigo grinned.

"So this is the famous Indigo," she murmured, looking him up and down, a strange expression on her face. "You look really familiar. I feel like we've met... but I don't know where..."

"You met him in the hospital, silly!" Matty piped up. "When *you* weren't in *here*," he said, waving his tiny hand up and down to indicate her body. "He made your spinny things better again, remember? And *I* helped!" he added proudly, puffing out his little chest.

"Ok, little man," Robbie interjected, rushing forward and snatching Matty up. Essie's brow was creased in total confusion. "You know Matty and his imagination," he said conspiratorially to her. "Always full of fanciful stories."

"I'm going to be a magic doctor just like Indigo when I grow up!" Matty cried over Robbie's shoulder as he carried him from the room.

Essie was still standing stock still, staring at Indigo as if trying to grasp onto something on the periphery of her mind.

"I think we met briefly at a New Year's Eve party a few years ago, right here in this very house," Indigo told her, shattering her reverie before she could catch what she was chasing. "Scar was pregnant with Matty? You were doling out the margaritas, attempting to get a bunch of doctors plastered."

"Oh," she said, pasting on an unconvinced smile. "That must be it."

"We're just about to have dessert, Ess," Cordelia said. "You'll join us, won't you?"

"Love to," Essie replied, shaking herself off and smiling warmly. "Who can say no to Scarlett's famous pudding."

chapter forty-three

girl I'm gonna miss you

indigo

He was changing in Cordelia's room when she came upstairs to find him. Sorrow gathered in her eyes when she saw him dressed for his flight, having swapped his boardies for tawny-brown pants. He was buttoning a chambray shirt over the top of a clean white tee.

"I can't believe you're actually leaving me," she said, leaning against the door jam, a forlorn look marring her exquisite features.

He held his hand out to her. "Come smooch me, angel face," he said, drawing her towards him and tilting her face to his with his index finger. She kissed him hard, her lips trembling, then buried her head in his chest, a deep shuddery exhale leaving her body.

"I know, I know," he whispered. "But it's only a week. We'll be together again before you know it." His lips moved over the top of her head as he smoothed his hand through her locks. He loved her hair, the smell, the feel. He was trying his hardest to be strong when, in reality, he was falling apart a bit inside. "God, I'm gonna miss you." He squeezed her tighter. They stood that way for moments on end before he asked, "Who's left downstairs?"

"Just Mum, Matty, Aurora, Rob and Essie. Essie's just whipped up a second jug of illusions and they're getting stuck into that, so they're pretty hammered. When's your driver coming?"

He glanced at the clock on her nightstand. "In about fifteen minutes."

"I only need ten," she murmured, pushing him back onto the bed and climbing on top of him, pawing at the buttons of the shirt he'd only just fastened as he pulled the top of her dress down. His lips travelled down the curve of her neck as his fingertips explored the soft mound of her breast, his mouth moving lower–

The door flew open with a bang and Matty came charging in. They both jumped up in shock. "A man's at the door for you, Indigo! He said he's gonna take you to the airport and that he's sorry he's early!" Cordelia quickly pulled up the front of her dress.

"Thanks, mate," Indigo said, hunching over and inching behind Cordelia as he readjusted himself, pulling up his fly and smoothing his hair. He flashed Matty an overly bright grin.

Matty stared curiously from Indigo to Cordelia. "What were you guys *doing*?" he finally asked, his little face scrunching up. He leant forward and whispered to Indigo, "Were you kissing Cora's boobies?"

"Of course not!" Cordelia cried.

"Oh… um, you see Matty, there was a …" Indigo looked to Cordelia for help.

"Bee?" she offered.

Indigo widened his eyes at her before adding, "Yeah… a big… bee."

"Cora's 'llergic to bees," Matty said.

"It flew down my top, you see, Matty Moo, and Inds was just helping me get it… out," she finished weakly. She looked at Indigo and shrugged.

Matty narrowed his eyes, looking from one to the other. "Well, you're lucky it didn't stinged your tongue, Indigo," he said earnestly.

"Mmm," Indigo said, turning to throw the rest of his stuff into his bag, including his denim jacket which she'd had since the night of the formal. The three of them went downstairs together, Matty in between them holding their hands.

cordelia

The moment they entered the living room, Matty announced to everyone, "There was a big bee in Cora's room!" They all began making their way over to Indigo to say goodbye.

"A bee?" Mum said, brows soaring. "In the house?"

"Yup, a *big* bee," Matty said, eyes wide. "It flied down Cora's top and Indigo had to take off her top and try to get it out!"

Cordelia wanted the floor to open up and swallow her.

"Oh my *God! Sprung!*" Robbie cried, guffawing so hard he bent double as Essie burst out laughing. Aurora smirked behind them.

Mum shot her and Indigo a look, and murmured, "A bit of discretion in the bedroom, please, you two." But her eyes were crinkling and Cordelia could tell she was trying to keep a straight face.

Cordelia covered her face with her hands.

"Was it a killer bee?" Robbie gasped, wiping his eyes.

"You're so lucky your big strong boyfriend was there to save you," Essie dead-panned. "*Ferris Bueller, you're my hero...*"

"Oh my God," Indigo muttered under his breath.

"Please stop," Cordelia said, teeth clenched. Mortified beyond belief, she wanted nothing more than for them all to stop talking.

"Oooh, we're just getting started." Robbie grinned. "If you ever think we're gonna let you forget it—"

Just as Indigo reached for Cordelia's elbow, she raised her hands in the air. "*Stop it*, Rob!"

And they all froze.

Everyone was suddenly statue-still and silent, Robbie mid-snark, Essie grasping his arm, her head thrown back in laughter, Mum standing, hands on Matty's shoulders, biting her lip in a lame attempt to stifle her giggles. Aurora stood at the rear, her hand covering her mouth.

Cordelia gasped. "Oh shiiiiiit. Why now?" She hadn't meant to.

She jumped when she suddenly sensed movement beside her. Indigo was glancing from her to the others in shock. "Um, Cora? How come they're frozen and I'm not?"

They both looked down at his hand on her elbow.

"Oh," he said, blinking. "So if I'm touching you, I'm immune?"

She shrugged. "It would seem so." Her eyes travelled from her mother to Robbie to Essie to Matty. "Craaap," she moaned. "What have I done?"

"Ok, ok, so you just froze your family," he said, moving to rub her back. "It happens to the best of us."

She raised an eyebrow at him and he grinned. "Anyway, thanks, babe, this is awesome, I couldn't take another minute of their shit. Sooo, since my car's here, I'm gonna head off," he joked, turning and taking a step towards the door. "If you could wait until I'm safely at the airport to unfreeze them, that'd be great."

"You're hilarious," she said, her tone thoroughly unamused. She stared him down, arms crossed.

He laughed and stepped back to pull her into a hug.

"I don't believe this," she said, frowning. "I'm being attacked by a knife-wielding maniac and I can't summon the power to freeze him to save myself, yet my brother gives me a bit of shit and all of a sudden I'm freezing everybody like there's no tomorrow?"

"It's ok, my love," he murmured into her hair. "Unfreeze Rory, would you?"

Indigo rubbed her back as she focused hard on Aurora. She raised her hands and threw them towards her. Aurora blinked rapidly, her eyes darting around the room, her mouth falling open. "So it wasn't a one-time thing," she said.

"Team talk," Indigo said, beckoning her over.

"I just assumed it was tied to Cora's emotions," Indigo said. "But she was pretty emotional when Sandy was trying to kill her, right? So why couldn't she do it then?"

Aurora stared thoughtfully at Cordelia. "I seriously have no clue. But leave it with me. We'll use this week to work on it. It's a shame we can't ask Raf, I reckon he'd probably have some ideas."

Cordelia looked at Indigo. "What if we never work it out? What if it's completely random?"

Aurora stiffly touched Cordelia's arm for a split second. "It's ok. We'll figure it out together." And for the first time ever, her eyes weren't hard as steel.

Cordelia stared at her for a beat or two, then nodded. "Thank you, Aurora."

Indigo put his arm around her, squeezed her tight. "Now unfreeze them, beautiful."

"If I unfreeze them, Rob's never gonna let us live the bee thing down."

"Well, you can't leave him like this forever," he said in exasperation.

"You sure about that?"

He shot her a look.

"Fine," she sighed, as they shifted back into position. "Ready?" He and Aurora nodded. She raised her hands again and threw them towards her family. They immediately reanimated.

"I gotta head out," Indigo said, letting go of her arm and jerking a thumb towards the front door. "So I'm gonna grab the rest of my stuff and... go."

"Why?" Robbie asked. "Is there somewhere you gotta BEE?"

"Oh, for Christ's sake," Cordelia muttered under her breath.

Robbie and Essie were draped over one another crying with laughter while Matty looked on with bemusement.

"Ok, Indigo sweetie," Mum said, composing herself and stepping forward. "Come give us a hug goodbye." She stood on tip toe to wrap her arms around him.

"Sorry, Scar."

"Oh, to be young and in love," she said dreamily. "Travel safe, ok?" She drew back to grip his hands and look him in the eye. He nodded, shooting her a sheepish smile.

"Nice to meet you again, Essie," he said. "See ya later, Rob." He curled his lip at Robbie who was gasping for breath.

Still chuckling, Robbie stumbled forward to hug him close. "Love ya, mate."

Aurora reached up to give him a quick peck on the cheek. "I got her, ok?" she murmured. He smiled and squeezed her arm in thanks.

Indigo held a hand out to Matty. "High five, buddy." Matty jumped up to slap his palm, then grabbed on tight to Indigo's thigh, wrapping himself around it like a monkey.

When Indigo finally managed to disentangle himself from Matty, having pinkie promised, sworn, and vowed on Buzz Lightyear he'd be back soon, Cordelia walked him out to the car where the driver waited discreetly behind the wheel.

Her stomach churned as tears threatened to spill down her cheeks. She could barely fathom that this was it. That in a few moments, he just wouldn't be there anymore. Two steps down the driveway, he suddenly tugged her into the shadows of the bushes at the side of the house. And she was in his arms. And she could barely breathe at the very nearness of him, his face inches from hers, his whole body pressed to hers, the electricity palpable.

"Well, here we are again," he whispered, his thumb caressing her lower lip, his eyes bright on hers.

Her breath caught in her throat. Her heart was beating so fast.

And then his lips were on hers, gentle at first – until she was kissing him back, and then not gentle.

When they finally broke apart, they were both breathing heavily.

"I love you, Cordelia," he whispered as she touched her fingers to his pinkie where her ring sat securely. "In this and every timeless now, 'til my last breath, and beyond." She caught her breath and gathered herself and told him that from the very depths of her soul, she loved him too. Always and forever, in this and every timeless now.

And then he was gone.

She smiled sadly as she watched the tail lights of his car disappear down the street until they were out of sight. She and Indigo had their whole lives ahead of them, so much to look forward to sharing together over the months and years and decades to come. Really, what was one week in the scheme of things? The two of them, they'd only just begun. The other night Indigo had whispered to her that real love stories never ended. And theirs? It had existed since the dawn of time and she knew with everything she had, it would continue to exist 'til the world stopped turning.

Because their love, it transcended all.

chapter forty-four

stuck on you

big sur, california, january 1996

raf

He sat on the damp earth, knees bent up, eyes cast down, listlessly watching a caterpillar humping its way through the leaf litter. Raf was deathly still, his back braced against the trunk of a majestic redwood. He'd ventured off the trail some time ago and was now deep in the forest where the emptiness of the silence seemed to echo.

He slowly raised his eyes to observe the sun seeping weakly through the thick canopy above. The air smelled of wood and water, and he drew that freshness deep down into his lungs.

Raf had needed to get out of there, out of that house, the house that had been his mother's. His mother whom he had loved and adored and trusted.

Before.

Before he knew better.

But now?

Now, at the very thought of her, his mouth went dry, his hands clenched to fists, his whole body trembled as though venom coursed through his veins.

How *could* she?

It was the betrayal that hurt the most. The selfishness and the betrayal. And that was in part his father's fault, because she'd become what he'd created, had been shaped by his disloyal ways. He'd damaged her so badly that her need to hold onto her men, to keep them with her at any cost, outweighed everything else.

And the cost… it had been astronomical.

She'd shattered Raf's life.

And he hadn't even known it.

He could have had everything. *Everything!* But she'd taken all that away, seemingly without a second thought, without remorse.

Although… the letter.

She'd had it on her when she'd died. Had she been on her way home from retrieving it? Was it to be her deathbed confession?

Raf had rented a motorbike in San Diego and just started to ride. He hadn't cared where. He'd ended up taking the coast road north, bypassing LA and heading past Santa Barbara, not knowing where he was going until he'd arrived in Big Sur, the giant sycamores calling to him, offering their comfort and solitude. He'd always loved it here.

He'd shrouded his mind, and he knew his family was worried about him so he'd called Dawn and told her he was ok, that he was just taking some time. He wasn't ready to talk about it yet, and he knew she'd pass his message onto the kids. That was weeks ago now.

Raf reached into his pocket and pulled out the water-damaged envelope, crumpled and worn. He held it in his lap, staring down at it. It had become a talisman, something he couldn't stop touching. It was a connection.

To her.

To *them.*

He knew its contents by heart. Well, the contents he'd been able to decipher, so much of it washed away by the flood that had damaged the parlour, by the passage of time. It was, what? Eighteen, nineteen years old, after all. He clutched it to his chest, as those legible excerpts ran through his head, tormenting him, hollowing out his insides so they ached.

It had been written by her mother.

Charley's mother.

Back then, so desperate, pleading for her daughter. For her unborn grandchild.

... 'We have been trying to track down a man by the name of Diego Rafael, and are writing to all the Rafaels in California in the hope this letter finds Diego or a relative of his...'

'... We want to let him know he's going to be a father...'

'... couldn't go through with the termination...'

'... baby will be born this year...'

'... wants him by her side throughout all this...'

'.... she believes they want the same things in life, and still loves him very much...'

'... still holds hope he will return to her before the baby arrives so they can welcome it together...'

'...If only he would come back to Australia, together they can start the life they so wanted...'

'...She can't do this alone. We've found a couple willing to adopt the baby, who can give it a good life, if Diego chooses not to return.'

'Time is running out... papers need to be signed...'

Raf still recalled that day back in 1977 when, through wracking sobs, she'd told him she was pregnant. He was delighted. She was devastated. She asked him to support her choice to terminate the pregnancy. But he just couldn't. He *wanted* to have a baby with her, a life with her, a home and a family. She was the only future he could see. Him, her, two or three kids, and a little cottage in the rural hinterland of Byron where they could raise their own chickens and grow their own vegetables yet be at the beach in minutes. That was all he needed in life.

He promised to stand by her, to support her, to love her until the day he died, and he meant it with all of his heart. He got down on one knee and proposed to her, offering her everything he had. But still she refused to see the pregnancy through, saying she was too young, that she wanted to travel, to explore, to finish school even, essentially to have a life before she had a baby. She loved him, too, so much, desperately, in fact, but she wasn't ready to be a mother. She was terrified of resenting him, or worse, of resenting the child.

She wouldn't even entertain the notion. Her mind was made up. And so was his.

It was a deal breaker.

He'd always been pretty laid back and felt pretty strongly that what anyone did with their body was their choice, but this... this was complicated. The issue wasn't that abortion was largely illegal in Australia back then; he'd never been one to take the law to heart. He'd seen plenty of unloved, unwanted kids in his time and, in his eyes, that was a far greater tragedy. The fact that backroom abortion wasn't safe, now that bothered him greatly, because if anything ever happened to her, he would want to die. And the thing was, this baby, *their* baby, it *was* wanted, so wanted. Well, wanted by him. It was like the moment she'd announced she was pregnant, he'd grown attached to the idea of this child, it was like he loved it already and he wanted it. He wanted it with her so bad.

He was twenty-two, he was immature and arrogant, and he took the fact she was willing to risk her life to not have his baby very personally. She told him in anger that if he couldn't find a way to support her, to see things her way, he wasn't the person she'd thought he was and he should just go.

And so the day she'd travelled down to Sydney to terminate the pregnancy was the day he'd left town.

He packed his stuff and hit the road, hitchhiking north. He sold his Kombi van before he left, leaving the money behind for her. He might not have approved of her choices, but he still had responsibilities.

But now... now he knew she hadn't gone through with it.

She'd kept the baby!

Raf tilted his head back, the dappled light playing through the boughs of the redwoods flickering upon his face. He'd never felt so lost, so disoriented, so unsure of which way to turn. So many years had passed. What must *she* think of him? What must they both think of him? The very thought hollowed him out, sucked all the air from his body so he could barely breathe. A letter like that, so raw, so emotional, so desperate, to have gone unanswered all these years...

All this time, he'd believed she'd gone ahead with the termination. She'd been so adamant about it, after all. And she'd left Byron, travelled down to Sydney with her mother to have the procedure... He'd seen them leave!

But she hadn't gone through with it.

What had made her change her mind?

He had a *child* out there somewhere.

A son? A daughter?

The letter said they'd found someone to adopt the baby if he didn't return. He could only imagine how heartbroken, how lost she'd felt when he hadn't shown up, hadn't stepped up. She must have been so alone, so scared… She'd been so young, oh so young to raise a child on her own. And he'd inadvertently left her with no choice.

He clutched his chest, his heart aching like it had never ached before.

Had she given their baby up? Had someone else out there raised his child? A child he'd wanted so desperately. He'd have travelled to the ends of the earth for her and that child. He would have been a damn good father, too.

But he'd been robbed of the chance.

By *her*. His mother. She'd stolen that from him.

He well knew what had triggered her actions: the request for him to move to Australia and start a life there. And it was a life his mother had known would keep him there, keep him on the other side of the world, from her, forever. He'd been travelling at the time, he'd seen the date on the letter, knew he'd been living outside of Cairns then, but his mother had always assumed he would eventually find his way back home to her. But something like this? It would keep him away permanently. And she couldn't handle that.

What was it she always said? *"My family is my world. May the Moon Goddess help any women who dare try to take either of my men away from me."*

She'd been true to her word. Utterly, brazenly, devastatingly true to her word. She wasn't who he'd thought she was. And that just added to all the hurt, all the pain, writhing and tumbling through every fibre of his being.

And now? He didn't even know what to do, where to start.

Their baby could be anywhere in the world.

Baby? Not a baby.

Far from a baby now.

Tears rushed to his eyes at the thought of the life he'd missed. He had so much to make up for, and he wanted to start making up for it as best he could. Starting now.

His best bet was to find Charley, and his heart leapt at the very thought of seeing her again.

But where to even start?

Byron Bay, where they'd first met?

He'd tried to call her there, so many years ago now, and he'd discovered her family had moved away. But someone there might remember them, might know of where they'd gone…

And if not? What were his options?

A thought came to him suddenly, and he pushed it away.

Because he couldn't do that.

To approach her, to ask her for help, he'd be in breach of universal law.

The Witch Queen.

She had access to information no one else did.

And surely she owed him a favour? After everything he'd done for her…

But he couldn't ask her. It just wasn't done.

"Micah," he moaned. "In all the years I've done your bidding, that I've committed to you without question, I've never asked you for anything for myself. But now I need for you to help me. Please help me, Micah, please help me find them!"

But Micah remained silent. Micah hadn't spoken to him directly since that day on the beach, the day before he'd prepared Raf so brutally for hosting him.

When darkness began to fall, Raf returned to his lodgings in a small cabin in the woods. His stomach was too knotted and torn to face food, so he simply laid his swag out on the saggy bunk and promptly fell into a coma-like sleep among the swirling dust-motes.

He pushed open the door to a dim room he didn't recognise, and there she was, curled up on her side on the bed, and she was crying, her silky hair splayed out on the pillow, her shoulders shaking as she wept. Charley. He gasped. She was so beautiful; he'd almost forgotten how so. Why was she crying? Was it because of him? Did she know he wasn't coming back?

There was a window behind her, and he glanced outside to see a kookaburra perched upon the branch of a banksia, its head tilted to one side as it seemed to regard him.

He crept further into the room, reaching out for her, wanting to take her in his arms, to comfort her, to tell her he was there, that it was all going to be ok, but before he could touch her, the room faded and vanished, and suddenly he was on a beach.

In the distance, he could see the silhouette of a woman walking with a small child. She wore a long dress, her hair loose down her back as they strolled towards the bright, setting sun. They passed a set of red and yellow flags spiked into the sand as they headed toward the rocky outcrop at the far end of the beach. The child was only small, and was scampering along the shore, stopping now and then to pick up a shell or a rock to present to her. Raf inhaled sharply. Was this his child?

Their backs were to him, and he tried to yell out to them, tried to ask them to turn around, to wait for him, but nothing came out. The glare from the sun was so bright, and he raised his hands to shield his eyes, but still they were distorted from his view so they shimmered like a mirage.

Raf watched as the woman suddenly stopped dead, but the child kept walking, picking up pace, posture changing as though hurrying towards someone special. The woman watched in silence, eventually raising her hand in a wave, as the child disappeared from view and vanished...

Raf woke disoriented, flailing for something to grasp onto. He sat up, drenched in sweat despite the frigid air in the tiny cabin.

It was just a dream.

Or was it more? It had certainly felt like so much more.

A glimpse into the past, perhaps? Into the aftermath of his leaving.

A past where she was so sad.

A past where she and the child were together... Until they weren't. She'd stopped, allowing the child to continue on without her. Was that an omen? Had they gone their separate ways?

He needed to know more. And he did have a pre-cog at his disposal, someone who was able to access the past. But Nash was in Aspen with Indigo and Sasha. He was sure Dawn had the number. But there was no phone in this cabin.

He could see through the grimy window that the sun had already risen, casting wan light through the gloomy room. He threw his swag back, climbing out and fumbling for a light switch. By the dim glow of the bare bulb hanging from the rickety roof, he hurriedly stuffed his things in his bag and strode for the bike. He had to find a phone.

He turned the ignition and the bike roared to life. He took off at speed, fishtailing out of the dusty driveway and onto Route 1 north, jaw clenched. At least he had some direction now, a course of action, something to cling to.

He would find them.

Both of them.

Charley.

His child.

No matter how long, no matter how far he had to search, even if it took the rest of his life, he would find them.

gratitude list

In the spirit of reconciliation, I'd like to acknowledge the Traditional Custodians of country throughout Australia, and their connections to land, sea, sky and community. I want to pay my respect to their Elders past and present and extend that respect to all Aboriginal and Torres Strait Islander peoples today.

From the very first time I visited the Northern territory when I was ten, I've been in awe of the beauty of Aboriginal culture. I've always been fascinated by the Dreamtime, and the synergy and connection our First Nations people have with this great land. Plant medicine and energetic healing are passions of mine, and so the way of the *Ngangkari* Healer is something I wanted to celebrate upon the pages of *transcended*.

I want to thank *Ngangkari* healer and First Nations Doctor, Wyarta Miller for assisting me with accurately and sensitively telling the story of Raf's time with Jedda, Jackie, and his mob. Wyarta, you are a true sensation and wonder, and I am in awe of you. Thank you for taking the time to share your experience, gifts and rich history with me. My gratitude knows no bounds. I also want to give a shout out to Harlan and Shia for sharing your amazing mum with me!

I want to thank the other two legs of the *descended* tripod, Juliet Potter and Lorelie Luna Ladiges: you two are my Ambassadors of Quan. Your unending belief in me and this series warms my heart and I am so grateful to have you both on my team and in my life. I love you guys. I literally couldn't do this without you.

Sherryl Clark for editing this book not once, but twice, and Sonia Spatino for lending me your amazing proofreading skills and for correcting my dodgy Italian (and my perfect Hawaiian! There definitely is no 'd' in '*shave ice*'). Ladies, this book wouldn't be what it is without your keen eye for detail.

My dear friends and fellow authors, Kim Barden and Em Greville – I feel like we've been through a *lot* together this past year... You gals have had my back in the trenches and I have so much gratitude for your encouragement and friendship. Thank you for sharing your wealth of knowledge and for making the author's journey feel a little less isolated. Oh, and, Kimmi, I hope this book gives you gooseflesh!

Candice Gunn, beta reader extraordinaire... Thank you, thank you, thank you my gorgeous friend. Your encouraging, sassy, constructive feedback is everything. You are my choreographer of fight scenes, sexy motorbike dismounts, and classy BJs, and my eradicator of potatoes. The extra layer of polish on this manuscript is thanks to you.

To the Bookstagram community, what can I say? I'm a private person and am not a massive sharer, so when I was told I had to be active on social media, I resisted. Little did I know what awaited me within this amazing bookish community, and how many wonderful friendships would be formed. The incredible support I have found from brilliant reviewers both overseas and in Australia has blown my mind, and I thank you all from the bottom of my heart for championing my book — you know who you are. You have all played an integral part in bringing this series to the world.

To everyone who read *descended* and took Indi, Cora and the gang into their hearts, I've loved every single one of your messages, DMs, your posts, fanart, reviews and comments. I'm sorry *transcended* took so long to get here, but I wanted it to be the best possible version of itself it could be. Thank you to everyone who reached out purely to hurry me up and demand to know what was taking so long…! I'm always happy to be nagged and held accountable.

This book itself wouldn't be the beautiful creation it is without the artistic talents of three special people. Nicolee Payne, your abilities blow me away. Thank you for painting the spectacular artwork that graces the front cover of *transcended*. I literally cried when I first saw it. You captured Indigo's heart so perfectly for book one, and now you've captured Cordelia's. Bea Brabante, for incorporating that artwork into a stunning cover I'm so proud of, and Kathy Shanks for ensuring *transcended* is just as beautiful as the inside as it is on the outside.

To my family on both the Du Vernet and Adamsas sides, and of course, to all my wonderful friends – there are so many of you and I can't possibly mention you all or this book will never end, but I love you all – Jacki Lang, because I can always count on you for holidays, hot fudge sundaes, and emergency school pick ups (but not Jon cos apparently you were too busy partaking in Mai Tai Time on some other continent to come to my book launch… kidding, I've forgiven you because of your undying *descended* fandom), Alex Price-Randall for your enduring support, Pam Wilson because you make all your co-workers read *descended*, Georgie Hookway: early draft reader and doubt-destroyer, and of course, three of my OGs: Jane Francis, Louisa Warr and Felicity McVay; you gals know what you mean to me, and I thank you for having my back at book launches, book festivals, and in book stores.

Mum and Dad, what can I say? You're the best in the business and I don't know how I got so lucky. Thank you for believing in me. I don't think anyone has read more drafts of these books than my mum, and I thank her for always being willing to dive back in and share her many, *many* thoughts. And then there's Dad, who's still reading my first book a year later and will probably never finish it, which is actually a good thing because there's no way he's reading *transcended* (because of the spicy scenes; yes I'm in my forties and I have four kids but Dad and I are both pretending I'm pure as the driven snow).

Last but definitely not least, my heart and soul, my husband John and my four boys, Xavier, Dash, Remy and Ted. I couldn't do this if you five didn't support and champion me. Thank you for making my life so wonderful and for making me smile every day. We truly are blessed to have one another, and I'm so grateful you chose me to be the woman in your lives. (And yes, Dash, because you're the only one who read *descended*, you're top of the favourite child leaderboard).

I love my life and the people in it, and I'm grateful for you all.

Ingrid x

Made in United States
North Haven, CT
25 June 2024

54037550R00321